THE
Grip Trilogy

USA TODAY BESTSELLING AUTHOR
KENNEDY RYAN

The GRIP Trilogy

FLOW (Grip #1)
Copyright © Kennedy Ryan, 2017 ALL RIGHTS RESERVED

GRIP (Grip #2)
Copyright © Kennedy Ryan, 2017 ALL RIGHTS RESERVED

STILL (Grip #3)
Copyright © Kennedy Ryan, 2017

*Audiobooks available for all 3 titles.
Check Audible Escape to listen FREE with subscription!

Cover Art: Najla Qamber Designs

Cover Photos: Sarah Zimmerman Photo

Editing: Angela Smith, Word Whisperer

Proofreading/Copyediting:
Ashley Williams, AW Editing
Paige Maroney Smith

Never miss sales, new releases,
and get a free book every month!

Join Kennedy's mailing list
www.subscribepage.com/kennedyryan

Author's Note

I'm so excited to share the Grip Trilogy in this box set. This is a really special journey that encompasses not only a timeless love story, but also touches on some of the most pressing issues of our time. I wrote these books a few years ago, and hoped issues like police brutality would be less relevant by now. Unfortunately, they are more pressing than ever.

When I decided to do a box set and new covers for the Grip Trilogy, I also decided to revisit the conversations around social justice to ensure I had clearly articulated what my characters believe and where they stand. Bristol and Grip's story has not changed. It is as I originally dreamt it, and is as epic as it was when I penned it, but with a few word choice changes for clarity.

If you have the e-books of the individual titles, *Flow, Grip* and *Still*, doing an update through Amazon should deliver the most current changes to your device. This box set includes, not only all three individual stories, but also a Grip short story originally featured in the *Cocktales* charity anthology, and BRAND NEW scenes exclusive to this box set. There is also some cool audio that exists only here!

Readers tell me all the time how this journey has touched them. To every person who has ever reached out, expressed how this story affected you, just know that *you* impacted me, and I'm so grateful Grip & Bristol's journey brought us together!

Thank you for reading!

ALSO BY KENNEDY RYAN

The SOUL Trilogy

Want Rhyson's story? Two musicians chasing their dreams and catching each other?

Dive into the Soul Trilogy!

(Rhyson + Kai)

(FREE in Kindle Unlimited)

My Soul to Keep (Soul 1)*

Down to My Soul (Soul 2)*

Refrain (Soul 3)

Available in Audible Escape!

ALL THE KING'S MEN WORLD

Love stories spanning decades, political intrigue, obsessive passion. If you loved the TV show *SCANDAL*, this series is for you!

The Kingmaker (Duet Book 1: Lennix + Maxim)

FREE in KU!

Ebook, Audio & Paperback

The Rebel King (Duet Book 2: Lennix + Maxim)

FREE in KU!

Ebook, Audio & Paperback

Queen Move (Standalone Couple: Kimba + Ezra)

The Killer & The Queen

(Standalone Novella—Grim + Noelani)

Coming Soon!

(co-written with Sierra Simone)

www.subscribepage.com/TKandTQ

Flow

I fell for her before the beat dropped.

USA TODAY BESTSELLING AUTHOR

KENNEDY RYAN

GRIP TRILOGY BOOK #1

If I could undo your kisses

If I could un-feel your touch

If I could unhook this heart from yours I would.

But I'm trapped in the memory of what we were Stuck with the reality of
what we are

Tempted with the promise of a future Afraid of possibility

I don't know how our story ends,

but this—this is where it started.

One

Grip

I**t's just one of those days.**

Monica's singing in my head. I'm relying on nineties R&B to articulate myself. I'm that hungry. My mouth waters when I think of the huge burrito I was this close to shoveling down my throat before I got the call. My stomach adds a rumble sound effect to the hunger.

I visually pick through the dense LAX crowd, carefully checking each baggage claim carousel. No sign of her. Or at least what I think she might look like.

Rhyson still hasn't texted me his sister's picture. If I know my best friend—and I do—he probably doesn't have a picture of her on his phone. He wouldn't want to admit that, knowing how important family is to me, so I bet he's scrambling to find one. They are the weirdest family I've ever met, which is saying something since mine is no Norman Rockwell painting. I've never actually met any of the Gray family except Rhys and his Uncle Grady. Rhyson's parents and sister still live in New York, and he hasn't seen them in years. Not since he emancipated. We don't "emancipate" where I come from. Nah. We keep shit simple and just never come home. Worked for my dad. He didn't even wait till I was born to leave. Less messy and fewer legal fees. But we didn't have a fortune to fight over like the Grays did.

My phone rings, and I answer, still scanning the crowd for a girl fitting Rhyson's vague description.

"Whassup, Rhys." I clutch the phone and crane my neck to see over what must be a college basketball team. Not one of them is under six five. Even at six two, I can't see the forest for the trees with trees this tall.

"Trying to finish this track. Bristol there yet?" That note in Rhyson's voice tells me this conversation only holds half his attention. He's in the studio, and when he's there, good luck getting him to think about anything other than music. I get it. I'm the same way.

"I don't know if she's here or not. Did you forget to send the picture?"

"Oh, yeah. The picture." He clears his throat to make way for whatever excuse he's about to give me. "I thought I had it on my phone. Maybe I accidentally deleted it or something."

Or something. I let him get away with that. Rhyson's excuse for sending me to pick his sister up from the airport is legit. There's this pop star diva who needs a shit ton of tracks remastered at the last minute before her album drops, but I suspect he's also nervous about his sister's visit. Maybe this emergency is a convenient way to avoid dealing with her for a little bit. Or inconvenient, if you were me and missed lunch rushing to get to the airport as stand-in chauffeur.

"Well, I don't know what she looks like." I push my sunglasses onto the top of my head.

"She looks like me," he says. "I told you we're twins. Lemme check the Cloud for a picture."

Did dude just seriously say 'check the Cloud'?

"Yeah, Rhys, you check the Cloud. Lemme know what you find." "Okay," he says from the other end, and I can tell he's back into that track. "I called to tell her you were coming, but I keep getting voice mail. I'll try again and send a pic."

Once he hangs up, I concentrate on searching methodically through the crowd. She'd be coming from New York, so I've narrowed it down to one carousel. "She looks like me" isn't much to go on, but I stop at every tall, dark-haired girl, and check for signs of Rhyson's DNA. Hell, she could be right in front of—

That thought fizzles out when my eyes land on the girl standing right in front of me.

Shit.

Black skinny jeans cling to long, lean legs that start at Monday and stretch all the way through next week. A white T-shirt peeps through the small opening left by the black leather jacket molding her arms and chest.

And the rack.

The leather lovingly cups the just-right handful of her breasts. Narrow waist and nice ass. She's not as thick as the chicks I usually pull, but my eyes involuntarily scroll back up her slim curves, seeking the face that goes with this body.

Fuck. This woman is profanely gorgeous.

I never understood the big deal with high cheekbones. I mean, they're cheekbones, not tits. You can't motorboat cheekbones, but now I get it. Her face makes me get it. The bones are molded into a slanting curve that saves her face from angularity and elevates it to arresting. Her mouth, a wide, full line, twists to one side as she scans the crowd around her with eyes so light a shade of gray they're almost silver. Dark, copper-streaked hair frames her face and slips past her shoulders.

The alert from my phone interrupts my ogling. It's a text from Rhyson.

Rhyson: Here ya go. This pic's old as hell, but she can't look much different.

When the photo comes over, it confirms in my nearly agnostic mind what my mother has been trying to tell me for years. There must indeed be a God. How did I ever doubt Him? He has sent me, little old me, a tiny miracle to confirm His existence. It isn't water into wine, but I'll take it. I toss my eyes up to the sky and whisper a quick thanks to the Big Guy. Because the girl in the family picture, though almost a decade younger and with braces and frizzier hair, is the gorgeous, willowy woman standing in front of me in baggage claims. One hand on her hip and a frown between her dark eyebrows, she leans to peer down the conveyor that now holds only a few bags.

"Dammit," she mutters, pulling her hair off her neck and twisting it into a knot on her head. "I don't need this today."

"We were on the same flight," a guy offers from beside her, his eyes crawling up and down her body in a way that even makes me feel violated. "My luggage still hasn't come either. Maybe we could—"

"Don't." The look she gives him should wither his hard-on. "It's so not happening."

"I was just thinking if you—"

"I know what you were just thinking." She turns away from him to search the conveyor belt again. "You've been just thinking it since we left New York, and not hiding it. So again, I'll say . . ."

She turns back to him with a look that would singe the fuzz off your balls. "Don't."

I like her already. The guy is sputtering and still trying, but he has no game. It's sad really. Guys who have no game.

"Bristol," I say her name with confidence because I can already tell that's the only thing she'll respond to.

Her head jerks around, and those silvery eyes give me a thorough up and down sliding glance. After she's made it all the way down to my classic Jordans and back to my face, she looks just behind and beyond me, as if she isn't sure she actually heard her name or that I'm the one who said it.

"Bristol," I say again, stepping a little closer. "I'm Grip, a friend of your brother's. Rhyson sent me."

Her eyes widen then narrow, the frown deepening.

"Is he okay?" she demands. "Did something happen?"

"No, he's just tied up." I smile to reassure her, hoping she'll smile in return. I want to see her smile. To see how those braces worked out for her.

"Tied up?" Those full lips tighten, still showing me no teeth. She shakes her head a little, huffing a quick breath and stepping closer to the conveyor. "Figures. So you're stuck with me, huh? Sorry."

"I'm not." At least not now that I've seen her. I wouldn't have missed this for my burrito.

She gives me the same knowing look she leveled on No-Game guy. Like guys have been looking at her like that for a long time. Like she can smell lust from fifty paces. Like she's telling me it isn't happening.

Oh, it's happening, baby girl.

I'm plotting all the ways I'll convince her to go out with me, and then who knows where that'll lead when I remember. This is Rhyson's sister. Shit. The hottest girl I've met in ages, and I should probably try not to sleep with her.

Okay. I'm agnostic again. Sorry, Ma.

"I'm waiting for my luggage." She runs a hand over the back of her neck the way I've seen Rhyson do a million times when he's agitated. I note all the other things about her that remind me of my best friend. Let's just say Rhyson's DNA looks a helluva lot better on her. I mean, he's a good-looking guy, but he's, well, a guy. If I rolled that way, maybe. But I roll her way, and dayyyyyum.

"Here's mine," No-Game pipes up with a smug smile when he pulls his big square suitcase from the line.

Bristol creases a fake smile at him that disintegrates as soon as she looks back to the belt.

"Mine shouldn't be far behind then," she says.

"Unless it's lost," No-Game sneers but can't seem to drag his beady eyes from her rack.

"You got your luggage," I say, looking down at him. "How 'bout you step off?"

His blue eyes hiding behind the round glasses do a quick survey of me. I know what he sees and probably what he thinks. Big black dude, arms splashed with tats, "First Weed. Then Coffee" T-shirt. He's probably ready to piss himself. He's like the Diary of a Wimpy Kid all grown up but still wimpy. I could squash him with my eyelashes. It seems we've arrived at the same conclusion because No-Game Wimpy Diary guy turns without a word and pulls his suitcase behind him, docile as a lamb.

"Impressive." Bristol smirks but still doesn't flash teeth. "Been trying to shake that jerk since La Guardia. I felt like spritzing every time he looked at me."

"Spritzing?"

She makes a spraying motion toward her face.

"Yeah, like to refresh your . . . never mind." She rolls her eyes and sighs. "Anyway, he may look harmless, but I bet under all that geek he is a nasty piece of work. Unfortunately, it only takes money, not actual class, to fly first class."

I've never flown first class, so I wouldn't know. Come to think of it, I've only flown once. Ma sent me to Chicago to visit her cousins the summer my cousin Chaz died. That was a bad summer. I don't know if it was the heat, but The Crips and The Bloods made our hood a jungle that year. They may have been hunting each other, but a lot of innocent blood ran down our streets. Not that they cared. Not that they ever cared. Ma took all the money she'd been saving from braiding hair to get me out of Compton that summer, and I think I flew Ghetto Air. Whatever shitty aircraft that little bit of extra money got me on, that's what I flew. Not that Chi-Town was less violent, but at least it didn't hold any memories for me. You don't dream other people's nightmares. And in my own bed, I'd wake up every night hearing the shot that killed Chaz just outside my window.

"Finally." Bristol's voice brings me back. "Here it is."

An Eiffel-tower sized Louis Vuitton suitcase ambles down the conveyor belt.

"I thought you were just here for a week?" I lift one brow in her direction.

"I am."

"You sure? 'Cause I could fit my whole apartment in that big-ass suitcase coming at us like a meteor."

"Very funny." A teasing grin pulls at the corners of her bright eyes. "Maybe that says more about your apartment than it does about my suitcase."

The one-room hovel I call home right now appears in my mental window.

"You might be right about that," I admit with a laugh, grabbing the colossal suitcase when it reaches us and setting it on the floor. "Shit. You pack your whole sorority in here?"

"I'm not in a sorority, but thanks for the stereotype." She reaches for the handle, and her hand rests on top of mine. Both our eyes drop to where her slim fingers contrast with my rougher, larger ones.

You know that electric tingle people talk about? That thing that zips up your spine like a tiny shock when your hands first touch? That isn't this touch. It isn't electric. It's something that . . . simmers. A heat that kind of seethes under my skin for a second and then explodes into a solar flare. I watch her face to see if she's feeling anything. If she does, she hides it well. If she's anything like her brother, hiding things is a habit. Her expression doesn't change when she tugs the handle until her hand slips from under mine.

"It's got wheels." She pulls the suitcase toward her and finally meets my eyes. "My feminist sensibilities tell me to carry it myself."

"Maybe my manhood won't let me walk idly by while a delicate lady carries her own suitcase." I shrug. "I got a rep to protect."

"Oh, I don't doubt you have a rep." Bristol's brows arch high and her lips twist into a smirk. "Where to?"

I grab the suitcase by the handle, pulling it from her grasp, and start walking. When I look over my shoulder, her narrowed eyes rest on the mammoth suitcase I've commandeered. The defiant light in her eye makes me want to commandeer her like I just did this over-priced baggage. This is Rhyson's sister. I need to keep reminding myself she should be squarely placed in the NO FUCK bin. But, damn, if all bets were off, she'd be feeling me every time she walked for a week.

If things were different. But they're not.

So I won't.

I'm just gonna keep telling myself that.

Two

Bristol

I'M MORE THAN CAPABLE OF DRAGGING MY LUGGAGE AROUND, BUT I appreciate the view as I watch Grip do it for me. My eyes inevitably stray to the tight curve of his ass in the sweatpants dripping from his hips. His back widens from a taut waist, the muscles flexing beneath the outrageous T-shirt hugging his torso and stretching at the cut of his bicep.

Ever since he called my name and I looked up into eyes the color of darkened caramel, I haven't drawn nearly enough air. Soot-black eyebrows and lashes so long and thick they tangle at the edges frame those eyes. Lips, sculpted and full. Some concoction of cocoa and honey swirl to form the skin stretched tightly over the strong bones of his face. I'm almost distracted enough by all this masculine beauty to not be pissed at my twin brother.

Almost.

Five years. I haven't seen Rhyson outside of a courtroom in five years, haven't even spoken to him since Christmas. I finally initiate this visit to him in Los Angeles, and he sends some stranger for me? I fall into step beside Grip so I can read his expression when I drill him. In profile, he's almost even better, a tantalizing geometry of angles and slopes. He tosses a quick look to me from the side, a caramel-drenched gaze that melts down the length of my body before returning to my face, stealing more air from my lungs.

"So, why couldn't Rhyson come get me?" I ask.

"Long story short," Grip says as we reach the exit. "The album Rhyson's been working on—"

"He's working on an album?" A grin takes over my face. "I didn't know he was working on new music. Piano, I assume? I can't wait to hear—"

"It's for someone else," Grip corrects. "He's producing an album for an artist, and her label wants all these changes before it drops. Some remastering, maybe some other stuff."

"Oh, I was hoping he was back to performing. Doing his own music." I narrow my eyes and nod decisively. "He should be."

I'm actually here in part to convince him of it. I'm staking my entire college degree and career aspirations on him seeing things my way. People usually do see things my way if I play my cards right. My mother taught me to play my cards right. She may not be much of a mother, but she's a helluva card shark.

"He will one day." Grip offers me a small smile. "When he's ready."

"You think so?" I hope so. "Yeah."

He drags my suitcase toward an ancient Jeep with a mountain-sized airport security guard standing in front of it.

"Thanks, man." Grip pounds fists and accepts keys from the guy. He glances up and down the busy sidewalk. "Anybody give you shit yet about the car being here?"

"Nah." The guard gives a quick head shake. "You know I run this place."

"Yeah right." Grip sketches a quick grin. "Well, thanks."

"No problem, bruh." The guard's eyes flick to and over me briefly before returning to Grip, brows lifted in a silent query.

"Oh, Amir, this is Bristol, Rhyson's sister." Grip waves a hand between us. "Bristol, Amir. We grew up together. He made sure my car wasn't towed while I came to get you. It was all kind of last minute."

At the last minute, Rhyson decided he would delegate me to strangers. I swallow my disappointment and spit out a smile.

"Nice to meet you, Amir." I extend my hand, and he brings it to his lips in unexpected gallantry.

"The pleasure is all mine." Amir grins roguishly, his eyes teasing from beneath a fall of dreadlocks. "You didn't tell me Rhyson's sister looked like this."

"Didn't know." Grip laughs and hauls my huge suitcase into the back of the Jeep. "The operative words being 'Rhyson's sister', so pick your jaw up and say 'Goodbye, Bristol.'"

"Goodbye, Bristol." A delightful smile creases Amir's face. "Goodbye, Amir." I can't help but reciprocate with a wide grin of my own. Amir salutes and makes his way back inside the airport. When I glance back to Grip, he's leaning against the dilapidated Jeep watching me closely, traces of a smile lingering on his handsome face.

"What?" I quirk an eyebrow as the smile melts from my face. "Nothing." His shoulders push up and drop, languid and powerful. "Just thinking those braces worked out well for you."

"Braces?" My fingers press against my lips. "How'd you know I used to wear braces?"

Grip hands me his phone, and if I didn't have enough reasons to string Rhyson up, sending "ugly stage" adolescence pictures to his hot friend gives me another. Once I get past embarrassment for my twelve-year-old, frizzy-haired, flat-chested self, I really study the picture more closely. It's a rare family photo, and I remember the day we took it with absolute clarity. Rhyson was home off the road for a few weeks. We'd known since he was three years old what an extraordinarily talented pianist he would be, but it was only around eleven that he actually started touring all over the world. Music is a family business for us, and my parents went with him on the road as his managers. I, however, had no talent to speak of, so I stayed home with a nanny who made sure I ate, went to school, and had a "normal" childhood. As normal as your childhood can be when your parents barely remember you exist.

"Rhys sent that so I could identify you at the airport." Grip holds out his hand for his phone.

I study the photo another few seconds. Rhyson looks like he'd rather be anywhere but with the three of us. Just a few years after that picture was taken, he would find a way to leave us. To leave me. As much as I told myself over and over that he emancipated from our parents, not from me, that never made me feel less abandoned or less alone in our sprawling New York home. After he moved to California to live with my father's twin brother, Grady, I'd sit in the music room at his piano, straining my ears for the memory of him rehearsing in there for hours every day. Eventually, I stopped going in that room. I draped his piano in white cloth, locked the door, and stopped chasing his music. Stopped chasing him. I told myself that if he wanted to be my brother again, he'd call. Except he never did, so I called him. It hurts to feel so connected to someone who obviously doesn't feel as connected to me.

"You okay, Bristol?"

Grip's question tugs my mind free of that tumultuous time in my family that felt like a civil war. His hand is still extended, waiting.

"Sorry, yeah." I drop the phone into his palm, careful to avoid actual skin-to-skin contact. Based on how my body responded to the brush of his fingers when he took my suitcase, I suspect he could easily fry me with another touch. "Just feeling sorry for that geeky little girl in the picture."

"Oh, don't cry for her," he says with a grin. "I have it on good authority when she grows up the braces are gone and she has a beautiful smile."

I roll my eyes so he won't think his lines are actually working on me, though he does actually make me feel a little better.

He opens the passenger door and I slide in, catching a whiff of him as I go. It's fresh and clean and man. No cologne that I can detect. All Grip.

"So where to now?" He starts the old Jeep but lets it idle while he turns radio knobs, searching for a station.

"Food." I blow out a weary breath as the long trip and lack of food hit me hard. "I hope Grady's got food at his house."

Grip's eyes widen just a bit before sliding away from me.

"Uh, there may not be a ton of food at Grady's place." Grip taps his long fingers on the steering wheel. "He's kind of out of town."

"Out of town?" I snap my head around to stare at his rugged profile. "He knew I was coming, right? How can he be . . .what?"

My father and his twin brother, Grady, weren't close before, but after Rhyson emancipated from my parents to live with him, our relationship with him grew even more strained. My parents resented him "taking" Rhyson away, and I haven't seen him either. I never had much of a relationship with my uncle, and it doesn't look like that will change on this particular trip.

"A colleague had a death in the family," Grip says. "He needed Grady to step in for him at a songwriters' conference."

A piece of lead rests heavily on my chest, constricting my breath for a second. Why am I even here? It's obvious I'm the only one looking for any connection, any reconciliation for our family.

"He couldn't have anticipated this," Grips adds hastily.

"I get it." I force a stiff curve to my lips and stare out the passenger side window so Grip doesn't see the smile never reaches my eyes. "This is gonna be some family reunion. Uncle Grady away and Rhyson . . . tied up."

"We don't cry in front of strangers."

My mother's voice echoes back to me from childhood. We don't cry in front of anyone, truth be told. I blink furiously and sniff discreetly, hoping a red nose isn't betraying the stupid emotion swelling in my belly and pushing up into my chest. I must be PMSing. I suckled at my mother's iron tit. Something this insubstantial after all I've been through shouldn't affect me this way. I know not to wear my emotions in places people can see them. And yet, here I am, against my mother's wishes and advice, clear across the country, risking parts of my heart with family who apparently don't give a damn about me.

"Bristol, Grady will be back soon and Rhyson will be around." I hate the deliberate gentleness of Grip's tone. It's as if he sees my cracks and knows that at any minute I might break.

Red nose and teary eyes or not, I'll show him I won't break. I'll make sure he knows I'm stronger that that. That I don't need my brother or my uncle. That they are the ones who missed out on knowing me.

I whip around to tell him so, to unload my defenses and assurances on him, but all my bravado slams into the compassion of his eyes. More disconcerting than how beautiful his eyes are, is how much they seem to see. How much they seem to know. The bitter words die on my tongue. I swallow the shattered syllables. I swallow the pain. With practice, it goes down easy, lubricated by tears I'll never shed. I've had lots of practice. I've had lots of tears, but this stranger, this beautiful stranger, won't see. I steady my trembling mouth and level my eyes until they meet his stare squarely.

"I'm hungry. Are we going to eat, or what?"

I know I sound like the spoiled sorority girl he assumed I was, but whatever. Talking about food is highly preferable to discussing my family drama, which goes back too far and down too deep. Especially on an empty stomach.

He shifts his glance back to the line of cars pulling away from the airport. Those full lips don't tug into the easy smile he showed me before. I regret making things heavy. Shit got too real, too fast.

"Sure." Eyes ahead, he shifts from park to drive and pulls away from the curb. "I know just the place. Food's great."

Maybe to distract myself from the familiar disappointment sitting alongside the hunger in my belly, I run my eyes discreetly over all six feet and however many inches of him. He's nothing like the guys I've dated, but gorgeous nonetheless. He tucks his bottom lip between an even row of white teeth, concentrating on the ever-hellish LA traffic. As much as I know I shouldn't, I imagine biting that bottom lip.

Am I hungry? Oh, yeah.

Three

Bristol

ALL THOSE CAUTIONARY TALES ABOUT STRANGER DANGER apparently didn't take because I'm currently cruising down the I-5 with a man I met only minutes ago, who may have the face and body of a lower level deity but has not provided any real proof that he actually knows my brother. Yet, how else would he have known my name? And he did have that hideous throwback picture on his phone. I'm fairly certain he's no Ted Bundy, but I could have at least asked to speak with Rhyson to confirm. I slide a surreptitious glance his way, studying the hands on the steering wheel. Those hands are grace and capability, rough and smooth. Doesn't mean they wouldn't wring my neck . . .

"So, how did you say you know my brother again?" I ask, deliberately nonchalant.

"I was wondering when you'd get around to asking some questions." His expression loosens into a grin. "You keep looking at me like I might pull over at the next rest stop and stuff you in the trunk."

"Who . . . what . . . me? Noooo."

He breaks away from the traffic long enough to give me a knowing look, accompanied by a smirk.

"Okay, maybe a little." A nervous laugh slips out. "I actually was thinking I should have asked for some proof or ID or something. Not just hopped in the car with a perfect stranger."

"Perfect?" Cockiness curves his lips. "I get that a lot." "You're so full of yourself, aren't you?" I laugh.

"Oh, I shouldn't be?" Even in profile, his grin is a little dazzling. "No, you're right. I could have offered more than 'I'm Grip. Let's eat.'"

He tips his head toward the phone in my lap.

"Why don't you call Rhys so you can breathe a little easier?"

I should have thought of that. What's wrong with me? Maybe subconsciously there's some part of me that's hesitant to call, dreading those first awkward moments when Rhyson and I have no idea what to say to each other. When it becomes terribly apparent I no longer know my twin brother and he no longer knows me.

If he ever really did.

"It's ringing," I tell Grip, phone pressed to my ear.

"Bristol?" My brother's deep voice rumbles from the other end. Even arranging this trip we talked very little, coordinating most of it by email and text. Hearing his voice, knowing I'll see him, affects me more deeply than I thought it would. He has no idea how much I've missed him. Emotion blisters my throat. Even though we haven't talked much the last few years, he sounds the way he always did when I would slip into his rehearsal room while he was playing. Exhausted and distracted.

"Yeah. It's me." I draw a deep breath and dive in. "So, you couldn't break away long enough to meet your long-lost sister at the airport, huh?"

"Lost sister?" Rhyson emits a disbelieving puff of air. "You? Lost? Never."

He really has no idea. No one does.

"I would have been there," Rhyson continues. "I made sure I'd be done with this by the time you landed, but this artist and her label are riding me hard about remastering—"

"Yeah, I heard," I cut in. "It's fine. I'll see you when you're done. You will be done soon, right?"

"Uh . . . soon? Sure. Relatively soon."

That could mean anything from tonight to next year when Rhyson's immersed in music. At least, that used to be the case, but I doubt much has changed.

"Then I guess I'll see you when I see you." I try to keep the disappointment and irritation out of my voice, but Rhyson's sigh on the other end lets me know I fail.

"Bristol, I'm sorry. I'll see you at Grady's tonight, okay? And I promise we'll catch up tomorrow."

"So you'll be done tomorrow?" My heart lifts the tiniest bit. I don't want to sound needy, but he's the whole reason I'm here. Against my parents' advice, against my better judgment, I'm seeking him out. I've crossed the damn country to try. If I don't try, who will in what's left of our family?

"Not sure if everything will be wrapped today or not," he says. "I'll send them the tracks, but they may have more tweaks. We'll see."

"Sure." I clip the word. "We'll see."

"In the meantime, you're okay?" Rhyson sounds half in the conversation, like the music is already siren calling him.

I flick a glance Grip's way. His expression is completely relaxed and impassive, and his eyes are set on the road like I'm not even there, but he doesn't fool me. There's this constant alertness that crackles around him, as if he's been trained to be on guard but is wily enough to let you believe he isn't. I think he's always completely aware of everything around him, and this conversation between Rhyson and me is no exception.

"Yeah, we're on our way to eat." I fiddle with the strap on my bag. "Since apparently Grady isn't home either."

"Yeah." Guilt drags Rhyson's one-word reply out. "That was completely unexpected. He—"

"Grip explained," I insert before he rehashes the story I've already heard. "The conference. I know. Things happen. Well, I guess I'll see you at Grady's place ...your place ...tonight," I finally say.

"Great. Can I speak to Marlon?"

"Marlon?" I frown, wondering if I really should have been more cautious before getting in the car. "Um ... someone named Grip picked me up."

Rhyson chuckles, and I notice Grip's mouth hitch to the side, even though he doesn't turn his head.

"Marlon is his real name. You think his mom named him Grip?"

"How would I know what his mom named him?" I laugh and meet Grip's eyes briefly, finding them smiling back at me.

"Here ya go." I proffer my phone. "For you, Marlon."

He stops my heart for a beat with a stretch of white teeth and full lips.

Wow. That's just not fair.

"'Sup, Rhys." He nods, his smile melting a little every few seconds and a small pull of his brows making me wonder what Rhyson's saying. "All right. Yeah. We'll grab something to eat. I got you."

He offers one more grunt and a mumbled "peace" before handing the phone back to me.

"Hey," I say once I have the phone back.

"Yeah. Hey," Rhyson says. "I actually did have dinner planned for us. You still like Mexican?"

"I love Mexican." I'm pleasantly surprised that he remembers.

"Well, maybe we'll get to try this place before you go back, but with the emergency on this project …" He sighs heavily. "Anyway, Marlon will take you to eat and then bring you to Grady's and stay with you till I get home."

"He doesn't need to do that." I hate feeling like a burden to anyone, and right now, I feel like the egg baby project Grip has to keep alive. "I'll be fine on my own."

"Marlon doesn't mind," Rhyson assures me. "He has stuff to do for Grady anyway. He helps with one of his music classes."

I just bet he does. Lies. I glance at Grip's profile, a study in impassivity.

"Gotta go," Rhyson says. "See you later if you're still awake when I get home. I'm sure you're exhausted."

"Yeah. More hungry than anything."

"Marlon will take care of you." A voice in the background interrupts Rhyson. "Hey, I need to go. See you tonight."

"Okay. Tonight." I hold the phone to my ear for a few seconds after he's gone just because I don't want to talk.

I finally drop the phone to my lap, processing the longest conversation I've had with my twin brother in five years. I have no idea what's going through Grip's mind. It's too quiet, so I break the silence with the lightest question I can think of.

"Marlon, huh?" I ask with a smile.

"Only Rhyson calls me by my real name." He keeps his eyes ahead on the road, grimacing good-naturedly. "And my mom."

"And Grip, where'd that come from?"

"I was in a talent show or showcase or some shit when I was a kid." He laughs, shaking his head at the memory. "I had to recite a poem and was so nervous, I kept holding onto the mic even after I was done. Just wouldn't let go. Maybe it was like my safety blanket. Who knows? One of the kids started calling me 'Grip' after the show, and it stuck."

"So even then you were craving the spotlight," I tease.

"I guess so." His smile fades after a few seconds. He looks briefly away from the road and at me. "I don't mind, ya know. Staying, I mean. There's things I can do in the rehearsal room at Grady's house."

I don't bother arguing, because I seriously doubt I'll change his mind now that Rhyson has asked him. I just nod and pretend to check the email on my phone.

"We're here." Grip pulls into a parking space and cuts the engine.

I look up from my phone, surprised to see the length of pier stretching from the shore out over the Pacific Ocean.

"Where's here?"

"Mick's. Jimmy, one of our good friends, works here. Food's good."

"Well, that's all I care about."

As we're walking up the boardwalk toward a sign that reads "Mick's" I feel overdressed. In my sleek leather jacket and ankle boots, both black, I'm so very New York. Everyone's milling around in bikinis, tank tops, board shorts, and flip-flops. Once we're seated at a window booth with an ocean view, I slip the jacket off. I sense more than see Grip's eyes linger on my arms and shoulders bared by the sleeveless shirt under my jacket. I force myself to keep my arms at my side and not cross them over my chest. I block his line of vision with the huge menu and feel as if I can breathe a little easier with it between the heat of his eyes and my skin.

"So what's good?" I ask.

"I get the same thing every time. Burger and fries."

I scrunch my nose, not seeing anything I want, but half-starved enough to settle. Before I can say as much, a set of perky breasts in a green bikini appear beside our table. My eyes do the slow crawl from the girl's hot pink toenails in her wedge heels, over the skimpy cut-off denim shorts and the bikini top, which barely bridles her breasts. Bright blue eyes and blonde hair complete the California package. If all the girls look like this, and a quick glance around Mick's dining room tells me a lot of them do, I may reconsider my secret plan to move here when I graduate.

"Hey, dude." Perky tits leans over to drop a quick kiss on Grip's jaw.

"Jim, what's good, girl?" He slaps her ass, aiming a playful smile up at her. "Been missing you."

Rewind. Jimmy's a girl? Her name tag reads "Jimmi." The "i" would be cuter if I wasn't so hungry.

"I know." Jimmi blows at the blonde bangs brushing her eyebrows. "Between shifts here and gigging all over town, there's been no time to hang."

"Yeah, Rhys and I were just saying the same thing," Grip says. "We need to get everybody together."

"My uncle's beach house!" The blue eyes light up. "He's out of the country and said I could crash there some."

"We need to do that for real."

"We could play Scrabble again," she says. "Remember how much fun we had?"

"You sure you want to play Scrabble?" Grip lifts a skeptical brow. "Why wouldn't I?" She looks confused, or maybe that's always her look. She's very blonde, even if it may be from a bottle, so I can't tell. "You're not really good at it," he says with a grin.

"Why would you say that?" Jimmi's hands go to her hips.

"'Cause you thought 'guffaw' was a character from *Lord of the Rings*."

"Ugh," Jimmi half-groans, half-laughs. "You weren't supposed to tell anybody that."

Oh, my God, guffaw.

Laughter bubbles up in my throat. I try to push it down, but it's no use. It springs from my mouth as a, well . . . guffaw. Jimmi looks a little embarrassed but manages a self-deprecating smile. Grip's laugh matches mine.

"Jim, this is Rhyson's twin sister, Bristol. Bristol, this is Jimmi. She went to high school with Rhys and me."

"Great." Jimmi gives me a wry look. "Now, she'll think I'm an airhead."

I don't deny it and just smile and hold out my hand. "Nice to meet you, Jimmi," I say. "I promise not to tell."

"Well, thanks for that." Jimmi squints an eye and tilts her head, considering me. "Did he say twin sister? I knew Rhyson had a sister, but I had no idea you guys were twins. I see the resemblance."

I'm surprised she's even heard that much about me.

"I live in New York." I attempt a natural smile. "We haven't seen much of each other lately."

Jimmi's smile shrinks, her eyes dropping to the floor.

"Oh, yeah." She nods, avoiding my eyes. "He doesn't get back to New York much, does he?"

"No, not much." I agree quietly since it's obvious she, like everyone else, knows how splintered our family is.

"So where is the maestro?" Jimmi directs the question to Grip. "Last minute remastering with that project he was working on," Grip says.

"Ah." Jimmi nods, a tentative smile on her lips. "I haven't seen him in weeks. I miss him."

"Okay, Jim, you know the deal." Grip's look seems to hold a careful warning.

"I know. I know. You don't have to worry about me." Jimmi waves a dismissive hand in the air and turns back to me. "Did you see anything you want?"

If I'm not mistaken, the anything she wants is my brother, but I just got here, so what do I know? I deliberately shift my eyes to the menu.

"What's good?"

"Let's see." Jimmi leans over my shoulder to consider the menu like she hasn't seen it before. One of her breasts nearly pokes my eye out. I lean back in my seat to avoid a nipple.

"Careful where you aim those things," I say before I catch my wild tongue. I'm great at keeping my thoughts to myself when it counts, but when it doesn't, I don't bother.

Startled blue eyes collide with mine, and I'm not sure if she expects an apology or what, but I just look pointedly from her torpedo tits back up to her face. For a beat, I think I've really offended her, but then she laughs until she has to bend over, giving the customers behind her an eyeful, I'm sure. Grip grins, his eyes affectionate on blonde and breasty.

"Oh, we're gonna be friends." Jimmi wipes the tears at the corner of her eyes. "Watch where I aim . . . that's priceless. Okay. You like seafood?"

"Um, yeah." I blink a few times at the speedy shift of gears. "I love it."

"You like scallops?" She drops her voice to a conspiratorial whisper. "Off-menu item."

"I would kill for scallops." My mouth is already watering, and my empty stomach is already thanking her.

"Your server will be over in a sec, but I'll tell her to hook you up." She winks at me before turning back to Grip. "I'm singing in a little bit. They're finally letting me on stage."

She gestures to a small space set up for live music.

"Nice." Grip's smile reflects genuine pleasure. "'Bout time."

"Don't leave before I'm done." She squeezes his shoulder. "I may have a gig for you."

"For real?" He glances down at his beeping phone, a frown wrinkling his forehead before he returns his attention to Jimmi. "My money isn't nearly long enough. I'll do anything but strip."

Jimmi gives him a head tilt and a come-on-now twist of her lips. "Okay, you got me. For the right price, I probably would strip." A devilish smile crinkles his eyes at the corners. "But not my first choice."

"It's deejaying at Brew. Maybe tomorrow night." Jimmi crosses her arms over the menus pressed to her chest. "Could be a regular gig, for a while at least."

"Cool." Grip's glance strays back to his phone, his tone distracted. "Everything okay?" Jimmi eyes the phone in his hand.

"Yeah." Grip lifts his eyes, splitting a look between the two of us. "Sure. Let's chop it up after your set."

"Okay. How long you here, Bristol?"

"Just a few days. I leave Friday."

"Good!" Jimmi beams. "We'll get to spend some time together." "I'd like that."

Now that I've gotten past the breasts stuffed into the bikini practically assaulting me, I mean what I say. She seems cool. "Good luck on stage."

We've bonded a little over scallops and tits, so my smile for Jimmi comes more naturally.

"Thanks!" she squeals and wiggles her fingers in a wave. "Gotta go get ready."

"So you and Jimmi went to high school with Rhyson?" I ask, watching Jimmi teeter off on her wedge heels.

"I'm sorry. I thought you knew that." Grip shakes his head. "I really did just kind of grab you and toss you in the car."

"It's fine. I appreciate your help." I peel the paper from the straw Jimmi left on the table, focusing on that instead of looking at Grip. "I actually know very little about my brother's life since he left."

"What do you want to know?" Grip relaxes, stretching one arm along the back of the booth.

"Lots I guess." I shrug, keeping my voice casual. "I'll let Rhyson tell me his stuff, but what about you? If you were at the School of the Arts, you must be . . .a musician? Dancer? What?"

"I'm Darla, your server," a petite girl says before Grip can respond. "How you guys doing today?"

"Fine, Darla." Grip flashes her a smile, not even trying to be sexy, but Darla melts a little right where she stands. I practically see the puddle. The lashes around her pretty, brown eyes start batting, and I might be too nauseated to eat my scallops.

"I'm fine, too, Darla." I wave a hand since she seems to have forgotten I'm here. "And actually really hungry. Jimmi mentioned scallops. How are they prepared?"

"Scallops?" Darla's brows pinch. "We don't have scallops on the menu."

"No, she said they were an off-menu item." I hold onto my patience even though my stomach is starting to feed on itself as we speak.

"No, we don't—"

"Darla." Grip grabs her hand, stroking his thumb over her palm. "Maybe you could double-check on the scallops because it seemed like Jimmi knew about them."

After Darla visibly shudders, her smile widens and she leans a little toward Grip.

"I am new," she admits shyly. "I could check on it for you."

"I appreciate that." I give her a gentle reminder that they were actually for me, not the man she's salivating over.

Darla's smile slips just a little as she uses the hand Grip isn't holding to retrieve the pad from her back pocket. Obviously reluctant, she drops Grip's hand to pull the pencil from behind her ear.

"And to drink?" She sounds like she'll have to trek to Siberia to fetch whatever I order.

"Water's fine." I look at the tight circle her irritation has made of her mouth. "Bottled, please."

I wouldn't put it past her to spit in it.

"I always get the Mick's Mighty," Grip pipes up. "And fries. Let's just stick with that. And that new craft beer you guys got in."

"A beer?" Darla squints and grins. "Are you twenty-one?"

"I don't know." Grip doesn't look away, seeming to relish how mesmerized our girl Darla is. "Am I?"

Darla eyes him closely . . .or rather even closer, her eyes wandering over the width of shoulders and slipping to crotch level where his legs spread just a little as he leans back. Darla bites her bottom lip before running her tongue across it. This is just sad. Exactly the kind of behavior that could set the women's movement back decades. In Rochester, New York, Susan B. Anthony is turning over in her grave as Darla licks her lip.

"Um, were you still going to check on the scallops?" I give her a pointed look. I mean, seriously. How does she know Grip and I aren't a couple? I'd be insulted if he were mine. Hell, I'm insulted, and he isn't.

Darla shifts hard eyes back to me, heaving a long-suffering sigh and straightening.

"Yeah. I'll go check on the scallops." Her face softens when she looks back to Grip. "And I'll get your order in."

"The beer?" His smile and those eyes wrapped in all that charisma really should be illegal.

"Okay." Darla giggles but still doesn't ask for his ID. "The new craft coming up."

"Well, that was sad for women everywhere," I mumble.

"Don't blame Darla." Grip's cheeky grin foreshadows whatever outrageous thing he's about to say. "Blame all this chocolate charm."

My laugh comes out as a snort. "I'm guessing that's a self-proclaimed moniker."

"I see you're immune to it, but you do catch more bees with honey." Grip offers this sage, if unoriginal, advice. "Or in my case, with chocolate."

"Where'd you read that? *The Player's Guide to Catching Bees?*"

"No, I learned it the way I learn most things." His eyes dim the tiniest bit. "The hard way."

I'm not sure what to say, so I don't say anything for a few seconds, and neither does he. It should be awkward, but it isn't. Our eyes lock in the comfortable silence.

"So before Darla buzzed through," I pause for effect, waiting for his quickly-becoming-familiar grin, "you were telling me about the School of the Arts. You're a musician?"

"I write and rap."

"As in you're a rapper?"

"Wow, they said you were quick," he answers with a grin.

"Oh, sarcasm. My second language." I find myself smiling even though it's been a crappy day with too many complications and not enough food. "So you rap. Like hoes, bitches, and bling?" I joke.

"At least you're open-minded about it," he deadpans.

"Okay. I admit I don't listen to much hip-hop. So convince me there's more to it."

"And it's my responsibility to convince you . . . why?" he asks with a grin.

"Don't you want a new fan?" I'm smiling back again. "I just doubt it's your type of music."

"We've known each other all of an hour, and already you're assigning me 'types'. Well, I'm glad you have an open mind about me," I say, echoing his smart-ass comment.

I halfway expect him to volley another reply at me, but he just smiles. I didn't anticipate conversation this stimulating. His body, yes. Conversation, no.

"So are you any good?" I ask. "At rapping, I mean."

"Would you know if I were good?" he counters, a skeptical look on his face.

"Probably not." My laugh comes easier than most things have today. "But I might know if you were bad."

"I'm not bad." He chuckles. "I think my flow's pretty decent." "Sorry," I interject. "For the rap remedial in the audience, define flow."

"Define it?" He looks at me as if I asked him to saddle a unicorn. "Wow. You ever assume you know something so well, that it's so basic, you can't think of how to explain it?"

"Let me guess. That's how it is with flow."

"Well, now that you asked me to define it, yeah."

"Just speak really slowly and use stick figures if you need to." Rich laughter warms his eyes. "Okay. Here goes."

He leans forward, resting those coppery-colored, muscle-corded arms on the table, distracting me. I think I really may need stick figures if he keeps looking this good.

"A rapper's flow is like ..." He chews his full bottom lip, jiggling it back and forth, as if the action might loosen his thoughts. "It's like the rhythmic current of the song. Think of it as a relationship between the music and the rapper's phrasing or rhythmic vocabulary, so to speak. You make choices about how many phrases you place in a measure. Maybe you want an urgent feeling, so you squeeze a lot of phrasing into a measure. Maybe you want a laid-back feel, and you leave space; you hesitate. Come in later than the listener expects."

"Okay. That makes sense."

"And the choices a rapper makes, how well the current of that music and his phrasing, his rhythmic vocabulary, work together, that's his flow. Cats like Nas, Biggie, Pac—they're in this rarefied category where their flow is so sick, so complex, but it seems easy. That's when you know a flow is exceptional. When it seems effortless."

"Now I get that." I give him a straight face, but teasing eyes. "I can see how you won your rap scholarship."

"Rap scholarship! It sounds so weird when you say it." He sits back in his seat, a smile crooking his lips. "I actually went for writing. Rapping was kind of Rhyson's idea."

"Rhyson?" Shock propels a quick breath out of me. "What does he know about rap?"

"I'm guessing more than you do." His smile lingers for a second before falling away. "I wrote poetry. That's how I got in. Rhyson was looking for a way to translate his classical piano sound to a more modern audience, so I helped him. And he convinced me that all these poems I had could be raps. The rest is history."

"So you have an album or something?"

"Not yet. Working on a mixtape." He clamps a straw between his teeth. "Also working on paying my rent."

"Thus the Deejaying?"

"Deejaying, sweeping floors for studio time, writing for other artists, doing stuff with Grady." A careless shrug of his shoulders. "Whatever comes, I do."

"You write for other artists?" "Yeah."

"I don't get it. Rappers don't write their own stuff? I thought it was so personal and rooted in where you're from and all that."

"To not know much about hip-hop, you have definite ideas about it," he teases.

"You'll find I have definite ideas about everything." I chuckle because it's true. "Even things I know nothing about."

"Ah, so that's a family trait."

He's so right. Rhyson and I are both obstinate know-it-alls. "Apparently." I nod for him to continue. "You were saying."

"So hip-hop's like any other genre. There are some guys who write everything themselves, and it's like what you're describing. But a club's a club's a club. Love is love. Anybody can write it. So sometimes guys like me, who are kind of writers first, we help."

"Would I know any of the songs you've worked on?"

"Probably not." He grins. "Not because they're not on the radio, but because I doubt you listen to those stations."

"You're making a lot of assumptions about someone you just met. Maybe I know all of them. Try me."

He rattles off four songs. I know none of them. Dammit. I'll have to eat crow, which if Darla doesn't get my scallops, I might gladly do.

When Darla returns and confirms that they can provide my scallops, I place my order. The hurried meal I ate this morning is a distant memory, so I dive in as soon as the food arrives, working my way methodically through every morsel on my plate. I eat the scallops so fast you'd think I sprinkled them with fairy dust to make them disappear.

"Remind me to keep you fed." Grip takes another bite of his burger.

"Very funny." I glance up sheepishly from my empty plate. "How's their dessert?"

We share a slow smile, and I can't remember when I've felt this way with another person. Laughing at each other's jokes, comfortable with each other's silences, calling each other out on our crap.

"Grip." A tall man with dark brown skin and eyes to match stops at our table. "I thought that was you."

"What's good, Skeet?" Grip stands, and they grasp hands, exchanging pats to the back. "Haven't seen you in months. Congrats on the new album."

"Man, thanks." Skeet's eyes flick to me. "Who's the little shawty?"

The little shawty? Does he mean me? Grip catches my eye, apparently finding it funny.

"This is Bristol," he answers with a laugh. "Rhyson's sister." "Rhyson, Rhyson. Who's . . ." Skeet frowns for a second before he remembers. "Oh. That white dude who plays the piano?"

Not exactly how I would describe one of the greatest living classical pianists, but we can go with that.

"Yeah, that's him." Grip's smile appreciates the irony of Skeet's description. "Bristol's visiting for the week."

"Nice." Skeet smiles politely before turning his attention back to Grip. "What'd you think of the album?"

Grip screws his face up, a rueful turn to his mouth.

"That bad?" Skeet demands.

"It was a'ight," Grip concedes. "Honestly, I just know you have something better in you than that."

"Well, damn, Grip," Skeet mumbles. "Why don't you tell me what you really think?"

"Oh, okay. Well, that shit was whack," Grip says.

"Um, I was being sarcastic," Skeet says. "But since we being honest . . ."

"We've known each other too long to be anything but honest. It just felt kind of tired." Grip sits and gestures for Skeet to join us. "Who'd you work with?"

"You know that guy Paul?" Skeet sits and steals one of Grip's fries. "They call him Low."

"That dude?" Grip sips his beer and grimaces. "Figures."

"Well, you ain't been around," Skeet says defensively. "I didn't know if you was still down or whatever."

"Am I still down?" Irritation pinches Grip's face into a frown. "I'm the same dude I've always been. I'm working with anybody who can pay, so don't use that as an excuse."

"Right, right, but you know how some of these niggas go off and get all new on you."

My eyes stretch before I have time to disguise my surprise when he uses the N-word so freely in front of me. I squirm in my seat, sip my water, and try to look invisible. That is one of the worst words in the English language, and I would never use it. I've never said it, and I never will. It's hard for me to understand how people of color use it even casually.

"Well, I ain't new." Grip pulls out his phone. "Let's get some dates down to hit the studio. See if we can write some stuff for your next one."

While they set up studio time, I happily consider the dessert menu. I was totally serious. It feels like I haven't eaten in days, and I have room for more.

"Sorry about that," Grips says once Skeet is gone. "But the struggle is real. Don't work, don't eat, so I work whenever the opportunity presents itself."

"Do you really think his album is weak, or did you just say that to drum up business for yourself?"

"Oh, no. The shit's weak as hell." Grip's deep laugh rolls over me and coaxes a smile to my lips. "I don't lie, especially about music. It's the most important thing in my life. It's my gift, so to me it's almost sacred."

"Now I understand how you and Rhyson became so close," I say wryly. "Music always came first with him. Or at least it used to be. I don't pretend to know him anymore. Not that we've ever been that close."

It's quiet for a moment while I pretend to read the dessert menu.

"You love your brother," Grips says softly, drawing my eyes up to his face. "I know guys like us aren't easy to put up with. We lose ourselves in our music. We neglect everything else in our lives, but don't give up on him. Cut him some slack. He's working his ass off."

"I guess I'm not doing a good job of hiding how hard this is, huh?" I manage a smile.

"Well, I'm also really perceptive."

"Not to mention incredibly modest," I reply.

Laughter comes easily to us again, and something about the way he's considering me across the table makes me think it surprises him as much as it surprises me.

"I am perceptive, though." Grip takes one of the last bites of his burger. "Like your face when Skeet—"

"Dropped the N-word in front of me like it was nothing?" I cut in, knowing exactly where he's going. "Yeah, like what's up with that? I don't understand anyone being okay with that word."

Grip looks at me for a moment before shuttering his eyes, shrugging, and picking up one of his last fries.

"Probably because to him it *is* nothing. I mean, if he says it. If we say it."

"But I couldn't say it, right?" I clarify unnecessarily.

He holds a French fry suspended mid-way to his mouth. "Do you want to say it?" He considers me carefully.

"God, no." My gasp is worthy of a Victorian novel. "Of course not."

"You can tell me." He leans forward, his eyes teasing me conspiratorially. "Not even when you're singing along to the hippity hop and they say it?"

"We've already established that I don't listen to the hippity hop very much," I say wryly.

This is such a sensitive topic, one I'd hesitate to approach with people I know well, much less someone I just met. In conversations like these, before we say our words, they're ammunition. After we've said them, they're smoking bullets. There seems to be no middle ground and too little common ground for dialogue to be productive. We just tiptoe around things, afraid we'll offend or look ignorant, be misunderstood. Honesty is a risk few are willing to take. For some reason, it's a risk I decide to take with Grip.

"I just mean, isn't that a double standard?" I pause to sift through my thoughts and get this question right. "It's such an incendiary word with such an awful history. I completely understand why Black people wouldn't be okay with it at all."

"Well, then you're halfway there."

I shoot him a look from under my lashes, trying to gauge before I go any further if he thinks I'm some weird, entitled white girl asking dumb questions, which I probably am. He's just waiting, though, eyes intent and clear of mockery or judgment.

"So why . ..why should anyone use it? Why put it in songs? Why does Skeet feel okay calling another Black man that?"

"First of all, I'm not one of those people who assumes because I'm Black, I somehow represent every Black person's perspective," Grip says. "So, I'll just tell you how I and the people I'm around most think about it."

He pauses and then laughs a little.

"I guess we don't think about it. It's such a natural part of how we interact with each other." He gives me a wry smile. "Some of us feel like we take the power away from it when we use it."

"Taking the power?" I shake my head, fascinated, but confused. "What does that mean?"

"Like we get to determine how it's used."

He pauses, and I can almost see him weighing the words before they leave his mouth.

"You have to account for intent. It was originally meant to degrade and dehumanize, as a weapon against us, but we reappropriate it as ours and get to use it as we see fit."

"I don't know that I really get that or agree," I admit, hesitant because I've been misunderstood before in these conversations. I'm too curious. I always want to understand, and don't always know when to stop asking.

"Because of our unique history in this country, that word will never be safe for anyone to use to us," he says quietly. "But with all that Black people endured, being able to take that slur back and decide how we want to use it feels like the least we should be allowed. And it's the very definition of entitlement for others to want to use it because we can."

"That I get." I hesitate, wanting to respect his opinion, his honesty even though I don't agree with parts of what he's said. "I guess to me, we have enough that divides us and makes us misunderstand each other. Do we really need one more thing we can't agree on?"

Grip's eyes don't waver from my face, but it's as if he's not as much looking at me, as absorbing what I just said. Processing it.

"That's actually a great point," he says after a few seconds. "I hadn't thought of it like that, and it's good that you ask that question. You're not asking the wrong question. Is it the most important question, though? To me, some guy calls me the N-word, we'll probably fight. I'll kick his ass, and we're done. It's over."

He slants me a cocky grin, and my lips refuse not to smile back. "But I want to hear the same dismay and curiosity," he continues, his smile leveling out. "About the issues that are actually eroding our communities. Let's ask why Black men are six percent of the general population and nearly forty percent of the prison population. Let's get some outrage over people of color getting longer sentences for the same crimes other people commit. And over disproportionate unemployment and poverty."

His handsome face settles into a plane of sharp angles, bold lines, and indignation.

"I can fight a dude who calls me the N-word," he says. "It's harder to fight a whole system stacked against me."

The passion and conviction coming off him in waves cannon across the table and land on my chest, ratcheting up my heartbeat.

"It's not bad that you ask why we call each other that, Bristol." The sharp lines of his face soften. "There's just bigger issues that actually affect our lives, our futures, our children, and that's what we want to talk about."

Nothing in his eyes makes me feel guilty for asking, and I think that he wants me to understand as much as I want to.

"When other people are as outraged and as curious about those problems as Black people are," he says, "then maybe we can solve them together."

It's quiet for a few moments as we absorb each other's perspectives. My mind feels stretched. As if someone, this man, took the edges of my thoughts and pulled them in new directions, to new proportions.

"Now that I get," I finally say softly. "You're right. Those things are more important, and that's powerful."

I look up and grin to lighten the moment.

"But don't think you've changed my mind about the N-word. That still doesn't make sense to me."

He leans forward with a wide smile, his eyes alive and dark and bright all at once. And I wonder if this is the most stimulating conversation he's had in a long time. It is for me.

"Is there anything that you don't completely know how it works or why it works, but you know the rules that govern it?" he asks.

"Um, Twitter?" I laugh, glad when he responds with a smile. "Then the N-word is your Twitter."

He sits back in his seat, long legs stretched under the table, arms spread on the back of the booth, and a smile in his eyes for me.

"You may have me halfway to understanding that," I say. "But you will not get me to be okay with the misogyny that is such a part of hip-hop culture."

"I don't disrespect women in my lyrics," he says immediately. "My mom would kill me."

"Well, maybe I'll listen to some of your stuff."

"I feel honored that you would deign to listen to my music."

I toss a napkin across the table at him, and it bounces harmlessly off his face. He throws it back at me and laughs.

"I mean, for real," he says. "What kind of self-respecting, white millennial doesn't listen to hip-hop?"

He laughs when I roll my eyes at him.

"Are you one of those people who thinks hip-hop belongs to Black people?" I ask.

"Of course it does." He smooths the humor from his expression. "We made it. It's ours in the same way jazz and the blues and R&B are ours. We innovated, making sound where there was no sound before. The very roots of hip-hop are in West Africa from centuries ago. But we share our shit all the time, so you're welcome."

I lift a brow at his ethno-arrogance, but he throws his head back laughing at me, maybe at himself.

"Art, specifically music, is a living thing," he says. "It isn't just absorbed by the people who hear it, but it absorbs them. So, we shared hip-hop with the world, and it isn't just ours anymore. The Beastie Boys heard it. Eminem heard it. Whoever heard it fell in love with it, added to it, and became a part of it."

"And that's a good thing?"

"Mostly. If that hadn't happened, if we hadn't shared it and someone other than us loved it, it'd still be niche. Underground. Now it's global, but that wouldn't have happened if it hadn't gone mainstream. Mainstream means more opportunities, so I'm all for white, Asian, Hispanic. We need everybody buying hip-hop, because ultimately, it's about that green."

He rubs imaginary dollars between his fingers before going on.

"I think some fear that when hip-hop goes mainstream, it's mixed with other influences. It's diluted, and I get that, but we have to evolve. That isn't selling out. That's survival."

The way he talks about music and art fascinates me. Rhyson's talent, his genius, always isolated him from me. I've been around musicians all my life, but with no talent of my own, I was always on the outside and couldn't figure out how to get in. Grip just shared that with me. He let me in.

Before I can dig anymore, Jimmi takes the stage for her performance. And when I say she takes the stage, she takes it. She owns it. She overpowers the small space, and you know she's something special.

"Wow." I spoon into the fudge brownie and ice cream I ordered during Jimmi's set. "She can back those tits up, huh?"

"She definitely can," Grip says. "And speaking of double standards, I think you have one criticizing hip-hop for its misogyny and then hating on another woman just because she has a great rack. Is it any worse when men judge women's worth by their looks than when women do it?"

He's serious. At first, I think he's joking, but then I realize his eyes hold a subtle rebuke. He's protective of Jimmi. Maybe they're together? The thought sours the ice cream in my mouth, and it shouldn't. I've known this guy for all of a couple hours. And he isn't my type. And I'm leaving in a week.

"I wasn't judging her."

His look and the twist of his lips say otherwise.

"Okay, maybe I was judging her a little bit." I laugh and am glad when he laughs, too. "She's a pretty girl, and sometimes they get a bad rap."

"They?" Grip lifts his thick brows. "Do you not realize how beautiful you are?"

I have no idea how to respond. I'm attractive. I know that. Guys have been hitting on me since middle school.

"Whatever." I shrug. "I just don't define myself by my looks. There's a lot more to me than that."

"I believe you," Grip says. "I'm just saying there's a lot more to Jimmi, too, so maybe you guys have a lot in common. And maybe you should withhold judgment until you know her better. If not altogether."

I'm quiet while I finish my brownie and think about what he said. He has a point. One I hadn't considered. I had to leave my Ivy League college to get the most thought-provoking, stimulating conversation I've had in ages. Maybe ever. And with a rapper. Jimmi isn't the only one there's more to than meets the eye.

Four

Grip

I FIGURED RHYSON'S SISTER WOULD BE ATTRACTIVE. I MEAN, THEY'RE twins, and he's one of those guys girls trip all over themselves for. And I knew she went to an Ivy League college, so of course she's smart. But Bristol is all kinds of things I could not have anticipated or prepared for. Her curiosity, her authenticity, and her honesty hook something in me and draw me closer. I didn't expect the conversation we had at Mick's to go where it did. I loved that she wasn't afraid to wade through the difficult questions of race, and that she gave measured, thoughtful responses and expected the same from me. Those are tough conversations to have with someone you know, much less with someone you just met, but it felt like nothing was off-limits. As if I could give her room to be naïve and she could give me room to be obnoxious. We both gave each other space to be misunderstood, because we really wanted to understand.

I admit only to myself that I'm drawn to her in a way that is dangerous because she's Rhyson's sister. Starting something that can't go anywhere could be awkward down the road. I'm not that guy. Usually I fuck them and then I leave them. That's it. That's all. And I can't do that to Rhyson's sister.

The string of text messages reminds me there's a girl I'm trying to leave even now. I've been dating Tessa for two months, but we haven't really talked in the last couple of weeks. She blew my mind the first time we had sex, and her pussy put some kind of hex on me and made me agree to "dating." Well, that hex has worn off. I told her we probably need to take a break, but she either wasn't hearing me or was ignoring me. When I tell a girl we need to take a break, that's code for there's this other chick I'm feeling so we should cut this off before I do something we'll both regret. I wish I could just let it fade, but I'm going to have to actually break it off. She keeps hitting me up, so it seems like that conversation will have to happen soon.

I steal a glance across at Bristol, who's slumped in the passenger seat with her head dropped to an awkward angle while she sleeps. She probably wouldn't give me the time of day anyway. Rhyson's so unassuming that you'd never know he comes from deep pockets. Old money and new. He turned his back on that life to emancipate from his parents, but Bristol still occupies that world. A guy like me, driving this piece of shit Jeep, sweeping floors, and doing odd jobs to make ends meet—no way would she check for me. She doesn't even listen to hip-hop. She probably hasn't ever dated a Black guy, and I wouldn't be the exception.

Now me? I like to think of myself as an equal opportunity connoisseur. My dick is not so much color blind, as it loves every color. And I have a rainbow coalition fuck record to prove it. If it's wet and tight, I don't really care what color it is.

Crude, I know.

Maybe that's an issue of race I won't explore with Bristol. I'm sure she has her limits.

I pull up in front of my apartment complex. I'm kind of glad Bristol's asleep. Maybe I can sneak inside and get back out to the car before she wakes up. I need to grab my laptop for the tracks I'll work on while I'm at Grady's. I wouldn't have stopped otherwise. We joked at the airport about her suitcase being bigger than my apartment. She isn't far off.

I'm carefully, quietly opening the driver side door when she stirs.

"Hey." She sits up and stretches her arms over her head, straining the tank top against her breasts. "Where are you going?"

My mouth goes dry when her nipples pucker through the thin material. I can resist her for my best friend. Bristol and Rhyson may not be close, but she is still his sister. A pretty face and a great set of tits aren't worth any possible static with him. I may need to sticky note that over my mirror this week, though.

"Oh, you're up." I lean through the window. "I just need to run inside my apartment and grab something before we head to Grady's."

"Can I use your bathroom?"

Shit. I mentally run through the disaster area that is my tiny apartment. I'll be lucky if a roach doesn't greet us at the door.

"Um, sure. Come on."

When we cross the landing, I remind myself I have nothing to be ashamed of. I pay my rent. I'm making my own way and not breaking any laws. I have the integrity of my art, not selling out for the quick buck, but holding out for the right opportunity. It all sounds hollow when Bristol, in her lambskin leather and designer distressed jeans, blows into my one-room apartment on a cloud of expensive perfume.

"Through there." I point to the tiny bathroom off the one room that encompasses the kitchen, living room, and bedroom. The brochure called it "studio," but hovel is probably a more accurate description.

Bristol's sharp eyes wander over the threadbare thrift store couch and the Dollar Store dishes in the drying rack. The disarray of my narrow, un-made bed, which is flush against a wall, mocks me.

"Could you hurry up?" I ask curtly. "We need to get going."

Her startled eyes stare back at me for a moment before she moves quickly to the bathroom. I grab my laptop and am already standing by the door when she comes out.

"There wasn't a towel." She holds up her dripping hands.

"Oh, sorry." I take the few strides to the kitchen and grab a roll of paper towels on the counter for her.

She dries her hands and tosses the used paper towels into the trash. Instead of following me back to the door, she leans against the counter.

"I thought you were tired." I shift from one foot to the other, back prop-ping the door open. "Let's go."

"I have that same print." She nods to the poster of Nina Simone hanging on the wall over my bed. "She was an excellent pianist, and my mother loves her."

My shoulders, which have been tight since we pulled up in front of my dump apartment, relax an inch.

"Yeah?" is my only response.

Bristol nods and walks over to my turntable against the far wall, running her fingers over the dust cover. "You use this to deejay?"

I'm standing here holding the door open for her to leave, and she's con-ducting an inspection.

"Uh, yeah."

"You're still deejaying tomorrow at that place Jimmi was talking about?" She looks up from the turntable, apparently in no hurry to leave. "Brew?"

"Yeah, that's what I'll use for some of the set. I prefer vinyl, but most setups nowadays are completely digital." I sigh and nod my head out to the hall. "Look, we better get going."

"What's the hurry? Rhyson's at the studio and Grady's at his retreat all week. Just an empty house waiting for us."

"I'm ready to go. I have better things to do than give a perfect stranger a grand tour of my place when I need to be working."

Hurt strikes through her eyes so quickly, I almost miss it. She lowers her lashes and walks toward me without addressing my rudeness. She's squeezing past me in the doorway when my conscience reprimands me. I grab her elbow to stop her from leaving, tucking her into the doorway, too.

"Hey." My hand slides down her arm to take her hand. "I'm sorry. I'm an asshole. I didn't mean to snap at you. I don't know why I did that."

She looks up at me, her back against one side of the doorframe, mine against the other. With her coming where she's from, and me coming from where I'm from, there should be a vast ocean separating us, filled with our differences and all the reasons we should never meet on shore. But there's only this wedge of charged space between our bodies that seems to be shrinking by the second. What should be foreign feels familiar. When I assume I know something, she surprises me.

"You have nothing to be ashamed of," she says softly. "I'm sorry I made that crack at the airport about my suitcase being bigger than your apartment.
"

"I actually said that," I remind her, pulling up a smile from somewhere.

"Whatever." She waves a dismissive hand, grinning just the smallest bit in return. "My point is that I'm a spoiled bitch sometimes. I can't blame you for assuming I would judge your place. I just want you to know that I don't. Hearing all the things you do on the side so you can pursue your craft, I admire that kind of commitment."

"Thank you." I look at her, cataloging her features one by one and realizing the most fascinating thing about this girl isn't visible to the naked eye.

"When you're rich and famous, you'll look back on this time—this apartment—and laugh. And appreciate how far you've gone."

"You haven't even heard my stuff." I scoff and smile. "How do you know I'll be successful?"

"My brother's a genius. You must be talented or he wouldn't make time for you." Her lips twist just the slightest bit. "Believe me, I know from personal experience how little time Rhyson has for the mediocre."

"So you don't sing or play?"

Her face lights up with genuine humor.

"Much to the dismay of all my music instructors. Everyone thought they'd get a female version of Rhyson."

"And you . . ." I lift my brows, waiting for her to tell me what they got.

"Can't carry a tune in a bucket or a note in my pocket to save my life," she says. "I tried the clarinet, and was only . . . I think the word my instructor used to describe me was 'adequate.'"

"It can't be that bad. I mean, Grady and Rhyson are both obviously incredible musicians. Your parents played themselves, didn't they, before they started managing?"

"Yes, they all play, which makes me the ugly duckling."

I don't even realize that my hand has lifted to brush my knuckle across the slant of her cheekbone until it's done. Her eyes widen, but she doesn't pull away. Her skin is like warm silk to touch.

"Ugly? I doubt that." My voice comes out all deep and husky. If I keep this up, I'll be excusing myself to jerk off in the tiny bathroom. "We better go."

I drop my hand from her face and clear my throat. I need to stay focused, not on her face and body and that clever brain, but on getting out of here without spreading her out on my unmade bed.

Five

Bristol

I'VE READ THE SAME LINE SEVERAL TIMES. MY LAPTOP COULD BE UPSIDE down and I probably wouldn't notice. I'm sitting here on the couch with my computer propped on my knees, not making any headway on the essay for my internship application. I could blame fatigue considering I haven't really stopped since I left New York this morning. And my body clock may still be on East Coast. And I am getting hungry again. I could use those excuses for my lack of focus, but there's only one real reason if I'm honest.

Grip.

He's an unexpected fascination, a tantalizing riddle I keep turning over in my head. I keep hoping he'll make sense eventually, but then I'm somehow glad he doesn't add up or behave the way I think he should.

If he were in the same room, I'd still be surreptitiously gawking, stealing glances at one of the most beautiful men I've ever seen, but he's in Grady's music room working on his own stuff. He went there almost immediately after we arrived, and I haven't heard a peep from him since. I guess he is as obsessed with music as my brother. Yet another reason not to venture too deeply into the attraction I feel for him.

"Not that he's here," I mumble. "He isn't much company."

I'm the one who said he doesn't have to keep me company, and now I'm complaining because he isn't. Maybe I imagined the charged moment at his apartment in the doorway. He touched my cheek. It was barely a brush of his fingers over my face, but it ignited ...something. Emotion? Desire? I'm not sure, but I haven't felt it before. Based on what I've seen of the player and his "chocolate charm," I shouldn't be feeling anything at all if I know what's good for me.

I learned early on that people aren't careful with your emotions. They're too self-involved to consider how their actions affect others. I saw it when my parents forced Rhyson to tour, even though it was ripping our family apart. I've seen it in Rhyson's own disregard for our relationship and how easy it was for him to walk away, forgetting he had a twin sister on the other side of the country. I've seen it in my parents' sham of a marriage. They're partners, but I'm not sure they genuinely care for one another at all. Certainly there isn't any love. I protect my heart because no one else will.

Sometimes I wish I didn't have a heart at all because, despite knowing what I know, I keep putting it out there to my family. Here I am, visiting Rhyson and willing to move after graduation if he'll have me. I used to be afraid I'd be like my parents, careless. Now, I fear that I care too much about people who don't give a damn.

"Machiavelli?" Grip's voice, as deep and rich as espresso, caresses the nape of my neck from behind, making me jump. "Interesting choice."

I look from the sharply hewn lines of his face to the flashing cursor behind Machiavelli's name on my screen.

"Sorry." He walks around to sit beside me on the couch. "Didn't mean to startle you."

I set my laptop on the coffee table and scoot a few inches away, tucking myself into the corner of the couch. I wasn't doing a good job focusing when he was in the other room. With the breadth of his shoulders, the stretch of his muscular legs, and the towering energy he brought with him, I give up. I'll work on it tomorrow. A thrill passes through me at the prospect of another conversation with him. I'm not one of those giddy girls who gets all breathless when a guy comes around. And yet, with those caramel-colored eyes resting on my face, I'm short of breath.

"Isn't this spring break?" Grip crooks a grin at me and leans into the opposite corner of the couch. "Seems like even Ivy League should get some time off."

"Oh, I'm taking some time off for sure." I tuck my legs under me.

Since I exchanged my jeans for some old cut-offs, I have to pretend not to notice him looking a little too long at my bare legs. The last thing I need is to get the idea that he likes me.

"So, you write essays about Machiavelli to relax?"

"Not exactly." I laugh and scoop my hair up into a topknot. "I'm applying for an internship. The application is due next week, and I need to finish the essay."

"What's the essay on?"

"I have to write about an icon of power from history."

"And you chose Machiavelli?" He chuckles, considering me from beneath the long curl of his lashes. "Remind me not to get on your bad side."

"You know much about him?"

He pulls his T-shirt up from the hem, and my heart pops an artery or something because it shouldn't be working this hard while at rest. I swallow hard at the layer of muscle wrapped around his ribs. One pectoral muscle peeks from under the shirt, tipped with the dark disc of his nipple. My mouth literally waters, and I can't think beyond pulling it between my lips and suckling him. Hard.

"Do you see it?" he asks.

"Huh?" I reluctantly drag my eyes from the ladder of velvet-covered muscle and sinew to the expectant look on his face. "See what?"

"The tattoo." He runs a finger over the ink scrawled across his ribs.

Makavelli.

"I hate to break it to you," I say with a smirk. "But someone stuck you with a permanent typo."

He laughs, dropping the shirt, which is really a shame because I was just learning to breathe with all that masculine beauty on display.

"Bristol, stop playing. You know it's on purpose, right?"

"Oh, sure, it is, Grip." I roll my eyes. "Nice try."

"Are you serious?" He looks at me like I'm from outer space. "You know that's how Tupac referred to himself on his posthumous album, right? That he misspelled it on purpose?"

I clear my throat and scratch at an imaginary itch on the back of my neck. "Um . . . yes?"

His warm laughter at my expense washes over me, and it's worth being the butt of the joke, because I get to see his face animated. He's even more handsome when he laughs.

"You're funny." He laughs again, more softly this time. "I didn't expect that."

"Why not?" I frown. "Did Rhyson make me sound like I wasn't any fun?"

"He hasn't said much at all, actually."

I figured I wasn't paramount in his mind, but it hurts to hear how little Rhyson has told his friends about me. Even when I resented my parents lavishing all their attention and love on my brother, I was proud of him. I told anyone who would listen about how talented he was. How he traveled all over the world. I wanted everyone to know. Again, my heart is a scale out of balance, with my end taking all the weight.

"I didn't mean it that way," Grip says after a moment of my silence. "I can tell you and Rhyson have a lot to work out."

"If he ever comes home, I'm sure we will." I search for something to shift the attention again. "So, you're a Tupac fan?"

"That would be an understatement. Fanatic is more like it."

"Even I know the Biggie–Tupac debate," I say with a slight smile. "I guess I don't have to ask where you fall."

"Oh, Pac, all day, every day." Grip's passion for the subject lights his eyes. "I mean, I give Biggie his props, but Pac was a poet, and truly had something to say. He was unflinchingly honest in his commentary on social justice and the state of his community. He was brilliant."

"You don't talk like most rappers I know." I smile because I hear how bad it sounds, but I somehow feel like I can say it to him even ineloquently.

"And we've already established that you know so many rappers." He crosses his arms over his chest, the cut of his muscles flexing with the movement. "Some of your best friends are rappers. You're so down."

His dark eyes glint with humor.

"Don't make fun of me." I fake pout.

"But it's so much fun." He fake pouts back. "I meant it as a compliment."

"Yes, but by comparison it would be an insult to other rappers, right?" He's half-teasing, half-challenging.

"I don't enjoy this logic thing you're doing. It's making me seem narrow-minded."

"If the mind fits," he comes back with a smirk.

"I should be irritated with you for calling me out." I try to keep my face stern.

"And I should be disgusted by your preconceived notions." He glances up from under his long lashes, his mouth relaxed, not quite smiling. "But I'm not."

"And why is that?" I ask softly, my breath held hostage by the look in his eyes under hooded lids. I want to look away. I should, but he should first, and he doesn't. So we're both trapped in a moment, unsure of how to do the thing we should do. When I feel like my nerves will snap from the heated tension, he clears his throat.

"Um, I thought you might be getting hungry again." He stands without answering my question, running both hands over the closely cut wave of his hair. "Wanna order something? Pizza? Thai?"

"Anybody do good empanadas around here?"

"You kidding me?" He pulls out his phone and smiles. "This is LA. If there's anything we have, it's good Mexican."

We order and are eating in Grady's kitchen within the hour. I sip the beer he grabbed from Grady's refrigerator.

"This is good."

"So you like Mexican," he says.

"Empanadas especially." I eye the last one in the Styrofoam tray on the marble island centered in Grady's kitchen.

"The way you're looking at that empanada is very *Lord of the Flies*. Like I might have to fight you for it. Like it's the conch."

"So are you Piggy in this analogy?" I pour false indignation into my voice and prop my fists on my hips.

"I ain't Jack."

I snatch the last empanada before he has a chance to, and he throws his head back laughing, shoulders shaking.

"To be so skinny, you put it away," he says once he's finished laughing at me.

"Skinny?" I glance at my legs in the cut-offs. "I'm not skinny."

"Okay, do you prefer slim?"

"I guess you're all 'I like big butts and I cannot lie.'"

"You know, that's the only hip-hop reference you've gotten right all day, and it's from like ninety-two."

"That's not fair." I clear away the cartons and paper from our delivery meal. "If I ask you about songs I like, you probably wouldn't know them, either."

"Wrong. I would shut you down." He takes his phone out of his pocket and puts it on the counter. "Check my playlists."

I look at him for an extra few seconds, and he tips his head in invitation toward the phone.

"Go for it."

I sigh but grab his phone and scroll through his songs. Coldplay, Alanis Morissette, Jay Z, Usher, Justin Timberlake, Lil Wayne, U2, Talib Kweli, Jill Scott.

"Carrie Underwood?" I glance up from his phone to meet his wide grin.

"First of all, the girl's fine as hell. Second of all, who doesn't like 'Jesus, Take the Wheel'?"

"Oh, my God! You're ridiculous."

"We've talked a lot about my musical tastes today, but not about yours. I showed you mine, now show me yours."

I will not think about him showing me his. I wonder, not for the first time today, if I packed my good vibrators.

"Let's just say my playlist would be a lot less varied," I offer, dissembling all thoughts of the muscular physique hidden beneath his clothes.

"White bread, huh?" His knowing smile should irritate me, but I find myself answering with one of my own.

"And what would you call yours?"

"Multi-grain."

I shake my head, dispose of the trash, and head back into the living room. I sit on the couch but don't make a move to pick up my laptop. When I look up, there's uncertainty on his face.

"Are you gonna work or . . ." His question dangles in the air waiting for me to catch it.

"No, someone told me even Ivy League should relax on spring break."

He laughs and takes his spot in the opposite corner of the couch. "Rhyson should be home soon," he says.

I'd almost forgotten to be irritated with my brother. Grip does a great job distracting me.

"It'll be good to see him again." I sit cross-legged on the couch and palm my knees. "I'm glad he found you guys out here. He needed somebody in his life."

"We're as close as brothers," Grip says softly. "I probably wouldn't have made it through those first few years of high school without him. That school was like a foreign country."

"Was it so different from your old one?"

"Uh, night and day. Growing up in Compton is no joke." The quick-to-smile curve of his lips settles into a sober line. "The School of the Arts required a completely different set of survival skills. I've learned to navigate any world I find myself in. Be whatever I need to be for every situation."

"You adapted?"

"Had to. Constantly." Grip chuckles just a little. "It was tough, but it taught me to be comfortable, even in environments where there's no one else like me. I got whiplash trying to be one thing at school and another thing at home with my friends and family."

He shrugs.

"So I just decided to be myself. To adapt, yeah, but never lose who I am."

"That's cool," I say. "It took me longer to figure that out. Sometimes I think I still am."

We both tuck our private thoughts into the silence that follows my confession.

"Well, being myself comes and goes." Grip gives me a smile that takes some of the heaviness out of the room. "We're always tempted to be something else when it's easier. My mom was determined for me to go to that school, but she always challenged me to stay true to who I was."

"It's just the two of you?"

"Yeah, always has been." He leans forward, elbows on knees as he speaks. "She is the single most influential force in my life. She demanded so much from me. Wanted more for me than most guys from my neighborhood end up having."

"Sounds like you guys are really close."

"We are. When my teacher realized I could write, she pushed for the scholarship. If it were left to me, I never would have tried. I didn't want to leave my friends and go to a school across town with a bunch of rich, uppity kids. That was how I thought of it then."

He glances up from the floor, his eyes crinkling at the corners. "My mom dragged me up to that school for the entry exams and sat there while I took every test."

My mother probably never even knew one of my teachers' names in school. I'm the "privileged" one, considering our wealth growing up, but I feel positively deprived as Grip talks about the active role his mother took in his upbringing, in his life.

"She used to give me a supplemental book list every school year. Books she said the schools wouldn't teach. She said, 'Don't wait for nobody to give you nothing. Even your education you have to take. If the one they offer you isn't enough, make your own.'"

"Is that how you're so well-read? Or at least seem to be." I raise my brows at him. "Or maybe that's just how you pick up the smart girls?"

"Are you a smart girl, Bristol?" His voice fondles my name.

"You can't turn off the flirt, can you?" I ask to distract myself from the fact that it's working.

"Was I flirting?" He lifts one brow. "I wasn't trying to. I wasn't gonna bother because I assumed you weren't into the brothers."

A puff of air gets trapped in my throat as I try to draw a deep breath. I cough, aware of his eyes on me the whole time.

"That isn't how I decide who I'm 'into', as you call it," I say once I've cleared my airway.

"You telling me you've dated a Black guy before?" Surprise colors the look he gives me. Surprise and something else. Something warmer.

I wish I could surprise him, but I can't.

"No, I've never dated a Black guy." An imp prompts my next comment. "What am I missing?"

The warmth overtakes the surprise in his eyes, spiking to a simmer that heats the gold in his brown eyes molten.

"Oh, you don't want to know." Grip's voice goes a shade darker. "It might spoil you for all the others."

"You think so?" A sensual tension sifts into the air between us. "They say once you go Black." He stretches out his smile. "You won't go back."

A laugh pops out of my mouth before I can check it. "And that's your experience? Have you been disappointed by the rest of the female rainbow?"

My pulse slows while I wait for him to respond, like if my heart hammers I might miss an inflection in his voice. He puts me on high alert.

"Oh, no. By no means." Grip leans back, considering me from under heavy eyelids. "I don't care what color a girl is. I like the color of smart, the shade of funny, and sexy is my favorite hue."

"If that isn't a line, then I don't know what it is," I scoff, but his words tie a band around my chest that makes it harder to breathe.

"I'm not wasting my lines on you. You're the kind of girl who wouldn't respond to bullshit anyway."

He assesses me shrewdly, and for a moment, I feel like he's pushed up under my shell, insinuated himself under my skin to see the very bones no one has ever been privy to.

"So what color am I then?" I ask before thinking better of it. He'll probably just say I'm white, obviously.

"What color are you?" he repeats, his eyes never leaving my face. "You, Bristol, are a freaking prism."

Six

Grip

/ NEED TO PUT THE BRAKES ON THIS.

It's one thing to be secretly attracted to Rhyson's sister. It's another thing altogether to encourage her attraction to me.

And Bristol is attracted to me.

I know when a girl wants a taste. Some girls I look at and immediately know they're slurpers. They'll eat the soup and tip the bowl up, slurping greedily till the last drop. Bristol . . . she would eat you slowly, savor you in delicate bites until there's nothing left of you but an empty plate. And then she would lick her fingers. She's very sensual. It's subtle, but I notice these things. The way she lifted her hair off her neck at lunch today to feel the ocean breeze. The way she explored the ridges of the empanada with her tongue before taking a bite, groaning when the flavors flooded her mouth. Her body seeks sensation, presses in to discover what the world offers to stimulate her. I don't think she knows it about herself, and it's a shame some man hasn't taught her, but I can't be that guy.

Though, I'd make an excellent instructor.

For the second time today, I find myself watching her sleep. I don't watch chicks sleep, not even after I fuck them. It's usually more of a . . . dilemma. More like . . . well, this is awkward. I really don't want her to stay, but she fell asleep. My dick put her into a semi-coma, so I should at least let her sleep it off. That kind of thing. Certainly not noticing how her eyelashes make half-moon shadows on her cheeks. Or the satiny texture of her skin. Or the constellation of almost indiscernible freckles splattered across her nose because she was out in the sun today. I certainly wouldn't be wondering if somehow she might be dreaming about me.

We talked. That's the problem with this girl. She doesn't just talk. She probes. She ponders. She wonders. She asks. She carries on a helluva conversation, which from my experience, is a lost art. We talked about our childhoods, high school, our aspirations, and our dreams. My favorite show of all time, *The Wire*. Her favorite show of all time, *West Wing*. How neither of us has ever seen *How I Met Your Mother*, and don't understand *Two and a Half Men*. She can't believe I've never seen *Swingers*. I can't believe she's never seen *Purple Rain*. We talked about things we don't understand and aren't sure we ever will. Things we thought we had figured out, only to realize we didn't know jack shit. It feels fresh like a beginning, but it also feels like we've known each other for years.

It's two o'clock in the morning, and her body's on East Coast, so of course, she eventually succumbed to exhaustion, but even then, she fought it, drifting off mid-sentence. And dammit, if I don't want to wake her up and ask what she was about to say.

This is bad.

This is really bad.

The garage door opening snaps me out of my own tangled thoughts. I get up from the couch, moving as quietly as I can so I don't wake her. Rhyson's coming through the garage door just as I enter the kitchen. Fatigue sketches lines around his mouth. His eyes are dulled by all the day behind him and the non-stop work it involved.

"Dude." He walks over and daps me up before slumping into one of the high stools at the kitchen island. "Shitty, shitty day. These execs don't know what they want, and don't know what they don't want until you've spent hours making it. Anyway, thanks for picking up Bristol and taking care of her today."

"No problem." I lean against the wall, noting all the similarities between his face and Bristol's. I was struck by how alike they are in other ways, too. Rhyson and I also connected right away when we were both new guys. I shouldn't be surprised to feel a quick and deep connection with his twin sister, but I still am.

"Where is she?" Rhyson gets up to open the refrigerator, staring at its contents for a few seconds before turning to face me.

"In the living room." I tip my head in that direction. "Knocked out."

"On that couch? She'll regret it in the morning. I'll get her to the guest room."

He closes the fridge and sits down again. I can't tell if it's nerves about seeing his sister after so long, or that frenetic energy we feel after being immersed in our music for so long. You're exhausted, but you're on this high and can't settle right away.

"Yeah, she was pretty tired," I say. "We had lunch at Mick's."

"For real?" Rhyson glances up, a slight quirk to his lips. "How's Jim?"

"Still feeling you." I roll my eyes but have to laugh. She's been into Rhyson since tenth grade, but he's never given her the time of day.

"Not gonna happen." He shakes his head for emphasis. "We're such good friends. Why does she want to spoil it with fucking?"

"I usually like it when girls 'spoil' things with fucking." We both laugh at my half-joke. "But in Jimmi's case, I know what you mean. Just friends."

"Right, and that isn't changing." Rhyson runs his hands through his already-disheveled hair. "How is she? My sister, I mean?"

"Go see for yourself," I say. "When was the last time you saw her?" "Four, five years," Rhyson mumbles, sliding his glance to the side, not so much, it seems, to avoid my eyes as to avoid something inside himself.

"Man, how'd you go that long without seeing your twin sister?" "You know how things went down with my parents after I emancipated." Defensiveness stiffens his voice and his back.

"Your parents, Rhys, not your sister."

"Same thing." Rhyson's shrug is supposed to look careless, but it doesn't. He cares. "She's been under their roof all this time. She's probably just like my mother."

The girl I spent the day with is nothing like the she-dragon Rhyson described his mother to be.

"Maybe she isn't," I say. "Or maybe you never spent enough time with her to know her in the first place."

"Is that what she told you?" Rhyson narrows his eyes. "If we didn't spend time together, it wasn't my fault. She got to go to school and parties and shop and have friends. Be normal. Do whatever the hell she wanted while my parents tracked my every step, dragging me all over the world like a show pony."

"I just can't imagine not seeing my family for that long, at least not my sister, if I had one, much less my twin sister."

"Yeah, but you've got your mom and Jade and your aunts. You have a normal family. I've got the Borgias."

"Normal?" A snort of disbelieving air whooshes past my lips. "I'm pretty sure my Uncle Jamal was a real life pimp at some point."

"Dude, you may be right." Humor lightens his expression for the first time since he came through the garage door.

"Seriously! You'd get arrested doing half the stuff he tells you to do to girls."

We laugh, recalling all the slightly disturbing advice my uncle often dispenses about women.

"Okay, so maybe your family isn't completely normal," he concedes. "But you have to admit, mine is the freak show that everyone had tickets to."

Even before I met Rhyson, I'd seen the news about the courtroom battle he endured to emancipate from his parents. The sensationalized details were inescapable, plastered on the front page of every tabloid for weeks.

"I just don't know what she wants from me," Rhyson says softly, his eyes unfocused as if he's asking himself.

"I think she wants her brother back."

I straighten from the wall and walk over to join him at the counter so I can talk softer in case she wakes up and hears.

"Seems like she's missed you," I say in a low tone, looking at him intently. "She seems hurt that you let it go this long and haven't been really responsive when she reached out before."

"I just didn't know where she stood," Rhyson says. "Battle lines were drawn, and I thought she took my parents' side. To survive, I had to distance myself from everything associated with them."

Rhyson looks haunted for a moment, like he's seen a ghost. I know the ghost is actually himself when he first left home, addicted to prescription drugs and barely able to function.

"Maybe you should just tell her that," I say. "Maybe that's the quickest way to a fresh start."

"Maybe." Rhyson rolls his shoulders and sighs. "So, what's she look like?"

Beautiful.

"Um . . . good," I say instead, clearing my throat and dropping my eyes to study the swirling pattern in the countertop. "She looks good."

It's so quiet that I finally look up to find Rhyson staring a burning hole through my forehead. We know each other too well.

"She's my sister, Marlon." A warning lights his eyes. "Don't mess with her. None of that chocolate charm shit you put on these other unsuspecting girls."

"I wouldn't." I steel my voice against the doubt I have even in myself. I should be able to leave Bristol alone, but after today, I'm not sure that I will. But I'm not admitting that to my best friend until I absolutely have to.

"Not that I have to worry about you since you're"—he throws up air quotes—"'taken'. Aren't you and Tessa still a thing?"

I just shrug, too tired to discuss the complication of disentangling myself from Tessa.

"Not for much longer," I settle for saying and leave it at that.

When we go back into the living room, Bristol's in the same spot as when I left her. She's pulled her knees under her and tucked her hands under the cheek laid against the couch. I draped a blanket over her, but it's slipped some, leaving visible her face, the slim shoulders in her tank top, all the dark and burnished hair falling down her back, tendrils clinging to her neck.

Rhyson gapes like he's never seen her before. If that picture was anything to go by, I guess she's changed a lot in five years. He approaches her with slow steps and then squats down by the couch. He stretches his hand toward her hair but then hesitates, dropping it back down to his side. A muscle knots at his jawline, and his lips clamp tight. He blinks rapidly and swallows whatever emotions he doesn't want her to see when she wakes up.

"Bristol," he says softly, shaking her shoulder. "Wake up."

Her eyes open slowly, lashes fluttering over her cheeks for a few seconds. She turns her head to see who woke her, and she doesn't have the time Rhyson had to prepare. Emotion soaks her eyes, and a wide smile comes to life on her lips.

"Rhyson," she whispers, none of the irritation and hurt I've seen her fight all day evident. "You're here."

"Yeah, I'm here." I wonder if she notices how his laugh catches a little in his throat. "You're here, too."

The seconds stretch into a minute as they stare at each other, taking in the face so like their own, but so completely different.

"You look . . ." Rhyson tilts his head, studying his sister with sober eyes. "You're beautiful, Bris."

Tears flood her eyes, one sneaking over her cheek. She swipes it away quickly.

"Stop." She smiles self-consciously. "I look the same."

Rhyson shakes his head, brushing her tousled hair back with one hand. "My little sister grew up."

"Little sister?" She quirks one dark brow, some of the spark I saw today returning to her eyes. "We're twins, doofus."

"I was born first," he counters, his crooked smile telling me he's enjoying this.

"And that one minute more in the world gives you so much of an edge?" she fires back.

"Whether you want to admit it or not, you're my little sister." The look he gives her already apologizes before his words do. "I'm sorry we missed the last five years."

"Me, too," she says, the smile dying from her eyes.

"And for missing today. I wish I could say tomorrow would be much different. I have to be in the studio a lot, but you can come with me."

"Okay. That sounds fun." She stretches, yawns, and tosses the blanket off, standing to her feet. "We can talk about it in the morning. I'm off to bed."

"Me, too." Rhyson stands, talking through a yawn. "Marlon, it's so late, you should just crash here tonight."

Bristol's eyes shift over his shoulder, widening like she just realized that I was still here. She offers me a smile more reserved than the ones we exchanged while we talked all night. When we made each other laugh.

"Thanks again, Grip, for keeping me company today."

"No problem." I take the spot and the blanket on the couch she just vacated, not looking up to meet her eyes. "Any time."

I feel her eyes on me. After all we discussed today, all we shared, my tone probably seems impersonal. She may not know it now, but she'll realize soon, that's for her own good. She's something rare—smart, classy, gorgeous, funny, opinionated, and under it all, where she tries to hide it, kind. And burrowed beneath all of that, vulnerable. She isn't the kind of girl you mess over.

I repeat that warning to myself for the next hour as I stare into the darkness of Grady's living room. No, she isn't the kind of girl you mess over. A guy needs to be very sure he wants her, and just her, before he makes a move.

Yeah. A guy would have to be very sure.

Seven

Bristol

"HMMMMM."

I moan as soon as the warm bite of syrup-soaked waffle hits my tongue. "Don't tell me you're a short-order cook, too, when you're not deejaying or sweeping floors or writing songs."

Grip laughs, not looking up from the waffle maker on the kitchen counter. Powder sprinkles his face, right above the corner of his mouth, sugary white against the caramel of his skin. I want to lick it away. That realization has me choking on my waffle.

"You okay?" Rhyson pounds my back like I'm a little girl.

"Yeah." Eyes still watering, I sip my orange juice. "Just went down the wrong way."

Grip brings another stack of waffles to the table.

"Send these down the right way," he says.

Our eyes catch and hold across the table. Sunlight floods Grady's well-appointed kitchen, and you'd never know Grip slept on the couch and hasn't showered. Damn, the man looks good in this light. He'd probably look good in no light. A thin layer of stubble coats his chiseled jaw, and I wouldn't mind rubbing up against it, feeling the scrape as he leaves a mark on me.

My vagina needs a serious pep talk.

"So what's the plan for today?" Grip slices into his stack of waffles.

"Well, I'm in the studio pretty much all day again." He glances at me while he chews. "Sorry about that. It's bad timing but unavoidable."

"It's fine." I pause with my orange juice halfway to my mouth. "You did say I could tag along, right?"

"Won't you be bored?" Rhyson spears a waffle square. "I mean, if you want to come, you can."

"And the alternative would be . . .what?" I ask. "Sitting here in Grady's empty house all day?"

I could make the uncomfortable expression on his face go away, but I won't. I want him to feel the discomfort. I'm spending my spring freaking break here so we can reconnect, and that's what I want us to do.

"You have to be in the studio tonight?" Grip asks.

"Yeah. The singer's coming in to lay some new vocals." Rhyson scowls. "I hope we can knock everything out tonight. Maybe go to Santa Monica Pier tomorrow. But there may be another short session or two."

"If you want, I can swing by the studio to get Bristol tonight on my way to Brew." Grip directs the comment to Rhyson, not looking at me. "Take her with me."

He's barely spoken to me all morning. We talked last night for hours, and if I hadn't conked out, we probably would have talked for hours more. Maybe he has this kind of connection all the time, authentic and easy. He probably stays up all night talking to girls all the time. To me, though, it feels exceptional to be able to talk with someone so openly in such a short time.

"That cool with you, Bris?" Rhyson asks.

"Sure." I check Grip's face for any sign that this is a pain in his ass. "If you don't mind. Aren't you working?"

"Just deejaying." He taps his fork against his lips. "Jimmi will be there, too. You guys can hang."

I chuckle and drag my fork through the sticky syrup on my plate. "She seems cool," I say. "And really talented. She blew the roof off Mick's yesterday."

"They finally let her on stage?" Rhyson rubs his eyes and yawns. "Good for her."

I read between the lines of fatigue on my brother's handsome face.

"You still seem sleepy, Rhys. Why don't you go catch some z's until you have to be at the studio?"

"You sure?" Rhyson's eyes already seem to be drooping at the prospect of crawling back into bed. "I only need like another hour or two, then we can roll out."

"No problem." I walk my plate over to the sink and rinse it off. "I can clean up in here."

"You don't have to clean up after me." A small frown lands between Grip's eyebrows.

"You didn't have to cook for us," I come back, loading my plate and utensils into the dishwasher. "But you did. It was delicious, by the way."

"Glad you enjoyed it," he says politely before looking away. I'm struck again by the contrast from last night when he was warm and open. This morning, he isn't so much cold as he is indifferent. I just met him yesterday and refuse to allow myself a sense of loss. I mean, come on. We had a few intelligent conversations and a couple meals. No big deal.

Keep telling yourself that.

"Take a change of clothes with you to the studio," Grip says. "You can get dressed there before we go to the club."

He comes to the sink, handing me his empty plate. When I tug, he doesn't let go, and we have a childish tug-of-war for a second between our hands and between our eyes. He finally relents, grinning and walking back to the table. Rhyson watches the byplay between Grip and me with eyes that are suddenly alert and speculative.

"I better get going." Grip grabs his backpack from the floor near his seat. "Stuff to do and people to see."

"Thanks again for everything," Rhyson says.

"It's nothing." Grip gives me a smile before waving at us both and disappearing through the kitchen door.

"You know not to get all giddy over Marlon, right?" Rhyson watches me with big brother eyes. "I mean, he's a great guy. My best friend, in fact, but he goes through girls like toilet paper."

"You mean he wipes his ass with them?" I ask with false innocence.

"Good one." Rhyson doesn't grin as he comes to stand beside me at the sink. "Seriously, Bris, all the girls fall for Marlon, and he isn't ready to be good to any one girl."

"And are you?" I challenge him with a smirk, disguising the pinch in my chest hearing him describe Grip. I should be glad he's telling me, though I don't need him warning me about his best friend. "Ready to be good to one girl?"

"Hell, no." Rhyson laughs, crossing his arms over his wide chest. "I want to be as good to as many girls as I can."

We laugh, but once the joke is over, I realize we're alone for the first time since I arrived in LA. Alone for the first time in years. This is nothing like the comfortable silences Grip and I shared yesterday. This is awkward, filled with the memories of the last time we saw each other. We were in a courtroom, and he'd just been awarded his "freedom" from our family. And, boy, did he take flight. He never looked back from that day forward. If I hadn't reached out, there's no telling when we would have reconnected. Maybe never. Maybe he would have been fine with that.

"So how are the folks?" There's a studied relaxation to Rhyson. I may not have seen him in years, but I still recognize the tension in his shoulders. The stiffness of his back belying his false ease. He isn't just waiting for news of our parents. He's braced for it.

"They're good." I load the last plate into the dishwasher. "They talk about you a lot. I know they miss you."

"Miss me? Or the money?" he asks bitterly. "Are they not getting their monthly royalty checks?"

"That isn't fair, Rhyson. I know they didn't handle everything the right way all the time when they managed your career."

"Is that what you call enabling my addiction to prescription drugs so I could get through shows? So they could build their fortune at my expense?" Anger flares in Rhyson's eyes and colors his face. "Spare me the song and dance about them missing me. They have fifty percent of every dime I've ever earned. That was the price they named to let me leave. They aren't getting anything else from me."

I'm quiet for a moment, wondering how much I can press on this wound before he lashes out at me even more.

"And me?" I blink at the tears blurring the vision of my brother in front of me. "Do I get anything else?"

"I didn't know you wanted anything in the settlement, Bristol." Rhyson frowns. "But we can arrange—"

"How dare you?" Indignation tremors through me and makes my voice shake. "I call you. I write you. I text you. I fly to freaking Los Angeles and am hauled around the city all day while you Liberace in the studio, and you have the nerve to think I want your money? I don't need your money, Rhyson. I have a trust fund that will take care of me for the rest of my life if I don't want to work, which I do."

His eyes lay so heavily on me I feel them like a weight. He never looks away from my face when he asks his next question, as if he might catch me in a lie.

"Then why are you here, Bristol? What do you want?"

God, I come here with my heart bleeding on my sleeve, and it's still not enough for him. He needs me to cut it out and hand it to him in chunks of flesh and blood.

"I thought it would be obvious what I want." I tip my chin up defiantly and meet the skepticism and mistrust in his eyes. "I want my brother."

Eight

Bristol

WHEN RHYSON SAID I COULD COME AND WATCH HIM IN THE studio, he wasn't lying. That's about all I've gotten to do. He certainly hasn't talked to me much, and I can't imagine the complete focus it takes to create music at this level. Rhyson hasn't budged in eight hours. He's obsessing over four or five notes that, to his ear at least, are not "falling right." Whatever that means. He's barely looked up except when I brought him a sandwich, which still sits half-eaten on the piano.

At least I've knocked out my internship application. Machiavelli is all done.

An irrepressible grin springs to my lips as I remember Grip's reaction to my thinking his tattoo was misspelled. Mental images of the muscled terrain the tattoo adorns melt my grin. I've had plenty of time to remember how much I enjoyed hanging out with him yesterday. Rhyson's warning wasn't necessary, but it remains fresh in my mind.

He isn't ready to be good to any one girl.

And I am but one girl.

I glance down at the cleavage on display in the dress I changed into. Definitely a girl and definitely ready to let off some steam. The painted-on black bandage dress shows off all my assets, especially the ones up top. It lovingly traces the curves of my waist, hips, and ass, leaving my legs bare from mid-thigh. I've left my hair hanging down my back in loose waves. My makeup is smoky eyes and red lips.

"I deserve a night out," I tell the girl in the mirror. "Three thousand miles and I'm closeted in a studio all day?"

The girl in the mirror mocks me with her smoky eyes. She knows as well as I do that I wouldn't have traded today for anything. It felt like old times. Rhyson may have forgotten, but I used to do my homework outside his rehearsal room. I loved hearing my brother play, replaying a passage until it was perfect. That hasn't changed. I may not make music, but I love it. My parents may manage musicians now, but they were both brilliant musicians when they were younger. Uncle Grady, too. I told Grip I was an ugly duckling in my family. Maybe I'm not ugly, but I'm certainly the odd man out.

My eyes drop to the shadowy cleft between my breasts. Correction. Odd woman out.

I slip back into the studio unnoticed, and my heart skips a stupid beat when I see Grip at the piano with Rhyson. Both of their faces, which are so different but so handsome, wear matching frowns of concentration.

"Did you try it here?" Grip points to a place on the pad Rhyson has been scribbling on all day.

"Yeah." Rhyson chews on the end of his pencil. "But it's a major third."

"Ahhhh." Grip nods since that apparently holds significance to him that I don't grasp. "I see."

Neither of them looks up when I step farther into the room, keeping their eyes trained on the pad.

"Oh!" Grip's face lights up. He grabs Rhyson's pencil and music pad, writing furiously, a wide smile spreading over his face. "What about that?"

Rhyson takes the pad, frowning for a few silent moments before laughing and slapping Grip on the back.

"That does it." Rhyson's shoulders slump with his relief. "Man, thanks. I've been looking at it too long. I didn't even see what was right in front of me."

"Glad I could help." Grip's expression shifts, amusement twitching his lips. "Hey, did that guy send you his demo or mixtape or whatever? The guy from Grady's class?"

"That dude." Rhyson grimaces and then shifts into an odd British accent. "I was gonna listen to that, but then I just carried on living my life."

Huh?

"That's one of your goofy ass movie quotes, isn't it?" Grip shakes his head, his grin teasing Rhyson. "Which one?"

"Russel Brand in *Forgetting Sarah Marshall*. You'd like that one." "That's what you said about *Little Nicky*."

"Okay." Chagrin wrinkles Rhyson's expression. "Upon further consideration, that was an Adam Sandler miss, I admit."

"I've never known anyone as obsessed with movies as you. You got a quote for every day of the week."

Really? I don't remember Rhyson ever watching movies. He never had time. It strikes me—again—how little I know this version of my twin brother. Grady, Grip, and Jimmi seem to all know more about him than I do. Maybe because they're his family now.

"Yeah. You know that's how I decompress." Rhyson returns his attention to the music pad, halfway gone already.

"I can think of several ways to decompress that . . ."

Whatever Grip planned to say goes unsaid when he catches sight of me. His eyes scroll over my body in a quick assessment and then go back up and down for slow seconds. When he finally reaches my face, his eyes burn into mine. His mouth falls open just the tiniest bit, and in that small space between his full lips, I see his tongue dart out for a quick swipe. Like he wants a taste of something. Like he wants a taste of me. It's a nanosecond, but it's real, and I see it before he stashes it away and schools his face into the indifference he showed me in the kitchen this morning.

"Bris, wow." Rhyson's brows disappear under his messy fall of dark hair. "You look . . .wow. Grip, you'll have to protect my little sister at the club tonight."

I saunter closer, my Louboutins adding another inch or so to my confidence and some sway to my hips.

"Maybe I don't want to be protected." I laugh at the nauseous look on Rhyson's face. "This is my spring break, brother, and I am all grown up. I've been in this studio all day working on my essay. I'm ready to be hair down, bottles up, and I'm glad you won't be there cramping my style."

"You finished?" Grip asks, speaking for the first time. "The application?"

"Yeah." We stare at one another for a few seconds before I untangle our eyes. The leftover heat in his gaze is still too hot for me. "I'll read over the essay one more time before I submit."

"What's this essay for anyway?" Rhyson asks from behind the piano, linking his hands behind his head.

"An internship I'm applying for with Sound Management." I watch his face to see if it sinks in for him.

"Sound Management?" Rhyson bunches his brows. "They manage some huge acts. What's your major?"

"Business. But my emphasis will be entertainment. Entertainment management is what I want to do."

I feel Grip's eyes on me. I hadn't mentioned that in all our discussions about music yesterday. I wanted to talk with Rhyson about this myself.

"Following in our parents' footsteps." Cynicism twists Rhyson's lips. "Shocking."

"Well, it is the family business." I shrug my shoulders nonchalantly. "Besides, maybe you'll need someone you can trust to manage you when the time comes. I want to learn everything I can. Maybe move here after graduation."

Two sets of eyes snap to my face, Rhyson's and Grip's. Even pointedly eyeing my manicure, I feel them both looking at me.

"What the hell?" Rhyson's face is somewhere between thunderstruck and thundercloud, shock and anger competing. "Manage me doing what? I'm not a performer anymore, Bristol, and I won't be."

I give up feigning interest in my nails and focus all my will on my brother, even managing to block out Grip's magnetic presence.

"You are a genius, Rhyson." I set my face in stone. "One of the most brilliant pianists to ever live. There is no way you're supposed to spend the rest of your life writing music for other people and producing their stuff."

"Did Mother put you up to this?" Rhyson levels a cold stare at me. "I knew it. You come here all 'I want my brother back', but this is your agenda. Their agenda. To get me under their control again."

"Fuck you, Rhyson." The words erupt from the pool of lava boiling in my belly. "I'm the one who has made any effort to maintain a relationship between us, not you."

"Yeah, and I know why." His anger, which matches mine, slams into me. "They couldn't get me back themselves, so they use you to manipulate me."

"Use me?" A bark of laughter hurts my throat. "Why would they ever think I had any influence over you? When have you ever cared about me, Rhyson? If they didn't know by the absolute disregard you had for me when you lived at home, surely they would have known by the way you cut me out of your life when you left."

The anger on his face stutters, going in and out like a bulb with a short.

"Wait. Known what?" Bewilderment puckers his expression. "What would they know, Bristol?"

"That you haven't ever given a damn about me." Emotion overtakes me, inundating my throat, burning my face, saturating my eyes. "They have to know that. I certainly do."

"That isn't true, Bris." He runs a hand through his hair, his movements jerky. "Look, this escalated fast. I shouldn't have—"

"No, you shouldn't have."

Someone entering the studio silences us both, curtailing our argument. A guy around our age wearing headphones looped around his neck pauses, watching the three of us cautiously.

"Sorry." He adjusts his black-rimmed glasses. "Rhys, am I early or . . ."

"No. We, um . . .I'm ready." Rhyson propels a sigh, looking at me. "Bristol, I—"

"Are we going to this club or what?" I cut him off, slicing a look Grip's way.

"Uh . . ." Grip's eyes skid from me to my brother. "Maybe you should—"

"Never mind. I'll go by myself."

I charge down the hall, my red bottoms making a meal of the carpet and eating up inches with every step. I'm almost at the studio exit by the time Grip catches me, grabbing my elbow and turning me to face him.

"You don't even know where you're going, Bristol." Concern and irritation blend in his eyes.

"I'm pretty good at figuring shit out." I tug on my arm. "Let go."

"Just calm the hell down." He scowls and doesn't let me go. "Come on. The car's parked out front."

I follow him to his Jeep, blinking at the tears rising up as I mentally replay the argument with Rhyson. How dare he question my motives? I've gone above and beyond to show him how important he is to me, and he insults me? Doesn't trust me? I'm tempted to demand that Grip stop the car and hitch a ride to the airport. Just leave all my crap at Grady's and go back to New York right now.

"You're both so damn stubborn." Grip negotiates the traffic, sparing me a quick glance.

"Me?" My harsh laugh bounces off the Jeep's interior. "He's the one."

"You know he's just hurt, Bristol."

"He's hurt?" I turn in my seat to face him, the seatbelt cutting into my chest. "He's the one who left five years ago. He's the one who acted like I was a nuisance every time I reached out. And then I come out here on my spring break, just to have him work the whole time. I swear he's using it as an excuse not to deal with me."

"He does have actual work," Grip inserts.

"And he's the one hurt?" I power on. "The hell." "You can't control him, Bristol."

"Contr . . .you're on his side." Even though Rhyson is Grip's best friend and I've only known him a day, I feel betrayed. "You think I'm trying to control my brother? I'm trying to help him fulfill his dreams."

"No, they're not his dreams." Grip shakes his head adamantly, eyes trained ahead. "Not right now. They're your dreams for him. The same way your parents worked him to death doing their dreams. It feels the same to him."

"It isn't the same." I say it even though what he says makes sense. I don't want to accept it. He takes my pause as the chance to speak some more.

"Think about it." Grip's voice gentles, and the look he sends me from behind the wheel gentles, too. "Their priorities weren't straight. They seemed more concerned with the career than with him. When you take the reins like you did back there, it makes him think that you're just like them, especially your mom."

I let that set in for a second, let it sink through my pores and trickle down to my heart. It hurts because, though I love my mother and have done all I could to please her, she's a hard-nosed bitch.

Am I?

"You're not like her," Grip says softly, as if he read my mind. "At least not the way he described her to me. You're not that."

I turn my head and look out the window so he won't see my lip trembling or the tears quivering on my lashes. It feels like I keep hiding from him when he seems to see everything.

"Maybe I am," I whisper. "I just . . .he's so talented. I will never believe he's supposed to be some hack who just writes for other people."

I whip my head around, eyes wide. "No offense."

"None taken." Grip laughs, the cocky smirk firmly in place. "I already know I got the goods. It's just a matter of time and the right opportunity before I'm on somebody's stage."

His smirk disappears when he glances at me.

"For me and for Rhyson. I actually am on your side in this. I believe he should be doing his own music, too, and he will. But he has to come to it for himself."

I bite my thumbnail and shake my head, turning my eyes back to the traffic crawling by.

"How do you guys live with this traffic?" I ask, needing to dispel some of the heaviness in the car.

"Like New York's much better?"

"True. But you don't have to drive in New York."

"Well, it sounds like you may have to endure it with the rest of us soon." We're sitting still, jammed in a tight line of vehicles, so he looks at me fully, a question in his eyes before he asks it. "Were you serious about moving here when you graduate?"

I nod and swallow my nerves as I wonder if he's asking for Rhyson or if he might have a personal interest in my relocating to the West Coast.

"That's the plan." A self-deprecating smile wrings my lips. "The ridiculous plan based on Rhyson doing something he has no intention of doing. You must think I'm crazy, huh?"

"It is crazy."

My heartbeat stumbles. I know it's farfetched. I know it's irrational to stake my entire college career, my future, on the dreams Rhyson isn't even dreaming, but to hear Grip affirm my lunacy chafes. Then his lips, which are a contradiction of soft and sculpted, curve into something especially for me. A smile just for me. When he turns to look at me, it warms his dark eyes.

"And I don't know what Rhyson did to deserve you," he says.

Nine

Bristol

'M NOT SURE I LIKE THIS CLUB.

Another scantily dressed woman walks over to the booth and passes Grip a slip of paper, presumably with her number on it.

That might have something to do with why I don't like this club. And it's ridiculous. I met the man yesterday. But in my defense, we've squeezed weeks of conversation into the last two days. Still, that doesn't excuse the jealousy gnawing my insides. When I add that to the lingering hurt from my argument with Rhyson, it makes it impossible for me to enjoy myself.

"Are we gonna dance or just hold up the bar all night?" Jimmi moves her shoulders and ass to the Drake song in Grip's rotation.

"Sorry. I'm not a very good dancer." I shrug, not really sorry. "And I'm kind of tired."

And horny.

My midterms took it out of me. The internship essay took it out of me. This trip has taken it out of me. I need a good drink and a good lay, in that order. I don't know Jimmi well enough to confess it. She'd probably hook me up with some stranger, and that isn't what I want.

That isn't who I want.

I glance over at the booth where Grip has been all night, keeping the music going.

I'm not letting myself go there. I purposely look away, only to clash eyes with some frat looking guy a few feet away eye fucking me. He flashes me a too-white smile. That smile would glow in the dark. I don't return it, but deliberately look away, hoping he gets the message.

The message being no.

"I love this song," Jimmi says. "Grip has great mixes."

"Yeah, he does." I sip my Grey Goose, waiting for the buzz that will numb the hurt Rhyson inflicted. Something to take the edge off this sexy itch I haven't scratched in months.

Months?

Well, damn. No wonder I'm horny.

"So what do you think of him?" Jimmi asks. I obviously missed something.

"Huh? Sorry." I set my hurt feelings and needy libido aside long enough to focus on Jimmi's pretty face. "Who? What do I think of who?"

"Grip." Jimmi sneaks me a curious glance. "All girls have thoughts about Grip when they first meet him."

"Um . . .he's nice?" I set my drink down and turn my stool to face the wall of bottles behind the bar. "He's my brother's best friend. That about sums it up."

"Oh, the two of them together." Jimmi fans herself. "They've been double trouble since high school."

She touches my arm, her eyes contrite.

"I'm sorry. That's your brother I'm talking about. Awkward." She gives my hand a reassuring pat. "Rhyson's nowhere near as bad as Grip, though."

"As bad?" I swirl the contents of my glass without looking at her. "What do you mean?"

"Oh, Grip goes through girls like it's nothing." Jimmi lets out a husky laugh. "They're disposable."

"I can imagine," I answer weakly. She's only echoing what Rhyson already told me. The guy I talked to for hours yesterday doesn't match the one they're describing, but they know him better than I do. "But I heard he makes it worth their while." Jimmi wiggles her eyebrows suggestively. "One of my girls got with him. She says he's hung like you wouldn't believe."

Not what my vagina needs to hear right now. I cross my legs and squirm in my seat, seeking some friction, some release. The alcohol is kicking in, and it only fires the need in me. I imagine all those inches stretching me and . . . I need to rub up against something.

"Are you not into Black guys?" Jimmi scrunches her nose. "I mean, I have some friends who aren't. I don't care. I'd screw a hole in the wall if it could make me come."

"Wow. That's a . . .colorful way to say it. No, I've never dated a Black guy, but I guess I just never had the opportunity." I shrug. "I don't really care."

Especially if he looked like Grip. I'd take green Grip. Pink Grip. Red Grip. If Grip were a bag of Skittles, I'd eat every one.

"Oh." Jimmi claps excitedly. "Grip's gonna perform."

"He is?" I perk up, spinning around on my stool. Sure enough, he's on stage with a mic. Under the lights, he seems even taller, even broader.

"What's good?" Grip spreads his smile around the club. "I don't get to do this as much as I'd like, but they're gonna let me spit a few bars for you tonight."

The cheering and whistles and catcalls explode from the audience.

"I see my reputation precedes me." Grip chuckles and nods to the drummer in the corner. "Lil' somethin' for you."

I wasn't lying when I told Grip I don't listen to rap much. I don't hate it. I've just always been indifferent. I can't make out half of what they're saying, and once I know, it's all bitches and hos and slurs. I wince through half of it and roll my eyes through the rest. It's just not my favorite music. But Grip is a different breed. I understand every word he says, and I'm hanging on every one. Literally waiting for the next syllable. The images he paints are so vivid that, if I closed my eyes, they'd be spray painted on the back of my eyelids. I'd be drowning in color, floating in sound. The richness of his voice floods the room, and I realize he has us all rapt. We're eating his words, a feeding frenzy of imagination. He's a storyteller and a poet.

I feel the same as I did listening to Rhyson growing up. Like the sun and the moon were in my house. Like I was a part of Rhyson's great galaxy, and he was the star. Grip is a star. Sweeping floors and doing all the things he does to survive are all just dues he's paying. He's lightning in a beautiful bottle, just waiting to strike. A pending storm. He's hypnotizing. Intoxicating. I'm as buzzed off him as I am off my Grey Goose.

"He's good, right?" Jimmi grins at me knowingly. "I felt the same way the first time I heard him. It's his writing. His stuff is so much deeper than most of what's out there. He's really saying something."

"Yeah." I clear my throat and try to appear less mesmerized. "He's really good. Wow."

"Don't look now, but we aren't the only ones who think so." She nudges me with her elbow and inclines her head toward a group of girls clustering around Grip. "Did you ride with Grip?"

"Uh, yeah." I can't force my eyes away from where he sits on the edge of the stage, girls buzzing around him. He did say you catch more bees with honey.

Or, in his case, chocolate.

"I may be taking you home," she says with a slight smile. "Those are what I like to call 'ground floor groupies'. They see his potential same as we do, and some of them want in on the action before the rest of the world gets a taste of him."

My muscles lock up as I watch several girls stroke his arms and press against his side. That he doesn't see through it makes me sick, souring my high after his performance.

"I think I do want to dance." I knock back my drink and turn to find frat guy, who's still a few feet away. "With him."

I point him out, and before Jimmi can ask me any questions or try to stop me, I'm gone. I walk up to glow-bright smile, and enjoy seeing his eyes get wider the closer I get. Yep. He's one of those. All bold and staring with no idea what to do with it.

"Hey." I step so close I smell the whiskey on his breath. "You've been staring at me all night."

"Uh, you're hot," he stammers, his eyes rolling over my body and sticking to my breasts.

Has it come to this?

"So . . .you want to dance?" I prompt. I'm not a great dancer, but the alcohol humming through my blood convinces me that I am.

"Sure."

I walk onto the dance floor, assuming he's following. Assuming he's staring at my ass as I pop my hips in a loose-limbed sway. His hands clamp my waist, his fingers drifting down to spread over the curves of my butt. I press my back to his chest and start moving, start reaching for a feeling, any feeling to block the emotions that have ravaged me over the last few hours. The hurt and jealousy. The disappointment and resentment. He gets stiffer and harder with every measure of the song, with every roll of my hips. He pulls my hair aside, and his breath lands heavy and hot on my neck. Whatever my body is reaching for, I'm not finding it with him. I'm about to pull away and go order another Grey Goose, when I hear a deep voice behind me.

"Dude, step off."

Gravel studs Grip's voice. Whether he's irritated with me or glowbright, I don't know. I whirl around to face them. My partner, apparently more a lover than a fighter, has obliged Grip's request and is already halfway back to his frat boy friends.

"What the hell do you think you're doing?" I demand.

"I was just about to ask you the same thing." The club lights stripe his handsome face, painting him in shades of pink and blue and green. "You were working that guy up for nothing."

"For nothing?" I raise both brows, hands on my hips. "It wouldn't have been for nothing. Have you forgotten? This is my spring break. Girls get drunk and they get laid. I'm already halfway to one, and you just ruined the other."

His face goes hard as cement.

"You're still hurt from your fight with Rhyson." He shakes his head. "I'm not letting you go home with anyone half-drunk and emotional."

"I wasn't going home with him. I would have fucked him in a bathroom stall. In the alley. We would have figured it out."

The light strobes the emotions on his face, flashing anger then frustration.

"I'm gonna excuse that because I know you're upset." "I'm not upset," I snap. "I'm horny."

"Shit, Bristol." He glances at the people dancing within earshot. "That is not what you say in a club full of frat boys trolling for ass. I'm trying to protect you from all these dicks."

"I like dick!" I say a little too loudly, drawing a few more stares. Boy, that Grey Goose has kicked in after all. "And you're cock blocking."

"Cock block . . ." Grip's mouth drops open then snaps shut. "Let's go. You're exhausted and irrational, so Imma give you a pass."

"I'm not going anywhere with you."

I slip past him and stomp off the floor as much as my Louboutins will allow. I have no idea how we got into the club, and I make several turns and detours. I'm sure I'm headed toward the entrance, but I end up behind the building instead of in front. I step out anyway, hauling in a cleansing breath and leaning against the brick wall to calm the tremors shivering through my body. Grinding into glow-bright did nothing for me, but catching a whiff of Grip's clean masculine scent, feeling the warmth of his body as he stood so close—that has me trembling.

"I told Jimmi we'll see her later." Grip walks toward me in the alleyway. "Let's get you home."

My anger has died off, and so has his, apparently. His voice is gentle, his eyes compassionate. He sees too clearly, too much. He detects all the hurt festering under my clingy bandage dress. I hate that he's so sweet and still a player. I won't forget about the bees. And the honey. And the chocolate.

"God, just leave me alone." Pressing into the brick wall at my back, I hold my head in my hands. "I've already told you I'm horny, and you just keep . . ."

I growl and fist my hair and my frustration in my fingers. "You're right." I stand straight. "Let's just go."

I push off the wall at my back only to collide with a wall of muscles and heat at my front. Neither of us makes a move to put any distance between us. My breath stutters over my lips as I fight the magnetic pull of him. We stand there in the alley, trapped in a sensual stasis, unmoving except for our chests heaving against each other's with each labored breath. His hands find the curve of my waist, the dip of my back. He doesn't press me to him, but his touch scorches through the thin material of my dress. He drops his head, pressing his temple to mine, and draws in a breath behind my ear.

"Did you just . . ." I search for the right word, "whiff me?"

His husky laugh leaves warm breath at my neck, skittering a shiver down my spine.

"It's better than the alternative," he says.

"Which is what?" I pull back to peer up at his face.

"Kissing you." His eyes boil from caramel to hot chocolate. Sweet, hot, steamy need spikes in the look he pours over me.

"I'm not doing this with you, Grip." I close my eyes, my hands covering his on my hips. I mean to push them away, but my fingers won't move. They trap his touch against me.

"We just met yesterday," I remind him and myself.

"I know." He shakes his head. "You're my best friend's sister."

"I live in New York."

"I'm here in LA."

"I don't even know you." I laugh a little. "And what I do know is not good. You're a player."

"Who told you that?" Irritation crinkles his expression.

"Um, you basically did." I roll my eyes. "And Jimmi. And Rhyson."

"They shouldn't . . ." He sighs, releasing his frustration into the stale alley air. "I understand why they would say that, but this isn't . . . you're not . . ."

He bites his bottom lip, a gesture that seems so uncertain when he's been anything but.

"Don't be upset with them for telling me the obvious," I say. "I saw all those girls tonight for myself. I know what it's like for musicians."

"I don't even know those girls."

"You barely know me, either."

He doesn't reply, but the way he looks at me—the pull between us—defies my statement. We know each other. Not in terms of hours or days, but something deeper. Something more elemental. I can't deny it, but I have no idea what to do with it.

"Look, I can admit I'm attracted to you." Grip surveys my body one more time before clenching his eyes closed and giving his head a quick shake. "Damn, that dress, Bristol. All fucking night."

An involuntary smile tugs at my lips, but I pinch it into a tiny quirk of the lips instead of the wide, satisfied thing sprawling inside me.

"Not all night." I firm my lips. "You had quite the fan base. Women lined up after your performance."

"Thirsty chicks." Grip grimaces. "Banking on the off chance that one day I'll be something they can eat off of. Maybe get themselves a baby daddy. Get some bills paid every month."

"It isn't an off chance," I say softly. "It's a certainty."

"What's a certainty?" A frown conveys his confusion.

"That you'll be something one day." I point toward the door leading back into the club. "When you grabbed that mic, when you took that stage, it was obvious you're as talented as Rhyson. It looks and sounds different, but you both have that special quality that makes people watch and listen. You can't teach that or train it. You either have it or you don't."

I offer a smile.

"And you have it."

Surprise and then something else, maybe self-consciousness, cross his face. For one so bold and sure, it's funny to see.

"Yeah, well, thanks." He shrugs and goes on. "Anyway, I know the deal. My mama schooled me on girls like that."

"Your mother sounds very wise."

"Very. She made sure I knew their game."

He waves a hand between our chests.

"This, what we're feeling," he says, his eyes going sober. "It isn't a game."

I hold my breath, waiting for him to tell me we should jump off this cliff. That as crazy as it seems, we'll hold on tight and break each other's fall.

"It's complicated." He lowers his eyes before lifting them to meet mine. "It's just an attraction, and we should probably resist it. I mean, you're only here a few days. If things didn't work out for us, it could make shit awkward with Rhyson, and I know you want to repair things with him. There's a million reasons we shouldn't act on this attraction. Right?"

"Right." I offer a decisive nod. "A million reasons."

As we ride back to Grady's bungalow in our first strained silence since we met at the airport, I realize he was wise to stop whatever could have happened in the alley. It would probably have been a half-drunken regret. There are a million reasons we should stop. But right now, I can only think of the one reason not to stop.

Because I don't want to.

Ten

Bristol

THE RIDE HOME FROM BREW IS MOSTLY SILENT. YET, IT'S A SILENCE filled with all the reasons Grip and I shouldn't indulge the attraction plaguing us. Grip's scent alone—more than clean, less than cologne, and somehow uniquely his—makes me close my eyes and take it in with sneaky sniffs. I wonder if he's taking me in, too. I still tingle from that alleyway alchemy, the chemistry that snapped and sizzled between us behind the club. It's all I can think of.

"We're here." His voice is deep and low in the confines of the car.

I glance at Grady's house, which is dark except for the porch light, and wonder if Rhyson is home, awake, interested in finishing the argument we started earlier. Because who doesn't want to scratch and claw with their sister at two o'clock in the morning?

"Thanks." I turn a grateful smile on him, not meeting his eyes. I fumble with the handle until the door opens, the cool air raising goose bumps on my arms. Or maybe that's his touch, the gentle hand at my elbow. I look back to him, waiting for whatever he has to say.

"Bristol, I ..." He bunches his brow and gives a quick shake of his head before turning to face forward. Both hands on the wheel of the ancient Jeep. "Never mind."

"Um, okay." I get out, ready to slam the door when his words stop me again.

"I had fun tonight." He leans across the middle console so I can see his face a little. His interior light doesn't work, so he's still basically in the dark.

The shadows smudge the striking details of his face, but I feel the intensity of his eyes.

"You had fun wrangling a half-drunk girl off the dance floor and arguing in a dirty alleyway?" I ask sarcastically. "Yeah, right."

I hear the little huff of a laugh from the driver's seat.

"I had fun hanging with you," he responds softly, the smile tinting his voice. I let his words settle over me for a moment before I pat the roof of the car twice and step back.

"Me, too," I finally answer. "Have a good night and thanks for everything."

Manners.

As Grip pulls away from the curb, I can't help but wonder why I'm being painfully polite when what I'm starting to feel for him is anything but well mannered.

A little wild. A lot unexpected. Completely unlikely, but definitely not polite.

I use the key Rhyson gave me and hope there isn't an alarm. I walk deeper into the house, still a little wired but unsure what to do. The door leading to the kitchen opens, and Rhyson steps into the living room.

"Hey," I say softly, watching for signs of lingering anger.

"Hey." His eyes fix on my face, and I'm guessing he's gauging me, too. "You too tired to talk?"

I sit on the couch and gesture for him to join me. He sits, elbows to his knees and eyes on the floor.

"I'm sorry for how out of control things got at the studio," he says, his voice quiet, subdued. "I . . .I don't feel like we know each other anymore."

A humorless laugh escapes my lips.

"And I'm not sure we ever did." I smile a little sadly when our eyes connect around that truth in the lamplight.

"You're probably right."

He sighs, raking his long sensitive fingers through wild hair. He has an artist's hands. Well kempt but competent and capable of creating.

"Do you remember when they insured your hands?" I ask.

"Yeah." He doesn't say anything more, but draws his brows draw into a frown.

"I overheard Mother discussing the policy. We were eleven." I bite my lip and smile. "I remember asking her why they insured your hands. She said you insure things that are too valuable to lose forever. She said your gift was irreplaceable and that made you incredibly valuable. They had to protect you."

"That sounds about right," Rhyson says bitterly. "Protect their investment."

I don't acknowledge his interpretation of it because he never saw it from my side.

"I was so jealous of you that day." I shake my head, feeling that helplessness and the frustration of having nothing to offer flood me again. "I had nothing to insure. I had nothing that valuable to our parents. They had shown me a million times, but that day she put it in words."

"Jealous?" Rhyson's incredulity twists his handsome face. "You were jealous of me? You had everything, Bristol. You had friends. You got to go to school with kids our age. You had a normal life. That was all I wanted."

"You had them," I counter. "The three of you would go off for weeks at a time, and I had nannies and therapists. You had our parents."

"I had them?" Rhyson demands in rhetorical disbelief. "Yeah, I had them riding my ass to rehearse eight hours a day, reminding me that I might be a kid, but adults paid good money to come see me play. I had nothing."

"You loved piano," I insist, needing to know that things are as I remember them, because if they aren't, what has been real?

"I loved piano, yes, but that just came to me. I don't even remember not knowing how to play. Piano I was born with. The career? The road and the concerts and the tours? That they made me do."

Condemnation colors his eyes.

"The addiction—I let that happen," he says.

"You were too young," I counter softly. "Too young to take the pills, and our parents should have stopped you, not enabled you. I see that now."

He scoots closer, looking at me earnestly.

"Bris, I had to get away from them." He shakes his head, and his eyes are bleak. "To survive. I needed to get better, and to do that, I had to put as much distance between them and myself as possible."

"But that meant me, too." Tears prick my eyes.

"Yeah, I'm sorry about that." He drops his head into his hands. "But you stayed. You were there. I didn't know whose side you were on."

"There wasn't a side, Rhyson." My words come vehemently. "You were all my family. They weren't perfect, far from it, but they were the only parents I had. I wanted them to love me. You were the only brother I had. The only family I had, and it was ripped apart. You didn't seem to want to repair it."

"Not with them, no," he admits. "Not yet. Maybe not ever." "And me?" My heart flutters in my chest as I wait.

"When you would call, I thought it was them having you check up on me or trying to get in so they could get me back to make money for them. Even when you called and told me you wanted to come here for spring break, I thought there was an ulterior motive."

He laughs, eyeing me with no small amount of doubt.

"And when you started talking today about moving here and managing my career—"

"I probably should have handled that better." It's the truth. "I know it seems crazy to you, but you're a star, Rhyson. Like once-in-a-lifetime genius star. I don't want to capitalize on it. I just want to see it happen, and for some reason, it isn't."

"I don't know if I can do that shit again, Bris. It takes so much, and I only got through it with the drugs. I don't want to create a situation where I need those again. If there was one thing I learned when I kicked the habit, it was that I have an addictive personality. Music is the only thing I need to be addicted to."

"I'm not trying to create a situation where you need the drugs," I say. "I just want to be your sister again."

"And my manager?" Skepticism lifts one of his brows. "You want to be that, too?"

"I still have two years left at Columbia. We could start with me just being your sister." A wide smile stretches across my face at the prospect. "And then see what happens."

Eleven

Grip

I HATE CARNIVALS.

My cousin Jade used to drag me to these things and make me stay until the smell of funnel cake wasn't even sweet anymore. We'd ride the Ferris wheel and run through the fun house. We'd play every game we could afford and some we managed to swindle our way into. Ring toss. Big Six Wheel. Ring the Bell. Skeeball. Jade's so competitive, I'd have to let her win the basket toss most of the time. Not so much she'd get suspicious, but enough that she didn't pout the whole damn time.

Something shifted between Jade and me along the way. I know it started with a secret shame we share, and over time, that deteriorated our closeness some. When I won the scholarship, leaving her in our local public school, things only worsened. We're still close, but it isn't what it was before. Maybe it's just a part of growing up.

All that to say, I hate carnivals.

And Jimmi's "brill" idea (her whack word, not mine) to show Bristol some fun before she leaves is this carnival. It could be worse. Rhyson could be stuck in the studio again, and I could be entertaining Bristol by myself. And that could get touchy . . .since I want to fuck her.

I mean, yes, talk to her till the sun comes up, laugh about the stand-up comedians we both like, exchange playlists, debate hot-button politics, explore all the ways we are different and just alike . . .but also I want to fuck her.

And never more so than last night in the alley. That sensuality I wasn't sure Bristol understood about herself gyrated on the dance floor. The way her eyes dropped closed when she took her first sip of Grey Goose, licking the drops from her lips and savoring their taste. The way she rolled her hips, even sitting on her stool, her body seeking out the primal beat of the music. She says she can't dance, but it wasn't skill that had her out on the floor. It was her body pinned up, searching for release. And she thought she would find it with that Zeta Delta Dick frat boy who had been scoping her all night. I could barely focus from song to song as I watched her. Watched him watching her. I knew I couldn't give her the release she wanted, but he certainly wasn't going to.

It feels like this has been building between us for months, but it's only been days. I had decided to squelch it, but when I heard her master plan about moving to LA and managing Rhyson, something turned over inside my head. A possibility? A maybe? Doing what she's doing, staking her college career, planning her future based on helping her brother's dreams come true, it's crazy.

And so completely right.

I've known since the beginning that Rhyson will have to play again. We use the word genius like it's nothing. I mean, seriously. Apple genius? But he is legit genius. Like playing Beethoven at three years old genius. And for him to neglect his gift, in whatever form it takes—classical, modern, pop, rock— is a travesty. Everyone around him knows it. Jimmi, our friend Luke, Grady. I know it, but none of us have called him on it. We have this silent pact to let him come to it on his own. He has to after what he endured for years under his parents' tyrannical management. But Bristol, who hasn't even seen him in five years, does it. She's so sure it's right that she's betting her Ivy League education on it. She's planning her future around it. She's challenging him in a way none of us were willing to do.

And that's my kind of girl. That abandoned passion. That bottomless commitment. You don't meet people like her often, and when you do, you never forget them. I couldn't get her out of my mind before, but now . . .

I glance over at Bristol and Jimmi, who are playing water guns with Rhyson. It's good to see the siblings laughing. Maybe they worked things out after I dropped Bristol off last night. They seem to be trying to enjoy the little time they have left. She leaves in two days. Why that feels so shitty this fast baffles me.

"Come on, Grip!" Jimmi eyes me over her shoulder as she sprays blindly at the target in front of her. "Grab a gun."

"Nah." I munch on the popcorn I grabbed a few booths back. "I'm good."

Carnivals do have good popcorn. But funnel cake? I ate so much of it with Jade, the smell nauseates me. When they finish the game, the girls want to do rides.

"Ferris wheel." Jimmi presses her hands together in a plea to Rhyson. "Please ride with me."

Rhyson carefully considers the girl who has been one of our closest friends since high school. She's also had a crush on Rhyson about as long as she's known him. He's very careful with her heart, though, encouraging her as little as possible. Rhyson gets as much ass as I do, but he's just on the low with his shit. He knows there should be a huge KEEP OUT sign all over him for Jimmi.

"Okay, we can ride." Rhyson holds up an index finger. "Once, Jim. I know how you get. All 'again, again.'"

"Cool." Jimmi's expression may be calm, but her eyes dance all over the place. "We can talk about that song I'm working on."

She knows him well. As soon as she says that, Rhyson is in. Talking music theory and asking about chord changes will occupy them for the whole ride.

"We're down to ride, too." Luke, the other guy we've been tight with for years and a fellow arts alum, hooks his elbow around his girlfriend Mandi's neck.

"I ate that Polish sausage." Mandi looks a little green. "Think I'll be okay on the Ferris wheel?"

I wouldn't trust it. You can't ever un-see projectile vomit, and there's nothing sexy about that.

"So, you'll ride with Grip then, Bristol?" Jimmi looks between the two of us with a gleam in her eye. Don't let the blonde hair fool ya. Jimmi's sharp as a new pair of scissors. She probably picked up on the vibe between Bristol and me last night. We don't need her matchmaking. I'm trying to figure out how not to complicate this situation more. The last thing we need is be alone on the—

"I'll ride." Bristol stuffs her hands into her pockets and looks at her feet. "I mean, if you want to, Grip. Since everyone else is. Up to you."

She looks up at me, wearing not much makeup at all. Just as beautiful. A threat to my peace of mind.

"Weren't you scared of heights?" Rhyson asks his sister, a reminiscent smile playing around his lips.

Surprise flits across Bristol's face.

"Uh, yeah. For a little while. Sometimes." She laughs, covering her mouth with one hand. "Mother sent me to therapy for it. Remember that?"

"God, yes." Rhyson's face lights up. "Didn't she send you to therapy for biting your nails, too?"

"And for wetting the bed. I was three! Since she was never there, therapy was Mother's parenting alternative," Bristol says dryly.

Wow. Their mom does sound like a piece of work, but Rhyson and Bristol are laughing about it as if it's nothing that their mother sent a three-year-old to therapy for bed-wetting. Just two prisoners, reminiscing about doing their time. Only Rhyson escaped, and Bristol stayed behind bars.

The ride is crowded, and there aren't any available cars near each other, so we're all spread out, leaving Bristol and me strapped into this small space and relatively alone. At first, the only sound is the whir of the motor and distant squeals from the ground below. After a few moments of quiet between us, Bristol snickers. I glance at her to see what's so funny, but she isn't even looking at me. She's looking down at the ground, which is growing smaller and smaller as we ascend.

"What?" I ask. "You laughed. What's up?"

She turns her head, and her laughter slowly leaks away until the only thing left of it is a shadow in her eyes.

"I was thinking about my mom sending me to therapy for biting my nails." She shakes her head. "I spent so much time in therapy, I knew the therapists about as well as I knew my nannies."

"You had nannies?"

"Sure." She laughs again, but this time bitterness tinges the sound. "Who else was going to raise me with my parents trailing Rhyson on the road most of the year?"

"That sucks."

I want to say more, but feel it might the wrong thing. Like how her mom should have stayed her ass at home with Bristol instead of forcing Rhyson to perform most of his childhood or leaving him addicted to prescription drugs. But that might be too much.

We reach the top of the wheel, and both of us look over our respective sides at the ground. When I turn back into the car, Bristol's face has gone pale, and her breath comes in little anxious puffs.

"Hey, you okay?" I lean into her space, grasping her chin to turn her face to me.

"Yeah. I just—" She closes her eyes and clamps her teeth down on her bottom lip. "I shouldn't have looked down."

"Are you still scared of heights?"

"Sometimes." Her eyes are still closed, and she pulls in deep breaths through her nose and blows them out through her mouth. "This used to help."

"If you're still scared of heights, why'd you want to ride this thing?"

When she opens her eyes, I almost wish she hadn't. There's a vulnerability at odds with Bristol's bold persona. There's a question there that she's afraid to voice, and I know just as surely as if she'd said it aloud that she got on this ride to spend time with me. She drops her lashes and fidgets, bending her body over the bar holding us in and folding her arms on top of it.

"Just don't look down." I clear my throat, looking away from her, too. "We'll be finished soon."

Only we don't move at all for the next few seconds. And then more seconds.

"What's going on?" Low-level panic infiltrates her voice. "Why aren't we moving?"

"They just kind of pause sometimes," I lie. "Probably just so we can get a good look at everything."

Her laugh catches me off guard.

"They just kind of pause?" She rolls her eyes, looking more like the confident Bristol I've gotten to know the last few days. "You're a better liar than that."

"I don't lie." I shrug. "Ask anybody. I'm honest as Abe. You know how you're in a group and someone farts? And no one claims it?"

"Don't tell me." She giggles, resting her cheek on her folded arms and looking at me. "You claim it."

"If I do it, then I claim it." I grin at her, glad to see some of the color returning to her face. "I have no shame, but at least I'm honest about my shit."

Just as I'm thinking crisis averted, an announcement reaches our ears from the ground that there is a technical problem they're working on, and we should be moving in a few minutes.

"Minutes?" Bristol peers back over her side.

"Don't look down, Bris." I've never shortened her name before like that, the way Rhyson does, and I shouldn't like how intimate it feels.

"Okay. I promise not to freak out unless they leave us up here much longer."

"And if we are up here much longer?"

"Then I can't make any promises." She runs an anxious hand through her hair. "I'm not scared of heights in general. I can go up elevators and stuff. This is the only thing left from my old fear. Being in an open ride like this and suspended over the ground. I just can't stop thinking that I could fall so easily."

The more she talks about it, the more the color vacates her cheeks and her breath chops up again.

"Okay, let's distract you until we get moving again." I roam my brain for something to take her mind off the imagined fall to our death. "What's the weirdest place you ever had sex?"

Yep. The girl I'm supposed to be not trying to screw, and that's the question that comes to mind. Live by the dick, die by the dick, I guess. No going back now, so I just wait for her response like it's not a moronic question.

"Um, how do you know I've had sex before?" Her eyes and her grin collaborate to tease me. "Maybe I'm a virgin."

"Weren't you the girl who screamed 'I like dick' at the top of her lungs last night on the dance floor?" I throw my head back and guffaw, in honor of Jimmi and her word-challenged self.

"Oh my God." Pink washes over her high cheekbones. "I can't believe I did that. It was the Grey Goose talking."

"And warned me that you were horny like you might pounce on me if I got too close." My laugh dies down to a smile, even though this conversation is making my jeans tight.

"Okay, you can stop humiliating me now." She's only half-joking but twists her mouth to the side. "Coat check."

"What?" Is the height going to her head already? "What's coat check?"

"That's the weirdest place I ever had sex. It was at my debutante ball, and—"

"You were a debutante?"

"Don't ask. My mother's doing." She sighs and offers a wry smile. "But my date and I snuck into the coat check closet and did it. I had on this huge white dress and he was struggling to find the condom and the heel on my shoe . . ."

She waves her hand dismissively and grins. "I guess you had to be there."

That would have been awkward.

"I think I get the picture," I say. "Your turn."

She sobers in a few seconds, and her mouth gradually flattens into a soft line.

"What's your greatest regret?" she asks softly.

"You're kidding, right?" I turn my knees in, pressing my back against the side of the cart so I can see her squarely. "I ask you a funny sex question, and you go for the jugular with this?"

"You didn't place any prerequisites on it."

"I didn't know I was dealing with a sadist, or I would have."

"Well, you didn't." She smiles a little, her eyes softening. "Greatest regret, and you have to be honest. Not something stupid like never seeing *The Goonies*."

"God, of course I've seen *The Goonies*." I run a hand over my face, scouring all the regrets crowding my past to find the one that's the worst. And once I have it, I'm not sure I want to be honest with her. If I am, it means I have to be honest with myself, too.

"Okay." I cross my arms over my chest, tipping my head back to contemplate the stars in the darkening sky. "I was like, twelve years old."

"Is this gonna count?" She drops a skeptical look on me. "That's pretty young for regrets."

"Not where I come from," I say softly. I unfocus my eyes, looking back through the years until I find that day on the playground. "This cop stopped me and my cousin Jade."

"For what?"

"For . . .nothing." I shrug. "It isn't like what you're used to. They didn't need a reason. And this was in the nineties, so drugs were huge in our neighborhood. And kids our age were slinging on the playgrounds. So, we didn't think anything of it."

"What happened?"

"He searched me, and of course, found nothing. I was a good kid." A staccato laugh comes quick and short. "I watched movies, went to school, and wrote poetry. Not exactly a gangbanger in the making. My mom made sure I kept my head down and kept moving. You didn't have to find trouble in my neighborhood. It found you."

I glance over my shoulder at the ground, which is so far away the people below like a colony of ants, and turn back.

"Then the same cop searches my cousin." I pause and swallow the heat blistering my throat. "He . . .she had on this dress, and he . . .touched her."

I'll never forget Jade's indrawn breath. He'd told me to stay against the wall, to face the wall, but when I heard her gasp, I looked at them. I wasn't a rule breaker, but I knew this one time, I should break the rule. I should step in when I saw his hand working under her dress, when I saw one tear slide down her face. He had a gun. He was a cop. I didn't know what to do. Jade just shook her head at me, thinking the same thoughts and holding the same fears. It was only a few moments, but that was all it took to turn the whole world upside down.

"I don't know why we never talked about it," I say to Bristol. "And we never told anyone. Jade didn't want to. She was ashamed, I think. I know I was."

"You were kids and he was in authority." There's a world of emotion in Bristol's eyes when they bore into mine. "That's awful."

I blink away the tears filling my eyes as that day suffocates me again.

"And some days, I look in the mirror, like just brushing my teeth or whatever, and I'll say it out loud. I'll say 'Don't touch her.' Just like that. Just that, and maybe he would have stopped."

But there's no rewind button. There are no do-overs. There's no delete key that undoes the damage or the guilt or the shame. I'm sorry, but I can't make it un-happen, and that's why it's called regret.

"Things just kind of changed after that, between me and Jade, I mean," I say. "I mean, we still talk, but . . ."

I shrug, giving up on words to articulate my complex relationship with the cousin I still love so much.

"We all make mistakes and do things we wish we could do differently," Bristol says softly, drawing my attention to her pretty face in the carnival light. "That's part of life. You and Jade should talk about it someday. Tell her you're sorry it happened, and that given the chance, you would have done things differently. We only get one life, but it's filled with second chances. That's why I came here to try again with Rhyson."

I don't reply, but we smile, and I want to tell her that I've never spoken about this before. I want to tell her how good it felt and that I could talk to her all day. That this wheel could be stuck up in the sky for hours, and I wouldn't get tired of hearing her talk or watching her listen.

I look over the side of the car again, wishing I could hurl this shame and hurt down to the ground but knowing I'll live with it forever. Even though it has faded through the years, it isn't gone. It won't ever go away completely, but at least today, for the first time, I shared this load.

And it feels lighter.

Twelve

Bristol

I SHOULDN'T HAVE ASKED THAT QUESTION. "I'M SORRY."

I whisper it, but Grip hears. He's looking over the side, maybe composing himself. There were tears in his eyes when he talked about his cousin Jade, and that dark, dirty day. When he looks back to me, his eyes are clear of tears but they are still shaded with emotion.

"Sorry for what?"

"For asking you . . ." I lift one shoulder, hoping it conveys things I can't put into words. "I'm nosy. It gets me in trouble. I ask too many questions, and then I—"

"I like it," he cuts in softly.

My breath swirls around in my chest and furiously circles my heart like a cyclone.

"You . . .you like what?" I ask.

"That you're curious and ask questions that make me think. That challenge me. People don't always do that."

There's a disparaging twist to my lips. "Because it's called casual conversation," I say with a husky laugh. "And I seem to have trouble keeping things casual."

With you.

I don't say the words aloud, but our eyes exchange them nonetheless.

"It just means I get to ask a tough question that will gut you." He delivers the words lightly, but the curiosity in his eyes is real. This will be a gutter.

"Okay." I release a long-suffering sigh. "I guess it's only fair. Hit me with your best shot."

"Toughest day of your life." He twists so his back is against the car and he has a clear view of me.

"Wow. Just go for it, huh?"

"Like you didn't?" He cocks one brow and props his chin in his hand, as if he has all the time in the world to wait.

"Right." I laugh nervously. "This is the last question. No more after this."

"And I was honest with you, so repay the favor." He says it easily, but the remnants of emotion on his face remind me it's true.

"Toughest day of my life." I twist a little to face him, too, which is probably good because, if I look over the side, I might start hyperventilating again. "Um, the day Rhyson left."

It's quiet for a moment, and I give him my face to search, not looking down or away. So he'll know it's true.

"Grady had been visiting us for the holidays." I look down at the anxious tangle of my fingers on the safety bar. "And he took Rhyson with him when he left."

Rhyson wasn't home much, but when he was, I could always find him in one of two places: his rehearsal room or the tree house in our backyard. I ran from room to room. I climbed that tree looking for him, but he was nowhere to be found, and no one had even bothered to tell me.

"What I remember most is the silence." I hush my voice like it's a secret, and maybe it is, because I've never told anyone this before. "Rhyson rehearsed constantly when he was home."

I laugh, but it costs me a pain in my chest right above my heart.

"I was such a goofball I would sit out in the hall and listen to him play for hours while I did my homework, painted my nails, or even talked on the phone with my friends."

I rest my elbows on the safety bar and prop my chin on the heel of my hand.

"That was when I felt closest to him. I know that sounds crazy since we weren't even in the same room when he was playing, but his music was the realest thing about him. And not in a concert hall or in front of an audience. It was most honest, most raw, when he was alone. It was just for him."

A sigh trembles across my lips and is absorbed by the cooling night air.

"And I would pretend it was just for me, too. So when Grady took him away . . ." I hear my mother's influence, her anger even in how I phrase that, so I amend. "When Rhyson left, the house was dead. No music, no life. He left without even saying goodbye."

Hot tears leak from the corners of my eyes.

"To me, I mean." My breath stutters as I struggle to get the words out. "I am his twin, Grip. Somehow I, this unremarkable in every way girl who couldn't even play a clarinet 'adequately', shared a womb, shared the beginning of my life with this genius person, and I feel it so deeply. It's like I feel his music, I feel him the way twins feel each other."

I bite my bottom lip to control its trembling. "But he doesn't feel me."

"He does, Bristol." Grip reaches over to grab my hands, his one hand, which is so much bigger, darker, and rougher than mine, is a comfort. "I know he loves you. He's just . . . like you said, a genius. Musicians, sometimes the art takes so much from us and we don't know how to save enough for the people around us. We pour so much into it, it's isolating, especially for Rhyson. He was a kid. Dealing with more shit than most adults ever have to. The kind of pressure that had him popping pills just to survive it."

I know truth when I hear it, and what Grip says is true. I just stare back at him, giving him permission to go on.

"Rhyson's addiction was a destructive path, and your parents weren't helping. They may not have realized it, but they were only making it worse." Grip dips his head to catch my eyes as he says the next part. "You said Grady took him, but he saved Rhyson. You know that, right?"

I do know that. For the first time, I allow the worst-case scenario to play out in my head. If Rhyson hadn't left, hadn't gone to rehab, or hadn't gotten the help he needed, what would have happened? God, I've made this all about me. All about how I felt when Rhyson left, not how desperate he must have been to go. All these years, I thought my heart was broken, but only for myself. For the first time, maybe ever, my heart breaks for the gifted, lonely boy who had nothing but his piano.

I mop my hands over my cheeks, gathering the wetness on my palms. So many tears. I've never told anyone how I felt that day. My mother tried to make me go to therapy for that, too, but by then I was sixteen with a strong will of my own and refused. I was tired of talking to strangers, and I wanted to keep this pain locked away, private.

Until now. Until Grip. His eyes rest on my face. I feel his compassion, and it weighs so much I want out from under it. I turn my head to escape the honesty between us for a few seconds. Just for a reprieve. As soon as I look over the side, I realize my mistake.

"Oh, God. We're so high."

Breath charges up my throat, panic pushing out the last few minutes of peace. My heart jackhammers. Blood rushes to my head, and the world spins. I grip my head to make it stop.

"Hey, hey." Grip scoots closer, eliminating the distance between us. "Put your head down as far as you can."

The safety bar keeps me from putting my head between my knees, but I don't think it would help anyway. Nothing helps. It's irrational. I know I'm safe, but fear mocks me and makes me its bitch. I hate it, but I can't stop it.

"My mom used to tell me to recite things," Grip says from above me. "Like to distract myself when I was scared. To give me something else to focus on."

It only makes me more anxious that I have nothing I can recite. Fear jumbles all my thoughts together, so discombobulated that I can't even assemble the digits of my phone number.

"I can't think of anything."

"Okay. Hold up." He rubs my back in soothing strokes that don't soothe. "I'll do it. Just listen to my voice. Focus on what I'm saying."

I can't focus. I can't stop the encroaching darkness, blurring my edges and knotting my interior. It's never been this bad, and it would happen right in front of Grip.

"I'll recite 'Poetry' by Pablo Neruda. My favorite, actually." Grip's voice is warm but disembodied as I press my eyes closed. "It feels like he was writing my life story. Like he knew there would be this kid who needed something bigger than himself, and he wrote this to guide that kid to a different path. This has always felt like more than a poem. It's personal. It feels like my prophecy."

The emotion, the honesty in his voice compels me to hazard a glance at him. In the faint light of the moon and the bright lights of the carnival, I see his face. Beautiful and bronzed, a sculpture of bold bones and full lips. His eyes are intent, never looking away from mine as he begins.

His deep voice caresses Neruda's sentiments of how poetry called him from the street and away from violence. Of how writing saved him from a certain fate and opened up a world he'd never imagined. And Grip's right. The poem could have been written for him . . . could have foretold the story of a boy called, not from the streets of a Chilean city, but from the streets of Compton.

Passion weaves between his words and conviction laces every line. He means these words. He loves these words. Amazingly, as he's reciting a poem I've never heard before, someone else's words illuminate Grip to me. I see him clearly. A man deeply committed to his craft and who views his gift as a miracle of circumstance. As cocky as he is, I see him humbled by the means to escape a path so many others never leave. And if the poem tells his story, his eyes are a confession, never straying from mine, holding mine in the moonlight, his voice liquid poured over something sweet. As he approaches the end, my fears are forgotten, but I'm still stuck on a Ferris wheel under a darkened sky, and nothing has ever been more fitting than the final words, in which the poet says he wheeled with the stars and his heart broke loose on the wind.

There are too few perfect moments in this life. Far too few of us get them, but I am privileged to have this one with this man. When he empties his chest of his heart and empties his body of his soul for me under a starry sky on a Ferris wheel. And I know. In this moment, I know that I'm lost to him. It has been a matter of days. It has been a string of moments. It has not been long enough to tell him, but in my heart, I know I am lost.

"Did that help?" he asks.

He searches through the dim light for my fear or my panic, but they aren't there anymore. He leans closer, so close his breath whispers over my face. I don't know when he realizes that fear has gone and that something else has come, but I see the change in his eyes.

I think he might be lost in me, too.

The inches between our lips disappear. At the first brush of his mouth on mine, I know this kiss will never end. It will live on in my memory for the rest of my life. His lips beg entry, a tentative touch that blazes through my defenses and hastens the rhythm of my heart. I clutch his arm, skin and muscle, satin over steel. A thousand textures collide. The hot silk of his mouth. The sharp, straight edge of his teeth. The firm curve of his lips. The taste of him. God, the taste of him makes me moan. He cups my face, fingers spearing into my hair. I press so close the heat of his body burns through the thin fabric of our shirts.

"Bris." He says it against my lips before trailing kisses down my chin. His mouth opens over my neck, hot and wet, and I arch into him, the pleasure like a train in my veins. Rushing. Vaulting. Exploding.

"Oh, God." I'm a panting mess. My hands venture under his shirt, desperate, nails scraping at his back. "Keep kissing me."

He's back at my lips, devouring, our tongues dueling, dancing. This kiss has a cadence, his head moving to the left and then right, on beat, a syncopation, a simultaneity of lips and tongues. His mouth slants over mine, hot and zealous, and I link my fingers behind his head, clinging, afraid this will end. Afraid to lose the enormity of this moment. At the top of the world, so close we could almost touch the sky and with only the stars watching, I found out what a kiss should be.

Thirteen

Grip

'M SO SCREWED.

I kissed Bristol last night, and nothing's the same. Our kiss ended once the wheel started turning, but nothing stopped. There's a momentum to this thing between Bristol and me that I can't stop. I don't want to stop. We held hands through the Ferris wheel's slow, rolling descent to the ground. By silent agreement, we let go when we saw the others. I don't want this examined, mocked, made light, and for now, we want to keep it to ourselves.

The rest of the night, we stayed with the group, but a quiet, untraceable intimacy linked us. We played silly games and won stupid prizes. She won me a black plastic watch. I won her a whistle. We got lost together in the fun house, and I pressed her against a wavy mirror. Even distorted, our shapes were perfect together.

I don't know what to do. I don't know what she wants or what I am to her. Is she slumming? Am I some exotic fruit or a novelty she sampled on vacation? Or does this feel to her like it feels to me? Like the beginning of something. Mr. Chocolate Charm himself can't get up the nerve to ask a girl if she really likes him.

I watch her and Jimmi running on the shore, laughing as the tide chases them. Jimmi's uncle has a small beach house in Malibu, and we're spending Bristol's last day here. Rhyson spent the day with us but got called into the studio for one more tweak. It's been a perfect day, except I've had no time with Bristol alone to ask her what she's thinking or feeling. She leaves tomorrow, and I don't know if we'll forget this ever happened, or if we'll make it something more.

"Whew." Jimmi collapses onto the beach blanket. "This day has been amazing."

"It's gorgeous here," Bristol smiles and sits beside Jimmi. "Thank you for bringing me."

Our eyes collide over the small fire we used to roast marshmallows and s'mores. She looks quickly away and lies down to close her eyes.

"We need to be heading back," Luke says, his arm around Mandi's shoulders. "One last swim before we go? Not too far out because it's already dark."

"Let's make it count," Jimmi says, a reckless glint in her eye. "Skinny-dipping."

Luke and I are already shaking our heads. No way am I going bare nuts into that freezing water.

"I'm not going naked into the ocean," Mandi says. "There's seaweed and fish and it's cold. No, thanks."

"What about you?" Jimmi nudges Bristol, who still lies back, eyes closed. "You chicken?"

"Those mind games don't work on me." Bristol sits up, a defiant smile curling the edges of her full lips. "Do you honestly think I'd let you goad me into such a stupid dare?"

They look at each other, exchanging wicked grins and then scrambling to their feet, a blur of long legs and flying bikini tops. My jaw unhinges. I can't believe she did that. It looks like she kept the bottom on, but I can clearly see her top, which is nothing more than two tiny triangles of fabric, on the beach with Jimmi's. Their squeals echo in the night.

"You wanna?" Mandi asks Luke, sporting a reckless grin of her own now.

For a moment, Luke looks like he'll resist, but his eyes wander to the bikini tops on the sand and then to Mandi's considerable rack.

"Hey, why not?" He shrugs, standing to his feet and shucking off his trunks. I look away, not needing to see his tan line or his junk. I deliberately avert my eyes when Mandi tosses her top and runs to the ocean's edge.

I look to the shore, making out their bodies, shadows in the fresh moonlight, frolicking and screaming and laughing. A smile settles on my lips, and I'm on my feet walking toward the water. Not naked, though. It's too cold for that shit.

I've waded in just a few feet, still adjusting to the temperature of the water, when an arm slips around my waist from behind. Warm, water-slick breasts press into my back.

"Bristol?" I ask in a voice that is husky and hopeful.

"No, it's Jimmi, you doofus." Bristol's voice is playful, her chuckle full of mischief as she slips away, deeper into the water, a little farther from shore.

We're not too far out, but I don't see or hear the others as I turn to face her. The night cloaks her. There isn't enough moonlight to see her clearly, but I sense her. I sense her craving because it matches mine. It's her last night here, and I'll be damned if she's leaving without kissing me again. I press through the water's resistance until our bodies are flush. Her nipples, tight from the cool night air, and maybe from desire, pebble against my chest. I dip my head and leave my words in her ear.

"I want to kiss you again."

Her sharp breath is her only reply, but I rest my lips against hers to taste her consent. Palming her sides, my fingers almost meeting at her back, I stretch my thumbs up to rub her nipples, alternating between strokes brisk then slow.

"Oh, God, yes." She spreads her hands over my shoulders and to my neck, urging my head down. "Kiss them. Please kiss them."

I slip my hands over her ass and lift her out of the water so she can lock her legs at my back, scooting her up until I can take one nipple into my mouth.

Shiiiiiiit.

I open wide, taking as much of her into me as I can, sucking the nipple and licking at the silky halo of surrounding skin.

"Grip, yes." Her hands claw at my shoulders and run up my neck. She dips her head to possess my mouth with hers. Her kiss woos me in the water. Her fingers on my skin are poetry. Her lips, prose. The rhythm of her heart against mine, iambic. Every touch, eloquence.

The current tugs at our bodies as the tide comes in, and clinging to each other, we let the flow take us. With our mouths still fused, legs still tangled, tongues hungry and twisting together, we drift into deeper waters.

Complex and effortless.

My own words come back to haunt me, describing a rapper's flow. I can't help but compare it to what's passing between us in the deep. The unexpected alchemy that's been flowing between us since the moment we met. It's layered and complicated, and yet, there's no struggle, no force. It feels easy. Effortless. It feels so good, I can't imagine this ending.

"I need to know," I mumble at the underside of her breast. "What we're doing, Bristol."

"What do you mean?" she gasps. "This feels fantastic."

I slide her down my body and frame her face in my hands. "Is this like some spring break fling for you?" I ask earnestly.

"Grip, I . . ." She drops her forehead to my chest, and I would give anything to turn up the wattage on the moon so I could see her face better. So I could see her eyes. "I don't know."

It shouldn't hurt. We shared a few days, a few conversations, and the best kisses of my life. That's it. That's all, but last night feels like the best night I've ever had. And to think it wasn't monumental for her or that she's "deciding" what we'll be when I feel like the decision was made for me almost as soon as I laid eyes on her, hurts.

"I'm not a casual kind of person." She sighs, and I can imagine the jaded look on her face. "And there's a lot that could go wrong. You're my brother's best friend. I'm moving here and it could be awkward if things . . .go south."

"They won't," I assure her. "Just give it a chance."

"What?" She lets out a cynical laugh. "A long-distance relationship?"

"Why not?"

"You're a player for one thing, Mr. Bees with honey and chocolate. You get bored, you move on, and you probably cheat."

There's a question in her voice, and I know this is the moment when I should tell her about Tessa. But I'm having such a hard time even getting her to consider making us an us, and I don't want to make it any harder by throwing that wrench in the works. I'll deal with Tessa as soon as Bristol is gone.

"It'd be different with you." I run a palm over her wet hair. "I know it would be."

"But I don't know it would be, and . . ." I see the shape of her head as she lifts it, shaking it. "Can we take it slow? I don't want to get hurt, and I think you could hurt me really badly."

Her answer is soft and honest, and it only makes me want her more.

"We can do that." I bend to kiss her neck, sucking at the salt-covered skin until she gasps, grinding her hips through the water seeking me. That's her spot. One of them. She wants to take it slow? I'm willing to take my time finding all the others.

Fourteen

Bristol

TAP, TAP, TAP.

I look up from the suitcase I'm packing. Someone's knocking on the door of Grady's guest bedroom. I hastily tuck the cheap whistle Grip won for me at the carnival into the bag and zip it up. When I open the door, Rhyson stands in the hall.

"Can I come in?" His dark hair, always a gorgeous mess, flops into his eyes.

"Sure." I step back and wave him in, sitting on the bed and waiting to hear what he has to say. We've had very little time alone since the night we talked after the club. We spent yesterday with his friends, and he had to go back to the studio last night.

"All packed, huh?" He eyes my huge suitcase.

"Looks that way." A small, sad smile touches my mouth. "I'll miss LA. Who'd have thought?"

"Will you miss LA, or will you miss your big brother?" he teases. "Not this big brother stuff again."

"I haven't been much of one." His smile fades. "A brother, I mean."

Instead of answering, I wait for him to go on.

He shakes his head. "It's so hard to know what to trust when it comes to them, to our parents."

"You can trust me to be who I say I am, Rhyson. Your sister." I tilt my chin and flash him some confidence in the form of a smile. "You'll see that when I'm managing that career for you."

"I don't have a career." He laughs and leans back on the bed, propped on his elbows.

"But you will. You should. And when you do, I'll be right there to help you."

"You can't build plans around something that hasn't happened yet."

"Idiot, what do you think dreams are if not plans we make based on things that haven't happened yet?"

We laugh a little, and I lie back beside him, resting my head on his shoulder. What I wouldn't have given years ago to have my brother like this. To have time with him when he wasn't rehearsing or touring or doing whatever was required of him.

"Don't you have any dreams of your own?" he asks.

Grip's face, his soft touches, and promises in the dark waters last night, come to mind. I want to believe him because those kisses on the Ferris wheel, in the fun house, in the ocean were the best of my life. The conversations we've had this week changed me. No controversy, no memory, no hope or fear was off-limits. They have woven themselves—he has woven himself—into the fabric of my dreams so quickly it frightens me.

"I do have dreams," I finally answer. "And they're all here now."

He smiles at me slowly and nods.

"We better get going." Rhyson glances at his watch, and it makes me think of the cheap watch I won for Grip last night. I shake off memories of the carnival as Rhyson rolls the Louis bag out of my room and down the hall.

"It's a shame I didn't get to see Uncle Grady this trip."

"Next time," Rhyson says. "But there are some people who want to tell you goodbye."

When we enter the living room, my new friends are all there. Jimmi, Luke, Mandi, and standing at the back of the group is Grip, his eyes a beautifully laid trap I stumble into and can't wriggle free of. "Oh, you guys." I wrap my arms around Jimmi, who squeezes me so tightly I can barely breathe.

"I feel like I found a new bestie." Jimmi blinks tears from her big blue eyes. "We have to talk every week, and you have to come back soon. And I can come to New York, too."

"Deal." I smile through a few tears of my own. "We'll stay in touch. Don't worry."

I haven't spent as much time with Luke and Mandi, but it's still sweet of them to show up to say goodbye to me. They're both cool, and Rhyson is lucky to have this tight-knit circle of people in his life. I don't really have anything like them in New York, and it makes me want to wish away the next two years at Columbia so I can move here right away.

And then there's Grip.

We take a few careful steps toward each other, and I feel like everyone's watching us.

"Thank you for everything," I say softly, leaving a few inches between us. His eyes burn a mute plea for more.

"No problem. Sure."

He glances down at the floor before slipping his arms around my waist and dragging me against his warm, hard body. Not caring what Rhyson or anyone else thinks, I tip up on my toes and hook my elbows behind his neck as tightly as I can. His hands spread over my back, fitting my curves to all his ridges and planes.

"You come back to me, okay?" he whispers in my ear. "Slow doesn't mean stop, right?"

My cheeks fire up, and I glance self-consciously at the others, but they aren't paying attention. Rhyson is rolling my suitcase out to the car, and Mandi, Luke, and Jimmi are talking about last night at the beach swimming nude. Or semi-nude. Jimmi was the only one brave/crazy enough to be fully naked.

"No, slow doesn't mean stop," I agree. "In fact—"

His phone ringing interrupts me telling him I plan to come back this summer when I have a few days off from my internship.

"Lemme grab this," he says, frowning at the phone. "It's Jade."

I remember her name from the story he told me on the Ferris wheel. The one he still feels guilt over.

"Hey, whassup?" He presses the phone to his ear, and his brows snap together. "Why'd you tell her I was here?"

I turn away, heeding Rhyson's call to come on or I'll miss my flight. We walk outside to load up the car so we can get on the road. Rhyson and Grip are taking me, and I'm not sure if we should tell Rhyson what has been going on or not. It feels like such a fledgling thing but still substantial enough that he should know. I'm still silently debating when a Toyota Camry pulls up to the curb, and a curvy woman with dark brown skin and black, curly hair gets out. A scowl mars her beautiful face, and anger has her arms swinging at her side with her long strides.

"Where is he?" she demands of Rhyson without any preamble. "Uh, hey, Tessa." Rhyson glances up the driveway and widens his eyes meaningfully at his best friend.

Rhyson may be looking at Grip, but Grip is looking at me, and if I didn't know better, I would say he's panicking. Before I have time to process what's happening, how my world is about to be ripped into tiny pieces, Tessa begins her tirade.

"How you gonna ignore my calls and text messages?" Yelling, she fits her hands to the swell of her hips. "For two damn weeks, Grip?"

"I didn't." Grip looks at me with troubled eyes over her shoulder and then back to her face. "We just kept missing each other. What's going on? What's this about?"

"This is about me trying to tell you something I wanted to talk about in person, not over some voice mail." Her strident voice pitches across the yard at him.

"Okay, damn, Tessa," Grips says, irritation evident on his face. "I'm going with Rhyson to take his sister to the airport. Can we talk later? When I get back?"

"Who is she?" I whisper to Rhyson.

"That's Tessa." Rhyson stretches his eyebrows until they disappear under his unruly hair. "Grip's girlfriend."

"His girl—"

I choke on the rest of the word as a tight hand vises my throat. That can't be. Last night's water-dappled promises and sea salt kisses. The perfect kiss under the stars at the top of the world. All lies? We shared deep, dark lonely things. We shared everything, and it was the most honest connection I've ever had with anyone. And under it all was the lie that he could be mine? That maybe I could be his? That he didn't belong to someone else? He would have said.

"No, we can't talk when you get back," Tessa snaps. "We need to talk now. I'm sick of chasing your ass down. You are taking responsibility for this."

"Responsibility?" Grip shakes his head and shrugs "For what?" "For this baby, that's for what," she retorts with harsh smugness.

His wide eyes snap to my face, and any doubt that she might be the one lying, that somehow this is all a prank, a hidden camera stunt, dissolve. That guard I forgot about and dropped all week falls back into place over my heart just in time.

We don't cry in front of strangers.

My mother's admonition, the voice of reason in my head that I ignored the last few days, slips iron discs between my vertebrae.

"Rhyson, can we go?" I ask. "I can't miss my flight home." "Bristol!" Grip yells over the screeching banshee with wildly gesticulating arms in front of him. "Wait. I can—"

I open the door to Rhyson's car and get in, not wanting to hear the dollar-late, day-short explanations disguising his lies.

Rhyson gets in, glancing over his shoulder at the spectacle on the yard, the beautiful woman screaming at Grip's rigid face and ticking jaw. He looks at me through the car window, his eyes begging me for something I won't give.

Second chances.

"Drive, Rhyson." My voice is rock and resolve. "Let your friend sort his shit out. I'm going home."

*If I break your heart,
I break mine.*

USA TODAY BESTSELLING AUTHOR
KENNEDY RYAN

GRIP TRILOGY BOOK #2

Resisting an irresistible force wears you down and turns you out.

I know—I've been doing it for years.

I may not have a musical gift of my own,

but I've got a nose for talent and an eye for the extraordinary.

And Marlon James—Grip to his fans—is nothing short of extraordinary.

Years ago, we strung together a few magical nights, but I keep those memories in a locked drawer and I've thrown away the key. All that's left is friendship and work.

He's on the verge of unimaginable fame,

all his dreams poised to come true.

I manage his career, but I can't seem to manage my heart. It's wild, reckless, disobedient—and it remembers all the things I want to forget.

"You are the perfect verse over a tight beat."
—*Brown Sugar*

Prologue

Bristol

Eight Years Ago, After Spring Break—New York

I FEEL LIKE A FOOL.

Like those foolish girls who fall for the tricks of beautiful men. Men who keep women on the side. Men who cheat and don't think twice about lying. I'm usually an excellent judge of character, but I was blinded by a charismatic smile and gorgeous body. By a brilliant mind and a silver tongue. So starved for attention, I mistook Grip's attention for kindness. Something I could count on. Something I could believe in. I forgot I can only count on myself. Only believe in myself. But now I remember. His girlfriend screaming on the front lawn jarred my memory.

"Cheating asshole," I mutter, rolling my mammoth Louis Vuitton suitcase through the front door of my parents' New York home.

My classes at Columbia don't start back up for another two days, so I'll hang here until I have to be back in the city. My apartment is cold and lonely. I glance around our foyer, checker-boarded with black-and-white tiles, and up the wide staircase. This crypt of a house is pretty cold and lonely, too. After the last week in LA, surrounded by Rhyson's friends, I feel the isolation more profoundly.

At least there's an elevator here. Because dragging this huge suitcase up the steps is not my idea of fun after a five-hour flight. I'm headed around the corner to the elevator when a sound above draws my eyes up the stairs again.

A moan?

I listen more closely, despite my suspicion that I shouldn't.

Grunting and cries of what sounds like intense pleasure.

"Well, well, well." I laugh despite the crappy day I've had. "At least somebody's getting some, even though it's my parents. Ew."

I'm not actually disgusted. I think I'm . . . happy. Happy that after all these years of thinking my parents didn't even want or love each other, they thought I wouldn't be home and are upstairs happily fucking in their glorious middle age. I'd always assumed their marriage was more of a business partnership than anything else, with Rhyson and me the two-for-one requisite heirs of a powerful arranged alliance. But it seems they do want each other. It makes my heart just a little lighter.

That's saying something considering I stayed in the bathroom crying until the flight attendant forced me out for takeoff. Over that . . . chocolate charm lothario. That cheat. That . . . liar. My eyes are still a little puffy, a situation I need to remedy before Mother's sharp glance starts probing. I'll already have to endure an interrogation about how Rhyson is doing in Los Angeles. They haven't seen my twin brother since that fateful day in court when he emancipated. They've talked to him even less than I have over the last few years.

"Oh, God! Yes. Yes!"

They're getting louder and more fervent. Okay, this is getting awkward. They obviously don't think anyone else is home, or they wouldn't be quite so uninhibited. I'll just slip into my room and come out later.

Someone walks through the front door behind me just as the elevator opens. Maybe Bertie, our housekeeper?

It's my mother. Oh my God.

Every auburn hair in place, her face as smooth and lineless as it has been the last twenty-one years. She sets her Celine bag on the table by the front door.

"Bristol, welcome home." She walks forward, her gait even and confident, so similar to mine it's like watching myself move. She air kisses, an insubstantial affection that falls short of my cheek. "I want to hear all about your trip, of course."

"Of course."

I mentally scramble for a way to get her out before the couple upstairs starts grunting and moaning again. Is it Dad? I can't even convince myself that my father is not upstairs fucking another woman. There's no other logical explanation.

"Mother, I want to tell you everything." I leave my suitcase by the elevator and walk to the front door. "Let's go grab coffee. That little place up the street. Pano's?"

"Coffee?" Mother has a way of injecting tiny amounts of scorn into just about anything, including the little laugh she offers at my suggestion. "You just got here. I just walked in the door. Why would we—"

"Fuck, yes!" The exclamation comes from upstairs.

Mother freezes and whatever drops of scorn she was poised to deliver congeal on her painted lips. Her eyes slowly climb the staircase before they return to meet mine. She looks as self-assured as she ever has, but there's a film over her eyes as fragile as blown glass.

"Mother, we could—"

"It's fine, Bristol." She nods to the suitcase by the elevator. "Take your bags upstairs and we'll talk at dinner about your trip to see your brother."

"But, Mother, we should—"

"Bristol, my God! Can't you just listen for once? Can't you just for once do exactly what I ask you to do and not make my life any harder?"

It isn't true. It isn't fair. I haven't made her life harder. Not ever. I've accepted the nannies who raised me when she and my father took Rhyson on the road. I lay on the couches of New York's finest therapists when Mother abdicated walking me through my "issues" as a child. I was an honor student. When she asked me to do the stupid debutante thing with the sons and daughters of all her Upper Eastside friends, I did it. I'm in an Ivy League college, like she wanted. If anything, I've bent over backward, pretzeled myself to please her when I could.

I turn to leave, but a door upstairs flies open, and a blonde girl, maybe a year or two older than I am, rockets down the hall. Nina Algier, a brilliant flute player and one of my parents' clients, stops and stares at us over the railing above, hair wild, eyes wide and horrified. Tall and coltish, she's a rising star in the Boston Symphony Orchestra. She looks back over her shoulder as my father joins her there.

Rhyson and I share his dark coloring, taking only Mother's gray eyes. He looks so much like Rhyson and Uncle Grady, handsome, distinguished, with just a little gray at the temples. His eyes flick to me before moving on. I never feel like I even register for him. I'm not musical; therefore, I'm worthless. That is how it's always felt. The hardness in his eyes softens just a bit when he sees my mother, maybe with remorse. I've never seen my father sorry for anything, so I wouldn't recognize it on him.

"Angela," he says so softly that his voice barely reaches us by the door. "You're home."

I bounce a look between my father and my mother and Nina Algier, certain that I'm in an alternative universe. That's all? That's fucking all he has to say?

Nina, who has been as still as an ice sculpture to that point, galvanizes into action, rushing down the stairs. Her white silk blouse is half-buttoned and hanging from the waistband of her skirt, and there's a flush painted on her cheeks when she cannons past us. She smells of my father's cologne.

"I'm sorry, Mrs. Gray," she mumbles, avoiding our eyes and fumbling with the door handle until it finally opens and she springs free.

"Go to your room, Bristol," my mother says, her voice the same low, even tone it's always been. "We'll talk about your trip later."

I'm torn between railing on my father, comforting my mother, and getting the hell out of here. I take door number three.

Or rather I take the elevator. As soon as I step off and start toward my bedroom, I hear their raised voices. Their anger, their contention, it was a sound I had never heard before that moment. Not even when Rhyson sued to emancipate did they present anything other than a united front. A cold front, but always united. My parents aren't prone to displays of affection or expressions of love, so I never expect the emotion that rises from downstairs before I hear the front door slam.

Damn this day. It has ravaged me.

I flop onto my bed and close my eyes. My room, which has been empty for months, is cold. New York is cold. It was only last night that I waded nearly naked into the waves, a hedonist seeking my pleasure with a beautiful man I thought I knew in no time. Even after only a handful of days, I thought I knew. How he got close enough to break my heart so quickly, I'm not sure, but I know it is not whole. Maybe I fell for the possibility of him. The idea that there was actually someone out there who saw me, flaws and all, and would accept me. "Got" me. That must be it. And yet, I can already feel those places around my heart that I stiffened and starched to forget him . . . softening. Giving some quarter and asking me if I shouldn't let him explain. If maybe he does deserve that second chance.

"Weak bitch." I'm the only one in the room to hear the admonishment. I'm the only one who needs to.

Exhaustion must have demanded her due, because I don't even recall falling asleep. When I wake, the room is darker and colder. I'm not in LA, the land of sand and sun. It's still New York, and it's still cold, and maybe that's as it should be. I slip out of the wrinkled clothes I flew and slept in and put on leggings and a Columbia sweatshirt before padding down the stairs in search of food. Surely Bertie made something for me.

I'm in the kitchen, foraging between the pantry and the fridge, when I hear the weeping. I drop a drumstick on the counter and follow that sorrowful sound. Seeing your mother cry for the first time is always hard for a child. I don't know that it's any easier because I'm twenty-one years old. I can't recall ever seeing her tears, not this way. Not sprawled on the living room floor surrounded by shattered glass and spilled liquor.

"Mother, let me help you." I reach for her, but she wrenches away.

"Leave." A broken sob drowns the word. "God, why can't you just leave me alone like everyone else does?"

Her words are always sharp, but I think she sharpens them to their finest point for me. And they always find their mark, bull's-eye in my heart.

"Get up." I grab her arm despite her efforts to keep it from me. "There's glass everywhere."

"Bertie will get it," she slurs.

I look more closely and realize she's drunk. Totally, sloppy drunk. I loop her arm over my shoulder, half-dragging her to the couch where I prop her up. Her head droops to the side, and I see the tracks of tears in her usually flawless makeup.

"Mother, he isn't worth this." I keep my voice soft but try to sound convincing.

"How would you know?" The words roll around in her mouth, a soup of consonants and vowels. "You have no idea."

"I know that if a man cheats once, he'll do it again."

"Once?" A bitter laugh cracks her face open. "You think this was the first time? Oh, God. I've lost count. There's the ghosts of a hundred Nina Algiers in our bed."

"Then leave him." I take a seat beside her, grabbing her hand to urge her. "You're stronger than this."

"No." She says the word sadly, quietly, helplessly. "I'm not."

When she looks at me, I see that it isn't just the decanter that's shattered all over the floor. My mother is shattered, and there are shards of glass, decades old, in her eyes.

"I love him," she whispers. "He'll have to leave me, because I love him, and I don't know how to stop. I don't know how to let go."

The strongest woman I know? Tough as nails negotiator? The enemy you never want to face, leveled by love?

"I can't believe you tolerate it, Mother."

"Oh, spare me, Bristol." Her disgust and anger trip over each other to get to me. "You'll be here one day if you're not careful. In this same spot, with this same broken heart."

"You're wrong." Something in my heart whispers that she's right, but I can't acknowledge it. I won't.

She sits up from her drunken slump and looks me right in the eyes with sudden clarity.

"You are just like me, maybe worse," she says. "You need too much. And you'll love too much, too, if you're not careful. I fell in love with the wrong man a long time ago, and people like you and me, we don't know how to stop."

"Stop saying I'm like that." The words throb in my throat before I can release them.

"I don't have to say it." She drags herself up and over to the bar, grabbing another bottle and pouring herself a drink. "You already know it's true."

Even knowing all that Grip has done, there is still some part of me that wants it to all be a cruel joke so I can forgive him. Give him that second chance. Maybe she's right. Maybe I am like her. But if I am, I'm learning her lesson here, today. She loves the wrong man so hard that even when he hurts her, she can't turn it off.

If that's how we love, then it's better to never start.

Grip

Six Years Ago, After Graduation—Los Angeles

By the time I arrive, Bristol's welcome party is in full swing. Maybe that's best. Maybe it will make things less awkward. We haven't seen each other in two years. When she wouldn't answer my calls or text messages, or even confirm she received the book of Neruda poems I mailed to her, as hard as it was, I had to let it go. I messed up, and she shut me out. I told myself I'd try again when she finished college and moved here to LA. Rhys and Bristol kept in touch and made progress over the last two years. Now, she's here to do what she said she would—manage Rhyson's music career.

I've entered Grady's house more times than I can count, but I've never felt nervous crossing this threshold. Like can't-eat-need-a-drink nervous. And there hasn't been anyone to really talk to about this. I know Bristol didn't tell Rhys what happened between us, and I took my cue from her. How we resolve this is our business, no on else's. I hope once we get this shit sorted, once she understands, we can see if there's anything left of what we started two years ago. If it's even worth trying. It wasn't long enough to be love. It's too deep, and I'm too old for a crush. It's too raw for infatuation. I may not be able to put a name to it, but it didn't vacate the premises when Bristol left. I can't evict it.

The living room is packed, crowded with people I don't think Bristol knows. They're our friends, and all they know is that Rhyson's sister is moving to LA. I walk in on some joke already punch lined because everyone is laughing. I slip in, wanting to go unnoticed. Jimmi immediately makes that impossible.

"Grip!" She unfolds herself from the cross-legged pose on the floor and throws herself at me. "I wondered where you were."

I squeeze Jimmi but look over her shoulder and directly into Bristol's silvery eyes. Only for a second before she looks away and dives back into a conversation as if I don't exist. But that second tells me a lot. It'll take more than an apology to fix things between us. She looked right through me as if I wasn't there. As if she wished I weren't.

She looks even better than before. Her hair is shorter and sits just above her shoulders instead of down her back. Her face looks leaner, like something chiseled all the illusions away from the soft flesh and striking bones, sharpening her. Black jeans, high-heeled boots, and a silk blouse that leaves her arms and shoulders bare and ties behind her neck. She had a high shine before, but now there's something more polished about her. The sophistication gleams even brighter. It could have been that big-time internship she got with Sound Management in New York. Or maybe she just grew up.

"Dude." Rhyson stands, too, coming to dap me up and grin. "How'd the session go?"

"Good." My eyes stray to Bristol, who is still in deep conversation with a small group of people. "We knocked out both verses in no time."

"Nice." Rhyson glances at his phone and grimaces. "I'm still waiting on that call from the label."

"For real?" I reassure him with a grin, though I know I can't unknot his stomach or calm his nerves while he waits to hear back from the record label considering signing him. "They'll call."

Rhyson's finally ready to perform again, but he's going back in as a contemporary artist instead of a classical pianist.

After a few minutes, I work my way over to the circle of conversation Bristol is embroiled in. I even take an empty spot on the couch facing her, restricting myself to a few furtive glances, though I'd rather stare.

"So, Bris," Luke, our friend from high school says. "What are you gonna do while you wait for Rhyson to make it big?"

"I'm not sure I'm 'waiting' for him to make it big." Bristol's laugh is husky and assured. "I think it'll be my job to ensure he makes it big."

She rakes her hair, cut into its stylish bob, back from her face. "But I'm doing some stuff with Sound Management's LA office while we work toward our goals." She goes to take a sip of her white wine, only to find it empty. "I'll be back. I'm grabbing a refill."

She doesn't acknowledge me, but stands and heads toward the kitchen. I could let this go. She's sending me clear signals. It's unlikely she wants to take up where we left off in the ocean that night, but my whole life has been a series of unlikelies.

I swing the kitchen door open soundlessly. I'm glad Grady oils his hinges because I get a moment to study Bristol before she realizes I'm there and that she isn't alone. She leans into Grady's kitchen counter, arms stretched to the side, both palms laid flat on the surface. Her wine glass sits empty beside a full bottle of white. She drops her head forward and expels a heavy breath. The ease she projected out there drops away. I know an escape when I see one. If she's running from me, I'll have to disappoint her.

"Hey."

I drop that one word in the quiet kitchen, and she jumps as if it were the report of a bullet. She rounds on me, and for just a second, everything about her whispers vulnerable. The wide, troubled eyes. The tremulous line of her full lips. An uncertain frown. She tucks it all away so quickly, you'd miss it if you weren't watching. One thing I got really good at the last time Bristol visited, was watching her.

"Hi." She picks up the bottle of wine, her excuse for leaving the room, and pours herself a glass.

"Salut." She lifts her glass and starts to walk past me.

I grab her elbow before she makes it to the door. Her eyes zip-line from my hand on her arm to my face.

"Did you need something, Grip?"

She raises both brows, disdain on her face. When she told me she had been one of those high-class New York debutantes, I couldn't reconcile that with who I met: the approachable girl with the easy laugh and curious eyes. I see it now in the frosty look she gives me. It's designed to put me off, but it'll take more than that.

"Did you get the book I sent you?" I ask, not letting her go, waiting for her to jerk away. She doesn't. She wants me to think our skin-to-skin contact doesn't affect her the way it affects me, but her pulse is a hummingbird flapping at the base of her throat with rapid wings. Pink washes over her cheeks. Her pupils swallow the silver in her eyes.

"The poems?" she asks calmly. "Yes."

"And?"

"Thank you." Her lashes drop. "I brought it back for you."

"No, I wanted you to have it. You never returned my calls or text messages. I emailed you. I—"

"I didn't see the point," she interrupts. She tugs at her arm to gently extricate herself and walks back over to the counter, putting a safe distance between us.

"You didn't see the . . ." I check my frustration. This is, after all, my fault. I'm the one who didn't tell her the whole truth. "I think we *were* the point, Bris."

"Then I'm glad I didn't waste my time or yours because there is no us." She looks me in the eyes, but I think it's only to prove she can. "You lied to me."

"Not really." I risk a few steps closer until I'm leaning against the counter beside her. "I was trying to figure out how to break things off with Tessa for a few weeks."

"You aren't still together?" she asks nonchalantly.

"Wasn't my kid." I suck my teeth and release a short breath, exasperated. "That's what I'm trying to tell you. If you'd just listen—"

"Listen?" she cuts in, showing a spark of anger. "To what? You cobble together some technicalities and semantics to disguise the truth?"

I prefer this, the honesty of her anger over that frigid, fake indifference.

"I should have told you," I admit softly, pouring all my regrets into the gaze we hold. "I was looking for the right time."

"The right time was somewhere between the airport and that Ferris wheel." She curves her lips into a fraudulent smile. "But that's okay. It doesn't matter now. It's worked out for the best."

"It isn't worked out. I tried to get in touch. You never responded." "Nothing to say." She lifts one slim shoulder, perfectly executing carelessness. "It's behind us now, and we can have a fresh start." Is she saying . . .

"You mean—"

"As friends, yes." She looks at me pointedly. "Look, I'm on a whole new coast and starting my new job. Figuring out where I'll live. Getting Rhyson's career off the ground. There's a lot of things I need to focus on. What might have been between us if you hadn't lied isn't one of them. Let's forget all the other stuff."

I roll back the sleeve of my denim shirt, showing her the black watch I wear every day. The cheap watch she won for me on a priceless night.

"Does that look like I've forgotten, Bristol?"

Surprise flits across her face before she cements it back into her designated expression.

"Look, we'll both be in Rhyson's life," she says with her eyes on the floor. "You trying to make that week something it really wasn't will only make things awkward."

"I'm not trying to make it something." My voice scolds and pleads. "It was something, and you know it."

"I know you lied to me." Her voice is flat, eyes steady. "And the only thing left for us is friendship."

Her face softens, and a smile warms her eyes for a moment.

"I actually think we could be good friends," she says. "Who else is gonna teach me remedial hip-hop?"

I can't bring myself to smile at her lighthearted comment. She's offering me crumbs when I want the whole loaf. I want so much more than she's willing to give me. If I'm honest, I want more than I deserve. Doesn't make me want it any less. We only had a week together, but the conversation, the connection—I never had it with anyone else before or since. It is real, and real is so rare, you can't ignore it when you find it. You don't give up on it.

The kitchen door swings open, and Rhyson rushes in, his face alight with excitement, his phone pressed to his chest.

"It's them," he whispers to Bristol. "It's the label about the deal." "Oh my God!" Bristol waves him over to the kitchen table and he lays his phone down on the table, putting it on speaker.

"Hey, I'm back." Rhyson glances at his sister, their identical eyes locked. "You're on speaker with my manager Bristol."

I half-listen as they start preliminary talks for what will be the foundation of Rhyson's first record deal. I know later on I'll be thrilled for him. Right now, though, as I glance at the cheap rubber watch on my wrist and remember that night at the carnival, the kiss when our hearts wheeled with the stars, I'm sad. And I can't help but think the watch is a perfect symbol.

Because I'll be biding my time.

One

Bristol
Present Day

THERE ARE DAYS YOU WANT TO JUST START OVER BECAUSE IT FEELS like every hour takes you into a deeper level of hell.

And there are days you wake up already scraping the very bottom of the pit, unable to claw your way up the fiery walls.

This week has pretty much alternated between the latter and the former. Today, I'm trapped in some purgatory between the two.

No matter how I look at it, this week's been hell.

"Sarah." I barely raise my voice, but I know my assistant hears through the open door connecting our offices.

At first, I managed everything for Rhyson's music career by myself. He translated his fame as a classical piano prodigy into a modern rock sound that made him one of the biggest stars in the music world. Now, in addition to managing Rhyson and helping with Prodigy, the record label he recently launched, I also manage the other acts on our fledgling label and our friend Jimmi, who isn't actually signed to Prodigy. Rhyson and I recognized once I took on those additional responsibilities, I would need help. We've made astounding progress in just a few years.

The things you can do when you have no personal life. "Yeah, boss." Sarah appears at the door. "You need me?"

I thought I was in hell. Sarah looks like hell trampled her face. She isn't so much standing as allowing the doorframe to prop her up. "Sarah, I hope we've reached that point in our relationship where I can tell you when you look like shit." Sarah nods weakly.

"Good." I grimace and gesture for her to sit down in the chair across from my desk. "Because you look like shit."

"I probably look worse than I feel." Sarah settles carefully into the cream-colored leather chair.

"Let's hope so." I glance back down at the multiplying mound of papers on my desk. "I'm sorry you're not feeling well. I'll make this quick so you can go home, but are you well enough to tell me what the hell is going on in Denver?"

"Denver?" Sarah blinks slowly back at me. I cling to my patience. I really do, and I remind myself she isn't feeling well.

"Yeah. Denver. They have snow and mountains and the Broncos." "Did something go wrong for the guys?" She frowns with pain-dulled eyes. "Everything was set up at the venue."

"Yeah, well, I just got off the phone with Danny from the band, and he says everything's screwed up. There are several items from the equipment list missing."

"I sent their rider two months ago." Sarah shakes her head, confusion drawing her brows together. "I spoke to Elle, our contact at the club, last week, and she confirmed everything."

"Have you talked to Morris?" I ask of the road manager who's supposed to be handling things. I tap my nails on the edge of my desk, but stop immediately. My mother does that. There are enough naturally occurring similarities between my mother and me. I don't need to cultivate more.

"No, but I'll call him right now." She pulls her phone from her pocket and dials, looking at me while she waits. "It's ringing."

"That's usually how it works. When things go really well, he actually picks up. Something he hasn't done for the last hour I've been calling him."

I don't mean to sound like a bitch, but Rhyson handpicked Kilimanjaro, and they're an incredible band. They could have signed with any number of huge labels, but they chose us. They don't have a studio album out yet and are still considered "underground." This tour is building a grass roots fan base for their first release.

Prodigy may be small and just starting, but my brother's reputation is on the line. So is mine.

"Hey, Morris," Sarah says, forcing a smile he isn't here to appreciate. "How're things going?"

How're things going?

I just told her they're going to shit. I need to get to the bottom of it, not find out if he's enjoying his day.

"Give me the phone," I whisper-shout, extending my hand.

"I've got it," she mouths, nodding as if that's supposed to reassure me. "Uh huh. That's great, Morris. Look, the band called and said things weren't quite what we'd asked for."

She listens for a second, finally biting her lip and clenching her eyes closed.

"I see." Her sigh sounds a little too resigned to me. "Well, I guess it is what it is. Not sure what can be done about that since we're not there and the show is tonight."

The hell.

"Give me that phone, Sarah." This time I look at her sternly enough so she knows it isn't optional. She reluctantly passes it to me.

"Morris, it's Bristol."

"Hey, Bristol." Nervousness creeps into his voice.

"What's this about things not being what they should be for the band out there? Their rider is very clear, and Elle signed off on everything."

"Yeah, I think there were a few things they wanted equipment-wise that we were told would be available that aren't."

"Then Elle needs to fix that."

"I've tried to talk to her but haven't gotten any movement yet." His shaky laugh from the other end irritates me. "She's one tough cookie, that one."

"Hmmmm. Okay, well, I'll call her right now, and if that cookie doesn't want to get crumbled, she better give my guys every damn thing in the rider."

There's a short pause after my statement. "Good luck," Morris finally replies.

"By the way, Morris." I pause until I'm sure I have his full attention. "If I have to do your job and mine, one of us is redundant. The next time I send you out as road manager, I expect you to manage. If you can't, I'll find someone who isn't intimidated by a small-town club owner."

I don't wait for a response. What can he say to that? I hate incompetence. I haven't had trouble out of Morris before, but this is strike one. I use Sarah's phone to call Elle so she won't see me coming.

"Sarah, hey," Elle answers after the third ring, sounding bored and distracted. "If you're calling about that outrageous rider, I'll tell you what I told Morris. Take what you get. The show is tonight, and we don't have time to get all the equipment they're asking for. They'll be fine with what we have."

"Not Sarah, Elle. It's Bristol."

"Bristol, hey." I can practically hear her sit up and take notice. "Well, you heard what I was just saying then."

"Oh, I heard you. Now you hear me."

I lean forward, planting my fist on my desk to support my weight. "There's a contract between you and me, lady. One you signed.

Not fulfilling those terms places you in breach." I pause before resuming. "Is that clear?"

"I can't possibly find those mics they want in a day, Bristol."

"I didn't expect you to, which is why you've had the rider for months. You assured us that was more than ample time to secure the guys' equipment preferences."

"Well, I was wrong."

"Did you even try?"

I know she won't admit that she didn't try, but she needs to know that I don't believe she did.

"Elle, I don't give excuses, and I don't accept them. Make it happen or you'll be hearing from my lawyer."

"This is ridiculous!" she screeches from the other end.

"What's ridiculous is that this conversation even needs to happen." I smack my lips together in disbelief. "You actually think I'll fall for that? Waiting until the last minute and then shrugging all c'est la vie when you don't have time to fulfill the terms?"

"No, I—"

"You will find that equipment," I cut in. "I don't care if you find it up your ass. Just clean it before you give it to my band."

I end the call before I threaten to come out there myself. Then I'd have to actually follow through, and after being in hell all week, the last place I want to be is Denver. I got enough snow living in New York most of my life.

"Thanks." I hand Sarah's phone back to her.

"You're so badass," she whispers with her hand pressed to her stomach.

"Only when I have to be."

She barely lifts a knowing brow.

"Okay, yeah. Kind of all the time, but you know people make me, right?"

Sarah lets out a low groan and squeezes her eyelids closed.

"What is it?" I walk around the desk and press the back of my hand to her forehead. "You don't have a fever."

"No, I have a period," she responds listlessly.

"Ohhhhhh." I sit on the edge of the desk, studying her pretty face, which is twisting with discomfort. "Bad month?"

"Do the words 'red wedding' mean anything to you?"

I grin at her *Game of Thrones* reference, and she slits one eye open and offers an anemic smile.

"Go home." I gesture at the daunting pile of papers that seem to be metastasizing on the desk behind me. "Believe me. I can attest to the fact that the work isn't going anywhere. I've been trying to get rid of it all week with no luck."

"Really?" She sits up from her slumped position, one hand open on her forehead, the other at her belly. "You sure you'll be okay without me?"

"Yeah. I'll probably just follow up with the band and make sure Elle came through."

I don't mention the dozen other things I need to do that have made this week hell because she might feel bad.

"Okay." She stands gingerly and is making her way toward the door. "I'll just close out this one last email and be out."

"Sounds good."

My cell rings, and I glance down to see who it is. Will Silas. A fellow manager.

"Will, hi. What's up?"

"Bristol, hey. Nothing much. I wanted to talk about tomorrow night."

"What about it?" I walk back to my desk and sift through a few contracts I printed and started marking up. "The venue is all set. I spoke with them earlier. Sound check is at seven. Everything else is in the email I sent."

"Yeah, the email you sent at two o'clock this morning." He chuckles, a note of admiration in his voice. "When do you sleep, girl?"

"When all the work is done." I give a little laugh and check my impatience. I really need to look at these contracts. "So if we're all set for tomorrow's performance, what can I do for you?"

There's a pause on the other end screaming Will's reluctance. "Uh, Qwest has a special request," he says after a few seconds more of screaming quiet.

"Okay. Let's hear it."

"I know you have that reporter Meryl scheduled to talk with Qwest and Grip after the show."

Grip's upcoming album is Prodigy's first release. Even though *Grip* will be his first solo project, his popularity has grown through features on other artists' singles, all of which went platinum. He built a sterling reputation as a writer and producer over the years, along with hugely popular underground mixtapes. Now an artist in his own right, there's nothing like him out there. He has *it*, and brings *it* to everything he does. His current single "Queen" featuring Qwest, currently sits at number one, and the album hasn't even dropped.

"Yeah. *Legit* is doing that in-depth piece on Grip," I tell Will. "And I agreed to a chat with the two of them before she flies back to New York the next day."

"Yeah, she has, um, some other things she'd like to do after the show."

This time the pause is mine. The reluctance is mine. Qwest doesn't have some things she'd like to do after the show. She has someone she'd like to do after the show.

Grip.

"Oh, yeah?" I drop the contract and run my hand over the back of my neck where the tension always seems to gather. "Like what?"

"She was thinking she and Grip could hang out after the show. They haven't seen each other since they wrapped on the 'Queen' video a month ago. So …"

Pairing Grip with Qwest, the hottest female rapper on the scene right now, was sheer brilliance. I wish I could take credit for it, but Qwest approached us about working with him.

"So …" I pick up where Will left off, waiting for him to voice the request.

"Could we cancel the chat with the reporter so Qwest and Grip can go out after the show?"

I swallow the big no that lodges in my throat. It's true that Meryl will be irritated if we cancel. She'll be shadowing Grip for the next few weeks leading up to the album release writing this piece. I don't want to start our working relationship not delivering the one-two punch of Qwest and Grip together. But, if I'm honest, that isn't the only reason I want to refuse Qwest's request to spend time with Grip.

I clear my throat before responding.

"Um, let me see what I can do, Will. I can't make any promises, but I'll try. I don't want to alienate this reporter. This piece she's doing is great exposure for Grip's album."

"I get that, but you know how Qwest is." Will laughs, probably to keep from crying, because Qwest is a handful. "If we make her do the interview, she'll probably say some outrageous shit and ruin it anyway."

Irritation prickles under my skin. Qwest is undeniably talented. And undeniably hot for Grip. I've seen it for myself. She practically engraved an invitation for Grip to screw her at the "Queen" video shoot. For her to put her libido above a commitment is highly unprofessional, but then, it *is* Grip. She wouldn't be the first woman I've seen lose all sense of decency where he's concerned.

"If I can't get them out of the interview without potentially damaging this piece," I say, stiffening my words just enough. "Then I'll expect your artist to be where I need her to be when I need her to be and to conduct herself professionally. If you can't control Qwest, don't make me do it."

"That won't be necessary." Will's tone stiffens a little, too. "It shouldn't be that big a deal. Promise the reporter something else. Something bigger."

"Like what?"

"Like what if she goes with us next month? She'd get Qwest and Grip performing in Dubai. The optics alone will be a great add to her story."

Damn. Wish I'd thought of that, too. Grip and Qwest are giving a sweet sixteen concert for the daughter of one of Dubai's ruling families.

"That's a great idea." My tone still makes no promises. "I'll pitch it to Meryl and get back to you."

"Sounds good. See you at sound check."

With a million things clamoring for my attention, demanding action, I stand still at my desk for a full minute, staring unseeingly at the work waiting for me.

Qwest and Grip.

They're perfect for each other. Not only that, but it would be good for business. Their fans would eat up a romance between them. They'd be the king and queen of hip-hop. All the ideas spin through my head of how to maximize on a relationship between my artist and Will's. I could spin a street fairy tale of it. It's what Qwest wants. It's what everyone would want.

But I'm the one thing I know without a shadow of a doubt Grip wants. Over the years, we've managed to become friends. Really good friends actually, and I was thrilled when he finally agreed to let me manage his career. But that's all. Grip has made it clear he wants more, but that's all I can give, and that's all we'll be.

So if you won't have him, Qwest can.

That little voice of conscience and reason whispers to me every once in a while. Depending on the circumstance, sometimes I listen. Sometimes I ignore. I know this time I should listen.

Sarah's groan from the outer office pulls me from minutes of contemplation I can't afford. Despite all the work I've already done, I still have so much to do.

"You're still here?" I call out, walking to the door.

I fight back an ill-timed smile when I see a Hershey's bar, a Costco-sized bottle of Midol, and a legion of tampons spilled on the floor from Sarah's purse. It's like a Menstrual Survival Kit.

"Yes." Sarah sighs, pressing two fingers to her temple. "I forgot about an errand I'm supposed to run. Ugh. I just wanna crawl between the sheets and die for a little while."

"Let me handle it." Another thing I can't afford. Doing other people's jobs, but it feels like I've been doing that all day. All week. "You sure?" Doubt pinches Sarah's pained expression even more.

"I know you have a ton to do."

"As you can see by the state of my desk," I say, pointing a thumb over my shoulder toward my office. "Work isn't going anywhere. Anything I don't finish today, will still be there tomorrow."

"Oh, good." She blows out a relieved breath. "Let me get Grip's bag."

"Let you get what?" Tiny thrills of panic and anticipation alternate through me. "Grip's bag? What do you mean?"

"He left his bag here earlier today when he met with Rhyson." She bends to gather the spilled items from the floor, shoveling them into her purse. "He needs it tonight, and I told him I'd drop it off on my way home."

Apparently, I'm back at the lowest level of hell. After a week like I've had, the last thing I need is Grip being all . . . Grip. He'll ask me out. I'll refuse. He'll try to kiss me. I'll evade. I'll leave, and he'll go screw some random girl, thereby proving I was right not to give him a chance.

It's what we do.

We've been playing this game that isn't a game for years. One day, he'll realize I mean it when I say there isn't a chance in . . . well, hell, that it'll ever happen between us.

"I need to give you the code for his loft. He texted it to me." Sarah pulls out her phone, scrolling through messages. "He says he misses the bell all the time. So just use the code and go right in because he'll probably have the music up or be in the shower."

Grip in the shower. My mind paints vivid pictures that involve Grip's powerful body, rivulets of water, and not much else. I may not want a relationship, but I'm not blind or dead south of the waist. My heart, though, last time I checked, was north of my belt. I don't let anyone near that thing. If I let Grip in, the compass goes out the window. North or south wouldn't matter. No territory would be off-limits with him. I see Grip all the time. Here at the label offices. In the studio. At shows and appearances. But alone. At his house. Freshly showered. And me vulnerable, and let's face it—horny, is a disaster waiting to happen. A disaster I've managed to avoid for a long time.

"Maybe he'll be fine without the bag tonight. I mean . . ." I falter, embarrassed at how husky my voice sounds, though Sarah would never guess it's because of the shower scene playing in my head. "It can't be that urgent."

Disappointment and resignation flicker across Sarah's face, but she covers it quickly.

"Don't worry about it." She pulls the purse on her shoulder and reaches under her desk to retrieve a black leather backpack I recognize as Grip's.

"He offered to come get it, but I said I'd bring it. I'll do it."

Guilt burns in my chest. Sarah lives around the corner. She'd really be going out of her way to take the bag to Grip. I, on the other hand, pass his exit on my way home. I really wish I was as much of a bitch as people think I am.

"Gimme." I flick my fingers for her to hand the bag to me. "I got it. You go home, dope yourself up with Midol and chocolate, and I'll see you tomorrow."

"You sure?" Relief slumps her shoulders and brightens her eyes.

"Of course." I take the bag and shoo her out the door. "Go." "You're the best boss ever." Sarah makes her way carefully toward the door like lady parts might fall out if she walks any faster.

"Yeah, yeah. Whatever." I manage a grin. "Remember this when I have you working till midnight next week."

Once she's gone and the office is quiet and it's just me and my never-ending pile of tasks, I get back to work. I can barely focus, though, with that bag sitting in the corner mocking me. Daring me. Taunting me.

I keep working until the angle of the sun through the window behind me shifts from shine to shadow, the only indication I have of how long I've been at it. Other than the growl of my stomach.

I touch the home button on my phone to check the time.

"Shit." I drop my head into my hands and blow fatigue out through my nose. "Food, Bristol. Food should have happened hours ago."

Sarah usually makes sure I eat. She's becoming invaluable to me in ways I didn't anticipate. Mostly personal ways. Slipping me food. Ordering my favorite coffee blend that I can only ever find online. Putting up with my bitching when things don't go my way. Being a friend. Generally, I only allow myself so many of those. Her continued proximity has me bending that rule.

The problem of proximity. It's exactly why, despite my working with Grip as closely as I do now as his manager, I still find ways to keep my distance. If anyone could make me bend and forget the rules, it's Grip. He doesn't know that, though, and I need to keep it that way.

It's getting darker in the office now, not quite sunset. The dimming light camouflages the bag tucked into the corner, but I know it's there, and it's time for me to deal with it.

And the man who owns it.

Two

Bristol

HE'S COME A LONG WAY.

When I first met Grip, he lived in a one-room hovel and subsisted on two-for-the-price-of-one street tacos. His pride wouldn't allow him to ask my brother for much help financially, and Rhyson respected him too much to force the issue. So Grip was sweeping floors in exchange for studio time, deejaying in clubs all over LA, writing for other artists. He paid his dues pursuing his dreams. As I pull into the underground parking lot of the exclusive loft complex where he lives now, I can't help but think he's finally getting paid back.

Even though Sarah said I should use the code and go right in, I can't make myself do it. In the lobby, I press the button to ring his place, waiting for a response over the intercom that never comes. With a heavy sigh, I shift his bag on my shoulder and punch in the code that opens the cage-like elevator that will take me to the top floor.

It's all very industrial and modern, an old warehouse renovated into upscale loft apartments. A rolling garage door of sorts faces me as soon as I step off the elevator. The blare of nineties hip-hop bleeds through the concrete walls. I pull out my phone again to check the instructions Sarah sent. Once I punch in the code, the door rolls up, and high-decibel Tupac gushes out like water from a cracked dam. The first night Grip and I met, we talked about Tupac. I barely knew any of his music. I barely knew anything about hiphop. Raised in a family of classical music aficionados, I'm still not a huge fan, though ironically, I'm managing one of its rising stars.

The loft consists of a large, open space with high ceilings, red brick walls, and exposed rafters. Pillows pepper an L-shaped sectional the color of molasses. The thick slab of wood serving as a coffee table is flanked on another side by a latte colored backless couch. Four barstools line up along the strip of matte steel converted into a countertop separating the living area from the kitchen. A set of rail-less steps float up to the second floor, where a length of walkway leads to a closed door. Grip's bedroom, I presume. Vinyl albums fill decorative mahogany crates stacked and lining the wall housing the fireplace. A multi-shelved arch is built into another wall and holds dozens and dozens of books. Grip is nothing if not well-read.

A beautiful brown leather journal on the coffee table catches my eye. I gave him that three birthdays ago. I walk over to brush my fingers over the supple leather. He says some of the best lyrics he's ever written were conceived between those sheets.

"Nosy bitches get shot."

The words are followed by the click of a gun being cocked. My heart slams against my rib cage when I see the girl standing just a few feet away in the open door of a bathroom, eyes and hand steady over the gun aimed at me.

"Don't shoot." My hands fly up automatically. "I'm a friend of Grip's."

"Not one I ever met."

She's a pretty girl. Her unblemished skin glows, smooth and richly colored mocha. No makeup that I detect. Her hair is cropped close to her head and worn with its natural texture. A plaid shirt hangs large over baggy jeans and Chucks. Big brown eyes, almost doe-like and framed by long, curly lashes, never leave my face. They lend her an air of innocence belied by the 9mm aimed at my heart.

"Jade." Grip's voice drops from above. He stands at the walkway rail, looking down at us. "Put that damn gun up."

"Some stranger rolling up in the house," Jade says, lowering the weapon. "I didn't know."

For a moment, I forget about the gun trained on my torso. With the arresting picture Grip makes, T-shirt looped at his neck and hanging over his bare chest, he's more dangerous than the armed girl in front of me. A stack of abdominal muscles trails down to the indentations carved into his hips. Drops of water bead the smooth slope of his shoulders and the arms splattered with vibrant ink. Beltless dark wash jeans hang low on the lean hips. I lift my eyes to his face, a dazzling arrangement of jet-colored brows and bold bones balanced with lips so sculpted you would never guess how soft they are.

I don't have to guess. I remember.

"Your hair," I gasp. Gone are the dreadlocks he's been growing the last few years. There's barely any hair at all it's cut so short, just a subtle dark wave shadowing his scalp.

He runs a hand over his head, a wry grin tipping one corner of his mouth.

"Just something different." He exchanges a look with the girl holding the gun at her side. "Jade cut the locs out for me."

"Jade?" I drag my eyes from his face to hers. "As in your cousin Jade?"

Her eyes shift to mine, adding another question about me to her gaze.

"Yeah." Grip slips the T-shirt over his head and starts down the steps. "Good memory."

Jade and I watch each other warily. Grip told me they grew up together in Compton. He also told me about a dark day on a playground when an officer went too far while searching her, crossed a line of innocence. Knowing that, my heart softens some, even though she's still giving me the same hard look.

Eyeing Jade, focused on her, I took my eyes off Grip. Now he stands right in front of me, looms over me. I'm usually braced for the raw sexuality that clings to him, so strong my knees have been known to go weak. But him being so near and looking so much like the guy I met eight years ago, before the dreadlocks. Before the underground mixtapes and concerts and record deals. Before his fame. The start of a beautiful friendship. Anything else we could have been ended almost before it started.

Almost.

"So, Bris, to what do I owe this pleasure?" Grip grabs a remote from the table and silences Tupac. In the abrupt quiet, his eyes make a slow voyage down my body, his perusal pouring over me like hot oil. The silk romper I wore to the office today suddenly feels too short as he takes in my legs. Even though the sleeves reach the elbow, my forearms prickle with goose bumps under his stare. By the time his eyes reach my breasts, my nipples are tight and beaded in the silky cage of my bra. His eyes linger there before lifting and roving over my face.

He knows.

Even though I ignore this awareness that always seethes between us, no matter how much I pretend it isn't there, he knows. Even with Jade standing just two feet away, his proximity, his nearness and heat, cloister us in false intimacy.

"Um, Sarah was sick so I'm just bringing . . ." I don't bother finishing the sentence. My voice is unnaturally husky. My breath, abridged. I just hold up his backpack as explanation.

"Oh, yeah," he says. "Thank you."

He takes the bag by the strap, his fingers deliberately touching mine. I glance from where our fingers mingle to the face that looks even more handsome with barely any hair framing it. He looks so much like the guy who picked me up from LAX when I visited for spring break years ago. Nothing has changed, and everything is different now. He looked at me that day the way he's looking at me now, as if I were some new mystery he wanted to lose himself in solving. Conversely, he looks at me like he knows my every secret.

Jade clears her throat before speaking, snapping the moment between Grip and me.

"Man, I hope you ain't trying to bring her home to your mama." Jade's eyes follow the same head-to-toe journey Grip's took over me, but derision weights her look at every stop. "You know Aunt Mittie would have a fit if you start shit with some white bitch."

"Bitch?" I have a low give-a-fuck threshold, and she just crossed it. "You've called me bitch twice, and you don't even know me. Or did we meet and I forgot you already? I see how that could happen."

"Bristol." Grip chuckles down at me, the warmth that probably made Jade suspicious in the first place evident in his eyes. "She does still have a gun."

I glance from the firearm at Jade's side to the smirk on her pretty face, feeling bold now that I know who she is and bolder still now that Grip is close enough to hide behind if necessary. He'd never let anyone hurt me. Except himself. I'm pretty sure Grip could crush me without noticing.

"Jade, ease up," he says. "She's Rhyson's sister."

"And Grip's manager," I add. "You and your Aunt Mittie can rest easy. There's nothing going on between us."

I feel Grip's eyes on me when I say there's nothing between us. I won't give him the satisfaction of looking, of letting him mock the defenses I wrap around myself to guard against anything that could develop. They've held this long, and I have no plans of yielding any time soon.

"Your manager, huh?" Jade studies me again, as unimpressed as the first time. "I see."

"You need to be thinking less about me and more about you. About what I said." Grip hooks an elbow around her neck and kisses her forehead. "Come to the studio next week. Lay some tracks."

Jade stiffens under his arm, observing him with narrowed eyes. Grip also told me their relationship wasn't as close after that day at the playground.

"Hmmm. We'll see." She pulls away and walks over to grab an Oakland Raiders cap from the countertop. "I'm out. Some of us still gotta actually work to make them ends meet."

Grip is one of the hardest working artists I know. He's what they call a studio rat. He's behind the board and in the booth every chance he gets. Not to mention the appearances, writing for other artists, photo shoots. Indignation rises up in me on his behalf. Before I can mount my defense, he's diffused it with a grin aimed at his cousin.

"Whatever, J." He tweaks her nose, his affection for her obvious and, from my perspective, inexplicable. "Just come to the studio. Maybe it'll keep you out of trouble."

"I am trouble," she bounces back with a sassy grin. "I'll think about it." She looks to me, raising her eyebrows like she's waiting for me to say something.

"Nice meeting you," I offer in her expectant silence. Even in the face of rude bullshit, the manners instilled in me are flawless. She ignores my comment and brushes past me and out the door.

"I'm gonna walk J out." Grip takes my wrist gently between his fingers. "Could you wait a second? I have questions about the email you sent last night."

I see right through this ploy. He knows that without a good reason to stay, I'd be right behind him and on that elevator. Except I've been in hell all week. Working myself to the bone for longer than I can remember. There's tightness across my shoulders, noosed around my neck, trapped in the fists balled at my side. I just want to unfurl, and as much as he makes me tense, there's no one else I can relax with the way I can with Grip. So, against the better judgment I've exercised for years, I stay.

When he comes back, the two takeout bags he's holding release tantalizing scents into the air. I'm settled onto the huge comfortable sectional taking up so much of the living room. I could fall asleep right here if I weren't so hungry. Starvation has eroded my sense of self-preservation, and as much as I dreaded coming here to see him, I dread going home to my empty cottage even more.

"Ran into the delivery guy." He raises the bags and gives me a measured look, like he knows I could bolt at any moment. "You hungry?"

"I could eat," I understate while the lining of my stomach feasts on itself.

"Empanadas?" He smiles because he knows they're my weakness. One of my many weaknesses.

"Baked or fried?" I ask, as if I'm particular.

"Which do you want it to be?" he parries.

"Fried."

"Then they're fried." He hooks the bag handles over one wrist and grabs plates from the cabinet with his free hand. "Come on."

In utter laziness, I watch him cross the large space to a door in the far corner.

"Make yourself useful and grab me a beer from the fridge and whatever you want to drink." He looks over his shoulder at me expectantly. "I can't carry you and the food up to the roof, Bristol."

"The roof?" I groan my exhaustion and settle deeper into the cushions.

"Oh, sorry." He pauses, concern sketching a frown on his face. "Is it too high?"

I have a selective fear of heights. Put me in a little bucket in the air on a ride that could plunge me to my death, I'm chop suey. But sitting safely on the roof, I should be fine. I do not, however, need him reminding me of our night on that Ferris wheel. Not tonight when I'm already feeling weak.

"No, the roof isn't too high," I answer. "It's too far away. I'm tired."

"Well, food's going up and so will you if you want some," he says, disappearing through the door.

Sigh.

I grab a beer for him and a bottle of Pinot Gris for me. If I were alone, I wouldn't bother with the glass I pull from the rack. It has been a straight-from-the-bottle day … week … month. But I'll save that for the privacy of my own home. And it'll probably be vodka, my self-numb-er of choice.

Damn these shoes. I've got a thing for heels. Even wearing the romper, I'm still sporting three-inch Jimmy Choos. By the time I make my way up the winding stairs to the roof, I want to toss the shoes off the building despite how much they cost.

The second I step through the door to the roof, I forget about my shoes, my empty stomach. I even forget the empanadas for a moment. We're just high enough to see the city's skyline in the distance, set ablaze by the horizon's last hurrah before sunset. There's no fear, and the view takes my breath. For just a second, the sheer scope of the sky makes all the problems that followed me home from the office seem small in comparison.

"This is gorgeous," I whisper, taking the last few steps to the center of the roof.

"Yeah, I can't take credit for the view or this setup. The decorator did it." Grip eyes his rooftop retreat with a pleased smile. "I don't get up here as much as I'd like, but every once in a while to eat or write."

I can see how it would be the perfect place to write. Padded benches tuck into the far corner, and slate-colored cushions rest against the brick wall. Four low, square tables stand in the center with candles of various sizes and shapes strategically dotted on them.

Grip sets the bags on one of the tables and walks to the wall to turn a few knobs. Soft music fills the air around me, and strands of fairy-tale lights now glimmer over our heads. It's all very romantic.

"You know this is just two friends eating dinner, right?" I flop onto the padded bench and put down our drinks.

"I do know that." The innocent expression is the only thing that doesn't look right on Grip's face. "But if you need to remind yourself, I understand."

I make sure he sees me rolling my eyes before tearing open the bags of precious fried dough.

Correction. Baked.

"You said these were fried," I complain around a bite of empanada.

"My bad." He stretches his brows up and takes a leisurely sip of his beer. "That's your second one, though, right? I guess you barely notice the difference when you inhale them."

"Very funny." I actually do laugh and polish off another one.

"Well, so much for leftovers." He leans back against the cushion beside me until mere inches separate our shoulders.

"You shouldn't have invited me to stay if you wanted leftovers."

"I think your company's a fair trade."

Our eyes connect across the small slice of charged space separating us. I sit up from my slouch, inserting a few much-needed inches between us.

"You mentioned needing to talk about the email I sent." My business-like tone clashes with the soft music and lighting, which is exactly what I need it to do.

"Yeah." He considers me for an extra moment, as if he may not allow me to steer our conversation into safer territory. "You mentioned that next Wednesday at three you have a sit-down scheduled with that reporter from *Legit*."

"I checked the shared calendar, and that block of time was free. Was I wrong?"

"It's my fault." He shoots me an apologetic look. "I forget to add personal stuff there sometimes. I'm talking to some students in my old neighborhood that day. Could we reschedule?"

Between my request to cancel tomorrow's interview for Qwest's would-be booty call, and nixing next Wednesday's sit down, Meryl won't be too happy with me.

"What if she tags along?" I sit up straighter, twisting to peer down at him. "She could see you talking to the students and then you guys could chat a few minutes maybe right there on the grounds. Get some local color shots."

"Local color?" A husky laugh passes over his lips. "There's four colors in Compton. Black, brown, red, and blue. In the wrong place at the wrong time, on the wrong street, any of those could get you killed. I don't know. And I don't want the talk exploited. Like headline shit. That isn't why I'm doing it."

"I know that. Of course it isn't. I'll make sure it isn't like that."

He glances up at me, wordlessly reading between lines.

"You'd be coming, too?" His voice is soft, but the look in his eyes is loud and clear. His eyes tell me he likes having me near. It makes my stomach bottom out like we're back up on that Ferris wheel, and if I'm not careful, I'll fall.

"Why not?" I give what I hope is a casual shrug, though it feels as stiff as my neck.

"You just haven't been around much lately." His eyes never leave my face, and I hope I drop my expressionless mask in place fast enough to keep him out.

"We connect every day." I look him straight in the face like it isn't hard to do. "So I don't know what you mean."

"We text, email, FaceTime, but we haven't seen each other much."

I rub at the knots in my neck, wishing a masseuse would magically appear.

"Are you tight?" His voice and eyes seem to simmer, both hot and steady.

The double entendre of that question is not lost on me. As little sex as I've had the last year . . . years, I'm probably as tight as a peephole, but he'll never know.

"It's just been a long few weeks."

"I know something that could relax you."

He bends over me, pressing me back into cushions. "Grip, what are you—"

"Relax," he interrupts with a laugh, stretching a few inches more to unscrew a jar sitting on the concrete pedestal beside my seat. He settles back into his space, freeing up my lungs to breathe again.

"My Uncle Jamal used to say if you can't have a good ho." He holds up a joint. "Have good dro."

"Have I mentioned that your uncle is a misogynist who subscribes to antiquated and archetypal notions of womanhood?"

"Yeah, more than once, but I'm pretty sure he was a pimp, so that makes sense."

What the what?

He says it as if he just told me his uncle was a fireman. "You mean like 'big pimpin', Jay-Z' kind of pimp?"

"No, like, 'bitch, go get my money on the corner' kind of pimp." A frown pleats Grip's expression. "By the time he came out west, no, but I think back in Chicago he may have been a pimp."

I'm having trouble processing this. I've met Grip's Uncle Jamal a few times, and he never struck me … maybe that is an unfortunate way to think of it considering he may have struck the women who worked for him … but he never struck me as a pimp.

"He's actually my great-uncle," Grip says. "My grandmother's brother. When she left Chicago to move out here in the seventies, he followed."

Grip shakes his head, blowing out a heavy sigh.

"The generation before him thought Chicago was the answer to Jim Crow, so they left the South. And then they thought the answer to poverty and crime was California and left Chicago," Grip says. "Always running. Stokely Carmichael said, 'Our grandfathers had to run, run, run. My generation's out of breath. We ain't running no more.'"

We have Grip's mother to thank for all the varied people he can quote.

"So your mother moved here for better opportunities?"

"My mother moved here because her mother moved them here." Grip considers me a few extra seconds before going on. "My grandmother was part of the Black Panther movement, which was huge in Southern Cali."

"What? I never knew that."

"It isn't exactly what I lead with when I meet someone." Grip laughs.

"Weren't they violent?" I ask carefully. "Like 'blowing up things' violent?"

"They were … complicated. They weren't perfect, by any means, but they were providing free lunch for kids in poor neighborhoods, tutoring students, teaching self-defense, doing a lot of good. That's what drew my grandmother to the movement."

"And your mother?"

"Ma definitely ain't a Panther." He chuckles. "But don't cross her because I wouldn't put it past her to blow shit up."

I have no plans to cross her.

He pulls a lighter from the pocket of his jeans, and I notice the black plastic watch on his strong wrist. I've never seen him without it since I won it at that carnival. I don't know what to think about that, so I don't let myself think about it.

"So you in or what?" he asks.

I drag my eyes from the plastic watch to the expectant expression on his face.

"You know I don't smoke weed."

"Oh, I'm giving it up, too." His sculpted lips stretch into a smart-ass smirk. "Next week. Come on. When was the last time you got high? Not high off contact, either."

"Columbia. Senior year. Finals." The memory of munching my way through my study sessions bubbles laughter from my chest. "I was lit through half my econ exam."

He leans into my shoulder, his deep laughter rumbling through me.

"Come on, Bristol," he cajoles, drawing on the joint, blowing a circle of smoke out, and then offering it to me. "It's legal in half the country now, ya know?"

"Medicinally."

"Well, it's all the way legal in Cali." White smoke halos his head, contrasting with the devilishly handsome face.

This is a bad idea. Even at my most vigilant, it's sometimes hard to stave off the attraction between Grip and me. If I'm … impaired … there's no telling what I'll give in to. But the string of tough days, the months of non-stop work getting the label off the ground, this hellish week—it all bombards me, and in a moment of weakness, I take one draw. And then another. And then another.

An indeterminate amount of time later, I'm feeling nice. Shoes off. Feet up. Hair down. High as a kite.

The wine conspires with the weed and my exhaustion to create a laid-back haze. My eyes keep closing, and my head keeps lolling onto Grip's shoulder. When I manage to crack my eyes open, he's watching me intently, alert. He's a creature who hides his weapons, lulling his prey into thinking he poses no danger. Maybe it's a survival mechanism he picked up from his childhood in a gang-infested war zone, camouflaging the threat, but he isn't hiding how dangerous he is now. The jet brows slant over eyes with the color and heat of melted caramel. His desire is a cloak, heavy on my shoulders, tight around my arms, hot on every part of me it touches.

He's such a beautiful man, his body a palette of precious metals—darkened gold, bronze, copper. I should remember that I'm not the only one who thinks so. If I took what that look offers, he would never be just mine. I'd have to share him. Not right away, maybe not the first time or the first year, but eventually. That's the way it is with men like him and women like me. I get it, but I don't have to choose it.

"I can't believe you cut your locs." Even to my ears it sounds like a diversion, nervous and chatty.

"Technically, I didn't." His steady eyes don't waver. "Jade did."

I follow the line of conversation like a lamp lighting my way out of a dark cave, hoping it will dispel the tension coiling around us.

"As many times as you've talked about Jade," I say. "I never envisioned our first meeting would be at gunpoint."

"She thought you broke in."

The corner of his mouth tips. I give him my "you're shitting" me look. "Yeah, because I look like such a criminal."

"Some of the worst criminals wear three-piece suits and have an Ivy League pedigree."

"Oh, you don't have to tell me. I grew up with half of them." I grimace and lean back, closing my eyes. "Just make sure I'm somewhere else if she ever does come by the studio."

"Bris, don't be sadity." His words and voice chide me.

"I don't even know what 'sadity' means, so I seriously doubt I'm being it."

"Sorry." His laugh rolls over me. "It means uppity. Stuck up. Jade's had it hard. Don't judge her."

"Me, judge her?" My eyes pop open, and I sit up, hand pressed to my chest and eyes stretched wide. "She's the one who called me a bitch before she even knew my name."

I lie back only to snap up into a sitting position again. "Oh, and again after she knew my name."

"She isn't the most polite, I give you that."

"And apparently, when I finally meet your mother it won't go any better."

That was the absolute wrong thing to say, and I don't examine what prompted me to say it. I've never actually met Grip's mother, but I know they're incredibly close. I never plan to be "the one" he takes home to Mama, but to think she would disapprove simply because I'm white is galling.

"My mom would adjust. She isn't narrow-minded, just . . ." Grip trails off, his long lashes dropping over clouded eyes. "You have to cut them both some slack. You can't imagine the things we experienced living where we grew up. I was lucky going to the School of the Arts. That was my exit. It could easily have been Jade. She just didn't apply. She's a better writer than I am."

"I doubt that," I mumble.

His gaze latches onto my face, narrowed and searching. "Why, 'cause she's hood? I'm hood, Bris."

"Maybe you are, but you never called me a bitch."

"At least not to your face." He doesn't even crack a smile.

Our eyes catch and hold. At the corners, my lips fight a smile. He stops holding his back around the same time I give in. Our laughter clears the air.

"And I didn't doubt Jade was better than you because she's hood or stupid." Eyes down, I circle the lip of the wine glass with one finger. "I doubt it because I've never met a better writer than you."

I inwardly slap myself. Why the ever-living hell do I keep saying things like this? As soon as things lighten, I say something stupid to let him know just how much he means to me. Must be the weed.

"You wanna know the real reason Jade didn't like you?"

Grip leans into me, pushing back my hair and rolling his still-icy beer bottle over my neck. I swallow, but don't dare look at him, hoping he'll drop it, but he doesn't.

"When you grow up on the streets, you don't just develop a sixth sense." He captures a lock of my hair and tests it between his fingers. "You have six, seven, eight, nine of 'em, because those instincts could be the difference between death or life. My mom and Jade have so many senses they almost know what you're thinking before you think it. And even though I've never told her, Jade only had to be in the room with us for a hot minute to know I want you."

I clench my eyes closed and pull in a stuttering breath, trapping my bottom lip between my teeth.

"Don't do this, Grip."

"Jade's right," he continues as if I hadn't spoken, hadn't asked him to stop. "My mom would flip if I brought a white girl home. If I brought you home. She knows I don't consider color when I date, but she'd love to see me with a woman who looks like her. You know better than most that we don't get to choose our family, but we still gotta love them."

I don't respond to that. He knows how contentious things have been between my brother and my parents. Beyond the headlines everyone else has seen, he knows how hard I've worked to reconcile them. I moved to LA to help Rhyson with his career, yes, but also to bridge the countrywide chasm between the two factions of my family.

"Like you, I'd do anything for my family." He comes in an inch closer, caressing under my chin and tilting it up with his index finger. "But if you'd ever give me a shot, I wouldn't give a fuck what anyone thought. I'd take you home to my mama."

I'm a little too high and a lot too horny for this conversation, for the stone-hard thigh pressing against me, for the heat coming off his body and smothering my resistance. I try to sit up, hoping it will clear my head so I can make my escape, but his hand presses gently into my chest, just above the swell of my breasts, compelling me back into the cushion. His lips hover over mine, and I will him to kiss me because I'll make the first move if he doesn't. After years of not moving, I have no idea how I'll explain that once the smoke clears.

Sometimes at night after the chaos dies, I think about our first kiss at the top of a Ferris wheel. Just like then, his lips start soft, brushing mine like wings in sweet sweeps, coaxing me open and delving into me. Sampling me, he groans into my mouth and chases my tongue. The rough palm of his hand cups my face, angling me so he can dive deeper. He doesn't come up for air, but keeps kissing me so deeply I can't breathe. He tastes so good, I'll choose him over air as long as I can. Why is it never like this with anyone else? I want it to be so bad, but it never is.

He releases my lips to scatter kisses down my neck. My back arches, and my nipples go tight. He knows that's my spot. After all this time, he still knows. My neck is so incredibly sensitive, a gateway to the rest of my body.

"You taste exactly the same." His words come on a labored breath in my ear. "Do you know how long it's been since I kissed you?"

Eight years.

"Eight years." He shakes his head, eyes riveting mine in light lent by candles and the moon. "And you taste exactly the same."

His words shiver through me, searching out my nerve endings and invading my bones. If I don't get out of here, we'll be fucking on the rooftop before I can draw another breath.

"I should go." I slide from under him, scooting down the couch as far as I can without falling off. "This is why I don't smoke weed."

I force a laugh, hoping he'll let me get away with it. I scoop my hair behind my ears and drop my chin to my chest. When I glance over at him, displeasure clumps his brows and tightens his mouth.

"It's not the weed, Bristol." His glance slices through the haze hanging in the air. "It's us. Don't pretend it isn't us."

"There is no us." My feet explore the floor, searching in the dark for my shoes. "You know that."

He puts a staying hand on my knee until I look at him.

"What I know is that neither of us has been in a serious relationship in years."

"That doesn't mean anything." I stand and slide my feet into the Jimmy Choos. "You haven't exactly been waiting around, have you?"

"Damn right I haven't been waiting around." He doesn't get up, but his firm hold on my wrist stops me from walking away. "I'm not Rhyson."

I look down at him, frowning my confusion. "What do you mean?"

"Remember when Kai put Rhyson in the friend zone?"

Of course I do. For a long time, my sister-in-law Kai denied the attraction between her and Rhyson.

"Yeah, so?"

"When Kai wasn't checking for Rhys, I assumed he had to be sleeping with other girls." Grip shrugs. "I mean, he and Kai were just friends. But, nope. He said he only wanted Kai and didn't sleep with anyone else."

"Then you're right." I tug at my wrist, but he holds on tight. "You're definitely not Rhyson."

"It was months, Bristol. She shut him out for months. Not years."

"I'm not shutting you out." I release a tired breath. "I'm living my life, and you're living yours."

"Right." He nods and turns his mouth down at the corners. "So, if you won't be with me, then I'll fuck whoever the hell I want. If you have a problem with that, you know what to do about it."

For a moment, our eyes tangle in the dimness. His words sink into my flesh like briars. Every word out of his mouth only proves that I'm right to get out of here. That I'm right not to give in. If I ever gave him a chance and he fucked around on me . . . I've seen what that looks like. It looks like a woman as strong as my mother reduced to pathetic, teary drunkenness.

"It's none of my business." I shift my eyes away from him and to the glittering city skyline just beyond the rooftop.

"It's none of your business until you say it is." I force myself to look back.

"Don't hold your breath, Grip." I say my next words with deliberation. "I mean, it's not like I'm sitting around saving it, either."

He pulls me forward, and I press my hand to the hardness of his chest so I don't fall into him. My knee supports me, pressed against his on the couch.

"Are you poking me?" One strong hand wraps around the back of my thigh, anger marking his expression. "Do you want to know if it bothers me when you fuck other guys?"

I just stare at him unblinkingly. He presses my leg, urging me forward until I'm fully on the couch, fully on him, one knee on either side of his legs, facing him. Straddling him.

"It makes me want to set the world on fire." His words come softly, but the truth roars in his eyes. "To think of you with them."

There haven't been nearly as many men as he probably assumes, but I don't reveal that. I can't offer him any relief.

"You wanna know what consoles me, though?" He looks up at me, calculation in his eyes. Before I can tell him I don't want to know, he goes on. "For one, I know when we're together, it'll only take once for me to fuck their memory out of you."

I shoot him an uncertain look. He sounds fierce enough to follow through on that threat right now. I manage to snatch my wrist from his grasp. I back off his lap, walking swiftly toward the steps that will take me back into his loft. I'm only a few steps down when he calls from the top.

"It also helps that I know how much it bothers you, too."

I freeze on the fourth step, my palm pressed to the wall.

"I don't know what you mean." The words echo in the narrow stairwell, sounding much more confident than I feel inside.

"The other women." He mock-sighs behind me like he's getting impatient. "Like I don't see it, Bris."

I know I should keep going, but I'm stuck on the stairs, afraid of what he has perceived. He slips past me and down onto the step below, his height still putting him eye level with me.

"You think I'm that oblivious?" He walks his fingers up my arm. "You always conveniently have somewhere to be when I'm with someone else."

"I'm busy." I study my shoes on the step, not looking up. "I have more to do with my life than hang around waiting for you to screw some groupie."

"And you watch me." He dips his head until he traps my eyes. "You watch me all the time. You can't keep your eyes off me any more than I can keep my eyes off you."

"You're delusional." I offer a hollow laugh. "Thanks for dinner."

I shove past him, squeezing between the stairwell wall and the taut muscles of his body.

"You don't want to know the third thing that consoles me?" he asks at my back.

"No," I fling over my shoulder. Only a few steps to go and I'll be in his loft and then out the door.

"They don't satisfy you." He plays the comment like a trump card. "Sexually, I mean."

My hand is on the knob to his loft, but I look up at him, anger overtaking the fear and confusion of the last few moments.

"Who the hell do you think you are?" I snap. "To presume you know anything about my sex life."

"Oh, but I do." He takes the few steps separating us until he's right in front of me, his hard body pressing me against the door. "Remember last year when you bought your cottage and invited us all over for dinner?"

I have no idea where he's going with this, but I can't pretend I'm not curious. I just stare at him, knowing he doesn't need my permission to go on.

"Everyone was playing cards, and then I left the room and was gone for a long time." He presses his forearm to the door behind me and over my head until our bodies are practically flush. "Remember?"

"You said my chili sent you to the bathroom," I say breathlessly.

I'm not a great cook and was surprised the chili turned out halfway decent. Grip was the only one who complained.

"I'm sorry about that." He grins at me, his eyes lighting with temporary mischief. "I lied. Your chili was pretty good. It really was. No, I wasn't in the bathroom. I went to your bedroom. Ya know. To explore."

"My bedroom?" I can't believe him. "How dare you?"

"Desperate times call for desperate measures. I have no problem playing dirty. I welcome it actually. But I stumbled upon something in the drawer by your bed that was very telling."

There are two drawers in my bedside table. One holds journals and a few items that would tell him too much about my feelings. That drawer remains locked, so he wouldn't have seen what was inside. But the other drawer . . .

"I've never seen so many vibrators in one place." Grip's grin is half-teasing, half-cruel. "Residential, of course. You've got your own black market sex store in there."

My face heats, and I cannot even form words. Embarrassment chokes me.

"I figure anyone with that many vibrators can't be coming on the regular. With a guy, I mean," he clarifies unnecessarily.

"Stop it." I fire the words at him, so angry, so humiliated I want to slap him.

"It's okay." With gentle fingers he brushes the heavy hair back from my forehead. "I think I understand the problem. It isn't you. It's them."

I push away from the wall, only to be blocked and gently but firmly pressed back against the door.

"Guys, we can be so clumsy." He shakes his head and sighs. "You know? Quick. Selfish."

He trails fingers down my arm to link our fingers.

"See, I bet they start here," he whispers, slipping his hand between us until his fingers lightly drift across the space just below my belly where my thighs juncture. My panties soak with the promise of his fingers. My breath catches at the brief contact where I crave him most.

"When they should start . . ." His hand glides up and over my belly and between my breasts. Over the curve of my shoulder and neck until he reaches his destination. He finally taps my temple three times. "Here. They should start here and work their way down because your mind is your most erogenous zone, Bris. I look forward to making you come with my words alone."

I fumble with the knob behind my back until the door swings open. I take several steps into the apartment. I can think more clearly now that I'm away from that tower of muscle, bone, and heat standing pressed against me. The strong girl who has resisted him all these years is regaining her composure.

"Whatever you think you know about me," I yell, not bothering to turn around. "About my sex life, about anything—you have no idea."

I stride over to the couch and retrieve my bag, determined to get out of here with the hard shell still around my soft places. When I'm at the front door, I glance back, surprised to see Grip still in the stairwell where I left him, the door standing wide open. Our eyes clash one last time, and there's a coalition of sadness and frustration and want in his gaze. I can't afford to look too long, so I make a dash for the door, hoping against hope that he won't come after me.

I'm nearly at my car by the time I realize I'm perversely saddened he didn't follow.

Three

Grip

I PROBABLY SHOULDN'T HAVE KISSED HER.

Second thought, hell with that.

I'd do it again if given the opportunity. That's just it. There hasn't been an opportunity, no opening for years. And then all of a sudden last night, a crack. Something inside of Bristol opened just a fraction, but it was enough for me to explore and exploit. I would have explored and exploited all night if she had let me, but that space sealed shut almost immediately. Something shut her down. I don't know what holds Bristol back from making us . . . an us. It has to be more than what happened with Tessa.

I saw that crack in the wall she's used to keep me out. Maybe my Shawshank plan is working. Rhyson, Bristol's brother and my best friend, would appreciate that, movie geek that he is. In *Shawshank Redemption*, Andy hangs a poster on the wall in his prison cell. At night for years, he secretly chips at that wall until one day, he's made a hole big enough to crawl through and escape. That's me. Chipping away at that wall for years, and last night may have been a breakthrough.

Or not.

Because as Bristol walks down the hall of the Prodigy offices, headed straight for me, there's barely a flicker of recognition in her eyes, much less desire. She nods to me before carefully brushing past to enter the conference room for our meeting.

There are already a few people here, including Bristol's assistant Sarah. They chat as Bristol sets her iPad and phone on the table, her movements easy and graceful. She wears her hair in one of those complicated braid things it looks like you need a degree to do, the dark and coppery length tamed to rest on one shoulder. She's paired dark skinny jeans with her trademark stilettos and a slouchy shirt hangs off one shoulder.

The seat beside her is occupied, so I take the one across from her. She glances up, catching my eyes on her. The tiny frown pulling between her brows is the only indication she gives that she even knows I'm here.

"Let the party begin," Rhyson says from the door, wearing one of the ear-to-ear grins he seems to have all the time since he got married. The fact that Kai is also pregnant ... well, let's just say it must hurt to smile that hard.

"You think you could tone down that smile, Rhys?" Max, Prodigy's head marketing guy and cynic-in-chief, asks. "It's too early for such joy."

Rhyson takes the seat at the head of the table, but his smile doesn't budge. Max just came through a nasty divorce, so he and Rhys are in very different places. So are we, for that matter. I won't lie. Seeing Rhyson settle down with someone who loves him the way Kai does and seeing them preparing for their first kid, it makes me wonder how close I am to any of that. I'm knocking on thirty years old. I'm in no hurry, though. My album drops in three weeks, and all my hard work is about to pay off. Is already paying off. Still, I'd like someone to share it with. Not just some groupie. A friend, a lover, a partner.

Bristol's head is lowered over an open folder. As hard as she works, as single-minded as she is about her job, you'd never guess family is everything to her. I've never met anyone who works harder than Bristol. She's ambitious, yes, but people don't realize what fuels it. She works hard for the people she cares about. I'm not even sure that Rhyson's career would have exploded the way it did without Bristol. She was the one who pushed him to get back to making his own music. When she and Rhyson were barely on speaking terms, she chose her degree based on his future and relocated from New York with no guarantees. She's sacrificed a lot over the last year building this record label not just for success, but out of love for her brother.

I always refused when she asked to manage me, too, because I didn't want to be just a job to her. I gave in a few months ago, hoping that working together so closely would force her to acknowledge the attraction, the connection between us. But she has somehow managed to keep me out, even as she propelled my career forward. I had success before she came onboard, but I know the unprecedented doors opening for me now are doors Bristol banged on and kicked in.

"Before we get started," Rhyson says, his grin now aimed at me and growing. "Marlon, dude, what the hell happened to your hair? Kitchen fire?"

He and my mom. The only ones who still call me Marlon. "Jokes." I nod, suppressing my grin. We pretty much bust each other's balls every chance we get, a fifteen-year habit. "Nah. Just wanted something different."

When Jade came over last night, we started reminiscing about old times in the neighborhood where I grew up. Hard times. Thinking about how far I've come since then, how much has happened, made me even more excited for this next chapter. I feel something fresh happening inside of me, and I wanted the outside to reflect it.

"Well, you look about twelve." Rhyson ignores the middle finger I slowly slip into the air in his honor. "Okay, Bris. Tell us what we're doing."

Bristol flicks a glance my way before diving in. I think she's still adjusting to the new hair, or lack thereof. I am, too.

"Okay. Just to put us on the same page." Bristol looks down the table at everyone. "We're talking about the Target Exclusive."

I still can't believe it. Target approached us about an exclusive edition of *Grip*, my debut solo album. Usually reserved for the likes of Beyoncé and Taylor Swift, an opportunity like this is something we can't pass up. But we'll have to work our asses off to get it done in time. Fortunately, working my ass off is one of my specialties.

"They want three bonus tracks that will be exclusive to their stores." Bristol checks her notes before going on. "We need to choose the songs today. Rhys and Grip have several songs not included on the wide version of the album for us to consider. We have to move fast, though, because we'll need to re-master the tracks and get that version of the project pressed and shipped out as quickly as possible." "And how exactly did this happen again?" Max frowns at the folder in front of him. "Are we rushing? Committing to something we can't pull off well in time? I'm not sure about this."

Before I can tell Max to go suck his own dick, Bristol beats me to it . . . if not more tactfully.

"Max, I don't have time for you to punch holes in something because you didn't come up with it." She rests a fist on her hip and looks at him impatiently. "It's a freaking Target Exclusive for a debut album. What's there not to be sure about?"

"I do have legitimate concerns," he replies firmly. "It isn't that I didn't come up with it."

Bristol tilts her head and gives him a knowing look.

"Okay, maybe that's part of it," Max admits with a laugh. "But it's a lot to turn around in a tight time frame. Can we do it with excellence?"

"Max, I get your concerns." Bristol tosses her folder onto the conference room table. "But have you ever known me to commit to something we couldn't get done? I'm not saying it will be easy. Between this, the shows we have with Qwest over the next few weeks, the reporter trailing Grip for the story, and let's not forget a trip to Dubai thrown in the mix, I'll probably have a bald spot by the time this is all said and done."

There are smiles, snickers, various expressions of amusement from everyone at the conference table.

"But it'll be worth it." Bristol's eyes land on me. "*Grip* will be one of the best albums of the year, and we're damn well gonna treat it that way."

I knew she believed in me, but the sincere passion resonating from her is deeper than I even thought. I wish she'd direct some of that passion to me, instead of my work.

"And that starts with positioning it for the best possible opportunities." Bristol's eyes shift from mine and touch on each person at the table. "This is something we can't let get away. I promise you we can do it."

"I say let's go for it," Rhyson says.

And if he says it, we're going for it. Rhyson and Bristol often disagree loudly and vehemently, but when they agree, it's done.

"Well, that's settled." Bristol shares a brief smile with her brother but then snaps her fingers. "I almost forgot. Grip?"

She turns to me, and we look straight at each other. I barely catch the flash of vulnerable uncertainty before she shutters it.

"Yeah?" It's the first word I've spoken since the meeting officially started, even though it's all about my album. It isn't that I don't care about this stuff, but I'm much more interested in actually getting the music to listeners, for them to connect with what I created.

"Target wants you to film a spot next week." She taps the iPad, her eyes roaming over the screen. "They sent over a treatment for the commercial. I have it here somewhere."

"Lemme guess," I say. "There's lots of red and big dots."

"Smart ass." She shoots me her first natural smile of the morning. "I'll show you later. Let's listen to these tracks. My contact is waiting. Grip and Rhys, you guys walk us through our options."

Rhyson dips his head to defer to me. Right.

"So this first song," I say, pulling up the file sharing where we've stored the bonus tracks. "It's called 'Bruise.'"

There's so much I could say to set up this song. I tell them bits and pieces of it. How personal it is. How cathartic it was to write about the tension and fear that marked my relationship with cops growing up. Before black lives or blue was preceded by hashtags, the debate dividing our nation, divided my family. There's so much more I could say to make them know what this song means to me, but I don't say any of it. I just play the song and hope it speaks for me. And while it plays, I can't help but remember the day that inspired it.

Four

Grip
12 years old

"**S**EXUAL CHOCOLATE!**"**

I've lost count of how many times we've watched *Coming to America*. My cousin Jade, my boy Amir, and I know just about every line by heart. Every week, we watch this bootleg copy Ma bought at the barber shop, and not even the shadows of people's heads in the shots or the sometimes-unsteady camera work make Eddie Murphy as Randy Watson and his band Sexual Chocolate less funny.

"'That boy good,'" Amir quotes when Eddie Murphy does the infamous mic drop and leaves the stage.

"'Good and terrible,'" Jade and I finish the quote. We all crack up laughing like it's the first time.

"Y'all and this movie." Jade's older brother Chaz walks through the living room in his jeans, no shirt.

His body is like one of the graffiti walls off Largo Avenue, inked with five-pointed stars declaring his Bloods gang affiliation, "186" scrawled on his chest signifying the code for first-degree murder. His other passion, the Raiders, vie for equal space on his arms and back. Ink stains every available inch of skin, but he left his face clear. Ma says thank God the boy is vain, otherwise he would have ruined that handsome face of his with tattoos. A teardrop or something.

Everyone says we look alike, Chaz and me. Ma and his father were brother and sister, but my uncle died before I was even born, so I never met him. Ma sometimes looks at Chaz with sad eyes and says if you've seen Chaz, you've seen his daddy. You've seen her brother.

"How many times y'all gon' watch this movie?" Chaz's bright smile flashes before he pulls his Raiders T-shirt over the muscular framework of his upper body. "If it ain't this, it's *Martin.*"

"Wasssssup!" Amir, Jade, and I parrot Martin's signature phrase on cue, laughing while Chaz rolls his eyes.

"Y'all little niggas a trip." The pager on Chaz's hip beeps, and he plucks it off his waistband to read the message. I love that we made him laugh before we lost his attention.

Jade's other brother Greg is LAPD, but we don't trust cops, so they aren't our heroes. Chaz is our hero. He may be a gangbanger, and he slings, but he's cool. He always has the latest Jordans, the freshest clothes, and the sound system you hear before you see his car bouncing around the corner, hydraulics on point. His mom, my Aunt Celia, doesn't ask where the money comes from when he pays her rent every month. She turns a blind eye, but Ma won't take Chaz's money, no matter how tight it gets at our house.

"Shit," Chaz mutters, a frown puckering his eyebrows. He usually walks slowly so everyone can see his fresh kicks, to make it easy for what Ma calls "fast tail girls" to catch him, but he runs to the back of the house like someone's chasing him.

"What's up with Chaz?" I ask Jade.

"Mmm-hmm." Jade shrugs, her attention already back on *Coming to America.* "No telling. Trouble probably."

Chaz has been nothing but trouble for a long time. Like most kids, he thought he'd be a baller, get drafted one day. If it isn't rapping, it's sports. In the hood, those are a boy's dreams when anything seems possible. Most dreams don't last long on this block of rude awakenings.

Our three sets of eyes stretch wide at the sound of a helicopter overhead outside. The cops have been cracking down lately. Sometimes it feels like they've forgotten us here in Compton, like they give up on trying to regulate the violence and death we've become numb to. One minute, you're on the playground swinging, hanging on monkey bars, and the next you're dodging bullets. The cops come on their terms, usually when they're looking for somebody. That bird in the sky tells us they're looking for somebody. I don't say it, but Chaz's response to the pager and the helicopter that sounds like it's right on top of us has me wondering if this time they're looking for him.

"Amir." Ms. Bethany, Amir's mom, stands on our front porch, her usually pleasant face stern through the bars over the screen door. "Bring your narrow butt home right now."

"But, Ma." Amir gestures to the television. "We coming up on the barber shop scene where Eddie Murphy plays all the different characters."

"And I'm coming up on that butt if you don't get to that house like I told you." She sends a worried look up to the sky. "Go to the closet."

The three of us exchange glances. The violence has been so bad lately innocent people have been getting caught in the crossfire. Just last week one of our neighbors caught a stray bullet sitting in his kitchen. Drive-by. After that, Ma and Ms. Bethany told us we should go to the closets when we hear gunfire or even helicopters. Most times, those birds are looking for guys who run and shoot first, not caring where the bullets land until later.

"Hey, Bethany." Ma walks up the hall from the kitchen, drying her hands on a dishtowel. "Everything all right?"

"That bird." Ms. Bethany flips her head up toward the sky. "They looking for somebody."

She aims a careful glance at Jade, pausing before going on. "Word on the street's they're looking for Chaz."

Jade's troubled eyes meet mine. Chaz bounces between our houses sometimes. I'm not even sure Ma knows he's here.

"For Chaz?" Ma looks down the hall. "Chaz, you back there?"

The answering silence tells me he's gone. Probably snuck out through my bedroom window. My heart starts banging on my ribcage, dragging back and forth like on prison bars. My breath goes short. Mama says we have extra senses, things the streets teach us to survive. We smell danger. Feel trouble disrupting the air. In just seconds, an invisible hand is choking our whole block as that bird hovers, and none of us can breathe.

"Amir, I said come on." Fear adds a few lines around Ms.

Bethany's tight lips. "Now, boy." Amir drags himself to the door.

"I don't want to leave," he gripes. "Ain't fair."

"Fair?" Ms. Bethany pops his head with her palm. "Get your fair butt 'cross that street."

She glances over her shoulder at my mother. They watch out for each other. Amir eats at our table as much as I eat at theirs.

"Mittie, let me know if you hear anything about Chaz."

With that, she's gone, retreating into the house to seek shelter until what we all feel coming passes over. Ma grabs the remote and turns off the television, standing to block the screen. She points back down the hall to my bedroom where we hid the last few times.

"Get to the closet."

Before we can groan and complain like Amir did, a tall figure in uniform at the screen door distracts us. My cousin Greg takes after his mother. He and Jade share the same almond-shaped eyes and walnut complexion, where Chaz and I have skin like deep caramel, like Ma and her brother.

"Aunt Mittie, I need to come in." Greg's face is sober. He darts looks around our small living room, alert. "Hey, Jade. Marlon."

I flick my chin up like I see the older boys do, trying to be cool. Jade just stares at her brother. His decision to become a cop divided our family, and she doesn't know from one day to the next whose side she's on.

"To that closet," Ma repeats, her lips set in a line. She opens the door for Greg, not checking to make sure we obeyed. We walk down the hall but linger to eavesdrop as soon as we're out of sight.

"What's going on, Greg?" Ma finally allows the worry to seep into her voice now that she thinks we're out of earshot. "This about Chaz? They say y'all looking for him."

"Yes, ma'am." Greg's heavy sigh covers all the scrapes and trouble Chaz has been in leading up to today. "He's wanted for questioning in that shooting yesterday off Rosecrans."

"Shooting? The kid?"

"He was sixteen. He was a Crip, Aunt Mittie."

That's all he has to say. Between Crips and Bloods, color is the only offense needed.

"He ain't here." Ma's voice goes harder. "And your mama is working a double shift, so she ain't home yet. Greg, you look out for your brother now."

"Aunt Mittie, I've been trying, but he never listens to me. He's always tripped about me becoming a cop. A lot of folks here in the neighborhood did."

"I understand, Greg. You wanted to change things. I get that, but you know cops haven't made friends here. It'll take some time, but folks will come around."

A shot cracks the air beyond the front porch.

"Go!" Ma's voice becomes urgent. "If Chaz did what they think, he'll have to deal with the consequences. Just protect him, Greg. Just . . . for your mama. Okay?"

"I gotta go."

Jade and I slide down the wall, faces turned toward each other, connected by our fear and worry.

"What'd I say?" Ma stands in front of us, her eyes fired up with frustration. "Get in that closet. Now."

She points to my bedroom, looking from Jade to me.

"I know you're scared for Chaz, but be scared for yourself. A stray bullet could take you out. Now, get in there."

We stand and start down the hall. Ma grabs my elbow, pulling me around to face her. At twelve, I'm almost as tall as she is, but I'm straddling childhood and adolescence. Half the time I think I know best and don't need her. This is the other half of the time when I want my mama to hug me and tell me it will all be okay. That we'll all be okay.

"Remember what we talked about?" she asks softly. "You go in that closet and don't be scared."

"You can't make yourself not scared, Ma." I stuff my hands into the pockets of my jeans.

"That's true, but you can distract yourself. You're a sharp boy. You got a memory like an elephant. Recite some of them poems you're always reading in Ms. Shallowford's class. Sing a song. Say the Pledge of Allegiance. I don't care. Just don't leave that closet until I say so."

I nod and enter my room. Michael Jordan, NWA, Tupac, and the Oakland Raiders plaster my walls. Other than a small bed and dresser, that's all the decoration the room requires. Jade isn't in the closet. She's standing by the window Chaz must have left open when he snuck out.

"In the closet, Jade." I walk in, expecting her to follow. For a second, her face defies the order. She glances through the window and out to our front yard. Both her brothers are out there. On opposite sides of the law, but both at risk.

"There's nothing you can do." I make my voice certain like I hear Ma's even when she isn't sure at all. "Get in here."

As soon as Jade sits beside me in the tiny closet, the wail of approaching sirens splinters the air. Fear widens her eyes, and she clenches skinny arms around her legs. She presses her forehead to her knees and quietly cries. Jade is more sister than cousin to me. Nobody messes with me if she's around, and nobody messes with her if I have anything to say about it. Her tears, I can't take.

What Ma says is true. My head is like a vault. Poems, lyrics, all of it gets locked in my head. Ms. Shallowford's class is the only place I'm rewarded for remembering poems, for loving poetry. For writing my own. I do it only in class because I don't want to catch it from the other guys, but for Jade, whose hands tremble as the sirens come closer, I'll do it.

I start with the question that launches Langston Hughes' famous poem "Harlem," asking what happens to a dream deferred.

When I quote the line, when I ask the question, Jade lifts her head. I feel stupid. I usually do this alone. I'm usually in my bed when the sound of bullets rips through the air, and the words that calm and comfort me, I'm the only one who hears. But Jade's with me now, and I taste her fear. It's bitter like aspirin dissolving on my tongue as I continue, posing Hughes' questions about dried-up raisin dreams. Jade blinks at me, her tears slowing. She swipes at her running nose. Feet scamper past my open bedroom window, a chase underway. Angry voices bounce off the walls.

"Hands in the air!" Greg's voice reaches us in the closet. "Chaz, man stop. Come on. Put the gun down."

Jade's chest expands and contracts with breaths like she's about to hyperventilate, her eyes round as plates.

I continue with the lines of "Harlem," comparing the delayed dream to rotten meat and syrupy sweets. The words barely penetrate my mind, but they keep my heart from falling out of my chest.

I'm not sure if it helps Jade, but the words anchor me, give me something to focus on besides the chaos on the front yard. Besides the threat of violence chilling the air. I blink back tears, but Jade's flow freely down her cheeks.

"Chaz, no!" Panic and pain wrestle in Greg's words. "Don't make me do it!"

Pop!

It's a silly word for the sound a gun makes. Ms. Shallowford taught our class about onomatopoeia last week, but none of the sounds she used for gunfire seem right.

Pop! Crack! Bang!

If you've heard shots as many times as we have, if you live with it, you know the sound a gun makes when it's fired is a moan. The moan of a mother, a father, a daughter, or son losing someone they love. It's the sound Jade makes when she runs to my window, her eyes scanning the front yard for both of her brothers. We find them there together. Chaz's lifeless head rests in Greg's lap on the patch of grass. Greg's face crumples, the brows bent with pain, his mouth stretched wide on a wail. He's covered in the blood spurting life from his brother's chest.

Jade scurries through the window, rushing across the yard and hurling herself into the grief, pummeling Greg's shoulders, slapping his head, screaming obscenities. Ma jerks her off, pulls her back and into her arms, eyes full of pain locked on the blood-covered brothers. My Aunt Celia runs up the street and into the small crowd gathering. A cop restrains her, but you can't hold back a mother's anguish. We all watch Aunt Celia's face collapse, her eyebrows buckling over eyes streaming devastation. Her mouth, a gaping hole of torment. She strains, arms outstretched for her dying son, hands clawed to scratch the other. Sobs rack her body, and she is a world of pain.

"You killed my boy!" Aunt Celia's voice, a dirge, booms over the eerily still street. "I hate you! I hate you! I hate you, Greg!"

His mother's mournful litany bounces off Greg's head and shoulders as he cradles his brother, rocks him, imprisoned by his own guilt and pain.

I can't move. My shoes stick to the thin, cheap carpet in my bedroom. The smell of death invades my nose like an enemy, and my heart trills in my chest, hammering a rapid beat. My breath wheezes from my throat, and my head spins. I grasp for consciousness, searching for the words that calmed me moments ago. Moments before a bullet split our world right down the middle.

I mumble the final lines of "Harlem," even though I'm the only one listening, and I reach the same conclusion Hughes does.

So here in these streets, in my neighborhood, what happens to a dream deferred?

It explodes.

Five

Grip

I T'S AS QUIET AS A MORGUE WHEN THE SONG ENDS. I HAVE NO IDEA WHAT the Prodigy team sitting around the table thinks. Verse one of "Bruise" is written from the perspective of a young black man, verse two from that of a cop. I'm the only black man in the room. As much as I love Rhyson, as close as we are, I'm not sure he can understand the indignity of being stopped for no reason by cops on the regular. Being forced to lie on the ground and get searched without explanation. Targeted. Profiled. Made to feel second-class. It isn't his experience, but all my life in my neighborhood, it was mine. I infused every line of that verse with the pain and frustration and resentment brimming over in my community. I hope I told Greg's story, too, my cousin who became a good cop. Who had to shoot his own brother and probably saved lives that day. I admire him as much as I admire anyone. Instead of running from the police force, he ran toward it and decided to do his part to make things better, though sometimes the system as it exists feels beyond repair.

"As much as I think it's a great social commentary," Max finally speaks first. "Are we sure this is what we want to bring up given how divided our nation is right now? I mean, will you be alienating half your listeners? I'm not sure it's the right song for the Target Exclusive."

I shrug like it doesn't bother me, but it does. Should I push? The song is special to me. I didn't even realize how much until now when it sounds like it might not make the cut.

"I agree with you, Max," Bristol says, her tone all business and brusque. "It isn't right for the Target Exclusive."

"I'm glad we can agree on something this morning," he says with a chuckle.

"It belongs on the wide version of *Grip*." Bristol has that defiant look she gets when she digs her heels in. "If it's on the Exclusive, fewer people will hear it, and everyone needs to hear that song."

She meets my eyes for a second before blinking away all softness.

"I agree," Rhyson says quietly.

My best friend and I stare at each other for moments elongated with the things we haven't talked as much about. We have so much in common—our passion for music, the video games we play, the books we read, our acerbic sense of humor—that we often haven't discussed the ways we're different. But the lyrics of "Bruise" paint a picture he's never seen up close.

"So what do we need to do to make that happen?" Bristol has shifted from any sentimentality she felt for the song to battle plan, figuring out how to make it happen at this late date.

Rhyson and I break down every step we must go through to get the song on the album in time. She doesn't blink, but Sarah scribbles frantically, jotting it all down.

"It'll happen." She looks at Rhyson and Max before her eyes land on me. "I promise I'll get it on there in time."

This is what I keep falling for over and over. Bristol is passionate and determined, one of those rare people who never accepts no for the ones she cares about. And whether or not she wants to admit it, she cares about me a hell of a lot.

We listen to three more songs. Bristol loves them all, but she likes everything I write. I'm not being conceited. I can't think of one song or poem I've ever shared with her that she didn't love.

"We need to nail this last song down." Rhyson glances at his watch. "And quick. Kai has an ultrasound today, and I'd much rather see my baby than go through eight more songs when we only need one."

He points to Bristol, his look only half playful. "You get no say this time, Bris."

"What?" She frowns and pushes out her bottom lip a little. "Why not?"

"Because you love everything Grip writes," he says matter-of-factly. "You're no help. We'll be here all day."

Her eyes flick to mine and then down to her iPad. She knows it's true. I've never been more certain of anything than I am that Bristol cares deeply about me. I wasn't guessing last night when I said she watches me. She does. I know she wants me, but a lot of girls do. None of them care about me the way Bristol does, though. The same bottomless devotion she has for her brother, for her few close friends—hell, even for her mother, who doesn't deserve it, she has for me. She hides it in friendship and excuses it with business, but every time I catch her looking, I know the truth.

"So I think I have the final song." Rhyson starts tapping the iPad in front of him until the first strains of the track fill the conference room. A song I never meant anyone to hear.

"Oh, not that one." I go into the shared folder, searching frantically for the file he's playing so I can shut it down. "Rhys, not that one. Let's not—"

"This one is the best option." Rhyson tilts his head, a look of consternation on his face. "Can we just hear it?"

I don't have to hear it. I know every word.

I fell for her before the beat dropped. Between the verses and
After rehearsal and
In sixteen bars I was intoxicated
After sixteen bars, me and her was faded
Had our first kiss on a Ferris wheel
We was on top of the world.

I'm on top of the world (When I love her)
Top of the World (When I hate her)
Top of the world
(When I take her or leave her)
With her I'm on the top of the world

I roll her up tight in my blunt paper
Inhale her like smoke, in my lungs she's a vapor 'Cause she always on the run
Making me hunt, making me chase
Making me run like it's a race
Making me work like it's my job
Even when she bottom she come out on top
She be on top of the world

I'm on top of the world (When I love her)
Top of the World (When I hate her)
Top of the world
(When I take her or leave her)
With her I'm on the top of the world

At the last note, Max starts a slow clap. Everyone around the table joins him. Everyone except Bristol, who stares blankly at the shiny conference room table.

Shit.

"I love it," Max says. "Rhyson, you're right. That's it. Man, the lyrics are so clever. It's infectious. Now that's a hit."

"And what's the song you're sampling?" Sarah asks. "Was it Prince?"

"Uh, yeah." I clear my throat. "'I Wanna Be Your Lover.'"

"As soon as I heard it," Rhyson says. "I knew it was the one. Maybe we should take this one to the wide release, too? Bristol, we should see—"

"If we're done," Bristol says abruptly, cutting off Rhyson's suggestion. "I need to get back to my office."

It goes quiet, and everyone stares at her, but she doesn't stop. She grabs her phone and walks quickly toward the door.

"Sarah," she tosses over her shoulder. "Could you go over that last item on the agenda?"

"Um, okay." Sarah's wide eyes scan the agenda Bristol left. "Here we are. Bristol wants to—"

"I gotta go, too." I push back my chair and stand. "Let me know if you need anything else."

Before anyone can stop me or ask questions, I'm out the door and racing up the hall to catch her before she leaves. I round the corner and come to a halt. Bristol leans against the wall, head down. I approach slowly, cautiously, like she'll run off if I startle her.

"Bris," I say softly once I'm right in front of her.

She stiffens, raising her lashes to reveal the accusation of her eyes.

"How could you?" she asks, her whisper knife-sharp.

"It was just for me." I grab the end of the braid hanging over her shoulder. "No one else was supposed—"

"But the song's about us." She jerks back, freeing her hair from my fingers. "About me. How dare you?"

"How dare I?" Now I'm pissed. "Those are my thoughts. My ideas. My music, Bristol. No one dictates how I express myself. Not even you."

"Even when those thoughts and ideas are about me?" She presses her eyes closed and flattens her palm to her forehead. "What happened then was private, and you've put us on display for anyone shopping at Target."

"I didn't mean to. I'd forgotten about that track until Rhyson started playing it." I squat until I'm eye level with her, even though she still doesn't look at me. I lift her chin until she has to. "It was for me, not anyone else. Music, writing—it's how I process what I'm feeling. Always has been. You know that. That's how I was feeling, what I was thinking, and I needed to get it out."

"How you were feeling." Now that she's looking at me, she isn't looking away, and her eyes sear me even before her words do. "You hate me? In the lyrics, you said when I hate her. That's how you feel?"

There's startled hurt in her eyes, but I won't lie to her.

"Maybe that day, that moment." I shake my head. "But no. I don't hate you. How you make me feel? I hate that sometimes."

"How do I make you feel?"

Alive. Tortured. Exhilarated. Hungry.

"Confused," I say instead. "Frustrated."

"What's so confusing about no?" She glances down at the shiny hardwood floor at our feet. "I've been telling you no for years. I mean it."

"What's confusing is that no matter what you say, I know what you feel."

"And you know this how?" She looks up, one imperious brow lifted. "A few kisses on the roof one night when I was high?"

All those walls are firmly erected. No gaps. No cracks. We're back at square one. Judging by the indifferent look on her face, we might even be pre-square one. Have I been fooling myself all these years?

But despite what my eyes tell me, my gut says she has no idea what to do with the way I make her feel. All my instincts tell me Bristol wants me, and fuck if I understand why she won't give us a chance. Maybe she suspects what I know for sure. If I ever get her, no way in hell I'm letting her go. That gap last night showed me what's behind that wall, and I want all of it.

She lures me closer without trying. Her scent, her warmth, her softness, her toughness entices me to lean into her. The feeling of last night, the want, rushes through me again. My hands find her waist, and I imprint my shape into hers against the wall.

"Grip, no." Her breath shivers over her lips, and she turns her head away from me.

"Why not?" I run my nose up and down her neck until she shudders under me. Her body is honest with me even when she hides the truth. I want her truth. I have to know.

She wriggles free, stepping away and pacing a tight circuit in the corridor.

"Bristol, about last night—"

"The other song, 'Bruise,'" she cuts in, stopping her pacing to face me. "It's fantastic."

Not-so-deft change of topic. I'm not sure if it was because she was genuinely interested in the song or afraid of what I would say next.

"Thank you." I slip a fist into my pocket and lean against the wall to watch her

"And your cousin Chaz who was shot by his brother, the cop." Her eyes fall to my left forearm where Chaz's name is inked into the skin. "They're Jade's brothers?"

"Yeah."

"I can't imagine what you described. When I think about that happening, you getting stopped like that over and over again . . ."

Bristol bites into her bottom lip. She turns her head to stare at me, sadness saturating her eyes. "Can you just tell me when all my privilege makes me clueless?"

Damn her. Every time I think I might be able to get past this girl, move on to someone who will actually tell me how she feels, she does this. Shows the tender under all that tough and reminds me why not one day has gone by in eight years when she hasn't at least crossed my mind.

"I can do that," I promise quietly.

"Good, I—"

"There you are. I was looking for you guys." Rhyson strides down the hall toward us. "You both bailed on the meeting. What gives?"

"Sorry. You're right," Bristol says, eyes cool again when she looks at me. "I have too much to do to be standing around. Gotta go. Grip, I'll email you about the Target spot. Should be later this week."

I just nod and watch as she walks away.

"What's wrong with her?" Rhyson asks.

"What's wrong is your timing is shit," I snap.

I love Rhys, but this is one time I want to strangle him.

"What's crawled up your ass?" Rhyson frowns and starts walking. "Can you tell me while we walk? I don't want to be late for Kai's appointment."

"Sure." I match my long stride to his. "I wish you'd checked with me before you played that song."

"Everyone loved it." He jabs the down button for the elevator several times.

"Not everyone." I give him a wry smile. "You do know that doesn't make the elevator come any faster, right?"

"Maybe we should take the st—"

The ding of the elevator doors opening shoots down that suggestion.

"Who didn't like it?" he asks as we board.

"Bristol didn't."

"What?" He frowns over eyes just like his twin sister's. "Why would Bris not like it?"

Do I really want to do this? All these years I haven't talked about this with Rhyson. After the drama with my almost-ex-girlfriend/close-call baby mama, Bristol wanted to put that week behind us, including not telling Rhyson about it. It was kind of awkward anyway, so at first, I was cool with that. Now it just seems stupid that he doesn't know after all these years.

"Bristol doesn't like the song because it's about her." I run my hand over the coolness of my scalp, half-expecting to encounter locs hanging down to my shoulder. "The song, it's about us."

We've reached the building's underground parking garage. As soon as he steps off the elevator, he stops abruptly.

"What the hell are you talking about?" Genuine confusion clouds his expression. "When did you ever kiss Bristol at the top of a Ferris wheel? Is that like a metaphor?"

"No. Dude, I literally kissed your sister at the top of the Ferris wheel."

Rhyson looks torn between losing his lunch and punching me in the face. This might actually make the awkwardness worth it.

"When was this?" he demands. "You and Bristol? Is this recent?"

"No, when she was here for spring break. Remember we went to that carnival?" I sigh. "Don't worry. It hasn't happened again. Unless you count last night."

"Last night?" Rhyson's mouth falls open a little, even as he starts moving in the direction of the Porsche Cayenne in his parking spot. "What the hell? Tell me."

I may be enjoying this too much. Rhyson always has his shit together, so seeing him thrown for a loop is rare and wondrous. To be the cause of it, even better.

"I left my bag here yesterday, and she brought it by my place last night." I pat the hood and deliberately turn to leave, not actually expecting to get very far. "Well, I know you're in a hurry so—"

"Marlon." Rhyson leans against the SUV with his arms folded and a frown on his face. "Cut the crap. Talk."

"We kissed." I lean beside him against his car and shrug. "That's it. That's all."

"That's all?" He lifts a skeptical brow.

"For now." I grin as salaciously as I dare considering Bristol is his sister. "There's always tomorrow."

"Let that shit go." Rhyson blows out an exasperated breath. "I don't want this affecting your working relationship at such a crucial time. Your album's about to drop, and Bristol's hand is in every aspect of it. If you pursue this, it could get awkward. We can't afford awkward right now."

His phone rings with his own song "Lost", Kai's ring tone. "Damn." He glances at the screen. "That's Kai. Probably wondering where I am. She'll feel better if I'm in motion."

"Then by all means get in motion." I step back when he starts the car and pulls out of the space, driver side window still down.

"Don't forget what I said about Bristol, okay?" He gives me one last worried look.

"What? You mean to go for it?" I ask, hoping to see some hackles rise. "Got it."

"Not go for it. Did you not hear a word I . . ." He studies my face and must see the humor there. "Screw you. You know I'm right. Leave it alone."

Leave it alone.

That's what my mom used to say when I'd pick at my scabs. She warned me it would only take longer to heal, but it was a compulsion, a fascination. It's the same way with Bristol. I've been pulling this scab off over and over for years.

If I have to leave her alone for this to get better, maybe I don't want it to heal.

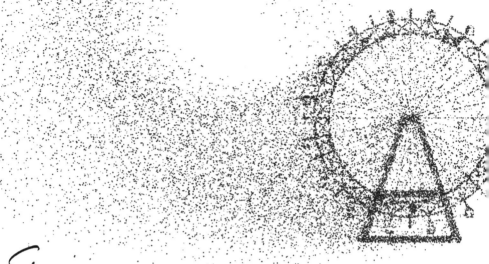

Six

Bristol

"YOU'VE DONE A GREAT JOB WITH EVERYTHING, BRISTOL."
The praise comes from Will, Qwest's manager, as we check the set list for tonight.

"Thanks," I murmur without looking away from the document detailing the songs and cues for the performance Qwest and Grip will give soon. "Are your rooms okay?"

"That would be an understatement." His dark eyes laugh at me when I finally look up. "The Presidential Suite at The Park-LA is a little over the top, wouldn't you say?"

"The Presidential Suite?" I frown, mentally scrolling through the email I sent Sarah about accommodations for Qwest's team. "I'm glad you like it. I just don't remember reserving it for you."

"Yeah. It's a three-bedroom suite." It's his turn to frown. "Is there a problem?"

"No. Probably just a mix-up. No problem." I catch Sarah's eye across the room and flick my chin so she knows I need her before looking back to Will. "Is Qwest settled okay?"

"Um, yeah." Will's face broadcasts his reluctance. "She really wants to hang with Grip tonight instead of doing that interview, though. Any update from the reporter?"

Translation. She really wants to sleep with Grip before she goes back to New York. That's her business and his, not mine, I remind myself and draw a deep breath to support the words I need to say.

"I'm trying. I've left Meryl a message and am just waiting to hear back."

"Waiting?" Will glances at the platinum watch on his wrist. "She needs to let us know soon."

"Believe it or not," I say sharply, despite the control I thought I was exercising. "My job description as Grip's manager does not include arranging booty calls. So yes, waiting to hear back. And if Qwest needs to hear that from me, it's a message I'm more than happy to deliver personally."

Will holds up both hands, his teeth flashing white against his goatee and dark skin.

"Whoa, whoa, whoa." He takes my hand and squeezes. "You handle Meryl. I'll take care of the booty call."

"Sounds good to me."

"You must admit," he says, his eyes persuading me to smile. "It is an awful lot of booty for one person to manage."

I laugh before I catch myself. Qwest's ass is the stuff of legends.

Jaws drop over it. My laugh withers in my throat when I think of Grip spending the night holding on to that ass.

"I'm just trying to keep my artist happy," Will says. "So don't flip."

"Flip?" I find a polite smile from somewhere. "You'll know when I flip, Will. I'm far from flipping. I'll have an answer for you before the show is over."

"Grip's lucky to have you." There's sincerity in his eyes, which is something we don't find much of in this business.

"Qwest is lucky to have you, too."

Because God knows she and I would kill each other.

Will knows hip-hop, but he knows business even better. Armed only with his MBA and hustle, he started a small management firm just a few years ago. Qwest was his first act, but he's parlayed that into several others, and recently merged with Sound Management, one of the largest firms in the business.

"Congratulations, by the way, on the deal with Sound," I add.

"Thanks." Will's smile is instant and tinged with pride. "Ezra Cohen asked me to tell you hello. I didn't realize you knew him, though I shouldn't be surprised."

"I interned with Sound in New York and worked some at their office here in LA when I first moved. Ezra's been a mentor of sorts to me over the years."

"I guess with parents like yours, making those connections is easy, huh?"

I stiffen at his words, resenting any assumption that my parents' success managing classical musicians fast tracked me.

"He actually wasn't familiar with my parents at all. He's mainstream. They move in classical circles." I clip each word. "I applied for the internship like anyone else and busted my ass once I got it."

"I'm sorry." Will's dark eyes search mine, and he grimaces. "Look, real talk. I'm the only minority at the Sound Management partner table, and most of them think I'm Ezra's answer to affirmative action."

The memory of fetching coffee for some of those assholes during my internship makes me grin.

"And a lot of folks at Penn State thought of me as some kind of token. Like I was taking the spot of someone who actually deserved it," Will continues. "I guess what I'm trying to say, and not very well, is that I know what it's like when people assume you got where you are using something other than hard work. Didn't mean to imply that."

"No problem." I relax my face until my smile becomes genuine. "Sorry I got defensive."

"Then we're both sorry." Will returns my smile, straightens his tie, and nods to Sarah as she walks up. "I need to check on something for Qwest. See you in a little bit."

Once he's gone, I gesture for Sarah to join me at a nearby table to go over a few details before the doors open.

"You're feeling better today?" I ask.

"So much better." Sarah grins, looking more like the perky girl I'm used to seeing. "I went to bed as soon as I got home and woke up a new woman. Thanks for taking the bag to Grip."

"No problem." I ruthlessly suppress the images and sensations that assault me when I remember being on that rooftop with Grip, and focus on the task at hand. "Did you, by chance, upgrade Qwest to the Presidential Suite at the Park?"

I sip my water. As badly as I need a drink, I've been trying to cut back. I'm known for holding my liquor, but that doesn't mean I should. If I'm not careful, I'll end up drinking vodka for breakfast like my mother.

"No." Sarah frowns and pulls out her phone, scrolling through emails. "The reservation is for a luxury suite, not the Presidential."

She whistles and lays her phone on the table. "Somebody messed up. Costly mistake."

"Hmmmm. Maybe." I have my suspicions about other scenarios, but don't voice them. I just open a few emails that might need my attention. "Did we hear back from Meryl about Grip's date with Qwest?"

Sarah clears her throat in a way that catches my attention. I glance up from my phone and wait.

"I haven't heard back yet," Sarah says. "But does Grip know about this um . . . date?"

"I think Qwest wants it to be a surprise of sorts." I keep my face impassive.

"She's wasting her time," Sarah singsongs the words, a small smile on her matte pink lips. "Grip only has eyes for one woman."

Sarah is more observant than I gave her credit for. I stand and smooth my hair.

"I don't think all the girls Grip sleeps with really care where his eyes are," I say, keeping my tone neutral. "There are other parts of his anatomy they're much more interested in."

"If that one woman he has eyes for would give him a sign, I'm sure he'd keep his anatomy where it should be."

"Well his anatomy has to be onstage in about an hour," I tell her. "So, I'm going to make sure it is."

Did I say I liked being friendly with Sarah? Retract that statement. I don't need her that close or seeing that much. She better be glad she's so efficient.

And that I like her so much.

I prepare a mug of lemon tea in the kitchen for Grip. He's been performing so much his voice must be tired. I'm walking down the hall to the dressing room, and the door is ajar. My brother's voice reaches me through the small open space.

"Call me whipped if you want." Laughter threads Rhyson's deep voice. "You're just jealous, Marlon."

Softer, feminine laughter joins Rhyson's.

"Rhys, don't tease him," my sister-in-law Kai chides.

"He knows it's true," Rhyson insists. "You want the wife and kid now that I made it look so good, right? I see it in your eyes. You're ready to settle down. You're tired of sowing all those wild oats."

"I haven't been sowing anything." Grip's voice when it comes has a little gravel in it. "I always wrap it up."

I clench my fist at my stomach. I know he sleeps with women. If I hadn't known, he made it abundantly clear last night.

"I don't mean literally sow," Rhyson says. "You already had one baby daddy close call."

"Not funny," Grip answers. "Too soon."

"How can it be too soon?" Rhyson demands with a laugh. "Tessa was eight years ago."

"Considering what she tried to pull on me," Grip answers. "It will always be too soon."

Tessa.

Tessa was my close call, too. I may have fallen hard and fast for Grip that week, but I've been getting back up ever since. My hands and knees may be scraped, but I'm otherwise in tact, if not a little tougher and smarter. Tougher and smarter should be the natural evolution of a woman. It's the only way we'll survive as the "weaker" sex in this world.

Weaker, my ass.

"Just admit you want this," Rhyson says with a laugh.

I carefully peer through the crack to see Rhyson's very pregnant wife sitting on his lap. He brushes Kai's long, dark hair away from her neck to drop a kiss there. I can't believe Gep, Rhyson's most trusted security guard, isn't out here keeping watch. Then I notice a shiny shoe only a few feet from Rhyson's. Figures. Gep is inside with them.

"You two do make it look good." The smile in Grip's voice stills my heart for a beat. "But it looks good on you because you found the right girl. A lifetime with the wrong girl is a sentence."

"Then find the right girl," Rhyson says. "And do not say it's Bristol."

A needle pulls through my heart at my brother's words. Grip and I aren't right for each other, but to hear someone else say it, to hear my own brother say it, hurts.

"Don't start." Now Grip's voice is tight. No sign of a smile.

"Yeah, Rhyson," Kai chimes in. "I believe Bristol will come around."

You're wrong, honey.

"I already told you who Bristol will marry," Rhyson says. This I gotta hear. My brother is notoriously obtuse about me.

"She'll marry some guy in a suit with a stick up his ass and who has our mother's approval."

Okay. Maybe not completely off base.

"Don't say that about your sister," Kai says.

"It isn't a criticism," Rhyson replies, his tone ringing with truth. "Just a prediction. Bristol wants more control than what she would have with a guy like you, Marlon."

"We'll see, huh?" Grip answers softly. "You might be right."

"I still have my money on Grip and Bristol." Kai's voice is light but a little defiant.

"Don't lose our money, Pep," Rhyson says. "Ow! Why'd you hit me?"

"Because you're being a jerk," she says, laughing a little. "And I'll kiss it better."

They would turn my stomach if I wasn't getting a niece out of this in the next month or so.

"Uh . . . I'm still here," Grip says. "Don't start making out. Remember Gep's innocent, virgin eyes."

Gep's gruff hack of a laugh joins the others. I'm positive the ex-CIA operative hasn't been innocent or a virgin in decades.

"In all seriousness," Rhyson continues. "Qwest likes you a lot."

"What gave you that idea?' Grip asks. "The way she practically dry humps me onstage every time we perform? Maybe I'll wear a condom for our set tonight."

I find myself smiling listening to them laugh. "She's a sweet girl," Kai defends.

Kai actually pointed Qwest my way when the rapper asked about meeting Grip. They've developed some kind of odd friendship. Odd because Qwest may be sweet in her own way, but she's a diva. She and I would still rip each other's hair out. Kai doesn't have a drop of diva in her body.

"She's very sweet," Grip agrees. "I've been surprised by how sweet she is. And smart. And gorgeous. And funny. She's actually kind of amazing."

That needle makes another pass through the fibers of my heart as I listen to Grip's glowing words for Qwest. Why wouldn't he think those things?

"And let's not forget that asssss!" Grip laughs.

Seriously. The girl's ass has its own hashtag. I'm pretty sure it's insured. Rhyson and Gep join in the laughter, but Kai refuses.

"Does it always come down to that?" Kai sounds only slightly outraged. She has room to talk since she has "assets" in that area herself.

"No," Grip answers. "I like legs and breasts, too."

"Both of which Qwest had the last time I checked," Rhyson says. "Oh, you checked, did you?" Kai asks.

"Not like that," Rhyson rushes to say. "I mean, not at all like that. It's just her—"

"Dude, just stop," Grip laughs. "That's a no-win grave you're digging for yourself. I may not be married, but even I know that."

"Rhyson, to misquote *Mean Girls*," Kai says. "Stop trying to make Qwest happen."

My brother and Kai are film geeks and could talk in nothing but movie quotes for days. How I ever thought they weren't perfect for each other, I'll never know.

"Maybe it isn't Qwest." Some of the laughter fades from Rhyson's words. "I'm just saying I know how important family is to you. I don't want you wasting any more time than you have to pining for my sister when she hasn't budged all these years. How long are you gonna wait?"

I glance through the crack again and see Rhyson holding Kai even tighter, his chin on her shoulder and her temple leaned against his head. With Rhyson's hand splayed across her baby bump, they're the picture of marital bliss. Happiness personified. Grip's eyes reflect the same emotions roiling inside me. Maybe a little envy. Maybe a little doubt. He's probably asking himself the questions Rhyson asked of him.

What is he waiting for? Me? To change my mind? I won't. It shouldn't be me. He needs to see that, and I know what I need to do to make sure he does.

Seven

Grip

THE LIGHT KNOCK ON THE DRESSING ROOM DOOR INTERRUPTS MY conversation with Rhys and Kai. And Gep, if I count his non-verbals as conversation, which I pretty much have to since he barely speaks.

"Come in." I expect a stagehand to tell me it's almost time, but it's Bristol. God, she's beautiful.

I'd like to kick everyone out, lock the door with us on this side, and fuck her against the wall. She could keep those heels on, too. I can imagine them digging into my butt while I tear that ass up.

I'm not a gentleman.

I feel like I'm channeling Uncle Jamal for a moment. Maybe Rhyson's right. Maybe she needs a guy wearing a suit accessorized with a stick up his ass. Tonight, she looks like the definition of class.

Those heels are the color of tangerines and match the cropped top showing off the golden skin of her stomach. The long sleeves cling to her arms, and the narrow white skirt hugs her hips, ass, and the infinity of her legs. The coppery streaks stand out in the dark hair parted down the middle and pulled back at her neck.

"Hey." She hands me a steaming mug of lemon-scented something or other. "For your voice."

It takes no effort to hold her eyes with mine when I accept the drink. I will her to remember our bodies pressed together on the roof under a full moon. She's wearing blush, so I can't tell if she's flushing or not under my stare, but she gives nothing else away so I can't know for sure.

"How's my niece today?"

She rubs Kai's little belly.

"She's good, Auntie Bristol," Kai says affectionately.

"What's up, brother?" Bristol musses Rhyson's hair with her knuckles.

"Nothing much. Just supporting our artist." Rhyson swats her hand away and grins at her. "Excellent job tonight, as usual."

"Thanks." Bristol checks the items on my dressing room table. She's anal about our riders, and I know she's making sure everything we requested is there.

"I talked to Danny today." Approval lights Rhyson's eyes when they rest on his sister. "He says you laid down the law and got things straightened out for their show when no one else could. He couldn't stop singing praises of your bad assery."

"It was nothing. I'll probably join them on the road for at least one stop. Maybe after *Grip* drops." Bristol leans against my dressing room mirror to face us. "Kai, if you weren't so preggers, we'd get to hear you tonight."

"Small mercies." Kai rubs her belly and allows herself a wry smile. "Or not so small. I'm sorry I can't perform our song, Grip."

My first single from the album was a collaboration with Kai. We got the video in the can, but she ended up pregnant and having some complications that kept her from performing live. The song still stayed at number one for weeks.

"Don't think twice about that." I grab her hand. "You just keep growing my niece in there."

"If she gets any bigger," Kai says, toggling a smile between Rhyson and me. "I'll pop."

"Soon," Rhyson says with a tender smile.

"Well, I love the single with Qwest." Kai's shoulders start moving to the song she must hear in her head. Not only is she a great singer but also an incredible dancer. One of Prodigy's most versatile artists, she'll start working on her debut solo album soon after the baby arrives.

"My favorite line of 'Queen,'" Kai continues. "Is the no one sees your crystal crown lyric."

"Neruda," Bristol and I say in unison.

Surprise locks my eyes with hers when she makes the connection between my current single and Neruda's poem "The Queen." Maybe the book I gave her meant something to her after all. Or am I doing what Rhyson said I do? Wasting my time and reading too much into things that don't mean anything?

"The poet?" Surprise blooms on Kai's pretty face, her tilted eyes sliding between the two of us. "You're a fan, Grip?"

"Huge fan." My eyes haven't left Bristol's face since she mentioned Neruda, my favorite poet. "I didn't realize you were, Bristol."

"Lucky guess." She shrugs and straightens from the dressing room table.

"You're still coming tomorrow, right, Bristol?" Kai tucks into the crook of Rhyson's arm.

"Tomorrow?" Bristol frowns and screws up her face. "I should know this, right?"

"Lunch at our house. The whole Prodigy team is coming over." Kai laughs and rubs her baby bump. "You have just a few things going on, so I'll give you a pass on forgetting."

"Oh, yeah. I'll be there. One o'clock?" Bristol asks.

"Right," Rhyson says. "You want your favorite? Empanadas?"

Bristol and I exchange a quick look. There's no way she isn't recalling last night on the roof. I hope she still feels my hands all over her because I still taste her. I'd back her into a corner and taste her again right now if it wouldn't horrify Rhyson. He swears up and down that Bristol would destroy me if we ever get together. He doesn't realize that's a risk I'd take every day and twice on Sunday. I'm not sure he really believes I'm serious about Bristol. Hell, Bristol may not think I'm serious. Kai would probably start cheering. She's pulling for us if no one else is.

"Whatever's easiest," Bristol says. "Grip, you're on soon."

She walks to the door, class and grace and elegance twined into one girl I can never get out of my mind. "I'm going to check a few last things."

At the door, she practically bumps into someone.

"Excuse me," Bristol says. "Oh, Qwest, hi. How are you?"

Qwest steps fully into the room, the energy that explodes when she performs on stage, latent and waiting for her to pop the top.

"I'm good." Qwest gives Bristol's toned body a head-to-toe inspection. "Damn, you look good, girl. You got a man I haven't heard about?"

Bristol's husky laugh drifts back into the room and caresses my ears.

"You never know," she says, injecting some mystery into her voice.

Tension grips my neck and shoulders. Even though I know she isn't dating anyone, our exchange last night about fucking other people has been haunting me ever since. I try not to think of her with other guys. Hell, I sleep with other girls, but if she even hinted we had a chance, that would be over before she could even ask. She knows that, right?

"How's the Park?" Bristol asks. "Your suite is okay?"

"That suite is the bomb!" Qwest's dark eyes glimmer with pleasure between the fake lashes she wears for stage. "Maybe the nicest I've ever stayed in."

"Good," Bristol says. "I've got a friend there who went the extra mile for me."

"You mean Parker, Bris?" Rhyson asks, a slight frown on his face. She looks over her shoulder to her brother. They aren't your typical twins, but every once in a while I suspect they're telepathically communicating things the rest of us are missing.

"Yeah, Parker," she confirms. "I need to go."

She's gone before Rhyson can ask the questions I see lining up in his eyes. I hadn't thought of Charles Parker since our artist showcase in Vegas. His family owns the Park Hotels all over the world, and when we held our showcase at the Park-Vegas, he was wrapped around Bristol like a damn vine. I haven't seen or heard any sign of him since, so he hadn't entered my mind. Now, I wonder if she has been seeing him and I was just that oblivious. If she hid it from me. Or worse, maybe she wasn't hiding it from me at all. Maybe I didn't occur to her and she was just living her life like she told me.

"Is Bristol dating Charles Parker?" Qwest asks Rhyson.

"Not that I know of." Rhyson shifts Kai so he can stand. "I wouldn't be surprised if he hooked her up, though. Our families have been close all our lives. Our mothers are best friends. Roomed together at Wellesley."

How did I not know this? I'll be following up with Rhyson later. But first . . . I need to deal with Qwest. Rhyson, Kai, and Gep tell us they'll see us out there, and all drift out of the room, presumably to give us some time alone.

"Hi," Qwest says as close to shy as she can get.

There's nothing shy or subtle about Qwest. Skin flawless and the color of nutmeg. Her trademark braids, which are usually pulled into a knot, flow down to her tiny waist. Her body is a series of highlights and exaggerations. The curve from her waist to her ass is positively hyperbolic. I used to wonder if that ass was real. Remembering how she invited me to touch it and find out for myself the first time we met crooks my lips into a grin. This girl makes me laugh. She's talented and beautiful. Smart as a whip. I should feel so much more for her than friendship. And maybe I would if it weren't for Bristol.

But there is Bristol.

"Hi, yourself," I answer. "You ready for this?"

"Ready to get it over with." She walks over until she stands directly in front of me. "So we can have a good time later."

"A good time?" I shrug. "Sure. We could get a crew and go hit Greystone."

"A club?" She shakes her head and reaches up and over my shoulders, pressing her body into me. "No, I had something much more private in mind for us."

She is tight and warm and curvy against me, and if she keeps doing this, my dick will get hard. But that's it.

"Okay." I rest my hands lightly at her hips to move her so I can step away. I grab the button up I'm wearing for the show. "More private, huh? Just remember we have that interview with the *Legit* reporter after the show."

"Didn't Bristol tell you?" Qwest's eyes heat up a few degrees. "She got it cancelled so we can hang out."

"Hang out" is a euphemism for screw me into next week. I'm sure Bristol realizes this, and yet, she cancelled a long-standing interview to accommodate the desire branded in Qwest's eyes.

"Bristol arranged it, huh?" My voice is plastered to the walls of my throat. "Well then it's settled. You just tell me where we're going."

She runs one long nail down the center of my chest, her eyes never leaving mine.

"Oh, I will."

Eight

Bristol

THE FIRST TIME I SAW GRIP PERFORM, I LITERALLY ALMOST CAME.

Standing in the wings, watching him charm the audience with his charisma, challenge them with his lyrics, and feed them from the palm of his hand. I've almost nodded off waiting for guys to find the spot, to get me off, and this man does it hands-free from fifty feet away in front of a crowd without even trying. It's embarrassing to be so aroused just by watching him onstage. A heat wave flushes my body. Tiny beads of sweat gather down the line of my back, across my lip, at the nape of my neck . . . from watching him. While the blood seems to slow to a languid creep through my veins, my heart hurtles in my chest. Fire-winged butterflies swarm in my belly. I'm wet.

Good God. When will this set be over?

Thank goodness it's the last song or I'd need spare panties. I must not be the only one feeling hot. When Grip brings Qwest onstage for "Queen" to close the show, her eyes rake his tall frame possessively, like he's already hers. Like she wants to jump him under the lights in front of everyone. When she sidles up to him before her verse begins and grinds her hips into his, the audience goes wild. They want this to be real. There's already rampant speculation about a romance between Grip and Qwest. Some even mistakenly assume the song honoring women from all walks of life was written for her. Tonight's sexually charged performance will only send it into overdrive.

She stuffs her mic into her tiny bra top, freeing up her hands.

Grip's denim button down shirt hangs open already, his chest and abs a map of muscles on display. Qwest slides her hands under the shirt at his shoulders and guides it down over his arms until it catches at his wrists. Squeals from the audience pierce the air. Grip laughs, his smile as bright as the stage lights overhead, and shakes the shirt free of his hands. Qwest ties his shirt around her waist before diving into her verse.

She's a powerful figure, the cocky feminism and hard flow of her lyrics juxtaposed with the soft curves of her body. She turns her back to Grip, pressing and circling that is-it-really-real ass into his groin. His hands at her tiny waist look huge and commanding, and I know exactly what every woman in this place must be fantasizing about right now.

Because I would be, except I'm no longer aroused. Seeing how perfect they look together, feeling their chemistry like a tangible thing permeating the whole room, cools me right off and leaves a painful lump in my throat.

"They're fire," Will says from beside me with a grin. "And it's burning up the charts. People want them to happen, and it's driving sales. Their chemistry is a huge part of why 'Queen' is number one."

"It would seem." I try to relax my face so I can smile back.

"And their night out will only fuel it. Thanks for getting the interview delayed. Qwest was very happy."

"Good. She can show her appreciation in Dubai. Meryl's expecting a one-on-one with her, too."

"She'll be more than happy to," Will says. "You should have seen her face when I told her about tonight. I haven't seen her like this over a guy . . . well, ever really."

"Grip has that effect."

He had that effect on me.

Had? Who are you kidding, Bristol? He still does.

And it's harder than I want to admit, seeing him have that effect on Qwest.

We both clap, adding our applause to everyone else's when the set closes.

My shoulders drop with relief. Not only because I'm no longer held captive to the burlesque show Qwest made of the performance but also because I didn't realize how much preparing for this show has stressed me out. It was televised, and every show, every shoot, every interview counts leading up to the release of Grip. In my gut, I know this album is special. I wake thinking about it, and it's the last thing on my mind when I fall into an exhausted heap each night. Unfortunately, that means Grip owns the first and last of my day. I keep a pad by my bed so when promotion ideas or things to do hit me, I can capture them right away. I don't know if I've ever felt this much anticipation and excitement for a project, for an artist. Whether it's because it's that great or whether it's because it's Grip, I don't let myself consider.

I'm at the bar ordering my well-earned, much-deserved vodka martini, when a hand presses against the small of my back, caressing the bare skin. I stiffen and look over my shoulder.

"Parker." I turn back to the bar and smile at the bartender as I accept my drink. "Well, that didn't take long. I texted you, like what? Twenty minutes ago?"

"More like fifteen." The hotel mogul I've known all my life grins and slides a steamy gaze down my body. "You have any idea how long I've been waiting for you to call?"

"Since Vegas?" I turn and prop my elbows on the bar. The action pushes my breasts forward in my cropped top, and his eyes predictably drop.

"A lot longer than that." He captures a lock of hair that's escaped from the knot at my neck, tucking it behind my ear. "And you know it."

"I just wanted to thank you for upgrading the suite." I force myself not to pull away from his hand and take a sip of my drink, closing my eyes in pure bliss. "God, I've needed this drink since I woke up this morning."

"We make the best vodka martini at the Park." He pauses, running a finger down my neck. "The Park-Vegas, I mean. Let's go."

"Now?" I take another glorious sip and cock an eyebrow at him. "Tonight?"

"Got a 'copter waiting on my helipad."

"I love that after all these years you still think your money impresses me." This time, my sip becomes a gulp that bottoms the glass out. "It's charming, really."

The bartender passes me another without my having to ask. "You, my man," I tell him, accepting my second drink gratefully.

"Are on your way to quite a tip."

When I turn back to Parker, the humor gathering in his eyes dissipates as he starts at my toes and takes me in, not stopping until he meets my eyes in the blue-green light of the club.

"I really miss fucking you, Bristol."

The glass stops halfway to my mouth, my breath catching. Not because his words turn me on. It's one thing to invite him here in hopes that Grip will see him and give Qwest a chance. It's a whole other thing to get entangled with Parker again. Our mothers have been planning our wedding since they discovered they were pregnant within days of one another. For some reason, Parker has always been onboard.

Onboard ... obsessed. Semantics.

"Parker, we've talked about this." I set my drink down on the bar. "We tried and failed at a relationship. I think we've satisfied our parents' misplaced intentions."

"This isn't about what our parents want." Parker palms my hip and pulls me closer, dropping his head until his lips brush my ear. "It never has been for me. I've always wanted you, and having you for a few months wasn't nearly enough. Give me another shot."

Parker and I dated for a while from senior year in high school until I went to college. When I chose Columbia and he went to Stanford, I took advantage of the long distance to break things off. We had zero chemistry, but I think something in me recognized the promise of what he's become—spoiled, entitled, and a bit of a bully. I could so easily have become those things. Hell, I may have even been those things at various points in my life, but I didn't want to be that. I certainly didn't want to be with that.

"Sorry to interrupt."

I look just past Parker's shoulder to see Grip standing there. To anyone else, he might look at ease, but I know him better than most. I know his face intimately, have every line of it memorized. I know how frustration thins his full lips. How his eyes narrow at the corners when he's annoyed. How anger ticks the strong line of his jaw.

"No problem." I gesture to Parker. "Parker, this is—"

"Gripe, right?" Parker extends his hand, which Grip leaves hanging in the air, his eyes fixed on Parker's face.

"It's Grip," I correct, breathing a little easier when Grip finally shakes his hand. "Remember Grip is one of my artists, Parker. He performed at the show in Vegas."

"I need a minute, Bristol," Grip says, not acknowledging my introduction. He walks a few feet away without waiting for my response.

"Be right back," I tell Parker. Parker catches me by the elbow. "I'll have them ready the 'copter."

I pull free without answering and step over to where Grip waits. "What's up?" I ask him.

"Next time, before you pimp me out," he snaps, eyes darkening to hot chocolate. "Give me a heads-up, would you?"

"What are you talking about?"

"You didn't set me up on a date with Qwest?" His brows push up. "Did she misunderstand?"

"I didn't 'pimp you out.' I thought it would be a nice surprise." I shrug nonchalantly. "That you'd enjoy some time to relax. Sorry if I overstepped."

"She wants to fuck me." He dips his head so his eyes wrangle with mine under the moving lights. "You do realize that?"

"You're consenting adults," I say around the fist in my throat. "Whatever you decide to do is up to you."

"This guy, Bristol?" He twists his lips derisively and switches gears without a clutch. "The guy with the irretrievable stick up his ass. This is the guy you give the time of day?"

"Don't start."

I turn to walk away, but he clamps his hand around my wrist. Just that contact sends a smoke signal up my arm. Parker can whisper in my ear that he wants to fuck me, and I'm dry as a bone. One touch from Grip, and I'm gushing in my panties.

Figures. My vagina, the contrarian.

He doesn't get to say more because Qwest walks up to us, her smile wide with anticipation.

"Hey." Her eyes drop to where Grip still holds my wrist. "Everything okay?"

"Just touching base before Grip leaves." I tug my wrist free, looking up at the neutral expression shuttering Grip's face. "You've got a couple of days off before everything goes even crazier. Enjoy them."

Grip's eyes cool to iced mocha and freeze when they shift over my shoulder. I turn to see Parker standing there, a sober-faced gentleman in a suit standing just a few paces behind him. The man with Parker is one of those people who carries just enough menace not to blend into the wallpaper but with a face you'd be hard-pressed to remember.

"Bris, we need to go if we want to make that flight." Parker's hands, usually possessive when in my vicinity, settle on my hips as he positions himself at my back.

"Um, okay," I say, though I'm still not sure I'm going with him anywhere.

"Thanks again for the suite, Bristol," Qwest says. "It's incredible."

"You actually have Parker here to thank for that." I force myself to lean back into him, knowing I'll pay later for encouraging him. "He's the one who upgraded you."

"Anything for Bristol's friends," Parker says smoothly.

"You two together?" A smile lights Qwest's sharp eyes.

"On and off since high school," Parker says.

Mostly off, but no need to split hairs right now.

"No way." Qwest's mouth hangs open a little. "I had no idea."

Neither did I.

"I actually escorted Bristol to her debutante ball." Parker tucks his chin into the crook of my neck. "That's how it started."

In my eighteen-year-old mind, sex in that coat check was such an adventure. Little did I know that would be the high point. I spent the next four months trying my damnedest to shake Parker and have been shaking ever since. That tic in Grip's jaw tells me he remembers the story I told him about screwing my escort, but until now, he never knew the guy.

"You were a debutante?" Qwest laughs, looking at me through the lens of my family's wealth and pedigree. "Wow."

"In another life, and at my mother's insistence." I put a little distance between my ass and Parker's dick, because apparently, trips down memory lane arouse him.

"We better go." Grip grabs Qwest's hand and turns to leave abruptly without saying goodbye.

Qwest waves over her shoulder and stutter steps to keep up with Grip's swift, long-legged stride away from us.

I should feel good that this is working even better than I planned. Qwest is with Grip. Grip saw me with Parker. All is going according to plan, but it feels so wrong. I watch Grip and Qwest slip through a side exit, hand in hand, and wonder, too late, if maybe I've made a big mistake. Actually seeing him with another woman—someone he could really fall for—saws at my insides. He was right, up on that roof. It hurts me to see him with someone else, every time. I know I could have him, but not on my terms. Probably not forever. Probably not to myself. It's ironic. People think I'm heartless. That I don't care enough. That isn't it. This ache, this wound bleeding on the inside of me, it tells the truth of how I really feel.

And I'm sick and damn tired of feeling. I want to forget that Grip is probably falling for Qwest tonight. Probably sleeping with her tonight. I want to be numb. I want the best vodka martini money can buy, even if I do have to fly to Vegas with Parker to get it.

"Hey." I turn to Parker, determined to feel less by the end of this night. "What about that drink you promised me?"

Nine

Grip

"Y OU DON'T LIKE STAND-UP COMEDY?"

Qwest's question pulls me out of my own head, where thoughts of Bristol with that punk ass Parker have tortured me ever since we left the club. So Parker's the coat check guy. And the man her mother has wanted her to marry since the cradle.

"What?" I frown and force myself to focus. "No, I love Chappelle. I can't believe we caught a show."

Dave Chappelle has been doing surprise shows in the city, and we were lucky to catch one tonight.

"Do you not like steak?" Qwest points her fork at the medium rare meat on my plate, nearly untouched.

"Love it." I take a bite. "This is delicious."

I survey the private dining room of the restaurant still open solely to accommodate us at this late hour. We're the only customers here. Qwest's security guard stands just outside the door.

"So do you not like me?" Qwest injects humor, but her eyes beg the question.

I feel like shit. She went to a lot of trouble to make tonight fun, exactly what I would have chosen. I've been half here the whole time. The other half of me can't stop wondering where Parker took Bristol on the "flight" he mentioned. I need to make more of an effort.

"You know I like you, Qwest." I toss my linen napkin on the table. "I'm sorry I've been so . . ."

I search my tired mind for the right word. "Preoccupied?" Qwest finds it for me.

"Yeah. It's rude, and you're great. It isn't you." I lob a smile across the table before lifting my water for a sip.

"Would you like to fuck me, Grip?"

I almost spew my water. I grab the napkin to dab at the corners of my mouth.

"It's a yes or no question," she continues unfazed.

"Um, maybe it isn't." I would laugh if this wasn't so awkward. "I'm attracted to you, yeah. Of course."

"I know that." She walks over, slides between the table and me, and straddles my hips. "But what do you want to do about it?"

Her wrists link at the back of my neck. I run my hands up and down her back. She's slim and tight and supple beneath her silk dress. She'd let me take her right on this table where her guard could hear her scream when she comes.

"Is there someone else?" Voice dropped, she runs a hand over my closely cropped hair.

"Yeah." I release a breath, my voice low and husky, too. I shake my head. "No."

"That's also a yes or no question." She slips her hand into the collar of my shirt and runs a long nail over my shoulder.

"I don't know." I try to focus on the conversation even as her touches distract me. "I'm just realizing that she may not feel the same way."

"Then she's a fool." Qwest rocks her hips into me, the heat between her legs like a furnace on my dick.

I gently push her back to put some distance between us.

"Qwest, I like you." I look her right in the eyes. I learned my lesson with Tessa. I'm not that dude who leads girls on anymore. "I respect you and think you're amazing. The last thing I want to do is hurt you. I'm afraid that's what would happen. We got business together. We're friends. Maybe we shouldn't mess with that."

"Let me worry about it." She scoots forward again. "I'm going into this with my eyes wide open."

She leans into me and sucks my earlobe into her mouth. Fuck. It's been too long since I had some. My dick rises to the occasion, and she pulls back with a satisfied chuckle.

"So what do you say?" She opens her lips over my jaw, mumbling against my neck. "We doing this or what?"

"Um . . ." My underserved libido and my anger over Bristol riding off into the sunset with that punk ass urge me to say yes.

Gripe? Motherfucker, you know my name.

"You have a few days off." Qwest slides her hands over my back under my shirt, lightly raking the skin with her fingernails. "Fly back with me to New York tomorrow night and I'll screw myself into your system."

A million, no more, guys would kill to have Qwest and her ass in their lap right now. I know this. It isn't her. I'm just so tired of being with anyone who isn't Bristol. In all these years, I haven't figured out how to move past what started between us. I know it was only a week. And we were young. And I mishandled the situation with Tessa. I get all that, but it wasn't just a few kisses on spring break. It's the friendship we've built since then. It's her passion about my writing, about my work. Her commitment to her brother. Her knife-sharp sense of humor. The soft, sweet side only a handful of people get to see. It's the way she tastes. The texture of her skin. Her hair. Her laugh. The conversations I can have with her and no one else. Everyone who thinks we're not right for each other doesn't know her, doesn't know me, or doesn't know how good we are together.

I want Bristol. Not anyone else.

And that's a problem, because for the first time, I have to consider the possibility that she doesn't, not even deep down where I thought she did, want me.

Ten

Bristol

THERE'S A MAN IN MY BED.

I barely know my name. I'm not sure who's leading the free world or what year it is, but I do know there is a man in my bed. I at least know that is unusual. I don't do sleepovers.

At least sober Bristol doesn't do sleepovers. Apparently, after one . . . or two . . . or eight vodka martinis, drunk Bristol does sleepovers.

The guy is naked. I do know that. Man parts poke between my butt cheeks.

My naked butt cheeks.

Dammit, I'm naked. He's naked. In my bed. At my house. The likelihood that we didn't have sex diminishes with every detail I absorb through my pickled senses. My thong and bra, a man's pants, suit jacket and shirt leave a sinful trail across the hardwood floor of my bedroom. To the left, a man's expensive watch rests on my mirrored nightstand. Under the duvet cover, which I'll probably burn later, a muscled forearm reaches across my hip, and a hand flattens against my stomach. He pushes my hair aside and trails kisses down my neck.

"Morning, Bris."

I clench my eyes closed and silently curse, dread lining my stomach. Or maybe that's nausea. There's a bass drum banging in my head, and I could vomit on my Egyptian cotton sheets any minute now. I struggle to bring the room into focus as the details swim in front of me. This is the worst scenario. I could have had meaningless sex with a stranger, but nooooo. Instead, I had meaningless sex with the man who has been obsessed with the idea of marrying me since we were ten years old. Meaningless sex that will mean something to him.

Oh, this will end marvelously.

"Parker?" I ask tentatively.

"I hope so." His husky laugh blows the hair at my neck. "Last night was amazing, Bristol. Even better than before."

"Before" set a low bar from what I recall. The orgasm I had in that coat check was the only time Parker got me off. And I think the threat of getting caught probably helped a lot then. After that, I touched myself more than he did every time we had sex. A girl's gotta DIY when he isn't getting it done. The story of my sex life.

I bet Grip would get it done.

Since when did my vagina start talking back to me? Maybe I'm still drunk. I hope so. God, please let this be a drunken hallucination. Parker's fingers wandering between my legs confirms it's happening.

"Um, Parker." I turn over, pulling the sheets over my naked breasts. "Last night is kind of hazy. I'm not sure how we . . . did we . . . you know."

"Fuck?"

Blond hair falls into his blue eyes brimming with laughter. He looks good in the morning. I remember that now, but it doesn't make up for how overbearing he is the other twenty-three hours of the day.

"Uh, yeah." My cheeks fire up. I'm blushing? Apparently, even I have some shame. Remembering who was inside you last night must be one of my standards."

Yes, we fucked." He leans over to kiss my neck. "We took the jet back from Vegas."

"I thought we took a helicopter?"

How drunk was I?

"We took a helicopter there and the Park Hotel jet back." He kisses my shoulder. "We kissed in the car."

Jesus, Mary, and Joseph. This is worse than I thought.

"And then we came here and made love." His hand explores under the sheet, gripping my thigh and pulling my knee over his hip. "You still give the best head, Bris."

Oh. Dear. God.

Do I still have disposable toothbrushes? No way I'm using my electric. I assumed my tongue felt furry and sticky from too much alcohol. Apparently

Parker's dick was down my throat last night. I don't typically swallow, but I also don't typically sleep with Parker. I want to purge the contents of my stomach just in case. I want to purge the contents of last night. To make it go away, flush it down the toilet like it never happened. All signs indicate it did happen, though. And from Parker's growing erection, he thinks it will happen again. Not when I have all my faculties.

I roll out of the bed, and it feels like my head keeps rolling. Dizziness assaults me, and I stumble back to the mattress. I look over my shoulder to find Parker watching me intently.

"You okay, Bris?"

Do I look fucking okay?

I nod as much as my pounding head will allow, grabbing the sheet and wrapping it toga style to cover my nakedness.

"Parker, I hate to rush you off," I lie. "But I have an appointment this morning."

He looks at me like I've disenfranchised him somehow. Like it's his inalienable right to screw me before breakfast.

"Re-schedule or—"

"No, sorry. This is can't-miss."

I shuffle to the bathroom, making sure the sheet covers the vital parts even though he's seen and sampled them all. When I look back, he's propped against my tufted headboard like he has all the time in the world, sheet down to his waist, hands folded behind his head.

"You should probably get going." I lean into the arched doorway of the bathroom. "I'm going to shower and then I'll be leaving, so …"

"You kicking me out?" His smirk works my last remaining nerve.

"Yes, Parker. I'm kicking you out. Men don't normally sleep at my house, and if I hadn't been plastered out of my mind, you wouldn't be here this morning."

The smirk dies, collapsing into a flat line.

"You're not implying that I took advantage of you somehow, are you?"

"Imply?" I shake my head. "I'm saying I'm disappointed you had sex with me knowing I was drunk and maybe not fully … aware."

I've known Parker literally my whole life. As slimy as he can be, I don't want to think he would drug me, but was I that drunk? To remember nothing? Everything after we arrived in Vegas is a blank sheet of paper, and as hard as I try, I can't sketch any details. I wanted a good martini. That's all. I know I had no intention of sleeping with Parker. Even drunk I can't imagine allowing this, wanting this. I've come as close as I can to an accusation without actually making it, but based on Parker's heavy scowl, it's close enough.

"Bristol, you were completely willing, and we did use protection, if that's your next question."

It was, but I still see a visit to my doctor in the very near future.

"I don't doubt that." Even sighing makes my head spin a little. "But we haven't had sex in over a decade, and you think the night I'm drunk is the night to get reacquainted?"

He climbs out of my bed, less modest than I was, not bothering to cover up. He's in good shape, but his dick is as underwhelming as I remember. I avert my eyes, embarrassed for him. Embarrassed for myself. No wonder it doesn't feel like I had sex last night.

"I know you're having a rough morning," Parker says as he steps into his pants. "So I'll excuse that. When can I see you again?"

"I think we should slow this down." I run fingers through the tangled hair hanging past my shoulders. "I didn't, um . . . anticipate any of this. I'm not in the market for a relationship right now."

"This is happening, Bristol." He buttons up his shirt, his eyes never leaving my face. "It's always been obvious that we're perfect for each other. Last night only solidified it."

"Forgive me for not agreeing since I don't remember much about last night." I turn into the bathroom. "We'll talk more later. Could you lock up on your way out?"

I don't wait for his response before closing the bathroom door and slumping against it, barely able to meet my own eyes in the mirror. Shame, frustration, disappointment swirl in my belly, joining the nausea. I feel violated, and as much as I want to put all the blame on Parker, there's really no one to blame but myself. I blink at the disheveled, puffy-eyed girl in the mirror who has tears filling her eyes.

"Bristol," I say to her. "What the fuck?"

After a few more moments of self-castigation, I start my shower. I wonder what time it is, but I left my phone in the bedroom. At least I presume that's where I left it. Hopefully, it isn't lost somewhere between here and Vegas. I have this appointment downtown, then errands, and then the Prodigy lunch at Rhyson's.

God, facing Grip after sleeping with Parker. Not that I haven't slept with other guys before, but the other night on the roof, our conversation in the hall yesterday, the confrontation in the club last night—we haven't talked this openly about what's between us in years, and now everything feels right at the surface.

An hour later, YSL Roadie bag on my shoulder and feeling only slightly more like myself, I walk into Chelle's, the high-end jewelry store I stumbled across downtown. Black skinny jeans ripped at the knee, black cashmere T-shirt, a knee-length camel-colored cardigan duster and nude ankle strap sandals. Hopefully no one will notice that I'm woefully in need of a pedicure. My head remains under attack, so I couldn't endure the blow dryer. My still-damp hair is scooped up into a topknot that I hope looks somewhat intentional. I wait until the last possible second to remove my sunglasses. My intolerance for sunlight is near-vampiric.

"Bristol, morning, love." Chelle, the owner of the exclusive, but lesser-known, shop air kisses my cheek.

"Morning." I clear my throat of the alcohol-induced Barry White effect. "How are you?"

"Not as good as you, I would imagine." Chelle pairs a knowing grin with her Stella McCartney jumpsuit. "You sneaky thing."

"Huh?" I slide the sunglasses farther up into my hair. "We have an appointment, right? My necklace came in?"

"Boy did it, you lucky girl." Chelle gives my arm a light slap and starts toward the back. "Come on. I've got it ready for you."

Either the lingering effects of my inebriation have dulled my senses, or Chelle has been imbibing, too, because she's acting strangely. I sit down at the small display table and wait. I special ordered this necklace a while ago and was giddy to get the message that it had come in. It's twenty-four carat gold with a diamond-encrusted vertical bar, which hangs just above my cleavage. The inscription on the bar is my favorite part.

"It's beautiful, Chelle." I bend over the table to examine it more closely and reach for the wallet in my bag. "Looks good. Let's settle up. I'm late for lunch at my brother's."

"Already paid in full." Chelle's smirk and teasing eyes mystify me.

"What do you mean it's—"

"She means it's my gift to you. I've already taken care of it." Parker stands in the door leading to the back room where Chelle keeps inventory. "I couldn't resist."

White-hot rage lights me up like a signal flare. I squeeze my eyes shut in a futile attempt to douse my temper.

"You didn't tell me you were dating Charles Parker," Chelle whispers in my ear. "You lucky thing."

I can't muster a smile, and my voice comes out so softly I barely hear it myself.

"Chelle, would you excuse us for a moment?"

"I get it," Chelle says. "You want to reward him in private. Just spill all the deets later."

"Oh, I'm going to reward him, all right." My eyes pin Parker where he stands, still wearing last night's clothes.

"Now don't be mad," he says. "You left your phone in the bedroom, and I saw the alert to pick up the necklace. I just thought it would be something I could do for you."

He lifts the necklace from its velvet box and goes behind me to clip it on. I step away and whirl around to face him.

"Don't you dare." Anger shakes my voice. "Who do you think you are? And what the hell do you think you're doing paying for jewelry I ordered for myself?"

His face registers what I'm saying slowly, the smile fading into confusion. "We had a great time last night, and I wanted to—"

"Thank me?" Brows lifted high, hands on hips, I cut in. "Is that what this is?"

"Well, not exactly. I just—"

"The other women you sleep with may require these little fuck tokens the next day as expression of your appreciation. I, however, do not."

"You're being unreasonable."

"I'm being independent. I'm being the woman who earned the money to buy this outrageously expensive necklace, chose it for myself, and has been looking forward to swiping my own damn card to pay for it."

"Bristol, I—"

"No, you will listen." My words butcher whatever he was about to say. "The bed you woke up in this morning? I paid for that. The house you locked up on your way out? I paid for that. The car I drove here in? All me."

I step as close as I dare and glare up at him.

"I will not be kept." My words whiz through the air like arrows. "That may be the road your mother chose, but it isn't the one mine did. Mine taught me not to rely on any man for anything, and I'm damn well not starting with you."

He blinks at me for a full ten seconds before he sighs, his tight expression relaxing into a smile.

"All that fight and pride." He grabs my upper arms and looks down at me intently. "You'll be my queen. With you at my side, we'll rule the world. Can't you see that?"

After last night's fiasco of lost memories, I can barely rule myself. He thinks I want to rule the world with him? Some replica of his committee-chairing, debutante-sponsoring, Vicodin-popping mother? She's my mother's best friend, and actually very sweet, but hell will freeze over before I become her.

"I need to pay for my necklace and go." I pull out of his hands and turn back to the showroom.

"I've already paid for it." His voice hardens. When I look back, so have his eyes. They're blue crystals in his handsome face.

"Then we'll get you a nice little refund."

I call Chelle back in and instruct her to refund Mr. Parker's card and to charge mine.

"I'll need the card you paid with." Chelle gives Parker a confused look but accepts his card. She probably thinks I'm crazy. On the surface, Parker is one of the most eligible bachelors in the country, hell, maybe in the world. Why wouldn't I want him and his gifts?

He and I stand in awkward silence while Chelle processes the transactions.

"I didn't mean any harm." He steps closer until his stale morning breath wafts over my lips. "I want to see you again. Soon."

"I don't know, Parker."

I step back and away. This is already out of control. I wanted to just wave Parker around a little so Grip would take that step toward Qwest. Somehow, I ended up sleeping with the guy I've avoided for the last decade. I grew up surrounded by people like the man Parker has grown into. Not just overbearing, but willful. Spoiled. Entitled. Combined with unlimited resources and unchecked power, that's dangerous.

"I fly to India tonight for business." He presses his hand to my back as we exit Chelle's. "Can we talk when I get back? About where we go from here?"

I'm so tired. I'm running late, and I don't feel like fighting with Parker in the street in front of half of Los Angeles.

"Okay, we'll talk when you get back," I concede. "But I'm not making any promises."

He steps closer until I'm pressed into the driver side door of the Audi convertible I treated myself to last year. Before I can object, he leans down to press a hard kiss against my lips. The contact is quick, but I still resent it.

"Fine," he says when he pulls back. "I'll make all the promises."

That doesn't reassure me. With men like Parker, there's a fine line between a promise and a threat. I hope I haven't set myself up for either.

Eleven

Grip

HAVEN'T SEEN THE PRODIGY TEAM THIS RELAXED IN WEEKS. WE'RE ALL chilling here at Rhyson's place. It's the quiet before a very big storm. Grip not only is my solo debut but also it's Prodigy's first release. It's a big deal for us all. We needed this small block of time to blow off steam. It's been so intense, and it will only intensify the closer we get to release day.

Max and Sarah are talking near the pool table. Neither of them knows how to actually play, so they just hold the cues and lean on the table, trying to look cool. Rhyson's playing Grand Theft Auto with Simon, one of the sound engineers. Several of the team members went swimming out back. The whole gang is here. Almost.

I check my watch again. I've been at Rhyson's for thirty minutes and still no sign of Bristol.

"She called to say she'd be late," Kai whispers, taking the spot beside me on the brown leather couch.

"Am I that obvious?"

Until I told Rhyson, no one else really knew about the week we shared. It was ours and no one's business, but after seeing her with Parker last night, I feel like the butt of an eight-year joke. Like everyone knows how I feel, and I was a fool for holding out hope. For still holding out hope. I'm not prepared to give up yet. I wonder sometimes what will convince me to give up on the possibility of us.

"It isn't that you're obvious," Kai says. "I just know how you feel."

"Our plan isn't working." I offer her half a smile.

Kai actually suggested I let Bristol manage me to get closer to her. That if we were around each other all the time, she'd have to acknowledge her feelings, my feelings, whatever. Bristol had been trying to manage me for years, but I didn't want to just be her job. Apparently, she's now not only my manager, but also my pimp. It still burns me up that she handed me over to Qwest like some prize at the fair.

"You mean Project Proximity?" Kai grins and reaches for one of the brownies Sarita, their housekeeper, made.

"Yeah." I shrug with phony carelessness. "Maybe Rhyson's right. Maybe she wants a guy like Parker, and I should just give up."

"Rhyson isn't right. Not this time," Kai mumbles around her brownie. "He's biased. He's so close to you both, he doesn't want things to go south and become awkward. Not just personally. He's thinking about the business, too, I'm sure."

Kai laughs, the husky sound drawing Rhyson's attention. He grins over at us . . . mostly at Kai, before returning his attention to the game.

"And he's afraid Bristol would destroy you." Kai's eyes meet mine in a careful stare. Maybe she's afraid of that, too.

"I know." I grin because I ain't scared. Not even a little bit. "Most brothers would be protective of their sisters, but I get it. Bristol's a handful."

I slant her a sneaky grin and hold my hands up for her inspection.

"But I got big hands."

"Oh, God." Kai shakes her head and chuckles. "Rhyson is protective of Bristol in his own way, but he thinks she's too much like their mother."

"She's not."

Kai pauses chewing to hold my eyes with hers.

"Bristol is like her mother, Grip. I think she's aware of that, and you should be, too. It isn't all bad." She shrugs. "I'm like my father in a lot of ways, and we know his history."

Kai's father, a pastor, left her and her mother in Glory Falls, the small Georgia town where she grew up. Ran off with the church secretary and never looked back.

"Just because she's like her mother, doesn't mean she *is* her mother," Kai continues. "Rhyson got away from that house, from his parents. Bristol wasn't so lucky."

"Are you saying Rhys doesn't trust her?" I frown, because I know he does now. They've gotten past that.

"Of course not. I think Rhyson is self-aware and recognizes how much he's like his parents, and how easily that can go badly if he isn't careful." Kai offers a tentative smile. "Maybe he's just afraid Bristol won't be careful with you."

"I'm willing to take that risk."

"Apparently, she's not." Kai leans over and squeezes my hand. "Yet."

"Why couldn't it be easy for us the way it was for you and Rhyson?" I wait for the incredulous look Kai gives me. Their journey was anything but easy.

"It's funny you mention us, though." Kai rests her hand on her belly. "Bristol reminds me a lot of myself."

"Really?" If there were ever opposites, it would be Kai and Bristol. "You'll have to elaborate."

"I believe Bristol has feelings for you," Kai says. "I've told you that before, but something holds her back. That's how I was. I knew I had feelings for Rhyson, but I let all my hang-ups keep me from doing anything about it. I didn't trust him or myself."

"You think Bristol doesn't trust herself?" I smack my lips derisively.

"Not just herself." Kai's eyes fill with sympathy. "I don't think she trusts you either, but I believe she will."

That's the very hope I've been clinging to for years, but now I'm not as sure. I can't believe I thought Kai was just another thirsty chick when Rhyson first started bringing her around. She's the opposite of that, and of all the amazing things my best friend has had in his life, she's the best. She's the only one who sees what Bristol and I could be together.

"It's about time you showed up," Max says from the pool table across the room.

Kai and I follow the direction of Max's smile. Bristol makes her way slowly down the steps to the rec room, still wearing sunglasses. The grim set of her mouth and faint lines bracketing her lips speak of a rough night. I wonder how rough it got with Charles Parker.

"Sorry I'm late." Her voice a tired rasp, she pushes the sunglasses up into the hair screwed into a knot on her head.

"I hate you, Bris," Sarah says, looking over Bristol's narrow, ripped-knee jeans and long cardigan. "You look great even hungover. You are hungover, aren't you?"

"Very much so." Bristol tips her head back and closes her eyes. "Gah. Sid Vicious is playing in my brain."

"Isn't he dead?" Max squints his eyes and frowns.

"Max, I can't with you today." When Bristol opens her eyes, she looks right at me for a few seconds before looking away to Rhyson. "Hey, brother."

"Bris, what's up?" Rhyson glances away from the screen briefly. "I didn't even know you could be hungover. You hold liquor like a bottle. I've never seen anything short of a tranquilizer lay you low."

"Apparently," Bristol says, settling onto the couch across from Kai and me, "they tranquilize vodka martinis now."

"Where'd you have these vodka martinis?" I ask, addressing my first words to her since our confrontation at the bar last night.

She becomes preoccupied with the handle on her bag for a few seconds before lifting her eyes to mine. They're slightly pink and puffy, more pewter than bright silver today.

"Um, Vegas actually."

"Vegas? Last night?" Sarah plops onto the couch beside Bristol, jarring them both.

"For the love of God, it's a couch, not a trampoline." Bristol winces and raises a shaky hand to her forehead. "Yeah. Just with a friend."

"Woman of mystery." Max squeezes between Sarah and Bristol. "Give us all the details."

"No." She scoots over, her flat voice and flat eyes opaquing her thoughts from them, from me.

"Did you take anything, Bris?" Kai asks sweetly.

"You know," Bristol says, mouth tipped to the left, "I didn't. I was rushing and didn't even think to."

"Come on. We'll get you something." Kai presses her hand into the couch for leverage, and Bristol stands to help pull her the rest of the way.

"Whoa. Careful there, little mama." Bristol smiles for the first time since she arrived. She's already got a soft spot for her niece. "Let me help you."

Rhyson's eyes leave the screen and fix on his petite wife with her hand pressed to the small of her back. He and Bristol exchange a quick grin. He's still watching Kai as she and Bristol climb the steps and leave the room.

"Dude!" Simon laughs triumphantly, pointing to his winning score on-screen. "That's what happens when you take your eyes off the prize."

"Oh, my eyes were on the prize." Rhyson tosses the controller to the floor. "I'm out. Food? Sarita left raw meat. I think I can manage to get it to and from the grill without the fire department intervening."

"Maybe I should handle the grill." I follow him out onto the patio adjacent to the rec room. "Remember the last time you tried to grill?"

"Nothing was lost or destroyed," Rhyson says.

"Unless you count Grady's eyebrows."

"God, he looked ridiculous for months." Rhyson's laugh booms over the memory of the uncle he lived with here in LA when he emancipated. "Too much lighter fluid. That was the problem."

"No, you not knowing what the hell you were doing was the problem."

Max and Sarah join us, stretching out on two lounge chairs and scrolling on their phones.

"Daaaaaaaaamn." Max sits up on the lounge chair and flips his legs around to face Sarah. "Did you see Spotted?"

"No, what . . ." She checks her phone, eyes stretching. "Oh my God. Is this true?"

"Photographic evidence." Max's delighted laugh lights up his face. "Well, at least now we know who Bristol was with and what she was doing."

My head snaps around when he mentions Bristol's name. So does Rhyson's. He beats me to the punch.

"What are you talking about?" He walks over to Max's lounge chair. "What about Bristol?"

Max and Sarah pick up on the fact that neither Rhyson nor I find the prospect of Bristol on Spotted, one of the most viral gossip sites, as amusing as they do.

"Gimme your phone, Sarah." I stretch my open palm to her, waiting until she reluctantly hands it over.

Well, shit.

Spotted has a pictorial chronicling Bristol's date last night. Bristol and Charles Parker climbing into a helicopter. The two of them drinking in an intimate nook, the Vegas strip lit up behind them. Parker deplaning at a private hangar and getting into his Viper. Him pulling out of her driveway this morning. And then him kissing her in front of a jewelry store not even an hour ago.

Really? A Viper? You can't tell me this guy doesn't have a small dick. He's overcompensating for something. Has to be. But my girl . . . or I thought she would be my girl one day . . . is sitting on his fucking lap in Vegas drinking vodka martinis. And it looks like he spent the night. Every detail is a poisonous dart piercing my skin, toxic to my system. Jealousy, rage, resentment crawl through my blood.

"Charles Parker?" Max looks impressed. "One of the biggest fish you can catch. Go big or go home, Bristol."

"What are you talking about?" Bristol asks, standing with Kai at the patio door. "Go big? Go home? What?"

"You dark horse." Max crosses over to her, his grin and eyes eager. "Your secret's out."

Her eyes fly to mine, and we have a wordless conversation. My eyes ask questions that hers tell me I don't want to know the answers to.

"What secret?" She frowns her confusion at Max.

"You're all over Spotted," Max drawls. "You and Charles Parker. How dare you keep all that juiciness from us."

"What?" Panic widens Bristol's eyes. "What the hell?"

"It's all here for the world to see." He hands her his phone. "Someone took the time to document your night out."

Bristol's expression darkens while she reads the Spotted post. By the time she hands Max his phone, she's smoothed her face into a blank, shiny surface.

"Wow." She takes the spot Max occupied on the lounge chair. "Must be a really slow news cycle if that's all they have to talk about. No news there."

"Are you kidding?" Sarah leans forward, her face alight with salacious speculation. "You're dating one of the most eligible bachelors, like in the world, Bris. How could you keep that from us?"

"Bristol's business is just that." Rhyson flips steaks over the open flame. "She works hard and deserves some privacy when she finally takes some time to play. So leave her alone."

His words come casually, but we all know he means it. He knows his sister as well as I do. She may be playing it cool, but this is not the kind of spotlight Bristol enjoys. She's uncomfortable, and he doesn't like it. They exchange a look, and I suspect there will be a follow-up conversation.

Meanwhile, I may as well be that steak Rhyson's flipping on the grill. *Raw. Tossed. Seared. Hot.*

I'm hot as hell. Riled like a horse with a bur under the saddle. If I don't get out of here, I'll explode all over this sunny day. And then there will be no secrets left. There won't be a person on our team who doesn't know how bad I have it for Bristol. Or how little she cares. And how sick to my soul I am of all this shit.

"I'm gonna head out," I tell Rhyson at the grill.

"Marlon, no." He stops flipping meat and gives me a searching look. He knows what this is about. "Dude, stay. Food's almost done. We can—"

"I actually have a flight to catch." I lean over and do the man pound-thump to his chest.

"Flight where?" His eyes move over my shoulder, I presume to his sister, before settling back on me.

"I got a few days off. I'm going to New York."

"But—"

I turn away from him and address everyone else.

"Yo. I'm gonna bounce, guys." I fist pound Max and Simon. Give Sarah a quick hug. "Got a plane to catch. I'll be back next week."

I head over to Kai, ignoring Bristol as she gets up from the lounge chair even though I feel her eyes on me. I feel her eyes on me all the time, but maybe I imagined it was more than it really is. After seeing those pictures of her with Parker, knowing he wants to marry her, knowing that she'll probably do it and be miserable for the rest of her life just like her mother, I'm sick of trying to crack her code. I'm done deciphering how what she actually wants differs from what she says she wants. She says she wants Parker? I'll take her at her word.

"Take care of my niece while I'm gone." I leave a quick kiss on Kai's cheek.

"Don't go." She grabs my wrist to stop me from pulling away, her dark eyes worried. "Grip, I'm sure that—"

"I'm not sure." I cut off whatever assurances she would offer.

"Not anymore."

Brushing past Bristol standing there as still as a statue, I head back into the house, through the rec room, and up the stairs. I'm in the foyer at the front door when the clack of heeled footsteps catches up to me.

"Grip." Bristol's voice at my back stops me with my hand on the door. "When were you going to tell me you were leaving town?"

I turn to face her but don't take my hand off the door handle. If I keep it in my hand, maybe I won't lose sight of the reasons I need to go.

"Bristol, I'm leaving town." I turn back to the door. "Bye."

"Grip, wait. Talk to me."

Her touch on my arm stops me. Scalds me. I hate wanting her like this. Constantly. Futilely. I lean against the door, indicting her with a narrowed glance. She wants to talk? Let's talk.

"You fucked him, didn't you?"

Her long lashes flutter in a rapid blink before lowering over her eyes. I've caught her off guard. She steps back, her hand falling away. A deep breath fills her chest and whooshes past her lips. She looks at me, biting her lip, but doesn't answer.

"Tell me." My words are chipped with stone. "Did you fuck Parker last night?"

She looks up at me, a spark of defiance lifting her chin like it's none of my business.

"Yes."

Such a softly spoken word, but it slices me down the middle like I'm a cadaver. A humorless stretch of my lips is all I can manage.

"You must have laughed at me."

"I didn't." She closes her eyes, shakes her head. "I never did." "On the roof the other night when I went on and on about how neither of us has been in a relationship in years, when you were already in one." A laugh hacks at my throat. "Can you believe I thought you were waiting for me? When all along you were waiting for him? Some medieval power couple alliance shit your parents drew up years ago."

"It isn't like that. You don't understand what—"

"Was it good?" I straighten, stepping close, invading her space. My voice, a dark rumble in my chest, boils over between us. "Did Parker figure out how to make you come? Did he fuck you again this morning at your house? In your bed? Did he find the vibrators in your nightstand? Did you show him how you like it, Bristol?"

"Stop." She tips her head back to watch me, bright eyes welling with hurt. "I hate the way you're talking to me, the way you're looking at me like you don't know me. Please stop."

I grab her hand and press it to my heart.

"Do you have any idea what we could be together? Hell, what we already are?" The hot words sear my lips. "It's rare and real and you just keep spitting on it. You just keep ignoring it. Ignoring me. And I'm so fucking over it."

She stands there in silence, eyes fixed on her hand over my heart, the muscles in her throat working as she swallows.

"You haven't asked me because obviously you don't care," I go on, my heartbeat kicking into her palm. "But I didn't sleep with Qwest last night."

When she looks at me, surprise flickers through her eyes before she veils them with her lashes again.

"You don't want to know why a guy like me would turn down top-shelf pussy?" I ask, deliberately crude.

"I don't want to know." She drops her hand from my chest and turns like she's leaving, but I grab her arm and turn her back to face me.

"I thought something happened on the roof the other night," I grit out. "I thought after all these years, it was happening. You were starting to realize we could do this. We could be an us. So, I turned Qwest down. I wanted to be able to look you in your face today and tell you that I didn't sleep with her. That I would never fuck anyone else ever again if you wanted to be with me."

The tears standing in her eyes must be for our friendship I'm going to ruin, for the hurtful words I keep making myself say. There was a time I'd fool myself that they were for something else, but that time is gone. I swallow a hot knot of hurt and pointless humiliation.

"But you don't want to be with me." I drop her arm and open the door. "So if you'll excuse me, I'm gonna get back to fucking who the hell ever I damn well please."

Twelve

Bristol

OUTWARDLY, MY MOTHER AND I COULDN'T BE MORE DIFFERENT. My cheekbones, wide mouth, dark hair—all my father. In contrast, my mother's hair is flame-bright, unrelieved red without a hint of gray, thanks to the bottle. She's like a cultivated pearl, breeding in every curve and class in every line. In the eyes, though, you find the resemblance. The silver-gray eyes I see in the mirror every morning, stare back at me from my mother's face this beautiful morning over brunch.

"I'll have eggs Benedict." Mother glances from the brunch menu for Afloat, the restaurant located on a yacht in Marina del Rey, to the server's conciliatory expression.

We've never eaten here before, and I was surprised when she suggested it. We typically eat at the home she and my father purchased when they relocated here from New York last year after his heart attack. From time to time, we'll eat in town, but never here. It's a nice change. I need the fresh air. My world has become claustrophobic since the Spotted piece outing my night with Parker. "And a Bloody Mary," Mother adds, closing the menu and handing it to the server.

Of course. Because it wouldn't be . . . a day . . . without my mother drinking. I've only seen her actually drunk once in my life. I learned more about my father, about my mother, and about myself that day than I wanted to know. I wish I could un-learn it, but I can't.

The server clears his throat, shifting his eyes from my mother to me.

"And you, ma'am?"

198 | KENNEDY RYAN

"I'll have poached eggs and smoked salmon," I tell him.

"And to drink?" The young man's eyes discretely tease me, bordering on flirtatious. "Bloody Mary for you, too?"

"No, this coffee is great, and I'll add orange juice, please."

I've avoided vodka, all alcohol really, since last week's Vegas debacle. If I thought getting drunk would make me forget the look on Grip's face when he realized I slept with Parker, I'd drink myself stupid. But nothing will make me forget that. I still feel his heart pounding into my hand. His words and the hurt in his eyes have haunted me since he left.

"There was another piece about you and Parker in the *New York Post* this morning." Mother's pleased eyes meet mine across the table as the server walks away with our orders. "You looked good."

"Those same shots from Vegas?" I sip my coffee. "I looked drunk."

"No, these were new ones." She laughs lightly. "Actually old photos, old memories. Someone dug up the pictures from your debutante ball."

A groan vibrates in my chest and throat.

"Great. That's all I need. More fodder for this ridiculous narrative they're spinning. We've gone from slutty night in Vegas to epic fairy tale. I wish they'd find some other couple to obsess over."

"Well, they did feature a piece on Rhyson's friend Marlon."

I go still for a moment at the mention of Grip's name. The speculation about Parker and me has only been matched by rumors of a budding romance between Grip and Qwest.

"They can report on that all day long as far as I'm concerned." I resume sipping, hoping my face is unreadable, though my blankest expressions have never hidden much from my mother. "That's good for business. That rumor sells records."

"Hmmm, yes. That's right. You're managing Marlon now, right?"

"Right."

It didn't take long for social media to latch on to the relationship it seems Grip and Qwest are pursuing full throttle. He's been in New York for the last two days, and pictures of them exploring the city have popped up everywhere. The latest of them leaving one of Grip's favorite strip clubs, Pirouette, surfaced last night.

Of course there's already a hashtag shipping the two high-powered performers. #GripzQueen has been trending since yesterday, connecting their hip-hop love affair with "Queen," the single still sitting at number one on the charts. With Grip's album dropping so soon, it couldn't be more perfect if I'd planned it. In a way, I did plan it. Will is ecstatic, as I should be. But the pictures I've seen of them holding hands in Central Park, kissing on the Brooklyn Bridge, and leaving Qwest's Manhattan apartment building for a morning run—they all turn my stomach. I'm not sure I'll be able to eat my eggs when they come.

I feel even sicker when I think of my last conversation with Grip. I may have done irreparable damage to our friendship. At least we still have his career. We still have work. I keep comforting myself with that, though it feels hollow. I knew it might come to this, but I had no idea it would hurt this much. His crude words keep playing over and over in my head. Even if Grip and his "queen" weren't trending, I'd still be unable to get him out of my mind.

"It's nice he's found someone of his own . . ." My mother trails off as she searches for some politically correct word. "Type. You know. Another . . . entertainer."

"Yes, they make a great couple," I agree neutrally.

"And much more appropriate than the crush he's had on you all these years." Mother says it matter-of-factly, as if we've discussed this many times in the past. We have not.

"What do you mean?" I pleat my brows in a facsimile of dismay. "What crush?"

"Oh, Bristol. It's me." Mother tilts her head, her eyes sharp and brittle. "I've seen him several times over the last few years with you and Rhyson. It was patently obvious he had feelings for you."

"He doesn't," I reply softly, fixing my eyes on the boats floating around us.

"And of course that you have feelings for him, too." Mother smiles her thanks at the server who sets her Bloody Mary on the table. "But you've always hidden those feelings well, thank goodness."

I sit quietly, biding my time until the server places a glass of juice in front of me with promises to bring our food in a few moments. I save my response until he has stepped away.

"I have it under control, Mother."

There's no need to deny it. That would be useless and foolish. Even as careful as I've been, at some point, I slipped, and she saw something that told her things I've never said. Pretending she has missed the mark would be futile.

"You'd better." Mother watches my face, her bright eyes as hard as diamonds. "Because Parker would not take kindly to you tossing him over for some . . ."

"Careful," I warn, clenching my jaw.

"Musician," she says, her tone defensive. "I was going to say musician."

"Rhyson is a musician. What's wrong with musicians? And it's none of Parker's business who I have feelings for. Despite all your plotting and best efforts, I'm not marrying Parker. I don't love him."

"Even better." A bitter smile twists the thin, painted red line of her lips. "If you don't love him, Parker's mistresses shouldn't bother you."

"Parker's mistresses won't bother me because I'm not marrying him."

"Then what are you doing?" Mother narrows her eyes at the corners and her lips pinch in the center. "Parker isn't the boy you grew up with, Bristol. Do not toy with him."

"I'm not toying with him. I was very clear that I didn't want a relationship. He refuses to listen, and this media maelstrom hasn't helped. He's in India on business." I roll my eyes and take another sip of orange juice. "Very conveniently, he's been so tied up he hasn't returned my calls. Someone from his team confirmed the rumors about us. They wouldn't have done that without his consent. He's the one toying with me, manipulating me through the media. Not the other way around."

"Of course he told them to confirm." Mother takes a draw of her Bloody Mary. "Hmmm. That's good. He probably tipped them off for the pictures in the first place. Men like him leave very little to chance, and he's probably tired of waiting for you to marry him."

The thought had occurred to me. For someone to be trailing us at every stage of the evening capturing those photos seems farfetched. The photos of him leaving my house the next morning and kissing me at Chelle's definitely required a "tip" or inside track. I wouldn't put it past him.

"Be very careful, Bristol. This thing with Marlon and his new girlfriend is the best thing that could happen," Mother says. "If Parker suspects you have feelings for Marlon, that you might choose Marlon over him, he'll find a way to crush him. Do you know that?"

"Yes, Mother. I know that. It won't be a problem." I meet her eyes with a sigh. "Like I said, I have it under control."

"Oh, yes. The same way you had your brother's career under control?" Mother's eyes flash silver fire at me across the table. "And yet, instead of him playing with the Pops, as he should be, he's starting some record label thing."

"That was a misunderstanding," I flash right back at her. "You chose to believe I was moving to LA to manipulate my brother for you, to get him back under your management, when actually, I moved here to help him pursue his dream. Not yours."

We both fall silent as the server places our plates on the table.

"And that record label thing is my job," I add when the server leaves. "One I'm very good at, by the way."

"Well, I guess you made do since you had no real talent to speak of." Mother takes a bite of her eggs Benedict. "Lemonade from lemons, they say."

The words I would fire back at her die on my lips. I can shake down crooked vendors and go toe to toe with the toughest people in one of the toughest industries, but my mother . . .

She always makes me feel inadequate. As if I failed her somehow being born less talented than my twin brother. Music connected the three of them, and I could never push my way into their circle. I was left out. Disconnected. That's what surprised me with Grip. How connected we felt, and the closeness that wasn't dependent on blood or even common interest. It came from how clearly we saw and accepted each other almost right away.

It's rare and real and you just keep spitting on it.

"Did I tell you we're managing Petra now?" Mother interrupts Grip's voice reverberating in my head. There's no trace of the hateful barb she just tossed at me left on her lips. Only a smile.

"No." I look out to the harbor again. "How nice for you."

"I still think it's a shame she and Rhyson never resolved their issues," Mother says, taking a delicate sip of her liquor.

"Issues?" I snort inelegantly. "She cheated on him, Mother, with one of his classmates."

"It was high school, for God's sake." Mother sighs her exasperation. "People make mistakes when they're young. Two piano prodigies. So young and in love. God, the classical world ate up their dueling piano tour. So much potential."

I'm pretty sure Rhyson dodged a bullet with that one and has no regrets.

"Well, all is not lost." I try to keep my smile from become smug. "Rhyson has Kai now, and their first baby is on the way. I think Rhyson is fine with how things worked out."

She didn't exactly approve of Kai for Rhyson, but he hasn't considered our mother's opinion in a very long time.

"Kai's due soon." I study my mother's unreadable expression. "Have you guys talked about that in your sessions?"

My parents and brother are in family counseling, still trying to mend what was broken when Rhyson left.

"We've missed the last few sessions," Mother admits, a hint of genuine sadness in her eyes. "Not that Rhyson would talk to me about my own grandchild."

"He'll come around."

Maybe? One day?

Rhyson has made a great deal of progress with our father but remains at odds with our mother.

"Why does your father get a pass and I don't?"

That's a complicated answer that Rhyson will have to give her because I can't.

"You'll have to ask him that." I shrug. "Maybe bring it up in your next session."

"By the way, Dr. Ramirez suggested we bring you in," Mother says casually.

I nearly drop my fork. They were supposed to bring me in "soon." That was over a year ago, and I still haven't been to one session. I've been waiting so long for this, to be heard. To have my say about how all the decisions they made affected me years ago. How I'm still affected by the civil war that splintered our family.

"When?" I keep my voice free of eagerness.

"Hopefully in the next week or so. Rhyson's been busy with that record label." Mother says it with such distaste I almost laugh. "And your father and I have taken on several new clients in addition to Petra."

"Just keep me posted. I'll adjust my schedule however I need—"

A hand on my shoulder cuts the sentence short. I look up to find my mother's best friend since college standing over me, her blue eyes and blonde hair a beautiful, older echo of her son's.

"Mrs. Parker." I cover her hand on my shoulder with mine, forcing a smile to my lips. "So good to see you."

"So formal?" The gentle rebuke in her eyes coaxes my lips into a genuine smile.

"Sorry, Aunt Betsy." I kiss the cheek she offers before she takes a seat at our table.

"Betsy, hello, darling." Mother sips her third Bloody Mary. "When did you arrive in LA?"

"I left you a message that I was flying in from New York last night." She smiles at our server. "Mimosa, dear. Thank you."

They don't fool me. Like mother like son. I have a feeling Aunt Betsy and my mother have done some orchestrating of their own to make sure even with Parker in India, speculation about us remains high. I cast a quick glance around the floating restaurant, my eyes peeled for cameras and paparazzi. Not giving a hint that I sniffed them out, I scoot aside to make more room for Aunt Betsy between my mother and me.

"Nothing to eat?" I ask.

"Trying to maintain my girlish figure." Aunt Betsy winks. "Do what we have to do to keep our men, don't we?"

If by "keep" she means watch helplessly as her husband screws half of the Upper East Side, then I guess she's doing everything she can. She and my mother didn't exactly hit the lottery in the fidelity department. At least my father is discreet. I would never have known about his indiscretions had I not come home early that day.

It doesn't take long for the conversation to circle around to what she and my mother have been planning since they compared ultrasounds almost thirty years ago: my "pending" nuptials to Parker.

"We need to have you up to the house in the Hamptons, Bris." Aunt Betsy caresses the diamond at her neck. "Maybe next weekend?"

"I'm really busy right now." I smile politely instead of telling her that I will never, ever, ever, ever, ever marry her son. She'll soon see. "One of the artists I manage is about to drop his first album."

"Oh, well isn't that nice?" She sips her Mimosa.

Between Mother's Bloody Mary, Aunt Betsy's mimosas, and the pictures stacking up of Grip and his "queen", I could use a drink. I'm caving and ordering a vodka tonic. Life's too short and too tough not to.

"Bristol, over here!" someone yells from the hostess stand at the restaurant entrance.

Here we go. A camera flash makes me blink a few times. When I look back , the photographer is gone. Great. I could write the caption myself: "Bristol Gray, manager to the stars, brunches with future mother-in-law."

I pretend not to see the smug looks of satisfaction the two conspirators exchange. On second thought, forget the drink. Vodka got me into this mess. More vodka won't get me out.

Thirteen

Grip

EVEN THOUGH I WAS ONLY HERE MY FRESHMAN YEAR BEFORE transferring to the School of the Arts, my old high school in Compton feels like home. As early as elementary school, Jade and I watched Greg and Chaz play football on Friday nights. Chaz was already dealing by then, already banging, but he was such a gifted athlete. Football was the last thing tethering him to school. Otherwise, he probably would have dropped out long before. Only blocks away from where Chaz died, the ink scripting his name into my arm seems to burn.

"Man, these kids are so crunk to see you today," Amir, my "security guard," says from his spot on the wall of the gymnasium beside me.

Since Amir worked airport security for years, he was a natural choice when Bristol insisted I have some kind of protection. I don't need security, but it means Amir and I get to hang all the time, and it puts him on my payroll instead of someone else's.

"Yeah. I'm pretty stoked to be here."

I slide my hands into the pockets of my jeans, studying the kids assembled. Shondra, the teacher who coordinated this assembly, told them we could do autographs after and to give me some space. I'm using this time to mentally rehearse the things I want to tell them. Things I wish someone had told Chaz. Or at least things I wish he'd listened to.

Shondra crosses the gym floor, twisting her hips like she has since the eighth grade. Only now she wears a skirt and silk blouse around those thick thighs and round hips instead of the booty shorts and oversize earrings she sported growing up. Her natural hair fans out in a curly afro around her pretty face. I watch Amir watching Shondra. He always crushed hard on her.

"When you gonna make your move?" I bump his shoulder with mine. "It's been years. Man up."

"I know you ain't talking." Amir reluctantly drags his gaze from Shondra's twisting hips to meet my eyes. "After you punked out and ran off to New York to get away from Bristol."

The teasing grin freezes on my face. The disadvantage of Amir working for me is the same as the advantage. He's around all the time. He sees a lot.

"I wasn't running away from anything." I shoot him a frown. "You telling me you wouldn't jump at the chance to spend two days and nights with Qwest? Any man would."

"Yeah, but 'any man' hasn't been stuck on Bristol forever." His face crinkles with a laugh at my expense. "You have."

"Was stuck. Past tense. I'm over it. She ain't the only girl in the world."

But she was the only girl I could think about. Even waking up with Qwest in New York, Bristol occupied my mind as soon as my eyes opened. I still feel her hand over my heart. I think it's branded there in acid.

"Please," Amir scoffs. "I was there when you met Bristol. The way you looked at her that day at the airport, I ain't ever seen you look at anybody else like that."

He pauses for emphasis, brows up in the air "Not even Qwest," he adds. "She's a great girl, but she isn't your girl."

"Neither is Bristol." My teeth clench around the words. "Haven't you heard? She's Charles Parker's girl."

"I ain't buying it."

I didn't before, but I do know. She's slept with guys in the past. I'm not an idiot. I know that, and I certainly have no room to talk. This is different. A relationship with this guy who's been chasing her for years, who her parents have always wanted her to marry. This is real, and the fact that she's with him makes me mad as hell.

"Hey, guys." Shondra finally reaches us and splits a smile between Amir and me.

I nudge him with my elbow the same way I did in eighth grade when he couldn't work up the nerve to ask her to the winter dance.

"What's up, Shon?" I bend to hug her and watch as Amir does the same.

"Thank you so much for coming, Grip." Her dark eyes shine her excitement. "It's so needed."

"Things are getting better, though, right?" I ask.

I've heard violence is down. Gang recruitment, too. I know there's still a long way to go, but progress has been made.

"Yeah, but not enough and not fast enough." Shondra's sad smile dims the shine in her eyes. "I lost a student last week, and another the week before. Both shot. Still too many funerals. And they have so much potential."

She punches my shoulder.

"Too many Crips, not enough Grips," she half-jokes.

Amir and I laugh, too, even though we feel the weight of what she's saying. I feel the responsibility of being here and doing things like this.

"You, Kendrick Lamar, guys who made it out of here, but still give back, still come back," Shondra continues. "We need you. We need more, so today means everything."

"Whatever I can do," I assure her.

"Well, there's this one student I really hope you get to talk to," she says. "He reminds me so much of you at that age. He's in my English lit class and is such a good writer. There's this writing contest I want him to enter that could lead to big things, but his friends called it 'gay.'"

I wince. We may struggle with a lot of things in the hood, but we have homophobia down. That, we're great at.

"So, of course," Shondra says, rolling her eyes, "now he won't touch it with a ten-foot pole. And both his brothers are Piru."

Amir and I exchange a look, knowing what that means. When your family is Piru, a Blood alliance gang, it probably won't be long before you are, too.

"They call him Bop," Shondra says. "What's his real name?" I ask.

"His name is Dudley," she replies with mischievous eyes.

"Dudley?" Amir laughs. "That ain't even gangsta. Your mama call you Floyd. Imma call you Floyd."

The three of us laugh at his *Coming to America* reference, and it feels good to be home. As hard as I've worked to get out, to survive it, being back here today feels right. Even though I can't ever think about *Coming to America* without thinking about Chaz's last day on earth, it feels right to be here.

Shondra's eyes shift just beyond me and light up with a smile. "Ms. James!" She reaches behind me to hug the petite woman with neat dreadlocks pulled away from her unlined face. "So good to see you. Now, it's a party."

"The whole neighborhood is buzzing about some superstar coming," Ms. James says. "I had to come see for myself."

"Ma." I reach down and pull my mother close, her small frame and fierce spirit burrowing into my side. "I didn't know you were coming."

"And I didn't know *you* were coming." Her eyes, golden brown like mine, hold a light rebuke. "I wanted to hear what you have to say about life and stuff, Mr. Superstar."

"I'm pretty sure most of it will be things you told me in the first place."

"We'll see." She studies my head, a frown on her face. "You cut out your locs. What else don't I know? I had to hear through the grapevine you were in New York with your new girlfriend."

Amir catches a laugh in his fist, and Shondra stretches her eyes with humor.

"Uh oh. Busted." Shondra chuckles and drops a kiss on my mother's cheek. "Good to see you, Ms. James. I need to go find the principal. Be right back."

"Shondra, don't be a stranger, girl," Ma says. "I can't remember the last time you came over for Sunday dinner. You ain't that grown."

"No, ma'am, I'm not." Shondra laughs and turns to leave, speaking over her shoulder. "I'll be taking you up on that. Nobody beats your greens, but don't tell my mama I said that."

"Um, is the b-bathroom still down the hall, Shon?" Amir stutters, looking all nervous.

"Yeah. Of course." Shondra looks back at him like he's crazy. "I'm going that way. You want to follow me?"

Amir grins at me over his shoulder as they walk away.

"Pussy," I mouth at him silently, laughing when he scowls and turns to follow Shondra's hips through the exit doors.

"I'm glad Amir is with you." My mom takes Amir's spot on the wall beside me. "You need somebody who's known you since jump to hold you down, to keep your head on straight the bigger you get."

"Ma, my head stays on straight. Don't worry."

"I do worry." She dips the arch of her brows into a frown. "Especially when you don't tell me things. Why'd I have to hear about you and Qwest on the news?"

"It's not . . ." I sigh, frustrated with how out of control things have gotten in such a short time. "The media's made it bigger than it is. We had a few dates. I spent two days in New York. That's all."

Any hopes I had of keeping things low-key and taking it slow with Qwest went out the window as soon as social media figured out I was staying in her apartment. In just a few days, our fans have made this into some epic love story.

"Well, maybe it should be big." A hopeful grin lights up her still-youthful face. "I need grandbabies. And Qwest seems like the perfect candidate."

"She's a great girl." I keep my tone neutral. "But I don't want you putting too much weight on this."

"It feels like a big deal because you haven't been with a girl in so long." She gives me a wry grin. "I mean like on dates and a relationship. I know you still been smashing."

I groan and close my eyes at her bluntness. She had me when she was just eighteen, and though there was never any doubt which of us was the parent, her youth often made us feel like friends, a unique closeness I usually love. Unless she's talking about me "smashing" chicks.

"Ma, please." My eyes beg her to stop because once she gets started, there's no telling how she'll embarrass me.

"Boy, what? I bought your first pack of Trojans." She smacks her lips, exasperated. "I'm the one who took you to the clinic that time you had that burning—"

"All right, Ma," I cut her off before someone comes and hears her over-sharing. "I got it."

"I thought I was #GripzQueen." She laughs at the face I make. "Seriously, when do I get to meet her?"

"She'll be here for the album release party in a few . . ."

My words trail off when two women walk through the gym doors, drawing the attention of the students waiting in the bleachers. For one thing, the girls are white. We pretty much only see black and brown here. Secondly, the girls are attractive. At least the taller one is. She's damn beautiful.

I assume that's the *Legit* reporter who's shadowing me for the next few weeks entering the gym with Bristol. I barely notice her, but I absorb every detail of Bristol's appearance, starting at her feet in ankle boots, rolling up her long legs in black leather leggings, over the denim shirt with sleeves rolled to the elbow. Hair hanging loose around her shoulders. Even angry with her, I can't ignore the elemental pull between us, like our bodies are in lock step as soon as she walks into a room. It's almost gravitational, and I need to figure out how to shut it down.

"Which one of those girls are you looking at like that?"

My mother's question snatches my attention from the gym entrance.

"Huh?" I make my face confused. "What do you mean?"

"Boy, don't play a player." She inclines her head toward the door. "You lost your train of thought mid-sentence, and looking at one of those girls like breakfast, lunch and dinner. Now which one is it?"

"I don't—"

"Marlon." Her lips compress. "I'm not asking you again."

Like I told Bristol. My mother has extra senses.

"The tall one with the dark hair." I roll my shoulders away from the wall, bend my knee to prop a foot against the wall. "Bristol."

She squints in Bristol's direction.

"She's pretty." Disappointment shadows her face. "White, but pretty."

"Don't start, Ma. And don't worry because she doesn't want to be with me."

"Why not?" Indignation straightens her back and rolls her neck. "She thinks she too good for you or something?"

"You're the one who only wants me dating Black girls, so why you tripping?"

"I never said only Black girls." She pats my shoulder. "I'd settle for Latina. Brown's a color, too, you know."

"Wow. Good to know I have options, but like I said, she isn't interested."

"Hmmmm." She considers Bristol, who's almost reached us. "I think I just saw her on the cover of some magazine in the checkout line."

"Yeah. She's dating—"

"That Parker boy!" Ma's eyes go wide when they meet mine. "His family's rich as hell, baby. So is hers. She's Rhyson's sister, right?"

"Yeah." I straighten from the wall as Bristol and the reporter draw closer. "Can we talk about this later?"

"One more question."

"Ma." Irritation huffs a breath from my chest.

"What?"

"So are you using Qwest to get over her?"

"Not exactly."

"I raised you better than that." Ma points a slim finger in my face. "Don't you play with that girl's feelings. You be honest with her."

"I have been honest with Qwest, Ma." I try not to feel like an asshole. "We were on the same page before Black Twitter blew up with #GripzQueen and #BlackLove hashtags and all that shit. In just a few days it's like … more. It feels like more than what she and I talked about it being."

"Shhh." Ma plasters a smile on her face. "Bristol's coming."

I turn my head to find Bristol's eyes flitting between my mother and me, questioning and wondering.

"Hey," she says when they stand in front of us. "Welcome home."

We stare at each other for a few electric seconds, caught in the memory of the last time we saw each other. Of the last hurtful words I hurled at her. The crude things I said. I feel bad for that, but I'm also still so damn frustrated with her. And yes, hurt. Hurt that she chose that Parker asshole over me when I know what we could have, what we could be.

The silence swells, Bristol slides her eyes away from my stare, uncomfortable waiting for me to respond.

"Uh, yeah. Thanks. Good to be back." I shift my attention to the reporter. "Hey. I'm Grip."

"Sorry. I should introduce you." Bristol grimaces and then smiles. "Grip, this is Meryl Smith. She'll be shadowing us . . . you . . . the next couple of weeks for the *Legit* story."

"Such a pleasure to meet you." Meryl pumps my hand enthusiastically. "I'm a huge fan. I've loved your music since that first underground mixtape."

I study Meryl with her pale skin, mousy brown hair, owlish glasses, and marvel again at the globalization of hip-hop. My music reaches the kids sitting in this gym, living in the hood, and somehow finds suburban girls like this one, who probably listened while studying for her finals at Ivy League colleges. I wouldn't have it any other way.

"Thanks." I smile at Meryl and squeeze her hand. "I'm looking forward to it."

Before we go further, Shondra and Amir return.

"Bristol, hey, girl." Amir pulls her into his side, his smile affectionate. Like he said, he was there the day I met her. She's known him as long as she's known me. "Been missing you."

"I've been around." She gives him a squeeze and leans her head on his shoulder. "You're the one who ran off to New York."

"Not me." Amir tilts his head in my direction. "Just following the boss."

My gaze wrestles with Bristol's until I break the awkward, heated moment.

"Bristol, this is Shondra," I say. "She teaches here and coordinated everything. Shon, this is Bristol, my manager."

I turn to find my mother has Bristol under her microscope. This should be fun.

"Bristol, this," I say, pulling my mother close, "is my mom."

"Your mother?" Bristol's eyes widen and swing to my mother. "But you look so young."

"You know what they say." Ma shrugs. "Black don't crack."

"They actually say that?" Bristol asks.

Shondra and Amir laugh right away. If you get Bristol, you like her. Amir's always liked her. Shondra must get her, too. Even irritated with her, I have to smile a little. Ma isn't prepared to laugh, but her lips twitch.

"I mean," Bristol rolls her eyes at herself, "I've heard so much about you."

"Have you now?" Ma looks Bristol up and down. "You're Rhyson's sister, huh?"

"Um, yes." Bristol nods, an uncertain smile on her lips at my mother's thorough vertical inspection. "We're twins actually."

"Hmmmm," Ma says. "I see the resemblance."

"Yes, well, it's great to finally meet you." Bristol glances at me briefly before turning back to Shondra, pouring all her charm into a smile. "Meryl needs to sit down with Grip once he's done, just for a few minutes. I was thinking there might be a place here on campus where they could do the interview?"

"Sure," Shondra says. "We can find a spot, easy."

"And we'll just need to get some releases signed." Bristol reaches into her bag and extracts a few forms. "In case we use pictures of any students or places here on campus. Could we scope a few possibilities?"

"We might be in *Legit* magazine?" Shondra's eyes light up. "That's great. We have a few minutes before Grip starts. Let's go."

She, Shondra, and Meryl turn to walk off.

"Amir," I say quickly. "Go with them."

"It's okay, Grip." Bristol looks over her shoulder with a small smile. "We'll be fine."

"Bristol, you're not home." I check my frustration, conscious of how closely the others watch me, especially my mom. "Things could pop off here without warning. Amir will know what to do if anything goes down."

"She'll be fine, Grip," Shondra reassures me.

"I know she will because Amir's going." I tip my head toward him . "You got it?"

"Yeah, I got it," he says.

"Amir," Bristol says pointedly, leveling annoyed eyes on me. "That isn't necessary. Really."

"Well, Amir works for me, and I told him to go with you."

A muscle tics in Bristol's jaw, but she turns without another word and starts walking swiftly toward the exit. Shondra, Meryl, and Amir trade uncertain looks before they take off to catch up.

"Oh, I see you have your emotions well in check," Ma says sarcastically, watching Bristol leave through the gym door. "No one would ever guess how you feel about that girl."

"Ma, please." Chin dropped to chest, I run a hand over my head. "Not today."

"You need to get over her." Ma shakes her head. "Just try with Qwest for me, okay?"

"It doesn't work like that." I shove my hands into the side pockets of my leather jacket. "I wish it did. I thought it could."

"Now, when did you say I get to meet Qwest?" She skips over what I've said. "You got . . . distracted before."

"She'll be here for the release party in a few weeks."

"I'll meet her then." She reaches one hand up to cup my face. "I know you don't understand, but I get sick and tired of our successful Black men ending up with women who don't look like us."

"Ma, I hear you, but you know I've dated all over and that's never been how I chose who I was with." I place my hand over hers against my face, wishing I could transmit my perspective to her through the touch connecting us. "That's not everyone and it's not me."

She drops her hands and lifts one brow. "You think I made all those sacrifices so you could be a cliché? Some Black man who thinks a white woman is the ultimate symbol of success? Like a nice car or a big house, but with blonde hair?"

"She isn't blonde, and you know me better than that. You raised me better than that." I'm losing the grasp on my patience the longer I have to defend my feelings for Bristol, since they won't be doing me any good anyway. "I didn't fall for her because she's white. I fell for her because she's . . . Bristol."

"You *think* it isn't a factor, but it is." Mama places her hand over her heart like I'm breaking it. "I was afraid of this. I wanted you to go to that fancy school, but I always knew this could happen, that it could influence you. And here we are."

"I've dated Asian girls, Hispanic girls, black girls, white girls. Why is this such a big deal to you?"

"But marrying is a different story."

"Who said anything about marrying? And it's a little late in the century to still be hating white people."

"Tell them that," she replies with fire. "And I don't hate all white people. Just like I don't like all Black people. All God's children, red and yellow, black and white get on your mama's nerves. Not hating them does not mean marrying them."

"Nobody's talking about marrying anyone," I reiterate. "She won't even date me, much less marry me. You have nothing to worry about."

If anyone should worry, it's me. Because after two days in New York in Qwest's bed, my feelings for Bristol are just as strong. My anger and my frustration lie on top of them in a thick pile, but I've come nowhere near snuffing them out.

Not for the first time I wonder if anything ever will.

Fourteen

Bristol

'M NOT SURE HOW MUCH MORE MY OVARIES CAN ENDURE TODAY.

As if Grip looking the way he does isn't enough, seeing him inspire these kids from his old high school is like a stick of C4 planted in my ovaries.

Boom.

It seems I'm not the only one. Meryl "the huge fan" reporter hasn't taken her eyes off him since we got here. So much for professional objectivity. She practically threw her panties at him.

Okay. I'm being ridiculous. I know it. I'm taking my frustration out on poor Meryl because the person who really deserves it can't take it. Not Grip for going to New York and sleeping with Qwest. Not Qwest for inviting him and being exactly the kind of girl he should be with. No, the person who deserves my scorn is me, but I think watching Grip fall for Qwest on every social media platform is punishment enough. So, Meryl it is.

"I know it feels like there's no way out sometimes," Grip tells the assembled students from his spot on the gymnasium floor. "I grew up just a few streets over, so I know what happens in Bompton."

Grip told me once that here when a word starts with the letter "C", you often substitute a "B" because this is Bloods, not Crips, territory. The possibility that wearing blue or saying "couch" instead of "bouch" could get you killed? I can't imagine human life being treated so cavalierly.

"Half the boys I knew when I was your age didn't make it past twenty." Grip drops his eyes to the wax-shiny basketball court before looking back to the students. "And too many others are locked up. I'm not gonna sugar coat it. The odds are stacked against us."

He steps closer, and the passion in his eyes and in his voice reverberates, reaching as high as the rafters. Reaching each student listening intently. Reaching me.

"You have to make your own way out. You're responsible for your future." He runs his eyes methodically up and down the rows of students. "You can't wait for somebody else to give you anything. My mom taught me that."

The warm smile Grip and his mother share telegraphs a closeness I envy. She's exactly as I'd imagined she'd be. Proud. Confident. Fiercely protective.

"She was the one who encouraged me to apply for a scholarship at the School of the Arts," Grip says. "Even though it meant leaving this school where all my friends were and taking a bus across town everyday alone. Even though it meant going to a new school that felt like a foreign country, where I felt like an alien. If I hadn't done that, you might not be hearing my music now. You probably wouldn't even know my name."

"He's amazing," Meryl whispers, her eyes fixed on Grip's expressive face. "I can't wait to write this story."

"Good," I whisper back with a forced smile.

My phone buzzes in my lap, and I look down at the screen. Parker.

I would ignore this call, but I've been leaving him messages for the last three days. He has to know I suspect he leaked that information to the media. I need to set him straight, and there's no telling when he'll stop avoiding me and call again.

"I need to take this," I tell Meryl quietly. "Be right back."

I bend at the waist and tiptoe, hoping I haven't drawn much attention to myself, though Grip couldn't miss me stepping out.

"Parker," I say as soon as I'm in the hall. "Why did it take you so long to return my calls?"

"Bristol, I miss you, too." His deep voice is part humor, part caution.

"Your people confirmed to the media that we're dating." I lean against the brick wall and plow my fingers through my hair. "They wouldn't have done that without your express permission."

"I've been in India. You know that. It's just a misunderstanding. A miscommunication."

"One I am fully capable of correcting if you don't do it." I pause for emphasis. "Soon."

"Is it really so far from the truth?" he asks. "Come on, Bristol. We did spend the night together just days ago."

"You know damn well I was too drunk to even know my name that night, much less choose to sleep with you. Now, everyone thinks we're practically engaged."

"I'll handle it."

"You better, or I will."

Something sinister uncurls and hisses in the silence on the other end.

"That wouldn't be wise, Bristol," Parker says quietly.

"You don't scare me." I push myself away from the wall, standing perfectly straight as if he were right in front of me to see. "I hope you know that."

"I don't want to scare you." He infuses his words with artificial warmth. "I want to love you."

"Love?" A bitter laugh leaves an aftertaste on my lips. "The way my father loves my mother? The way your father loves yours? No, thank you. If I ever do marry, it won't be to a man who needs other women like they do. A man who humiliates me with his infidelities."

"I'm sure you can persuade me not to stray," he says, sounding pleased that it matters to me. "I had no idea you were so possessive."

"I'm not possessive of you, and any man I have to persuade not to stray is welcome to do so. If I have to convince him I'm worth his fidelity, then he isn't the one for me."

"I love your spirit, Bristol." He sounds a little like he's . . . panting? "It turns me on."

"All right." I wish he were here to see my eyes rolling. He's like a hound dog after a rabbit. A swift rabbit he won't get ahold of again. "On that note, I'm gonna go."

"But, baby—"

"I'm working," I say, cutting into whatever bullshit he planned to say. "And don't call me baby."

I hang up before he has the chance to protest further and quietly ease back through the gym doors so I don't disturb Grip's talk.

Only he isn't talking. He's at one end of the court, poised to shoot the basketball. He's no longer wearing his black leather jacket and Kelly green hoodie, but just a plain white T-shirt and black jeans. One of the students, as tall as Grip and with an athletic build, guards him with a hand in his face.

"What's going on?" I ask Meryl. "What'd I miss?"

"It was great." Meryl's eyes glimmer with her eagerness. "One of the kids challenged Grip when he talked about the value of an education. He said Grip didn't go to college, but he's still, and I quote, 'stacking dollars'. Then Grip said everyone doesn't have to go to college, but an education is something that cannot be taken away."

"Wow. Sounds intense." I watch the two guys run back up to our end of the court. "How did they end up playing basketball?"

"Then Grip said he's enrolled in online courses now." Meryl gives me a curious look. "Did you know that?"

"Uh, no." I shake my head, watching the student make a difficult shot. "I had no idea."

He never told me. Why would he not tell me something that huge?

"So then Grip calls him out about some writing contest he apparently won't enter," Meryl says. "Before I knew it, Grip said he'd play him for it, one on one. If Grip wins, the student—I think they called him Bop—has to enter the contest."

"And if Grip loses?"

"If Grip loses, Bop wins his shoes."

"His shoes?"

Grip has a massive tennis shoe collection, and the classic Jordans in his closet are his prized possessions. I recognize the pair he's wearing now as especially expensive and rare.

"We haven't even sat down for the interview yet," Meryl says gleefully. "And I've already gotten a lot."

I notice Grip's leather jacket and hoodie on the floor. I pick them up so they won't get stepped on or dirty. As soon as they're within sniffing distance, his clean, masculine scent surrounds me. I hold the material to my chest and surreptitiously inhale, closing my eyes to absorb this small part of him. The items still have the warmth of his body, and holding them, even for a few seconds, warms my chilled places.

When I open my eyes, I encounter Ms. James' golden brown gaze locked on me. Even fully dressed with Grip's jacket and hoodie hugged to my chest, I feel naked under her stare. She sees everything. I clear discomfort from my throat and turn back to the court.

Grip takes one final shot, which apparently puts the game away, and the students go crazy, emptying the bleachers and rushing the basketball court. Even Amir, Shondra, Ms. James, and Meryl join the exuberant knot of students surrounding Grip on the court. I hang back, observing. He's laughing, at ease, at home, the basketball pressed to his hip.

I've never been in this position with him. On the outside, out of favor. It's awkward, and it hurts. Maybe I could mitigate this by telling him that Parker and I aren't dating. Parker should be telling everyone soon enough himself anyway. But do I have the right? Grip finally seems to be moving on and giving someone a real shot. I'm still not going to be with him, so what would telling him accomplish? I should give them a chance, him and Qwest.

I skirt the edges of the crowd, waiting while he signs autographs, all the while encouraging Bop to keep writing, to enter the contest. I've never seen this side of him. Listening to the songs he writes about his childhood and his old neighborhood, I suspected it, but seeing it firsthand is an entirely different thing. An entirely better thing.

Meryl steps out of the crowd until she's standing with me.

"I'm glad you invited me." Her broad grin pushes the glasses up on her cheeks. "This is a great add for the piece."

"Speaking of which," I say. "Grip has a session soon, making some last-minute adjustments for the album. We better get him into the courtyard for your interview before it gets too late."

I make my way through the crowd until I'm standing right behind Grip, waiting for him to finish the last few autographs.

"You enjoy managing my son?" Ms. James asks at my shoulder.

I turn my head, startled to find her so close, those eyes, so like Grip's, trained on my face.

"Yes, very much." I clutch his leather jacket and hoodie a little closer. "I manage several artists, but Grip definitely has a special place. He's like family, being so close to Rhyson."

"So he's like a brother to you?" Ms. James asks.

"Something like that." I lick the lie away from my lips, turning to offer her a smile. "We've known each other a long time."

I see a good stopping point, and know I have to dive in and get him out before he starts with another group.

"Excuse me, Ms. James." I smile politely and press my way to Grip's side.

"Hey." I touch his elbow, drawing a sharp glance from him. The smile on his face, the light in his eyes dies when he realizes it's me. That look drags a serrated knife over an open nerve.

"Sorry to interrupt," I say softly. "But we need to get into your interview with Meryl. I think you have a session this afternoon, right?"

For a moment, it seems he may not even acknowledge my question, but then he nods and turns back to the crowd.

"Gotta go, guys." He raises his voice to be heard by all who are around. "I'll stay longer next time."

"Sorry to break things up." I look up at him, searching the rigid lines of his face for any softening. He flicks a glance my way with a barely discernible nod.

"Oh, here's your stuff." I extend the jacket and hoodie to him.

"Thanks," he mutters, slipping the hoodie over the plain white T-shirt he played basketball in.

"Sure." I look over at Shondra to give myself something to do while things feel so weird. "Hey, can we head to the courtyard for the interview now?"

"Of course," Shondra responds. "Follow me."

Meryl gets a call on our way to the courtyard. While she's on the phone and Shondra is a few paces ahead of us, I search for something to break this awkward silence between Grip and me.

"I didn't know you were taking online courses."

"And I didn't realize it had anything to do with managing me." He looks straight ahead. "So, why would I tell you?"

He quickens his steps to catch up to Shondra, to get away from me. I notice his shoulders relax, the handsome profile lit with a smile as they talk about old times in these halls.

It's like a slap across my face, his indifference. Or was it rejection? It all feels the same now. In giving him his chance with Qwest, I wasn't prepared for what I would be giving up. Whatever existed between us, even the friendship I've grown to treasure over the years, will never be the same.

Fifteen

Bristol

H E'S GOING TO BE NUMBER ONE. HE'S GOING TO BE NUMBER ONE. HE'S going to be number one.

That thought buzzes around my head as I obsessively check the numbers on *Grip*. It's Prodigy's first release. It's the thing I've poured everything into for months. With two number one singles already under its belt, topping the album charts would be a crowning achievement. It's critically and commercially beyond anything we could have hoped for. Reviews are glowing. Sales are shockingly good. By the time Meryl's story goes to press, Grip will be in another stratosphere.

I rarely cry, but tears stand in my eyes because no one deserves this more than he does. He's worked hard for years and is one of the most talented artists on the scene. So happy tears, but tears nonetheless.

"Knock, knock." Rhyson raps his knuckles against my open office door and pokes his head in. "Got a second?"

"Sure." I sniff and sneak a thumb under my eyes, hoping runny mascara doesn't give away too much. "Come on in, brother dearest."

"Did you see the numbers?" The eagerness on Rhyson's handsome face matches the unassailable joy leaping in me since I saw the first batch of sales figures.

"What numbers?" I blank my face, but probably can't suppress the happiness in my eyes.

"What numbers, my ass." Rhyson huffs his disbelief, collapsing into the leather chair across from my desk. "I bet you've been checking every five minutes."

Try every two.

"*Grip* is outpacing sales of my last album," Rhyson says. "You're telling me you don't already know that?"

"It's pretty freaking awesome, right?" I burst out, unable to hold it back any longer.

"Yeah, it is." His smile softens with what looks like affection . . . for me. "We did it, Bris."

"Grip did it," I reply immediately.

"Of course, he did, but this is Prodigy's first release. This is our baby, and we did good, kid."

It means everything to hear Rhyson talk about the label as ours and the work as our shared project. This feeling, this accomplishment, the possibility of it, is what compelled me to focus my college degree on business and entertainment. It spurred me to move here for Rhyson's solo career, even when he wasn't sure he wanted one after all the drama with our parents. Hell, he wasn't even sure he wanted me in his life.

"It's pretty incredible." I push the words past the pesky lump in my throat.

"So where's the man of the hour?" A grin curves Rhyson's lips. "He's your best friend." I shuffle some papers on my desk, avoiding Rhyson's eyes. "You don't know?"

"Are you kidding me?" He barks a laugh out. "You know where all your artists are at all times."

"True." I twist my lips into a wry grin at how OCD I can be. "He's got a full day. He started off super early this morning with a call into The Breakfast Club in New York, and he's everywhere. Several instore appearances. He's even on Seacrest, in studio."

Rhyson gives a low whistle, sitting back to cross an ankle over his knee.

"Wow." He studies my face. "So why are you here and not with our biggest star?"

"Sarah's got it." I stand and take a small stack of papers to the shredder I keep in the corner. "We do have other artists, and I've been giving so much to Grip, there's lots to catch up on. Kilimanjaro is still out on the road. Luke is finishing his album. There's a few movie scripts coming in for Kai, after the baby of course."

"No nudity." Rhyson frowns. "Like at all. Preferably no love scenes. We need final approval on the script. Aren't there any great, meaty nun roles out there? Remember Audrey Hepburn in *A Nun's Story*? She received an Oscar nomination for that."

I chuckle because my brother is notoriously possessive over his little wife. The nun stuff sounds ridiculous, but he isn't even kidding. I look back, and his face is completely serious. Poor Kai.

"Uh, got it. Nuns. I'll see what I can do." I sit again, hoping he's lost his previous line of questioning.

"So, about Marlon."

Damn, he's persistent.

"I promise you Sarah's got it. She's more than capable."

"I'm sure she's capable. You wouldn't keep her if she weren't. We're not known for tolerating incompetence. Guess we got that from our parents."

Among other things.

I leave that on the shelf because Rhyson and I have never gotten far discussing our parents. Come to think of it, there are a lot of things we don't get far discussing outside of our business dealings.

"Besides Marlon, you've worked harder on this than anyone, Bris." Rhyson leans forward. "You should be with him today, and you know it. So why are you here?"

"Drop it. Geesh." I open my laptop and pull up my checklist for Grip's listening party and release celebration. "Everything's covered."

The only sound in the office is my fingers flying over the keys. I glance up to find his cool eyes on my face. I pause my typing and lean back in my seat to cross my legs.

"What?" I lift a brow.

"Can I ask you something?"

"You just did." My lips move a degree in a smile.

"What's up with you and Marlon?" There's no trace of a smile on his face, and his eyes hold only questions, no humor.

"Rhyson, leave it." I sigh and lean toward my desk, back to my typing.

"I wasn't going to bring this up because I didn't think it would be a problem." Rhyson frowns and runs a hand over the back of his neck, uncharacteristic discomfort on his face. "But Marlon told me about . . . you know."

I stop typing to give him my full attention. "Not yet, I don't know. He told you what?"

"He told me about you guys hooking up when you were here on spring break that time." Rhyson pushes the words out like they burn his tongue.

"Oh, did he?" Irritation blisters beneath my skin. "I should go check the restroom. Maybe he wrote 'for a good time call Bristol' on the stalls, too."

"Bris, it's been a long time. He probably wouldn't have told me now if it hadn't been for the song. I had no idea 'Top of the World' was about you."

"It doesn't matter." I fix my eyes on the screen. "Water under the bridge. Water that never went anywhere anyway."

"That's what I thought, but things have been weird lately," Rhyson says. "And it's none of my business."

"Right." I don't look away from the sales report in one of my open browsers. "It's not."

"Until it affects my business," Rhyson finishes, his tone stiff. "If things weren't tense between the two of you, you'd be with Marlon today. We can't have whatever is going on with you personally affecting business."

"So what?" My eyes jerk to his face. "Are you here to write me up? Put a warning in my file? Give me a demerit? Whatever you came here to do, do it, say it so I can get back to work."

"There's no need to get defensive."

"There is when you tell me you think I'm not doing my job because of some shit with Grip."

I open yet another browser. Anything to avoid the curiosity in my brother's eyes.

"Do you have feelings for him, Bristol?" Rhyson asks softly.

In all these years, he's never asked me. Not once has Rhyson ever asked if I returned Grip's feelings. He's always assumed that when I brushed aside Grip's advances, his flirtations, there was nothing to it on my end. Any hope I have that I'll get out of this conversation without telling him something fades when he doesn't drop it.

"Bris, look at me," my brother demands.

I finally abandon my laptop, meeting his eyes. "Do you have feelings for Marlon?"

I still can't make myself admit it aloud. Even though he isn't in the room, it's like as soon as I say the words, they'll land on my sleeve for Grip to read. But my silence says it all. I've never had to deny my feelings to Rhyson, and I find it harder than when I lie to Grip.

"What the hell?" Rhyson leans back in his seat, resting his head on the back of the chair and staring up at the ceiling. "All these years and you never . . . why?"

"It doesn't matter what I feel."

He sits back up, spearing me with the frustration in his eyes. "How can you say that?"

"Because I'm not doing a damn thing about it. That's why."

"But if you . . ." He pauses, obviously taking great care with the next word that comes out of his mouth, as he should. "Care about Marlon, and he's made no secret of how he feels about you, then why not?"

"Weren't you the main one afraid I would destroy him?" I pinch my brows together. "Seems you'd be the last person encouraging a relationship between poor, vulnerable Grip and your sister the man-eater."

"What?"

"Oh, please, Rhyson." I steady my voice for the next words. "Just a few weeks ago, I overheard you warning him away from me. Telling him that he should pursue Qwest instead. So, don't act as if Grip and me would be some match made in heaven. You know we wouldn't be good together."

Rhyson is quiet for a few moments, studying the clasped hands in his lap.

"I admit there are risks involved." Rhyson looks up at me from beneath his dark brows. "I have been concerned that you might hurt him."

"It never once occurred to you that he might hurt me?" A bitter laugh darkens the air around me. "That maybe he had already hurt me and I wasn't willing to risk my heart being broken?"

"You mean the stuff with Tessa? It wasn't his baby, Bris."

"It could have been." I shake my head and twirl my chair away from him to face the view through my window. "That wasn't even the point. He lied to me. He never once mentioned he was in a relationship that whole week we were . . ."

Together. To even think of us as "together" pains me.

"Whatever we were doing that week," I finish lamely. "If he would cheat on Tessa, he'd cheat on me."

Rhyson comes to stand in front of me, propping himself against the windowsill.

"You think Marlon would cheat on you?" Rhyson looks at me disbelievingly. "He was a kid!"

"He hasn't exactly been chaste since."

"Neither have you," Rhyson tosses back. "You can't hold anyone he's been with against him when you weren't together, Bris. That's ridiculous."

"You say that so easily because you'd never cheat on Kai."

"Of course I would never cheat on Kai." He looks offended that I even brought it up. "I couldn't."

"Well you're the exception to the rule. Most men have no trouble cheating." A laugh sours in my mouth. "Our father certainly doesn't."

"What did you say?" Rhyson peers at my face like he's never seen me before. "Dad cheats on Mom?"

"Oh, God, Rhyson." I lean back in my seat, part horrified, part relieved that he knows. "Yes. Dad cheats."

"When?"

"When not?" I meet the confusion in his eyes. "Almost since the beginning."

"I mean, I figured they didn't have what you would call a typical marriage." A frown settles on Rhyson's face. "But I hadn't thought about ..."

He shrugs, his expression clearing.

"She probably cheats, too," he says. "It isn't like they have some grand passion."

"She loves him," I say softly. "She's never cheated on him." "How do you know all of this and I don't?"

"Because I've been there, Rhyson." Pent up emotion pushes my voice out louder than I intend. "You left and never looked back. I'm the one who stayed. I saw what happened."

"What did you see?" His eyes never leave my face. Maybe he's really seeing me for the first time since we were kids.

I hear my father screwing that girl as if I'm standing down in the foyer again.

"I heard him." I draw a deep breath, releasing it on a shaky exhale. "I went home after spring break but didn't tell them I was coming. As soon as I walked in the house, I heard them upstairs. Someone having sex. Like loud, so I knew they didn't think anyone else was in the house."

I lean forward, propping my elbows on my knees and scooping my hair away from my face before going on.

"There was this part of me that was happy." I shake my head, remembering the goofy grin I wore thinking I'd caught my parents making love. "I never thought they loved each other. I knew they were . . . partners, but I didn't think of them as having sex. Of enjoying each other."

"Yeah, neither did I." Rhyson clears his throat. "And then what happened?"

"Then Mom walked through the front door." I meet Rhyson's horrified eyes. "Yeah. She walked in and heard him fucking someone upstairs. And I was standing right there, thinking the whole time it was her."

I pop up, on my feet and pace around my office, because even the memory agitates me.

"She wasn't shocked." A staccato laugh chokes me. "Devastated, but not shocked. She was used to it. She accepted it."

"Why doesn't she just leave him?" Rhyson asks. "If it hurts so badly, why not just leave? Is it the business?"

"No, that's what I thought." I walk over to join him at the window, setting one hip on the windowsill and leaning my shoulder against the pane. "She brushed it off like it meant nothing, but later that night, I found her drunk and crying. Just . . . this pathetic person, nothing like our mother at all."

I bite my lip, as if I can physically hold back the last of a dirty secret, but it's about to spill out of me.

"She loves him. She doesn't leave because she can't. She loves him desperately."

I tip my head back, preferring the ceiling to the perplexed look on my brother's face.

"She has vodka for breakfast to get through the day," I say. "Did you know that? Bloody Marys if she's in public, but at home, she just drinks vodka first thing in the morning."

"Are you saying our mother is an alcoholic?" Disbelief, horror, smudge the clear gray of Rhyson's eyes. "How could I not know all of this?"

"Like I said, you weren't around." A wry grin tilts my mouth. "And you were already running from us. As if you needed more reason to stay away. I didn't want to tell you now that you're finally trying with our parents. I didn't think any of this would endear us to you."

"I don't know what to say." Rhyson pushes his fingers through his unruly hair. "What to think. It's like there was this whole world going on that I knew nothing about. Our parents. The cheating. Mom's drinking."

He gives me a direct look that probes for anything else I might be hiding.

"You and Grip. What does all of this have to do with the two of you?"

I lean my temple against the cool glass and don't respond. I don't want to talk about this with him. We go years without talking about anything but music and business and shit that doesn't matter, and he wants to go excavating my brain while our first release rockets up the charts.

"Grip isn't our father." Rhyson turns my chin with his finger until I have to meet his eyes. "And you're definitely not our mother."

"Aren't I?" I shake my head, lowering my eyes to hide anything else from him. "You don't believe that. You know how alike we are."

"Not in the ways that count," Rhyson says. "I'll be the first to admit that I didn't trust you when you first came back into my life. I thought she could manipulate you. You know that."

"So did she. That's why she didn't completely lose her mind when I left New York to come here. She thought she could get to you through me."

Rhyson's jaw becomes granite.

"I know that." He looks at me, his eyes losing some of their stoniness. "But she couldn't. She didn't. You're not her."

"She's a foolish woman who feels too much for a man who doesn't feel enough for her, and she can't make herself walk away." A hollow laugh grates in my throat. "And I'd be just like her."

"No, you wouldn't. You're not."

"I am," I fire back, holding his eyes by sheer will. "You have me pegged so wrong, Rhyson. You always have."

"What? I . . ." He dips his head to get a better look at my face. "What do you mean?"

"You think I'm this hard ass who doesn't care."

My voice wobbles, dammit. I swallow as much of the years-old weakness as I can before continuing.

"That isn't me." The words barely make it out, singed by the hot tears in my throat. "I'm the girl who cares too much. When you and our parents walked away from each other, who fought for our family? Who actually cared that we weren't a family?"

"Well—"

"Me, Rhyson." I dig my finger into my chest, pressing my point. "And when we didn't see each other, literally for years, who took the first step? Reached out? Called? Came here to see you?"

"Bristol, I—"

"That's right. Me." I can't hold back the tears that leak over my cheeks. "Who was the idiot who hadn't had a real conversation with you in years, but chose her college major based on your dreams? Bet the whole farm that you'd let me back into your life if I could help your career?"

"You did," he says softly.

"Don't you see? Can none of you see how much I care?" A sob breaks into my words. "How damn starved I am? For anything from you, from Mom, Dad."

"From Grip?"

His question slices into the quiet like a knife through butter.

Softly. Smoothly, but it still cuts.

"It didn't even take a week with him," I whisper, sniffing and letting the tears roll over my chin, down my neck, and into my collar unchecked. "I knew I was in trouble after three days."

A chuckle at my own expense vibrates in my chest.

"Maybe less. Two days." I shrug. "We talked about everything that first night. There was nothing off limits. We were so different, but I'd never felt so . . . connected to anyone."

"I guess I was working on that project, huh?" Guilt floods Rhyson's eyes.

"That was the excuse you gave, yeah." I give him a knowing look. "We both know you were avoiding me. You had no idea if I was legit. You didn't know what to make of me after all those years apart. You always thought, and rightly so, that I was too much like Mother."

"I'm sorry."

"No it's true. I am." I smile, reminiscing about that week. "But Grip didn't know that. He just got to know . . . me. For me. He was smart. So smart. And such a good writer. Sensitive. He wrote poetry, for God's sake. What grown man who looks like him writes poetry? That's just not fair."

Rhyson and I share a smile, tinged with sadness.

"And he was so comfortable with himself," I say. "So confident, and it didn't come from having money or fame or anything else. Just confident in himself. It came from somewhere I couldn't even relate to, but it was completely authentic and magnetic."

"And?" Rhyson prompts when I stop myself.

"And I didn't stop it." I blow out a breath laden with my own incredulity. "For once, I decided I was going to free-fall. I was going to kiss at the top of a Ferris wheel, swim naked in the ocean—"

"Naked in the ocean?" Rhyson does a double take. "I wasn't gone that much. I missed all that?"

"We didn't let anyone know. It was just . . . us. I knew Grip was falling for me, and I knew for sure I was falling for him, and it felt so good. Just to let it go. To just fall felt good."

"If you and Grip were together, he'd be faithful."

"You think so. He thinks so." I laugh harshly. "But I'm not so sure. What makes me so special?"

"What makes you so special?" Rhyson leans over and gently pushes the hair out of my eyes. "How much time do you have, little sister?"

"We're twins, idiot," I hiccup through the last of my tears. "Once and for all, I'm not your little sister."

"Well, I came out first."

He pulls me into a hug. My throat swells with heat, emotion closing the passageway and making it hard to swallow, to breathe. I've longed to talk like this with my brother for years. And no matter how much business we did, it never became this personal. This vulnerable. I fight it back. I pull away.

"I'm sure at some point Mother thought she was special, too, but I flew back to New York and caught our father fucking one of his clients upstairs while our mother listened in the foyer," I say in a rush. "She didn't feel special that night when I was mopping her up off the floor, drunk and miserable. She feels things so deeply she has to make you think she feels nothing to protect herself."

"And that's what you're doing?" Rhyson's question comes softly but harshly. "Denying to Marlon that you feel anything when you feel everything? Is that why you're dating Parker?"

"God, you really don't know me if you think I'm actually dating Parker," I say, my response flat.

"You're not dating Parker?" A baffled frown settles between Rhyson's brows. "I knew it! What the hell, Bris?"

"If I won't be with Grip, he should be with someone like Qwest." I swallow the hurt even linking their names in the same sentence does to me. "And he wouldn't even try as long as he thought I was . . . possible. So, I let him, along with the entire known world, think that I was dating Parker when the media reported it."

"But he . . . didn't he . . ." Discomfort tightens Rhyson's words. "Him leaving your house that morning, that was—"

"Oh, no. I slept with him. That happened." I shrug. "I guess. He says I did."

A loaded silence stretches between us as Rhyson processes that information.

"You don't remember?"

"I was taking a page out of Mother's playbook, numbing with vodka so I didn't feel." My heart twists like a knife in my chest as Grip's cutting words before he left for New York come back to haunt me. "That kind of backfired."

"Wait. Let me get this straight." Anger bunches the muscle along Rhyson's jaw. "Did Parker take advantage of you? Like sleep with you while you were—"

"I can't, Rhyson," I say so softly I'm not sure he heard me. "He says I was willing. I just don't remember much."

"He says you were . . ." Rhyson narrows the rage in his eyes to slits. "That motherfucker."

"That motherfucker," I agree with a little laugh, even though it isn't funny at all to wake up and have no memory of having sex with someone. "I mean, I've let that go. You need to let it go, too. It won't accomplish anything."

"You say you aren't dating Parker," Rhyson finally says after he's composed himself some. "Does Parker know that?"

"Kind of." I laugh at the expression on Rhyson's face. "I've tried to tell him. He insists that I'm going to marry him one day and we're going to rule the world."

"Asshole," Rhyson mutters. "Exactly."

"You should be careful of him, Bristol. All that power and money make him dangerous."

"No, thinking he's God's gift is what makes him dangerous, but I've got it under control."

"What does that mean?"

"Meaning it was convenient for me to let him play this little fantasy out in public so Grip would finally move on." I toy with a loose string on the sleeve of my blouse and bite my bottom lip. "Thinking I'm with Parker moved him on to Qwest, but I've told Parker. He hasn't accepted it fully yet, but he'll tell the media the truth soon."

"If you really think Grip is over you that fast, then you don't know him."

For a moment, hope flares inside me. Hope that maybe I didn't completely burn the bridge between Grip and me. But it's a bridge I'll never cross anyway, so what's the use?

"He has the right to know the truth." Rhyson's worried eyes hold mine. "To know how you feel."

"The right?" I scoff. "They're my feelings, and I choose not to act on them, so what good does it do for him to know?"

"So what? You just watch him fall harder for Qwest? Give him to someone else?" Rhyson's voice is so full of disappointment and disapproval I almost flinch. "You're braver than that, Bristol. You're the most fearless person I know. And you let the threat of something keep you from what you really want?"

"You don't understand what—"

"I do," Rhyson cuts in. "It's the same kind of bullshit that kept Kai from being with me. Allowing her past and the mistakes her parents made to dictate her future. Imagine if she'd just given up? Not taken a chance on me? She had every reason not to."

He takes both my hands in his, squeezing as he looks at me, through me.

"We wouldn't be married. She wouldn't be pregnant." A bleakness enters his eyes. "The prospect of spending the rest of my life without her would destroy me. Why would you choose that?"

"You think I'm fearless?" The words get hung up on the tears flooding my throat. "I'm not. I'm scared shitless, Rhyson. I care so much about the people I love. I'd do anything for them. If I let myself . . . have Grip, there would be no boundaries. Do you understand what I'm saying? What if I end up like our mother? A strong woman whose man is her Achilles' heel? A drunken fool who takes whatever scraps he leaves and shares him to have whatever he'll give her?"

"You would never allow—"

"Neither would she, but she does." I shake my head. "I've seen it. How weak she is for him. She kept it from us for years because she's ashamed."

"All I know is the very thought of Kai with anyone else drives me insane," Rhyson says. "And we may not be typical twins, but I do know we're alike in that way. Actually having to watch her be with someone else, to see her fall for someone else and know that I allowed that to happen? I would be miserable, and so would you."

Images of Grip holding Qwest's hand and of them out in New York laughing and kissing twist around my mind, squeezing like a boa constrictor. My imagination fills in the dark gaps of what they're like in bed together. Of how she runs her hands over his broad chest, over the whipcord muscles of his arms and legs. How she strokes him, takes him in her mouth, takes him in her body. Of her satisfying him in a way I never will. She knows him now in a way I don't. They've passed secrets between their bodies.

The unrelenting flow of images floods my mind, torturing me. Rhyson thinks I would be miserable?

Oh, God, I already am.

Sixteen

Grip

POETRY HAS LONG BEEN A HABIT AND A COMFORT FOR ME. EVER since I was a kid, I would recite my favorite poems when I was afraid, nervous, excited.

Sad.

The words pull me into a rhythm. Something set and predictable, yet brimming with the potential to break wild and free.

In my favorite poem "Poetry", Neruda said he wheeled with the stars and that his heart broke loose on the wind. It seems particularly appropriate tonight because I do feel as if, with my debut album sitting in the number one spot, I'm tumbling through some galaxy I never thought to explore. A dark sky pelted with stars, with promises masquerading as constellations.

I quoted that poem to Bristol at the top of the Ferris wheel all those years ago when we got stuck. She was frightened, but our kiss chased her fears away. She flipped my heart upside down, upending everything I thought I wanted in a girl. That Ferris wheel was maybe a hundred feet off the ground, but with Bristol's lips so soft, first hesitant then urgent, her fingers twisted around mine like she was just as desperate to hold onto me as I was to hold onto her—I was on top of the world. I didn't have two pennies to rub together or a pot to piss in, but I was happy.

So fucking happy.

And tonight, I am at the top of the world, more successful than that pauper on the Ferris wheel could have imagined. I can see Bristol on the other side of the club where we're holding my release celebration, but she may as well be in another hemisphere there's so much distance between us. I'm a fool because given the choice, I'd take the Ferris wheel with her any day over tonight. That kiss, not this celebration, feels like the best night of my life.

"You do know you have the number one album in the country, right?" Qwest walks toward the edge of the stage where I'm seated. We just finished sound check for tonight's performance. "You got nothing to look sad about, baby."

"I'm not sad." I curve my lips into something close to a smile to prove it. "Just taking a quick breather. It's a lot to take in."

"How about you take me in." She stands between my legs hanging over the lip of the stage. One hand touches my chest through my shirt and moves down while her lips wander over my jaw and down my neck. Her hand searches between my legs. I'm limp as a noodle. It's embarrassing to have a woman hot enough to melt butter practically molesting you, and your dick doesn't care.

"Sorry to interrupt."

Bristol's voice snaps my head up, our eyes catching in the dim light of the club over Qwest's shoulder. She's scraped her hair back tonight so she's all high cheekbones and matte red lips. I permit myself a glance over the naked shoulders in her strapless black pantsuit. The tight silk coaxes her breasts higher until they spill a little over the cups. A scarlet sash cords her waist, and her bright red heels scream "fuck me." But it's Bristol, so they could whisper it, and I'd still hear.

My dick presses against my jeans, poking into Qwest's hand and putting that knowing grin on her face. She assumes my sudden hard-on is for her, not my manager. I'm a fraud. This thing with Qwest has gone too far, and I'm going to have to do what I never wanted. I'm going to have to hurt her.

"Could we talk for a minute?" Bristol's eyes drop to Qwest's hand on my dick before popping back up and staring just past my shoulder. "I just need to go over a few things for tonight."

We've hardly spoken this week. All the hard work we both poured into this release over so many months, and when the project is colossally successful, we can barely look at each other.

"Sure," I mutter, not bothering to check if she's finally managed to look at me. "Pull up a seat."

"I need to go find Will anyway." Qwest kisses my cheek and steps away. "See you backstage."

She and Bristol exchange polite smiles on her way to climb the stage steps and disappear in the wings.

Bristol shifts from one foot to the other, touches the silky bare skin at her throat, bites her lip, moves her iPad from the crook of one elbow to the other. I sit in silence, waiting for her to settle and tell me what this is about. Finally, she sets her hip against the edge of the stage beside me.

"I know it's been a crazy week." She clears her throat, long lashes lowered and eyes fixed to the floor. "How are you?"

"Good." I keep my tone brusque. "What'd you need?"

She hesitates, probably still unused to the indifference I've displayed since our confrontation at Rhyson's house. Since the Spotted post.

"So for tonight," she says, glancing at her iPad. "We have you slated to do three songs."

"Yeah, we just rehearsed them."

"About that." Bristol sets her iPad on the stage. "I know you're doing 'Queen' with Qwest, obviously."

"Yeah, and 'Bruise.'"

"For the third song," Bristol says, tracing the edges of her iPad without looking up. "The Target executive was wondering if you'd perform a song from their Exclusive deluxe version."

I already know where this is going, but I stay quiet, waiting for her to gather the audacity to ask me to do that song.

"They want 'Top of the World,'" she says softly, hazarding a glance up at my face.

"I'm not doing that song." I give an adamant shake of my head. "Not tonight."

"Of course tonight." Bristol huffs an exasperated breath. "It's the perfect fit obviously. Your album is at the top of the charts. The song is called 'Top—"

"Do I look like I need you to break it down for me, Bristol?" The only thing moving on my face is one brow lifting. I'm barely breathing. "I understand why they want it. I'm just not doing it."

"We have a track for it. The band—"

"My not doing that song has nothing to do with having a live band or a track, and you know it." I hold her eyes captive with mine. "You didn't even want the song on the album in the first place."

"I know, but it's so good," she admits grudgingly. "It's their favorite of the ones we added. They want people to hear it and know they can only get it there."

"Too bad."

"How long are you going to do this?" Bristol asks.

"Do what?" I fold my arms across my chest, a physical barrier over the heart she jerked around like a kite for years.

"You know what."

"No, I wouldn't have asked if I knew what."

This feels good. This is my first real opportunity to growl and snarl at her since the album dropped. She's been so deliberately ghost, and I resent it. That she made this dumb decision with that dickhead and drove this wedge between us when I want to share all of this success with her. But I can't stand to look at her for more than two minutes without working myself into a rage.

"You're letting this thing with Parker color your decision making."

She dared to actually bring it up. To actually say his damn name to me.

"This 'thing with Parker', as you call it, is not the point." I slip razor blades between each word. "I'm not doing that damn song, and you and those executives can kiss my black ass."

"Wow." Irritation narrows her eyes to slits. "That's real professional."

"Professional?" I drop a laugh loaded with sarcasm. "And was it professional for you to go MIA the week of my debut release and send your junior flunky to handle me?"

It's strangely satisfying to see her cheeks flush the color of not-quite-ripe raspberries. I know I'm not being fair. Sarah did a great job, and not once did I have reason to complain. But I can't complain to Bristol about the thing I want to—the fact that she chose that entitled prick over me—so I'll complain about things that don't really matter.

She's right. Real professional, and I don't give a damn. "Hey, what's going on?" Rhyson asks from a few feet away.

Bristol and I glare at each other while we wait for him to reach us. How it got this bad, I'm not sure. I'm only sure that I'm making it worse. Every time I'm near her I want to pour accelerant all over my anger so it burns us both to ash.

"What are you fighting about?" Rhyson looks between us, his frown deepening the longer he studies our faces.

"I was telling Grip that the Target executives want him to do 'Top of the World.'" Bristol sighs like I'm a thorn in her side. "But he won't."

"Bristol, could you give us a minute?" Rhyson asks.

"What?" Her expression climbs from irritated to outraged. "This is my job, Rhyson. I don't need you to—"

"If this is your job, then I am your boss." Rhyson's tone and face brook no argument. "And I said give me a minute with my artist."

"With your art . . ." Bristol folds her lips in to stem her words and draws a calming breath that doesn't seem to be working since she's still glaring at me. "Have at it, boss man."

She stalks off, her precipitously high heels clack clacking her indignation with every step she takes across the floor.

"You know you need to do this song, right?" Rhyson hops up beside me.

"No, I'm not . . ."

Reason swallows the rest of my sentence. Of course I know I need to do the song. But the last thing I want to do is get up in front of all these happy faces and sing about the first time I kissed Bristol or how she turns me inside out like a sweater running through the spin cycle.

"I'll do it." I run my hands over my face, exhaustion from the demands of the week landing on me like a brick house. "Whatever."

"This is exactly what I warned you about." Rhyson points a finger at me.

"I know you better get your finger out of my face." Involuntarily, my lips lift at one corner, and so do his. He laughs first, a small sound that loosens some of the tension bunching at my neck and shoulders. "I don't think this is going to work, Rhys," I say quietly after the short-lived laugh.

"What won't work?"

"Bristol, us working together." I tip my head back to look at the lights overhead with their multi-colored gels. "I don't want her to manage me anymore."

"Dammit, Marlon." Rhyson leans back, arms straight, heels of his hands pressed to the stage and supporting him. "You and Bristol work incredibly well together. Look at what you've accomplished."

"I know. I just . . . I can't do it. I don't want to do it." I look at him frankly. "I'll just keep antagonizing her until everything blows up, and we'll ruin even the chance to be friends some day."

"Is that what you want?" Rhyson asks. "To be her friend?"

"You know what I want." I tap out the bass line to "Top of the World" on my leg. "Wanted. But I'm finally accepting that won't happen. I only agreed to her managing me in the first place to be closer to her. Kai and I thought it would help my chances."

"Kai was involved in this shit storm?" He shakes his head. "That's what she gets for playing matchmaker."

"Her heart was in the right place." A bitter breath gushes past my lips.

"Mine wasn't, I guess. You were right all those times you said I should give up on Bristol and let it go."

"Yeah, well. What do I know?" Rhyson shrugs carelessly, but when he meets my eyes, he seems more careful than a few moments before. "I mean, what if I was wrong about Bristol? I've been wrong before. Like that one time in high school I was wrong."

"We both know you've been wrong a lot more than that." My smile starts but melts before it's fully formed. "But about this you were right."

"But, maybe if—"

"What are you saying?" I bunch my eyebrows into a scowl. "It's settled. I'm not working with her anymore."

I lace my fingers together behind my neck and heave a defeated breath.

"Dude." I meet his eyes with complete honesty. "I just can't."

Rhyson searches my face for a few seconds before nodding and sliding off the stage.

"So when?" he asks.

"After Dubai." I glance at my watch to see how late it is and hop off the stage, too. "I need to get ready."

"What do you want me to tell her?"

"Nothing." I bite the inside of my jaw, enjoying the slight pain. "I'll tell her myself."

"You sure?"

"If we're ever going to be friends again, then yeah. I need to talk to her about it. Right now, I can't be her anything. Not with things the way they are. Once I'm over her and have really moved on . . ."

I leave the thought half-done and shrug, heading back to get ready for the show because I have no idea what that will feel like.

Seventeen

Grip

HIGH SCHOOL. SENIOR YEAR. SCHOOL OF THE ARTS THEATRE. Empty except for Rhyson and me. We'd snuck up to the catwalk and, legs kicking over the sides, dreamed out loud. Compared to the success he'd had early in life as a concert pianist, Rhyson's dreams to write and produce music for other artists seemed modest. Mine, which were to be a voice to our generation, hear my music on the radio, and reach fans all over the world, seemed loftier than the catwalk we sat on that day.

Now Rhyson's onstage introducing me, applauding with everyone else in the packed club as I join him. I can't help but wonder if he ever thinks about the dreams we spoke into existence that day, the ones we worked into existence over the last decade.

"Here's the man with the number one album on the charts," Rhyson says, his smile wide and familiar. "How's it feel, man?"

"Surreal," I say into the mic. "I can't even believe it." "Well, believe it," he says. "You deserve it."

And I don't have to wonder if he thinks about that day, about those dreams. It's sketched on his face. The pride in his eyes and the excitement that practically vibrates off him. It isn't just my album. It's his label, something we're building together.

"Anything to say before you perform for us?"

"Just thanks to everyone for all the support." I look out over the crowd, straining to pick faces out of the clumps of people. I shield my eyes with one hand from the glare of the lights. "My mom's here somewhere."

"Over here, baby!" she screams from the left corner, making everyone laugh.

"You believed in me against every odd, Ma." I struggle to keep a smile in place, swallowing the emotion thickening in my throat. "There's no telling where I'd be if it weren't for you and every sacrifice you made so I could be here today."

"I love you," she yells back.

"Love you, too, Ma." I scan the room, packed but not so big it doesn't feel intimate. "Max and Sarah, all the engineering guys. Everyone who worked on the project, Prodigy's first, you guys are amazing. Thank you for all your hard work. Let's keep doing it."

Whoops and cheers come from the corner of the room where I know a good portion of the Prodigy team are gathered.

I could leave it there, move right into the three-song set and get this over with, but I can't. Even when we're barely speaking, when I can hardly look at her without getting pissed off, I can't ignore that so much of this night and of my debut album's success, I owe to Bristol. I don't have to scan the room or search the crowd. She's the compass in every room. I always seem to know exactly where she is. Where she always is when I perform. Backstage left.

"And Bristol."

I swing my head around to that spot where she usually watches from backstage. She's standing there, all business and sex in her suit, with her phone and those lips and those breasts and those heels that would dig into my ass with a sweet sting. Hearing her name catches her off guard, and she doesn't have time to pull that mask in place or blink away that vulnerability from her eyes. She's waiting, unsure of what I'll say considering how things stand.

"You take everything to another level," I say softly into the mic, unable to look away from the promise of storm in her cloud-gray eyes. "You're the hardest working, most committed person I know. Your passion for my work has been evident since the day we met. Tonight wouldn't be tonight without you."

"Thank you," she mouths, blinking rapidly and biting her lip.

There's no one in the room but her right now. We may as well be alone at the top of that Ferris wheel, lips seeking and hungry, trading breaths and heartbeats. The cheers, all eyes in the club on me, none of it registers. There's a web that traps us together, silky and fine, tensile and fragile. A sticky mess I've never wanted to escape until now.

Maybe it's time to let go …

I turn my attention back to the crowd before it gets awkward and make my smile as natural as possible. I have to shake this off. Truly this is the moment I've been waiting for and working for, and I'm not going to let my obstinate, misplaced feelings for Bristol ruin it.

"Where's Qwest?" I boom into the mic.

The room explodes with wolf whistles and catcalls and suggestive remarks as Qwest swaggers onstage, one hand wrapped around a mic, the other hand wrapped around her hip. Oversized safety pins tenuously hold scraps of material together on her tight, curvy body. Very little is left to the imagination, and I bet every man in here is imagining.

Except Rhyson, of course. He's backstage cuddled up with his wife, I'm sure.

The first hard beat of "Queen" drops, and it's like opening the gate on a charging bull. As my first verse starts, Qwest circles me in a sensual stalk that elevates the sexual tension so high the whole audience is probably lightheaded. When I reach the chorus, she bends over in front of me and starts twerking. I can barely get the words out I'm laughing so hard, and the audience is eating it like dessert. Camera phones flash all over capturing this. It'll be on YouTube, Instagram, Twitter, and anywhere else they can find to upload it before the night is through.

When our song is over, Qwest wears my outer shirt as usual tied around her waist. At least tonight I'm wearing a T-shirt under it. I don't want to perform this next song with chest and abs out. "Bruise" means too much. I don't want to set it up, explain it, excuse it, defend it, or make either side of the black and blue debate feel better or worse.

"This song is called 'Bruise,'" I say simply and quietly once Qwest has left the stage. "It's my next single, and I hope the lyrics speak for themselves. I hope they speak up for the kids in my neighborhood who get pulled over for nothing or whose dignity is dinged and chipped from the time they understand what those flashing blue lights mean. I hope my words rise up on behalf of my cousin Greg and other cops who put themselves in the line of fire every day, running toward the dangers the rest of us flee. I hope this song is a dirge for lives lost on both sides of a debate that has divided us, when we should unite. I hope this song is common ground."

The last chorus is more spoken word than rap, with the music and the beat falling away. A capella. When the final word leaves my mouth, disappearing into thin air, it lands in the total silence I've come to expect when people hear the song for the first time. A silence loaded with contemplation. The sound of walls dropping and assumptions combusting. Ignorance running from the room. The trickle of applause swells to the loudest it's been all night in here, and now, my smile is real. That dream I sketched in the air with Rhyson, suspended above a theatre, to be a voice for my generation, that just happened.

I check stage right where I saw Rhyson last. He wears the same look he did the first time he heard "Bruise", like his eyes open wider every time. He grins and tosses his chin up. Amir stands just behind him, and I'm struck by the two friends who have been mainstays in my life. They come from completely different paths and are completely different types of men, but they are both exactly what I need them to be.

Seguing from "Bruise" into the last song I'd ever want to perform tonight is tough. I'd usually talk a little about the story behind the song, but "Top of the World" is no one's business but mine and Bristol's. Or I'd share what it was like to write it, but it wrote itself on a night when I couldn't sleep. I'd fucked some random chick, whose name I'm ashamed I can't even remember. The smell of her perfume clung to my sheets, hung on my body. She lay curled up beside me, sweaty, naked, and sated. Disgust and frustration and loneliness and longing waged a blood war in my veins while I wondered what Bristol was doing at that very moment. If she was in bed with some other guy, thinking of me. Or if she was in bed with some other guy, and I wasn't on her mind at all. And, yeah, I hated her. For a sliver of a second, I hated her for throwing up road blocks and smoke screens and barriers every time I got close enough to see she felt the same way. And there was just enough hate and too much passion to hold in. So, I'd rolled out of bed, lit a joint, and these words puffed from my lungs and fell from the burnt tips of my fingers.

I can't say any of that, so I just signal the drummer to drop the beat. And my tongue is a stiletto that breaks the seal of my lips. It cuts the lining of my jaw, every word slitting my throat. I'm bleeding out over the infectious sample of Prince's "I Wanna Be Your Lover," in a room full of people, and none of them know.

I exit the stage with the sound of their applause battering my ears. I hope the executives are happy with the pound of flesh I just carved out of myself for them. I hope Bristol's happy, too, hearing my feelings spread out and tied down on an altar like a still-breathing sacrifice for slaughter. I brush past her in the wings, deliberately not looking at her face. It's the first time I've performed the song live, and I hate it as much as I did the night I wrote it. And I love it just as much, too.

With the hard part—the performance—behind me, I'm determined not to waste another moment brooding over the woman who wants someone else, or at the very least, doesn't want me. We're popping bottles and celebrating in earnest. Only my mother would look right at home in VIP and with her very own bottle of Ace of Spades.

"Baby, I'm so proud of you." She takes a delicate sip straight from her bottle. "When Marlon was growing up, I always said my baby won't have any strikes. That was all I wanted. My dream for him was just staying out of jail and not having a bunch of nappy headed kids running wild all over the neighborhood."

"Ma, in your stories, why my imaginary kids always gotta have nappy heads?" I tease her with a grin, drawing from the bottle of Cristal on the table beside me.

"Because your imaginary baby's mama has no idea what to do with their hair." She cackles and passes a fresh bottle to Amir. "Then Grandma has to come in with bows and brushes to save the day."

Everyone cracks up. Kai and Qwest sit on either side of my mom, and her hilarious commentary keeps them in stitches. Luke, our friend since high school and a certified pop star in his own right, has been in the studio nonstop recording his next album, so he looks like a convict on furlough. He signed to Prodigy shortly after Kai. Bristol manages them both.

"Luke, where's Jimmi?" I ask. "I miss her crazy ass."

"She's in London." Luke's blue eyes are slightly glazed, maybe from smoking a little something. "She'll be back in a couple of weeks. Hates she missed it."

"She texted me, but I haven't had a chance to open it," I tell him. "She's actually back next week," Bristol pipes up from the corner of the velvet sectional taking up the entire wall of the VIP section.

Jimmi is the only non-Prodigy artist Bristol manages. They met on that fateful spring break trip, too, years ago and have been close ever since. If there's trouble to be gotten into, they'll get into it together. Jim's one of the few people who can corrupt Bristol into outrageous behavior.

Like walking naked into the ocean at midnight.

I didn't ask for the image of Bristol's long, slim body nearly naked plunging into the Pacific between waves and moonlight, but it floats to me unbidden. I wonder if she ever thinks about that night. About that string of nights when she pulled me into her unexpected depths where I've been drowning ever since.

"Well, if it isn't The One!" a slightly accented voice yells from a few feet away.

Hector, the owner of my favorite strip club in New York, Pirouette, crosses the space with sure, swift strides. His real name is Martin, but "Hector" suits his image of the first-generation Cuban-American who pulled himself up by the proverbial bootstraps. He launched his first high-end strip club in Miami, and New York soon followed. "Hector" has become infamous. His own mama probably doesn't call him Martin anymore.

"This is amazing, Grip." Hector squeezes into a small space between Amir and me, gaining a deep frown from my friend/bodyguard/babysitter. "Feels like just yesterday you were in the strip club spinning for my grand opening in New York."

"That didn't even feel like work." I laugh because it's been a long time since I deejayed, and I miss it. "I haven't done it in forever."

"Come do it again!" Hector pushes an impatient hand through the dark hair that keeps flopping into his eyes. "You know we're opening a Pirouette here in LA in two weeks."

"For real?" I take another swill of my drink. "You doing big things."

"Be bigger if I had Mr. Number One spinning on opening night." Hector's already-impassioned expression brightens even more if that's possible. "And you and Qwest could perform 'Queen.'"

His VIP visit feels less spontaneous and more calculated with every idea he unpacks. I glance over at Qwest, but she's so deep in conversation with my mom, she didn't hear Hector's proposition.

Great.

Now I'll never convince Ma that Qwest and I aren't planning weddings and baby showers.

"We'll have to check Qwest's schedule." I take another look around our group. "I don't see her manager Will right now, but I can put you in touch."

"I hear Qwest's people drive a hard bargain," Hector says.

"Not as hard as Grip's people do," Bristol inserts, scooting down so she can hear the conversation.

"Well, hello there, mami." Hector's eyes touch every inch of Bristol from her bare shoulders to the heels stretching her already-long legs out farther. "I don't believe I've had the pleasure."

"Hector, this is my manager Bristol," I say, my tone void of any warmth. I know Hector. I may not get to have Bristol, but there's no way I'm letting a sleaze bag like Hector anywhere near her.

"Nice to meet you." Bristol extends her hand, giving me an "is this guy for real" look when he lingers over her hand with a kiss. "When does your club open?"

"In two weeks." Hector drops his glance to Bristol's chest. She pretends not to notice but slides a few inches away from him and discreetly wipes her hand against the side of her pants.

"We'll be just getting back from Dubai." Bristol frowns and squints one eye. "But we may be able to make it work. I'll talk with Will to check Qwest's schedule."

"Did I hear my name?" Qwest excuses herself from the conversation with my mom and Kai, heading over to our corner where she plops on my knee. On reflex my hands go to her hips, steadying her. Bristol's eyes linger on my hands touching Qwest, but I refuse to read into it like I've done in the past. I refuse to think it bothers her.

"I have a few things I need to check." Bristol stands, smoothing a few wrinkles from her pants. "I'll reach out. Grip has your info, right?"

"He does, but I don't have yours." Hector's glance slides from her breasts and over her hips and legs before crawling back up to her face.

"Like I said, I'll reach out," she says wryly before turning to walk away.

Hector leans back to watch her go.

"Damn, Grip," he mutters, eyes still glued to Bristol crossing the room. "Your manager is fine as fuck. She like a little color in her life?"

He rubs his chin and waggles his eyebrows. "Like the color brown?"

"Not happening." The words come out like pellets, and irritation tightens my hands on Qwest's hips. She turns her head to study my face, which I know must look like a tundra.

Hector eyes Qwest in my lap.

"Seems to me you got your hands full, bruh." He laughs. "If you ain't hitting that, somebody needs to."

"She's got a man." Qwest leans back on my chest so her head snuggles into my neck. "She's dating Charles Parker. Right, Grip?"

Hector's face lights up with a cocky grin. "I got something for her I bet he ain't giving her."

"The hell you do," I snap. "Don't even think about it, Hector. Keep your greasy hands and beady eyes to yourself."

For a few seconds, our tight circle goes quiet. I feel Qwest studying me closely. The rein I've had on myself all night, all week, is slipping. I want to get out of here and take this face off. Take these reins off and just . . . rage in my loft playing something angry like Public Enemy at full blast. As much as I want to ignore it, forget about it, I'm still mad as hell that Bristol isn't mine. And pretending I don't care is wearing my ass out.

"She's Rhyson's sister and my friend." I harden my eyes when they meet Hector's. "And if you want me performing at your opening, take her off your hit list."

"You got it." Hector's hands go up defensively. "I wouldn't be a red-blooded male if I didn't try. You say she's off limits, she's off limits."

I jerk my head in a nod and gulp down a mouthful of Cristal and irritation.

"You okay, baby?" Qwest leans back and turns her head so she can whisper in my ear, her back pressed to my chest, her ass pressed into my crotch.

"Yeah. I'm good. Just tired." I roll my neck against the tension vising it. "It's been a long week."

I rub her arm, regret nipping at my insides because I don't think I can let this thing go on with Qwest much longer. It's gone deeper than it was supposed to. She's gone deeper than she was supposed to, and the longer I put this off, the worse it will be.

"I've got something to make you smile." She sits up, clapping as Will comes into our section. "You made it!"

"Yes, barely." Will hands her a black velvet box. "Traffic was a beast because of some accident."

"Thank you." Qwest takes the box and then turns to me. "A little gift to celebrate the number one spot."

"Oh, wow." A surprised breath escapes my lips. "I didn't expect anything. You didn't have to do this."

"I wanted to, and don't say wow till you've seen it." Qwest puts the box in my hands, eyes lit with anticipation. "Go ahead. Open it."

It's gotten quiet, and everyone's conversations have died out as they watch and wait for me to open the box. When I pop open the lid, I'm nearly blinded by the bling.

"Shit." My jaw drops. A diamond and platinum watch glints against the black velvet bed. "What the . . . Qwest, you really didn't have to do this."

"Well, I noticed you wearing this thing." She gestures to the non-descript black watch I always wear. "And I knew I needed to light that wrist up."

I bite back an objection when she undoes my old watch, which is made of nothing but cheap rubber and vivid memories. That day at the carnival, I won Bristol a whistle and she won me this no-name watch. We joked that they were the worst carnival prizes we'd ever seen, but I can count on one hand the times I've taken that watch off since that carnival. And now this mammoth, glittering hip-hop cliché is strapped to my wrist, and I already can't wait to get home so I can shove it to the back of a drawer.

"I don't know what to say." I turn my arm back and forth, the overhead lights bouncing off the watch and making me squint. "It's . .

. I've never had anything like it."

"Lemme see," my mother says. She comes over, grabbing my arm and admiring the watch. "Ooooh, Erica. So nice."

"Erica?" My eyes flick between my mother and Qwest.

"She told me to call her by her real name," Ma crows. "Ain't that sweet?"

"That's great." I look around on the floor and the couch, unreasonable panic ripping through me. "Where's my watch?"

"What do you mean?" Qwest frowns, looking down at my wrist. "You're wearing—"

"No, the other one." I move her off my lap and bend to search the darkened floor. "The black one. It was just here. Where . . ."

It doesn't take the strange looks from Qwest and Ma to know I sound like an idiot. I've barely glanced at the expensive new watch, but I'm on the verge of losing my shit because I can't find some cheap watch no one would even want.

But I want it.

"Do you see it?" I ask my mother. "Check down by your feet." "Baby, I don't see it," Ma says with a laugh. "But I doubt you'll miss it."

I don't answer as I continue to scan the floor and couch around me.

"Got it!" Amir says from the floor on his hands and knees. "I guess it fell."

He hands it back to me, and my heart slows. I almost had a stroke when I thought I'd lost the thing. Losing Bristol has left me in even more of a panic, only it isn't evident on the surface. It's like pins under my skin. Needles under my scalp.

Of all things, my stomach growls loudly. I frown and realize I'm starving.

"Do they have actual food here?" I ask no one and everyone. "Or is it all libation?"

"See he always had a way with words," Ma brags, touching Qwest's hand. "You know he started with poetry. Won a poetry contest in the sixth grade and has been writing ever since."

"Ma, don't," I groan. I know she's going to embarrass me. That's a given. It's just a matter of how much.

"I actually think I have a picture here." She digs around in her purse and pulls out a falling-apart wallet. "Here we go."

"I wanna see!" Qwest laughs and settles down beside my mother. "So do I." Kai shoots me a wicked grin. She knows I hate this stuff. "Are there any naked baby pictures in there?"

"Food?" I repeat. "Is there any?"

"Why don't we go back to the house?" Ma doesn't look up from the stack of pictures ranging from toddlerhood to adolescence she must carry in her purse. "I could make chicken and waffles."

"I vote for that," Amir says, smacking his lips. "I haven't had chicken and waffles in a long time."

"Boy, you came by the house last week and had chicken and waffles," Ma says.

"I know." Amir rubs his stomach. "A week is a long time in waffle years."

"Did that actually just come out of your mouth?" I raise both brows. "For real, bruh? Waffle years?"

He doubles up, flipping me off with both middle fingers.

"Okay." I stand up. "I'm gonna go grab my stuff from the dressing room before we head out."

Amir stands with me, but I wave him back to his seat.

"Please don't try to 'guard' me," I say. "I hate it when you do that."

"It is my job."

"Well, right now you're getting paid to sit your ass back down and leave me alone for a few minutes."

"Give a man a little money." Amir grumbles, grins, and takes his seat. "And he gets all new on you."

I'm still smiling about that when I enter the dressing room to collect my bag and the clothes I wore to the venue. I almost run right over Bristol leaving as I enter.

"Sorry." I grab her to keep her standing upright. I intend to let her go, but my palms linger on the warm, silky skin of her shoulders.

"No problem." She steps back, looking up the few inches to my face, her eyes guarded. "I was just, um, leaving. Straightening up and then leaving."

I notice her hands behind her back, and the shifty look on her face.

"What you got there?" I reach behind her, but she steps back, deeper into the room and out of my reach.

"Nothing." She shakes her head, a self-conscious smile tugging at the fullness of her lips. "It's just . . . nothing."

"If it's nothing, why are you hiding it?"

I slide my hands down her arms until I encounter her death grip on the handles of the bag. I don't bother actually reaching for the bag, but give myself a few seconds with her pressed against my chest. She swipes her tongue over her bottom lip. I'm riveted by the motion of her tongue and how her breasts lift against my chest as her breath shallows. Her lashes flutter closed, and her sigh lands heavily in the quiet dressing room. She steps out of my hold and offers the bag to me, breaking the moment fusing our bodies together.

"For me?" I glance from the brightly wrapped box in the bag to find her gnawing on her lip, a tiny frown sketched above her eyes.

"Just a little something for, you know." She gestures vaguely in the air. "Congrats or whatever."

"Oh, you shouldn't have," I murmur, setting the bag on a side table so I can open the box.

She starts toward the door. "Well, I'll just—"

"Hold up." I gently shackle her wrist, pulling her up short and stopping her from leaving. Our eyes collide over her shoulder. "Don't you want to stay while I open it?"

"Obviously not." She tugs on her wrist uselessly. "Grip, come on. Let me go."

"I've been trying to," I say softly. "It's harder than you think."

She stops struggling, going still in front of me and pulling a breath in through her nose, huffing it past those cherry red lips. A fiery chord bridges the distance between our bodies, and I want to pull her close enough to burn me, to hurt me, to destroy me. Sometimes I don't think I care as long as she's close. I just want to feel her, even if it burns me alive.

But she pulls away.

"Like I said, it isn't much." She shrugs, clasping her hands in front of her while I rip the paper away. "Just something I kind of picked up on a whim."

When I open the box and see what's inside, I'm like a kid at Christmas. The limited edition silver Jordans with the black sole and laces are like polka dot unicorns for a collector.

"You say you got these on a whim, huh?" I take them out and resist the temptation to remove my boots and put them on right now.

"Yeah." She shrugs, but I don't miss the anxiousness in her eyes or the way she twists her hands. "Just thought you might like them. I know they're not—"

Her words fall off a cliff when I hook an arm around her neck and pull her against me. I drop the shoes and bring my other hand to her waist.

"That's some whim." My voice dips to a husky whisper that disturbs wisps of hair escaping by her ear. "Considering there's only maybe ten pairs of these ever made."

"Really?" The word comes out high and breathy, and the controlled line of her mouth melts and softens. "I had no idea."

I drop my head until my forehead presses against hers.

"Thank you, Bris." I sneak a kiss into the hair pulled back at her temple. "I meant what I said tonight. I know how much you've done for this project. How much you've done for me."

She only answers with a nod, but her lashes fall to cover her eyes, and her hand holds me at my hip as if she might fall if she lets go. I'd love for us to fall together.

But we can't. Or she won't. Whatever it is, I refuse to let this feel like something it's not. Or something she won't allow it to be because I'll go to my grave believing Bristol cares about me. That doesn't do me any good when she chooses to be with someone else. And at least for now, so am I.

"I better get going." I pull back, but somehow, my hand finds her neck, and my thumb caresses the warm skin over her hammering pulse. Somehow, her hand is still at my waist. "My mom's making chicken and waffles."

"Sounds good." She looks at me, and though we both keep asserting that we need to go, we can't seem to separate.

"You wanna come?" I know she won't, but the question is out before I can stop myself.

"Um, I doubt your mother would appreciate that." Bristol looks at the ground, a wry grin teasing one corner of her mouth. "She and Qwest seem to be getting along well, which is great. I'm glad. I'm happy for them ... for you."

She nods, like she's convincing herself as much as she's convincing me.

"I'm ... yeah. Okay." She raises her glance from the floor. "Maybe I'll come another time. I've never had chicken and waffles together."

The smiles we trade carry traces of sadness. I don't know what we will become. I'm not looking forward to telling her she won't be my manager anymore. Obviously, any hope that we'll be lovers is fading fast. And I can't stand by and watch her with that asshole, so even friendship feels like torture. Whatever we will be, for a few minutes, we're ... us. All I've ever wanted was for Bristol and me to be an us. I don't know what that looks like anymore, but I'll fight to keep her in my life.

Later.

But not while I can still taste her wild kisses in the fun house from years ago, where even distorted in mirrors, our bodies looked right together. So letting go of the us I always thought we would be . . . it's too soon for that.

"I better get going," I say. "They're waiting for me."

My hand falls from her neck, and the fluorescent lights glint off the watch on my wrist. Bristol's eyes follow my arm down to my side.

"Nice watch," she says, her eyes set on the gaudy thing that feels like an albatross tied around my wrist.

"Yeah." I lift it for my own inspection.

Her lips concede a smile before leveling out.

"Grip, Ms. Mittie said come on!" Amir's voice reaches us just before the door opens and he appears, flicking a surprised glance between Bristol and me. "Oh, sorry. I didn't know you were in here, Bristol."

"It's okay." She smooths her hair. "I was just going. I assume you're in for chicken and waffles?"

"Best believe it." He grins a little uneasily, still not sure what he walked in on. "You coming?"

"No, I need to go," she says, glancing at her watch.

"Parker waiting for you?" I ask grimly. The thought of him at her house, in her bed, or her in some penthouse with him, erases the goodwill of the last few moments.

"No." She looks back over her shoulder, one brow lifted at the return of my censure. "He's still in India."

She makes her way to the door, stopping to give Amir a hug. He's one of those few she loves. They couldn't be more different, but they get each other. In the beginning, I was their common denominator, but they've formed their own friendship over the years.

"Your passport is current, right?" She pulls out of the hug and pats the side of his face affectionately. "You ready for Dubai?"

"More than ready." Amir rubs his hands together. "I hear they got some of the most beautiful scenery in the world."

"I have a feeling you're not talking about the landscape." She laughs and heads for the door. "Sarah will get you all the details."

"Hey, Bris," I say.

She turns to me, the ease she shared with Amir evaporating as she waits for me to finish. "Speaking of Sarah, why don't you let her reach out to Hector?"

"Sarah?" She frowns, but nods. "Okay. Why?"

I could tell her that soon Sarah will be handling all of my day-to-day. Or I could tell Bristol that Hector has a thing for her, and I don't like guys who have a thing for her.

"Why not?" I counter, since we don't already have enough to argue about.

"Because it's my job." She rests a fist on either hip. "Because I'm usually the first point of contact, and—"

"How did Rhyson put it earlier?" I touch my chin and glance up at the ceiling like I'm trying to remember. "Oh, yeah. If this is your job then I'm your boss, and because I said so."

That goes over about as well as it did when Rhyson said it, but the irritation clouding her expression when she leaves is better than what we were feeling before Amir came in. A bristly Bristol is safer than the vulnerable one who makes me want to kiss her and make her scream my name.

"So?" I grab my box of one-of-ten kind Jordans and head for the door, checking to see if Amir is following. "Chicken and waffles?"

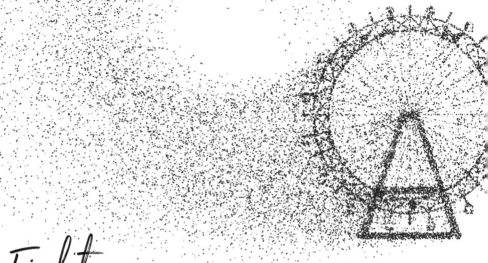

Eighteen

Bristol

ARE YOU THERE, GOD? IT'S BRISTOL.

Please make it stop.

For the love of all that's holy, if Qwest kisses him one more time, I'm breaking out my Dramamine. And the woman has a perfectly good, overstuffed leather seat. Must she perch on Grip's knee the whole time? The poor man's leg must be asleep by now. I mean, sure she's small, but still ... all that ass ...

Whoever said traveling by private jet was "flying in style" was never trapped in close quarters with the hip-hop lovebirds, also known as Grip and Qwest, for sixteen hours.

They look great together. Perfect together. I get why their fans still have #GripzQueen trending and want more of them as a couple. It's great. He's moved on. He looks happy. She's happy. Hell, even his mother is happy. In a small way, I helped orchestrate this. The least I can do is watch my handiwork unfold.

Only I can't.

I pull my sleep mask over my eyes and lie back. I'll just drift off into the darkness, take advantage of the quiet.

"Excuse me, Bristol." A low whisper comes from beside me. So much for quiet.

I lift one corner of the mask to peer at Meryl in the seat beside me.

"Sorry." She nudges her glasses up the bridge of her nose with an index finger. "I had a few questions."

Of course you do.

"Yes?" I draw on my dwindling reservoir of patience to respond with some civility. The girl has been our freaking shadow, and I'm regretting bringing her with us to Dubai, but I don't see where we had much choice. The price you pay for publicity.

"When do I get my sit-down with Grip and Qwest together?"

"It will be the middle of the night when we arrive in Dubai," I reply. "So we'll go to sleep, acclimate our bodies some. I thought you guys could do the interview over brunch tomorrow?"

"Oh, that works." Meryl jots something down in the notebook I've never seen her without. "And the desert shoot with Grip? Can that still happen?"

"Yes. I just need to confirm details with my liaison there. I think it can happen tomorrow afternoon, if your photographer will be ready?"

"Yeah, should be fine." Meryl looks down the aisle to where the photographer she brought along snores faintly. "I think he wants to keep it simple."

"Simple we can do." I lower the sleep mask and cross my fingers that she'll leave me alone.

"I've never flown on a private jet," she says. "Hmmm." I refuse to encourage her.

"I guess you have, huh? I mean, you're dating Charles Parker, so of course you've been on a private jet. We saw the pictures."

"Hmmm."

My monosyllable won't give this little newshound anything she doesn't already have. Parker said he would "take care of" the media's impression that we're dating. He needs to deal with it soon.

I've never been sure I believed in God.

My family wasn't religious in the least. In a clan of prodigies and pianists, a concert hall was our cathedral. But here in a vast desert of Dubai, I'm positive that only the deft hand of a higher power could have crafted beauty like this. Not the rolling landscape of sand and sun, but the right angle of jaw lightly dusted with shadow, the bold slant of cheekbones, the heavy sweep of brow and lashes, the lavish spread of soft lips and white teeth.

"Grip, could you turn a little to your left for me?" the photographer asks from behind his rapidly clicking camera. "That's it, and just prop your foot up?"

Grip bends his knee, setting his foot against the quad bike he's leaning on. Wide rips in his dark wash jeans flash the sculpture of muscles in his thighs. The slashes in his Straight Outta Compton T-shirt give glimpses of the bronzed skin wrapped around his ridged torso. Even in the hour we've been out here on the glorious Red Dune, the sun has bronzed him, heated the rich, caramel-colored skin to a deeper hue. "We almost done?" Grip asks for maybe the tenth time. "It's hot as hell out here."

"Sorry." Meryl scrunches her expression into an apology. "Paul, how close are we to getting what we need?"

"Just a little bit longer," Paul says distractedly, still snapping photos. "I want to get a few more before the light changes."

"If by light you mean that sun beating down on my head for the last hour," Grip says, a grin tipping one side of his mouth. "I'm ready for it to change."

"Sorry." I say. "Almost there."

His eyes flick to me briefly, sliding over my arms and shoulders in the tank top I've tucked into my black jeans. He hasn't looked at me, has barely spoken to me since we landed in Dubai. As much as I've pushed him away, avoided him, I miss looking into his eyes and seeing the things we don't say to each other, but feel, even though I've never voiced those feelings to him, and probably never will. One day I'll look into his eyes and they'll be void of whatever he felt for me before. It'll be gone because I killed it. Maybe it's already dead.

"And we're done." Paul lowers his camera and squints up into the bright sun overhead. "Just in time."

Grip relaxes against the ATV, running big hands over his head. His hair has grown just a little since he cut out the locs. Still not long enough to pull.

Right. Must stop thinking of someone else's man in terms of pulling his hair when he comes inside me since . . . he never will.

"Any chance I could take this thing out?" Grip asks the guide who brought us out here, patting the huge ATV.

"To-to ride, yes?" the man asks in his stilted English, his expression uncertain.

"Yeah." Grip's smile is all persuasion. "Come on. I'll sign a waiver or whatever anyone else would do."

"Alone?" the guide asks with a frown.

"I was gonna take her with me." I'm knock-me-over-with-a-feather shocked when Grip tips his head at me. Since he's barely acknowledged me in days. "You down to ride, Bristol?"

Maybe it's the desert heat suddenly beading sweat on my neck, sand in my throat so I can't breathe easily. Maybe I didn't eat enough at lunch, and

I'm lightheaded. More likely, it's Grip's gorgeous eyes waiting on me, resting on me when he's barely looked at me in what feels like forever.

"Um, well . . . I guess so." I search his face for some clue in this puzzle.

"Good." He nods and turns to the guide. "There's a set path, right?"

"Yes, but . . ." The poor little man still isn't sure, but sighs and relents. His supervisor probably told him to give the rich Americans whatever they want. Being guests of the prince probably doesn't hurt our case. "I'll get papers."

"And you'll take them back?" Grip points to Meryl and Paul. "Yes, of course."

I glance at Meryl because I feel her glancing at me.

"So I guess I'll see you guys back at the hotel," I direct my comment to Meryl and her curious eyes. "The party is at eight o'clock."

"I'm not sure how to dress for a royal Sweet Sixteen Party," Meryl says, splitting her attention between me and Grip, who's signing paperwork.

"I'd skip it if I could. I'm so ready to go home tomorrow."

"I guess I'll have everything I need for the story," Meryl says. "I think it's going to be awesome, especially with Grip hitting number one, and this gorgeous setting for the cover."

"Yep." I listen to Meryl with half an ear as Grip walks over. "Thanks for everything, Meryl."

Grip's slow smile makes a little bit of color bloom on her cheeks. I, unlike him, am not oblivious to her crush. "I can't wait to see how it turns out. See you at the party tonight."

Without waiting for her response he returns to the guide who has the helmets for him.

"Come on, Bris," he yells, swinging his leg over the ATV.

"See you tonight," I tell Meryl hastily as I go to join him.

The guide gives us some quick instructions. Grip nods, but it's obvious he's only half-listening. He and Rhyson love these things. The prospect of riding one on the Red Dunes has him excited and impatient to get on with it.

I climb on the back, not sure about this. Not sure why he asked or why I'm going. I slip my arms around his warm, hard body. My fingers brush against ladders of muscle peekabooing through the rips in his shirt. I jerk my fingers back, unprepared for the jolt the intimate touch sends through me.

"Hold on," Grip says, his voice a little muffled by the helmet. "Or fall off. Those are your options."

Riding wrapped around that hot, hard body, my thighs bracketing the power of his? The center of my body fitted to the curve of his ass? And the primal growl of this desert beast carrying us over the sand, vibrating beneath me for the duration of the ride? As horny as I am, I'll come before the ride is over. Not a good look. Using the electric boyfriend in my suitcase would be less mortifying.

"Another option would be not to ride at all." I scoot back and lift my leg to get off.

"Too late."

Before I can get any further, Grip revs the engine and takes off.

I'm forced to hold onto him tightly or get dragged by one leg. "Motherfucker," I mutter through my helmet.

"What was that?" Grip shouts over the engine.

"I said you could have warned me," I scream back.

I've seen Rhyson and Grip ride at the beach, but this is so far beyond that. The dunes climb so high and drop so low, making my stomach loop with each crest and valley. No matter how much I try to put some distance between our bodies, the motion of the vehicle, the speed of our ride pulls me inexorably into him. My breasts flatten against the wide, solid expanse of his back and shoulders. His muscles shift and flex beneath my arms with every rise, fall, twist and turn. Involuntarily, my limbs stiffen as I fight the pull toward his body, not just gravitational, but the sensual tug he always exercises on my senses.

"Relax, Bristol," Grip shouts over his shoulder. "Or you'll take us both down."

I give in, allowing the force and speed to collide our bodies. My legs mold to him, my nipples pebble at his back. I know I'm wet, and him securing my arm tighter around his waist with a rough hand doesn't help. To distract myself, I take in the scenery rushing past us. We soar over this mountain of scarlet sand, so high if I reached up to touch the azure sky, my palms might come away blue. The sun, high and saffron, splashes violet and pink through the clouds, a child playing with watercolors. Vivid color saturates the landscape, like a fresco stretched and painted, left out to dry in the sun.

We stop at the pinnacle of a dune, and just sit there for a few moments, the quad an idling beast beneath us. Grip kills the engine, swinging one leg over to get off. I carefully follow suit.

I steal a glance at Grip, who has walked a few feet away and surveys the same vibrant vista that captivated me during our ride, the helmet hanging from his hand. I take a few steps until I'm right in front of him, ready to ask what we're doing out here and why he brought me if he has nothing to say.

The guide gave him a black bandana to wear over his nose and mouth, protection from the sand flying from our wheels. With just his dark eyes and the slashing, inky brows visible above the bandana, he looks part outlaw, part Bedouin prince. He stows the helmet and pulls the bandana beneath his chin, revealing the rest of his face, the lips finely chiseled and full, the strong, square chin. He squints against the sun, his bold profile sketched into the horizon behind him, and my heart performs a perfect ten somersault.

It's so quiet, the air rides a fine line between peace and desolation. It's like we're in a vacuum, void of time. Like we're the last two people on a deserted planet, and everything except him and me and what's between us dissipates. Every thought escapes me, except one.

"I miss you," I whisper.

His head jerks around, his eyes meeting mine, going so narrow his long lashes tangle at the edges.

"You don't get to say that to me, Bristol."

I know why he says it, but it still feels like rejection.

"Grip, I just mean … your friendship. With things the way they've been, I miss us as friends."

"My friendship?" He cocks his head, a humorless laugh escaping him and echoing over the dunes. "We're not friends. Not right now."

"We are," I insist. "I need that."

"You need." Grip wads the bandana up in one hand and clenches the back of his neck with the other. "I've let you have that, let you do that, for too long. Ignore what I need. Fuck what I want. I've settled for whatever I could get from you for years."

I want him to stop, but anything I could say to stop him stalls on my lips, so he just keeps going.

"Even this setup, you managing me, was an attempt to be closer to you," he says, anger powering his words. "And what do you do? Go off and start dating that asshole. Choosing him when I've been patient. When I've been here."

The explanation I should have given him weeks ago fills my mouth, collects on my tongue. I know if I tell him the truth about Parker, it could mess things up with Qwest. And I want to. Even though it may mean the end of them, I want to. I'd rather have the back and forth of him wanting and me resisting than not having him at all. It isn't fair, but sometimes we do things that aren't fair to protect ourselves. To survive.

"I've let you make all the rules, but I'm changing them. I have to," Grip says before I can decide what I should say. "I was going to wait, but now's as good a time as any. You won't be managing me anymore."

And just like that, the words I would say are sawdust in my mouth.

"Wha-what?" I never stammer. I have this one part of him, of his life I've allowed myself, and he's taking even that away, and it makes me stutter. "What do you mean?"

"Sarah's going to handle my day-to-day—"

"Sarah?" My strident voice punctures the surrounding quiet. "Sarah isn't a manager. She's my assistant."

"I know." Grip nods, his expression pinched. "Like I was saying, she'll just handle the day-to-day stuff till I find a good fit for my manager."

"I'm a good fit!" Stupid tears dampen my eyes, and emotion watermarks my throat as the hurt rises inside me. "You have the number one album in the country. I'm not saying that's because of me, but—"

"Of course I know you're a huge part of that." He frowns and tosses the bandana back and forth between his hands. "This isn't about that."

"I did a good job." My voice falls to a dismayed whisper.

"I don't want to be your job." He blows his frustration out in an extended sigh. "I never wanted that. I wanted . . . more, and know that we're both with other people and it's obvious what I wanted can't happen . . ."

"What?" I demand, crossing my arms under my breasts, steeling my heart. "Then what?"

"I thought if I couldn't have a relationship with you, I didn't want anything."

His words crash land in the pit of my stomach. I grasp desperately at my composure, determined he's got as much of me as he'll get. My dignity at least is mine.

"But I was wrong, Bris."

His anger fading, his voice almost gentle, he reaches for my hand and dips his head to catch my eyes. I resent how my insides start melting.

"I do want us to at least be friends," he continues. "Right now I don't like who we are. Sniping at each other. The arguing and antagonism. It isn't us. I think we just need to go our separate ways and let things even out, so down the road, we can be friends again."

"So you just ruin a great partnership?" I shake my head and snatch my hand away, refusing to believe this is his solution. "When we talk to Rhyson about this—"

"He already knows."

"He knows?" Betrayal chokes my words. "You talked to him about this already? You decided this without talking to me first?"

"It isn't a decision we're making together," Grip says. "I decide who manages me, and it just can't be you right now."

I'm done with this shit. I shove my helmet back on and take my spot on the back of the ATV, waiting for him to get on.

"Bristol, let's talk about this."

"Oh, now you want to talk?" I snap. "After you've gone to my brother and gotten me fired?"

"Fired?" He frowns. "Come on. It isn't like that. You have plenty of other artists you're managing."

He doesn't get it. Of course I have plenty to do. Between Kilimanjaro, Luke, Kai, Rhyson, and Jimmi, I could have two more assistants and still need help with everything I do for all of them. But if Grip and I aren't lovers, and we're not working together, and we can't even be friends, then we're nothing. I haven't been "nothing" to Grip since the day we met.

"Take me back to the hotel," I say woodenly. "Bris."

I pour my anger into the look I level on him. "Right. Now."

He probes my eyes, and I make sure all he sees is anger. I stuff the hurt, bury the pain, keeping an impenetrable shield over my face, over my heart. He finally climbs onto the quad and starts the engine.

As we ride back, I resist the forces, physical and otherwise, that would slot our bodies together. He doesn't encourage me to hold him any tighter. He doesn't urge me to relax, to hold on, now that he's letting go. Maybe he senses that anything he said would bounce off me like a coin from a sheet drawn taut. I just want to get through this ride and back to the States. The glamour that shrouded these ruby-tinged dunes on our ride here lifts, leaving stark reality. What I thought was peace is actually the loneliness of an arid land. The Bedouin prince doesn't want me anymore, and all that's left is this dry, barren desert.

It's nothing but dust and sand.

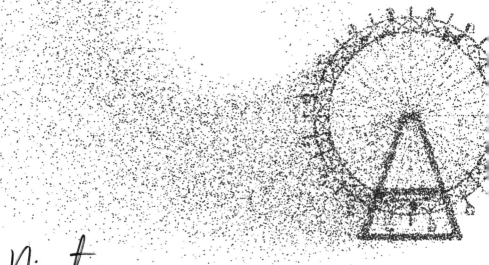

Nineteen

Bristol

HELL HATH WINGS.

This airplane is pretty much airborne hell. If I'd thought the flight to Dubai was torture, the flight home would give Dante new inspiration.

"Grip, what's wrong, baby?" Qwest asks . . . you guessed it . . . sitting on his lap.

"Nothing." He sits with his hands on the armrest while she snuggles into the nook of his arm and shoulder. "I'm good."

"You sure?" She squeezes his shoulder. "You're so tight."

"Just a long few weeks." His head drops back against the seat. "I'll be glad to get home."

"I know how to loosen you up." She inches closer and whispers in his ear, a husky laugh invading the space where Will and I sit across from them. Grip's eyes open to clash with mine. Despite my best efforts, I can't look away. I can't help but remember what he said to me that night on the roof. That I can't keep my eyes off him. It's true, but it shouldn't be an issue any more since he won't have me around. I deliberately look away and down to the phone in my lap.

"Great idea," Grip says.

They stand and walk to the back where there is a bed. I don't look up even at the sound of the lock turning. I guess it's the Mile High Club for them. My jaw clenches. My lips tighten, but otherwise I show no sign that it bothers me.

"What's wrong with you?" Will asks from beside me.

Okay. Maybe I'm not hiding it as well as I thought.

I convinced Meryl that Will and I needed to discuss a few things, so she should probably sit with the photographer. Looks like I won't fare much better with Will.

"Oh, nothing." I roll my neck and stretch in the wide legged jeans I chose to wear for the flight. "Just tired, I guess. You must admit it's been a lot lately."

"Yeah, Grip's on top."

"Qwest, too," I murmur, rubbing the denim covering my legs. "'Queen' is still number one."

"She'll want Grip for her next album. You know that. We'll need to coordinate."

A gust of air imitating a laugh rushes past my lips. "Oh, there's no doubt she'll want him."

Will turns in his seat to stare at my profile. I ignore him, taking my laptop from the bag by my seat and answering a few emails.

"What's up with you and Grip, Bristol?"

My fingers pause over the keys for just a second before I resume typing. "What do you mean?"

Will's fingers cover mine over the keyboard.

"Stop." He waits for me to look at him. "I know there's something going on. If it affects my artist, I need you to level with me. Are you guys . . ."

I fill in the blanks. He has picked up on something obviously. I'm glad I can look him straight in the eyes and tell the truth. Though, I can look people straight in the eyes and lie just as easily.

"Grip and I have been friends for a long time, Will, but it isn't like that."

"You sure?" Will asks. "Sometimes I think I pick up a vibe between you guys."

"Like I said, we've been together a long time." I shrug, slamming my laptop closed. I don't feel like faking work right now. "Friends for a long time. That's all."

"Okay, good." Will laughs his relief and leans back in his seat. "'Cause I'm pretty sure Qwest's in love with that guy."

His words spear me right through the middle. I could see that for myself, of course. She's completely into Grip. And he really likes her, but I know he doesn't love her. I don't want anyone to get hurt. If Grip stops trying with her, breaks things off, she'll be hurt. If he keeps trying and really falls for her,

I'll keep hurting. In neither scenario am I brave enough to do anything about it, to stop this train I'm at least partially responsible for setting on its course.

Sixteen hours just fly by when I don't have to stare at Grip and Qwest the whole time. They never came back out. I guess they put that bed to good use. The thought of him inside her, of her wrapped around him takes my breath with a sharp pain. I grab my bag and head toward the exit. As soon as I step onto the tarmac, I spot a black SUV with a vaguely familiar figure standing to the side. The man who accompanied Parker that night in Vegas. I think Clairmont was his name. I already know who will step out of the vehicle before Parker appears.

"You're a lucky girl." Meryl comes to stand beside me. "We can't all have billionaire boyfriends to come home to."

"Lucky me." I give her my fakest smile ever.

Will joins us, accessorizing his roguish grin with a wolf whistle. "No wonder you looked at me like I was crazy when I asked about you and Grip," Will says. "I almost forgot you have one of the richest men in the world on a string."

Right about now I'd love to choke Parker with said string.

"I'll touch base about the Pirouette gig in the morning," I say, not acknowledging his comment. I scrounge up a smile slightly more sincere than the one I offered Meryl. "I'll see you there tomorrow night. Get some rest."

I start toward the SUV like I had expected it to be there waiting. Halfway to the SUV, Parker covers the ground between us swiftly, stepping into my path.

"It's been too long," Parker says. Equal portions of ownership and lust mix in the eyes studying me. He takes my bag and snakes an arm around my waist, pulling me into him. His erection pokes my stomach, and I draw a shallow breath.

"Someone's happy to see you," he whispers through my hair, into my ear.

I can't take it. I didn't want to cause a scene, especially with Grip and Qwest deplaning behind me, but I instinctively pull out of his body lock.

"What are you doing here, Parker?" I leave my irritation close to the surface where he can see it. "How did you know I was landing today?"

"I have my sources," Parker says with a smile. "I have my ways."

He wraps possessive fingers around my elbow, and I jerk out of his hold again.

"Don't." I chop the word up and serve it cold. "You said you would fix this. To spare you the public embarrassment, I've left it to you. You've done nothing to address the rumors and then show up here like my long-lost lover. Who the hell do you think you are?"

"Who do I think I am?" His voice is a brick in a kid leather glove, a buttery soft blow. "You know who I am, Bristol, and I'm here to remind you who you belong to since you seem to think this is a negotiation. It's not. I've waited. I've been patient. That's over."

"Belong?" I keep my voice low and trap my outrage between Parker and me. I can practically feel Grip's eyes on us, and this could get ugly quick. "Parker, you're right. This isn't a negotiation because I'm giving you nothing, and I want nothing except for you to leave me the hell alone."

He grabs me again, and I jerk my arm, but this time Parker doesn't let go.

"Bristol." Grip's deep voice rumbles from behind me, and I go still, my eyes snagging with Parker's. The less contact he has with Grip the better.

I turn to face Grip, still clamped to Parker's side.

"Hey." I curve my mouth into a smile that I hope fools him. "What's up?"

His eyes move from Parker's iron hold on me to my face. The concern, the question in his eyes, doesn't bode well for things remaining drama-free.

"Everything okay?" he asks. "You need a ride home?"

"She has a ride home," Parker answers before I can. "It's Grip, right?"

Grip's icy eyes freezer burn Parker's face.

"Bristol can speak for herself." Grip's answer comes dangerously soft.

"Of course she can." Parker leaves a soft kiss at my temple. "Tell the man, Bristol."

The muscle knotting along Grip's jaw tells me I need to diffuse this. Even as angry as I am with him, I can't have him caught in Parker's crosshairs. He's mad with me, and I'm mad with him, but we're both still trying to protect each other.

"I'm fine, Grip." I loosen the hold Parker has on me so I can loop my elbow through his. "I'd forgotten Parker was picking me up."

"You sure?" He makes the mistake of touching my hand, and I feel Parker stiffen beside me. He's inspecting Grip with new, alert eyes.

"I am." I pull my hand away and pat his shoulder. "Your girlfriend is waiting. It's sweet of you to check, but I don't want to keep you away from Qwest."

He glances over his shoulder to find Qwest walking up with Will in tow, her eyes inquiring about the tableau playing out on the tarmac.

"Okay." He still doesn't seem sure, looking at Charles Parker like he might be Charles Manson. "We'll touch base about Pirouette tomorrow then?"

"I'll have Sarah call you." I inject a little venom into the statement, a small jab that he'll feel, but no one else will notice. "May as well start as we mean to go, right?"

He sighs and turns to join Qwest and Will without saying another word.

I keep my silence until we reach the SUV. I stop in front of Clairmont who stands guard at the door.

"Take me home right now." My voice and glare are low-level radioactive.

I don't wait for Clairmont's response before climbing through the open rear door and waiting for the reckoning that's long overdue between Parker and me. As soon as the door closes, I turn on him.

"Let's get something absolutely straight," I bite out. "You and I are not in a relationship. We aren't dating. We aren't getting married. I had to be so far under the influence of hard liquor I didn't even know I was in the world to fuck you again after a decade, and I guarantee that was the last time you get anywhere near this pussy."

Maybe I went too far, too hard. I've seen Parker's eyes cold, but they've always held a warm center for me. There aren't even trace amounts of heat in the subzero look he directs my way.

"Careful, Bristol." He covers my hand with his, a gesture intended to smother. "You don't want to make me angry."

"Why?" I elevate my brows to the appropriate level of disdain. "Would I not like you when you're angry? Who are you? The Incredible Hulk? And like I've told you before, you don't scare me."

"Maybe I should. Love and hate and fear and respect are all bedfellows."

"That sounds like one messed up orgy, if you ask me."

"Huh." His casual shrug comes at odds with the whipcord tension of his shoulders. "Maybe you and I will try the real thing once we're married, and you can tell me how you like it."

"I'm not a doll in the window." I shove his hand away from me and press my body into the leather seat as far from his as I can. "You don't just decide you want me and expect me to fall in line. How many ways can I tell you it isn't happening?"

"Is there someone else?" The question falls from his tongue so smoothly, but I know there's a dagger tucked into the silk of his words.

"If there were someone else, it wouldn't be any of your business."

"You know, through the years, I've given you space to sow your oats, so to speak, but I need to settle down. You've been groomed for me, Bristol, since we were kids. I'm ready for this to happen."

"You're crazy, and I don't want to see you again, Parker."

"And I want to see you for the rest of my life." He crooks stiff lips into a one-cornered smile. "Is that what they call an impasse?"

"No, an impasse is when there is no apparent solution." I channel all my frustration into my words. "I have a solution. Leave me alone. It's something stupid our parents dreamt up. Let it go."

Through the tinted window I see that we're already in my driveway. My cottage is my refuge. I need to get inside, lick my wounds from the disagreement with Grip, and shower Parker's touch away from my body.

"This is over," I tell him. "Don't call me again. Our families will, of course, remain close, but we don't have to. I don't want to."

"You don't decide how this ends, Bristol." A fiery tongue of rage licks through the cold eyes. "I do."

I nod to Clairmont, who opens the door and holds my luggage. I take the bag from him, not wanting him or Parker anywhere near my front door.

"Either you address the rumors in the press," I tell Parker, who watches me stonily from the back seat. "Or I'll do it. That's the only end you can control."

I don't look back as I make my way up the cottage drive, but I know he's still there and he's still watching. He won't let this go.

My cottage, though empty and completely quiet, welcomes me home like a friend. This place is all mine, from the decorations I personally chose to the plants I potted myself. Of all the things I've accomplished, my home is one of the things that makes me most proud.

I drag the luggage back to my bedroom and collapse onto the bed I didn't get the chance to make before I left for Dubai. The last few hours land on me like bricks. I don't even bother stripping away my clothes, but crawl in just as I am, under the fluffy duvet. I toe my boots off under the covers, leaving the shoes in the bed with me.

I have no idea how Parker will retaliate. That nefarious brain of his is hatching a plan to either trap me or to make me suffer for defying him. Not wanting him, not grasping the privilege of his desire is, in his mind, my gravest infraction. If he had an inkling of my feelings for Grip, that would add insult so egregious to an injury so deep, I have no idea how he would retaliate. But I know it would be swift and unreasonable.

On top of that, the full implications of Grip firing me unravel the last of my fraying composure. I'll have no place in his life. He wants us to "go our separate ways."

Separate?

When I've felt more connected to him than to anyone else? Even when I was spitting mad over Tessa, I felt his guilt and his regret. I felt how it tore him up that I left and gave no sign we would ever make good on the promise of the week we shared. Wanting him, pushing him away, watching him with other women, knowing I could stop it but too afraid to try. What I want more than anything, I deny myself. I deny him.

I sit up in bed, longing for all I have left of that week we shared. I open the drawer housing all my vibrators and sex toys, reaching to the very back until I touch a key. I carefully unlock the bottom drawer and pull out the worn leather volume of poetry a boy gave a girl years ago, a guarantee of his affections. The page corners are dog-eared, and the margins are filled with notes written in a brusque, masculine hand. I trace the bold strokes of Grip's handwriting, the audacious hope in his g's and p's, the impatience of the I's he took no time to dot and his hastily half-crossed t's.

I flip the page to a poem so familiar I could almost recite it backward, Neruda's "Sonnett LXXXI." In one of my favorite lines, the poet tells his love that already she is his, and implores her to rest with her dream inside his dream. That he alone is her dream. The note of possession, the inextricably linked futures, speak to me, especially with Parker's possessive claims still ringing in my ears. I would never belong to him, but how would it feel to love someone so deeply you relinquish yourself that way? To embrace the responsibility of them belonging to you. And to know whatever the future holds, you face it together. Whatever you accomplish, you celebrate together. When there is pain, you endure it together. I'm not sure I'll ever know.

Grip's scrawled note written to the side in black Sharpie cuts my heart.

Bristol, never forget our ocean. Remember our last night together. Your dream was inside my dream. Please believe that I would never hurt you. Give me a chance to explain. I need that second chance.

I can't read anymore. Not that I need to. I've read each poem, each note countless times since he mailed this book to me. By then I understood the curse I carried in my blood. Loving too deeply, too fiercely, too wholly. A love like that for the wrong man would ruin you.

I'm about to replace the book of poems when something silver in the drawer caches my eye. It's a cheap whistle, tarnished by age. I pull it out by the discolored string from which it dangles. I don't have to blow it to hear its piercing shrill. It's as sharp and clear in my head as the smell of funnel cake and the cool night air on my face at the top of a Ferris wheel.

I fall back into my bed, placing the whistle and the book of poems on the pillow beside me. They're like artifacts from another age that was marked with the promise of love. Marred with the agony of loss. It wasn't eons ago. It wasn't a light year away. It was eight years, and now the man who scrawled in these margins and presented this whistle to me like a piece of his heart, is cutting me out completely. This is all I have left of that night, of those days. Of the man who begged me to never forget.

Twenty

Grip

MY BODY HAS NO IDEA WHICH DAMN TIME ZONE IT'S IN. I COULDN'T sleep last night, but it wasn't the jet lag. I kept thinking about the interaction with Bristol on the tarmac. Something's off with Charles Parker. When Bristol jerked away from him, I knew it. I think I've known, but that one moment confirmed the suspicion I hadn't allowed to fully form until yesterday. I tried to dismiss it as a lover's quarrel, but I still found myself standing in front of them on the tarmac, prepared to punch Parker if he grabbed her like that again, even with that meathead security guard standing there.

I check my playlist one last time. Typically when celebrities deejay, there's little pressure to be any good. They don't have to actually know what they're doing. All they have to do is pick great songs and press play. But I used to live by the spin. Deejaying in between the songs I would write for other artists kept a roof over my head and ramen noodles in the pantry.

"We ready?" Hector asks from the floor.

I save the playlist I have loaded on the laptop set up for tonight before hopping down off the stage to join him.

"Yep, let's get it."

"You laced tonight, bruh." Hector points to my feet. "I heard your shoe game was beast. Which ones are those?"

"The Space Jam Blackouts." I grin and bow at the waist. "I broke out the classics for your grand opening."

"I feel honored." He laughs and looks around the stage. "Where's Qwest? She here?"

"Yeah, she's already in our dressing room and we've sound checked."

I look around the mostly empty club for anyone from my team. Sarah is at a table, her curious eyes glued to the scantily clad strippers onstage rehearsing their routines.

"Hey, let me introduce you to Sarah from the label." I start across the room with Hector falling into step beside me. "If you need anything tonight, she'll be your contact."

"Not Bristol?" Mischief sparks in Hector's eyes. "Does Qwest know you're sprung for your manager?"

"Shut up, man." I shoot him an annoyed glance that just makes him chuckle.

I'm more annoyed that he brought up my dilemma with Qwest than I am that he peeped my feelings for Bristol. I'm getting through this performance, and then I'm ending things with Qwest tonight. I have to. The flight home was a disaster. I didn't want to have sex with her, so I didn't, which definitely raised her suspicions. We shared a room in Dubai, but nothing happened. I told her I was tired and that my body was off because of the trip. Lame excuses. My dick would be ready in an outer space time zone if the need arose. It's not that she isn't beautiful. She's fine as hell.

It's that she isn't Bristol.

And as much as I wanted to try with someone hoping to get over Bristol, it isn't working. And it isn't fair. Not to Qwest. Hell, not to me. This isn't about convincing Bristol to be with me. I'm done with that shit, too. If she wants me, wants to dump Parker, she knows where to find me. That doesn't mean my feelings have changed for her. Bringing Qwest into this only made a bigger mess. One I have to clean up tonight.

"Sarah, hey," I say when we reach her table.

"Hey." She hugs me and smiles politely at Hector. "Is this Mr. Abrentes?"

I already gave her a heads-up that she would be the contact for anything Hector needs. I'll let Rhyson and Bristol determine when she finds out she'll be handling a lot of things for me until I find a new manager.

I give her and Hector a moment to talk through a few details before asking her the question that's been on my mind since I arrived.

"Sarah, have you heard from Bristol?" I ask. "Seen her?"

She's always at venues well ahead of her artists, and I've been here for more than an hour with no sign of her.

"She told me she'd be here by the time the show starts," Sarah says.

"Why so late?" The frown feels heavy on my face, so I can only imagine what it looks like. "She's usually here hours ahead."

"Oh." Sarah bites her lip and blinks a few times too many, betraying her nerves. "She said this would be a good training opportunity for me. Is that not okay?"

"No, no, it's fine." I squeeze her hand and reassure her with an easy smile. "I was just curious."

I ignore Hector's knowing grin. He's got my number now. But that's okay. Hector may be a dog, but he knows not to shit where his friends eat, to be crass about it. And even though Bristol and I aren't together, in his mind, that's where I eat. Nasty code, but it works.

I notice Sarah keeps looking back to all the nipples and ass onstage. I'm betting this is her first time in a strip club.

"Don't get any ideas, Sarah," I tease her. "Prodigy pays you well.

Don't be working that pole tonight."

She gasps her shock but laughs when she realizes I'm playing with her.

"I think I . . . no, that wouldn't . . ." Her cheeks burn pink. "I mean, I won't."

I'm halfway through spinning the first set when I spot Bristol at one of the bars. Damn, she looks good. The dress shouldn't look good. It has no shape. It just hangs off one shoulder, but every time she moves, it molds to the curves and lines of her body beneath the blue silk. The hem doesn't even hit mid-thigh, and her long, toned legs go on forever, the high heels emphasizing the cut of her calves. My mind goes blank of every image except those legs wrapped around me as I pound into her. I don't need this hard-on within fucking distance of Bristol.

The blonde beside her makes me set aside my reservations about going over. If it weren't for her, me and my hard dick would run in the opposite direction.

"If it isn't my favorite rock star," I say from behind Jimmi. She turns, squealing and hurling herself into my arms.

"I won't tell Rhyson I'm your fave if you don't." She lets out that rich, husky laugh that hints at her top-charting singing voice. "How the hell are you, Grip? I mean, besides having the number one album!"

"I definitely can't complain." I press a kiss into her soft blonde hair, which is flying all over the place. "Missed you, girl."

"I'm sorry I didn't make it to the release celebration." A grimace crosses Jimmi's pretty face. "I think I was in London that night. Great show, but I would rather have been here."

She links her arm through mine, and we lean against the bar. I don't speak to Bristol, who's sitting on a barstool with her legs crossed, and she doesn't speak to me. Jimmi bounces a glance between the two of us but doesn't comment on how tight the air is around us. Jimmi knows the score. She knows I've always had it bad for Bristol.

"Can you even believe this?" Jimmi's blue eyes soften, losing some of their usual cynicism. "When we were at the School of the Arts painting backdrops for musicals and dreaming of making it big, we had no idea. You, me, Rhyson, Luke. It's crazy."

"Right." I shake my head. "I still wake up some mornings thinking I'm supposed to be sweeping studio floors and rent's past due."

"Same here!" Jimmi's laugh mixes with the heavy beat of the Future song playing in the club. "I still have my name badge from Mick's."

"I would have starved those first few years without all the free food you hooked me up with from that place."

"Like your mom would ever let you starve." Jimmi turns to Bristol, who has been considering the stage intently ever since I walked over. "That's where we first met, Bris."

"Huh?" Bristol turns slightly glazed eyes to Jimmi. "Sorry, what?"

"Bris, what planet are you on tonight?" Jimmi bumps Bristol's shoulder with hers. "Grip and I were just talking about the good old days. Remember how we met at Mick's that first day you came for spring break? Grip brought you to lunch."

"You had on a bikini top and heels and cut-offs." Bristol scrunches her nose, her throaty laugh rich with affection. "You were such a skank."

"Yeah, well you were an uptight asshole prude." Jimmi leans into Bristol, her grin wide. "Who thought she was better than everyone else."

"I totally was." Bristol's mouth opens in a silent laugh. "I totally did."

"And Grip kept looking at you like he'd discovered chocolate." Jimmi bends at the waist, laughter shaking her shoulders.

The humor drains from Bristol's face. The club is so dark I almost miss the anger, the residue of hurt in Bristol's eyes from our argument.

"No, he didn't," Bristol murmurs into her vodka martini.

Yeah, I actually did.

Jimmi grabs Bristol's drink and gulps down most of it.

"Hmmm. That's good. I shoulda been drinking that." She licks her lips and wiggles the nearly empty glass before handing it back to Bristol. "Be a doll and get me one."

Bristol leans back, catches the bartender's eye, points to her glass, and then holds up two fingers.

"I was looking for you earlier, Bris," I say.

"Why?" Over the rim of her martini glass she spears me like the toothpick through the olive in her drink.

"You're just usually early, and I didn't see you."

"Didn't Sarah take care of you?" She cocks one brow. "I thought that's what you wanted."

"Bristol, yeah, but we need to talk about—"

"I could totally do that, Jim," Bristol cuts over my comment, gesturing with her glass toward the strippers onstage.

"Do what?" I demand, deciding not to pursue the Sarah conversation right now.

"Yeah, do what?" Jimmi asks.

"That upside-down move she's doing and make my ass clap," Bristol says, taking a sip of the new drink the bartender just gave her.

"Me, too." Jimmi sips on hers. "It isn't as hard as it looks. The one girl in the red … what was her name, Bristol?"

"Champagne," Bristol says. "I'm pretty sure she said her name was Champagne. It was something … festive."

"I think you're right." Jimmi tilts her head, her eyes never leaving Champagne as she hangs upside down on the pole, legs straight in the air. "Though they are rather athletic and well-trained, you must admit. I think one day stripping will be an Olympic sport."

"If strippers were men," Bristol says with an inordinate amount of conviction. "It already would be."

"There are male strippers," I remind her.

Bristol's withering glance makes me want to guard my testicles. "Don't you have a performance to get ready for?" She looks past my shoulder. "Where's your girlfriend? I almost didn't recognize you without her in your lap."

"Is she clingy?" Jimmi whisper-shouts as if I'm not standing right there listening. "I hate clingy girls."

"Clingy like ivy." Bristol stares into her drink, her mouth sullen. "Like a particularly aggressive strain of rabid ivy."

"Don't talk about her that way," I say. "She doesn't deserve that, Bristol, and you of all people should know that."

"Oh, me of all people?" Bristol leans across Jimmi until her nose almost touches mine. "Why me of all people?"

"You know why," I grit out.

"Why?" Jimmi interjects, round eyes ping ponging between Bristol and me.

"I didn't make you fuck her," Bristol snaps. "No one twisted your dick to sleep with her or any of the hundreds of other girls you've been with over the years."

"Hundreds?" I shake my head. "Not hundreds, but at least none of them had a stick up their ass."

"Oh, I bet there was a stick up somebody's ass at some point along the way." Bristol signals for another drink. "Maybe even yours."

"Musicians do like to experiment," Jimmi agrees. "Believe me. I know."

"Nothing has ever been up my ass," I say harshly. "And, Bristol, I think you should slow down on the drinks."

"You're not my father." She laughs bitterly. "Or maybe you are. You probably are. Yeah, you're my father."

"What the hell does that even mean?" I demand.

I don't get to the bottom of her glare because Sarah comes over to get me.

"Hey, you ready?" she asks. "Qwest is already backstage. You guys go on soon."

"Ooooh! I get to see you and Qwest perform live." Jimmi claps her hands. "I've heard you're fire together onstage."

"Oh, three-alarm fire," Bristol says sarcastically. "We had to add a hose to Qwest's rider."

"You're becoming a bitch, Bris," I snap.

"I'm factory order bitch." She toasts with her martini. "I came like this. Maybe you just never noticed."

"Grip, we gotta go," Sarah reminds me, but her worried eyes rest on Bristol.

"Stay out of trouble, Jimmi." I hook an elbow around her neck and whisper. "Watch Bristol. She's drinking too much."

"But drunk Bristol is so much fun," Jimmi whispers back.

"What are you guys whispering about?" Bristol asks, her eyes narrowed on Jimmi and me.

"You," I say without missing a beat. "Now I have to go do my job."

"How nice for you to still have a job," Bristol says, her words slurring more than they did four martinis ago. "Some of us got fired."

"Okay, Jimmi." I grab her by the shoulders to look her in the eyes. "I'm counting on you to keep her safe."

"You snot it." Jimmi cackles and sloppily covers her mouth. "I mean, you got it."

"Are you drunk, Jim?" I note her glassy eyes and flushed cheeks. She's a very functional drunk. You never realize she's drunk until she starts breaking shit and hooking up with strangers in port-a-potties. I've had whole conversations with her and not realized she was lit. I think I just had one.

"Just a little." Jimmi holds up her thumb and index finger, the smallest sliver of space separating them. "Lil' shit. I mean, lil' bit."

I search the club for Amir. I usually hate having him with me as "security", but I need him now. When I spot him talking with a very limber stripper, I know he'll hate me for breaking that up, but I wave him over.

"What's up?" He glances back over his shoulder at the girl now giving some dude a lap dance.

"Keep an eye on Bristol and Jimmi." I tip my head in their direction. "You know how they get when they drink together. It's never good."

"Got it." Amir assesses the two girls who are slumped against each other laughing over nothing.

"Break a leg, Grip," Bristol says, sober enough to be snide. "No, really. I hope you break your leg while Qwest is humping it."

I can't do this with her right now. With one more death stare, which she returns in triplicate, I head back to join Qwest in the dressing room. She's already in her skimpy costume, fake lashes on, braids spilling down to her waist. Her eyes light up as soon as I enter the room. I can't help but wonder if that's how I look when I see Bristol. If maybe sometimes, just maybe, she's ever looked that way when she saw me.

"Where've you been?" Qwest slips her arms around my waist. "My friend Jimmi is here, so we were just catching up." I set my hands at her hips, putting a little space between us. "Look, Qwest, can we talk after the performance? There's just some stuff I need to get off my chest."

"I was hoping you'd say that." She smiles up at me impishly. "I think we're on the same page."

By the mischief and lust in her eyes, I doubt that very seriously.

I'm grateful we're only doing one song. We power through "Queen," which is as energized and sexy as usual. Qwest actually steps up her game and is borderline indecent being that we're in a strip club. When in Rome.

When we come offstage and head back to the dressing room, I can tell the performance turned her on. She locks the door and presses me into a wall before we've said one word. Her tongue is so far down my throat it would take a Saint Bernard to retrieve it. I'm horny and it does feel good, but I can't do this again. I can't do this to her any more.

"Qwest," I say against her lips. "We need to talk."

Her mouth slows over mine until the kisses are just pecks on my lips and across my cheeks.

"I know." She nods, looking down at the floor. "I figured after what happened . . . or rather didn't happen . . . on the plane."

"Yeah, that's what I want to talk about."

"You don't have to. Hectic schedule. Crazy week." She gives me a sly look. "I even wondered if you might be bored."

"No, it isn't boredom. It's—"

A knock at the door interrupts.

"Who could that be?" Qwest asks in mock innocence before opening the door.

Champagne stands in the hall, her shy grin at odds with the cupless bra displaying her pierced nipples.

"Hey, Qwest." She wiggles her fingers, and her words are directed to Qwest, but her eyes are on me.

"Come on in." Qwest steps back, looking at me like I should be thanking her. "Voila."

"Sorry?" I run a hand over the back of my neck. "What is this?"

"It's your surprise." Qwest locks the door, stalking over to me and dragging Champagne with her. She leans up, kissing my neck, and nods to Champagne to get to work on the other side. Champagne's overachieving ass reaches straight for my dick, running her hand up and down my stiffening erection. I've had my share of threesomes, but having sex with Qwest hasn't solved anything. Having sex with Qwest and some random stripper certainly won't. I know how to fix this, and as much as it may hurt Qwest, I'm fixing this tonight.

"Whoa." I step out of their clutches. "What the hell? This isn't happening. Qwest, we need to talk."

"Not happening?" Champagne pushes out her bottom lip. "You promised I'd get to fuck Grip."

"Well, Grip didn't promise that you'd get to fuck Grip." I walk swiftly to the door, wrenching it open and gesturing to the hall. "Bye, Champagne."

"But will I still get—"

"See my boy Will out front." Qwest sighs, watching me as if I were a house pet who just bit her. "He'll pay you."

Once Champagne leaves, there's just Qwest and me, and all the things I need to say that may hurt her.

"I'm sorry." She walks over and loops her arms at the back of my neck. "I just thought when you couldn't get it up on the plane—"

"Hey. Don't be telling people I couldn't get it up." A sharp laugh slices the corners of my mouth. "That's how rumors get started."

"Sorry." Her smile makes a brief appearance before disappearing again. "What's going on?"

"Let's sit down." I lead her over to the plush couch in the center of the room, never letting go of her hands. "Qwest, you're an amazing girl. You're smart, funny, talented. Total package."

"If there's one thing I know," Qwest says, her full lips twisting wryly. "It's big butts, and I hear a huge *but* coming."

"But." I pause meaningfully and squeeze her hand. "This isn't gonna work between us."

"Why?" The dismay and hurt on her face drives a knife into my heart, making me feel like an even bigger jerk. "Things have been good, haven't they?"

"Yeah, but it's going so . . . fast." I shrug and look at her apologetically. "Once the media got ahold of us, it just went so damn fast. And before I knew it, we were being hashtagged and shipped and made into something other than what we said we would be. Bigger than what we said we would be."

I look at her frankly.

"I was honest from the beginning that I wasn't sure we should do this."

"But we're so good together." Tears stand in her brown eyes. "I thought we were . . . that maybe things had changed."

She bows her head, swiping at a tear.

"Things changed for me, Grip," she whispers. "I love you."

Even though my mom warned me, even sensing it myself, to actually hear her confirm it makes me feel worse.

"I told you not to do that, Qwest. You know I don't feel that way."

"You also know the heart doesn't always do what we tell it to." She lifts her head, eyes wide. "That's what this is about. It's that other bitch?"

Anger sparks life in her dulled eyes. "Grip, if you cheated on me—"

"No, I wouldn't do that to you."

Even if Bristol had turned to me, I would have broken things off with Qwest first.

I hope I would have.

"Did she finally decide she wants you?" Qwest asks, the flare of anger yielding to the hurt again. "That's why you're breaking up with me?"

"No, she still won't be with me."

The words are barely out of my mouth before Qwest is on the floor between my knees, her hands pressing my legs apart.

"Then let me have what she's missing." She pulls my zipper down, slipping her hand inside, her fingers going by memory to cup and stroke my balls.

"Qwest," I groan, pushing at her shoulders. "No. Stop."

"But you want it." She looks pointedly at my growing erection. "I know you do."

"No." I shake my head and zip my jeans. "That doesn't mean anything."

"But if she still doesn't want to be with you then—"

"But I still want to be with her." I lean my elbows on my knees and wipe a hand across my face. "Only her. Feeling this way, it isn't fair to be with somebody else. Not fair to you, and not fair to me."

"She doesn't deserve you," she whispers, leaning her head on my knee, tears now freely streaking down her face.

"But she has me." A sad smile rests on my lips as I swipe a thumb over her tears. "Whether she deserves me, whether she wants me, I'm hers, and I want her. I've tried to stop, but I can't. While that's the way it is, I can't be with you. I won't do that to you anymore. I won't do that to anybody. You deserve better."

A heavy knock at the door interrupts. "Who is it?" I shout, frowning.

"It's me, Grip." Amir's voice comes muffled but urgent through the door.

I cross the room to let him in, and Amir's eyes drift over my shoulder to Qwest still on her knees wearing her barely decent costume. "Sorry, man." Amir's wide eyes zip back to mine. "But that, uh, project you had me watching is a little out of control."

"What project . . ." My eyes snap to his. Bristol. "What's up?"

"Um . . ." Amir glances at Qwest. I look back to see her standing, eyes watchful and antennae up.

"Hey." I walk back to her, gently cupping her face and kissing her forehead. "I need to check on something. You'll be okay getting back to your hotel? Should I send Will back here?"

"Yeah, send him." She folds her hands over mine at the curve of her neck. "I guess I'll go back to New York. Nothing's keeping me here now."

"We still have some shows scheduled," I say carefully. "Will you be okay for them?"

"If you know anything about me, Grip, it's that I don't let nothing mess with my money." A choked laugh escapes her lips. "Not even my stupid heart."

"Your heart isn't stupid. It's a good heart, and some guy's going to be really lucky to have it."

She nods, fresh tears springing to her eyes and streaking through the heavy stage makeup on her cheeks.

"Be safe." I drop another kiss on her forehead and walk out into the hall where Amir waits.

"What's going on?" I ask once the door is closed. In the light of the hall, I notice some slight puffiness around Amir's eye. "What happened to you?"

"Bristol happened to me." He touches around his eye. "That's what I was trying to tell you. She's turnt up out there. I tried to check her, and she hit me in the face. Jimmi jumped on my damn back. You know that lil' white girl scratched me? You think I'll have to get a tetanus shot?"

"What the hell, Amir?" I push past him and barrel down the hall. "I told you to watch her. You know how Bristol and Jimmi are when they get together."

"Uh, I was watching her until she and Jimmi climbed up onstage with the strippers and started talking about making their asses clap."

I keep moving forward but glare daggers over my shoulder at him.

"If she's out here naked your ass is mine."

She isn't naked, but pretty close. She and Jimmi are on one of Pirouette's three stages along with a few professionals who are "coaching" them. Bristol's blue dress lies in a crumpled mound of silk at her feet, leaving her in a nude-colored strapless bra and matching thong. She's a hair from naked, and all the guys clustered around the base of the stage are salivating for that last hair to fall out. Jimmi isn't much better, also in bra and panties.

By the time Amir and I make it to them, one of the guys with a hundred dollar bill clutched in his fist has his other hand wrapped around Bristol's leg. Fury erases caution and discretion. I grab him by the shoulder and shove him to the side.

"Get your damn hands off her." The guttural growl of my voice barely registers above Lil Wayne's "Lollipop" blasting through the system.

"Nigga, who you think—"

The anger melts away from his face, morphing into a wide grin. "Grip!" He reaches to dap me up. "You did it tonight, dawg. And that song 'Bruise' you got out is deep. You telling our story, bruh."

"Uh, thanks."

With a curt nod, I reach up and grab Bristol's hand. I can only hope Amir has made more progress with Jimmi.

"Bristol, get your ass off that stage," I yell up at her.

She tugs at her hand, glazed eyes squinting down at me.

"No." Her other hand goes to the front closure of her bra. "I'm trying to get this thing off. It won't . . ."

She looks so confused by the uncooperative clasp, pouting and frowning down at her fingers that don't seem to want to work properly.

"I can do it," she yells at me. "Just give me a sec."

"Fuck this." I scramble onstage, pull the chambray shirt over my head, not bothering to unbutton it. "Bris, put this on. We're getting out of here."

"I'm not going anywhere with you," she slurs, pointing a loopy accusatory finger at me. "You fired me. Asshole."

I pull the shirt over her head, shoving her arms through the sleeves. I bend at the knees and haul her over my shoulder, ignoring her pounding on my back. Fortunately, a few "amateurs" were onstage trying their hand at stripping, so most people weren't paying as much attention and were focused on the main stages. Hopefully, I was able to stay under the radar as much as possible and none of this will land in tomorrow's news cycle.

I make my way through the crowd back toward the dressing room, Bristol still bouncing against my back. Farther down the hall, Amir has Jimmi propped up against the wall. Like me, he had to sacrifice his shirt, and we face each other, both wearing wife beaters and jeans.

"Does Jimmi not have security with her?" I ask.

"She said no, but she isn't exactly reliable right now." A tiny beaded clutch looks incongruous in Amir's beefy hands. "I found a valet ticket in her purse, so looks like she drove."

"You take her home, and I'll get Bristol to her place." "You sure? I don't know if I should leave you."

The skepticism on his face is like a straw breaking the camel's back of this night.

"I grew up same place as you, Amir." I hitch up my wife beater to show him the 9mm tucked into my waistband. No way I'd be in a club like this without it. "I'm strapped, same as you. You may be on the payroll to shadow me, but don't forget who you're dealing with. Now, you get Jimmi home. I'm pretty sure I can make it to Bristol's house without getting jacked."

He nods and starts herding Jimmi toward the private exit. By the looks of Jimmi's face, he'll be lucky if she doesn't vomit on his bright white Nikes before it's all said and done. With Bristol still slung over my shoulder like a sack of potatoes, upside down with as much liquor as she's consumed, I'm surprised she hasn't vomited down my back already. She's gone quiet and still. She may have passed out.

I carefully bend and flip her back, sliding her down my body until she's pressed to my chest, my arms folded at the small of her back to keep her upright. Her hands go to my shoulders, and she slumps against me.

"Bris," I say softly, saving the anger urging me to lambast her ass for later when she'll remember it. "Let's get out of here, okay?"

"No." She shakes her head, the burnished hair tangling around her shoulders and over her eyes. "It's fun. Don't . . . don't wanna go."

"Bristol," I say firmly, glaring down at her. "We're leaving right now."

"It's fun," she whispers, her face crumpling and tears rolling over her smooth cheeks. "I'm having so much fun. Can't you see I'm having fun?"

Still in my arms, she drops her head into the curve of my neck and shoulder. Her tears rain over me, dampening my skin, and her heaving sobs jackhammer my heart. I rub her back in soothing strokes.

Dammit, I can't take Bristol's tears, not even the drunk ones. "Hey, it's okay." I try to pull her back so I can see her face, but she presses closer.

"Don't." Her broken whisper is muffled into my neck. "Don't push me away again, Grip."

"I wouldn't." I palm the back of her head, rubbing the soft, wild hair. "I didn't."

"You did." Her tears come faster, her erratic breaths hiccupping her words. "You don't-don't want me-want me-around. You f-fired me."

"Bristol, you know—"

"You just want her." She trembles against me, folding her arms between her chest and mine. "You just want Qwest."

I know she probably won't remember this tomorrow, but as much as it cuts me open to see her like this, it's this raw, vulnerable version of Bristol that will tell me the truth. And I'm not noble enough not to take advantage of it to finally hear her confession.

"Does it hurt you when I'm with her?" I peer down at Bristol's face in the muted hallway light, hunting down the truth in her eyes.

"So much," she whispers, fat tears squeezing from under her clenched-closed-tight eyelids and leaving trails of mascara. "It hurts so much."

"Why does it hurt so much, Bris? Do you . . ." I swallow around the emotion clogging my throat at the sight of her tears, unsure if I really want to hear her say this knowing that tomorrow she'll probably just deny it. "Do you have feelings for me? Do you care about me, Bristol?"

With eyes the silver of moonlight, illuminative, so clear and unprotected, not fogged by her fears, insecurities, or questions, she tells me.

"So much." Another tear skids over the silk of one high cheekbone. "I care so much."

Something breaks free in my chest. Knowing I'm not crazy loosens a vise from around me. Knowing I haven't imagined that the connection we had all those years ago never went away.

"Bris, then why do you—"

My question never makes it out. With green tingeing her tear-streaked face, Bristol doubles over, clutching her stomach and puking all over my Blackout Jordans.

Twenty-One
Bristol

I HAVE TO STOP DOING THIS.

Not that drinking myself into a coma is a regular occurrence, but when the pain and pressure are too much, I find myself reaching for the same bottled oblivion my mother favors. And there's no doubt I've been drinking. Demons are line dancing in my skull. My furry tongue clings to the roof of my mouth. The morning chill creeps under my duvet, and I pull the chambray shirt I'm wearing closer around me. I tug the collar up to my nose, inhaling the clean, masculine scent. It's familiar. It smells like . . .

"Grip," I say into the quiet of my bedroom. "What?"

I literally jump and screech, flipping onto my back to find Grip staring at me unsmilingly, wearing a white tank undershirt. I have no idea how I came to be wearing his shirt from last night, or how he came to be sitting in my bed, broad shoulders overpowering my tufted headboard.

"You scared me half to death." I clutch his shirt over my pounding heart and touch my bare legs. My dress is nowhere to be seen, and under Grip's shirt I'm wearing only a strapless bra and a thong. I have to wonder if I did anything regrettable last night.

"Did we . . . um . . ." I lick my dry lips, not sure how to ask this question. The same one I had to ask Parker just a few weeks ago. Shame curdles in my belly that I'm repeating this destructive cycle. "Did we have sex?"

Grip cocks one dark brow, his lips not even twitching. "Do you feel like you could walk straight?"

I nod and move my legs experimentally to check for partial paralysis. "Um, yeah."

"Then there's your answer." He shrugs. "We couldn't have had sex."

"Very funny." I drag myself up to sit beside him against the headboard.

"Not being funny. Just stating fact."

His eyes remain sober. There was a time when he would have made this easier for me, allayed some of my discomfort with a joke. But there's no levity in his expression.

"Did you roofie me or something?" I try to lighten the heavy atmosphere since he won't.

"You roofied your damn self with that bottle of vodka you poured down your throat." If anything my attempt at a joke makes things worse. A scowl forms on his face. "What the hell were you thinking?"

"I wasn't thinking." I shield my eyes from the light intruding through my wide windows, curtains undrawn. "I was drunk, in case you didn't notice."

"Yeah, what the hell were you thinking getting drunk?" He shakes his head as he lifts a knee under the duvet and props his arm on it. "In a strip club. Do you have any idea how vulnerable you were in a place like that drunk off your ass?"

"I don't need a lecture." I swing my legs over my side of the bed, pausing for my head to spin. "What I need is . . ."

The words trail off when I see the water and aspirin on my bedside table.

"Thanks," I mumble around the two pills before gulping down water. I lift a hand to touch what feels like involuntary pageant hair. "My hair situation seems dire."

I try to run my fingers through the nest tangled around my head, but they stall at one knot after another.

"Yeah, your hair looks like shit. Your lipstick is smeared all around your mouth, and you have mascara running down your face like some emotionally unstable clown. You look like a circus refugee. Also, you reek."

I swing him an affronted look over my shoulder.

"Why are you being so mean to me?"

"Because I'm pissed, Bristol." He flings the covers back and stands, facing me with my unmade bed between us.

Even at this time of morning and under these circumstances, he looks highly fuckable in his jeans and undershirt, with a shadow coating the chiseled jawline. There isn't enough alcohol in my system to wash the horny away. I need to have actual sex with an actual person and actually remember it. Being this close to the sexiest man I know isn't helping.

"If I hadn't been there," Grip continues, blissfully unaware that I'm mentally dry humping him. "It could have been much worse."

Worse than what? I try to reconstruct the events from last night. I remember still being angry at Grip for firing me. I remember drinking lots of vodka with Jimmi. We asked that nice stripper Champagne to show us how to make our asses clap. And then ...

"Oh, God," I gasp. "Did I take my bra off? Like in front of people? Did I make it rain?"

He sucks his teeth, exasperation in every chiseled line of his handsome face.

"You were damn close," Grip snaps. "If I hadn't pulled you off the stage, you and Jimmi both would have been butt naked in there."

"Where's Jimmi?" I ask, my voice constrained by embarrassment.

"Amir took her home." Grip walks to the bench at the foot of my bed to grab his backpack. "You owe him an apology, by the way. You hit him in the eye."

"What?" I slap my forehead and close my eyes, mortified. "Oh my God, no."

"Oh my God, yes, and you owe me an apology." He gestures to his shirt covering my almost-naked body. "I want that dry cleaned, by the way."

"Yes, sir. Right away, sir." I load the words with a double helping of sarcasm and stumble toward the bathroom. "If you'll excuse me, I need to figure out what died in my mouth."

I'm practically brushing my teeth with eyes closed to avoid the road kill of my reflection in the mirror.

"You just keep getting better and better, don't you, Bristol?" I mutter around my electric toothbrush. I splash my face, but don't even bother with my hair and the rest of my bodily disaster. I'll shower once Grip's gone. I walk back into my bedroom to find Grip on his knees, ass up, looking under my bed.

And what an ass it is.

He glances over his shoulder from the floor, one brow lifted when he sees my head bent at just the right angle to peruse his butt.

"Um, can I help you?" he asks.

"Oh ... no." Embarrassment at getting caught checking him out fires up my cheeks. "Were you looking for something?"

"My shoes." He stands and glances around the room. "Did I mention that you threw up on a pair of thousand dollar vintage Jordans?"

"I'm sorry." I walk around to the side of the bed, joining the search for his shoes. I spot the worn leather book of Neruda poems and the tarnished whistle on the floor. My heart, my thoughts, my whole body goes still.

"Have you been going through my things again?" I snatch the book and the whistle up and cram them into the bottom drawer, which is usually locked. "How dare you?"

"How dare I?" Incredulity widens his eyes. "I didn't have to go through anything. That was on your pillow when I brought you in here. I just moved it out of the way so I could fall asleep."

Maybe he didn't recognize it. I know it's a feeble hope, but it's the only one I have. He quickly disabuses me of any possibility that he doesn't remember those items. Doesn't recognize their significance.

"I'm surprised you kept them." Grip hitches his bag onto his shoulder and steadily watches me.

"Well you kept the watch," I say defensively before I realize this only pulls me deeper into a conversation I'm too addled to have.

Grip's lips thin, and his jaw clenches.

"I kept the watch because that night at the carnival was one of the best nights of my life, Bristol. That night with you meant a lot to me." Grip crosses his arms over the muscled width of his chest. "But you already knew that. So, why did you keep a worthless whistle from that night? Why is the book of poems I mailed to you beside your bed?"

Anxiety prickles my scalp and heats my skin. I'm exposed, and my habit is to hide.

"No reason. I wouldn't throw that away," I mumble. "That would just be rude."

"Not only did you not throw it away," Grip says, walking to stand in front of me. "You highlighted. You folded down pages. You circled. You starred."

"You did go through my things." I glare feebly up at him. "I knew it."

He tips his head toward the drawer where I stowed the book and whistle.

"You've obviously handled that book, read it over and over. I'm asking you why, Bris." His voice drops and his eyes soften. "I've told you what that watch and what that night meant to me. Can you tell me what that night meant to you? What it still means to you?"

My defenses slam over my heart like a gate. He's much too close. Much too dangerous to someone like me who would not know how to stop loving him when he hurts me. When he cheats on me, lies to me. And he would. How could he not? I refuse to be my mother.

"It was a long time ago." I caress the buttons of his chambray shirt I'm wearing, fixing my eyes on my trembling fingers. "Don't read too much into a drawer full of old memories."

When I glance up at him, his face has cemented into a mask. His eyes are like iced coffee.

"Forget it." He turns abruptly and leaves the room, tossing the last words over his shoulder. "Never mind."

His proximity was causing my anxiety, but seeing him walk away only increases it. I sense that if he leaves this house, if he walks out that door, that's it. I'll lose him forever. He's already fired me, so we won't have work. We can't be in the same room for five minutes without fighting anymore, so we can't be friends. And I've made sure we'll never be lovers.

And why the hell not?

It's a rebel cry from my heart. That stupid thing pounding with angry fists against my ribs, demanding attention. Demanding him. Commanding me to find a way to make him stay. I'm not sure what I could say at this point as he crosses my living room with swift strides that take him closer and closer to the front door, but I have to say something, even if it's the wrong thing.

"I guess Qwest is waiting for you, huh?"

Yep, the wrong thing.

He's at the front door but turns to face me, irritation and disappointment on his face.

"It wasn't cool, Bristol, you talking about Qwest that way last night with Jimmi. She's been nothing but nice to you."

He's right, but him defending her only agitates me more.

"Well, it's the truth." I assume my face is resting bitch, but I can't fix it. "She is clingy. The girl doesn't know how to sit unless she's on your lap."

He stiffens, eyes hard and lips set in a flat line when he crosses his arms over his chest. "You sound jealous."

"Of her?" I bark out a disdainful laugh. "I don't think so."

"At least Qwest doesn't have to be high or drunk to tell me how she feels."

That low blow lands just above the belt in the vicinity of my heart.

"Fuck you, Grip."

"I already know you wanna fuck me." He raises both brows and tilts his head to the other side. "I'm wondering if you'll ever tell me how you feel about me."

He drops his bag to the floor and settles against the door, as if he has all the time in the world to wait.

"Or are you such a scared little girl you can't?"

"Scared little girl?" Indignation starts at my feet and works its way up to my head. "I'm not . . ."

I can't even finish the sentence. The truth smacks me across the face, and Rhyson's words ring as clearly in my head as if he's standing beside me.

You're braver than that, Bristol. You're the most fearless person I know. And you let the threat of something keep you from having what you really want?

Am I? Brave? Fearless? In most things, yes. But with this, with Grip, there's too much at stake. Too much to lose. If I give him a little, I'll give him everything.

Grip's waiting for me to finish, to respond, but whatever I was going to say flies right out of my head. While I'm standing here, trying to figure out how to hide from him, he's hiding nothing from me. There's so much raw longing in his dark eyes. There's so much emotion on his face it punches right through my heart. I've taken years to build a fortress against this man. I've learned to resist him. And he has over and over, time and again, put his heart on the line. Worn it on his sleeve. Persisted when I turned him away.

He's been brave. He just kept coming after me like a tank, even when I refused. Even when my brother told him he shouldn't. Even when I steered him in the direction of someone else. He even let me manage him for the chance to be closer to me. While I've drawn my armor tightly around myself, Grip stood naked in the heat of battle, stripped all of his armor away and made himself vulnerable. In my fear of becoming my mother, I think I'm becoming my father instead. The one who takes and takes, risking nothing. Always defining the relationship and expecting Grip to take whatever terms I offer. To take whatever's left. It's so selfish and so weak and so unfair, I feel sick, not because of the alcohol, but sick of myself. Sick of living in fear.

He wants to know how I feel? As if seeing that book of poetry didn't tell him. As if finding that worthless whistle didn't show him. As if I haven't already told him in a million silent ways. He already knows, but he wants to hear me say it.

I want him.

For the first time, watching him poised to leave my front door, poised to walk out of my life, my want feels stronger than my fear. The threat of Grip breaking me weighs less than the possibility of never having him. Before I know it, I'm swallowing my pride. I'm eating my words and mustering the courage to tell him everything and praying it isn't too late. I'm walking to stand in front of him.

"You want to know how I feel?" I can barely push the words past the tumbleweed in my throat.

He doesn't nod. Doesn't speak, but I know him too well not to recognize something flicker in his eyes. Hope? That I'll finally be brave enough to be honest?

"I want you so much it scares me," I say in a rush before my fear stops me. "The way I feel about you terrifies me."

I train my eyes on his Jordans because I can't look at him.

"I'm afraid you'll cheat on me, take advantage of me, and that I won't know how to stop wanting you. I'm afraid I'll settle for less than I deserve because I'd take whatever you'd give me."

He's completely silent, but his chest in front of me rises and falls with deeply drawn breaths.

"You want me?" he finally asks, voice husky, making no move to touch me.

I nod, sliding my glance to the side, looking for an escape route, though I already know there's nowhere left to hide.

"You want to be with me?" he presses.

I hazard a glance up, not sure how to take his impassive expression.

"I know you're with Qwest, and this is awful timing, but I—" "I broke things off with Qwest last night," he cuts in softly. My eyes zip up to meet his head on.

"You did?" His words kindle a small, fiery hope to life inside me. "Why?"

He tilts his head, a smile tipping one side of his mouth.

"You know why, Bristol." A small frown bends his eyebrows to meet. "It wasn't fair letting her think there was a chance when I couldn't get over you."

The blood slams against my wrists and at my temples in a frantic rhythm. My breaths grow shallow, fear and excitement and possibility mingling in my veins. He tilts my chin up until I'm forced to meet his eyes again.

"I won't be getting over you," he says softly. "And I would never cheat on you. As long as it's taken me to get you, you think I would jeopardize that with some piece of ass that doesn't mean anything to me?"

His words, his reassurances, loosen some of what's been tight inside me since I walked in on my father.

"You don't have me yet," I whisper, managing a tiny teasing smile.

He takes me by the hips, pulling me into his big body against the door, dipping his head until he hovers over my lips.

"Keep telling yourself that, Bris."

Anticipation crackles between us as I wait for him to take me, to claim me. Because there's no way I can stop him now. Despite any fear that may still linger, I don't want to stop him, but he's made every move for years. It's time for me to move first.

I tip up on my toes and press my lips to his, tentative as if it's our first kiss. I'm careful, as if he might turn me away, but he doesn't. With a groan, he spreads one hand over the small of my back and slides the other up into my wild hair. He angles my head just the way he wants and commandeers the kiss, nothing tentative or uncertain about him pulling my lips between his. Nothing careful about the way he plunges into me, his mouth slanting over mine, his tongue sweeping against mine. On repeat. Over and over. Avid. Desperate. Hungry.

He slumps against the door and takes me with him, searching hands venturing under the chambray shirt to cup the bare cheeks of my ass. With one foot he kicks my legs apart until he's between my thighs. I gasp at the stiff erection pressing into my panties. Involuntarily, my hips roll into him. We groan into each other's mouths at the heat, the hardness, the wetness of us touching. Of us together.

"Bristol." He trails his mouth down my neck to the spot that's basically a blank check to my body. "I want to hear the whole sordid story of why you've put me through all this shit all these years. I really do."

I nod, hastily loosening the buttons of the chambray shirt and sliding my arms out until I'm only wearing the strapless bra and the thong.

"Damn, baby," he whispers, dipping his head to nudge the sheer material of my bra down, baring my breast. He takes my nipple into his mouth, drawing on me so hard it's almost painful, but I'm glad he doesn't stop when I whimper.

"Grip." I clutch his head to my breast and grind myself into him over and over, a hurricane building inside me. "Please."

"Please what?" He paints my areola with his tongue. "What do you want?"

"You know." I'm almost in tears it feels so good and I want it so bad. "You know, Grip."

Without asking for more, his fingers slip into the sides of my panties, rolling them over my hips and down my legs. His eyes eat up my nudity. I feel exposed, and realize that my head may not be pounding as badly and I managed to brush my teeth, but the rest of me still looks and smells like last night. I'm a wreck from head to naked toe.

"Grip, wait." I pull back, reaching down to grab the shirt from the floor and sliding my arms in.

"You're going in the wrong direction, Bris." Grip shucks his shoes off again and rips the tank over his head, revealing his sculpted chest. "Clothes should be coming off."

"I . . . well, um . . ." My breath stutters when the jeans slide down his powerful thighs. Through his briefs, I see what he's working with, and it's more than I've ever had.

Shit.

My poor pussy may not be ready for this. I feel like I should have been in training to fuck him, the way I would for a marathon. Surely, all that dick isn't something you just wake up one morning and take.

He hooks an arm around my waist and drags me against him, his erection announcing his intentions. He teases my lips apart and sucks on my tongue until my knees turn to rubber. For a second, my brain is gooey with desire, and I can't think past the throbbing heat between my legs. I pull back to speak before I lose the ability.

"Remember I reek?" My lips lift at the corners with the relief of not having to hide from him anymore. "And our first time will not be with me looking and smelling like drunken debauchery."

His eyes are so open and tender on my face, and he laughs with me, dropping his lips to my ear.

"Okay, Bristol." His warm breath in my ear makes me shudder. "We'll do it your way. First I wash you."

He steps back, sweeping a smoldering look over my nearly naked body, his desire stroking me like a physical hand.

"Then I fuck you."

Twenty-Two

Grip

I've had some pretty wild dreams about Bristol Gray. But in my wildest dreams, I couldn't imagine that, not the nakedness of her body, but the nakedness of her soul, would be the thing that tempted me the most. Her eyes, so open and vulnerable—I couldn't have known that would be what was most precious to me. I feel like the guy who ran around for years screaming that the world was round when everyone insisted it was flat. I knew I wasn't crazy, that Bristol cared about me. I knew there was something undeniable between us. The greatest validation lies in those silvery eyes, completely unshielded for the first time in years.

"I guess I'll shower," she says once we're in her bathroom, reaching into the spacious, tile-walled unit to turn on the water.

"That's a great idea."

I peel back the flaps of my chambray shirt, which she has folded over her chest instead of buttoned. Her bra is right where I left it, tugged under her breasts so her nipples are exposed. We left the thong at her front door. I push the shoulders back, watching the sleeves skid down her arms. The shirt puddles around her feet. I take my time surveying the finely boned ankles, the infinite legs, tanned and toned. I devote a moment to appreciate the smooth triangle of flesh at the juncture of her thighs. I'm planning to gorge myself on that pussy. When I force my eyes over the curve of her hips and the dip of her waist, the tight tips of her breasts, it's her cheeks that make me smile.

"Are you blushing, Bristol?"

292 | KENNEDY RYAN

She's so bold, so brazen. I would never expect a little nudity to embarrass her.

"Shut it. Don't make fun of me." Her nervous laugh floats away on the steam from the shower. "I'm just . . . self-conscious."

"Maybe it's because I have on too many clothes."

I tug my briefs down, freeing my rampant erection. Her eyes drop to my dick and go wide. Under her stare, I get harder, my balls feel heavier as the seconds tick by. I've been with a lot of girls, but never has anyone made me feel like this without even touching me. I'm so ready, Bristol could breathe on me and I'd probably come all over her. I need to get this under control because from what I've inferred, the men in her life, in her bed, have not impressed her. I don't want to think about them too much because it makes me slightly insane. If she can put up with all the women I've been with, the least I can do is pay her the same courtesy.

But that doesn't mean I have to like it.

"If you're wondering," she says softly, lifting her eyes to my face. "You don't have to worry about Parker. There's nothing . . .we're not together."

I can get details on that later. It actually hadn't even occurred to me to ask.

"I wouldn't care if Parker was in the next room." I take her hand and place it on my bare chest, dipping my head to whisper in her ear. "I'd make sure he heard you scream."

She scans my face for any signs of distress, curiosity—I don't know what she's looking for, and I don't care.

"Parker and I aren't together," she says again.

"I know you're not, because you're with me."

"But what I'm saying is that we . . ." she lowers her lashes over cheeks still marked with faint mascara tracks. "We aren't—"

"Bris." I press a finger over her lips. "The last thing I want to talk about is the last asshole in your bed. He's rearview, just like Qwest and anyone else I've ever been with."

She nods, and her eyes lock with mine as she kisses my finger. I trace around her lips, tugging them open, touching her tongue, her teeth, the lining of her jaw. It's painful how badly I want this warm, wet mouth around my cock. I take her hand and lead her into the shower, gently setting her against the tiles to kiss her. Her arms climb over my shoulders and clench behind my neck. She's pressing against me, her breasts straining against my chest. She's wet and slippery, and I could lift her legs around me and take her right now, but I have no plans to rush.

Instead, I turn her to face the wall, reach for her shampoo, and slowly work the lather into her tangled hair. Her head falls back, and she sighs as my fingers massage her scalp. I pull the showerhead off the wall, rinsing out the shampoo and repeating the process with her conditioner. Still with my front to her back, I soap up my hands and run them over her firm thighs, tight waist, under her arms, and over the slender bones of her shoulders. I squeeze her breasts, rubbing my thumbs over the distended nipples until she cries out. Languidly, my hand journeys between her breasts and over her hipbone to palm her, my middle finger sliding into her slit and over the bud of flesh tucked inside.

"Grip."

My name on her lips when she's on the verge of coming hums through my blood. Knowing it's me doing this to her. Hoping that no other man ever has the privilege of touching her this way again, it's almost more than I can stand. I trap her clit between two fingers, rubbing up and down between the lips. My other hand roams over her ass, and I slip a finger between the firm cheeks. She stiffens, unsure of what I'm about to do. I sip at the water flowing in rivulets over her satiny skin. My teeth nip at the curve of her neck, at the elegant slope of her shoulder.

I match the rhythm I set in her pussy with the rhythm between her cheeks, caressing that puckered hole with each stroke, gathering her wetness and then slowly inserting my finger.

"Oh, God." Her face crumples as she pushes against my finger, urging me deeper in. "You have to … I'm going to …"

Her words twine with the steam, hotter than the steam. She slaps one hand against the wall, her head tipping back on a silent scream. Her knees buckle, and I catch her under her arms, seating her on the small bench tucked into the corner of the shower. Her head lolls back, eyes heavy-lidded, mouth slack, breasts heaving. She looks undone, but I'm far from done with her. I go down on my knees between her thighs.

"Spread your legs for me, Bris."

It's part plea, part command. Either way, she complies, her long legs yawning open for me. I swallow deeply at the sight of the thick, slick lips, pink and wet. Her clit is swollen from her orgasm. I have to resist the temptation to take it in my mouth and suck until she comes again.

"Hold your lips open." I can barely get the words out. My teeth slam together and my jaw clenches painfully as she obeys, opening herself with her fingers, her hungry eyes watching and waiting.

I set the showerhead to massage and let the warm water flow between her legs. She jerks, her eyes going wide and her mouth gaping on a sharp cry.

"That's it, baby." I roll the showerhead up and down and over her, watching her eyes squeeze closed and her face collapse when she loses the fight to maintain control. I twist the setting to vibrate and press it into her. Leaning forward, I capture one piqued nipple between my lips, rolling my tongue over it, drawing it deeply into my mouth.

"Grip, oh God. Please."

Her fingers tremble holding the lips open. Her head thrashes against the tiles. All the while her hips gyrate into the spray desperately, her rhythm uneven and broken with her desire. I need to taste that desperation. I drop the showerhead to the floor, not bothering to turn it off before I bend at the waist and pull her clit into my mouth.

"Bristol," I groan against the plump flesh. "You taste . . . Fuck."

I shove her fingers aside, spreading her as wide as she'll go, nipping at the lips with my teeth, slipping my tongue inside.

"Ahhhh." One of her hands clutches my shoulder, the other grabs my head, pressing me deeper into her rocking hips, deeper into her sweetness. Her taste intoxicates me. I hook her legs over my shoulders and devour her, my head bobbing furiously between her thighs. I want my mouth right here waiting to receive her when she comes. I take her nipple, rolling it between my fingers while I continue licking and sucking and supplicating at her altar.

She comes, shattering against the wall, shoulders shaking with dry sobs, her thighs trembling on my shoulders. I drink from her like a fountain. I'm thirsty, zealous. She claws the skin off my back, but I don't care. I want her wild, and the pain of her unleashed passion is worth it. I want her unhinged. I want her to feel what I've felt every day since we met. I've dreamed of having her a million times, and when she jerks and weeps and writhes under my hands, my name coming to life and then dying on her lips, I finally do.

Twenty-Three
Bristol

O BVIOUSLY I'M DEAD.

I can't feel my body and a dark angel hovers over me, so this must be heaven. The fluffy white duvet covering my bed is a cloud at my back.

"Bristol, baby." Grip's gruff voice reattaches me to the present, to the memory of what just happened.

Me, the queen of DIY orgasms, just came twice in the shower without a dick or a vibrator, or even at my own hand. Unless you count the massaging showerhead as vibrating. I try to speak, but my throat is scratched out from the hoarse screams Grip took from me.

"Yeah?" I finally croak.

"Before we do this," Grip says, a tightness around his eyes and his mouth. "I need you to believe I would never step out on you. I—"

"Grip." It's my turn to hush him, resting my finger against his lips. "You don't have to explain. We weren't together."

Anything else he would say stifles in his throat when I stroke him with a tight-fisted, steady rhythm.

"You were saying?" I whisper, lowering my head to suck on his nipple.

"Bristol, I'm not going to last long." His head drops. "Please don't take that as a sign of how it will always be, but watching you come in the shower has me halfway there already."

A shaky laugh breaks up his words.

"I've waited so long for this." The laugh dies, giving life to a tenderness in his eyes that pries my heart open another inch. "I've waited for you."

He pushes my damp, tangled hair back from my face, his touch rough and reverent.

"I've thought about this moment almost every day since we met. Not just the sex." His smile is so beautiful it literally hurts to look at it knowing it's for me. "I mean, yeah, of course, the sex. But the first day I met you, I wondered what kind of man it would take to win you. I wondered if I could be a man like that."

I slowly shift, nudging his shoulder until he's on his back and I'm looking down at him. I kiss a hard pectoral muscle and dip my head to lick between the ridges of his abs, his sharply indrawn breath making me smile against his skin.

"And what kind of man are you?"

His expression sobers, his eyes a mesmerizing night I lose myself in.

"The kind who would do anything to keep you." He brushes a thumb across my cheekbone. "Be sure because I won't let you go after."

I bite my lip to keep the tears at bay. He has no idea what it means to hear him say that. For the girl who had to beg for scraps of affection, for attention from the people she's loved the most, hearing him say that sets my fears free. All my life I've been the chaser. Chasing my parents' approval. Chasing my brother's love and friendship. I went to extremes to make them notice me, to make them love me.

I was right to be cautious. This heart of mine that has no borders, no bottom, no ceiling, would be crushed by the wrong man.

I could easily end up a shell bent to his will and settling for leftovers and reheated affection, but Grip is not the wrong man. He may be the only man I can trust with a heart like mine.

And I finally do.

"I'm sure." I rest my chin on his flat, hard stomach, reaching up to trace the bold bones of his face, the soft lips and thick, curling lashes. "Are you sure? I'm not like other girls, Grip. You have no idea."

He props up on one elbow to probe my eyes, palming my head and running his thumb over my brows and across my cheeks.

"Tell me what I'm in for," he says softly, his eyes serious, really asking.

"I'm going to be unreasonably possessive." I scatter kisses across his stomach, and the muscles clench beneath my lips. "I won't hesitate to destroy any bitch who tries to take you away from me."

"Okay." His breath hitches. "What else?"

I sit up, settling my legs on either side of his magnificent naked body, the narrow waist widening to the sleek muscles of his chest, the heavier muscles of his shoulders and ink-splattered arms. I admire the contrast of my thighs against his skin so deeply bronzed.

"I will hurt anyone who tries to hurt you." I laugh self-consciously. "If you hadn't figured it out, I'm kind of protective of the people I care about."

"I had noticed that, yeah." Grip caresses my hip, his fingers splaying possessively over me. "Anything else I should know?"

I lean forward until our flesh is flush, positioning myself over him, poised to inaugurate our bodies.

"Yes." I lean to reach my nightstand, grabbing a condom and barely fitting it over the thick, swollen head. "I like to be on top."

I slide slowly onto him, unprepared for the stretch. Not only am I tight, but Grip is wide and long. I breathe through the initial pinch, determined to take all of him, even if my body has to accommodate him inch by slow inch.

"You okay?" His concerned eyes scan my face. I offer a wobbly grin, biting my lip.

"Why is your dick so big?"

He chuckles, sitting up to kiss along my jaw and piercing his fingers into the hair at the base of my neck.

"You'll get used to it. It's the one stereotype about black guys that I'm glad is true, at least in my case. I can't speak for the rest of the brothers."

Our laughs meet between us, and I rest my temple against his.

"Besides," he groans when I roll my hips to sheath him completely. "You were made for me."

Our breaths catch, our chests press together, our bodies interlock. He caresses my back and then spreads his hands across my butt in ownership. Gently at first, he takes control of the pace. I pant with his every thrust up and into me, tightening my thighs around him. A blistering hunger burns away all discomfort as my body molds to his, as if we were carved to fit, as if I truly was fashioned to take him. I swoop to kiss the chiseled line of his jaw, and he turns his head, highjacking the kiss. Our mouths battle, each of us going deeper into the other with every parry of our tongues. The taste of him obliterates everything else. I can't see. I can't hear. I'm consumed, blindly grabbing his hard body anywhere I can—his biceps, his back, his thigh. There's so much of him and not enough time.

My frantic touches seem to shred his control. With a growl, he flips us, reversing our positions so I'm on my back, the bed cushioning my fall. He drags my leg over his hip and opens me up, grinding back in, his cadence merciless, all gentleness gone. He stares down at me, and it's hypnotic, our eyes locked as intensely, as intimately as our bodies. I hook my ankles at his back and meet every thrust, enslaved to the pace he sets. He's dictating my heartbeat, governing my pulse, holding my next breath cupped in his hands. I'm at his mercy, and it doesn't frighten me. With our bodies meshed, our hearts sharing beats, there's no room for fear. He lifts me up to pull my breast into his mouth, every tug of his lips, every delicate bite, lures me deeper under his spell.

"God, Bris." He groans against my swollen nipples, his breath a glorious burn on the sensitive skin. "I can't get enough of this. Baby, of you."

I don't want him to ever get enough, because I already know my desire for him is a bottomless well. He reaches between us to rub that cluster of nerves that combusts me in his arms. I cling to him as I explode, particles of myself floating in the air around us and settling onto the sweat-dampened sheets.

Guttural, groaning, he stiffens and floods me. My waters rise, and like a river bursting free of its banks, I overflow.

Twenty-Four

Grip

"**S**O YOU CAUGHT YOUR DAD BANGING ONE OF HIS CLIENTS," I SAY to Bristol over the large steaming pizza recently delivered to her door. "And that made you mistrust me?"

"It isn't that simple." She picks off a mushroom that landed on her half of the pizza. "Halving never works. The crap you don't like always ends up creeping to your side."

"One mushroom does not constitute creeping." I pop the discarded mushroom into my mouth. "Don't get distracted. You were explaining why you kept me and that tight, sweet pussy apart for so long."

The slice she's holding pauses on its way to her mouth. Her eyes smile back at me, though she censors the rest of her expression.

"Just because we're sleeping together doesn't mean you can objectify me."

"How is that objectifying you?" I laugh before taking a bite of my pizza. "I said it was sweet and tight. That's high praise."

"You're ridiculous."

She rolls her eyes but laughs and stretches on the living room floor, her back against the couch. She looks completely relaxed, wild hair tucked into the neck of her Columbia University hoodie, legs bare in her boy short underwear.

"And you're stalling." I tweak her big toe. "You were telling me about your dad."

Any humor drains from her face. She tugs one string of the hoodie, folding her legs under her.

"I was already wrestling with my feelings for you." She puts the pizza down, dusting her hands of crumbs. "I knew I felt too much too fast."

"It wasn't too fast."

"It was a week, Grip." Bristol reaches for the bottle of red wine, giving me a wry look. "I'm not saying it wasn't real. Just that it was fast. Throw the drama with Tessa into the mix, and I was already regretting letting my guard down."

Hearing Tessa's name replays that scene at Grady's house before Bristol flew back to New York. Tessa screaming at me about being her baby's father. Bristol witnessing it all with wide, devastated eyes.

"I didn't handle that well." I capture her hand, tracing the love line in her palm. "I should have officially broken things off with her before letting it go as far as it did between you and me."

"I didn't know what to think." She runs her thumb along my finger. "I felt so connected to you, but Jimmi and Rhyson had painted you as this player."

"And I was a little bit." I shrug, my smile rueful. "I was young and feeling myself. Just because I wasn't a cheat doesn't mean I wasn't a player."

"I know." She pours a glass of red, offering it to me, before pouring one for herself. "I was this close to writing you off anyway after Tessa, but when my mom and I walked in on my dad with that girl . . ."

She tips her head back, the wine untouched.

"That wasn't it, though." She grimaces. "It was seeing my mother after we caught him. She just . . . let it go. She put up a good front, but later I found her drunk and weeping because she loved him and couldn't make herself walk away. It was pathetic what she was willing to take from him. All those years Rhyson and I assumed she didn't love him, and the whole time she loved him too much."

For the first time since she said she wanted me, her eyes become guarded again.

"And I realized that I'm like that." She releases a disparaging puff of air. "That's what I did with my parents, with Rhyson. I took whatever they had to give, scraps, and even when they hurt me, like a broken spigot, I couldn't turn it off."

"You group Rhyson with your parents?" I hate hearing that because he would hate to hear it.

"Not him as much as how I responded to what I processed as rejection." She sips her wine, cynicism coloring her laugh. "And yet after years of silence,

I still wagered my future on him, on the possibility that he would take me into his life."

I'm silent, giving her space to express this her own way while my pizza goes uneaten, growing cold.

"It's like I only have a few spots in my heart, but the people who have one, I'd do anything for. I'd accept anything from them because they mean so much to me. It's needy and weak and I hate it about myself."

Emotion blurs her eyes with tears.

"I knew you were one of those people, Grip. That you had one of those spots, and when I saw how giving that kind of power to the wrong man has destroyed my mother, I just couldn't risk it with you."

Hearing her refer to me as "the wrong man" hurts, but I understand her caution. I just hate it took this long for her to trust me. Or for me to prove myself to her.

"I guess it didn't help that I've been smashing everything that moves since you came back to LA." I tear a slice of pizza into crusty confetti.

"And guys in your line of work aren't known for staying faithful." "I ain't gonna lie. You know I've had my fair share of . . ."

Ass.

"Fair share of girls," I amend. "But I promise you I always let one go before I grabbed another."

"You're not helping your case," she says wryly.

She's probably right. I should move on. "What changed your mind?" I ask.

She shrugs, picking pepperoni from her side of the pizza and chewing it slowly.

"I think seeing you with Qwest was a big part of it." Her lashes shield her eyes from me. "And Rhys calling me a coward."

"He knew about this?" I'm stunned for a moment. He wouldn't have let me suffer for years this way.

"Only a few days ago. He confronted me about it when things started falling apart between you and me. When I wasn't with you for the release, he kept digging until he figured out what I felt."

That's my boy! I owe him something overpriced or inebriating.

"I still have reservations." She draws her legs up to her chest, resting her chin on her knees. "We've only been together once, and I already feel like it would be impossible to walk away."

Her admission is a huge step, one I relish, but I think she's looking at this all wrong.

"Bristol, having the capacity to love that way, as fiercely as you do, is not in and of itself a weakness."

She doesn't reply, but that curiosity that first drew me to her sparks behind her eyes.

"My mom has it." I chuckle and shift to lie on my side, propped up on my elbow. "I think every strength has a dark side, can be a weakness. She's learned to manage hers."

I think of how hard it will be for Ma to accept my relationship with Bristol because of her desire to see me with a Black woman. Or Latina. She did say brown was a color.

"Well, she's learned to manage most of her weaknesses." I shake my head. "There wasn't anything she wouldn't do for me. She always said sacrifice is the essence of love. It was the same for her sisters and her brothers, but I saw her draw lines, set limits as she got older and more mature. She didn't take shit from anybody, especially if it affected me."

I lift up to lay a soft kiss on her lips, and she opens up, tangling her tongue with mine for a few seconds before I pull back.

"And you won't take shit, either, not even from me." I cup one side of her face. "Not that you have to worry."

I rest my forehead against hers.

"Bris, you have to know how crazy I am about you."

The lingering uncertainty in her eyes tells me, as much as I've chased her, showing all my cards for years, she doesn't really know. She doesn't know it's her and no one else. And who can blame her with my dick waving like the state flag for the last few years?

"The thing you think is your greatest weakness," I assure her. "Is your greatest strength. That capacity to love, everyone doesn't have it. That grit to fight for the people who mean the most to you, it's priceless."

"You think so?" she asks softly, not looking away from my face.

"I know so, and I feel honored that I have one of those spots in your heart." I lay a palm against her neck. "I promise I won't abuse it. You can trust me."

She closes the space separating us, taking my chin between her lips, meandering over my jaw and finally touching my mouth with hers.

"You know what I want?" Her question lands on my lips in a husky breath.

"Yeah. Me, too."

I sit up, reaching for her, my dick solid as a rock, but I come up with thin air. She's on her feet and walking toward the kitchen.

"Ice cream." Over her shoulder her eyes tease and torture, but I know she needed to change the conversation. So, I let her.

The sweatshirt hits the top of her thighs, and the occasional glimpse of her ass in the white boy short underwear isn't helping my erection. I follow her to the kitchen like she knew I would. When I swing open the kitchen door, she's bent over, her upper body buried in the freezer, the sweatshirt hiked up to show off the firm lines of her thighs and curves of her butt.

"I know I have ice cream in here somewhere." She shifts frozen meat and vegetables until she finds what she's looking for. "Aha!"

She turns to face me, bumping the freezer door closed with a hip.

"Found it." She shakes a quart of Ben & Jerry's Cookie Dough ice cream. "This is my fave, not that I can afford it."

I inspect the lean grace of her body, punctuated by subtle curves. There's so much more to Bristol than her body, but it's a really great place to start.

She hops up onto the kitchen island, swinging her legs and banging bare feet against the base.

"Want some?" She proffers a large spoon loaded with ice cream to me.

I definitely want some. I stalk over to her, insinuating myself between her knees and leaning forward, my mouth open and waiting. I can tell the moment she realizes it isn't ice cream I really want. Her eyes go smoky and her pink tongue swipes over the fullness of her lips. She takes the large spoonful into her mouth instead. I lean into her, my palms pressed into the island surface and my arms bracketing her slim body. She brushes our noses together once, twice before opening my lips in a frozen kiss that shivers through my whole body. Her icy tongue plumbs the recesses of my mouth, brushing the back of my throat in chilly strokes. She cups my chin and holds me still to control the tempo of our tongues twisting together. When we finally pull away, harsh, frosted breaths gust the air between our lips.

She slides off the counter and maneuvers me slowly until my back is against the island. Without ever looking away, she scoops another spoonful of ice cream into her mouth and drops to her knees. She holds the ice cream in her mouth while she deftly unzips the jeans hanging low on my hips, already unbuttoned at the waist. The pants drop and collect around my ankles.

Please let this be happening.

She touches my hips under the briefs, coaxing the underwear down my legs, too. With no preliminary, she stretches her mouth to take my dick between her lips, rolling her cold tongue around the throbbing head.

"Oh, dammit, dammit, dammit, Bris." I clench my fingers in her wild hair.

The wintry mix of her tongue taking me in rough strokes and the smooth sides of her throat clamping around my dick push me to the edge. Brows knit, eyes press closed, her blissful groan vibrates around me. She clutches my ass with one hand and takes my balls, heavy and tight, into her other hand, caressing them.

"I'm gonna come," I rasp in case she doesn't swallow. A lot of girls don't. Groupies tend to swallow because they want to leave an impression. They'll do whatever they think you want to get another night with you. I only want Bristol to do what she wants to do. She doesn't have to perform. I'm hers already, and I want her to enjoy everything we do as much as I do.

Because I'm enjoying the fuck out of this blow job.

Never pulling back, she reaches up and finds the quart of ice cream again. She pauses only to load her mouth with another scoopful of the frigid creaminess before she possesses me again, her head bobbing at a deliberate pace between my legs. It's apparent to me that Bristol will, like she does all things, finish what she starts, but I'll have to watch her swallow me down to the last drop some other time. I want to be inside her again. Now.

With gentle fingers, I tug on her chin until her mouth drops open. She looks up at me from her spot on the floor. I reach down under her arms and raise her off her knees.

"Rain check." I hoist her onto the kitchen island and yank the underwear down her legs. I lay her back flat and lift the heels of her feet to the marble surface, leaving her knees up and her legs wide open.

"Hold on, baby." I push into her, and we groan when the cold from the ice cream melts into her wet heat. I pound into her so hard she has to latch onto the counter to keep from sliding away. I break rhythm to check her face for pain or discomfort.

"Don't you fucking stop," she moans, her neck exposed, back arching, pushing her breasts up under the thick cotton of her sweatshirt. I shove the material over her torso, scrunching it at her shoulders and below her neck so I can watch her breasts bounce with every thrust. I bend to take one in my mouth.

"Take it," she pants. "Baby, take it."

The exquisite slide of flesh against flesh is like nothing I've ever felt, and I realize I'm in her with no rubber.

"Bris, I'm in raw." I grit the words out because I want to stay right where I am, flesh on flesh. "I need to pull out."

"No, you don't." She pants, her nails digging into my ass. "I'm clean, and I'm covered. You?"

"Yeah," I answer unhesitatingly. "I'm clean. So we can ..."

She nods frantically, shifting her hips forward on the counter to change the angle, to deepen penetration. She wants deeper?

I pull her legs straight up on my chest until her feet rest at my shoulders, leaving me nothing but ass and pussy. I slam into her at a bruising pace, hoping I'm not hurting her, but unable to imagine stopping. It's a primal mating—a feral rutting, and I'm the wild beast reduced to a clump of nerves and instincts.

"Grip." Her hands climb her chest to touch her breasts, twisting her own nipples. Watching that, there's no way I'm not coming, but her next words do the impossible. They stop me.

"I love you." Tears slip from the corners of her closed eyes. "Oh, God, I love you so much."

My breaths are choppy, my heart seizing in my chest. "What'd you say?"

Her eyes pop open, briefly touching on my face before fixing to the ceiling.

"Um ..."

I pull her up so her legs fall alongside my hips, our bodies still joined at the center, but her chest pressed into mine.

"Did you mean it?" I demand, cupping her butt.

"Grip, I—"

"Don't play games with me." Desperation sharpens my voice. I need to know she means it. She lifts her lashes, and fear saturates her beautiful eyes. Linking her fingers behind my head, her thumbs caressing my neck, she nods.

Not good enough.

"Say it again." I resume pumping in short and shallow thrusts that will stoke the fire, but won't satisfy.

"I'm scared to death." Her words come on choppy breaths. Without breaking rhythm, I bend to her ear.

"You have nothing to be afraid of." I press her hand to my chest, over my heart. "This is yours. No one else's."

I dip my head, slowing to nothing, but keeping her eyes.

"I'm yours. No one else's." I scatter kisses over her cheeks. "Even when we fight, I feel you. Your anger, your frustration. I feel your pleasure like it's mine. Your emotions like they're mine."

I peer into the flushed beauty of her face. Her sweatshirt is still pushed up so her breasts press into my naked chest. I give her a moment to recognize the syncopation of our heartbeats.

"Don't you feel how connected we are?" I ask. "If I break your heart, I break mine."

A sweet smile spreads over her lips and she nods.

"I love you." She laughs, shaking her head. "Eight years in the making, but I love you."

"I love you, too," I whisper into her hair. "You're everything to me, Bristol. You gotta know that."

Her tears come even as our bodies resume a ferocious pace. We splinter into a thousand pieces in her kitchen, becoming more together than we were apart. More than we were alone. With whispered promises and words of love, we exchange hearts.

Twenty-Five

Bristol

RIGHT SUN BEAMS THROUGH GRIP'S WINDOWS, LETTING ME KNOW we've slept later than I usually do even for a Sunday. We spent the night at the loft, and as I shake off a veil of dreams, lines from Neruda's "Night on the Island" filter through my consciousness. The poem follows a long night between lovers. Though I've read those lines more times than I can count, they were always beautiful hypotheticals. I never expected to sleep through the night with Grip or to wake with the possessive weight of his arm around me, welcome and beloved. I never expected any of what has transpired over the last two days.

And I almost gave him away.

I would have forfeited the perfect weight of his body over mine. Would never have felt the sweet heat of him wrapped around me, or the bold sweep of his hands over my nakedness under our covers in the morning. These are the things that cost nothing but are precious. And I almost never had them.

"What are you thinking about?"

Grip's whispered question mists the sensitive skin of my neck, and I scoot back to snuggle under the covers and against his hard, naked body.

"'Night on the Island.'"

"Fitting." He opens his mouth over the curve of my shoulder in a kiss. "Because you were definitely wild and sweet last night."

"You weren't so bad yourself." I turn over to run my thumb over his full lips. "Neruda was so romantic. I'm glad you introduced me to him."

"Dude had serious game." Grip laughs. "No one writes about love and sex and passion like Neruda."

He grins down at me, a hint of mischief in his eyes. "The original Chocolate Charm."

We both laugh at that. I haven't heard it in so long. It's our own inside joke, from the first day we met, but Grip really could charm lint from your pockets.

"I believe you promised to make me come with words alone." My husky laugh puckers the smooth quiet of the room. "Will you be using his words or your own? Or was that an empty threat?"

"You'll just have to wait and see," he teases me.

He pauses before going on with a more solemn tone.

"When I saw the book and the whistle on your bed, I didn't know what to think. Even though I knew the connection between us was undeniable, the last few weeks had me questioning everything I believed was possible for us."

"I'm sorry." I swallow my uncertainty and force myself to tell him things I've kept for years. "When it first came in the mail, I wanted to burn that book. I was furious with you over Tessa. I didn't want it to mean anything to me."

Despite his hand caressing my hip, I sense a stillness in him behind me, an alertness that tells me he's listening with every part of him.

"But even after I told myself I would put that week behind me, put you behind me," I continue. "I found myself reading it at night."

"Yeah?" He pushes my hair aside and traces the downy line of my nape with a finger. "Why?"

I shrug, reaching for the ease we shared yesterday at my house. In my shower. In my bed. Sex has always been much easier than intimacy, but with Grip they're inextricable. One giving rise to the other. One and the same. Sex with other men never meant much to me, but taking Grip inside my body shook me, rearranged me. Sharing the thoughts I've kept private for so long, I feel just as naked as I did in the shower when he commanded me to open myself for him. I feel more exposed.

"I kept going back to the book, reading your notes in the margins and searching between the lines for what it could tell me about you," I say. "When I moved to LA after college, the memories and emotions from that week all came back, and I had to freeze you out or I knew I'd give in to the pressure you put on me."

"You acted like we'd never been anything to each other," he says softly. "And despite my part in screwing things up, it pissed me off."

"Oh, so was that hate fucking you did with all those other women?"

I turn onto my back to look into his eyes, the lighthearted note in my voice forced. There's more than a granule of truth in most jokes, and this one is no exception. It's levity with talons, and I take the chance to dig in, even if it isn't entirely fair.

There's regret, but no apology in his eyes. "Nope. Just plain old fucking fucking."

He props up on one elbow and splays his hand possessively over my stomach.

"At first, I told myself I would win you back. I would remind you of how it had been between us, but you wouldn't budge. After a year or so, I promised myself I wouldn't give up on you, but I also assumed we'd circle back to each other when the time was right. In the meantime . . ."

"I get it." I rub the soft heather-colored comforter pulled around us. "It wasn't cheating, but it still felt like a betrayal."

I hastily glance up at him, spreading my fingers over the hand resting on me.

"I know that isn't fair, but it's how I felt."

"You felt that way because even though we weren't together," he says, caressing my collarbone. "We were supposed to be. Inside you knew us being apart wasn't right. Me with them wasn't right, and you with anybody other than me sure as hell wasn't right."

His chuckle loosens some of my tightly wound places. He settles his eyes, still slightly sleep-glazed and growing more solemn, on me.

"I don't want to rehash everything." He cups the side of my face. "We've wasted too much time. I want us moving forward from now on."

"Starting today." He drops a quick kiss on my lips. "I've got a surprise."

"A surprise?" I trail fingers over the carved strength of his shoulders and down the hard biceps.

He shifts until he's over me, notching his hips between my thighs. With both of us naked, we're one deep breath away from penetration. His lips wander down my neck and to my breast. He takes his time with each nipple. The suction of his mouth, thorough and voracious, stirs desire low in my belly.

"We are not having sex." I moan, wetness pooling between my legs and my hips circling beneath him, seeking friction. "I can barely walk."

He releases my breast with a pop, his smile triumphant. "What'd I tell you?"

"Like your other head isn't big enough, you had to go and have a big dick." Our laughter shakes us under the covers.

"If you're not giving up that ass," he says, the smile lingering. "Get dressed so we can go. I don't want to be late."

"Go where? Late for what?"

"Pretty sure I said surprise, and last time I checked, you don't know about those before they happen."

The thought of leaving the loft freaks me out a little for more reasons than one, but I'll start with one.

"Grip, as far as the world is concerned," I say carefully. "Qwest is still #GripzQueen. I don't want to embarrass her, or for people to assume we've done something wrong."

"We know we didn't cheat." Grip's frown and the hard set of his lips indicate this is as important to him as it is to me.

"I know, but I pushed you guys together, and I feel bad that she's gotten hurt in this process."

"So do I." Regret shades his eyes. "She cried when I broke it off. She thinks she's in love with me, and I feel like an asshole."

"So do I. And she *is* in love with you. It's obvious." I trace a thumb over the thick brows and chiseled bone structure that have fascinated me since the first time I saw them. "I know how much it hurts to love you and think someone else has you."

"You were jealous?" He echoes my caress, his thumb tracing my features, his eyes searching mine, his fingers working through my hair spread on the pillow.

I nod, biting my lip.

"And scared that you would fall for her. I know that sounds stupid since I pushed you together, but the reality of you wanting someone else . . ."

My words die around the painful lump in my throat. "Bris, I've never wanted anyone the way I want you."

He kisses me deeply, long strokes of his tongue inciting the same insatiable desire we've indulged in over the last day and a half. When he finally releases my mouth, we face each other on the pillow, foreheads pressed together, exchanging short, heavy breaths.

"We'll be careful," he concedes. "But I want you to do this with me today."

"But, Grip—"

"As far as the world's concerned, you're my manager, and it won't be unusual for us to be seen together."

"True." I still hesitate.

"Should we coordinate a statement with Will? Formally notify the press that Qwest and I aren't together anymore?"

"That feels . . . I don't know. Slimy. Like we're shoving her out the door."

"So we what?" A frown knits above the frustration gathering in his eyes. "Just wait for someone to ask me or her if we're together and then deny it? That's too passive. I'm not waiting for that."

He presses my hands over my head, his rough palms scaling the sensitive skin inside my arms and wrists. He dips his head to hover over my lips.

"I'm ready to be with you."

He pulls my bottom lip between his, nipping the softness and then trailing kisses down my neck. He pauses when the intercom system buzzes. Someone wants in. They must know the code to have gotten all the way up the elevator.

"Probably Amir," Grip mumbles, rolling out of bed, treating me to the glorious sight of a taut bronzed ass, the flare of muscled thighs, and the tempting breadth of smooth back and shoulders. Two columns of abdominal muscle stack above his navel and the fine trail of hair leads down to his long, semi-erect south pole. He slips on a pair of gray sleep pants flung over a bench at the foot of the bed.

"Shame to cover that." I drag myself up, resting my shoulders against the headboard. "I was really enjoying the view."

He looks at me from under a dark line of brows, his sculpted lips tilting at one corner.

"I thought you didn't wanna fuck." He leans one hand on the bed for support and palms my throat with the other, gently tilting my chin. "Them's fucking words."

"I am a little sore." I release the sheet tucked under my arms, the rush of cool air when it falls piquing my nipples. "But who needs to walk?"

The heat in his eyes scorches my bare shoulders and breasts. He pulls one knee onto the bed and captures my nipple between his lips, his tongue like fire licking around me. His thumb teases the other nipple tight.

"Grip." His name rushes from my mouth. My head falls back, and my fingers find his neck, pressing his teeth and lips harder into my flesh. "Please."

"Shit," Grip mutters against the underside of my breast. He pulls me down flat to the bed, rips the sheet back and pushes my legs open, his eyes locked on my center.

He presses my knees up and drops to his elbows, his long legs stretched behind him on the bed. I'm writhing at the first long swipe of his tongue.

He's lapping at me. There's a fire hidden in my slit, and every nip of his teeth and tug of his lips fans a desire in me so strong it clenches my belly. To want him this badly and not have him buried inside me hurts. Even knowing Amir could be on his way in, I clutch Grip's head. I roll my hips into him, a hungry undulation. Amir could walk in right now and I'm not sure I could stop. In an instant, in a matter of a few touches and kisses, I'm starved for Grip like the first time, like I've never had him before.

The buzzer comes again, insistent and extended.

"Grip, you know I got a key." Amir's irritated voice comes through the speakers. "Got me standing out here waiting on your ass. I'm coming in."

The front door beeps when it opens, and the sound of Amir's heavy footsteps climb the stairs ahead of him.

"Dammit." Grip pulls the sheet over me and bounds off the bed, crossing swiftly to the open door of his bedroom.

"Grip, you taking a shit or what?" Amir reaches the door just as Grip does, his wide eyes connecting with mine over Grip's shoulder. "Oh, hell. I'm sorry, bruh."

My cheeks burn. I tug the sheet tighter over my breasts and lift my chin, refusing to hide. From the rest of the world, yes. From one of Grip's most trusted friends who has seen all the bumps in our road, no.

"Out." Grip shoves Amir's shoulder, pushing him back onto the landing overlooking the open floor below. He gives me a quick glance over his shoulder, his mouth set. "Sorry 'bout that."

The door closes behind them, and my embarrassment whooshes out of me on a lengthened breath. The door pops open, and Grip sticks his head back in.

"Shower and get dressed. If we leave soon, we won't be late." Chagrin twists his lips and pushes his brows up. "And I'm sorry again about . . ."

He points a thumb out the door.

"It's okay." I muster a weak smile. "How should I dress? Where are we going?"

"Remember? Surprise." A devilish grin widens on his face. "Just be beautiful."

I slip on a silk robe against the slight morning chill. When I walk into Grip's massive closet, his prized shoe collection takes up an entire wall. My eyes immediately go to the gap he left for me to hang the things he suggested I bring and leave at his place. This is happening fast. I mean, I know it's been coming for years, but still.

"What are you doing, Bristol?" I ask myself, dropping to the bench planted in the middle of the closet, toying with the belt of my robe. "Are you sure about this?"

Amir showed up, the first contact we've had with the outside world in two days, and all my insecurities and doubts followed him through the front door. Are things really so different than they were before I told Grip how I feel? He's still a star with an all-access pussy pass. Still the kind of man who, even if he weren't famous, would attract women effortlessly. I'm still the girl who can't draw lines around her heart where he's concerned.

"Hey." Grip props a shoulder at the arched entrance of the closet. "You're supposed to be in the shower by now. I was hoping to ambush you all wet and naked."

"Um, I was just wondering what Amir said?" I wrinkle my brows. "What did he think?"

"I'm pretty sure his exact words were, 'Took you long enough, pussy.'"

His teasing grin melts when I don't manage a smile back, too disoriented now that the sex haze has cleared. He walks deeper into the closet and sits beside me, taking my hand. He kisses the inside of my wrist and clasps an arm around my shoulder.

"What's wrong?"

"I don't know." I shrug and press into the warm strength of his chest. The longer I'm tucked into his arms, the faster my fears drain away. "I guess seeing Amir just reminded me that there's a world out there that will be hard for us to navigate."

"Just out there?" He lays his lips against my temple. "What about the world in here? In your head?"

I glance up at him and hate seeing the guard going up in his eyes.

"I told you I'm not letting you go again, Bristol." The strain in his voice tightens his lips. "You don't get to have second thoughts. You can't—"

I grab his neck and slant my lips over his, invading the warm silkiness of his mouth, aggressively thrusting and seeking. Passionate. Certain. I've allowed these fears to rule me for years, to delay this for years. I'm not giving into them again. I won't ruin this. Grip said my capacity to love can be a strength. I'll let him show me how.

He hums against my lips, a greedy sound as his hands brand my back through the silk robe. He digs into my hips, molds my thighs and arms, possession in every touch. He pulls out of the kiss, cupping my chin and forcing my eyes to his.

"You can't take this away from me. Not again." His jaw clenches. "You start having doubts about me, about us, we talk about it. It's one thing to have to negotiate the Qwest situation or the pressures that come with this industry. Those aren't the things that kept us apart. I can fight all of that. I can't fight you."

"I know," I whisper. "I was having doubts for a minute."

"Was?" He's watchful and waiting. "Not anymore?"

"Not anymore." I lean in for another kiss, and his hand presses at the back of my head when I would pull away, maintaining the sweet contact. Ravishing my lips until they throb in time with the rhythm of our kiss.

"Don't doubt me, Bris."

A fist closes around my heart at the plea on his lips, in his eyes.

"I won't." I cup the side of his face and give him one last kiss. "I promise."

"Good." The tight line of his mouth eases. "Now we really will be late if we don't get cracking."

"I'm not gonna ask again." I stand and walk over to the bag of clothes I brought.

"Good, 'cause I still ain't telling you nothing." He laughs, but there's no mistaking the quiet satisfaction in his eyes as he watches me hang the few items I packed in his closet.

I've finished my shower and am wiping steam from the mirror when he comes into the bathroom, still wearing the sleep pants hanging low on his hips. I'm tempted to tug on the drawstring holding them up so I can see all his bare magnificence again, but his frown quells all my playful instincts.

"Now what?" I scrub cleanser onto my face, leaving untouched circles around my eyes.

"You said you and Parker are done, right?" His question and his tone ring abruptly in the bathroom.

My fingertips go still on my cheeks, and my eyes meet his in the mirror. Before I can answer, he reaches into his pocket and pulls out a phone. My phone.

"You left this downstairs." He places it on the bathroom counter. "Why's he blowing you up?"

"Is he?" I carefully re-tuck the towel under my arm, at least making sure it is secure since this conversation could quickly become less than safe. "I don't know."

I splash water onto my face, wishing I could wash away all those messages and the last few weeks with Parker altogether.

"Like four missed calls, text messages, voicemails." He rests a hip against the counter, waiting, expecting an explanation from me.

"Were you snooping, Grip?" My smile in the mirror as I dry my face is strained.

"I heard it ringing downstairs when you were in the shower." Grip crosses his arms over the width of his chest, biceps flexed with the motion. "Does he understand that it's over? Why all the calls?"

I dot moisturizer on my face and shrug.

"I'd have to listen to the messages to know what he wants for sure."

He picks up the phone and extends it to me, one brow cocked. "No time like the present."

My short laugh sounds uneasy even to me. I grab the phone, but set it back on the counter.

"Later. Aren't you the one who said I need to get ready?"

I run a brush through my hair and don't look at him even though his scrutiny in the mirror never wavers.

"I said I didn't want to re-hash everything," Grip says. "But just tell me what happened with Parker."

Shit.

"Um, what do you want to know?" I drop the question but walk away before he has time to respond, heading into the closet and flicking through my limited wardrobe options. "You really should tell me what to wear for this surprise of yours. Is this okay?"

I hold a romper to my chest, taking his "I don't give a damn" expression as a no and discarding it to search the rack for something else.

"Okay, maybe this one?" I hold up a cotton candy pink belted tunic dress with a high-low hem for his inspection. He still doesn't respond with anything other than the exasperation on his face. "Yeah, I like this one, too."

He snatches the dress from my hand and tosses it onto the padded bench in the center of the closet.

"Stop avoiding my question." Impatience disrupts the rugged beauty of his face. "What happened with Parker?"

"I thought we were short on time." I turn my back to dig in my carryall, searching for ankle boots. "I know I had a pair of—"

He pulls me around by my shoulders to face him. His hands glide down my still-damp arms to link his fingers with mine, the warmth of his bare chest emanating to my chilled skin.

"Tell me. Now."

I sigh and slump my shoulders before starting.

"I used Parker to push you to Qwest." I chew the corner of my mouth for a second. "We weren't ever actually in a relationship."

I roll my eyes and gesture vaguely.

"I mean, we dated a few months, yeah, back in high school."

"And fucked in the coat check." Grip's words emerge controlled, but a savage objection flares in his eyes, a warning that beneath the placid surface, a beast bides its time.

"Yeah." I rake my fingers through my hair. "But it didn't take me long to figure out it wasn't gonna work. I broke things off when I started at Columbia and he went off to Stanford. He's been trying to wiggle back in ever since."

"So you fucked Parker, after all these years, just so I would try with Qwest? You went that far to manipulate me?"

The scariest part of what he says is what he doesn't say. The things that, even though not voiced, take flight behind his eyes. Disappointment. Anger. Disgust.

"Not exactly. I—"

"Then what exactly?" he slices over me.

"Give me a chance to explain."

"That's what this is. The chance to have your say." He narrows his eyes. "I just hate everything you're saying."

I sit on the bench and press my knees together under the thick towel, trying to keep my back and my facts straight.

"That night on the roof you said neither of us had been in a serious relationship, and that seemed to make you think there was a chance when I really didn't think there should be. Then before the show, I overheard you talking with Rhys and Kai in your dressing room."

"You eavesdropped on us?" It comes as a quiet demand.

"Not on purpose, but I could tell that you wanted . . . more. That you wanted to be with someone the way Rhyson is with Kai, and you were held up with me."

I lean forward, resting my elbows on my knees.

"When Parker upgraded Qwest's room at his hotel that night, it was perfect timing." I dip my head until a fall of hair hides my face from him. "So I invited Parker to the club. I wanted you to see us together and thought it might give you a little push in the right direction."

The silence swells with all the emotions he's suppressing, but they bubble up to the surface anyway, tightening the air in the closet until it feels like a tomb.

"I can tell you're frustrated with me," I say softly. "You don't have to hide that. I can take it."

"You wasted more time." He walks over to the few of my items hanging in the space he allotted for me, back turned to me. He lifts the sleeve of a dress and lets it fall. "And we involved Qwest. She got hurt because of us. And Parker?"

He aims a hard look at me over his shoulder.

"You fucked him to advance this dumb ass plan of yours?"

"No." I squeeze my eyes shut, but that doesn't keep me from seeing myself clearly. "I had no intention of sleeping with Parker. I was so drunk I didn't even know what had happened when I woke up with him in my bed the next morning. He had to tell me we had slept together."

"Don't tell me that." He squeezes his eyes shut, a growl rumbling in his chest. He links his hands behind his head, pacing back and forth in front of the bench. "If you were anywhere near as drunk that night as you were at Pirouette, I can't believe you had sex with someone in that state. Do you have any idea how irresponsible that is? He could have done anything to you. You're supposed to be the rational one. The level-headed one, and you pull this shit."

I surge to my feet, reaching for anger. Anything to distract me from the shame and regret weaving together like a chain-link fence around my self-respect.

"I never claimed to be perfect and you aren't my keeper. I don't need a lecture, Grip. I'm just trying to tell you what happened."

"And I'm telling you it's fucked up!" Grip's voice reverberates in the confines of the closet. "All of it. You pulling in Parker to get me to sleep with Qwest."

"I didn't force you to sleep with her."

"You getting drunk," he continues as if I didn't correct him, "and riding off into the night with that asshole."

"Riding off into the night?" I scoff. "Glad we're not resorting to the dramatic."

"Sleeping with him when you weren't even lucid enough to remember." He pauses, giving me space to object, but I don't have an objection. He can't be anymore disappointed in me than I am in myself for that. My anger deflates as quickly as it rose, and so does his. He steps close and brushes a knuckle over my cheek before cupping my face.

"Bris, what's up with all the drinking lately?" His voice is a balm over the self-inflicted wounds of my own actions. "I mean, we've always joked that you can outdrink us all, that nobody holds their liquor like you, but it was never like this. Should I be worried?"

A heavy laugh tumbles out of my mouth. I lean into his warm palm and close my eyes against the concern on his face.

"I'm not an alcoholic if that's what you're asking." I step even closer to him, so close I can drop my head to his chest and mumble my words into the smooth skin. "Lately I just needed to be … numb."

"Why?" When I don't respond for a few seconds, he lifts my chin and searches my face. "Numb to what?"

I pull away to show him the truth in my eyes.

"You and Qwest. That night I sent you off on a date with her, I was miserable. And I knew I did it to myself. Not just involving Parker or arranging the date with Qwest, but letting my fears rule me. Denying myself the one thing I really wanted."

"And what was that?" His eyes rest intently on my face. He already knows the answer, but I know he needs to hear me say it. After all I've put him through, he deserves to hear it. "What do you want?"

"You," I whisper.

There's no gloating, no smugness in his expression.

"You've got me." He presses his forehead to mine, angling my chin to kiss me with quick tenderness. "I just hate how we got here."

"So do I."

I place my hands flat to his chest, hesitating before going on. "If it's any consolation, Parker and I were never actually dating. I'm pretty sure he leaked everything that night to Spotted. He thought the media storm and all the coverage would somehow pressure me into giving in and making it real."

"Giving in?" The muscle tenses beneath my palms. "What does he want?"

"He wants what he's always wanted." I shrug, frank when I meet his eyes. "He wants me. Ever since we were kids he said he would marry me. Our mothers started it, and he just latched on. He sees himself as the king of his family's empire, and me as his …"

I stop short of the word so closely associated with Grip and Qwest.

"Queen?" The word trips, loaded with irony, off Grip's tongue.

"He's crazy." I dig my fingers into my hair. "I keep telling him I won't marry him, but he won't take no for an answer."

"Why did you let it go on for weeks?"

"He was in India almost the entire time, and the media had, for the most part, lost interest." I force myself to tell him the truth; though, I know it will only anger him. "I knew you gave Qwest a chance because you thought Parker and I were serious. I'd just started pressing him to tell the media the truth."

"When I think about you basically unconscious, of Parker taking advantage of you like that . . ."

He holds my hand, his gentle grip tightening around my fingers. He lifts his lashes to reveal the leashed violence in his eyes, and he doesn't have to finish the sentence. It's written there what he wants to do to Parker.

"Then don't think about it." I stretch up to kiss him, deliberately stroking my tongue deeply into his mouth, an exclusive, intimate exchange I don't want to have with anyone else. "Think about us. Think about what we feel, what we've said to each other. Think about today."

"Today he's still calling you." A bunched muscle interrupts the smooth, lightly scruffed line of his jaw. "You told him it isn't happening, but he's still calling and texting."

"I know. I'll—"

"I want it to stop."

I blink a few times, waiting for the ferocity to clear from his eyes, but it only intensifies the longer I stay silent.

"Okayyyyy. I'll check the messages, and I'll handle it."

"If you don't handle him, I will," he warns.

Oh, the fuck no. That's the last thing I need. "That isn't a good idea. He's . . ."

I focus on our bare feet just inches apart, our toes pointing to each other.

"He's a very powerful man, Grip, and I don't want you hurt."

There's an ominous quiet before the storm I should have known my comment would stir.

"You think I'm scared of that son of a bitch?" A dark cloud breaks on his face, his voice a boom of thunder. "You think you have to protect me from him? Is that what you're saying?"

"You don't know him. He—"

"You get one shot." He clips the words, anger still brimming in his eyes. "Listen to the messages. Deal with him or I will."

"You don't boss me around." My words land heavily between us. I hate to say it, but I have to say it. I have no plans to be anyone other than who I am. "Let's be clear about that."

The bands stretching tightly over his expression loosen just a little bit. His eyes crinkle at the corners, and he drops a kiss at the corner of my mouth.

"That's my girl."

A confused laugh pops from my mouth. I assert myself, expecting resistance, and it only draws him closer.

"I have no desire to boss you around, Bristol. I love that you're a boss. It's sexy as hell."

"Well, thank you for—"

He cups my pussy under the towel tucked around me, his eyes heated, holding me hostage.

"This is the only part of you I want to boss around." His middle finger strokes along one side of my clit and then the other.

"There won't be any doubt who's the boss right here between these legs."

The lazy motion of his finger snatches the breath from me. I'm wet and anaerobic, unable to even pant while he tends to my clit, brushing a rough finger pad along the slickened nub. One thick finger breaches me and retreats. Breaches me and retreats, a rough repetition that soaks his hand and makes my thighs tremble. Holy hell, I may not want to be bossed around, but Grip is Commander-In-Clit. He can get it anytime he wants.

The unapologetic possession in his eyes as he watches me unraveling, my knees weakening so badly I have to hang on to his shoulders, tells me he knows it. I can't even care. If he does this to me when no other man has been able to, he gets to be smug about it. He's earned that shit.

The orgasm propels harsh breaths from my mouth. I come hard and with a crash, landing limply against his chest. The pleasure so overwhelms me that tears christen the corners of my eyes.

"That's right. That's my girl." He licks at the tears as if they're an offering, like they're his due. He palms the small of my back, and the possessive weight of his hand alone has my most hidden, private muscles clenching again. He holds complete sway over my body.

"You're right, Bristol," he whispers into my hair, humor rich in his voice. "You're the boss."

Twenty-Six
Grip

ROWING UP, DRIVING A RANGE ROVER LIKE THIS ONE—OVERLOADED, latest model, and just over two hundred thousand dollars—seemed about as likely as scoring a ride in Cinderella's pumpkin. But here I am. Or rather here we are.

"This car's gorgeous." Bristol caresses the stitch pattern perforated leather seats. "I didn't even know you were in the market for one. You've never cared much about cars before."

"True." I merge onto the 5, shrug, and shoot her a quick grin. "I'm good with my Harley and my six four."

"And what's so great about the six four?" Bristol laughs when I look at her like this should be self-evident.

"They don't make 'em like the '64 Impala anymore," I say. "That's when American cars were the bomb. It takes more than money to appreciate them. You gotta maintain and know your way around that beautiful body. She won't purr for just any dude."

"Why am I not surprised this became a thinly veiled conversation about sex?" Bristol laughs, opening the bag in her lap and finishing her makeup since I rushed her out of the loft.

"What can I say?" I grin. "Amir rolled through to drop it off."

"It's yours?"

"I'm test driving it."

"Hmmm." She flips down the visor mirror and applies lipstick. "I'd never picture you with this car, I guess."

"Maybe I'm full of surprises."

She'll soon see that for herself. I know she's gonna kill me for what I'm doing today, but she loves me. They say love covers a multitude of sins. We'll see. In the words of that great comedic philosopher Kevin Hart, "We gon' learn today!"

"And what is this surprise?" Bristol follows up predictably.

I only give her a shrug and grin in response. If she weren't distracted, she'd probably pay closer attention to the route we're taking.

"You'll have to wait and see."

She rolls her eyes and takes off her seatbelt to reach her purse on the floor, putting the makeup bag away.

The loud "whoop" from behind freezes my blood, and for a second, my heart isn't sure it's safe to beat. The flashing blue lights in the rearview mirror confirm what my body has already warned me of. Growing up in Compton, guys like me have an almost Pavlovian response to cops. Instead of salivating, we auto-perspire and run through the mantra our mothers drilled in our heads before we could even drive.

Keep your hands where they can see them. Never make sudden movements.

Have license and registration already out so you don't have to reach into any pockets or compartments. Always answer with respect. And most important.

Do whatever it takes to make it home.

"Put your seatbelt back on." I slap my license on the dashboard. "Now, babe."

I feel her eyes boring into me, but I'm too focused on getting through these next few minutes to address her questions. It feels like the gun I stowed in the glove compartment, the one I carry for my own safety, just turned its barrel on me, adding a complication to a situation I always hate finding myself in.

I resent the sheen of sweat covering my skin. Adrenaline pours through my system, spiking my blood, crashing my heart behind my ribs. No matter how much I remind myself that I've done nothing wrong, that I have the number one album in the country, and that I could afford to buy this car several times over and not even dent my bank account, I can't undo years of conditioning that tell me I have reason to fear. To be cautious. Even before that summer day with Jade on the playground, I had an uneasy relationship with law enforcement. We all did in my neighborhood. After that, it only worsened. After that, it was never the same. Since Greg joined LAPD, I've met many good cops, and things have changed a lot in my neighborhood, but it's still a deeply rotten system. When the cop taps the window, that's something I can't forget.

"Is there a problem, officer?" I ask through the half-open window.

His assessing eyes flick past me and over my shoulder, roaming over Bristol. I don't have to look at her to know what he sees. I've memorized her. The burnished hair is wild and loose around her shoulders. Her lips, pink and soft. Her dress reaches mid-thigh, but sitting, the hem rises even higher. His glance, though impersonal, lingers on her long, toned legs. The longer his eyes rest on her, the less I feel like dealing with this shit. I'm relieved when he looks back to my face.

"There's been suspicious activity in the area, so we're doing some routine stops." He steps back. "License and registration, please."

Suspicious activity my ass. I am the suspicious activity. My driving a two-hundred-thousand dollar Rover in this neighborhood is grounds enough. My driving this car here with a white woman in the passenger seat? An imperfect shit storm.

"Any weapons in the vehicle?" he asks.

Here we go.

"A 9mm in the middle console." My eyes don't stray from his. "I have a permit for it."

"I'd like to inspect the firearm and conduct a search," the officer says. "Could you step out of the vehicle?"

I could refuse, but the last thing I need is for him to feel like I'm being "uncooperative" and that he needs to call for back up. I pass the license and my permit through the open window.

"What's this about?" Bristol leans over to demand of the police officer. "He isn't getting out until you tell us what this is about."

"Bris," I say through clenched teeth and fraying patience. "I've got this."

"But he hasn't even really told us why we—"

"Be quiet." The words come out sharp and short. The hurt in her eyes twists my heart around, softening the shell that started forming as soon I saw that blue light. "Please. Just let me handle it."

She sits back, rebellion in the tight line of her mouth. She studies her nails as if she couldn't care less what happens next, but I know her better than that.

I open the door and step out.

"Sorry about that, officer, she just—"

"I'm putting these cuffs on as a precaution," he cuts in. "Just while I search the vehicle."

Cuffs? Shit.

He turns me roughly, rocking my chest into the car, pulling my arms behind my back, and clamping the cuffs on my wrists.

Bristol isn't pretending to be fascinated by her nails anymore. I feel her eyes latched onto me. I asked her to be quiet, but her shock and dismay at how quickly the situation has changed create a choking silence. He pats down my shoulders and arms, at my waist, inside my thighs and all the way down to my ankles. Rage boils up from a long-stirring cauldron in my belly, but I hear my mother's voice.

Do whatever it takes to make it home, Marlon.

When he's done, I turn and stand toe to toe with him for a few seconds, towering over him, dwarfing him. I have every advantage except the one the badge affords him

"The car isn't mine yet," I say calmly, ignoring the chafe of the cuffs. "I'm test driving it."

"All right." He tilts his head toward the curb. "Why don't you test drive that curb while I check the vehicle?"

A battle cry shreds the inside of my throat, desperate to escape. But it isn't time for fighting. I have to maintain control in what could, with one wrong word or move, become a volatile situation. I can't afford to lose control.

How many times did I sit on some damn curb, my boys and me? Pulled off basketball courts, out of cars, laid on our stomachs, stretched in the middle of streets like animals? Humiliation and rage linking us like some urban chain gang. If I think about it too long, I'll do something stupid. I just want this over so we can be on our way. I keep telling myself that, but the longer this goes on, the harder it is to remember.

"Ma'am, you can join him on the curb while I conduct the search," the officer offers.

Bristol scrambles out of the car, walking swiftly to sit on the curb beside me, the pink dress falling back to show another inch of her tanned thighs.

"Pull your damn dress down," I say around the gravel in my mouth.

She glances from the expanse of legs back to my face. She drops her knees and tugs at the hem of her short dress.

"We didn't do anything wrong," she says.

"This isn't about we, Bris." I look at her meaningfully, keeping my voice low even as bitterness rises in me. "This is about me. Driving that car in this neighborhood with you in the passenger seat."

"You think he stopped you because I was in the car?"

"Remember you asked me to let you know when your privilege makes you clueless?" I ask. "Well, that just happened."

Contrition pinches her brows together, and she lowers her eyes to the road before going on.

"I'm sorry." She shakes her head and then searches my eyes for answers. "I want to . . . I'm trying to understand. Can you just tell me why you have that gun in the car? I hate guns."

"I carry it all the time. You just never knew, I guess."

"Why? You have Amir."

"Yeah?" I ostensibly look around the surprisingly calm street. It's a Sunday afternoon, and I would expect at least a few kids popping wheelies. "And where's Amir now?"

"If you need him to—"

"That's my point. I don't need him to. I can protect myself."

"Hey." She presses a gentle kiss on my mouth, her soft lips opening briefly under mine. She rests her cool, soft palm against my face, and I lean into her, needing the contact. "I'm sorry if I was insensitive. I know this makes you think about what happened with Jade, but it isn't the same thing."

Ancient guilt cuts off my air for a moment, gagging me. I was a kid, just like Jade was. And he was a cop. I don't know what I could have done, but it kills me all the time that I did nothing.

"I know that." But the helplessness feels familiar. It feels the same. "But I'm never gonna be caught in a position where I can't take care of someone I care about again."

"I'm done," the officer says, walking toward us. "Well, almost. I've searched you. I've searched the car." His eyes light on Bristol.

"Ma'am, would you stand against the car for me?"

"No." My voice is an abrasion in the pleasant Sunday afternoon quiet. I'm cuffed, but I lean my torso in front of Bristol's chest so she can't stand. "She's clean."

The officer's brows lift at my challenge.

"I'll be the judge of that." He nods to Bristol. "Ma'am, may I search you?"

"I said she's clean." I swallow the helpless frustration bubbling in my throat, scorching the lining of my stomach. "Don't touch her."

Those are the words I said in my mirror for weeks after that officer crossed the line with Jade.

Don't touch her.

Words I never said to him that summer day.

Bristol glances from me to the officer, concern knitting her eyebrows. She understands my fear, as irrational as it may seem. She tries her best not to flash the officer when she stands from the curb. I surge to my feet and step between them, ready to beat him if I have to, literally with my hands tied behind my back.

My fists clenched behind me belie the calm forced into my voice and onto my face.

"I've cooperated fully with you, though you still haven't even given me a reason for the stop," I say. "You and I both know you don't need to search her. And you won't."

Am I imagining the touch of satisfaction in the look he gives me? That I may have the expensive whip and the beautiful girlfriend he could never pull in a million years, but today he gets to feel like the bigger man? In this neighborhood, just a block away from that playground where Jade lost a measure of her innocence, it's hard for me to tell where my preconceived notions end and reality begins. Is it as hard for him to look at me and not see what he expects instead of who I really am?

That moment of clarity doesn't change our circumstances. That he wants to search Bristol, and whether I'm right or wrong, he isn't touching her if I can help it. I need to calm down. I know the rules, I hear the mantra.

Do whatever it takes to make it home. Always answer with respect.

But there is no respect, not for me from him. Not for him from me. There is an unspoken feud pitting us against one another, and every cell in my body rebels against following the rules.

I try the old trick from my childhood, reaching for poetry—for Neruda, Poe, Cummings, anyone whose eloquence will calm the clamor of my heart and ease the riot in my chest. But all I find is the revolt of NWA's "Fuck Tha Police," chanting that a young nigga got it bad because he's brown. The lyrics gather in my brain like an unruly mob. Every word uproarious and disorderly. They swell in my head and crack my skull like a Billy club. My wrists strain against the cuffs, and the outrage of a million men who've sat on curbs and lay in the streets on their bellies strikes a match in my heart.

If I'm not careful, it could burn me to the ground.

The officer and I face off, an unbridgeable distance between us, when another cop car pulls up. Relief flashes over the officer's face to see one of his own arriving at the scene just in time. My anxiety doubles seeing another set of blue lights. Another cop to compound my trouble. But when the car door opens, it isn't just one of the officer's own. It's one of mine.

My cousin Greg gets out of the car like a guardian angel, and my shoulders sag. I didn't realize how painfully tight I held my muscles until he stepped out with his badge and all the tension drained from me.

"We got a problem, Dunne?" Greg triangulates a look between the officer, me, and Bristol.

"Routine stop, sarge," Dunne says. "I was just about to search the other passenger, but was getting resistance from the driver."

"That right?" His mouth kicks up at one corner. "You causing trouble, cuz?"

"Cuz?" Officer Dunne looks from me to Greg and back again.

"You know this one?"

"So do you." Greg laughs and shakes his head. "You told me you liked his song when I was playing it in the locker room this morning."

"What song?" He searches my face and then looks at my license he's still holding. "Marlon James. You're—"

"Grip," my cousin finishes for him. "Get the cuffs off, Dunne."

Officer Dunne reaches for my wrists.

I jerk back, trapping his eyes with mine, silently showing him my resentment

"Don't," I tell him with deadly calm, my brown eyes locked onto the cop's blue. "You've touched me enough."

An awful quiet follows my words. I don't look away from Dunne even while Greg removes the cuffs himself.

"I'm a huge fan," Dunne says awkwardly. "I wouldn't have . . . well, I didn't recognize you with your hair different."

Like that should make any damn difference. I don't respond. I can barely breathe, suffocated by my own vulnerability. Living in my luxurious loft, driving my expensive motorcycle, performing for sold-out crowds. This lifestyle insulates me from just how vulnerable I am when it comes down to it. Just breaths away from helpless. Herded and branded like cattle, emasculated, unable to even properly shield the woman I love. Fully clothed but naked on the side of the road, stripped of all dignity. No matter how many albums I sell, no matter how much money I make, I will never forget this feeling.

Officer Dunne mumbles another apology for any inconvenience. When

I keep stone facing him, he wisely gets in his car and drives away. I watch his taillights until he turns the corner and they disappear.

"Sorry about that, cuz." Greg daps me up. "We're working on it. Retraining the force and making sure we're in the community, not just policing it. It's slowly getting better. I hope. Dunne isn't a bad guy. Just still conditioned to make some assumptions."

"You mean conditioned to profile."

Greg doesn't address my comment. He knows it's true, but there's no good answer. He and I both know his colleague was wrong for that. His eyes urge me to let it go. I'm one of the few in my family who has a relationship with Greg. The others can't forgive him for Chaz. Even knowing Chaz probably would have killed others that day, even if by accident, had Greg not taken that shot. Greg joining the force always felt like a betrayal to them. Cops were in our neighborhood to harass and arrest, not protect and serve. They couldn't comprehend Greg crossing enemy lines. I understood why he wanted to change the problem from the inside. Despite the run-in with Officer Dunne, maybe because of it, I still understand, but we have a long way to go. It will take more than him on the force and some "retraining" to fix a system this broken.

"Who's this?" Greg smiles at Bristol, and she offers a stained smile in return.

"You know my boy Rhyson, of course. This is his sister, Bristol. She's my manager." I capture and kiss her hand before she can stop me, pulling her into my side. "And my girlfriend."

Bristol's surprised eyes clash with mine. I squeeze her hand, mouthing, "He's cool," to her.

"Ohhhhh." Understanding and confusion wrestle in Greg's eyes. "I thought you and—"

"Nope. Not anymore." I convert my grimace into a smile. "Look, we're keeping this on the low for now. If you can keep your big mouth shut until we want the cat all the way out the bag."

"Got it. You can trust me." Greg's grin grows wide, pride in his eyes. "You doing it big, ain't ya? Number one album. Got that top spot."

I welcome the change of subject, chuckling, shaking my head. "Still can't believe it myself."

"And this whip." Greg whistles, running a hand over the glimmering black paint covering the Rover. "Nice."

"It's actually for Ma." I smile at Bristol's look of surprise. "I've tried to give her like four cars, and she hasn't taken any of them. I'm hoping this one will be too much for her to resist."

"Good luck with that." Greg shakes his head. "She's about as stubborn as you are."

"I prefer to think of it as determined."

"That you were. You had to be. It's in everything you write. And that new track 'Bruise' is deep." He looks at me directly. "Made me proud."

After what just happened, my own words, the lyrics to 'Bruise' that urge us to understand and empathize, mock me. Do I really think I should try to walk in Officer Dunne's shoes? I notice the impression the cuffs left on my wrists. You don't see the impression they've left inside me, not just this time, but the time before and the time before. How can I walk in his shoes? How can he walk in mine? He's never lived with this constant threat, and I've never lived without it. Living those lyrics is so much harder than singing them from the safety of a stage.

Greg looks over his shoulder at his idling car. "I need to go. I guess you're on your way to Aunt Mittie's for Sunday dinner."

He glances at his watch, unaware of the bomb he just dropped on Bristol's world.

"You know how she hates it if you're late."

"Sunday dinner?" Bristol gasps when Greg climbs into his car, her eyes storming and hands balled at her sides.

I know what's behind her anger. Fear. Fear that my mom will reject her. Keeping it one hundred, Ma probably will reject her at first, but the woman who raised me will eventually see in Bristol what I see. And maybe not today, maybe not right away, but she'll be happy for me. She'll fall in love with Bristol like I did. Even with the humiliating confrontation still smarting like a third-degree burn on my pride, I'm excited about the two women I love the most starting the process today.

"What the hell, Grip?" Bristol demands. "You can't do this. Not like this."

I'm determined to shake off the unpleasantness we just experienced. I refuse to let that shit ruin a day I thought would never come. I lean my back against the passenger side door and bring her close until we are flush, front-to-front.

"Are you okay?" I ask softly.

"No, I'm not okay. You can't just spring this on me. I—"

"Forget dinner for a sec." I push her hair back from her face. "What just went down with the cop. Are you okay?"

Her irritation fades, concern taking its place.

"Am *I* okay?" She rests her elbows against my chest, leaning into me. "You were the one in cuffs. That wasn't fair. I'm sorry if I made it harder for you."

"You being here made it harder, but only because I couldn't protect you the way I wanted to."

"Not my privilege making me clueless?" she asks weakly, her eyes only half-joking. "I'm sorry."

I don't need her apologies right now. I need her. I slide my hands down her back leaning in a few inches and hovering there until she comes the rest of the way. As soon as our lips touch, all the tension, frustration, anger, and yes, fear—I let it go. She opens for me, taking me in. The world falls away, and I'm lost in her. We kiss until I feel her lose herself in me, too. Until the tension leaves her shoulders and her hands come up to frame my face.

"You're still in trouble for springing dinner on me like this," she says against my lips.

"I did say if you ever gave me a chance," I drop one last kiss on her lips. "I'd take you home to my mama."

Twenty-Seven
Bristol

ONLY HAVE MY OWN VANITY TO BLAME.

If I hadn't been so concerned about my makeup, I probably would have realized where we were headed.

I would have demanded he turn the car around, or as a last resort flung myself into traffic on the 5. Now I have no recourse but to endure this. The woman will hate me. She hates the very idea of me with her son. She loves Qwest because . . . Black. She hates me because . . . white. I know that's an oversimplification. There are a lot of things Mittie James loves about Qwest that have nothing to do with the color of her skin. But I could be Mother Theresa and she wouldn't approve of me because of the color of mine, or so it feels.

At least having to deal with this distracts me from the clusterfuck of that "routine" stop. I've never seen anything like it. That officer cuffed Grip for no reason, with no provocation. It's the kind of thing I might have doubted at one time if I read on Facebook. I might assume the driver exaggerated for the sake of the story. But I saw it with my own eyes, and I'm still holding my previously held notions up against what just happened and wondering how to reconcile the two.

"It's gonna be fine." Grip's hand braves the space across the console to capture mine.

"You should have asked me or at least warned me."

"I'm sorry."

"No, you're not."

His wicked laughter fills the car until his shoulders shake and he bends over the steering wheel.

"Yes, by all means wreck us. That would be a reprieve," I mumble, looking out the window to study my surroundings.

The community teems with life. A cohort of guys riding dirt bikes pop wheelies down the street. Young girls play hopscotch, their braids bouncing as they jump the squares. A man wearing a bright red apron stares appreciatively at the Rover through the steam rising from his front yard grill. I don't see the war zone Grip has often talked about when he was growing up. But we are sometimes in the most danger when we let our guards down, when we let peace deceive us and trick us into forgetting. Being at Grip's old high school, hearing about the funerals, the gangs, the volatility—it all tells me there is more to Compton than what this Sunday drive reveals.

A man in conversation with two others leans against an Impala, not as well kept or tricked out as Grip's, but a six four all the same. A blue handkerchief encircles one thickly muscled, ink-marked arm. Nothing's amiss in his actions, but maybe there's violence in the eyes tracking us. Something about him seems lost, desperate, dangerous. Or is that just my perception of him? Am I as bad as Officer Dunne? Fear and ignorance driving my assumptions? I'm discombobulated in this zip code, on this block, and the only things familiar to me are the opulence of this car and the man driving it.

I love him. Grip's fingers wrap around mine, and he darts concerned glances my way when he thinks I'm not looking. His beautiful words. His outrageous humor. The way he looks at me and makes me feel. Ms. James may not like me, but her son loves me. Obstinately, unwaveringly loves me. I'll hold onto that like an anchor.

"We're here."

Grip kills the engine in front of a small house in a row of houses that look almost identical, differentiated only by color and the front porch decorations. Ms. James' house is blue. A tributary of cracks run through the short span of concrete leading to the entrance. Three chairs squeeze onto the tiny porch, a vibrantly colored pillow in each one. I envision Ms. James and her friends seated there, inspecting the neighborhood and keeping watch. The wooden door stands open, leaving only the black-barred screen between me and Grip's childhood home.

"Stay right there." Grip gets out and stands just outside. "I have to open the door for you. We have an audience."

"An audience?" I peer through the tinted windshield.

It's a sci-fi movie out there, with all the inhabitants frozen in some time warp, and apparently this expensive Range Rover is the spaceship from outer space. And when I step out, I am the alien.

"Um, I feel like everyone's staring," I side-whisper as we approach the house.

"Yeah." He gives me a cocky grin. "I'm a pretty big deal." "Oh, God." I have to laugh. "Your conceit knows no bounds."

"Well, and it isn't every day they see a car like that." He turns to me on the front porch. "Oh, and you're the only white chick for miles."

Great.

"Anything I should know?" I ask.

"Nah, Ma's easy." Grip shrugs. "Oh, just remember it's sweet potato pie, not pumpkin."

That matters?

"Okay. Got it. Sweet potato."

"And the greens, they're collards, not kale."

"I've never had collard greens. You think I'll like them?"

"If you don't," Grip says, eyes stretched for emphasis. "Pretend you do. And eat. This ain't the day to diet, baby. Ma doesn't trust people who don't eat."

"Why is every tip you're giving me about food?"

"Food's her love language. Everything you need to know about my mother is on her table."

My palms are sweaty. Why does this feel so important? I glance at Grip's strong profile, and I can't help but think of all it took for him to emerge from this neighborhood as the man he is today. The talent. The strength. The intelligence. The perseverance. The kindness.

He wouldn't be the man I love without the woman on the other side of this door, and against the odds, knowing she wants him with a woman who "looks like her," I want her to want him to be with me. I want her to like me.

"Collard greens. Sweet potato pie," I rehearse under my breath.

"Hey." Grip grasps my chin, his touch gentle and his eyes intent on my face. "Scratch all that. I fell for you. Not the edited, censored version of you. That's who I want my mom to see today. I want her to meet the real Bristol."

The tightness in my shoulders eases, and the breath I was holding whooshes over my lips.

"Thank you." I lean a few inches toward him, poised for a quick kiss.

He puts his hand between our lips, the look he gives me completely serious. "But for real, though, eat those greens."

He opens the door and pulls me in behind him by the hand. "Ma!" He steps into the immaculate and modest living room.

"I'm home."

There's energy in the steps shuffling up the hallway. The closer they come, the tighter my nerves. I wiggle my fingers free of Grip's, ignoring his chastening look.

"You're late is what you are," her disembodied voice tosses up the hall. "You ain't been to church in I don't know how long, barely make it home for Sunday dinner, and when you do come you're . . ."

Mittie James' feet stop abruptly at the threshold, but her curiosity leaps into the room ahead of her and seesaws between her son and me. She's still wearing her church clothes and stockings with her bedroom slippers.

"You're late," she finishes, her eyes locked with mine. "Hello, Bristol. This is a surprise."

I want to look away, but I can't. A weak smile hangs limply between my cheeks.

"Sorry, I'm late, Ma." Grip closes the space separating them, scooping her petite frame into his broad chest. "It's okay that I brought Bristol, right?"

The caramelized eyes, so like Grip's, do a slow slide from me to her son.

"Of course. Welcome to our home, Bristol." She smiles politely and starts back the way she came. "Dinner's ready. Come on."

"You heard her." Grip smiles, takes my hand, and turns up the hall, dragging me along. "Dinner's ready."

"Hey, wait." I dig my heels in, making him stop, too. "Was it pumpkin or sweet potato?"

"Babe." He sighs and deposits a quick kiss on my nose. "Just come eat."

The small dining room feels full, even though there are only a few people at the table. I've met everyone here, but they receive my presence with varying degrees of surprise, curiosity, and animosity. Fortunately, Amir is here, and so is the sweet teacher from Grip's old high school, Shondra. I'm guessing Jade's in the animosity camp. Even with her hard, almond-shaped eyes tracking my every move, I feel a tug of sympathy for her. How could I not after what Grip just withstood? Knowing at such an early age, Jade was violated by one who was supposed to protect her. When I think of all these things, I see Grip finding it in his heart to write a song like "Bruise" as a miracle.

"Here's another plate." Ms. James rearranges the place setting by Jade to accommodate me. "Amir, grab that other chair out of the kitchen."

He jumps up to do her bidding but offers me a reassuring smile on his way. I look at the chair beside Jade, unsure if I should take it or let Grip have it and wait for the one Amir is bringing.

"We don't bite." Jade nods her head to the empty seat, her lips twisting derisively. "Sit down."

I offer her a small smile, which she doesn't bother returning. I take a deep breath, sit, and try to relax my shoulders.

"Good to see you again, Bristol," Shondra says, her smile warm and genuine.

"You, too." I'm so grateful for even that small kindness. "How have you been?"

"Good." Shondra sips from the glass of iced tea at her elbow. "Kids crazy as ever, but good. Still talking about Grip coming to see them a few weeks ago."

"It was fun." Grip leans back and drapes an arm across the back of my seat. I sit up right away, leaving plenty of space between his arm and my back.

"Well, fix your plates." Ms. James gestures to the table crowded with enough food to feed ten more people. "Nobody serving you here, Marlon. You know how to get your own."

"Yes, ma'am." His grin comes easy, and where I'm strung tight, he's as relaxed as I've ever seen him. There's a comfort, an ease, to him like I've never seen.

He's home.

He stands, stretching to scoop generous portions of everything. I'm about to do the same when he picks up the plate in front of me and replaces it with the full one.

"Here ya go," he says softly, his smile down at me intimate and affectionate.

He served me.

Oh, God. It shouldn't be a big deal, but it feels deliberate. He's expressing something. He's telling them all, without saying a word, that I'm special to him. I glance around the table, noting the smirk on Amir's lips, his eyes teasing me. The speculating surprise in Shondra's glance. The narrow-eyed resentment coming off Jade beside me like a radioactive wave. The disappointment on his mother's face before she stows it away.

"Thanks." I muster a smile for him. "You didn't have to."

"No problem." Grip metes out his own portions, sits in the extra seat, and turns his attention to the people still watching us closely. "So, catch me up. What's been going on?"

His question seems to crack the wall of tension some, and everyone eats and laughs and talks. I dig into the food. I've never tasted any vegetable like collard greens. I'm tempted to scoop up what's left with my fingers and turn up the plate to slurp the juices. Everything tastes so good, and I don't care if the greens are collard, kale, or Crayola, I want seconds.

They talk about people I don't know and things I don't quite grasp. I never watched *Martin*, so when they reminisce about a particularly funny episode, I smile and try to follow. Even without context, it's hilarious the way Jade tells it. I find myself laughing along.

"What you laughing at, Bristol?" The laughter drains from her face. "Have you ever even seen *Martin*?"

Busted.

"Um, no." I bite the inside of my jaw. "It just sounded funny the way you were telling it."

She rolls her eyes and sucks her teeth.

"Don't start, Jade." Grip's voice holds an unmistakable, quiet warning.

"What?" Jade grabs the Raiders cap off the table and shoves it on her head, leaning back in her seat. "Just didn't seem like her kind of show."

The sound of forks and knives scraping over the plates is magnified in the deep pool of silence following the exchange. It's because of me. Everyone is uncomfortable because I'm here, but I have no idea how to fix it. I'm just a girl having dinner with her boyfriend, as desperate for his mother to like me as you'd expect.

"You missed a great party, Jade," Amir finally says while serving himself another helping of everything. "Grip's release party, I mean."

"Girl, it was incredible." Ms. James beams with pride, her eyes set on her son.

"Yeah, sorry I couldn't make it." Jade doesn't sound sorry to me. "I guess you supposed to be a big deal now, huh?"

Grip bends a longsuffering look on his cousin and keeps eating without responding.

"Anybody can sell records," Jade continues. "But is it quality? I mean, is it real hip-hop?"

Grip tightens his lips, but there's otherwise no sign that what Jade says bothers him. I'm beginning to understand the dynamic between the cousins better now. Knowing about the incident with Jade and the police officer when they were kids, and Jade missing her chance to apply to the School of the Arts, I wonder if she's jealous. And maybe Grip knows it, but his guilt eats away at him, so he let's her get away with things no one else would.

"Grip's shit is legit, Jade," Amir says. "You still haven't heard the album?"

"I'm sure I heard everything he has to say before," Jade says. "No one's original anymore."

"Grip is."

It's out of my mouth before I think better of it. I really wish I'd thought better of it, because everyone, including Grip, turns a collective stare on me.

"I just meant, um . . ." I bite my lip while I collect my thoughts. "Grip's writing is excellent. His lyrics are incredible. As a matter of fact, the reviewer from *Rolling Stone* called the album innovative and revelatory. It's still the number one album in the country, and actually not just anyone can sell records in this market. In a climate where sales are down everywhere, Grip's are up. And that's because his work is stellar and resonates with a wide audience."

Grip's mouth tips at the corner, and I know he's laughing at me the way he and Rhyson always do when they say I love everything Grip writes. I do. And I probably sound like an infomercial, but it's all the truth.

"It's good, Jade." Ms. James addresses Grip's cousin, but her eyes rest on me, a little softer. "And you know I'm old school. I don't cut no slack, even for my own son. If it was weak, I'd tell you."

"And at this party I missed," Jade says. "Did you perform with Qwest, your girlfriend?"

She throws it out as a challenge, a dare to Grip to explain our situation.

"Qwest and I did perform," he says simply. "But she isn't my girlfriend anymore."

A bubble of silence swells, and Ms. James pops it with her next words.

"What do you mean?" She looks like Grip just kicked her puppy. "But she was just—"

Her eyes meet mine, and she cuts herself off, leveling her mouth into a flat line and pouring another glass of tea for herself.

"Ma, I told you not to get attached like that," Grip says softly with his eyes on his plate. "It just didn't work out."

He looks at me, taking my hand under the table and linking our fingers on his knee.

"I'm with Bristol now."

Shit. Fuckity shit.

Looking for something to do, I pour more gravy over my mashed pota-toes, drowning the poor side dish. I'm so flustered my hand shakes and I spill the thick, hot liquid in my lap.

"Oh!" I scoot back from the table, fanning the scalding spot on my thighs.

"Are you okay?" Grip grabs a napkin from the table and starts mopping at my lap.

Embarrassment and discomfort constrict my throat until I can't swallow or breathe. I manage to stand under the weight of everyone's scrutiny and choke out a few words.

"Where's your bathroom?" I gesture to the spot on my dress. "I'd like to clean up a little."

Really I just want to get out of this room where it feels like I'm being bludgeoned with their stares.

"Right through there." Ms. James points down the hall, her voice flat, her eyes sad.

"Thank you," I whisper, moving in the direction she indicated.

"Can I help?" Grip follows me into the hall. "Do you need—"

"No, just go back." I don't turn around because I don't want him to see the tears in my eyes. The stupid tears of rejection. I knew she wouldn't like me. Why was I not prepared for this feeling? "Please. I'm fine."

I know he's still there. His concern wraps around me from behind. I feel his solid warmth at my back and his breath in my ear.

"Baby, it's okay," he whispers.

I take a step forward, putting distance between my back and his tenderness, which will only break me down more.

"Grip, just ... I'm fine."

I don't wait for anything else before I step gratefully into the small bath-room. As soon as I'm behind the door, hot tears stream down my cheeks. I'm a fixer. It's what I do for a living. I fix everything for everyone, but there's nothing I can do to fix my skin. To fix the fact that everyone wants Grip with Qwest, and I can't ever be what his mother wants me to be. I know what she means to him and that he wouldn't be the man he is today without his mother's influence and guidance. That he disappoints her by loving me burns more than the gravy I spilled in my lap.

I allow myself a few moments of the lavatory pity party before wetting my napkin and wiping the dress, which is probably ruined. That's the least of my concerns, though. I splash water on my face until it looks sort of normal and steel myself to go back out there. It would be wonderful if Ms. James and Jade liked me, but they don't. I tell myself that Grip likes me, he loves me, so it doesn't matter.

I'm walking up the hall but stop when I hear my name.

"And you tried to tell me you and Bristol was just friends. Like I'm blind, dumb, and stupid," Jade says sarcastically. "You a trip, cuz."

"Oh, I'm a trip?" Irritation coarsens Grip's words. "Why?"

"You weren't satisfied with the fancy loft and the motorcycles and the cars and flying around on private jets," Jade says. "You just had to go and get you a white girl, didn't you? She's the last piece for your collection."

"Jade, lower your voice," Ms. James says softly.

"No, Jade," Grip snaps. "Shut the hell up."

"You had a queen but just had to go get you a Becky." Jade loads her voice with contempt before pulling the trigger. "Just like all them other niggas. Forgetting where they came from."

"I haven't forgotten a damn thing." Grip's words scrape against each other like iron sharpening iron, slicing into the thick air filling the house.

"Forget *who* they came from." Jade presses on like he didn't speak. "Like the sisters need another reminder that we ain't good enough. Ain't pretty enough. You sorry ass sellouts gotta stay true to form and choose them every time you get a little cash."

"My being with Bristol has nothing to do with you or anyone else," Grip says.

"Doesn't it?" Ms. James counters softly. "I'm sorry, but Jade's right. I didn't raise you to be a cliché, Marlon. Some man who thinks he needs a white woman on his arm to be successful."

"If you think that's what I'm doing," Grip replies softly, disappointment heavy in his voice. "Then you don't know the man you raised at all."

"I know you had a good woman, a beautiful Black woman who understands where you come from," Ms. James replies. "Who understands our challenges and knows how to support you."

The incident with Officer Dunne haunts me. How Grip had to guide me. Calm me. Correct me. How I had no clue about any of it. She's probably right. Qwest probably would have had Officer Dunne in his own cuffs when it was all said and done. In this moment, I feel completely inadequate.

"And last we heard, you were with Qwest," Ms. James says, her voice unapologetic. "Next thing we know you bring her in here uninvited and unannounced like some trophy we should put on the mantel. What am I supposed to think?"

"A trophy, Ma? Come on. This is me," Grip fires back. "You're right. I should have handled it differently and eased into it, but this is happening, whether you found out today or later."

"But you chose today to rub her in our faces," Jade cuts in.

"I'm not rubbing anything in your face," Grip says. "You're a part of my life. Bristol's in my life. I just want you guys to get to know each other."

"We should at least give her a chance," Shondra speaks up for the first time.

"Shondra, don't act like you don't feel the same way," Jade says. "When that basketball player got married last week, first thing you asked was did he marry a Black woman."

"Well, I like Bristol," Shondra says, not addressing the reminder of what she said before. "She's good people, and if you want to be with her, Grip, I got your back. It's fine with me."

"Well, it ain't fine with me," Jade says.

"Jade, come on now," Amir interrupts. "You don't even know Bristol."

"So what are you, Amir?" Jade challenges. "Another nigga with his nose wide open for this white chick? You know they freaks, so she might take both of you at the same time."

"Dammit, Jade!" Grip slams the table, rattling the plates and making the glassware sing a dissonant note. Anger edges his words. "You don't talk about her like that. What the hell is wrong with you? With both of you? You can't just be happy that I found someone I love? No matter if she's black, brown, white, whatever?"

"Love?" Ms. Mittie scoffs. "Once the novelty wears off, we'll see about love. For you and for her. Not to mention you'll undermine your credibility with a lot of people who saw 'Queen' as their song, our song. You'll lessen the impact you could have had in the community."

"Just because I love someone of a different race doesn't mean I'm not passionate about my own," Grip disagrees sharply. "About the causes that affect my community or the things that need to be said on our behalf."

"Well, you should ask yourself would she even give you a second look if you weren't who you are now?" Jade spews. "Would she have given you a second look if you weren't rich, famous? If you were just another nigga washing her car or changing her oil?"

Every insult, every assumption, every preconceived notion fell on me like a bag of stones. My arms are heavy with them. My neck, bowed. My back about to break. It took a lot for me to even admit I loved Grip, and I had to overcome so many fears to be with him. I'm trying to understand how his mother and Jade feel. I want to, but I can't listen to another word. I walk into the room, and for the first time, feel like myself. Feel like the girl I know Grip needs at his side.

"Bristol, hey." Grip tries to fix his face so I don't realize what I'm walking into. Tries to make this less uncomfortable for me, but it's too late. I'm well past discomfort.

"First of all," I start softly, spreading my glance between every one at the table, but ending with Ms. James. "Let me just say dinner was delicious."

Contrition darkens her eyes, but she doesn't look away.

"I'm sorry you heard all of that, Bristol," she says. "You're a guest in my home, and that isn't how I treat guests."

If Qwest had come here today, she probably would have been welcomed not like a guest, but like family. I remember the ease between her and Grip's mother at the release party. Like they had known each other for years even though they had just met. Jealousy stabs my heart. It's familiar, this stupid longing for someone's love, but I still hurt when it's withheld.

"I came here not sure if I should say sweet potato or pumpkin, kale or collards." I continue, shrugging and laughing a little. "Hell, I'm still not sure. I had no idea what to expect, but that was some of the best food I've ever had in my life."

Grip looks at me like he wants to check me for a fever or slip me a Valium.

"Also," I say, turning my glance to Jade. "You don't have to wonder if I would have given Grip a second look if he wasn't rich or famous because I fell in love with him when he was neither."

I look at Grip and don't give a damn that they can all probably tell how gone I am for him.

"He was sweeping floors and living in an apartment that quite possibly should have been condemned."

The jagged line of Grip's mouth softens just the tiniest bit, and he doesn't look away from me and I don't look away from him.

"It took me years to let Grip know how I felt, not because I didn't think he was good enough for me, or because he was Black. I can honestly say I never cared. He spoke to me in poetry and listened to my opinions and argued with me when he didn't think I was right and admitted when he was wrong." I smile, remembering my first night here in LA when we talked half the night away. "I started falling for him the day we met."

I look to his mother.

"You're right, Ms. James. I don't know how it's been for you, for your family. Our challenges may be different, but that doesn't mean I haven't known struggle. I may have grown up with plenty of money, but I know what it's like not to have."

My mother's coldness, my father's infidelities, my brother's distance all mock me, reminding me that no one in my family ever wanted me as badly as I wanted them.

I look at Grip's mother frankly, openly, a small smile pulling at my lips.

"I was so nervous coming here today," I tell her, my voice barely clearing a whisper. "I wanted you to like me. I didn't want to say or do the wrong thing to offend you, but now I understand that it isn't about anything I say or do. You're offended by who I am, by the things I can't change about myself. As I listened to you, I heard a pain that, you're right, I've never experienced. And for a moment, I said maybe they're right. Maybe Grip does need to be with someone like Qwest, but that was only for a moment."

I lift my chin, will it not to wobble, and will my words not to shake.

"Grip told me he wanted you to meet the real Bristol. Well, the real Bristol doesn't give up on the people she loves." I shrug, biting the inside of my jaw and blink rapidly, but a tear still escapes down my cheek even though I swipe at it impatiently. "I don't know how to. I can't stop loving your son. You wonder if I'll leave him. I won't, and if he leaves me he knows I'll probably chase him."

I allow myself to glance at Grip, but his familiar grin is not there. His eyes are sober, and I can't gauge his thoughts.

"And Qwest may understand where Grip is from, where he's been, better than I do. I can work on that. I *will* work on that." I look back to Ms. James. "But I know where he's going, and wherever he's going, I'm going with him. So, you and I should get used to each other because I'll be around."

I call on the impeccable manners of Miss Pierce's Finishing School.

"Thank you again for a lovely dinner, Ms. James," I say. "If you'll excuse me, I think I'll wait in the car."

I brush past Grip, who's probably going to skin me alive for talking to his mother that way. I rush down the short hall decorated with pictures of Grip from infanthood through high school, through the living room, down the cracked pavement, and to the car. When I yank the door handle, I realize my grand exit can only be so grand with the doors locked.

I'm not sure if Grip will be another five minutes or twenty, but I'm determined not to go back in there, even though I fidget when a few neighbors stare at me leaning against the passenger door. He emerges almost immediately, swift strides eating up the space between the blackbarred door to the Range Rover. His face is grim as he clicks the remote to open the car. I scramble to get in and away from any prying eyes. Grip climbs behind the wheel, draws and releases a deep breath, and pulls away from the curb without looking my way once. The quiet is killing me slowly, like Chinese water torture, but with drops of silence.

"Grip, I—"

"Don't." His voice comes husky and heavy. "Not yet."

I swallow my hurt. People say they want the real you, but when you give it to them, they reject you. I should know that by now. I've encountered it all my life, but I hoped it would be different with the man I loved. And I do love Grip. He can be angry with me. He can give me the silent treatment. He can try to shut me out, but there's no way he's getting rid of me. He thinks he loves me? He hasn't met a love like mine. My love is Pandora's box. Grip snapped my hinges and pried me open. He let this love out. My love has a wild streak. Good luck trying to tame it.

I didn't pay attention on the way here, but I do recognize we're not getting on the 5. Just two minutes from his mother's, Grip pulls behind a building that seems completely abandoned.

He's quiet, eyeing his hands on the wheel. I brace myself for his anger, his displeasure. I don't know what I expect to see when he finally glances over at me, but it isn't the look on his face. A look that says he loves me. A look that says he's proud of me. He says so much with just a look, but I want the words. And after a few moments he gives them to me.

"That was amazing," he says softly. "You're amazing. There's nobody else I'd choose."

Relief and gratification burst in my chest and push out on a long breath.

"You're not …" I swallow the lump that's refused to leave my throat since I heard the truth of what they thought about us, about me. "You're not mad?"

"At you?" He rests his elbows on the steering wheel and drops his head into his hands. "If anything, I'm mad at myself. I was so eager for you and my mom to …"

He trails off, shaking his head and grabbing my hand, linking our fingers on the middle console.

"I messed up." His eyes offer an apology. "I put you and my mother in an awkward situation. I should have handled it differently."

"It's okay. Hopefully in time . . ." A fragile laugh slips from me. "Like I said, I'm not going anywhere."

Grip's tender smile reaches across the small space separating us, and he kisses my fingers meshed with his. The brush of his lips drops feathers in my belly. I pull in a breath to suppress the shivers even that soft touch sets off across my skin.

Grip's smile fades, and the air thickens between us, making it harder to breathe. He leans across the console, takes my chin between two fingers, and kisses me, softly at first. As soon as I open, inviting him into me, his mouth demands my surrender. With a needy moan, I open my heart wider, taking as much of him in as I can. The kiss becomes compulsive, something I couldn't stop if I tried. My lips, my hands, seeking and hungry. His response, possessive, ravenous.

Grip hauls me over the middle console, squeezing me between his chest and the steering wheel, fitting my thighs on either side of him, shoving my dress up around my waist to expose my lacy panties. His hand wrings in my hair, pulls my head back, holds me still.

"I love you." His eyes probe mine so long I'm sure he plucks my thoughts from my mind, the emotions from my heart. "What you did back there, what you said . . ."

He presses his lips to mine, groaning against my mouth, his tongue diving in over and over until my head is spinning. I hold onto him, my arms clamped about his neck. He digs into my hips, urging me over him in a rolling rhythm, in the groove he sets. I assume the pace, riding the hot beam of flesh and steel behind his zipper. He lifts me to capture my breast through the thin cotton. He doesn't nibble at me like a delicacy. He gobbles at my nipple, pinching with his lips, nipping with his teeth. He shoves the collar aside with his chin, suckling me, singeing me through the sheer layer of my bra for long seconds before pulling my arms out of the dress, leaving it a strip of bunched material encircling my waist. He jerks the bra straps down to cage my elbows and finally takes my naked breast into his mouth.

"Oh, God." I rise and fall over him, my thighs trembling. "I need this."

"I know." He slides a hand into my panties, rubbing my slickness between his fingers. "Please say you're ready for me."

"I am." I drop my lips to his neck, sucking the skin roughly. "Get it."

He doesn't bother removing my panties, but shoves them aside. I can't wait, fumbling with his belt and zipper. He's hot and hard in my hand as I position myself and slide down, the scrape of flimsy lace against our joined flesh only intensifying the pleasure. He's wide and thick, and there's still a sting when his body insists past my tightness, still a kiss of pain underlying the rapture as he drills all that dick to the bottom of me. Oh, but God, it's worth it.

"Shiiiiiiit." Grip's brows scrunch, bottom lip trapped between his teeth, head dropped back against the headrest. "I wanna die this way. In here. Inside you. Just like this. Promise you'll fuck me on my deathbed."

Laughter erupts in the luxurious confines of the car, mine and his.

"Oh my God," I gasp, laughing but so close to coming I already see spots. "You're crazy."

I twist him impossibly deeper into my body, wanting to feel him where no one has ever been. Where no one's ever touched me.

"Bristol." My name bursts from his mouth as he explodes inside me, his passion warm and liquid. "God, what are you doing to me?"

Making you more mine every time.

A smug, satisfied smile rests on my lips a few moments later. He's still inside me, and I'm slumped onto his chest, the steering wheel digging into my back. I know we need to move. There's a sticky mess between my legs, and we could get caught at any moment, but I can't stop kissing him, my tongue in his mouth sustaining our intimacy like a note held at a conductor's command.

"We need to go," he whispers, his breath still labored, his palms starting at my feet folded under me and sliding up my thighs and under the panties I never took off. He fills his hands with my ass, the leisurely caress of a satisfied man, and I revel in the fact that I did that. That I satisfy him.

"Hmmmm." I snuggle deeper into him.

"Bris." His hands wander over my back and then coax my bra straps into place on my shoulders. "For real, we need to leave before we get caught. We already had one close call today, and that wouldn't exactly be the low profile we're supposed to be keeping."

"You're right. I'll move in a second." I chuckle, eyes closed and depriving my other senses so I can fully absorb the scent of him. "You were the one who couldn't even make it home."

"True." He pauses, lifting my head from his chest. "What you said at my mom's house . . ."

"I meant every word." I frame his face between my hands, my eyes latched with his. "I'm going wherever you go."

"And you think I would object?" He tilts his head, his eyes so warm as he looks at me. "You're everything I wanted before I even knew what I was getting."

I kiss him thoroughly, deeply, surrendering everything before pulling back to smile down at his contented expression.

"You wanted me, you got me." I kiss him one more time, branding him mine as surely as I'm branded his. "Be careful what you wish for."

Twenty-Eight

Grip

I T SHOULD SCARE ME HOW MUCH I MISSED BRISTOL AFTER JUST ONE DAY away from her, but it doesn't. I fully embrace my addiction to the girl. Luke and I flew out to join Kilimanjaro for the show in Chicago, their hometown. Bristol's brilliant last-minute idea of Prodigy solidarity, but even that one day without Bristol has me fiending. We've only been official a few days, and I don't sleep right without her. I'm so bent out of sorts waking up alone in an empty bed that I had Sarah change our flight to the earliest out this morning so I could get home sooner.

I need my girl.

"You don't wanna go home first?" Amir asks from the seat beside me.

The SUV picked us up at the airport, and I told the driver to go straight to the Prodigy offices.

"Nah, I'll take my stuff home later."

A knowing grin spreads across Amir's face. His eyes drop to my bouncing knee. "You got it bad, don't you?"

My knee stops bouncing long enough for me to scowl at him, but I can't hold back an answering smile. He's watched Bristol and me from day one. Knows the full story. I turn my head to watch the cars zooming by on the interstate.

"Damn right I got it bad," I mutter. "Look how long it took to get her."

"How was she after … well, you know?" Amir lifts his thick bushy brows. "Dinner."

"She's Bristol," I say wryly. "She's fine. Ask me how my mom is. That's a better question."

"You guys talked since Sunday?"

"Have we talked?" I pffft. "She's called me like eight times. She felt bad about the way things went down, but she still wants to talk sense into me. She thinks I'm in some kind of phase with Bristol. It's not like I haven't dated white girls before. I've dated Black girls, Asian, Latina. Everything in our species."

"Yeah, but you ain't ever brought a girl to Sunday dinner. Ms. Mittie knows you're serious about Bristol. She knows you think Bristol is the one, and she ain't okay with you marrying a white woman. She told us that when we still thought girls had cooties."

"Ma has been consistent, but Bristol is the one. She always has been. She just had to trust me to be her one."

"It's like that?" Surprise stretches Amir's face from top to bottom. "So, y'all are already talking marriage?"

"Hell, no." I laugh at the thought. "Do you have any idea how long it'll take to convince Bristol to actually marry me?"

"It was obvious on Sunday she's into you. I mean, I wanted to salute after the speech she gave."

I saluted her, all right. My dick was at attention under the table the whole time she was talking and was not "at ease" until I had her bunched up against that steering wheel with every inch I got fucking the hell out of her.

"I've made studying Bristol Gray my life's work." I lean back in the comfort of the SUV's leather seat. "Marriage will scare her to death. She's seen too many bad ones. The worst up close. It'll take some time, but I think I've proven I'm a patient man."

"And what about Qwest?" Amir's frown comes quick and heavy. "You heard from her?"

"Nah." It pains me to think of how Qwest got caught in the drama between Bristol and me. "I ended things almost a week ago, and we agreed we wouldn't talk for a while."

"So does she know about Bristol? Does she know you're already with someone else?"

"I never gave her a name, but I told her there was someone I wanted to be with who didn't want to be with me." I shake my head. "Then Bristol and I got together the next day. We're keeping things quiet until it's public that Qwest and I called it quits."

"Yeah, if it comes out about you and Bristol while folks still think you're with Qwest ..." The look he gives me has "oh shit" written all over it.

Qwest in the role of woman scorned, even if I didn't technically cheat, would not be a good look. For any of us.

"Yeah, we need to get ahead of it," I say. "I'll bring it back up with Bris."

"Does Rhyson even know yet?"

"No." My cocky grin comes fast. "Serves him right, too. Bristol told him how she felt about me weeks ago and he never let on. Asshole."

"You think he'll be happy for you?"

"Yeah, but Rhys can't figure out if he should protect me from Bristol, or Bristol from me. He knows for sure he wants to protect the business in case anything goes wrong between us. He doesn't have to worry about that. Bristol and I are solid now. Ain't no going back."

"Is she back to managing you?"

"Yeah, no reason not to now." I shrug and turn my mouth down at the corners. "She's so damn good at it."

"And that dude she was, um, dating?" Amir asks the sentence like he's tiptoeing over a minefield and Parker is a trip wire.

"They weren't dating."

I trap the truth behind my teeth. I can't even tell Amir that Parker slept with Bristol while she was basically unconscious. I can't get it out of my mind, the way he grabbed her on the tarmac. All the messages he's left, even though she's told him it's not happening. The extra senses my mama says we have tell me this dude's nature is fundamentally crooked. He won't hesitate to play dirty to get what he wants, and he wants Bristol. I may have grown up in the hood, but I've been straight as an arrow all my life. For this man, I won't hesitate to get a little bent if it means protecting her.

"Hey, you still got them contacts with Corpse's boys?" I ask.

Amir looks at me like I'm smoking crack and just offered him the pipe. Our moms steered us clear of the Crips, but Amir's cousin Corpse crossed over to the dark blue side. With a "b" name like Brandon, he changed his name when he joined, and became Corpse when it was clear he had a talent for assassination.

"I ask you about Charles Parker—one of the richest dudes in the world, by the way—and then you ask me about Corpse? Uh-uh. Nah, bruh."

"I'm not putting a hit on Parker." I run my tongue over my teeth, squeezing my hands into fists on my knees. "But he isn't taking Bristol from me. And I'll be damned if he's gonna hurt her. I just want options."

"Corpse ain't an option. Ever." Amir glances at the raised glass partition insulating our voices from the driver's ears. "And I'm gonna forget we had this conversation."

"I don't want you to forget." I level a hard, narrow look at him, everything in me pulled tight. "He's your cousin. Just reach out to him."

"I don't fuck with Corpse, and you know it."

"I got pulled over for no damn reason Sunday before we got to Ma's, Amir." My voice carries the bitterness of that memory. "Bristol was right there while some no-nut cop threw me against the car and cuffed me. He had me hemmed up, sitting on a curb. He could have hurt her. He could have touched her, and I wouldn't have been able to do a damn thing about it. Do you know how that made me feel?"

It's quiet in the car while Amir studies me with grave eyes. He's been beside me on that street before. The two of us in a line of our friends, bellies scraping asphalt, plastic cuffs cutting off circulation, dogs sniffing around us like hounds scenting prey. All while cops searched the car for drugs. And me, a music student making straight A's.

"The power we have, the control we think we have, it's an illusion. We can lose it in an instant." Cynicism roughens my voice. "Now, I'm a lucky man with more blessings and opportunities than most people, no matter what color they are, but in the end, it comes down to this skin I'm in. And I know all cops aren't bad, but it's the damn system. I can't even call it broken because it's functioning exactly how it was designed to—profiling us, prosecuting us for shit other people get away with, scot free."

We pull up to the imposing glass building housing Prodigy, but I'm not getting out until I know Amir understands how serious I am about this.

"You know how it is, Amir. There's a whole system stacked against me, and this motherfucker who's out to get my girl has every advantage. I just want options. Ya feel me?"

I sit with a stony face while Amir weighs what I just told him.

"I'll call Corpse," he finally says softly.

"Good." I open the car door.

"But," Amir reaches over and grabs my arm, "I'm talking to him, not you. We can't have any of this shit anywhere near you if things . . . if anything ever happens."

I stare at the face I've seen evolve from acned adolescence to the grown ass man still trying to protect me.

"It won't come to that," I assure him. "These are just precautions, but yeah, you can deal with him. Unless I need to."

Amir drops my arm, sucks his teeth and shakes his head. "Fool."

"You the fool." I chuckle. "And don't think I didn't see you tryin' to holla at Shondra Sunday."

He groans, but a smile illuminates his face. "We're going out this Friday."

"No way." I lean into the open door, arms braced against the car. "You finally grew some balls and asked her out."

If his skin wasn't so brown, I bet his cheeks would be red. Chagrin and embarrassment sit together awkwardly on his face. "She actually asked me out."

"She . . . so wait. You been crushing on this girl half your life, working up the nerve to ask her out, and she . . ." I press my fist to my lips to stifle the laugh. "So what you're saying is Shondra's balls are bigger than yours."

"Hey, some might say the same about you and Bristol," he says defensively.

"Oh, no, homey. Bristol loves these big balls. Trust." I propel myself away from the car with a deep laugh and yell, "Deeze nuts!"

Twenty-Nine

Bristol

"**B**RISTOL, GIVE ME YOUR PHONE."

Sarah is posted against my office door when she makes the odd request. She came in, closed the door behind her, and demanded my phone.

"What?" I return my attention to my laptop with a laugh. "My phone? Why?"

When she doesn't answer, I look back up. She's still standing there, back pressed to the door as if she's keeping something at bay. Her eyes are round. Her lips are tight. Her hands wring around one another at her waist. She catches sight of the phone on my desk at the same time as I do. We both dive for it. Somehow from across the room, that little ninny manages to snatch the phone that was only two inches from me.

"Give me my phone." I hold out my hand. "Right now."

"Bristol, let me just paint a picture for you first." Sarah tucks my phone behind her back.

"Let me paint a picture of you in the unemployment line if you don't give me my phone."

"Are there actual lines anymore, though?" Sarah stalls. "I mean, it's all computerized now, right?"

"You'll know for sure tomorrow unless you give me my phone." I sigh, exasperated. "How bad can it be, whatever it is?"

Her silence and the eyes shifting from me to the floor tell me it's bad. The worst things I can imagine immediately leap to mind.

"It's Grip? Rhyson? Kai? The baby?" Sarah's unchanging expression gives me no assurances. "Just tell me."

Sarah blows out an extended breath and starts tapping keys on my phone. When she finds what she's looking for, she turns the screen around for me to see.

"Let's start here," she says.

I take the phone, my eyes still trained on her face. At first, I'm not sure what I'm seeing. It's surveillance footage from the "routine" stop on Sunday with Officer Dunne.

"What is this?" I search Sarah's face for an answer. "This happened Sunday when Grip was stopped by a cop."

"Yeah, someone got ahold of the surveillance footage and posted it." Sarah bites her bottom lip. "There's a lot of talk about the irony of Grip being stopped DWB when 'Bruise' is just coming out. But there's a lot more . . . discussion about you and Grip. Keep watching."

I look again, and then I see it. I get out of the car and join Grip on the curb. I remember this moment when his forehead presses to mine and we whisper to one another, the intimacy between us obvious. Our lips touch and our eyes hold onto each other.

Oh, God, please no.

Our lips touch and linger. We kiss.

I slowly lift my eyes to meet Sarah's. Hers are wide and questioning. "It's just a . . . an itty bitty kiss, right?" False hope lilts my voice.

"Well, yeah," Sarah agrees and bites her lip. "But there is that other part."

"Other part?"

I look back to the phone. There's another clip after Officer Dunne leaves. A different feed, different angle. Maybe from a nearby pole. Who knows. We're chatting with Greg, and Grip kisses my hand and presses it to his chest. He pulls me into his side. I lean into him. There's nothing platonic about any of it. We look like we're in love, but it's nothing too incriminating until Greg leaves. The footage shows the long kiss we shared against the Rover. If there was any doubt we're more than friends, this kiss eliminates it.

The first few comments, like Sarah said, focus on the stop itself. But slowly, comments about me, about Qwest start trickling in. The comments become accusations about the white bitch with Grip. Dozens of commenters post about Grip cheating on Qwest. About him caught "creeping." With every comment, the vitriol, the outrage on her behalf increases. The hashtags stack up.

#GripzQueen. #BlackLove. #CheatingAss. #SellOut.

The room tilts. The floor beneath my feet becomes Jell-O. I stumble to my desk, perching on the edge.

"How long has this been up?" I ask between hyperventilating breaths.

"Um, maybe fifteen minutes," Sarah answers cautiously. "It's getting a lot of traffic, though."

"I can see that."

I scroll and scroll and scroll, but still haven't reached the end of the comments. Every once in a while, one commenter will mention the stop itself and how this is exactly what "Bruise" talks about, but it's drowned in the sea of speculation about Grip and me.

"What's a thot?" I look up from the phone, eyebrows bunched. "They keep calling me a thot."

"Um . . ." Hesitation is all over Sarah's face and in her answer. "That Ho Over There."

My mouth drops open. I was a damn debutante in the most exclusive circles of Upper Manhattan, and I'm a thot?

"Qwest." I look at Sarah with horrified eyes. "Oh, God. What must she be thinking?"

"Yeah, that's kind of its own thing, so to speak," Sarah says carefully. "I think that's why some of the comments are so vicious."

"Oh, my God." I pull up Qwest's Twitter account.

@YesItzQwest "When he get on, he'll leave your ass for a white girl." Kanye ain't never lied. Bruhs, don't forget the sisters who put u on. #QueenWithNoKing

The humiliation, the hurt, and dismay I experienced at Ms. James' dinner table Sunday has magnified, globalized. It isn't one, two, three women side-eyeing me because I'm with Grip. It's an entire socialsphere. I don't want to be pitted against them. Grip and I aren't what these comments suggest we are. I'm not some trophy to him. And he didn't choose me because I'm a symbol of unattainable success. I want to chase down every comment, recall every retweet, share and like. To tell them he quotes poetry to me. I know his favorite foods. I know he'd rather have Classic Jordans than a gaudy watch. We talk about real things, and even when I don't understand everything, he's patient with me because he loves me. I know him. I knew him first. I had him first. I loved him first. He's mine.

I want them all to know.

Sarah and I both jump when the office door swings open. Rhyson's hair stands all over his head like he's been plowing his fingers through it.

"Bris, have you seen—"

"Yeah." I collapse into the chair behind my desk. "Sarah just showed me."

"How are we dealing with the calls?" He sits on the edge of the desk, eyeing me with a mixture of caution and sympathy.

"Calls?" I split attention between my brother and my assistant. "Already?"

"I hadn't gotten to that quite yet." Sarah winces. "The front desk is flooded. Press, bloggers, news outlets asking for comments on the incident and the . . . status of you and Grip."

"It's all a misunderstanding," I tell them.

In synch, both of them stretch their eyebrows as high as they'll go. I get it. There's no mistaking that Grip and I are more than friends in that footage.

"By misunderstanding, I mean that Grip had ended things with Qwest by the time that footage was taken."

"But they performed at Pirouette together Friday night, and were by all accounts, still together at that point, right?" Rhyson asks.

"They broke up right after the show." I look at them helplessly. "We didn't want to hurt her. We wanted to give her some time to process everything and release a statement later. We were being careful."

"You call this careful?" Rhyson's sigh is powered by frustration. "How do we handle it? Where's Grip?"

"Oh his way back from Chicago," Sarah says. "He caught an earlier flight."

That's welcome news to me. Maybe my heart will stop hurting once he walks through that door.

"He needs to address this," Rhyson says. "'Queen' is such a huge part of his brand now, and like it or not, Black women took that as theirs. As an affirmation, and him cheating on Qwest with you—"

"He did not cheat on her." My voice cracks like a whip. "Are you not hearing me? He broke it off with her before we started . . . seeing each other."

"I get it. I know your history," Rhyson sighs. "But from the outside it looks like he cheated."

"Qwest certainly seems to think so," Sarah offers, her voice weak.

"This is just one tweet. There's a series of them and Instagram posts. And there are a few FaceTime Live posts from fans calling Grip a sellout and expressing their disappointment."

"This will start affecting sales, Bris." Rhyson shakes his head.

"Sales?" A humorless laugh comes out with my gasp. "You're thinking about sales?"

"Okay. Let's just start with you knowing me well enough to assume you and Grip are the most important parts of this for me, okay?" Rhyson's brow pleats and his mouth flatlines. "Now that we have that established, of course not just sales, but it is our job to protect the interests of the people who've invested in this label. The people who make their living from this label. They rise and fall with us, and right now we have one album out. Grip's. So yeah. I have to think about sales."

"I know, I just . . ." I've lost my bearings. There are so many important things competing in my head. I want to strategize about sales. I want to figure out how to correct this PR fiasco. I want to figure out who the hell did this to us. I want to protect Grip. He's worked too hard and for too long for this to derail his success.

"Yes. You're right, of course." I press my head into the supple leather of my seat. "Let me think about this for a second."

But any strategizing I would do goes right out of my head when Grip walks into my office. The worry in his eyes wrenches my heart. I'm jeopardizing his success. He has to be questioning whether or not this is worth the trouble. Whether I'm worth the trouble.

"Grip, I've been calling you, dude," Rhyson says.

"I literally just turned my phone back on after the flight from Chicago." Grip answers Rhyson, but his eyes never stray from me. "Could you guys give me a minute with Bristol?"

"We need to talk about how we'll handle this," Rhyson says, but his voice has lost some of its heat. "We need a plan because this has gone the worst kind of viral."

"Yeah, I know." Grip sits on the couch against the far wall in my office, stretching his legs out in front of him like we're not standing naked in a shit storm. "But I need to talk to my girl first."

Sarah immediately heads for the door, but turns just before leaving.

"His girl!" A sudden bright smile illuminates her face. "I know things look bad right now, but I just want to say yay. Like it's about time and yay for you guys!"

She scampers into the outer office, and if I wasn't feeling like the whole world is pointing out the stubborn cellulite on the backs of my thighs, I'd muster a smile.

"I'm not trying to be the hard ass," Rhyson says. "I hate having to think like this, but we do need to deal with it. It goes without saying that I'm happy for you guys."

"You could still say it." Grip's comment comes softly, but with a mild rebuke. "Your sister needs to know you support her and that she's more important to you than how this affects my sales."

Grip's so right. I hadn't realized how fragile I was feeling or how anxious I am about Rhyson's response.

"Bristol." Rhyson searches my eyes, his softening at whatever he sees there. "You're more important to me than all of this. I'm sorry if it didn't feel like it when I came tearing in here. You know how intense we are. You, me, Mom, Dad."

"It's okay." I push the hair behind my ears. "I get it."

"It isn't okay." He leans down to take my hand. "I've screwed things up with you more than once. I lumped you in with our parents and didn't stay in touch. I've been an awful brother most of the time, but I love you, Bris."

He flicks his head toward Grip without looking away from my face. "I'm happy for you, but I'm really just glad this guy can stop moaning like a little bitch about how much he's into you. It's so fucking awkward."

The three of us laugh, and the tension eases some.

Rhyson pulls me to my feet and into a tight hug. He kisses my hair and dips to catch my eyes.

"We all know you're a badass and don't need to hear this kind of thing," he says, even though I do. "But I love you, and you're so far beyond the best sister a guy could have it isn't even funny. The investors, this place, so many things that have happened for me wouldn't exist if it weren't for you. I want you to know I realize that."

Tears sting my eyes. Hearing him voice the things I've needed to hear, to know for years, moves me deeply, even in the midst of this craziness.

"I'll give you guys a few minutes," Rhyson says. "When you're ready, come to my office and we'll hammer out a plan to deal with all this."

Rhyson looks at Grip for a long moment, one brow lifted.

"And you," Rhyson says to Grip, his voice serious, but his eyes laughing. "Try to keep your hands to yourself."

"I'll see what I can do. Lock the door on your way out," Grip replies. "Or you might see more than you want to see."

"Oh, I've already seen more than I wanted to see. Believe me."

Grip tosses up both middle fingers, and Rhyson's laugh taunts us as he leaves the room. It's quiet in here, incredibly quiet as we stare at one another. What's felt so special, so intimate, so *ours* is being maligned and memed. Hashtagged and reposted and ridiculed. In here it's just us, but it feels like everything and everyone beyond that door is against us.

"Come here." Grip extends his arms, concern evident in his eyes. I drag my feet to get to him, not because I don't want him, but because I feel awful. As soon as I'm within grabbing distance, his hands encircle my waist, and he pulls me to his lap.

"Hey." He nuzzles his nose into my neck, behind my ear. "It's okay."

"I'm so sorry." I turn into him, tucking my head in the warm sleek curve of his neck and shoulder.

"This is on me." He shakes his head, a self-directed frustration on his face. "You didn't want to go to my mom's. You said be careful. I should have listened."

"I guess we won't know who leaked it, huh?"

"Does it really matter? It could have been anyone with access to those tapes. Who knows."

"It feels like the worst thing that could have happened," I whisper.

"No." Grip leaves a kiss in my hair. "The worst thing would be if you decided not to be with me. If you regretted us. That's my worst-case scenario. Not sales or any of that other shit."

"But you've worked so hard. I just hate being the reason it's diminished in any way."

"Listen to me." His hand splays across my hip and he brings me so close I feel his heart thumping into my ribcage. "Remember the release party? We were celebrating the album going number one?"

"Of course I remember." I cup his face and lay my head against his chin. "I was so proud of you. We all were."

"Yeah, well I was miserable."

I pull back to peer into his face.

"I mean, yeah. I was happy, excited for the album, but you know what my mind kept going back to?"

"What?" My voice is hushed, my heart waiting.

"Our first kiss." A smile crooks the corner of his full lips. "That night at the carnival, no one knew who I was. My bank account was sad. Not one of my dreams had come true yet, but I had you. That night I had you, and it was the best night of my life. And the night of the party, when I thought you might marry Parker, that we might not ever get back to what we started on that Ferris wheel, I could barely focus on the songs. That let me know what is the most important thing to me, and it ain't sales."

I don't know what to say. I thought I would. I'm rarely speechless, but him saying these things and hearing that I'm the most important thing in a life like his, when I haven't been anyone's most important thing ever before, something inside of me that has always been searching, settles. Something that has always been circling, lands.

"You are just making things worse for yourself," I finally whisper into his neck.

"How so?" He feathers kisses around my hairline, down my neck.

"You'll never get rid of me now."

"Good. That was the goal." He tips my face forward and kisses me lightly. "Now that we have that settled, let's go tell Rhyson how you're gonna make this all better. I know you have a plan."

Now that I've had a second. Now that the man I love has settled any lingering doubts ...

"I might have a few ideas."

Thirty

Bristol

"**Y**OU'LL OWE ME BIG TIME FOR THIS, BRISTOL." EZRA COHEN stares over his thick-rimmed glasses, the New York skyline sprawled behind him. "I'm also not entirely sure this is the best way to handle such a . . . shall we say, delicate matter."

"Will and Qwest haven't left me much choice. I need to staunch the bleeding on this, and they won't take my calls." I hesitate before giving him my most grateful smile. "Thank you so much for your help."

"If I didn't love you so much, kid, there's no way I'd even entertain a scheme like this." Ezra points a bony finger at me. "But in all my years knowing you, you're right ninety-nine percent of the time. This better not be that one percent."

He's right. This could backfire badly. If I miscalculate, I'll only make things worse. Before I have time to reconsider, Ezra's assistant opens his office door, showing in Qwest and Will. Qwest pulls up short as soon as she sees me, tilting her sunglasses down to look at me disdainfully over the cat eye frames.

Will comes in right behind her, shock flickering across his face when our eyes catch. "Bristol, what the hell are you doing here?"

"This bitch got some nerve." Qwest adjusts the Louis Vuitton bag on her shoulder. "I'm outta here."

"No, you're not." Ezra stands to his full five foot seven. His towering authority has nothing to do with his physical stature, and everything to do with the reputation he's carved out for himself and the business he's built. "You've been very publicly critical of the man who has the number one album in the country. And the two of you have the number one single in the country. That feud is bad for business, and I want it put down."

"I'm sorry to handle things this way," I interject. "But you wouldn't return Grip's calls, Qwest, and Will, you haven't returned mine."

"That's 'cause I got nothing to say to cheating sellouts or their skinny white bitches." Qwest's voice rings hard and harsh in the understated luxury of Ezra's office, but I see the hurt behind her eyes. Grip isn't an easy man to lose.

"He didn't cheat, Qwest," I say softly. "We need to clear the air."

"So he sends you to do his dirty work," Will scoffs. "This is highly unprofessional, Bristol."

"What's unprofessional is you not responding to my calls or emails for the last two days while your client went on a Twitter tour denigrating my client's character." I tilt my chin and remind him with a glance that he does not want to mess with me. "And Grip doesn't know I'm here."

He does know I'm in New York, but he thinks it's just to see Kilimanjaro on tour.

"Oh, so you go behind his back, too, not just mine," Qwest says sarcastically. "Good to know."

"I'm here to apologize," I say softly. "Not for cheating, because we didn't. We wouldn't, but for how you found out about our . . . relationship. For how things happened. Please give me a chance to explain."

For a moment, it looks like she won't yield. Her lips pull into a tight line, and her long nails dig into her palms.

"Five minutes," she finally says. "That's all you get."

I look to Ezra, who takes my cue and walks to the door. "Will, let's give the ladies a few moments alone," he says.

Irritation and indignation gather on Will's face, and he's torn between following his boss' orders, and protecting his client.

"Go on, Will. I'll be fine." Qwest looks me up and down.

Once we're alone, Qwest settles onto a couch across from the Ezra's desk and leans back, stretching her arms behind her.

"Clock is ticking," Qwest says.

"I know Grip told you from the beginning that there was someone he had feelings for," I say, sitting on the couch, crossing my legs. "He had reservations about getting involved feeling that way for someone else. He was honest about that."

"Yeah, but he also told me he didn't cheat on me."

"He didn't. He ended things with you at Pirouette Friday night, right?"

Pain breaks through the ice of Qwest's eyes for a moment before she tucks it back under and nods.

"You trying to tell me what I saw on that footage happened between Friday and Sunday?" she scoffs. "I wasn't born yesterday at ten o'clock, honey."

"We talked Saturday, the next day," I say. "About things we should have discussed years ago and decided we would try."

I look down at my hands folded in my lap and then force myself to meet her eyes again.

"I've loved Grip a long time and let stupid things keep us apart. We never meant to hurt you, and were trying to work out the best way to handle the public finding out about you and Grip since your relationship became such a huge part of everything."

"He should have told me it was you." Something beyond anger rises in the heated glance Qwest flicks my way. Resentment. "He's just like all the rest of them. He couldn't choose someone who really understands him."

"What makes you think I don't understand him?"

"He needs a sister who knows how to fight at his side and fight for him."

"So it would make it better if I was Black?"

"You have no idea what it's like seeing the best of our men always choosing you. As soon as they get a little something, make something of themselves, they need to go get a white woman to feel validated."

"That isn't Grip. That isn't what this is."

"Oh, please tell me what it is, Bristol," she says, her words soaked in sarcasm.

"I *have* experienced rejection," I say, my voice quiet.

"Rejection?" A harsh laugh erupts from her and she crosses her arms over her chest, tips her head to the side and cocks one disdainful brow. "Is this where you tell me about your *struggle*, Bristol? About all you've endured in your privileged life?"

Even the feigned amusement fades from her expression, leaving only cynicism, hurt.

"Let me tell you what rejection is. It's being told by an entire culture outright and in a million subtle ways that you're not good enough, not beautiful enough. These athletes and musicians, actors—most of 'em raised by single Black women, and when they find success, do they choose someone from their own community? No, they want someone who's nothing like the very women who sacrificed to make their success possible."

As she articulates it, I see not just her pain, but the pain behind what

Jade and Ms. James said. What Shondra didn't voice to me, but felt, too. I see the truth of it and for a moment, nothing I would say feels good enough, feels right, but I have to say something.

"I hear you," I finally tell her. "And I'm sorry, but that isn't what this is. Not what *we* are. We aren't a statistic or a trend. I've had these feelings for years, and Grip wasn't successful or rich or famous when I met him. He was just . . . himself. And I loved that about him."

"I do, too." Qwest blinks at the tears accompanying her soft response.

"I'm so sorry it happened this way." Tears come to my eyes, too. I look down at the carpet to hide them. "I know you care about him."

"I do. That's why it hurt to think that he . . . well, that he cheated." Her bark of a laugh cuts into the air. "It still hurts that I lost out to a white chick. Maybe it shouldn't make a difference, but if we're being honest, it does."

I can't change or apologize for what I am anymore than she can change who she is.

"Qwest, I—"

"Your five minutes are up." Her voice wavers just the slightest bit. She sneaks a finger under one eye to catch a tear.

"Okay. Thank you for listening." I stand and grab my purse. "Grip is doing an online interview with *Legit* tonight to address all of the craziness that's been going on. I wanted to give you a heads up. Once you knew how how things actually happened, I thought you might want to . . . well, put out your own statement so your stories line up."

"You've got all the bases covered, don't you?" Qwest's eyes remain averted, her mouth pulled tight.

"That's my job."

She looks up and sees right through me.

"Only Grip's a lot more than your job, isn't he?"

She knows he is, or I wouldn't have made this risky move. There's nothing more to do here, so I head for the door.

"Bristol," Qwest says, causing me to turn at the door. "You're a very lucky woman. Any woman, Black, white whatever would be lucky to have a man like Grip."

I don't think anything I could say would be the right thing, could ease the pain I see behind her eyes, so I just nod and close the door behind me. But in my heart, despite all the crap we've waded through over the last few days, I agree.

I just might be the luckiest girl in the world.

Thirty-One

Grip

BRISTOL'S IDEA FOR ME TO ADDRESS THE RUMORS AND misunderstandings directly in an online sit-down with Meryl from *Legit* helped a lot. It was short and to the point, mostly me laying out that I didn't cheat on Qwest and made sure to end one relationship before beginning another. Some will still call me a sellout, but I think most people get that it isn't about the color of our skin.

I wish my mother were one of those people. We've gone from me dodging her calls, to her ignoring mine. After the *Legit* Exclusive aired, I reached out, but she hasn't called me back. It's always been us. We've never fallen out this way, and I can't pretend it doesn't hurt. I keep telling myself I'll go to the house Sunday for dinner and we'll chop it up. Work it out over her sweet potato pie, but there's a part of me that knows it won't be that easy.

All of that aside, right now I can't pretend I'm not excited for my first night out with Bristol. Even if it is just a charity dinner, not a real date. I was scheduled to appear at this fundraiser weeks ago. After the *Legit* interview, Bristol wants me to be business as usual and show people I have nothing to hide. Of course I insisted that if we really have nothing to hide, she'll attend this event with me. It's been over a week since the footage leaked, and a few days since the interview. Surely people have moved on to something else. Something that has nothing to do with my girlfriend and me.

Who looks so damn gorgeous tonight.

I come out of the shower, towel tied at my waist, to stand behind her, settling my hands at her hips as she's putting on makeup in my bathroom.

"I've changed my mind." I kiss her neck. "This event's a waste of time. We should stay home and make love."

She smiles at me in the mirror, pausing in applying mascara.

"I could stay home and you could go."

There's hope on her face and in her voice.

"No way. I thought we had a point to make tonight." I squeeze her waist. "That we have nothing to be ashamed of or to hide."

I turn her around to get a proper look at her. She's wearing this green dress that cuts low between her breasts. The quarter-length sleeves cling to her arms, and the rest of the dress flows freely to her knees. A fragile gold chain adorns the bare strip of skin just above her cleavage.

"This is pretty." I lift the delicate gold links.

Her breath catches when my knuckles brush against the warm satiny swell of her breast. Looking into her eyes, I slip my hand into the bodice of the dress, cupping the weight of one breast, bringing the nipple taut with my thumb.

"Grip, don't start or we'll be late." Her voice is husky, her eyelids half-mast over the desire building in her eyes.

"Uh huh." I squat until I'm level with her chest, pushing the dress aside to expose one full, berry-tipped breast. I lock eyes with her when I take the nipple between my lips, sliding my hands down her waist and spreading both palms over her ass.

"Grip, stop." Her hands contradict her words, pressing my mouth deeper, urging me to scrape my teeth over the nipple. My hand wanders under her dress, skates over one silky thigh and into her panties.

"Shit." I massage her clit, plumping it between two fingers before slipping them inside of her with shallow pumps. "How am I supposed to get through this dinner knowing your panties are soaked?"

"I've got a solution for that," she says breathlessly. She reaches under her dress and slides the panties off, letting them ring around her bare feet. "No more wet panties."

I step back, gripping the knot of terry cloth at my waist, and pointing a warning finger at her.

"You know you're getting fucked so hard when we get home."

"Promises, promises." She turns back to the mirror with a smile, her cheeks and the soft skin of her throat and chest still flushed.

I'm dressed when the buzzer sounds. It's probably Amir. As much as I typically discourage him from "guarding" me, there will be a lot of people at this event tonight. For whatever reason, much of the shade seems directed at Bristol. I want him along more for her safety than for mine.

"That's Amir." I kiss her cheek on my way to the bedroom door. "I'll be down in a sec. Just finishing my hair."

"'K. We're downstairs."

Amir comes in, surveying my black dress shirt, gray slacks and short black boots hidden under my pants.

"Nice." He nods like I pass inspection.

"I try." I walk back into the loft. "Bris'll be right down. You want something to drink before we hit the road?"

"Nah." He glances up the staircase at my closed bedroom door and then back to me. "I do have an update on that thing we talked about."

"What thing?" I ask absently, strapping on my old black plastic watch. It's become a habit I can't break, and it feels good to wear it again even if it does seem cheap and out of place.

"You know," he says, voice barely audible. "The thing."

I sit down on the couch across from him and give him a puzzled look. "Why you talking in code?"

"Corpse, dude." He looks cautiously up the stairs again. "I talked to my cousin."

"Oh." I lean my elbows to my knees, now on high alert. "And?"

"I just asked him if he was still, you know, handling things for people."

"And is he?"

"Yeah." Amir looks like I'm pulling his back teeth. "But on a very limited, exclusive basis."

"I can be limited and exclusive." I pause to catch his eyes. "You know I'm not asking him to kill Parker, right?"

"Man, are you crazy?" Amir eyes the corners of the room, searching the ceiling, I presume for cameras or other devices. "You can't be saying that shit out loud."

"It's my house," I say wryly. "I think if there's anywhere we can safely talk about this, it's here. And I just want options. It would be a drastic situation. He'd have to do something pretty stupid for me to need Corpse, but I just want to know what's out there."

"Well you may have provoked him in that *Legit* interview," Amir says, mild reproach in the look he gives me.

"I just told the truth." I shrug. "When Meryl asked about Parker, I said I'm the only man Bristol's in a relationship with. End of story. It's true. What was I supposed to say?"

We shut the conversation down when the door above opens and Bristol comes out on the landing. For a moment it's just the two of us, her smile for me and me alone. Yeah, Corpse is just insurance, but I'd use him and anything else at my disposal to protect her. I glance back to Amir, wondering if he can read my mind as my girl comes down the stairs. The grim set of his mouth and the concern in his eyes tells me that he can.

Thirty-Two
Bristol

"INTEREST HAS DIED DOWN, HUH?"

I throw that lightly in Grip's face as we pull up to the charity dinner where there's a small mob of fans and media behind the ropes flanking the red carpet.

It isn't a ball or gala, thank God. Just your standard sit-down, five-thousand-dollar plate dinner. Grip was invited to talk briefly about the importance of giving back to the community. Meryl included parts of his talk at his high school in the *Legit* piece, along with a clip from her phone of him playing basketball with the student. Between that piece, and all the publicity "Bruise" is getting in the debate over tensions with law enforcement, Grip's being perceived as an artist with a conscience. I love it because I think it reflects who he truly is.

"It is crazy out there." Amir considers the crowd lining the red carpet leading to the hotel where the charity dinner is being held.

"It'll be fine." Grip gives Amir a pointed look. "Stay with Bristol if we get separated."

"He's here to guard you, not me." I adjust my dress before the door opens and we have to get out. I'm terribly conscious of the decision to leave my panties on the bathroom floor. I've been exposed enough without flashing my naked girl parts to the world.

"Amir, you heard me." Grip looks from me to his friend. "I'll be fine."

"Gotcha, bruh." He looks at the throng of people pressing closer to the car with cameras and microphones. "Bris, stay close."

I roll my eyes, but nod. I know it bothers Grip that a lot of the hate has died off for him, though some of the more vocal critics call him a sellout, but the lion's share of the vitriol seems to be for me. They've called me so many names, I may as well be doing business as "That White Bitch" by now.

"You ready?" Grip grabs my hand and doesn't wait for me to confirm.

We're on the red carpet sooner than I want to be. I don't answer any of the questions hurled at us, but one question makes me stiffen, and has the same effect on Grip.

"Bristol, what about Parker?" one reporter yells. "How does he feel about your new relationship?"

I hope I've adequately dealt with Parker. All of his messages were the same. I want you. You're mine. We're meant to be. You will marry me. Blah, blah, fucking blah. I left him a voicemail telling him to seek professional help and leave me alone. I haven't heard from him since, even after the police footage was leaked, but that doesn't mean anything. This man has persisted for years. We're into decades now that he's believed some day we'll get hitched and endure years of miserable matrimony just like our parents have. I'm not naïve enough to think one voicemail will kill that delusion.

"Bristol, are you with both of them?" another reporter asks.

I ignore the horrible question, but Grip turns in the direction of the reporter, glaring, his hand still holding mine, tightening around mine.

"What did you ask her?" His voice, a dark growl, has the reporter looking like a mouse caged with a snake. "Does it look like she's with him? She's with me."

"Grip, don't." I tug on his hand, pulling until he's walking with me. "Let's just go in."

The hotel entrance is a blessed end to a walk that only took a minute, but felt like forever with the glare of the spotlight. As soon as we're inside, I pull him into the nearest discreet corner. I reach up to frame his face, undeterred by the irritation stamped there.

"Hey, don't let those stupid questions get to you, okay?" I whisper. "You know I'm with you. You know what happened with Parker. That's all that counts."

"I know." He closes his eyes, turning his head to kiss the inside of my wrist. "But the Parker thing . . ."

Displeasure rattles his throat in a low rumble.

"You're mine. You're with me." He squats a little to kiss me, his lips possessive and commanding. He presses me into him, splaying his hand across my lower back. Even though we've stepped to the side, I know there have to be people watching us, but I sense he needs this, so I tamp down my self-consciousness and surrender. His kiss slows, his tongue doing a languid sweep inside like he's marking my mouth. He drops his forehead to mine.

"I know I'm overreacting." He sighs, tipping his head back and studying the chandeliers dotting the high ceilings. "I just hate that anyone would even think he has a claim on you."

"Hey, from their perspective, it was a blur." I take both of his hands in mine. "All of this—you and Qwest, me and Parker—it's all really tangled in their heads. They don't know I've been in love with you for years."

His eyes soften, like I knew they would, and he laughs, cupping my neck.

"You think you can charm your way out of that hard fuck you have coming tonight, don't you?"

"When have I ever run from a hard fuck?" My voice comes out low and sultry, my smile slow and only for him. "I'm earning it."

A hand on Grip's shoulder pulls us out of each other.

"They're going in," Amir says, eyes discreetly lowered. "Just letting you know."

"You ready for this?" Grip asks.

"You're the one who has to speak. I just look pretty and eat rubbery five-thousand dollar chicken."

Apparently I know my stuff, because that is all that is asked of me for the rest of the night. Our table is full of people much older than we are, community activists who probably couldn't give a flying fig about what's trending on Twitter. I doubt any of them know what a "thot" is either. And I'm so grateful.

Grip is extraordinary in this context. His background and childhood mean that he is in touch with real need like many celebrities aren't. It isn't just something he shouldn't forget. His mother still lives in the house where he grew up. His cousins and aunts and family are all still in that community. He talks about how he would have gone hungry at school if there hadn't been a free lunch program, and about the years when he was younger and his mother was on welfare. He smiles when he tells us how proud she was when she no longer needed it.

I marvel again at how we found each other, at how natural it has felt with us from the beginning, considering how vastly different our lives have been. Like someone gave him the answers to a test, as if he had a Bristol cheat sheet that no one else received. I can't take my eyes off him. He thought I watched him before. Now that he's mine, now that we're together, it's even worse. He rivets me, and it doesn't scare me anymore. Maybe I do love him too much and don't have boundaries. I don't care. This love is the stuff of magic, of fantasy, but so raw and real I can touch it. I can taste it. If for some reason I fall, how many can say they soared this high?

"You were excellent," I whisper to Grip as we stand from the table to leave. Amir sat at a separate table designated for security and bodyguards, so we wait for him to make his way over to us.

"Thank you, baby." Grip leans down to my ear, his voice dark and dirty. "Knowing you are naked under that dress has been driving me crazy all night. The napkin was barely big enough to hide my hard-on."

There is some secret switch he planted in my body that responds to him instantly. Heat and wetness collect between my thighs. For a moment, I consider dragging him to the nearest bathroom stall and slaking my lust before we make it home, but a voice from behind me dumps ice all over the flame building inside me.

"Bristol," my mother says. "Good evening."

I turn to face her, braced for her censure. I may have ignored several of her calls when the footage of Grip and me leaked.

"Mother, hello. I didn't know you were here."

"Well, it's a big crowd." She glances around the ballroom. "Betsy's here, too, somewhere."

She shifts her eyes to Grip.

"That's Parker's mother, by the way." She looks at my hand linked with Grip's. "We've been best friends more than forty years."

"It's good to see you again, Mrs. Gray," Grip says politely.

He and my mother haven't been around each other much, but he knows more about my family's dark secrets, dirty laundry and skeletons than just about anyone else.

"Marlon, good speech tonight," Mother replies stiffly before look-ing back to me. "Maybe my messages got lost in the . . . chaos of your life, Bristol. I needed to speak with you quite urgently."

"Really?" I frown and twist my mouth to the side in concentration. "Not sure how I missed that. What did you need?"

She squeezes her eyes at the edges, shoving as much condemnation into her narrow glance as possible.

"Maybe we could speak privately," she says.

Amir walks up, his eyes moving between the three of us before finally connecting with Grip. He lifts his brows and tilts his head, a silent query. Grip just nods, but keeps his eyes on my mother.

"Mother, this is our friend Amir." I give Amir a warm smile, hoping it defrosts the atmosphere my mother is creating. They exchange brief pleasantries, but the ice remains untouched.

"We need to get going, Bris," Grip says softly. "But there was a room they had for me before I got up to speak. If your mother wants to talk before we go, we could swing that."

I search his face, tightened into impassivity, giving nothing away.

"That isn't necessary." I dip my head, trying to catch his eyes. I already know what my mother wants to talk to me about. So does he. Why does he even think I want to listen?

"It actually is, Bristol." She looks to Grip, her eyes unthawed. "Marlon, show us where."

When we reach the small room, Mother walks in ahead of us. I linger in the hall and step close to Grip. Amir takes a few steps away, out of earshot, but within helping distance.

"Why are you accommodating her?" I lean into his chest, running my hands up to his neck. I lift up on my toes to whisper in his ear. "You could be fucking me by now."

"She's your mother." He pulls back a little, setting me away from him and gently nudging me toward the room. "Give her a few minutes."

It means something to him it's never been for me, the connection to a parent. I know the distance between him and his mother bothers him. As close as they've always been, discord isn't natural, when for me that's par for the course.

"Okay," I agree. "But can we work out some signal so if I need you, you'll come rescue me from this lecture?"

"Just hurry up." He turns me toward the door and swats my bottom. "So I can keep my promise."

I'm still thinking about how good that promise kept will be when I face my mother. I don't bother closing the door, even though I know Grip and Amir are in the hall. Maybe that will deter her from saying anything too insulting.

"What the hell do you think you're doing, Bristol?" Her voice thwacks me like a wet towel as soon as I enter the room.

"I'm giving you your private moment, Mother. What's this about?"

"You know exactly what this is about." She gestures toward the hall. "Is this what you call having things under control? Being broadcast kissing that . . . man all over the world?"

"That . . . man is my boyfriend, Mother," I snap. "And if you say one disrespectful word about him, I warn you, this conversation is over."

"Bristol, Parker—"

"I told you before I don't want Parker. I don't want anything to do with him."

Her expression cracks, irritation rearing from behind the protection of the smooth mask.

"Bristol, let me speak frankly. You aren't your brother. Rhyson is a musician with a rare gift. That is not your strength."

The words I've always known she felt even when she didn't express them land heavily on my chest, suspiciously close to my heart.

"I know you're playing around with this management business," she continues. "But you need to think about your future."

"Mother, you're a businesswoman with your own money. Why would you want anything different for me? Expect anything less from me?"

"Park Corp is worth billions, Bristol. You don't ignore that.

Charles Parker is a once and a lifetime opportunity."

"Opportunity?" I shake my head disbelievingly. "Is that how you went into your marriage, Mother? How's that worked out for you?"

As much as I believe my words, I regret them. I don't want to see my mother in pain, and the hurt that pinches her face before she can hide it hurts me, too.

"Don't turn this on me, Bristol. We're talking about you. I told you not to toy with Parker."

"And I didn't. I was clear with him that we weren't going to happen."

"Well Betsy asked him about this . . . scandal you're in with . . ." She gestures out toward the hall. "Him. Parker pretended to be fine with it, but I don't believe it. I can see Marlon holds a certain appeal. You want a good lay, a man with a lot in his pants, go for it. Understand the consequences, though. Parker won't give up."

"Bristol." Grip comes to the door, that muscle bunched in his jaw that usually means he's pissed. "Baby, let's go."

"We aren't done," my mother says testily.

"Yes, you are." Grip's fists are in his pockets, tucked away with his patience. "I couldn't imagine turning my mother down if she asked for time with me. I'd have to at least hear her out. So, I encouraged Bristol to do this, but I'm not going to stand out there while you insult her."

"I'm trying to protect her," my mother says. "Parker isn't easily deterred. I just want Bristol to understand what she's giving up having this . . . affair with you."

"Affair?" Grip glowers. "I've been in love with your daughter for a long time. For years. I didn't wait this long so we could have some affair, as you call it."

"Oh, and you're serious about Bristol." My mother rolls her eyes. "Because of you, my daughter is the butt of jokes. The names she's being called. The way people are talking about her. It's beneath her."

She doesn't say it, but her eyes do.

You're beneath her.

"Mother, I have put up with your shit for a long time." My voice vibrates with the anger overtaking every inch of me. "I can take it. I have taken it. I've listened to you tell me that I'm not as talented as Rhyson. You've made me feel worthless."

"I've never—"

"Yes, you always have, but no more. I'm in love with Grip. Not only do I want to be with him, I'm proud to be with him. And anyone who doesn't like it, that goes for you and any idiots hiding behind their Instagram posts or trolling Twitter, can go to hell."

I turn to leave the room, and am at the door when Grip's words stop me.

"Mrs. Gray," he says softly. "I've heard a lot of things about you over the years, and I can't say much of it has been good."

"Excuse me?" Mother's indignation blares in the two words.

"You have an awful relationship with Rhyson, and from what I can tell, it's just as bad with Bristol. The only difference is she stayed and he left."

"You don't know anything about our family, Marlon."

"Actually, I do. Your son and I have been best friends for over fifteen years." He pauses. "And I'm going to marry your daughter one day."

I swing around, my chin dropped to my chest, shock trilling through me.

"Not today," he goes on like he didn't just topsy-turvy my world. "Not tomorrow. We'll know when the time is right. That isn't my point. My point is despite all the evidence to the contrary, I think you love your daughter very much."

"I do." Mother's bottom lip quivers before she pulls it back into the disciplined line I'm accustomed to. "I'm only trying to protect her."

"You're trying to control her," Grip counters. "You tried to control Rhyson, and you lost him. If you don't want to lose Bristol, don't make her choose between us, or you'll lose her, too."

She and Grip stare at one another for elongated seconds, reading one another. My mother reads people like a polygraph. She smells lies and eats their weaknesses. They don't make peace. I don't think I've ever seen my mother make peace with anyone, but I think they understand each other. But who knows because she walks toward me, giving me a brief look, and then sweeps into the hall and out the door.

Very rarely am I speechless, but I don't know which words are the right ones. I know Grip loves me, but I can honestly say I haven't seriously thought about marriage. That's crazy, I know. Marriage is not the end all, be all to me. Rhys and Kai are rare. Happy marriages are rare from my experience. My parents' marriage is an unnatural disaster, a lame horse that should have been put down years ago, and yet it keeps limping on.

Grip walks over to me and lifts my chin, his eyes scanning my face.

"Breathe." A small smile tilts one corner of his mouth, but serious eyes search mine.

I draw a deep breath in and exhale long and slow. He's right. I think I've been holding my breath since I heard the word "marry."

"I didn't say tonight." He cups my face. "I didn't mean to freak you out. That was the worst way to bring it up. I just . . . I'm not going anywhere. Are you?"

"No, of course not." My voice comes out from whatever rock it was hiding under. "I see nothing but you in the future. No one but you. You know that."

"Then don't freak out on me."

"I guess I . . . we just haven't talked about it, and we haven't been together long and—"

He presses a finger to my lips. "Bris, it's okay."

"I guess I just didn't know what to say."

He dips to take my lips between his, exploring me, searching me until he's satisfied with the answer my body gives. He pulls back, his eyes taking me in.

"When I do ask you, just say yes."

Thirty-Three
Grip

'M SO HUNGRY I COULD EAT MY TIRES. IF I DIDN'T NEED THEM TO GET home to Bristol, I probably would. I pull the Harley into the underground parking garage of my loft. Bristol's Audi convertible sits in the neighboring spot. An involuntary grin works its way from the inside to land on my lips. Seeing her here at my place makes me think about the future. After last night, I've been thinking about the future a lot.

I couldn't have chosen a worst way or time to bring up marriage than during a confrontation with her mother . . . who happens to hate me.

It's beneath her.

Angela Gray's words echo back to me. Yeah, I got the message, lady. I'm some Boyz n the Hood thug rapper and your daughter will come to her senses when the novelty of how I lay down this pipe wears off.

Got it. Loud and clear.

Bristol's mother is the high priestess of veiled messages, though she wasn't hiding much last night.

Billions?

Damn. That's a lot of money Bristol's walking away from.

I look around the lobby of my loft building. It's nice. Luxurious even. Nicer than anything I ever would have imagined for myself growing up. Better than anything anyone in my family has ever owned.

But billions? Parker is worth billions.

I've been wrestling with this unfamiliar sense of inadequacy ever since last night. Unfamiliar because my mother raised me to assume I was up for any challenge, as if I could accomplish anything. That kind of confidence in a kid from my circumstances is rare, and not for the first time, I thank my mother. She'll come around. She has to. I told Mrs. Gray that Bristol would choose me. I know this because I would choose her. It wouldn't be fair, and it would cut me open and gut me, but if my mother insists on this attitude—on treating Bristol the way she did—I'll have some choices to make, too.

An odd, bitter smell hits my nose as soon as I enter the loft. An investigative sniff doesn't do much good. I still can't place that awful smell. Is it garbage or . . . what?

"Grip." Bristol bends over the rail up on the landing. Her dark hair hangs a little wild and completely free down her back. She rushes down the stairs and hurls herself into my arms. I stumble back, laughing with an armful of my girl.

God, yes. This.

Parker can have his billions and his hotels and his helicopters. This is all I want. I squeeze Bristol so tightly our hearts converse through our clothes. I lean into her, sliding my hands down to her waist and kissing her.

"Are you hungry?" she asks against my lips. She's wearing a simple black dress with short sleeves. She's barefoot and has on no makeup. I could eat her for dinner she looks so good. Or actual food and then just make love to her afterwards. I like that option even better.

"Starving." I peck her lips and squint toward the take out menus under magnets on the refrigerator. "We can order whatever you want, just make it fast."

"No need to order." Bristol pulls back, her eyes gleaming with anticipation. "I cooked."

So it wasn't the garbage.

"Um, why?" I pose the question cautiously because . . . why would she try to cook? That one good pot of chili hasn't convinced me.

"Grip." She pouts her lips so prettily that I'd eat her shoe if she pulled it out of the oven. "I wanted to make something you'd enjoy after that long photo shoot. How was it by the way?"

"It was great. I missed having you there, but Sarah did great."

"She did? Good. You were wrong for firing me. Of course, you were, but it made me realize that Sarah needs broader experiences. And if I don't recruit some help, I'll be working eighteen-hour days for the foreseeable future."

"The hell you will. Some of those hours are mine," I mumble against her neck.

"Not the neck." Her husky protest is half-hearted at best as she arches her neck to give me easier access.

"I really am starving." I laugh when she looks disappointed that I don't have her up against the wall yet. As hungry as I am, I'd probably drop her.

"Well, like I said." She pulls back, humor restored and eyes gleaming again. "I cooked."

She takes my hand and pulls me toward the dining room table. It's set beautifully with dishes I've never seen before, and lit with candles I know I didn't buy.

"What's the occasion?" I take the seat beside hers.

"Us." She leans down to kiss me. "Us is the occasion."

"I like the sound of that." I pull her into my lap, ignoring the hunger pains. She wiggles, which does not soften my dick any, until she squirms free.

"Dinner first." She's practically beaming.

"And what's for dinner?"

"Collard greens. Like the ones your mother made."

Her grin stretches across her face, and I don't have the heart to tell her how hard they are to get as good as my mom's. It's a start.

"Oh. Great." My mouth is already watering. Even knowing how other-abled Bristol is in the kitchen, I'm sure something turned out edible. "And what else?"

"Um ..." Her face falls. "Else?"

"Yeah, you know. Like meat, potatoes, or whatever. I'm really not picky, just hungry."

"I spent a lot of time on these collard greens." She bites her lip. "I wanted to cook something I knew you liked, and they were so good at dinner that Sunday. And I think they turned out great."

"Are you telling me you only cooked greens?" My stomach howls like a coyote.

"But it's a lot of them." She grimaces and shifts from one bare foot to the other. "I guess I didn't think this through."

"Babe, it's okay." I stroke one cheekbone, tracing the few almost undetectable freckles scattered over her nose. "I can't believe you went to the trouble of making one of my favorite dishes. Let's eat."

How bad could it be? I mean, they're greens, not escargots.

Can I just say ... damn.

At least now I know how bad they could be. I run my fork through the leathery green leaves on the pretty plates Bristol set. They also taste like I imagine leather would taste . . . but not as well seasoned. Meanwhile, my stomach is at my back. I should have eaten the Craft service on set today. I will suffer in silence because there is no way I'm telling her how bad these greens are.

"They're not great, huh?" she asks.

"They're the worst," I say before I can stop myself.

We consider each other across the table and the steaming crap pile of collard greens and laugh together. She gets up and climbs into my lap, sliding her hand into my jeans pocket to get my cell phone.

"Pizza?" She rests her forehead against my chin.

"With every meat known to man and some that haven't been FDA approved."

Once the pizza is ordered, she doesn't leave my lap, which is fine with me.

"I really wanted to make dinner special for you," she whispers into my neck, dotting kisses into the edge of my shirt and across my collarbone. "Those greens at your mom's were so good."

"It's taken her a long time to get those right. She used her mother's recipe, and her mother used her mother's recipe. They can taste really awful if not done right."

"So I discovered." She shakes against me with laughter.

"Maybe my mom can share her recipe one day," I venture softly. I know the things Bristol overheard my mom say hurt her, but she hasn't brought it up.

Bristol's laugh this time is a humorless huff of air.

"That would be an interesting development since she can't stand me."

"She'll come around, baby. She has to. She's just recalibrating her expectations. Like I'm sure your mom is doing."

Bristol shrugs one shoulder. Sending one side of the dress down her arm and leaving her shoulder bare.

"What your mother said last night about what you're giving up to be with me, to not be with Parker."

"What about it?" She doesn't know where I'm heading.

"Billions, babe." I kiss the top of her head, cupping the back and tugging my fingers through the soft strands. "It's a lot, right?"

She's silent for a few seconds before she glances up at me through her long lashes. Her fingers drift to the necklace I noticed last night. The thick gold bar hangs from the chain. It's obviously fine craftsmanship.

"You admired my necklace last night," she says. "But you didn't read the inscription."

I study her face while I lift the gold bar and turn it over.

Etched into the gold is the inscription "My heart broke loose on the wind."

For a second, the space of a heartbeat, I can't breathe. This means so much to me I literally cannot breathe.

"When did you get this?" My voice is hushed, reverent with the thought of what that night on the Ferris wheel must have meant to her, too.

"Months ago." She cups one side of my face. "We didn't even seem to be a possibility when I ordered this."

"But why . . . even then?"

Months ago, Bristol was deep freezing me, so it's hard to imagine that night was on her mind then. That I was on her mind then.

"Even if we hadn't gotten together, I was still going to wear this next to my heart because I knew I would never love anyone else that way." She shakes her head, eyes bright with conviction. "Not the way I felt that night. That night was awesome, magical, but it was just a glimpse of the man you would become. And I knew even if I couldn't have you, I'd carry this piece of you with me. This piece of your prophecy."

That poem inspired me in a way I have only ever put into words for one person. The woman sitting in my lap. The woman who has held my heart for years when I wasn't sure she even wanted it. And the whole time, this night, these moments, burned in her memory like they did mine. I'm torn between spreading her on the table and having my appetizer before the pizza arrives, or kissing her until she's limp in my arms. Before I get the chance to do either, the buzzer sounds.

"Pizza," we say together with grins.

"I'll get my wine," she says. "And your beer."

I clear my throat of the emotion still clogging it.

"Sounds good." I take one more look at her, how naturally she fits here, but she'd fit anywhere I was, and I'll fit any place she'll be. I guess we'll spend the rest of our lives chasing each other.

And getting caught every night.

I swing open the door, cash tip already in hand, but it isn't the pizza guy.

"Officers." I suppress the Pavlovian response. Obviously they're here for a reason, and I've done nothing wrong, so I'll just wait to hear them out. "What can I do for you?"

There's no answer from either of them, and they look like undertakers.

"Something wrong?" I ask.

"We um, need to search the property." One of them flashes his badge, and I note the name Officer Mars.

"Search?" I frown and glance over my shoulder into the loft. "For what exactly?"

"What's this about?" Bristol comes to stand beside me, hands already on her hips.

"We were tipped off that there may be a significant amount of cocaine in the residence connected to a recent bust over on Rosecrans."

"What?" I give an incredulous laugh. "In here? Nah, you got that twisted."

"You have search warrants?" Bristol demands. "You won't be searching anything until you show me one."

Amazingly they produce one.

"It was a huge bust connected to one of the largest operations on the West Coast," Officer Mars says. "We have to follow every lead in a case as significant as this."

"That may well be," Bristol says, eyes glowing the color of gunmetal. "But that has nothing to do with Mr. James."

"Ma'am, we have this warrant." He shifts his weight and hooks a thumb in his belt loop. "And we need to conduct a thorough search."

"This is ridiculous." I shake my head dazedly. "A tip? From who?"

"We aren't at liberty to say," Officer Mars asserts. "May we come inside?"

"No, the hell you may not," Bristol says. "I'm calling our lawyer. This is ridiculous."

"Bris, it's obviously just a misunderstanding." I lead her over to the couch and sit. "Just let them get it over with. They won't find anything."

"Sir, we're just doing our jobs," Officer Mars says softly. "It isn't personal."

"Not personal?" Bristol shouts. "What the hell do you mean it's not—"

"Babe, it's okay." I wrap my fingers around hers and pull her to wait with me on the couch. I wave a hand to the room. "Knock yourselves out for nothing. Waste our tax dollars doing this when you could be doing something real."

"I don't like this," Bristol whispers to me as they search the room systematically, finding nothing, of course. "I'm calling our lawyer."

"They're almost done. They won't find anything."

"What's this?" Officer Mars pats the back of my backpack, which I notice for the first time bulges more than usual. "I'm going to have to open this."

He pulls out a pocketknife and slits the back off the bag.

"This is outrageous." Bristol's voice stings like a scorpion. "Now you'll have to replace his bag ..."

Her voice trails off as a huge block of cocaine in an oversize Zip Lock bag falls from the lining of my backpack.

Officer Mars swears softly, flicking a surprised glance my way. I surge to my feet and point to the bag.

"That shit isn't mine."

"It's in your bag, in your residence," the other officer says carefully. "Your ID and other items that clearly belong to you are here."

"Grip, don't say another word." Bristol has her phone to her ear. "I'm getting our lawyers on the phone right now. I knew this was some kind of setup. God."

"Tell the lawyers to meet him down at the county jail."

"Jail?" The word torpedoes from my mouth at full speed. "The hell I am. I've never been to jail a day in my life, and I'm not going now. Not for some shit that isn't even mine."

"I'm sure we'll straighten it out then," Officer Mars says, his face set in impassive lines, though I can tell it isn't what he wants to be doing. "We have to take you in, Mr. James."

It's all surreal, and none of it sinks in. Not the officer reading me rights I promised my mother I'd never have to hear. Not Bristol's urgent conversation with Prodigy's lawyer. Only the cuffs feel real, enclosing my wrists again for something I haven't done.

"No cuffs," Bristol's hard voice batters the officers. "You'll take the private exit where no one will see, and keep this off the radar as long as you can."

"Ma'am, with all due respect—"

"You left respect behind when you came into our home and found drugs that don't belong to us."

"This isn't a negotiation," Officer Mars interjects almost gently.

"Oh, you better believe it's a negotiation." Bristol folds her arms over her chest, managing to look imposing even in her casual dress and bare feet. "Here's the terms. You follow my instructions for getting him out of here and keeping this off the radar as long as possible. How well you follow my instructions determines, when I bring a wrongful arrest suit against LAPD, how deeply I drag the two of you into it."

There's no sign of the soft, pliant woman who was in my lap just minutes ago. In her place stands a coldly enraged Valkyrie who looks fully prepared to escort them to the afterlife.

"Which exit did you want us to use?" Officer Mars asks reluctantly.

While Bristol goes over the plan to get me out of the building and down to the county jail, all I can think of is my mother telling anyone who would listen that all she ever dreamt was that I'd have a clean record and never spend a day behind bars.

Sorry, Ma.

Thirty-Four

Bristol

"**T**HIS CAN'T BE HAPPENING." No matter how many times I've said that over the last several hours, this is happening.

Grip is behind bars, and we can't get him out on bail. With all the money and connections at our disposal, he's still stuck in county jail with no chance of getting out tonight.

"It's the weekend," Barry, the lawyer says again. "There won't be a hearing until Monday."

"You're telling me Grip has to stay in jail until Monday?" The disbelief and fury on Rhyson's face may match mine, but I doubt it. "For something we know he didn't do? Hell, even if he did it, we should be able to get him out."

"He has no criminal record whatsoever. He should be released on his own recognizance." I've said this over and over, and Barry's answer remains the same.

"They found a lot of cocaine in his possession. Enough to bump this up to a felony." Barry polishes his glasses and shakes his head. "Because they have reason to believe it's connected to a larger case, to a case they've been working and a group they've been trying to prosecute for years, the typical strings I would pull aren't working."

Barry stands to his feet and gathers his briefcase and jacket. "Where do you think you're going? Rhyson, he isn't leaving." I grab Barry's briefcase and hold it hostage behind my back. "You're not leaving."

Rhyson and Barry stare at me, mouths hanging open. "Bristol, listen," Rhyson says. "I know you—"

"No, you don't know." My voice breaks. My heart breaks. "If you're willing to leave this place, to let Barry leave this place with Grip still behind bars, then you don't know."

"Bris, I get it." Rhyson says. "He's my best friend."

"But he's my . . ."

I drop the briefcase and turn my back on the two of them, my heart like a spinning speedometer, completely out of control and reckless. I cross one arm across my waist and chew my thumbnail. The sound of Barry leaving the room barely registers. A horrible suspicion sprouted like a weed as soon as the officers found that cocaine, and has grown into venomous certainty. It's choking every lucid thought and killing off my reason.

"Bristol, we have to go home." Rhyson turns me gently by the shoulders to face him.

"I want to see him." Tears flood my throat and emotion weakens my mouth into a trembling mess. "He didn't get to . . . to eat . . . and I need . . . I need to see him before we go."

"We can't tonight, Bris. It's . . ." he pulls his phone out of his pocket and grimaces at the screen. "It's one o'clock in the morning. Tomorrow. He's asleep anyway."

"Asleep in jail, Rhyson. We can't leave him."

"Look, we'll be back at it first thing in the morning. I am ordering you to go home, get some rest so you'll be ready to fight tomorrow. We can at least try to find some way to get him out before Monday, despite this hearing thing. But nothing more will happen tonight."

He heads for the door, looking over his shoulder at me.

"Let's go, Bris. I need to get home to Kai anyway. She's so close now, I hate leaving her alone."

Guilt pricks me as I think about my sister-in-law home alone, ready to deliver at any moment.

"You're right. Of course, go. I'll work on this tomorrow morning."

"Make no mistake about it," Rhyson says gently. "So will I. If there was more we could do tonight to get him out, you know I would do it."

I nod and walk with him into the hallway outside of the room we've occupied the last few hours, crawling up walls and shaking trees to make headway.

"Rhyson, what if I told you I think Grip being here has something to do with me?" I ask softly, finally voicing the noxious thought that has been scratching the inside of my head the last few hours.

"You mean Parker?" Rhyson slides a glance my way and nods. "It occurred to me."

I stop, grabbing his elbow to stop him, too. "So you do think this is my fault?"

"No, not your fault." Rhyson squeezes my hand. "But I wouldn't put it past Parker to be involved somehow. This was all too orchestrated. It smacks of foul play. If Parker is involved, I bet some high-ranking judge is in his pocket."

"My thoughts exactly."

"Bristol, promise me you won't contact Parker." Rhyson looks down at me sternly. "We knew he was dangerous, but now we know the lengths he'll go to. Or at least we think he'll go to. We'll work on this together tomorrow."

All the pieces start coming together in my head while I'm driving home. Once I know for sure that Parker is behind this, I'll feel better. He never does anything unless there's a gain. A measurable gain. I know what, or who he wants to gain. For the first time I feel some control. Steel enters my spine. I can fix this. I don't know what I'll have to do to fix it, and I honestly don't care as long as I can get Grip's name cleared and him out of this ridiculous situation.

I should be surprised to find the same black SUV that met me on the tarmac after Dubai in my driveway, but I'm not. Clairmont steps from the driver's side and crosses around to open the rear door for me. I don't look at or otherwise acknowledge him, but climb in, taking the seat across from Parker.

"You twisted motherfucker." I keep my voice even and calm despite the violent emotions howling inside of me. My fingers spasm with the base compulsion to claw his throat out.

"Bristol." Parker's blue eyes gleam with dark smugness. "Now is that any way to greet the man who holds the key to setting your lover free?"

"How soon can you get him out?"

"It took me very little time to break it. I can fix it just as quickly, with your cooperation, of course. And you should call your brother's lawyers off. They're wasting their time, though I must admit I am enjoying blocking them at every turn. I have the right judges so deep in my pocket they lick my ass."

"Who are you?" I lean forward, searching his face for an answer, looking for the monster hiding behind the polished mask. "What is wrong with you? Ruining an innocent man's life for what? Me? To marry me, a woman who doesn't love you?"

"Why would I care if you love me or not?" The razor edge of Parker's laugh slices through my nerves. "But a marriage offer isn't on the table anymore. How could it be now that the whole world knows you've soiled yourself with that thug?"

I watch him with no expression, waiting for his terms. It doesn't matter what they are. I'll do them to clear Grip's name. Parker may not realize it, but he has me exactly where he wants me. He can bend me, position me, do whatever the hell he wants with me. He's found my weakest point, and I'll say 'uncle' before he even asks.

"Just tell me what you want and stop playing games."

"Oh, but the games are the fun part." His lust pollutes the air. It's thick, a heavy fume filling my nostrils, gagging me. "And you know what I want, Bristol."

"Sex."

My steady eyes and matter of fact tone don't betray my insurgent heart, bawling at the thought of anyone but Grip inside of me.

"Well, of course. That's a given." Parker smiles at me like I'm a slow child. "You could have been my queen, but now you have to bow to me."

He drops the smile and nods to the spot in front of him. "I said now, Bristol. On your knees."

Teeth locked painfully and eyes hot with tears I will not give him the satisfaction of shedding, I drop to my knees and face him. He reaches out, pushing down one shoulder of my dress and then the other, until my breasts lay bare except for the gold chain dangling between them. My nipples go hard in the cool air, and I hope he'll take it for desire. A man like Parker needs to feel wanted, and my heart may have no limits where Grip's concerned, but my body does. And it refuses to want Parker.

He licks his lips, eyes brimming with greed, and cups my breast, squeezing with no mercy. I swallow a cry of pain, knowing it would only feed his appetite for my suffering.

"This body was made for me," he says huskily. His eyes lift to mine, hard as blue crystals. "Mine, and you humiliated me in front of the whole world, flaunting your sordid affair with him."

"There's nothing sordid about my relationship with Grip."

I stiffen when his hand slides down my torso, slipping past the material puddled at my hips and into my panties. His fingers play between my legs, but I remain obstinately dry. There is nothing about this, about him that excites me. I'm disgusted I ever shared my body with this man. Even as a naïve girl still in high school I should have recognized him as a monster.

"You're not as . . ." He withdraws his hand. "Ready for me as I would have hoped."

"I can get myself ready, if you like." I barb the smile before I give it to him. "It'll be like old times."

I'm not the only one holding back my true feelings. Despite the calm veneer, I see barely restrained rage in Parker's eyes. I'm just waiting for him to take it out on me.

"The whole world is laughing at me, Bristol."

"They aren't."

"To the world, you played me with that thug of yours."

I don't defend Grip. That would only make him angrier.

"I asked you to tell the press, Parker. I wasn't cheating on you, and you know it. Now let's get this over with." Urgency to free Grip, to clear his name, rides me. "Tell me what you want. I'm on my knees here. You want head? You want to fuck me in the ass? You want to invite a couple friends? I don't care, just tell me you'll clear his name and do it as soon as humanly possible."

Though I have my doubts about Parker's humanity.

"God, all that loyalty and fire. That was supposed to be mine, too." Parker runs a finger down my cheek, smiling when I flinch. "You think I'll make this simple for him? For you? No, he needs to be humiliated the way I was. Everyone has to know."

A cesspool of dread stands in my belly.

"Just tell me what I have to do, and give me the assurances I need that you'll get him out as soon possible."

"So impatient." He pushes my hair back from my face, his touch lingering at my neck with deceptive gentleness. "You and I leave for the Amalfi Coast tomorrow."

"All right." I have no idea why this is necessary, but I also can't care anymore. I just need to get Grip free.

"We'll fuck on my yacht, out on the upper deck."

My acquiescence freezes on my lips, horror seeping slowly into every fiber of my body.

"The upper deck?"

"Yes, the same reporter who leaked the Vegas pictures is standing by." His frigid smile is an icy warning. "The whole world will know that you may be with him, but you're on vacation fucking me. More importantly, he'll know."

I don't know if I can do it. For a moment, my will wavers.

"Do you think I've done my worst, Bristol?" Parker's smile is a sutured curve, a jagged row of stitches stretching over a wound. "Oh, it could get worse for him. What if there's a body somewhere connected to these drug deals of his? What if his DNA can be matched to any number of crimes? He could be put away for life, if I try just a little harder."

I think of Grip behind bars, possibly for years, life in ruins because he loved me.

"So tomorrow?" I pull my dress up over my shoulders, forcing the words past the heart trapped and bleeding in my throat. "What time?"

"I'll pick you up at two."

"I'll be ready."

I start to get up from my knees, but he grabs my elbow and turns me back to face him.

"One more thing, Bristol."

He jerks me into him, his mouth rough and cruel, and his teeth sharp on the tender swell of my bottom lip. My own blood rushes into my mouth. He flattens his hand to my chest, and my heart tattoos fear into his palm. A smile slashes his face before he snatches the chain from my neck.

"You really should have let me buy you this necklace."

Thirty-Five
Bristol

"T HE LAWYERS ARE WORKING ON IT, BUT WE KEEP HITTING A
wall." Rhyson shakes his head, dismay darkening his gray eyes
to slate. "It's the weekend, so that's part of it, but these guys can
usually break through anything. Even getting this private meeting room was
near impossible, and usually a good bribe can pull that off easily. Some high
ups must be monitoring your case really closely."

He splits a careful glance between me and Grip, who faces us from the
other side of the table, dressed in royal blue scrubs with "LA County Jail"
emblazoned on the back. It's incongruous. Awful and incongruous to see my
brilliant poet in this garb. This man whose record is cleaner than mine when
so many things where he grew up could have left smudges on him. That was
the thing his mother was most proud of, and because of me, that's gone.

Grip has been uncharacteristically quiet. Anger dulls the eyes usually lit
with humor, intelligence. For me—desire, love.

"My mom's coming?" he asks, not acknowledging Rhyson's comment at
all. "She knows to come here, right?"

Rhyson and I exchange a concerned look.

"Yeah, Gep made sure she knows we got this room. Did you hear me,
Marlon?" Rhyson presses. "We keep running into walls, but we're working on
it."

"Any idea what's behind it all?" Grip asks the question of Rhyson, but
his eyes rest on me. "Why I was set up in the first place?"

With a look, Rhyson and I silently agree to tell him.

"We think it may be Parker." I clear my throat and drop my eyes to the imitation wood of the table. "So, it's probably my fault."

"Not your fault, Bristol," Rhyson says quickly. "But I do agree that Parker is the only person with motivation and power enough to throw up the kind of road blocks the lawyers keep encountering."

"They won't make any headway." I run a trembling hand through my hair.

"How would you know that, Bristol?" Grip's question, his voice so hard it hurts my ears. "You sound really certain."

"I mean, I'm guessing." I shrug one shoulder, toying with the bangles on my wrist "If it's Parker, he'll have thought of everything."

"I bet he has." Grip's eyes rest so heavily on me I feel them even though I'm still not looking at him. I tuck my swollen bottom lip in my mouth, hoping he won't notice.

"Well, we're not giving up. Gep's calling in favors with all his old fed contacts. See what we can find." Rhyson glances at his watch. "I gotta run. Luke's got a session he needs me to sit in on, but the lawyers will keep working."

He stands and crooks a grin at us.

"Besides, I assume you guys want a few minutes alone." He tips his head toward the cameras in the corner of the ceiling. "Don't give 'em too much of a show."

I glance at Grip, but there's no answering smile. No acknowledgment of Rhyson's joke. He stands, and they do that man hug thing, pounding on each other's backs.

"I'm gonna get you out of here," Rhyson says. "I'm sorry you're not out already."

"Not your fault, man." Grip fist pounds Rhyson before taking his seat, his eyes latching on to me again. "Thanks for all you're doing."

"Bye, sis." Rhyson drops a kiss on my hair. "Stay out of trouble. Let me handle this Parker shit."

I nod but focus on the hands in my lap. I'm usually an excellent liar, but the dilemma with Parker has stripped all my guard away, and I don't trust my own subterfuge to hold under their sharp eyes.

Once Rhyson leaves, I'm not sure what to do with myself or with Grip. I lay my hand on the table, in hopes that he'll reach for it, but he doesn't. He's quiet and intent, dissecting me with his stare.

"What?" I hazard a glance up to meet his eyes. "Why are you so quiet? You're angry. I understand. You wouldn't be here if it weren't for me."

He doesn't reply, but the expressive curve of his mouth is stiff as wax. He slumps in his seat and links his hands behind his head, the muscles of his arms flexing.

"Say something." I gnaw at my bottom lip. "I promise I'm going to fix this."

He reaches into his pocket and pulls out his closed fist. Slowly, his eyes never leaving my face, he opens his fist and drops a delicate gold chain on the table.

"Did you lose that, Bristol?"

My hand flies to my throat. I know the necklace isn't there. Parker took it from me last night, and now Grip has it. I can't assemble these pieces into anything that makes sense.

That son of a bitch.

"Grip, where'd you get that?"

"Oh, it came with my breakfast this morning." He slides a slip of paper across the table to me. "Along with this."

Your queen or mine?

Parker's scrawled words may as well be carved into my skin. That's how much they hurt, how badly Grip reading them hurts. I must be bleeding subcutaneously. Just under my skin, I'm hemorrhaging pride and self-respect.

"I can explain." I look from the damning note, the gilded evidence glimmering against the cheap wood. "Parker and I, we aren't—"

"I know you aren't cheating, so don't even bother explaining that," Grip says. "We're so far beyond that. What does he want? Besides for me to know he's using me to get to you?"

How much should I tell him? I have no idea.

"Don't think about lying to me." His glance peels my skin back, and any lie I would tell him crumbles under that stare.

I have to tell him everything. I wanted to do this on my own because I knew Grip and Rhyson would try to stop me. Of course, they would. It's insanity to even consider what Parker has proposed. It's demeaning and soul-destroying.

And I have every intention of doing it and whatever it takes to get Grip out of here and his name cleared.

"Parker was at my house when I got home last night."

He flattens his hands on the table. His fingers twitch, but there's no other indication that he hears. That my words might infuriate him.

"He . . . he admitted that he did this. That he has at least one high-ranking judge, probably more, in his pocket. This case isn't going any-where unless he says so."

"Again I ask, what does he want?"

There's no curiosity behind the question. He already knows and just wants to hear me say it.

"He wants what he's always wanted." I force myself to look at him. "He wants me."

"He wants you to marry him?" Grip asks dispassionately.

"No, he says he'd never marry me now that I've 'soiled myself publicly with you.'"

"Well, at least there's that." The tight line of Grip's mouth loosens just a little. "So then what?"

"He wants to take me to the Amalfi Coast today."

All pretense that he doesn't care, that he knows everything, disappears. Urgency charges the stale air in the small visiting room.

"Today?" he demands. "What's his plan?"

"We'll have . . ." The word sits so foul, queued up and rotting on my tongue. I press my lips together against emotion and tears so I can go on. "Sex, we'll have sex on the upper deck of his yacht."

I push the words up my throat, as heavy as a boulder up a hill. "And the reporter who leaked the Vegas pictures will leak pictures of us . . . together."

"Fuck!" He bangs the table, the sound echoing like a clanging cymbal. It rattles my teeth. "You won't."

I keep my head lowered. I figure it isn't a good time to remind him he isn't the boss of me. We have so little time before I have to go, and I don't want to spend it arguing about something that, in my mind, is done. Is happening.

"Look at me, Bristol."

I clutch my conviction and raise my eyes to his.

"You are not doing this. Not for me." He does take my hand then, both of them between his, and squeezes. "We'll find another way."

"No, we won't. You don't know him."

These dull concrete walls are closing in on me, and the thought of Grip in here even another day traps my breath in my chest. Panic crushes me from the inside out.

"There isn't another way." I lift his hands to my lips, kissing his knuckles, his thumb, turning his hand and leaving a dry sob in the palm of his hand. "He's made sure of that. If there was a way, Rhyson would have found it by now."

"I won't let you do this."

"You can't stop me." I pull my hands clear of his, my resolve weakening the longer I touch him. The thought of anyone else touching me the way these hands did, with love and reverence, turns my stomach. "I told you. I warned you that I'm not like other girls."

My laugh leaves traces of poison on my lips.

"I don't have those limits." One tear at a time scalds my cheeks. "I'd do anything for you. It sounds romantic until it crosses your lines, huh? Until it goes too far."

I look at him, my smile ironic.

"Are you afraid, that like Parker, you won't want me either, after I've 'soiled' myself with him?"

"I'm afraid it would destroy something in you that I can't ever get back," he says earnestly.

I haven't admitted it even to myself, but so am I.

"If that happens," I say, dropping my eyes to my lap. "Whatever's left is yours."

"Don't, Bris." He crosses around the table, sits on the corner, and pulls me to stand between his legs, his hands running up my arms. "I'd stay before I'd let you do that."

"That's ridiculous. Oh my God. Don't even . . ."

I drop my head to his shoulder, horrified he'd even entertain sacrificing his career or years of his life for something he didn't do. That he would do that to spare me this indignity.

"I would never let you do that for me," I say, my breath hiccupping in my chest.

"I won't have to, but now you know how I feel." He bends his brows over the torture in his eyes. "You think you're the only one who loves without limits?"

"That makes no sense, Grip."

"Like it made sense for me to wait around for years while you figured out you loved me." His mouth pulls into a warped smile. "But who did that? This guy."

A breathy laugh breaks through my tears.

"I love you," I whisper, stepping back and giving up the warm safety of his arms. "There's nothing . . . nothing I wouldn't do for you."

The vestiges of his smile fall away. He runs his thumb over my lips, tugging at the flesh I know to be red and swollen.

"He did this?" There's brimstone in Grip's demand, fire in his glare.

"It doesn't matter." I pull away from his hand, embarrassed that Grip's seeing the results of Parker's rough kiss. It's a dim reflection of what he'll do to me later, I'm sure. "I need to go."

"The thought of him touching you . . ." Grip swallows, his voice falling into a dark abyss. "Of him hurting you, kills me, Bris. That I can't protect you, it kills me."

There's blood thirst in his eyes, and I have no doubt if Parker were in this room he'd be dead. But he isn't here. He's out there wreaking havoc on our lives, and I have the means to stop him.

"I need to go."

He catches my elbow, his touch firm and gentle. In his outstretched palm he holds the gold necklace.

"Don't forget this." He proffers it to me.

"Keep it till I get you out of here." His handsome face wavers as tears fill my eyes but don't fall. "If you still want me . . . after, I'll take it back."

I glance up at the camera in the corner before leaning in to lay my lips against his, pouring everything into that brief contact. When my lips would cling to his, I force myself away and out the door without looking back. Tears blur everything ahead of me, and I slam into someone right outside the door in the hall.

"I'm sorry," I mumble to the person I almost ran down. "Oh, Ms. James, excuse me. I wasn't . . . watching."

"How is he?" She skips past my apology, looking over my shoulder to the closed door.

"He'll be better when he's out of here." I brush the useless tears away, reaffirming my commitment to this course.

"This is some bullshit." Ms. James' righteous anger shines from her dark eyes. "My boy has never done drugs, much less would be carrying enough to sell."

Her mouth pulls into an unexpected grin.

"A little dro every once in a while, yes, but slanging 'caine? No way."

"I know. We all know. It's a setup, but we're getting to the bottom of it. I promise you he'll be out soon."

"A setup?" Her question is a rapier pressed to my neck, a threat to draw blood if she doesn't get answers. "Who set my boy up?"

"My ex-boyfriend." I face her head on, knowing this will only add to the myriad other reasons she has to dislike me and want me away from her son.

"You ain't been nothing but trouble to him," she says harshly, tears lique-fying the chocolate eyes. "I knew it. I knew him being with someone like you would only mean trouble."

"You were right."

"First the traffic stop and turning my son's community against him."

"I wouldn't say they turned against him," I disagree carefully. "Calling Marlon a sellout?" Her head tips, her brows lift. "Saying he disrespected Black women when he chose you over Qwest? That ain't turning against where you come from?"

Every one of her accusations is a tiny arrow that finds its mark. "I'm sorry." I force myself to meet her eyes. "Not for being with Grip, but that be-ing with me brought this on, but I'm going to fix it."

"The damage has been done. My son's record—"

"Will be cleared."

I look at her. I feel so hard right now inside. I'm marbleizing my heart to get through this ordeal with Parker. I do that to protect myself, but I crack the shell long enough to say what I need to say more gently.

"Ms. James, I'm going to do whatever it takes to get him out, to fix this," I say. "But when he's out, I'm still going to be with him, if he wants me. All the things you love about him, I love about him. He isn't a sellout because he loves me. And I'm not just after him for whatever you think the novelty is. We love each other."

I dredge up a smile and hope she doesn't notice the tears I can't seem to clear from my eyes.

"I need to go, but he wants to see you, and our 'favor' only extends so far. He won't have much more time to visit."

Even with her looking at me as if I've committed a crime or personally put her son here, I want to ask her for a hug. For a touch that tells me I can go through with this. That as abhorrent as it will be taking Parker into my body, having him leave his filthy fingerprints on my soul, that it will be worth it. That Grip is worth it. I want that from her because she's the one who taught him that sacrifice is the essence of love. She's the only one who would love him as much as I do and would do anything for him, too. I see it in her fierce eyes, in her warrior stance.

But of course she doesn't offer a touch or a word. She doesn't know I need it, and if she knew, I'm not sure she would care.

Thirty-Six

Grip

'VE BEEN IN THE LA COUNTY JAIL ALL NIGHT AND MOST OF THE MORNING, but this is the first time I've felt truly caged. I prowl the tiny visiting room like a starved beast. And I'm so hungry. I need to feel my sharp teeth tear into Charles Parker's skin. I want to eat him alive and spit out his bones for putting Bristol in this position. There has to be another way, something I'm not considering.

Like a dark shadow, Corpse looms in my brain. I wanted options for desperate situations. Am I willing to go that far? I can't even allow myself to imagine what I'll feel if Bristol goes through with this. She thinks she has no limits? I'm not sure of mine anymore. Fury blots out everything else. I clutch my head, pacing from the table to the wall, back and forth, the problem winding around my brain like a serpent. Looping, coiling, poised to strike. I bang my head against the wall, impervious to the pain. I'm just praying the blow will jolt me; show me a way out of this.

"I always said you were hard-headed."

My mother closes the door behind her. She crosses over to me quickly and wraps her arms around me, collapsing and sniffing against my chest. She's the toughest woman I know and only has one weak spot.

Me.

This is the first time we've seen each other since the fiasco of Sunday dinner. This shit situation has hurdled any awkwardness between us. She knows I need her, and any differences we have we set aside at least for now.

"Are you okay?" She explores my arms and shoulders. "Did they hurt you?"

"Ma, this ain't exactly *Letter from Birmingham Jail*." I manage a weak chuckle. "The guards have been getting my autograph and taking selfies. They asked me to freestyle at breakfast. I'm good."

"Good?" She rears back, running disparaging eyes over LA County's standard issue blue scrubs. "This ain't good, Marlon. I never thought I would see you here. Not you."

"And I haven't done anything to be here, so I'll be out before you know it," I tell her with more confidence than makes sense.

"You know I didn't do this, right?" I dip to catch her eyes, not thinking I would even have to defend myself. Not to her. "Somebody set me up."

"I heard." Her glare is a laser cutting through any secrets I would keep from her. "I saw Bristol in the hall."

I close off my expression. I can't hear any shit she would say about the woman willing to sacrifice her dignity, her body, pieces of her soul to get me out of here. I can't even wrap my brain around the money and power at Parker's disposal. Abuses like these, he's probably been inflicting his whole life.

When I get out of here, however it happens, I'll make sure he regrets this one.

"She told me this is her fault." Ma's disapproval is palpable.

"It isn't her fault," I say impatiently.

"I know it isn't the best time to bring it up," she says, her elevated brows indicating it must be said. "But if you had stayed with Qwest, this wouldn't be happening."

"I don't love Qwest, Ma." I blow out a weary breath. "And I don't need this right now."

"You didn't give her a chance. You could have—"

"I fell in love with Bristol years ago," I break in. "In a week. Did you know that?"

I grasp her hands and press them to my heart. "She's here, Ma. In my heart. In my head. I can't get rid of her."

I shake my head, a sad smile on my lips.

"I don't want to. I want to spend the rest of my life feeling this way, like I'm only half alive when she isn't here. There's nowhere she could go I wouldn't chase her. Have you ever felt that for anybody?"

Shock rounds my mother's eyes, and her fingers tremble against my chest.

"No," she whispers, her eyes searching my face. "I don't think most people ever do."

"It's painful." A hefty sigh heaves from my chest. "It's precious, though. I won't give it up."

Pain tears my heart in half as I look at the woman who, on more than one occasion, went hungry sitting across the table making sure I ate—who literally went without so I could have.

"I won't give her up for anyone." I lean to kiss her forehead. "Not even you."

"I only wanted . . . I only want what's best for you." Her bottom lip trembles, but she traps it in her teeth, eyes to the concrete floor. "A woman who knows how to fight. Who will stand with you and understands you. Who would do anything for you."

The irony of it runs me through like a sword.

"You always said you prayed I'd find someone just like you. As fierce as you, ride or die like you, as strong as you." I shake my head, rubbing her fingers between mine. "You don't realize your prayers were answered, exceeded. Why do you think I fell for her? Bristol's just like you. Don't miss that because she doesn't look it on the outside."

"I can't make myself want her for you, Marlon." She doesn't waste tears, but her eyes are sad. "I've always had this idea of who she'd be, and a debutante from New York isn't what I was expecting. I guess we mothers always have expectations. We always assume we know exactly what to do in every situation."

"Well, most of the time, mothers do . . ."

My words open up a path in my mind I hadn't seen before.

Dammit. I'm an idiot. Why am I just now considering this?

"Ma, I need you to do something for me. Someone I need you to call right away."

Thirty-Seven

Bristol

WHAT DOES ONE PACK FOR A TRIP LIKE THIS? WILL IT REALLY matter? The whole world will end up seeing my ass on Parker's upper deck off the Amalfi Coast.

I hold the pantsuit I bought at Fashion Week last year up to my chest. I'm not sure that Alexander McQueen's fall line is fitting for what amounts to rape and ignominy.

"Needs must when the devil drives," I mutter, tossing the grandma period panties that cover my whole butt into the pile. I'm not wasting my good lingerie on Parker's sorry ass. As long as my things are on the bed and not in the overnight bag, it's easier to pretend this isn't happening. That I'm not going anywhere.

The doorbell startles me since Parker isn't due for another hour and a half. I've been relishing every minute I have before he comes to get me. I peer through the small window of my cottage door.

"Mother." I stand there staring at her. She's been to my home exactly once since I moved into the cottage last year. After our fight the other night, I wasn't expecting her to darken my door anytime soon. "Is someone dead or giving birth?"

She walks past me, not waiting for an invitation.

"Don't be vulgar, Bristol."

Mother's eyes trace over the warm simplicity of my living room. I can't imagine where she would find fault in the understated elegance, but then she never ceases to astound with her innovative ways to find fault.

"I didn't realize death or birth were vulgar. My apologies." I gesture for her to sit, but I remain standing. "What can I do for you? I thought we said all we had to say the last time we saw each other. I don't have much time to spare."

"Packing for your trip, are you?" Mother's eyes heap disdain on my head. "Speaking of vulgar."

My breath hovers in my throat, drawn but not released. How does she know? I mean, soon everyone will know, but I was clinging to my last days of dignity.

"Trip?" I choose to play dumb, but I've never been good at pretending to be anything but intelligent.

"Oh, God, Bristol." Mother sets her Celine bag on the couch beside her. "From what I understand, we don't have much time, so dispense with the games. What time will Parker arrive?"

I blink at her, disoriented like I'm an actor in the wrong play. I flounder for my line and wonder who this character is in front of me.

"Mother, what are you talking about?" I perch on the edge of the love seat across from her.

"Marlon's mother called me and told me everything, so let's figure out how to save you."

"Ms. James?" It could be no worse than Grip's mother knowing this about me. Knowing that her son's girlfriend, whom she already dislikes, will be bartering her body for all the world to see. "She knows . . . she called . . . what's going on?"

"Bristol, do keep up." Impatience wrinkles my mother's smooth brow. "Marlon asked his mother to call me about your predicament. Wisely, I might add. How could you even consider such nonsense? I raised you better than that."

With everything else I've had to endure the last twenty-four hours, my mother's selective memory is more than I can withstand right now.

"Actually nannies were primarily responsible for my upbringing, if you'll recall, since you were managing Rhyson all over the world and couldn't be bothered to actually parent."

The temperature in the room drops so drastically, my words crystallize in the air as soon as they leave my mouth.

"Maybe I should have been more involved if you think this is acceptable behavior." Mother tsks and studies her wedding rings. "Debasing yourself this way for a man."

Laughter stirs in my belly and spills over, shaking my shoulders. I throw my head back and howl with it. I may be hysterical, but she is absolutely blind if she can say that to me with a straight face.

"The joke?" Mother asks with quiet dignity. "Please share it." "You accused me of debasing myself for a man."

My laughter does a slow leak until it's all spent, leaving me hollow and insulted. "At least I know the man I debase myself for is worth every minute of it. I'd debase myself for Grip every day if I had to. And the man you've been debasing yourself for the last thirty-odd years? Is he worth it?"

Mother's hostile eyes narrow on my face. Her hands clench into slim, beringed fists.

"You have no idea what my marriage is, what your father and I have."

"Don't you think I got an inkling when I caught him fucking a girl my age in our house? In your bed, and you did nothing but get drunk and cry about it?"

"How dare you." Mother snaps to her feet. "I came here to help you."

"Help yourself, Mother." I stand, too, needing to be on level ground with her. "Do you know how much time I wasted trying to please you? Trying to be you? Trying not to be you? You were such a contradiction, I wasn't sure if I should emulate you or eradicate you from my nature."

"Only you can't, can you?" Her eyes are solemn. "You think I wanted to fall in love with a man who cared so little for my feelings?"

Her bitter laugh echoes in the empty living room.

"It doesn't pay to love, Bristol. I had hoped you learned that lesson from me with your father. With your brother."

"Is that what happened?" I blink against tears that have nothing to do with Parker and everything to do with my mother standing in front of me telling me not to love. "You gave all your love to them and there was none left for me? They were worth the risk and I wasn't?"

"What in heaven's name are you talking about?" Mother frowns but takes her seat again by the Celine bag. "I guided you as much as you would let me."

"I didn't want to be guided, Mother. I wanted to be *loved*, but there was always a distance. You would only allow me so close."

"That was for your own good. You were already too much like me."

"It doesn't have to be a weakness, you know," I say softly. "With the right people, with the right man, love rewards hearts like ours."

"Oh, so it's strength that has you ready to fuck Charles Parker?" Mother asks, the crudity so at odds with her refined appearance. "Is that your reward?"

"No, Grip is my reward," I volley back without hesitation. "For him, I'll do whatever needs to be done."

I look down at my bare feet sunken into the plush rug covering my hardwoods.

"I love him. He loves me. You do crazy things for the ones you love sometimes. You accept things you thought you never would. You know that better than most."

Mother studies me appraisingly for a few moments before speaking.

"I do know." She twists her wedding band. "It's liberating knowing there's nothing you wouldn't do for him, to keep him. And it can also be a dark lonely trap, with love as your prison cell."

"Not for me," I say softly. "Not with Grip. It's taken me years to realize that I'm like you, but I'm not you. And Grip is nothing like my father. I almost lost him running away from this kind of love, but it's giving me the strength to do what has to be done."

"Let me tell you something about your father, Bristol." Usually I'm not even sure if my mother is breathing she's so serene, but today she draws a deep breath. "I don't talk about my marriage. Not with anyone."

This I know. I fasten my eyes to her lips like I might miss something and need to catch every word.

"I know what you saw that day." She looks down at her lap and licks her lips, the only sign of discomfort she allows. "It wasn't the first time, and I wish I could say it was the last. Do you remember when your father had his heart attack?"

I nod. We thought he would die. It was the impetus for Rhyson and my father to start repairing their relationship.

"I said I was away on a business trip," Mother says. "But I was actually leaving your father."

Mind. Blown.

And like a child the only thing I can think is I can't wait to tell Rhyson.

"Yes." She nods, a regal movement that barely disturbs her hair. "I'd had enough, and thought I could finally do it. I could leave him. I could *not* love him just enough to go."

My cottage is quiet, like even the furnishings, the walls, the bulbs hold the same bated breath as I do waiting for her next words.

"When I got the call that he'd had the heart attack." Mother pinches her lips together and blinks rapidly. "I knew I'd never leave him. It was like fate or some force didn't want me to go."

She looks at me frankly, her eyes as vulnerable as I've ever seen. As unguarded as mine when I'm alone.

"Things changed between us after that. Slowly, but they changed."

My father had a difficult recovery, but my mother stayed with him throughout.

"When he told me he was working on things with Rhyson and wanted to move out here, I jumped at the chance." Her knuckles whiten through her skin as she clutches the expensive handbag. "I thought maybe I can finally have my husband back."

She swallows. "My children."

Shock skitters over my nerves and short circuits my synapses.

Say what?

"When we started therapy sessions with Rhyson, we also started counseling for our marriage." Her laugh is truncated. "Can you imagine it? After thirty years? But we are trying."

"I had no idea, Mother."

"Why would you?" Mother's haughtiness snaps back into place. "It's private between your father and me. I didn't run to you every time he cheated, so I'm certainly not running to you now that he's trying not to."

"So you're in family therapy with Rhyson and marriage counseling with Dad, making things right with them, but didn't bother with me."

I will never figure out how not to be hurt by this woman. It's like some claw dug into my heart in vitro, and I don't know how to free myself from feeling anything for her.

"We have brunch," she says defensively.

"Brunch?" My voice pitches to the ceiling with my outrage. "You mean those regular intervals when you find new and inventive ways to criticize me over vodka and a meal? Oh, very healing, Mother."

"It's different with you, Bristol. You're . . . you're all the best parts of me," she says softly. "The tender parts, the tough parts, the smart and fighting parts. I've damaged you enough, and I don't know how to fix it between us."

"Well, manipulating me into marrying a tyrannical pervert isn't best place to start, if you're taking suggestions."

"I just . . . I don't know. I thought you could have all of that. That everyone wants all of that on some level. I didn't want you to turn it down."

"Maybe if I hadn't met Grip I would have settled for that." I shake my head, fresh tears burning my eyes as time disintegrates, and the time to go with Parker approaches. "I love him, Mother. You saw that even though I tried to hide it."

"I recognized the signs, yes," Mother says, a wry twist to her lips. "You were just like me when I met your father. I tried to hide it, too."

"Is that why you didn't want me with Grip?" I ask softly.

"Maybe in part." Mother shrugs elegant shoulders, turning clear eyes to me, or as clear as hers can be. "At any rate, he must love you to come to me after our confrontation the other night."

"He loves me very much." Just saying the words and believing them thaws some of the ice collecting around my heart.

"If you love him, then don't give yourself to Parker, and in such an undignified way." The distaste in her voice matches or exceeds the distaste on her face.

"I can't just stand by and watch . . ." My words drown in my guilt. "Grip's there because of me. His life, his career, his good name—all on the line because of me."

"Then don't stand by and don't give in." A touch of the pride I've always known my mother to hold gleams in the glance she gives me. "I may not have been baking brownies for your class or braiding your hair, but surely I taught you how to fight."

"I can't." Tears scald my throat and blur my vision. "I've been around and around this, over and over, and I don't see another way. I don't want to give in to his demands, but "

"Then don't."

"But I have to help Grip. Leaving him there is not an option." My mother's eyes soften some, and her stern mouth relaxes.

"Then let me help you."

Thirty-Eight
Bristol

"W HERE ARE YOUR BAGS?" LUST AND IMPATIENCE AND arrogance ménage in the glance Parker gives me. "Why aren't you dressed? I thought I was very clear that I'm in a hurry."

Parker stands in my living room, outfitted in power and his Gucci suit.

"I've decided against it." I slump on the love seat, a study in lassitude, wearing distressed denim shorts and my Columbia T-shirt. "You go on without me."

Violence flares in Parker's eyes before he tamps it down. He's one of those careful monsters who won't show his true form until absolutely necessary.

"I'm sure Grip will be sorry to hear that."

"So you do know his name." I grin at him, crossing my legs. "He'll be glad to know. I'll make sure to tell him once he's back home."

"You seem to forget who holds the cards here." Parker thins his already thin lips.

"I started thinking." I study my manicure before looking back to him. "Maybe I gave in too easily. It's a little cocaine. Grip has no previous convictions. We have the best lawyers. Why should I let a few dead ends stop us?"

"Do you have any idea how easy it was to have those drugs planted during your boyfriend's photo shoot?" Laughter lights his glassy blues. "And if you think I only have one judge in my pocket, you sorely underestimate me."

"Is that so?" I ask noncommittally.

At my lackluster response, frustration flares his nostrils, anger mottles his cheeks. The smug smile dissolves into petulant slackness. "Don't make me do it." His voice is practically a hiss. "I'll ruin him. Completely."

My heart tailspins behind my ribs at the certainty his words carry. He could do it. There's no doubt. I just watch him, knowing my stoic silence will provoke him. He feeds off fear, and I've turned over his plate. Even seeing his composure fraying, I'm unprepared when he grabs my arm and jerks me to my feet. He seizes my ass, pressing me into his erection.

"This is how I've felt every time we were in a room together for the last ten years." He narrows his eyes. "I get what I want, and I'm finally going to fuck you again. I'm done waiting."

My mother didn't raise a fool, but I realize in this instant that I have been a fool. I allowed this man to deceive me.

"We didn't have sex." I lean into him, breathing the words over him. "You just said you've been waiting ten years, even though we supposedly slept together that night in Vegas."

That black hole in my memory always felt deeper and darker than a drunken lapse, and I just figured out why.

He blinks, mouth falling open. The prey fights back. He wasn't expecting that.

"You were so determined to get drunk that night." He shrugs. "Adding a little something to one of the Parks' famous martinis was merely expeditious. You would have passed out anyway. I just helped you along, and you bought the story."

I snatch my arm from his grasp, indignation rising in me as I recall my confusion, my frustration, my shame that morning.

"You should have fucked me while I was unconscious." I hurl the words at him. "That was your best shot."

"Really?" He embeds slivers of glass in that one world. "We'll see about that."

He shoves me back onto the couch so hard my head bangs against the armrest, and for a second, the pain is celestial, inspiring stars in front my eyes.

He gathers my wrists above my head, one knee thrust between my legs. His face distorts, florid with his rage. Panic takes flight in my chest, flapping wildly around my heart.

"You thought you could give him what was mine?" The words are projectiles, the force behind them throwing spittle in my face. "Let him have you, fuck you and get away with it?"

He balls the collar of my T-shirt in his hands and jerks, ripping the shirt and exposing the wire taped to my bra. His shock-stretched eyes find mine beneath him.

"Should we add rape to the things you've already confessed to?"

He snatches the wire from my bra and crushes it under his foot. Without a backward glance he rushes across the room. As soon as he hauls the door open, he comes face to face with Greg.

Greg looks past Parker long enough to find me, lifting his brows over anxious eyes, silently asking if I'm okay. I nod, gathering the ripped edges of my T-shirt to cover my breasts. Even though my knees are so weak it feels like they're filled with méringue instead of cartilage.

Parker looks over his shoulder at me, his mouth distorted into a self-assured smile.

"You stupid bitch." He turns his back on Greg, pointing to him over his shoulder. "You think some beat cop can take me down? Even with what you think you have recorded, it won't be enough to keep me. Real power. That's what I have. You have no idea."

"I think I have an idea, son," Aunt Betsy says from the door leading to my bedroom.

All of this was worth it if only to see the consternation and shame briefly flash across Parker's face.

"Mother, what are you doing here?" His eyes flick between Aunt Betsy and me like she caught us playing house or doctor. Like she caught him with his hands down my pants.

"I'm here to do what your father should have done years ago." She hands him a manila envelope, her eyes sad and condemning. "I'm here to stop you."

He doesn't open the envelope immediately, caressing the seal instead.

"Whatever is in here, Mother, cannot touch me."

"Your father is a fool who believes our money makes him invincible and above the law, and he raised you to believe the same. I should have intervened long ago." Aunt Betsy nods her head to the envelope. "I didn't know all the awful things you've done, but I know now, and it's never too late."

Parker's eyes flicker from me to his mother before settling on the envelope still unopened in his hands. I have no idea what's in there. My mother and Aunt Betsy do, though. It's their plan, and since the only alternative involved me baring my nether parts for the world's inspection, I've yielded to their infinite wisdom.

When Parker opens the envelope, he pales, his face a white flag of surrender before he's said one word.

"Where did you get this?" he asks too softly. "Does Dad know you have it?"

"The combination of his safe is our anniversary date." Aunt Betsy's laughter is a peal of sarcasm. "He must have been feeling sentimental that day since this is the only way he's chosen to honor our marriage."

"When Dad finds out—"

"Then what, Charles?" Aunt Betsy draws up to her full height. "You and your father seem to forget half of everything is mine. More than half since the original hotels came from my great-grandfather. Renaming them 'Park' doesn't change where they came from."

"When he hears about this—"

"Oh, he's already heard." Aunt Betsy comes to join me on the love seat. "I believe there's a note from him in there, too. Something about you still not learning your lesson and abusing girls. That one was a very costly mistake. It'd be such a waste of the money he spent covering it up if I were to bring it out myself."

"You could actually leak it through Spotted," I pipe up. "Parker has a guy on standby. He's always got a guy."

"I am deeply sorry I ever thought my son was good enough for you, Bristol." Aunt Betsy brushes the hair back from my face and drops a kiss on my forehead. "I'm glad you've found someone worth your time."

"Worth her time?" Incredulous rage mottles Parker's handsome face. "That thug? That . . . rapper? You would give Bristol to him over me? She humiliated me, and she should pay."

"What am I paying for exactly, Parker?" I cross to stand in front of him, my anger propelling me just inches from his face. "Did I leak pictures of you drunk to the press? Did I drug you and lead you to believe we had sex when I was for all intents and purposes unconscious? Did I coerce you to have public sex to satisfy my own outsized ego? Did I plant drugs on an innocent man and blackmail judges to manipulate his case?"

"You chose him over me," Parker says grimly. "With all I could give you, you wanted some rapper from Compton over me."

"Even if it hadn't been Grip, it would never have been you," I hiss.

"I think this has gone long enough," my mother says from the same entrance Aunt Betsy used. "We have enough to prosecute you, Parker. Not for life, but you'll serve some time. We're only giving Officer James what he has on tape, but we have a never-ending stream of evidence from your father's safe. We'll just keep sending it to Officer James until enough sticks to keep you behind bars."

"You've already given us enough to free Marlon and clear his name." The tears gathered at the corners of Aunt Betsy's eyes leak down her face as she contemplates her only son. "And enough to prosecute you."

My heart breaks for her. I can't imagine how she wrestled with this decision before settling on the right course of action to set an innocent man free. I set all the soft feelings aside, though, to step right into Parker's face, my lips curling with deliberate wrath.

"If you ever, and I mean ever, you cowardly asshole, come near me or Grip again," I say. "More of that information will come out. Call it our insurance policy. If Grip even has a suspicious paper cut, I'm coming after your ass."

"So will I," a deadly soft voice says from behind me.

I look back and almost collapse when I see Ms. James leaning against the doorjamb, arms folded, lips set in stone, eyes lit with fury and indignation.

"My son is a good man." Her eyes drift from Parker for a moment to me. "And Bristol is a good woman. Just try to hurt them again. You find a way to slip from the law, I got some street justice for you. Bet you won't get out of that."

Greg steps into the fray before Ms. James can say anymore about "street justice", whatever that means, and pulls Parker's arms behind his back.

"Charles Parker, you have the right to remain silent . . ."

The Miranda Rights, the other cops streaming into my home, the flurry of activity all fade to the peripheral as I look at the three mothers who made my escape possible.

"Aunt Betsy, I'm so sorry." I pull her into a hug, and she sniffs softly in our embrace. She did what was right, but Parker is still her son. Without the information she took from her husband's safe, none of this would have worked.

"No, I'm sorry." Aunt Betsy pulls back, shaking her head. "The things he's done to other women, to so many people all these years, we failed him somewhere along the way. He has to pay. I just hope he heeds our warning and doesn't come after you again."

"Oh, he won't," my mother interjects. "What he did to Marlon is child's play compared to the things in that safe and the things your husband has covered up for him through the years. We'll make sure he doesn't forget what we have."

"Thank you, Mother." I'm not sure what else to say as our eyes lock and hold and soften. I know everything won't be repaired between us in a day, but today was a big step.

"I do love you, Bristol." Her voice doesn't waver, but her eyes, so like mine, for maybe the first time show me a little of what's in her heart. "I'm sorry Marlon believed that more than you did, but I know I'm to blame."

The flawless red line of her mouth pulls into a grimace.

"I think it's past time you joined your father, Rhyson, and me in sessions with Dr. Ramirez," she continues. "If we ever hope to be a real family, that is."

Her words ripple emotion through me, a tectonic shift in my own heart. I've disciplined my emotions over the last twenty-four hours, held in so much because I knew Marlon's freedom depended on it. The possibility that the relationship I've always wanted with her is something she might want, too, unravels me. The tears that have been bound behind a wall of control trickle down my cheeks. A sob unleashed in my chest takes me by surprise. Before I know it, I'm in my mother's arms. It's still awkward. She pats my back and holds me stiffly, unrelaxed, her walls not fully down, but all that matters is she doesn't let go.

I've always wondered if she'd lavished all her devotion onto my talented brother; if she'd squandered her deepest love on my unfaithful father, and there was nothing left for me. I know what it's like behind that wall. It's cold and lonely. It's barren with no sun. God, I'm so glad I finally let Grip in. And as my mother and I regard each other with new understanding, with new respect, I hope that someday soon, she'll truly let me in, too.

Over her shoulder, I encounter a darkened caramel gaze that's warmed and melted with sympathy, with compassion, maybe with understanding. Through my own tears, I offer Ms. James a tentative smile, and slowly, she returns it.

Thirty-Nine

Grip

Bristol: I'm on my way.

READ BRISTOL'S TEXT AND SLIP A SOFT CASHMERE SWEATER OVER MY head. Freshly showered, I fall back on the bed and respond.

Me: I'm home. Upstairs.

Our exchange is brief, but the air buzzes with anticipation. The last time I saw Bristol, she was on her way to Parker. I wasn't happy with her. I'm sure when I took matters into my own hands and had Ma call Mrs. Gray, Bristol wasn't happy with me. This morning, I woke up in County, ate powdered eggs, and wore jail scrubs that scratched my skin. Tonight, I'm in my luxury loft, wearing a cashmere sweater and chilling a bottle of wine that costs more than I used to pay in rent. An astounding turn of events.

I've never been angry enough to actually kill someone, but if Parker were standing in front of me right now, I might toss him on my rooftop grill and watch the flames consume his carcass. Maybe I would drink my two thousand dollar bottle of wine with the aroma of his charred flesh wafting in the air. There is some base level of my soul that would prefer primitive justice over the legal route we've taken.

We'll have to depend on the bounty of "insurance" Mrs. Parker found in that safe to keep her son on a leash. Though, I hope my conversation with him earlier dissuades him from bothering us, from bothering Bristol, again.

I wrestled with what to do about this menace. Street justice calls for me to use Corpse or any means available to protect myself, to protect my girl. I won't pretend I wasn't tempted to use Corpse. I was, but I wanted a better way. Greg and Mrs. Gray came up with a legal option, for which I'm grateful. If Parker ever tries to hurt Bristol again, directly or through someone she loves, I can't promise them, or myself, that I won't find another means. I wanted to tell him that to his face.

It pays to have a family on the force, connections of my own. Greg managed to get me into the "special" private holding cell where Charles Parker is being kept, separate from general pop, of course.

He was taking a piss when I entered his cell. He studied me warily over his shoulder, and I smelled his fear. It curled around my leg like an anxious cat.

"There are cameras everywhere," he warned. "Hurt me and you'll be caught."

"Just one for this room. It's looping for two minutes. That's all the time I need."

"What do you want?" He managed a sneer, even though I could see the terror in his eyes. "Money? I can give you that."

"You dumb shit bastard," I snapped. "I don't need your money. I have my own money."

"Not as much as I have."

He sounded like a spoiled little boy grasping for a leg up. I glanced down to his tiny dick still hung over his pants.

"Put your dick away." I injected pity in my voice. "How you ever thought that little bit of twig and berries would satisfy my girl, I don't know."

His eyes went reptilian, slitted, and a growl rumbled in his throat. He's used to being the one with all the power. I had a tenuous hold on my temper. The illusion of flippancy cracked the longer I was around that asshole. The longer I had to look into his fucking blue eyes, his entitlement and superiority still bleeding through jail scrubs. I prowled over, crowding him until he was forced to the porcelain behind him. With a handful of the rough scrubs gathered in my fist, I brought his chest to mine, slamming him into the urinal. His head banged against the wall with a satisfying thud.

"Don't think that all your money and power and fucking hotels will protect you from me if you ever touch her again," I said through my teeth.

The façade of his false calm cracked at the ferocity in my voice, and I saw his fear.

"And you sent me a note asking if Bristol was your queen or mine," I continued. "I came to answer your question."

I ran him through with a look, and slammed the wadded up, half-destroyed note against his chest.

"She's mine."

The sound of the door opening downstairs jars me back to the present and the comfort of my home. I banish all thoughts of Parker, and brace for the rush of seeing Bristol safe and unharmed. I'd like to make a GIF of the moment when she walks into my bedroom. Just replay these few seconds over and over again.

Bristol is wearing almost no makeup. Her hair streams loose down her back, dark and wild and streaked with copper. Her clothes are simple—white tank top, leather jacket, and ripped-knee jeans. She looks so much like the girl I picked up at the airport that day, the one I kissed on top of the world and chased into the tide. In her eyes, though, the color of smelted silver, something tried by fire, I see a woman who would walk through flames for me. Someone who would sacrifice anything to protect me.

I'm seated on the edge of the bed, legs spread and straining against my jeans. Bristol walks over slowly, her eyes holding mine above me. I trace her features with my eyes and imprint her on my heart. The slant of her cheek. The slash of her brows. The full curve of her mouth, now unsteady with emotion.

"Grip." She climbs onto my lap, knees on either side of me, head buried in my neck. "Oh, God. I'm so glad you're okay."

I slide my hands under her jacket, needing her warmth, her flesh and bones.

"Bris." I clench my eyes closed, relief flooding through me. "You're the one I was concerned about. You're okay. He didn't . . . God, if he had . . ."

I can't even finish the sentence, can't even complete the thought.

Today isn't for my rage, and that's all those thoughts lead to.

She pulls back, tear-clumped lashes spiking around her bright eyes.

"It would have killed me to give myself to him."

"I know that, baby." My palms at her back flatten the soft curves of her breasts against my chest.

"But I would have done it if I had to," she whispers. "For you, I would have done it and lived with the consequences."

I know that, too.

"I have something that belongs to you, Bris."

I scoot her back only far enough to reach into the pocket of my jeans and extract a black velvet jewelry bag. She looks from the bag to my face, pressing her lips together, drawing and exhaling a deep breath. I fasten the necklace in the front and turn it until the gold barrel hangs just above her breasts. I flip it over, and for the hundredth time since my mom dropped it off from the jewelry repair shop, read the inscription.

My heart broke loose on the wind.

This necklace affirms what I always knew. Even in our years apart, that day carved itself into her heart. It inhabited her memory as surely as she occupied mine. There isn't a scrap of me she can't have or doesn't already own. And my mother can condemn it, others can question it, but I'm so damn proud to be hers, and so humbled that she is mine. The world can go to hell with their opinions and notions of what fits and what doesn't. My heart is in Bristol's grip, my happiness in her hands.

"Thank you," she whispers shakily.

"My mom got it repaired." She stiffens against my chest.

"She did?" She lowers her lashes, shielding her eyes. "She was at my house when everything went down."

"I know." A laugh forces its way past my lips. "Once she knew the plan, nobody was keeping her away."

"She and I kind of had a moment at my place." A small smile touches Bristol's lips. "It was just a look, but I think it was a good moment. I know it won't happen overnight, but I think maybe she'll come around."

A little laugh slips from her, but I know it hurts her that my mother doesn't want us together. As tough as she wants me to think she is, I know it hurts her that during the scandal with Qwest, so many people came out saying we shouldn't be together.

"Bris, look at me." I wait for her to comply so she's looking into my eyes and I can look into hers. "My mom will come around. She's already starting to, but there's something you should know. Something I want you to believe."

I frame her face between my hands and tenderly run a thumb over her mouth.

"You're the most important thing in my life," I tell her. "I would leave everyone for you."

Her tiny gasp tells me that on some level she didn't realize that. The line of her mouth wavers. Her brows knit and tears slip over her cheeks. She presses her forehead to mine, and her shoulders shake. She folds her arms between us against my chest and surrenders to the emotion she's been fighting, maybe for years. I roll my palms over her arms and back, wanting to send my love through her pores, giving her no choice but to believe down to her bones that she's the most important thing in my life.

"Grip." She sniffs and swipes tears from her cheeks. "No one's ever . . . that means the world to me."

She bites her lip to suppress emotion, but it does no good. Emotion suffuses the air around us, reaches inside and clutches my heart. Head lowered, she touches the gold links Parker tried to chain her with, and chews the corner of her lip.

"Grip, if it didn't work, if I'd had to—"

"I would have loved you just as much." I tip her chin up and force her to look into my eyes and see the truth of it. To see the irrevocable nature of my love for her. "I would never have let you go."

She nods, sniffing and smiling.

"I'm still mad at you." With a teary laugh, trying to lighten the moment, she loops her arms over my shoulders and strokes the back of my neck.

"Really?" I frown and cock my head. "You don't look mad to me."

"How do I look?" A grin tips her mouth.

"Like you wanna fuck me."

Her eyes widen and she scoots forward, pressing herself into me. "That, too." She laughs. "But I'm still mad at you for telling my mother and your mother."

"I have a feeling I can persuade you to forgive me."

I fit my hands to her waist, flipping her back onto the bed to brace myself over her. With one finger, she traces my mouth, my cheekbones, my eyebrows.

God, her touch feels so good.

My lips are just shy of hers, and we swap breaths and promises. I study her face like an artist, painting each feature—her eyes, her lips, her cheeks—with love. She leans up, touching her lips to mine, and the stress, anxiety, indignity of the last few days disintegrates. Our love is powerful enough to shrink the world down to this moment, down to a circle no wider than her arms around me. The circumference of her and me. So powerful, but her eyes, if you know what you're looking for, can't hide her secret vulnerability.

Bristol has always watched me. I know because I was watching her, too. I observed her for years like an anthropologist untangling the mysteries of a new tribe. There's something in her eyes when she watches me that isn't there for anyone else. I was never sure what it was. Now I know. It's a passion so wild there are no borders. A limitless, loving fealty beyond what I could deserve. Not my music, not my money, not fame, or anything I dreamed would satisfy comes close to what I feel when she looks at me like that.

She feathers kisses over my lips, down my neck. We start slow and tender, but every touch, every long, lush stroke of our tongues together tosses kindling on this kiss until we're grunting and hungry.

She pulls back, seducing me with her eyes, and reaches down to my waist. Her fingers tease the waistband of my jeans before pushing the sweater over my head. She kisses my neck and shoulders, all the while undoing my belt and sliding my jeans and briefs over my hips.

She peels off her leather jacket and tugs the tank top over her head, sharing herself with me in erotic inches. Her breasts, tipped with plump nipples, come into view.

I ghost my palms over her nipples until they tauten into ripe berries. I squeeze them between my fingers and massage the fullness of her breasts until her breath labors and her head tips back, exposing the column of her throat. I trace the fragile framework of her ribs, gliding my hands down to her hips. I tug the panties down, and palm her center. My fingers tuck into the hot, silky slit, running up and down until she's dripping wet.

"Oh, she missed me." I grin and invade her with two fingers.

Bristol's breath catches in her throat, and she squeezes her top lip between her teeth.

"Did you just personify my pussy?" She laughs in between hitched breaths.

"I *am* a writer." I dot kisses under her chin and any reachable skin. "Take it as a sign of respect."

"I'll take this." She grabs my bone-hard, stretched-out dick. "As a sign of respect."

Her hand clamps and slides over me, thumbing the wet tip. Our eyes connect, and humor falls away, leaving the intensity that always rears between us. I'm working between her legs, and she's working between mine. She drags air in, gasping, churning her hips, fucking my fingers. I suck one berry-tipped breast, watching color blossom over her neck and cheeks.

"Oh, God." Her back arches off the bed, sheets knotted in one fist. "Yes, Grip."

Her hold tightens on me, her fingers dropping to roll my balls in her palms.

"This pretty pussy." I gather her wrists in my hand over her head and ease her knee back to her chest, opening her up. "It's mine, right?"

"Yes. God, yes." With dry sobs, she strains up to my lips, leaving kisses wherever she can. "You know it's yours. Please take it. Just take it."

Her submission, her admission unleashes an unquenchable thirst, an in-exhaustible hunger. I need some part of her in my mouth. I bite down on her shoulder and push inside, my breath hissing between my lips at the wet, tight fit. She meets every thrust, and we are fervent, fevered. Pleasure excruciating. Twined together, her heel digging into my ass, my arm hooked under her knee, urging her open to the compulsion of my body pistoning into hers. I cannot possibly in this life be deep enough inside her. I want so much more than her body. She has thieved my soul, and I need to feel the reciprocity, the exchange. To know I've pilfered her and taken everything that she would offer and anything she meant to hold. Because that's what she's done to me.

I loosen her wrists to grab her ass, angling her. Both legs wrap around my back, and she works her hips up, eager to meet every hard thrust. I sit up, bringing her with me, and she hooks her ankles behind me.

"Ride, Bris."

Her eyes, possessive, there's no doubt I'm hers. Her hands, urgent and everywhere at once. Our breaths heave raggedly between our lips. Our bodies are lock and key, and we're transfixed on each other. Inseparable. Insoluble. I seize her tongue, pulling her in, sucking her, wringing every drop of sweet-ness from the kiss. She whimpers, her hands clawing at my shoulders, my neck, scraping over my scalp.

"I love you." Her words drop hot in my ear with her breasts flattened to my chest and her thighs clenching at my hips. She tightens her pussy around my cock, a deliberate, hungry grasp and release.

"Bris." My eyes roll back. I'm at the mercy of those muscles. "I love you, too."

She tucks her head into the curve of my neck, her breaths short and sharp as she recites from "Sonnet LXXXI", telling me I'm already hers, to rest with my dream inside her dream, that we are joined by forever itself, and that we'll travel the shadows together. She pants, sitting up straighter, leveraging herself with one arm behind her on the bed, changing the angle, deepening the penetration. In the lamp's light, I see her head flung back in abandon, her muscles straining with the unrelenting ferocity, the rigor of our bodies.

"You alone are my dream," she says, adapting the quote, tears in the eyes she refuses to pull away from me. "And I alone am yours."

It is a pledge of persistence, hidden in the poems I sent her. It's a vow that she won't ever give up on us. Knowing she held the poetry in her heart when she wouldn't even consider me, when I wasn't even sure there was any hope, undoes me.

"Bristol, oh God."

I touch my forehead to hers, twisting my fingers into the damp hair at her neck. Pressed together, our heartbeats ricocheting, the universe tips, a dazzling lurching. A spectacular axis spinning beyond my restraint, just beyond my control. I once threatened to make her come with my words, but as the stars go blindingly bright and then dark behind my eyes, I realize she's the one who did it.

Epilogue

Bristol

I HAVE AN EYE FOR THE EXTRAORDINARY.

I can spot something special a mile away. That's how I knew the day I met the man onstage that he was something special. I just had no idea how much he would change my life. Had no idea I would love him this way. I certainly didn't have any idea he would feel the same.

"I think this is the best song he's ever written," Rhyson says to me as Grip sets up "Bruise" for the listening audience.

"You may be right about that." I lean close to the baby cradled to my brother's chest. "What do you think, Aria? Is it his best? Is that god-daddy's best song?"

My niece squeals, and Rhyson and I look at each other with wide eyes in case it disrupts Grip's performance.

"Here." Kai sticks a pacifier into her daughter's little mouth. "Figures you two would get her riled up."

Rhyson holds his daughter in one arm, and pulls Kai close to him with the other. The contentment on his face squeezes my heart in the best possible way. After all the tumult that marked the first part of his journey, private and public, he somehow managed to make a normal life for himself. As normal as being a rock star married to another rock star can be. Though, intercepting the look Rhys and Kai exchange over Aria's dark curly hair, I'm not sure there's anything "normal" about a love that deep.

Glad I'm not the only one drowning. Grip once told me the capacity I have to love could be my greatest strength. Over the last few weeks, I've come to believe him. Especially when that love is for the right man, a man who wouldn't exploit a heart like mine. He never ceases to amaze me with all the ways he proves he's exactly the one for me.

"So you may have seen some footage of me a few months ago during a 'routine' stop," Grip says from stage, a slight smile on those full lips I love so much. "It got just a little bit of coverage."

The audience laughs, but there is an underlying tension in the room. The whole night feels like that, as if it's on the verge of going wrong, though so far everything has gone right. Given Grip's complicated history with LAPD, the organizers of this event weren't sure he'd accept their invitation to perform at the Black and Blue Ball, held to promote better relations between communities of color and law enforcement. Maybe that's why they sent his cousin Greg to ask. With "Bruise" so closely reflecting the message of the event, Grip didn't hesitate to accept.

"I grew up in the part of the world that gave rise to the Watts riots and Rodney King. I was five years old when Rodney King was beaten." He gives a quick laugh. "I barely knew my name, but I knew his. He was a cautionary tale for us, and our mothers made sure we knew."

He grabs a stool and props himself there before going on.

"Even with all that, I thought police officers were dope." He disarms the crowd with a bright smile. "They had flashing blue lights and sirens. What could be cooler than that?"

The crowd laughs a little, some offer smiles. A few expressions remain tense because some people aren't sure where he's headed or what he'll say. Which side of the black/blue line he'll land on, and if he'll come down like a hammer.

"That footage showed me getting stopped in the neighborhood where I grew up. Some wondered if I would do this show tonight." He looks out at the crowd, eyes dark and earnest. "I'm here because the system needs radical reform. Unarmed men and women are dying. And there are cops who, if they don't do it, see it and remain silent. Do nothing, making them complicit."

He looks out over the crowd.

"And then there are cops like my cousin Greg, who has dedicated his life to actually serving and protecting, not just policing the communities we grew up in. I'm here for him and all the cops who say enough is enough and are ready to do something about it. I want to reimagine the system, rebuild it from the ground up."

Grip clings to the mic as if it's grounding him. He laughs, shaking his head.

"The best way to tear down the walls that divide us is to meet someone, to know someone on the other side of that wall," he says. "Cops were a 'they,' a 'them' until my cousin Greg became one. White people were a 'they,' a 'them' until I went to school with them. Until one of them became my best friend."

Grip turns his head toward stage left where he knows I always stand, his eyes tangling with mine.

"Until I fell in love with one of them," he says softly.

My heart contracts. I blink at the tears he inspires in me all the time. With his words, with his hands, his kisses. He has so many weapons at his disposal to break me down, every one more effective than the last.

I look out over the crowd, faces of every shade and walk of life, and wonder if they'll understand, if they'll hear what I heard from the moment Rhyson played "Bruise" in our meeting months ago. We'll see. Grip signals the drummer to drop the beat.

"This one's called 'Bruise,'" he says softly.

Am I all of your fears, wrapped in black skin, Driving something foreign, windows with black tint
Handcuffed on the side of the road, second home for black men Like we don't have a home that we trying to get back to when PoPo pulls me over with no infractions,
Under the speed limit, seat belt even fastened, Turned on Rosecrans when two cruisers collapsed in Barking orders, yeah, this that Cali harassment Guns drawn, neighbors looking from front lawns and windows I know cops got it hard, don't wanna make a wife a widow
But they act like I ain't paying taxes, like your boy ain't a citizen
They think I'm riding filthy, like I'm guilty pleading innocence.
They say it's 'Protect & Serve', but check my word
Sunny skies, ghetto birds overhead stress your nerves,
They say if you ain't doin' wrong, you got nothin' to fear, But the people sayin' that, they can't be livin' here . . .
We all BRUISE, It's that black and blue
A dream deferred, Nightmare come true
In another man's shoes, Walk a mile or two
Might learn a couple things I'm no different than you!
You call for the good guys when you meet the bad men,

Grip | 423

I'm wearing a blue shield and I still feel the reactions
When I patrol the block, I can sense dissatisfaction
There's distrust, resentment in every interaction,
Whether the beat cop, lieutenant, sergeant or the captain We roll our sleeves
*   up and we dig our hands in*
I joined the force in order to make a difference,
Swore to uphold the law, protect men, women and children,
These life and death situations, we make split-second decisions
All for low pay, budget cutbacks and restrictions
Not just a job—it's a calling, a vocation,
My wife's up late pacin', for my safety—she's praying,
I see what you see on all the cell phones
I'm just a man with a badge trying my best to make it home.

We all BRUISE, It's that black and blue
A dream deferred, Nightmare come true
In another man's shoes, Walk a mile or two
Might learn a couple things
I'm no different than you!

Grip

"You were amazing."

Bristol's soft encouragement soothes some of my uncertainty about the performance. Performing "Bruise" in a roomful of cops and community activists is much different than in front of screaming fans.

"She's right." Greg, who is dressed in his uniform, smiles, even though his eyes remain solemn. "We still have a lot of work to do so people feel like we're a part of the community. To protect them, not out to get them. 'Bruise' is exactly the kind of message both sides need to hear."

They're holding a reception for me to meet and greet people. I think I've shaken every hand here tonight. The stream of traffic is finally slowing down some, but I smile when I see my mom walking toward me. I didn't even realize she would be here tonight. The smile freezes on my face when I notice who walks with her. My cousin Jade and my Aunt Celia, who hasn't spoken to Greg in years.

"Hey, Marlon," Ma says softly, reaching up to hug me. "Bristol, Greg."

Greg lowers his eyes to the floor, not meeting my mother's eyes and certainly not his mother's.

"Hey, son," Aunt Celia says, her voice hesitant.

Greg looks up, and suddenly, he isn't the decorated officer. Not the strong man in uniform. In his eyes I see the young man he was all those years ago, wailing on my front yard with his brother dying in his arms. That young man's guilt and pain saturate the air around us. The look he gives his mother seeks something that only she can give him, and she does. She stretches her arms up, and he doesn't hesitate, folding his height in half to burrow into her neck, his tears and hers making peace, forgiving.

"Let's give them a minute," Ma says softly, tilting her head for us to step away.

"It's good to see you, Ms. James," Bristol says once we're a few feet from them. "You, too, Jade."

"Thank you for sending the tickets." Ma says.

Surprised, I look at Bristol, who just nods and tells my mom it was no trouble. I didn't know she sent tickets. Even after Bristol's "moment" with my mom, we haven't talked as much as we should. I've been giving her room to get used to Bristol and me. Maybe she was giving me room to change my mind. I hope she's starting to accept that won't be happening.

"That song 'Bruise,' it is dope," Jade says softly.

"Thanks," I answer. "I still want to get you in the studio writing. For real, Jade, it's past time you put all that talent to use."

"I'm always looking for new talent," Bristol interjects with a hesitant smile. "I won't know if you don't show me anything."

Jade's almond-shaped eyes narrow, like she's ascertaining if we're tricking her. I've never met anyone warier than Jade, but she's had lots of reason in her life to mistrust. She and I finally talked about what happened on that playground all those years ago. I won't say it changed everything overnight, but things have been a little easier between us.

"A'ight," Jade finally says, adjusting the Raiders cap she's never without. "Maybe this week."

"Good." I hook my elbow around her neck and kiss the top of her head, making her squirm and punch my arm. "Rhyson will be in the studio with me Thursday. Why not come ready with something for him to hear?"

Jade's eyes stretch. She may prefer hip-hop to Rhyson's modern rock, but she knows he owns Prodigy. She knows how famous he is, how successful.

"Seriously?" she asks.

"Seriously." I grin and drop another kiss on her head, one she doesn't dodge this time.

"I was hoping to see the baby," Ma says. "Where is Rhyson?" "They left right after I performed," I say. "They needed to get Aria home."

"Since you're the godfather." Ma laughs. "What's that make me? The grand-godmama?"

"I'm sure they'd love that." I glance at Bristol, who usually gets quiet around my mother. "Bris, that would make your mom the grandmother and the grand-godmama. It's a mouthful."

"True." Bristol smiles stiffly, her fingers tight around mine.

"Guess that'll have to do for me," Ma says. "Till y'all give me some grandbabies of my own."

Bristol and I share a shockwave as my mother's words sink in. It's been a few weeks since that first Sunday dinner, and we haven't gone back. I've seen my mother, of course, but after that first disaster, we haven't been back at her table. I need to be sure it won't happen again, and when we go back, we can make new memories that eclipse the painful ones Bristol has now. Is this my mother signaling that she understands that?

"Um . . ." I'm not sure what to say, but it probably needs to be more than this.

"Marlon tells me you liked my greens, Bristol." Ma interjects, her expression softened, smiling. "I even heard you tried to make them yourself."

I casually mentioned that once to my mother, hoping to show her how sweet and funny Bristol can be. I feel Bristol's irritation reaching out for me. Shit. It might be angry sex for us tonight. No sex is not an option ever.

"Yes, well they didn't turn out very well." Bristol looks at me pointedly. "As I'm sure Grip mentioned."

"They couldn't have been any worse than the first time I tried." Ma cackles, shaking her head. "My mama took one bite and threw them in the trash."

"She did?" Bristol's smile comes a little easier.

"Oh, yeah. They were awful." Ma pauses and offers Bristol a tentative smile. "Why don't you come over a little early on Sunday, and I'll show you how I make them?"

Bristol's mouth drops open a little, and she blinks several times. I elbow her on the sly.

"Um, yeah. Yes. I mean, that would be awesome." Bristol's mouth stretches to its maximum smile capacity. "I'd like that very much."

Ma nods, her smile not as wide but sincere all the same. She turns her eyes to me, and they water. Even when we've spoken recently, this has stood between us. Her inability to accept that I plan to spend the rest of my life with someone she saw as wrong for me and perceived as an insult to the sacrifices she made for me.

"I've missed seeing you on Sundays, Marlon." She offers the words like an olive branch.

"I'll be there this week." I reach down and pull her small frame close. "We'll be there this week. I wouldn't miss you teaching Bristol to cook collard greens for the world."

She laughs against my chest, but her arms tighten around me, and I know she's missed our easy closeness as much as I have. She pulls back, sniffing, but still linking one arm around my waist.

"Bristol, I owe you an apology." Ma never has been one for wasted time and bullshit, so I shouldn't be surprised that she dives right in. "What Marlon said tonight is true. I've treated you like a 'they'. I don't anticipate my son giving you up anytime soon, so it's time we fixed that. Time we get to know each other."

Bristol blinks several times, her eyes filling.

"I used to pray that God would send my son a fighter like me," Ma continues. "A woman like me. I thought she would have to look like me, but that isn't true. When I saw what you would do for my son, I knew God had answered my prayers in you. I'm just a stubborn old woman."

Ma laughs, characteristic sassiness lighting her face.

"Not that old now." She rests a fist on her hip. "Don't get it twisted. Mama still got it."

Only my mother would manage to make even this moment funny.

"But I was nearsighted about you." Ma's laugh fades, but the smile still crinkles the corners of her eyes. "I hope you can forgive me for that."

"Yes, of course," Bristol says softly. "Thank you very much."

"No, thank you." Ma reaches up to kiss my cheek, patting my back before she pulls away. "Come on, Jade. Let's check on your mama and brother. I'll see you both on Sunday. Don't be late."

She takes a few steps before looking back over her shoulder. "Oh, and you can bring my car, too."

We stand there for a second after she's gone, both quiet. An airy laugh from Bristol breaks our silence.

"Did she really say grandbabies?"

I turn her into me, linking my fingers through hers and pressing our temples together so I can whisper in her ear.

"You have a problem with grandbabies? Beautiful, café au lait grandbabies?"

Bristol pulls back, one brow lifted.

"Did you just refer to my future children in terms of beverages? Coffee? Milk? I don't think so."

"Babe, that's what they call kids who—"

"I don't care what 'they' call them." She links her arms around my neck. "Aren't you the one who said no more they?"

That takes my mind back to the performance tonight.

"You think people heard what I was saying?" I don't often show uncertainty when it comes to my music, to my writing, but I can show Bristol every part of me. Even the parts that aren't sure. "I felt like I was performing on eggshells sometimes. Like they expected me to offend them."

"Think about the first time we talked at Mick's that day." Her smile grows reminiscent. "I asked you about people using the N-word."

"Ah, yes, your Twitter," I say, referring to her analogy of things she didn't understand, but made them work.

"Why do you think that conversation worked?" she asks. "Because you had a great rack, and I wanted to impress you?"

"Um ... try again." She shakes her head and laughs up at me. "We wanted it to. We gave each other the benefit of the doubt. We wanted to understand. That's what 'Bruise' says. Walking in each other's shoes. Seeking to understand so we can change things. They couldn't have missed that."

"I'm the writer, but it seems like you always know what to say to me," I tell her softly.

"Is that so?" She kisses my chin and cups one side of my face. "I think you're just sweet talking me now with all that ... chocolate charm."

Haven't heard that in a long time. I was a cocky son of a bitch back then. In many ways, I probably still am.

"Oh, no." I turn to kiss the inside of her wrist. "If I was spitting game, I'd say something like this.

A storm could come, the winds will blow The rain can wash away
But what we have will stand forever, to last another day. The world can rail,
      their weapons clatter
Let them wage their wars
But peace I've found, and all that matters Everything here in your arms."

"Wow," Bristol whispers, eyes wide, mouth softened into a smile. "That isn't Neruda, is it? Who wrote that?"

I tip up her chin and lay my lips against hers. No need to tell her yet that it could be part of my wedding vows.

"Just something I'm working on."

Always. Evermore.
Even After. **Still.**

Still

USA TODAY BESTSELLING AUTHOR
KENNEDY RYAN

GRIP TRILOGY BOOK #3

I'll be there.
Through thick and thin. Ride or die.
You can count on me.
The promises people make.
The vows we take.
Assumptions of the heart.
Emotion tells us how we feel, but life . . .life has a way of plunging us in
boiling water, burning away our illusions, testing our faith, trying our
convictions.
Love floating is a butterfly, but love tested is an anchor.
For Grip and Bristol,
Love started at the top of the world
On a Ferris wheel under the stars
But when that love is tested, will they fly or fall?

Dedicated to the Innocent

Part I

"An artist's duty, as far as I'm concerned, is to reflect the times."

—Nina Simone, Musician & Activist

One

Bristol

"**Y**OUR CLIENT APPEARS TO BE LATE."

I glance from the pasty face across the table to my phone, noting the time. This guy could use some of our LA sun before he goes back to New York, though it is summer there, too. Maybe he just doesn't get out much.

"A little late," I tell Kevin, the rep from Barrow Publishing. "But he'll be here."

"Our team's excited about the possibility of working with Grip." Kevin gestures with his fork wrapped in angel hair pasta. "He'll be great for our urban imprint."

"Your urban imprint?" My own fork is halfway to my mouth, but I place it back down in the bowl of my half-eaten salad. "Why would you think that?"

"Well, he *is* a hip-hop artist." Kevin shrugs and chews his pasta. "Seems like the reasonable placement."

"He's also the guy whose debut album went double platinum and who sold out the largest venues across three continents while headlining his first world tour." I challenge him with one lifted brow. "You don't get numbers like that reaching a niche demographic. Grip has proven global appeal and would be best placed with your flagship imprint."

"We'll see." Skepticism colors Kevin's otherwise pale face.

"Oh, I *know*, because I won't settle for anything less." I spear a cucumber with my fork and him with a glance sharpened to a fine point. "Charisma knew that when she approached me with this offer."

My friend Charisma and I went to high school together and were room-mates at Columbia. She's now a powerful editor at a huge publishing company. I would much prefer lunch with her instead of this junior editor, but her schedule didn't allow for that.

My phone dings with a text on the table.

"Excuse me." I grab the phone to check the incoming text.

Grip: Hey babe. Sorry. About to get on the road.

Me: ETA?

Grip: Huh? Is that dyslexic for eat? LOL

Despite my irritation that I have to spend more time alone with this sun-deprived dickhead, my lips twitch.

Me: Estimated time of arrival, smartass.

Grip: Like 10, but if you send me a tit pic, I might be able to shave a couple min off.

I shake my head and lose the battle with my lips, surrendering a wide grin. I try to ignore dickhead's eyes on the tits in question. This guy is a bit of a lecher; I'll have to ask Charisma what she was thinking sending him.

Me: Not funny. Get here so we can be done with this.

Grip: I'm coming, but you know I come faster when you show me your tits.

I walked right into that one. I don't bother responding, instead setting the phone down and turning my attention back to Kevin the lecher.

"That was Grip." I wait for his eyes to lift from nipple level. "He got held up at his previous appointment, but he's en route."

"It's fine." His slick smile lubricates the space between us, leaving a greasy film in the air. "Gives us a little more time alone."

"Do we need more time alone?" I take a sip of my mineral water. "For what?"

"So I can persuade you to have dinner with me."

Is this guy for real? I glance into the eyes behind his square glasses. Everything about him screams metrosexual, pretty much the polar opposite of Grip. I guess I'm self-absorbed enough to assume everyone knows Grip and I are together. We were outed in the worst possible way just after he and Qwest broke up—via a surveillance video leak and Black Twitter feud—but we've managed to keep a pretty low profile ever since. Apparently, Kevin missed that bit of juicy gossip.

"I think we should stick to business," I offer with a wry smile.

"But what about pleasure?" He reaches across the table to rub the back of my hand.

"Pleasure?" I snatch my hand back. "Kevin, you wouldn't know where to start pleasing me."

He looks nonplussed, but it's the truth. Some women have trouble admitting they love sex; I'm not one of them. I love it, but I'm a woman of discriminating tastes and hard-to-please nethers. Fortunately, my voracious appetite extends to exactly one man who's figured it all out, and he's probably ... oh, less than ten minutes out.

Maybe I should have sent that tit pic after all.

"I just meant I'm only in LA for another day, and haven't seen much of the city," Kevin says. "I know you and Charisma are friends, so I thought maybe you could show me around before I go back to New York."

Maybe I misjudged him.

Except his eyes are x-raying through my blouse again. "Kevin, eyes up."

"Sorry." The lust in his eyes practically fogs up his glasses. "What?"

This is so not the way to get Grip on board with the book deal Charisma and I have been brainstorming. I'm killing Charm next time I see her—not that I'll see her any time soon. Barrow has her anchored to the East Coast, and Prodigy has me anchored to the West.

"Kevin, there's something you should know. Grip and I—"

"Sorry I'm late." The voice rolls over me like syrup, thick and sweet and sticking to my skin.

I glance over my shoulder, meeting the eyes I wake up to every morning, the color of chocolate flecked with caramel. Grip's slow smile is that extravagant curve of full lips that has stuttered my breath since the day I met him. Even if he weren't handsome, he would draw attention, reaching beyond sexuality, though sexual energy seeps from this man's pores. It's something more fundamental than sex appeal. Whatever it is, it's raw and compelling and in his very bones. I've never been able to completely put my finger on it, but wouldn't mind spending the next fifty years or so figuring it out.

"Grip, right?" Kevin stands and reaches past me to shake Grip's hand. "Kevin."

"Hey." Grip glances from me to Kevin, accepting his outstretched hand. "Like I said, sorry I'm late."

"Oh, no. It's fine." Kevin offers what is probably supposed to be a roguish grin, but comes off slightly creepy. "Gave me a little alone time with your manager here."

Oh, please spare me this.

Grip cocks his head and narrows his eyes a centimeter. "Alone time?"

"Grip, I was just about to tell Kevin that—"

"Ah ah ah." Grip silences me with a gesture, his eyes still locked on Kevin. "Let the man talk, Bris. And what did you use all this time alone for, Kevin?"

"I was persuading this beautiful lady to have dinner with me." Kevin seats himself, dipping his head toward the empty seat awaiting Grip at the table.

"Oh." Grip sits, nodding and setting his motorcycle helmet on the floor. "And how was that working out for you?"

"Between you and me"—Kevin slants me a knowing grin—"I think I was getting somewhere."

"Uh, Kevin, you really should—" I try again.

"Was he, Bris?" Grip cuts in over me, crossing his arms—vibrantly inked and roped with muscle—over his chest. His white shirt reads *HABITUAL LINE STEPPER*; no telling what that means. "Getting somewhere, I mean?"

Though well disguised, humor percolates behind his polite inquiry. Grip is possessive, but he knows this guy would never be anything but a joke.

"No, I told him we should keep things strictly business." I turn my attention from Grip to Kevin. "And I was just about to say I have a boyfriend."

"I'm sure he'd understand." Kevin flashes a conspiratorial wink Grip's way.

"I'm sure he wouldn't." A vein of steel runs through Grip's good-natured response. "He doesn't like her having dinner with other guys."

"What he doesn't know won't hurt him, eh?" Kevin leans forward slightly to elbow Grip's arm.

"Might get you hurt, though," Grip says, elbowing Kevin back with a little more force. "Eh?"

"Ow." Kevin rubs his arm, frowning at the spot Grip poked roughly.

This has gone on long enough. Every word out of Kevin's mouth imperils this book deal.

"Kevin, Grip *is* my boyfriend," I tell him, annoyed and tired of stretching this out.

Kevin's poor jaw nearly unhinges.

"*Grip* is your boyfriend?" Behind the designer spectacles, his eyes widen and dart between Grip and me.

Grip links our fingers on the table.

"As fuck would have it, yup." Grip raises our hands to his lips, kissing my fingers, but keeps his eyes trained on Kevin. "Is this your strategy for signing new authors? Hitting on their girlfriends? 'Cause I gotta tell ya, it's kinda brilliant."

I can't help it—I snort. My inelegant laugh draws Grip's dark eyes and wicked grin, fanning heat low in my belly that slides even farther south. I went years barely being intimate with anything that wasn't battery operated, and now I can't go two hours without wanting to be horizontally naked with this guy.

Though we *did* do it vertically in the shower this morning. I squirm in my seat remembering the slice of steamy heaven we had before the sun was all the way up. The sooner we get this over with, the sooner I can get back to the office and then home for more of that, whichever home we choose tonight. At some point, I guess I'll sell my place, or Grip will sell his? We'll live together, but will we get engaged first? Married? He did tell my mother he would marry me one day.

Oh, Bristol, please don't become one of those women obsessed with getting a ring, I self-admonish.

Because if you can't admonish yourself, who can?

We're in no hurry, and I actually appreciate our pace. The last few months have been . . . I don't even have language for how happy I am. It's contentment sheathed in passion, twisted around the deepest, most honest connection I've ever known. I wish everyone could taste this, could have this. That's when you know you're far gone—when you start wishing everyone else had what you have. I know what it's like to live without it, to live without *him*. It's lackluster, a pale parallel existence I have no intention of revisiting. We got just a taste of it this summer when he was on tour and I needed to stay behind in LA.

Miserable.

"Does that sound good, Bristol?"

Kevin's question snaps my attention back to the conversation at the table. Now I'm *daydreaming?* In the middle of a meeting? About proposals and engagement rings and fairy-tale endings?

"Uh, sorry." I split an apologetic glance between Grip and Kevin. "I got distracted. Does what sound good?"

"Grip wanted to reschedule the meeting." Kevin considers the calendar on his phone. "He has a session to get to at the studio, so maybe we can talk about the deal when he has more time."

Does Grip really have a session? Or is he just writing Kevin and this deal off? I try to read between the impassive lines of his face. I want him to give this a chance, despite the awful first impression Kevin made.

"You have a session?" I probe to see what he'll reveal.

His mouth kicks to the left, which usually indicates he's privately laughing at someone.

"Yeah, and don't you have that thing to get to?" He stands, grabbing his helmet and me, gently pulling me up by the elbow. "We both probably need to get out of here. Nice meeting you, Kev."

So that's a no on the session.

"You go to the studio." I pull away, narrowing my eyes at him so he knows I have his number. "I'll close things out with Kevin."

A quick frown clouds his expression. Joke or no joke, he doesn't want to leave me with some guy who was hitting on me just a few minutes ago.

"I can probably skip it." Grip's smile settles into an unyielding line.

"No need." I turn to Kevin. "I'm just gonna walk Grip out. I'll be back to discuss alternate dates."

"Sounds good. Great meeting you, Grip." Kevin picks up the menu and offers a quick smile. "I'll look at dessert."

Grip doesn't move, just keeps staring at Kevin, so I hook my arm through his and lead him out of the restaurant and to the parking lot. Once we reach the spot where his motorcycle is parked, Grip's hands settle on my hips and he pulls me into his chest, locking us together.

"What's up, little shawty?" he teases, running his nose along my neck. "What's your name? You got a man?"

"I do," I answer huskily. "But I could be persuaded. He'll never know."

"The hell." Grip chuckles, nipping my ear and sliding his hand to the small of my back.

"You don't really have a session, do you?" I ask abruptly, breaking the spell he's trying to weave.

"I'm not dealing with this guy, Bris." He pulls back to peer down at my face. "And neither are you. He's trying to have dinner with you? I'm not doing business with that—"

"In his defense," I cut in before he works himself into a lather. "He didn't know I'm taken."

Something flares behind his eyes when I use the word that says I'm his. I knew he'd like that; I'm nothing if not deliberate.

He leans down the few inches separating us until his lips are at my ear. His hands inch up to span my waist, his thumbs subtly, secretively brushing the underside of my breast. My breath hovers in my throat, suspended, and my mouth waters as I remember the taste of him this morning. Me on my knees in the shower, water beating on my shoulders, the long, rigid length of him hitting the back of my throat. His fingers screwed into my hair, holding my head still while he pumped over my tongue, scraped against my lips.

"So you're taken, huh?" He breathes against my neck. As calm as he looks from the outside, I hear the hitch in his breath, feel him hard and pressed into my belly. "I don't see a ring."

I shoot him a sharp glance. We haven't talked about rings and proposals in a while—it hasn't mattered. We practically live together, though we both still have our own places. Anything other than together isn't an option, but his teasing statement makes me wonder if he's started to think about it the way I have. I find myself holding out my hand a few times a day, studying my ring finger, wondering what he would choose for it . . . wondering when he'll ask.

Wondering when it started to matter so much to me. The last thing I want is to make him feel pressured. We've loved each other for years, true, but we haven't been official for long at all.

"Grip, I'm not—"

He palms my throat, thumb on one side of my face, fingers on the other, commanding me, coaxing my mouth open. His tongue sweeps the sensitive lining inside my jaw, over my teeth, around my lips. The sun is high in the sky. Patrons walk past us, coming to and leaving the restaurant. A few gawk. I'm not sure if they recognize Grip or if our PDA al fresco just disconcerts them. The kiss slows to mere brushes of our mouths, my lips pulled between his with tiny tugs and hungry bites. The firm hold he has on my chin softens, and his fingers slide into the hair falling around my neck.

"I had to shut you up because every time I mention rings you start stuttering and saying stupid shit." His eyes smile down at me. "And your mouth kind of hangs open. It's not a good look for you."

A laugh breaks free from me. It's a happy sound, like a caged bird free and singing. That's how I feel sometimes, like for years I walked around locked up, guarding my heart against this man, and now I've been let loose, liberated, kissing in broad daylight on the street and spilling laughter that sounds like a bird's song.

And not giving a damn what anyone thinks about it.

"Oh really?" My smile widens an inch. "I seem to remember you liked my mouth open this morning in the shower."

His chuckle rumbles in the small space separating our bodies. "Damn, Bris. What am I gonna do with you?"

"You'll figure something out." I prop my forearms on his shoulders, caressing his neck. "You always do."

He studies me for a few long seconds, something changing in his eyes. They sober, the cocky grin falling into a straight line.

"What's wrong?" I cup one side of his face, the slight scruff tickling my palm. One minute we're flirting and teasing, verging on horny, and the next we're ... not.

"Nothing." He sets his hand over mine against his jaw. "I just missed you today. I miss you when we're apart."

His words settle over my heart, refreshing like rain falling on dry, thirsty ground. I feel it, too. I'm not sure how I kept him at bay for eight years when eight *hours* away from him makes my chest ache. The look in his eyes ... there's more to it than what's on the surface, but I'm not sure what. He traces the corner of my mouth.

"You're just trying to distract me," I turn my mouth to kiss the hand touching my face, "from getting back to Kevin."

Grip rolls his eyes, some of the humor returning.

"You seriously think I'm dealing with that dude?" He scoffs a quick rush of air.

"Don't judge the deal by Kevin. I wish you could meet my friend Charisma. She'd be your editor, but she's tied up in New York, and Kevin just happened to be here in LA."

"Maybe we could meet her in New York." Grip's tone is careful and his glance is searching, but I'm not sure what he's looking for. Am I missing something?

"Not any time soon." I sigh, running my thumb over the dark arch of his brows. "Charm's stuck there, and things are way too hectic for me to get away right now."

"Yeah?" Grip twists his lips into a grimace.

"Yeah. Kai's finally about to drop her debut album, and Rhyson's in the studio working on his next project." A sudden smile takes over my face. "I forgot to tell you I got Luke that reality show about the making of his next album."

"Wow." Grip's eyes drop to the ground before he looks back to me. "Yeah, you've got a lot going on here."

"The show's filming in LA for the most part. I need to be on set at least for the initial footage, and don't get me started on everything happening for Jimmi. I may have to hand her off to Sarah, though she'd kill me."

"I get it," Grip says with a small smile. "You're too busy to go to New York."

There it is again. What's that look? Am I talking about work too much? I do that. I get caught up in my career, but I'm lucky enough to make dreams come true for the people I love the most. I never knew how fulfilling it would be, how damn good at it I would be. With every accomplishment, the opportunities double and my ambitions multiply. It's never bothered Grip before, but maybe now that things are busier than they've ever been, he's tired of hearing about my work and how much I love it.

"I'm sorry, baby," I say. "Here I am going on and on about Prodigy and all my stuff, and I didn't even ask about school. You registered for classes today, right?"

He goes still for a second, his expression becoming unreadable. "I'm still looking at classes. There's a little time before I finalize things for next semester."

"Well I want to hear all about it tonight." I tip up to leave a kiss on his lips. "But now I need to get back to Kevin."

Grip's face loosens into a grin.

"Tell his goofy ass you already have dinner plans, and to back off my girl."

"Oh, I have dinner plans?" I take a few steps backward toward the restaurant entrance, my eyes never leaving the handsome face with its stark planes and bold bones. "And what are these plans?"

"Dinner at my place."

"Am I bringing dinner?"

That's usually what happens—neither of us is exactly gourmet chef material.

"No, I'll grill up on the roof."

Ah, the roof, one of my favorite places in the world. Overlooking everything but isolated from it all, just my love and me. Add medium rare red meat, and it's my own private utopia.

"Then I'll see you after work." I smile and turn to go.

"Hey Bris," he calls.

I look over my shoulder to find that sober look back in his eyes, tightening the skin over his high cheekbones, making me nervous.

"I love you."

He says it to me every day, several times a day, and it never gets old, never frays around the edges or fails to palpitate my susceptible heart.

"I love you, too."

I don't try to lighten the moment with an easy smile or a flippant comment. Whatever is bothering him, he'll tell me, probably tonight. I'll let him come to it on his own.

In the meantime, Kevin.

Two

Grip

I HAVE TO TELL HER TONIGHT.

I've been putting it off, but I need to register for next semester. Getting my degree online has always worked for the busy pace of my life, but Dr. Israel Hammond, renowned criminal justice activist, will be a guest professor at NYU, and I need to be on campus. His book about racism in America completely rocked my world, and I need to take that class.

Rationally, I know it won't wreck us if I spend a semester in New York and Bristol stays here in LA. We survived eight years of games—chase, hide and seek, pin the tail on the donkey, with each of us playing the role of jackass from time to time. You name it, we played it. We survived Parker's sick attempts to destroy us, and he's stewing in a minimum-security resort-like prison suite because we figured out how to shut him down. We survived contempt and condemnation from people as distant as Black Twitter trolls and as close as members of my family who didn't want to see us together. They are slowly, surely, one by one, coming around. Jade will be the hold out; I know this, but eventually she'll see the light, too.

We win. Love prevails. I get it.

But that doesn't make the reality of me being on one coast while Bris lives on the other any easier to accept, even for a few months—not with the way I need her.

I flip our steaks, losing myself in thought and the smoke rising from the grill. Do I *have* to go? I'm a rapper, an entertainer ... do I really want to uproot my life for five months just to sit at the feet of some professor I don't even know?

Hell yeah I do.

When I'm forty years old, I don't want to still be just rapping. Jay-Z is a hip-hop unicorn. Who else is out there rapping and relevant at almost fifty?

I'll wait . . .

Yeah. Like I said. Dude's a unicorn.

I'm passionate about the causes affecting my community, and I'm educating myself now, equipping myself now so I don't squander this platform I've been given, but use it to do some kind of good. We have problems, and Dr. Hammond may have solutions. He's a brilliant man who, even as he rails against the system, is smart enough to work within it, who cares enough to reform it.

"Mmmmm, that looks good."

The comment grabs my attention, and I find myself smiling for the first time since I left Bristol. As she walks toward me, the approaching sunset paints the roof in shadows, but I see her clearly. Dark hair, burnished in places, falls around her shoulders. She has already discarded the dress she wore at lunch today in favor of a T-shirt and nothing else; it's the one I just tossed into the hamper.

She tugs at my *HABITUAL LINE STEPPER* T-shirt, the hem landing at the top of her thighs. Where the T-shirt stops, my eyes keep going, past the lean muscles of her legs and the cut of her calves, the delicate bones of her ankles and to her bare feet. I love this girl, head to toe. Beyond this gorgeous packaging, it's everything beneath that makes me beyond grateful she's mine. The loyalty, the bottomless pit that is her heart, her sense of humor. The toughest girl I know is also the most tender, and I'm so honored I get to see both sides, all her sides.

"You out of clean clothes?" I nod to my T-shirt. "You gotta wear my dirty stuff now?"

An impish smile tugs at her bare lips. She's washed away her makeup, and with it, all the sophistication she wraps around herself for her job. Up on this roof in my T-shirt, she's just my girl. I love her in every iteration, but this is the one only I get to see, so it's probably my favorite.

"I have clean clothes." She steps close enough for me to smell her scent and mine mingling in the fabric. "I like the way this shirt smells."

I drop a look over her, my eyes resting on the curves of her breasts in the soft cotton, where her nipples have gone taut under my stare.

"How does the shirt smell?" I ask, my voice as smoky as the steaks I should be paying attention to.

"Like you." She leans forward until her breasts press into my chest. "It smells like you."

My hands are twitching to touch her, and I finally surrender, slipping under the shirt to grasp her waist, pulling her up the few inches until our lips meet. I've been thinking about these steaks all day, and before Bristol arrived, I thought I was starving—but this, what I feel having her in my arms after hours apart, *this* is starving. It starts in my balls and tunnels up through my chest, infiltrates my heart, and presses its way to my mouth, which is open and devouring in a lips-searching, tongues-dueling kiss. I grip her by the ass, grinding our bodies together until the texture of her skin and mine, the scents of her skin and mine meld into this one panting, voracious thing that never seems to get enough.

"You better not burn my steak," Bristol pants in between kisses.

I angle my head to send my tongue deeper into her mouth, holding her still, teasing her until she's straining up, open and begging when I pull back.

"Grip." My name is a whimpering complaint. She cups my neck and tugs my head back down.

"Oh, no." I resist, laugh, and turn to the grill. "You were so concerned about me burning these steaks, Ms. Medium Rare."

"I am." She slides her arms around me from behind and I feel a sweet sting, her teeth gently biting my shoulder through my T-shirt. I love it when she bites me, but I'm not giving her that satisfaction yet. "But that doesn't mean you get to stop kissing me. You have to multitask."

One slim hand slides over my abs and past my belt to cup me through my jeans.

Damn. Not sure how long I can keep up this charade that I don't want to screw her into the wall on the roof where anyone with half a telescope could see.

"Wow," I say, keeping my tone unaffected, though she's gotta feel me getting longer and harder in her hand. "Somebody's horny as hell."

She makes a sound that's half outraged laughter, half indignant grunt before stepping around to stand in front of me by the grill.

"I will not be slut-shamed by my own boyfriend." Amusement lights her eyes, turning them to quicksilver.

"Shamed?" I put down the grilling fork I'm using for the steaks and reach for her again. "No shame in being horny for me, baby. I wanna give you a gold star."

Her eyes slide down to the erection poking her in the stomach. "Is that what we're calling it now? Should we name it?"

"Guys who have to name their dicks probably aren't using 'em right."

"So I ask again ... should we name it?"

I cock a brow and press our hips together.

"Are you implying that I don't know how to use mine? Because that's not the impression I got this morning when you came so hard you were singing like a bird."

She tilts her head, her eyes wide and considering. "Did you say like a bird?" A small smile plays around her lips. "What made you say that?"

"I don't know." I give a careless shrug. "Why?"

"It's silly," she says, rolling her eyes in self-derision. "I was thinking today when I laughed it sounded like ..."

Bristol blushes about once every Halley's Comet, so the color washing across her cheeks makes me wonder.

"What?" I probe. "Your laugh sounded like what?"

"Like a happy bird," she mumbles, peering up at me like I'm going to laugh in her face.

Which I do.

"Stop laughing at me." She narrows her eyes in mock warning.

"Right." I dip my head to catch her eyes and tease her. "Because when you tell me you laugh like a happy bird I'm just supposed let you get away with that."

"I'm not telling you things anymore." She narrows her eyes and folds her arms over her chest.

"Yeah, right. I'm your best friend." I pull her back into me. "You'll tell me everything like you always do."

"You are, you know." Her voice softens. "My best friend, I mean."

When she looks at me like this, her eyes stripped of every defense, no guard in sight, completely honest and open and vulnerable, I feel slightly invincible. It's a trick of the heart, I know, but I can't help but think that as long as she looks at me like this, there isn't anything I couldn't survive, that our love is the stuff of legends, rolled in Teflon, disaster-proof. I'm as fanciful as Bristol, my laughing bird.

"You're mine, too," I echo her sentiment. "My best friend."

"I won't tell Rhyson," she promises with a grin.

"I'm pretty sure he spits the same line to Kai." I keep a straight face. "We have to say that shit to get laid."

"I hate you."

"Orrrrrrrr do you love me and want to blow me after dinner?" I shrug and lift my hands, my palms up. "Just saying. Listen to your heart, Bristol. Listen to your heart."

"I'm listening to my belly right now, smartass, and it's growling. Feed me."

"Like my mama used to say, ain't no freeloaders in this house. What'll you give me for feeding you?"

"Um ..."

"I do have a suggestion, if you're searching."

"Let me guess—you have a 'Will fuck for food' sign up here somewhere?"

"I used bubble letters." I laugh and give her ass a light smack. "You can barter that booty."

It's so damn easy with Bristol—our banter, the chemistry, the perfect rhythm of our conversation. It was one of the first things I noticed when we met all those years ago. We didn't read each other's minds or finish each other's sentences. It wasn't cosmic, but it was a connection that seized me by the brain and grabbed me by the balls. She was as smart as she was sexy, as curious as she was forthcoming. There were years in between when we made things complicated, when things were strained, but now with our hearts settled on each other for good, it's simple.

This.

Her.

Us.

I'm as sure of her as I am that every night the moon will show up, the stars will shine down, and hours later, the sun will rise again.

This is my favorite part of every day. The sun is down, and we eat by fairy lights strung overhead. We both devour the steak and salad I prepared. When our plates are scraped clean, I'm on my second beer and Bristol has gone through half a bottle of red wine. We're cracking each other up and just sharing what happened during our day, which leads her back to lunch with Kevin.

"Your fans would eat up a poetry book from you." Bristol pours another glass of red. "And it would showcase the breadth of your talent beyond hip-hop."

I stand and gather our plates. Bristol, bottle in one hand and wine glass in the other, follows me to the door that leads back to the loft.

"I'll think about it." I gesture for her to walk ahead of me down the steps, mostly so I can catch glimpses of her ass under my shirt.

"Don't just say you'll think about it." She looks over her shoulder, rolling her eyes when she catches me checking her out. "Really? You see me naked every day. Don't guys ever mature beyond tenth grade?"

"Chronologically, yes." I drop a kiss in her hair as I pass her propping the door open for me. "In dick years, no."

Her phone dings from the coffee table in the living room. I hate that phone sometimes. Managing entertainers, her work is around the clock and all over the globe. Bristol's clients are usually spread across a few different time zones and never take into account the one she's in.

"Hmmmm." She takes another sip of her wine without glancing up from her phone. "You still interested in that panel in New York? The Artists as Activists thing?"

As soon as she says 'New York,' I'm reminded of my quandary. I have to talk to her about next semester before the night is over.

"Uh, yeah." I load our plates and utensils into the dishwasher, watching her across the open space. "Definitely."

"Hmmmm." Bristol continues scanning whatever she's reading, a slight dip between her brows.

"What's up?" I ask. "Something wrong?"

I cross the room to read over her shoulder. It's an email from the organizer, a popular New York-based radio personality named Angie Black with an army of loyal followers. I'm pretty sure Black isn't her real last name, but she's a titan on Black Twitter, #BlackGirlMagic at its best. I study the details, trying to figure out what has Bristol grunting and scowling, and then one name leaps from the list of panelists Angie provided.

Qwest.

"I didn't know Qwest was invited." I keep my voice casual, pull Bristol's hair back, and tuck my chin into the crook of her neck and shoulder.

"Hmmmm," she non-comments again, stepping away to set her wine glass on the counter, her monosyllable speaking volumes.

"You okay with that?" I grab her wrist, forcing her to face me. I cup the smooth line of her neck and lift her chin so I can see her expression. "I don't have to do the panel."

She squints in consideration for a few seconds, her lip between her teeth.

"No, it's fine," she finally says. "Qwest performed on tour with you this summer for a few shows and everything was okay, right?"

Qwest joined me on tour for two shows and everything seemed fine, but then I did avoid her like syphilis when we weren't on stage together.

"Yeah." I nod, keeping the syphilis qualifier to myself. "And you have to work on her next album, right?"

We struck a deal from the beginning—Qwest featured on my album, and I'd feature on hers. I also agreed to produce two of the other songs on her project.

"Those are all things I'm legally committed to do, though." I kiss the corner of Bristol's mouth. "If you don't want me to do the panel, I won't."

"But you really *want* to do the panel."

It's a statement, not a question. She knows I'm taking every opportunity I can to talk about criminal justice reform and improving relations with law enforcement . . . so yeah, I really want to do the panel, but I don't want Bristol feeling some type of way about Qwest and me doing this event together.

"I want to, yeah. It's important." I link our fingers and dip my head so we're looking into each other's eyes. "But not more important than you." I settle our linked fingers over my heart. "Not as important as us, Bris."

After a moment, she yields a smile.

"I'm fine with you doing the panel—on one condition." "Name it."

"Piggyback ride."

I fake exasperation, allowing her to shift the subject and lighten the air around us.

"Carry you up them steps?"

"Yes, up *them* steps."

She turns me around and presses on my shoulder until I'm squatting. When she jumps on my back, my hands hook under her long, smooth legs. I pretend to struggle under her weight and she laughs.

She sounds so happy I can't help but grin thinking of my driven, sarcastic girl describing herself as a bird.

"If I give you a piggyback ride," I tell her at the bottom of the staircase, "you give me a blow job. We'll call it even."

"What's so special about a blow job?" She tightens her arms around my neck when I start up the stairs. "I give you one like every other day."

"First of all, I can't believe you actually just asked me what's so special about a blow job. You may as well ask what's so special about the Taj Majal. A blow job is practically an eighth wonder." I press on as she laughs into my neck. "Second, the operative words there are *every other day*, so obviously, there's room for improvement."

"No, the operative word is blow *job*." She lightly smacks the side of my head. "Sounds like work for me."

"Well you're employee of the month."

"I better be the *only* employee."

"Oh, you don't have to worry about me cheating." I squeeze her thighs. "I like my balls *attached*."

Her husky laugh draws an answering chuckle from me. We've reached the bedroom and she slides off my back, walks around me to stand at the foot of the bed, mischief in her eyes, and smiles.

"What's a habitual line stepper?" She tugs at the hem of my shirt, emblazoned with the tagline, flashing black silk panties at the apex of her thighs. My eyes are glued there in case she lifts the shirt again—wouldn't want to miss that.

"Huh?" I burn a look over her breasts taunting me through the white cotton. "What was the question?"

"Habitual line stepper?" she asks patiently, pointing to the front of the T-shirt.

"Oh, uh . . . it's from a Dave Chappelle sketch, the one where Prince slaps Charlie Murphy."

"Prince slaps who?" She shakes her head. "I don't get it. I watched an episode and wasn't that impressed. He just makes a bunch of racial jokes."

"At least he makes fun of all races equally, and religion and politics and everything in between. Nothing and no one is safe. He's a master of satire and social commentary, and funny as hell. You must have seen a weak episode."

I take a step closer, lifting the hem to expose the smooth skin of her waist. I pull the shirt over her head and toss it into a corner. Her hair settles back around her shoulders, falling forward so her naked breasts poke through the dark strands.

"Forget Dave Chappelle," I say huskily.

I could write a sonnet to Bristol's nipples, the way they tip her breasts, the blend of pink and brown, roses and chocolate, shading her areola. I lean down to hover over them, my eyes snaring hers. Anticipation thickens the air.

"I wanna do to you what spring does to the cherry trees," I whisper, paraphrasing the Neruda poem before taking one nipple in my mouth and laving it with my tongue. Like a flower waiting for spring, she blossoms. She blooms like sweet fruit ripening between my lips. I pull away, but her hands urge me back to her breast, pleasure tightening her pretty features.

I ghost my lips over the other neglected nipple. Where at first I was sweet, now I'm all teeth and rough suction, stretching my mouth, wide and hungry, over the other breast. Where I laved the other nipple, this one I lash with my tongue. Her nails sink into my shoulders and she fills the room with whimpers. I release her nipple, satisfied by the vivid red marks slashing the delicate skin. Breath fights to free itself from her lungs, laboring past her lips, heaving her breasts. I gently turn her around by the hip to face the bed and almost bite my fist at the sight of her.

Thong.

Teeny, tiny thong. Ass out.

I coax her panties down her legs, inch by torturous inch. When she's a naked, lithe stretch of lines and curves, I reach around to cup her breasts, tugging on those nipples until they peek between my fingers. Bristol's breathing grows more ragged and she presses her back into my chest, circling her ass into my crotch.

I really wanted that blow job, but I'm not sure there will be time for that tonight. One hand stays right where it is, toying with her nipple as the other hand dips between her legs.

"Can you open for me?" I dust kisses across the elegant slope of her shoulders. She widens her stance no more than an inch, but I'll take a mile. I press the flat of my hand between her legs and the thick, wet lips of her pussy press into my palm. I vary the cadence of strokes over her clit until she's pumping into my hand, her hips chasing every thrust and her cries dying in her throat before they hit the air.

"Oh, God, Grip." Her voice verges on a sob. Even when she vises around my fingers, I don't let up the passionate pace between her thighs.

"That's it, baby." I drop to my knees, dragging my tongue down the smooth center of her back and over her ass. I clip the sweet flesh of each cheek between my teeth, relishing her startled gasp. Slowly, I press my hand to her back, bending her at the waist until she bows on the bed, on her knees. I scoot her forward, tilting her chest down and her ass in the air. With a rear view of her spread wide for me, I swipe my tongue down the inside of her thighs, drinking from the silky skin, wet with her juices.

"I'm getting drunk on you," I mutter.

"Grip." My name shatters on her lips, but it's not enough. I want her unintelligible. I suckle her clit and slip two fingers in, smiling against her pussy when she pants into the duvet. I stand and strip then run my cock up and down her divide, soaking in her wetness as she presses back into me, offering me more.

"You have to fuck me now." Her plea is breathless and urgent. She looks over her shoulder, her eyes glassy. "Please, right now."

Her eyes beg me. Her pussy weeps for me. The complete surrender in every line of her body undoes me, the last strands of control snapping and popping as they give. The wild, loose parts of me grab her hips and flip her onto her back. I push her legs wide until her knees almost touch her shoulders and run my finger over the hot, wet pleat of flesh between her thighs. Her eyes flutter closed.

"Open your eyes, Bristol," I say huskily. "Look at me when I fuck you."

When she looks at me, her hair like a dark river twisting behind her on my bed, my damn knees feel weak. That's what Bristol does to me with one look. That's how weak she renders me without even trying. Her eyes are the color of moonlight and her love glows like stars. My whole universe is right here, and I don't want to leave her and go to New York when the time comes.

Restless arousal shudders through her while she waits, while I stare. I shake off worry and uncertainty, dropping to my knees on the bed and lifting her by the hips. The sound of her breath hitching when I push in, when I invade that sacred space, tightens my balls. She's a tight, slippery tunnel, and after one stroke, I lose my mind. Body overtakes brain, a coup of instinct usurping reason. I push her knee farther back so I can go deeper. I twist our fingers together, pressed into the pillow by her head. I'm vaguely aware of Bristol moaning, of her tightening around me, of her coming again, the evidence of her pleasure spilling all over me, and then it's building in me, drawing my balls tight, flexing the muscles of my abs.

My love erupts. It blows.

I'm a geyser, a constant flow until the unrelenting rhythm of my body slows into something gentler, something tender. We press together, and beneath me she is crushed silk. My hot flesh and hers are slickened with the rigor of our passion, the sweat that bathes our skin. I don't know if it's mine or if it's hers, but this moment, this perfect glass-blown moment where our bodies unite and our souls intersect, this moment belongs to us.

Three

Bristol

I'VE SURVIVED A STORM.

That's how I feel every time Grip makes love to me, like a hurricane swept through and instead of taking shelter, I stood in the eye of it, the powerful wind whipping over me. I begged it to lift me. I let it love me. And this, the moments after, when the city lights shine through Grip's wide windows and play over our naked, sweat-slicked bodies, when Grip's fingers trace my back, playing over the vertebrae like keys on a piano, this is the quiet after the storm.

"I pulled your hair." Grip's voice comes quiet, still slightly hoarse. I screamed his name. He shouted mine. Our throats are raw from passion. My scalp still prickles from his forceful tugs of my hair. It's not quite pain, and in the moment, it felt good enough to make it worth it.

Grip works his fingers through the hair spilling onto his pillow until he reaches my scalp to soothe and massage.

"Did it hurt?" He leaves an offering of kisses between my shoulder blades.

"No." I lean back into his affection. "You know I love a rough fuck."

He chuckles at my neck, his warm breath caressing the sensitive skin.

"Just making sure."

He goes quiet again. We both do, for several long moments, where the only sound in the room is our breathing, and I swear I can hear his heartbeat . . . or maybe it's mine. Maybe they're the same, one not beating until the other does.

"I love sleeping with you." I don't say it to fill the quiet—we don't need that. I just want him to know.

"Me, too. Every night. Every morning." I hear him swallow, feel his fingers go still in my hair. "Bris, there's something we need to talk about."

Finally.

"I know." I roll onto my back and turn my head to catch whatever the city lights and the moon can show me on his face.

"You know?" He searches my eyes the way I'm searching his. "What do you know?"

"Not what you need to talk to me about." I pull the sheet up from my waist and tuck it under my arm. It's not cold at all, but as our bodies cool, I shiver. "I could just tell something was bothering you today in the parking lot."

He nods, inching close enough to drop a kiss between my eyebrows, then in the hair at my temple.

"Do you remember me talking about a book I read while I was on tour called *Virus*?"

"Are you kidding?" A smile turns up the corners of my mouth. "You read it like three times and said it changed your life. It's about criminal justice reform, right? Dr. Hammond?"

"Right." Even in the dim light, I see that Grip is pleased. "You remembered."

"Of course. I'm sorry I haven't read it yet. It's on my Kindle, I've just been so busy lately. I'll get to it."

"Hey." A frown pinches his brows the tiniest bit. "You don't have to read it because I did. I don't want you trying to be something you're not. Who you already are is exactly who I need you to be."

"I know." But it still feels good to hear it. Grip remains the good guy his mother raised to be a great man, the one who never forgets where he came from, but he's evolving. Maybe there's this little corner of my heart afraid I'll somehow get left behind, and his words go a long way to assure me I won't.

"Good." He looks at me for an extra few seconds, like he's checking to make sure I believe him. "Anyway, Dr. Hammond is a guest professor at NYU this semester."

I sit straight up in bed, grinning down at him lying on his side, propped on his elbow with his head resting in his hand.

"Grip, that's amazing."

"Yeah." He grins back at me, his eyes carrying answering excitement. "It's pretty dope. Reading his book opened my eyes and shifted my priorities in a lot of ways. It provoked me to not only do more, but to figure out what I want to do."

"So, with you enrolled online, how does that work?" I ask. "I mean, do you like audit the class by video? Or teleconference?"

Grip's smile falls away and he licks his lips, dropping his eyes to the sheets between us.

"It's not set up like that." He looks back at me, emotions wrestling in his eyes. "I think I'll have to move to New York for the semester."

Air rushes past my lips. How did that not occur to me? It makes sense that he would move to New York. I know Grip's ambitions go far beyond the stage, beyond music. He wants to have an impact, and the more involved he becomes, the more he requires of himself.

"Wow." Even knowing that, the thought of him living in New York for months shipwrecks me. For a moment I'm flotsam, inwardly adrift, flailing. I'm really excited for him, but I know my voice is dull when I speak.

"You should do that." I nod, convincing myself as much as him. "I think that's awesome."

"The class is three days a week." Even though I'm staring at the anxious tangle of fingers in my lap, I know Grip's eyes don't leave my face. "But it's Monday, Wednesday, Friday, so just the weekend between."

Not much time to fly back and forth between coasts.

"I'll come back to LA, of course," Grip continues. "And you can visit me in New York. I figure we'll see each other four, five times a month or so, sometimes more."

I'm a punctured tire, all the air hissing from me. The excitement I felt, I can't sustain at the prospect of so little time with him for the next several months.

"Hey, I know it's not great." Grip props his chin in my lap and wraps a wide palm around my hip, warming me through the sheet. "I don't have to go. Maybe I should reconsider and—"

"No." I shake myself out of self-pity and lean down to frame his strong jaw and high cheekbones, the face of a king, between my hands. "It's right. It's good. You need to do this, and I want it for you. We'll figure it out."

Grip tucks his head into my waist, kissing my stomach through the sheet and running his hand over the bare skin of my back.

"I know things are crazy at Prodigy right now, and that means more responsibility," he says. "Rhyson's trusting you with so much. It's everything you've worked for, and I'm happy for you."

I angle my head, studying him. If there's one thing I know, it's when Grip wants something. He's never held back from me, never left me wondering what he wanted from me, but now, I sense that he's withholding something.

"What do you want?" I slide back down the headboard until we're both lying down, facing one another. "From me? Grip, tell me what you want."

Hesitation clouds his expression, and then he shutters his face altogether.

"Like you said." He pushes the wild tumble of hair back from my face. "We'll figure it out."

"*Tell me what you want.*" I brush my thumb over the dark slash of his brows. "Can you do that for me?"

"Bris." He drops his lashes, covering whatever is hiding in his eyes. "I don't think—"

"Right—don't think, just tell me."

He scans my face. I know my expression is a blank check, offering him whatever he wants, but I don't care. All hesitation falls away. Staring back at me is the persistent man who pursued me shamelessly for eight years, who wore my resistance down to nothing.

"I want you to come with me." A muscle clenches in his jaw. "I know it's selfish and might seem like I'm asking you to follow me across the country, but—"

"Yes."

"I'm still asking," he goes on, like I didn't speak, like he didn't hear me. "I don't know how we make it work. We'll figure that out together, but the thought of seeing you only a few times a month . . . I know we *can* do it, I just don't want to."

"Grip."

"And maybe I *am* a caveman. Maybe it *is* sexist to ask you to be the one who moves. It's just, with classes three times a week, I don't see how I can—"

"Grip." I press my fingers over the soft lips that were making love to my nipples not even an hour ago. "Baby, I said yes."

"You did?" he mumbles into my fingers, his eyebrows shooting up in surprise.

"I did." I laugh, not exactly sure how I'll make it work, but knowing that I will. For him, I will. "I mean, I'll have to come back and forth some, but I have to try. I don't want a long-distance relationship. That sounds like torture."

Grip's smile dims and his brows draw together.

"But Rhyson needs you here now more than ever. He won't be happy to hear you're moving to New York at such a crucial time."

"Rhys will understand. He's got Kai." "What does that mean?"

"That he knows how it feels to have someone who means more than everything else."

Grip's expression softens. His eyes are intent, like he's memorizing the way the light strikes my face the same way I'm memorizing him. He slowly, painstakingly peels the sheet back from my breasts, the cool air raising goose bumps on my naked skin . . . or maybe that's just Grip.

"I know you said you like a rough fuck." Grip shifts until he's leaning over me, his weight supported by the muscles flexing in his arms. He slots his lean hips between my thighs, and I feel him eager and ready again through the sheet covering my legs. "But how do you feel about long, slow, grateful ones?"

I widen my thighs so he sinks deeper into me.

"The longer," I say, reaching between us to grab his growing erection, my hand fisting him, lengthening him. "The better."

Four

Bristol

ME: Hey! I know it's Sunday morning, but I need to talk to you about something.

Rhyson: Sure. You wanna call?

Me: I was actually thinking about coming over.

Rhyson: See you when you get here.

Me: I'm kind of already here.

No message bubbles appear, and a few seconds later the front door to Rhyson's stately home flings open. My twin brother stands in the entrance, grinning at me as I lean against my baby girl, the Audi convertible I bought a few years ago.

"Aren't you polite this morning?" He steps back, gesturing for me to walk past him into the house. "You usually just barge in."

He's right. I have all his codes and keys, full access to his life. "That was before Kai moved in." I pause in the doorway to give him a quick hug before walking through to the foyer. "If you didn't like to screw your little wife all over this place at all times of the day, maybe I would risk showing up unannounced."

He offers no apologies, only that cocky grin that used to strip women of their panties. Now he just uses it to tell me he's a happily married man with one set of panties to worry about.

"Probably a good idea." He tips his head toward the kitchen. "Come on. I'm eating breakfast."

Sunshine brightens the room, the marble counters and modern

state-of-the-art appliances—which Rhyson's probably never touched—gleaming. His housekeeper has always taken good care of him, and now Kai cooks any time her schedule allows.

"Hungry? Coffee?" Rhyson glances at me, his eyes silvery under a sweep of dark hair. He's my brother, but even I can appreciate that he's a beautiful man.

Of course he is—we're twins.

He and I tell Grip that all the time to make him roll his eyes and laugh. Speaking of Grip . . . I'm here for a reason, and I hope this goes well.

"No, I'm good." I cast a disparaging look at the orange mash in the food processor on the counter. "Especially if that is breakfast."

"That's Aria's baby food. Kai makes it herself." Rhyson laughs and settles onto a bar stool at the counter, a croissant on the plate in front of him. "Today was sweet potato."

I find myself smiling too as I take the stool beside him. "Where is my adorable niece?"

"You're not gonna believe this." Rhyson slants me a wry grin. "Don't laugh."

"I won't." Though I'm laughing a little inside already because he told me not to. I'm perverse that way.

"Kai took her to church." He gives me a *don't say a word* look.

Rhyson would be an atheist if he cared enough to actually declare himself something, and the irony of him marrying the daughter of a Southern Baptist preacher is not lost on any of us.

"Kai took Aria to church?" A half-laugh, half-breath leaves my lips. "Did she go with Aunt Ruthie?"

Kai's Aunt Ruthie lives with them and helps out with Aria since Kai's schedule can get crazy. One of the first things Aunt Ruthie did when she relocated from Glory Falls, Georgia, was find a church here in LA. I can't pretend to understand why this is urgent for anyone, but apparently it's a thing for church people.

"No, that's just it." Rhyson takes a sip of coffee and shrugs. "She doesn't like Aunt Ruthie's church, so she's looking for the 'right' one. She wants Aria to grow up in a progressive church, an oxymoron if I ever heard one."

"So Aria will grow up believing in arcs and angels?" The smile I give him holds genuine curiosity. "Are you okay with that?"

Rhyson tips his head to the left, actually considering it.

"I trust Kai. She won't go overboard or get Aria into anything crazy." He shrugs and goes back to his croissant. "Besides, that's how Kai was raised, and it didn't screw her up too badly."

"That's definitely true. You married up, brother."

As I knew he would, Rhyson almost spits out the coffee mid-sip, his expression incredulous.

"Oh, now I married up, but not too long ago you swore Kai was a conniving gold digger." Rhyson narrows teasing eyes at me. "Excellent judge of character, by the way."

"In my defense, I was looking out for you." I smile brightly, ignoring just how wrong I was about my now sister-in-law. "It all worked out beautifully."

"Can't argue with that." Rhyson offers a quick smile before turning eyes the exact shape and color of mine in my direction. "But you didn't drag your ass over here on a Sunday morning to celebrate my marriage."

I hadn't realized how much I was dreading this conversation until I was right in front of it.

"I think I will have some coffee after all." I walk over to the counter, to the coffee machine that looks like it came with launch codes. Rhyson waits patiently, but his curiosity crackles in the kitchen while he takes the occasional bite. Once I'm settled beside him again with a cup of coffee I don't want or need, I turn to face him.

"Do you remember the book Grip couldn't stop talking about this summer?"

Rhyson snorts and cocks one dark brow.

"It was unavoidable." He leans back and crosses his arms over his chest. "*Viper* or *Sickness* or—"

"*Virus*, by a guy named Israel Hammond."

"Right." Rhyson's face animates. "When I went to Marlon's show in Paris, he quoted like half a chapter to me back at the hotel."

"That sounds right." I smile, my heart swelling a little with pride in Grip's passion, his convictions. "He says it was life-changing."

"That's our guy." Rhyson chuckles, affection for Grip coloring his smile. "Somebody's gotta change the world."

"Yeah, well …" I bite my lip, training my eyes on the swirling pattern in the marble countertop. "Dr. Hammond is guest lecturing at NYU this semester."

It gets quiet enough for me to hear the hum of the shiny appliances in the kitchen.

"He's going to New York then?" I feel Rhyson's eyes on my face but don't look up to meet them quite yet.

"Yeah," I answer before biting the bullet and looking up to meet his gaze. "And I'm going with him."

Rhyson nods slowly, turning his mouth down at the corners. "Never thought I'd see my little sister dropping everything to follow some man across the country."

I'm too on edge to detect the teasing in his voice, so I'm already poised for battle, mouth locked and loaded with ammo, only to find him laughing at me.

"Bastard," I mutter, fighting a smile.

"I'm not sure our mother would appreciate that."

Rhyson's smile holds, but his face ices over the way it always does when my mother comes up. My relationship with her isn't nearly as complex and convoluted as his, and overall, on a scale of one to fucked up, my relationship with her has always been pretty fucked up. That said, I'll never forget how she intervened to get me out of the mess with Parker. I'll always remember those moments of naked vulnerability she and I shared that day we took him down. Things have continued to slowly thaw between us, even though we're still not besties. It takes effort and patience and forgiveness—three things Rhyson has never had for our mother.

"You cut Dad some slack, Rhys," I say, reminding him of the progress he and our father have made over the last few years.

"Maybe you could cut her some, too."

"Maybe you could mind your own damn business." He shifts his cool stare over my shoulder.

I just keep looking at him because he knows that I, unlike half the people in this town, am not scared of him and can give as good as I get. He also realizes that I know how deeply our mother injured him. She injured me, too. They all did, but I kept on fighting to have them in my life. As hard as it's been, it's also been worth it.

"Bris, I'm sorry." Rhyson runs an agitated hand through his already rumpled hair. "I . . . can we just talk about what you came here to talk about and leave her out of it?"

"Sure." I lick my lips and set aside my fix-it reflex, that part of me that wants to get to the bottom of everything and make it work properly. Our family has never worked properly, so why I—who spent half my life on a therapist's couch—think I can fix us, I have no idea, but I never stop trying.

"So you want to go with Marlon to New York, huh?" Rhyson forces a smile, deliberately shifting us to safer ground.

"Yeah." My smile comes more naturally just because he said Grip's name. There are two things absolutely right in my life: my career and my man. I would prefer not to ruin one for the other, but if Rhyson forces me to choose, I have every confidence I can find another way to make a living—though I know it won't come to that.

First of all, I'm his sister.

Second of all, he needs me too badly. I've become indispensable. That, even beyond the blood and DNA we share, is my insurance policy.

"Look, I know there's a lot going on with Prodigy," I begin, prepared to build my case for why I could work from the moon as long as I have Wi-Fi.

"But nothing you can't handle from New York," Rhyson says before I can mount my defense.

"Right." I sketch a quick frown before continuing. "And I know I need to be on site for certain things."

"But you can just fly here for those and then go back to New York when you're done." Rhyson sips his coffee, regarding me steadily over the rim. "Between video conference, Wi-Fi, and every other technological advance at our disposal, shouldn't be a problem."

"I was hoping you'd see that." Though I thought I would have to be the one to make him see it.

"And it's just for the semester, right? Next semester you guys would be back in LA?"

"Yeah." Out of habit I rub at my neck to ease the tension, but there's no tension there. This conversation is going much better than I had hoped. "We'll be back in December after finals."

Rhyson kind of stole my thunder, took some of the wind from my sails. I was fully prepared to persuade, convince, and cajole him to my point of view, but he anticipated everything I had lined up. I do at least have one thing he probably didn't see coming.

"I was thinking while I'm in New York, I could feel out some Broadway possibilities," I say nonchalantly.

"Broadway?" Curiosity lights up his eyes. "For who?"

"Well, I know Kai wants to get into acting, and after her album drops, we've been talking about movie roles."

"No nudity," he cuts in, wearing his *I mean it* face. "I told you, Bris. Don't even bring us a script that calls for her to do some fifty shades of fucked-up shit with some dickhead actor. If I haven't been clear—"

"The last time we discussed Kai's movie career, you asked me to look for nun roles." I layer my look and my words with sarcasm. "I think you were pretty clear."

"Good," Rhyson mutters, either not seeing or not caring how ridiculous he sounds. My sister-in-law will thank me later for saving her from wearing a habit onscreen.

"Kai's one of those rare talents who can do it all," I continue. "She sings, dances, acts, and is gorgeous."

"Yeah, she's pretty amazing." Pride and love fill his eyes, and I'm so happy my brother didn't listen to me when I questioned Kai's motives, so happy neither of us settled for the matrimonial farce our parents showed us all those years.

"There aren't many Broadway roles that require nudity." I shrug and widen my eyes innocently. "Maybe my time in New York could open up a whole new avenue for Kai."

The cogs are turning so hard in my brother's head, I think I smell smoke.

"I love that idea, Bris." He leans over to hook his arm around my neck and pull me closer. "And I think it's great that you're putting your relationship with Marlon first."

"You do?"

"Yeah, and I know it's your choice. He's not that guy who would drag you across the country by your hair."

"I had to force him to tell me he wanted me to go with him." I smile at the memory. "He's so concerned with me being happy and doing what I love."

"Unlike me who would just say Kai, pack your shit, you're coming with me to New York?" Rhyson laughs, but his voice rings with truth.

"Your words," I say with a grin. "Not mine."

He almost destroyed their relationship trying to control Kai. Our parents set that pattern managing his career as a piano prodigy, using love as control, and it's taken him twenty years to break out of it.

"I've gotten a lot better, too," Rhyson asserts. "Just ask Kai."

"Ask me what?"

Kai stands in the kitchen doorway, Aria perched on her hip. Her petite frame is perfectly lit by the sun shining through the windows, and for a moment, my brother looks dazzled by the dark hair hanging almost to her waist and the tilted eyes that are even more beautiful because they are kind. My niece is such a perfectly adorable blend of Rhys and Kai, I can't resist going over and snatching her up immediately.

While I'm cooing to Aria, Rhyson is thoroughly kissing his wife, pulling her much shorter frame up and into his.

For a long damn time.

"Ahem." I clear my throat meaningfully. "You think you two could wrap this up before Aria graduates?"

Kai turns dreamy, love-dazed eyes my way, a bashful smile on her pretty face. You'd never know this unassuming girl in her simple jeans and T-shirt is about to blow the music industry wide open. Her sweetness cloaks a driving ambition that is backed up by immense talent. She's going to be the biggest thing since . . . well, Grip, and it's my job to make sure that happens. No one deserves it more than Kai; she's lost so much over the course of her life, and it's good to see her happy, especially with my brother.

"Sorry." A faint blush colors her cheekbones. "Rhys, what were you saying Bristol should ask me when I came in?"

He winks at me conspiratorially over her shoulder.

"We were just wondering how you feel about Broadway."

Five

Bristol

"THIS COULD BE THE ONE, BRIS."

I glance from the clean modern lines of the beautifully decorated Tribeca apartment to Charisma Simmons, my friend since high school. Her mother, Bridget, one of New York's most elite realtors, has shown me several properties this week, and none of them made me feel like this one does. There's something special here. Even though Grip and I will only be leasing it for the semester, it has its own permanence, like it has only ever been someone's home. There's a warmth that wraps around me; it feels personal. It could be that this one comes fully furnished while the others were cold, stark, empty boxes—albeit expensive empty boxes. You have to mortgage your soul to live in New York. I shouldn't be surprised; I grew up here, and LA isn't much better. We had an apartment on the Upper East Side, where I lived during the school year, close to the private school I attended. When I wasn't there, I was at our estate a few hours outside the city. My parents and Rhyson were rarely at either since they were usually on the road, and those places never felt like home—but this, this was someone's home. I can feel it.

"It *is* beautiful." My gaze drifts over the sprawling space, the exposed rafters, the red brick wall fitted with wide windows overlooking the city, and the slatted staircase leading to the upper floor. "Your mom said the owner wants to meet us, right? How close are they?"

"Oh! Let me check."

Charisma, or Charm as we chopped her down to growing up, pulls her phone from the latest Birkin bag. She looks every inch the New Yorker, shaded in black and gray, swathed in leather, accessorized and name-branded from head to toe. The knife-sharp points of her precisely bobbed hair slice into her skinny shoulders. The Gucci eyeglasses framed by her perfectly arched brows say more about how smart she likes to look than they do about her nearsightedness. I know her secret. In the cutthroat publishing industry, a woman as delicate and lovely as Charm does whatever necessary to be taken seriously by the intelligentsia, including wearing glasses she doesn't actually need.

My wardrobe has adapted to New York, some, too. There's always an edge I don and doff depending on the coast. Today I've paired my black tulle-ruffled mini skirt with a tight black leather jacket and ankle boots. If we're spending the fall here, I need to shore up my sweater-weather game.

"My mom's fifteen minutes out. She got stuck uptown," Charm says, slipping her phone back into her bag and flashing the impish grin that landed us in the principal's office more than once. "But that gives us a few minutes to catch up before she arrives. How is it that you've been here all week and we haven't even had dinner?"

"Your author released a book." I run a finger over the mantel topping the glass-encased fireplace, noting its dustless-ness. "And it was a huge week for several of my clients. Me being here instead of LA, managing the time difference, trying to see properties . . ."

I shrug carelessly, used to our dynamic by now. Charm and I have kept in touch some, but we have demanding careers we've been completely dedicated to since graduating. It's paid off. Both of us hold pole position in our respective industries, but there's been little time for long-distance friendships, and missing each other has become a habit over the years. The two girls who grew up together and knew each other's secrets are now women who have a lot to learn about who the other has become.

"Well we have a few minutes now." Charm pats the cushion of the slate-colored suede sectional. "Come talk to Mama."

I sit beside her and smile involuntarily. My affection for Charm has stubbornly hung around since we searched for ways to make our modest school uniforms sexier.

"Tell me about this man of yours, the one you're dropping everything to follow." Charm purses her lips and wiggles her brows with salacious speculation. "I must admit, I was surprised to see you with a Black guy."

Charm's eyes stretch and she gasps, covering her mouth with one perfectly manicured hand.

"Oh, God. Did that sound bad? You know I'm a progressive."

"Of course you are, Charm." I pat her hand while holding on to my humor and patience. "Grade A liberal."

"I just meant . . . well, you never dated Black guys in college." My shrug is easy, my laugh less so. This feels weird.

"I never really thought about it. It didn't matter—it *doesn't* matter."

"No, it doesn't." She puckers her perfectly plucked brows. "I sound like those people assuring you that they really do have Black friends."

I don't answer, just lift both brows. Sometimes when you're quiet, people hear themselves.

"I really do have lots of Black friends." Her tinkling laugh pokes fun at herself.

"I'm sure you do." I grin and decide to let her off the hook for now.

"I've seen pictures, of course. He's . . . wow." Charm licks her lips, anticipation all over her face. This is more her speed—talking about how hot a man is rather than the sticky issues of race.

"You have to tell me everything," she says, practically flushing. "Don't hold back. Remember the Dick Diaries?"

How could I forget our regular debriefs after sexual encounters and misadventures?

"I'm not talking about this with you, Charm," I say with neutral determination. "It's not appropriate."

"Oh, Bris, come on." Charm levels a knowing look at me because in a past life, she *did* know all my dirt. "Remember we had a threesome with that guy from Penn? The one with the bumpy dick? I know how you sound when you come. I'm pretty sure telling me if your boyfriend is well hung doesn't cross any lines we didn't cross a long time ago."

I groan because I try to forget that night with Crooked Dick. "Please don't mention that when Grip gets here."

I haven't seen him in two weeks, and he's coming straight from the airport. He did a few shows in Europe and recorded with some Danish producer Rhyson has been raving about. Needless to say, after not seeing him for thirteen days, under Charm's watchful eyes, I'll have to restrain myself from dry-humping him.

"Also," I tell Charm, "I faked that orgasm, so don't presume you know how I sound when I come."

"You faked that?" Charm looks aghast then impressed. "Damn, you're good."

"Lots of practice." I glance at my phone one more time to make sure I haven't missed a text from Grip. "I'm serious, no talk of threesomes in front of Grip. His plane landed thirty minutes ago. I sent him the address and he should be here any minute."

"He doesn't know you did threes?"

"He doesn't *like* that I did. Believe me, I do *not* want to hear about his either. We're both pretty possessive, but I know he's had his share." I give her a flinty look. "Speaking of sharing, I don't anymore, not him, so don't even think about it."

"Okay, okay." Charm throws up her hands in defense. "I get it."

"What do you get?" Charm often thinks she "gets" things about which she's actually clueless, and I'm guessing my relationship with Grip qualifies as one of them.

"You're exploring your options." Charm's smile is as dirty as a smudge on pristine paper. "Trying something different."

"He's not some exotic experiment." I wince at the picture I think she's forming in her head.

"You're not . . ." Charm's eyes narrow, speculate, and then widen. "You don't think he's, like, *the one*, do you?"

Before I can assure her he most definitely is the one, she goes on. "I assumed you'd land with someone like Parker." She pours scandal and conjecture into her glance and shakes vigorously. "I mean, before he went to prison, of course, but anyone with that much money can always be redeemed."

"Parker?" Revulsion is on spin cycle in my stomach. "Parker is a miscreant who cares only about himself. He's cruel and perverted."

I sit up straighter and tell her what used to be the unpardonable sin in her book.

"And he fucks like a boy. I practically had to hold his hand when we had sex." I look at her meaningfully. "I mean that quite literally. I got myself off more often than not."

"Through the years, my standards have lowered by necessity. I could live with DIY if I had all his millions." Charm laughs at the disgust I know is evident on my face. "I'm just saying, men like Parker, that's who we marry. We know what it is. We're UES, Bris."

"I may have grown up on the Upper East Side, but you know it's not all it's cracked up to be."

"Actually, it was every bit that it was cracked up to be for me." Charm laughs in that way that always made me want to join in. She is outrageous, and what Grip would call "siditty," but underneath all the posturing, she's a good friend.

"But that was never enough for me," I remind her quietly with a sad smile for the holiday breaks I spent at her house when my family was on the road. Our eyes exchange those memories before she goes on.

"And he's enough?" she asks. "Grip is enough?"

"Oh, he's more than enough." I chuckle, a rich, satisfied sound even to my own ears.

"Is that your subtle way of telling me he has a big dick?" Her eyes light up with humor and curiosity.

"Believe me, there's nothing subtle about it." We share the kind of secret grin I only have with Charm and Jimmi, my two wildest friends.

"Now *that* I understand." Charm's glance turns contrite. "I didn't mean to sound . . . like I sounded before, but you must admit, he's a bit of a departure from the guys we've dated, the guys *you've* dated in the past."

"I know that, but you have these labels for us. Everyone does. I'm Upper East Side, Hamptons, debutante, Ivy league. I'm Angela Gray's daughter." I lift my brows in expectation. "And he's a rapper from Compton, right?"

"Well, that's oversimplified, but from the outside looking in, yeah."

"But what you don't know is that he's an incredible son. Seeing him take care of his mother showed me how he'll take care of me."

I press my hand to my heart, touching the place where the truth about him glows like a filament.

"He's a loyal friend, and he has a conscience even when it's not convenient," I say. "You don't know that when we make love, he whispers poetry. He makes me feel treasured. He'd die for me, and without thinking twice, I would die for him, too."

My words dangle in the air, defying gravity, and Charm is looking at me like she's never seen me before, like I'm a stranger. Compared to the self-absorbed, vapid girl she knew years ago, I probably am. I'm a new creature, and Grip has undoubtedly had a hand in refashioning me. I'm a little embarrassed when I replay my words. Charm and I haven't really talked like this in a long time, and I just poured my heart down her throat like a vodka tonic.

"I get why you're tempted to define him with easy labels, but he . . . well, Grip defies defining." I shrug and offer a self-conscious laugh. "You'll get it when you meet him."

"Then I'm about to get it." Charm's eyes lock onto something over my shoulder and light up like a kid sniffing cotton candy. "Hello there. Grip, I presume?"

I glance over my shoulder to the apartment entrance. Grip stands there, a huge suitcase on wheels trailing him.

How long has he been there? Did he hear me gushing about him like a lovesick teenager?

Lines of fatigue bracket the decadent spread of his lips, like he hasn't had much sleep. A thin layer of stubble hugs the jut of his jaw, like he hasn't had a shave, and his dark eyes rove over my breasts, my legs, and my face, like he hasn't had *me* in thirteen days. From ten feet away, he's eating me alive, and the memory of our last morning together crowds out the present. The phantom strokes of his hands over me, how he licked greedily at my body's secrets—it all rushes back. If Charm weren't here, I'd already be wrapped around him like a koala in heat.

"Guess I'm in the right place." He spares Charm a quick glance and a polite smile before looking back to me, his eyes going gentler and hotter. "Hey babe."

The hell if I care what Charm thinks. I'm up and across the few feet separating us. My arms slink up behind his neck and I press into him, so solid, so *here* after two weeks of absence. He drops the handle of the suitcase to lock his hands low on my hips, barely a decent distance from my ass, and lowers his head to kiss me. It should be quick. I'm aware of Charm watching us and of her mother and the owner of this lovely apartment mere minutes away, but as soon as I taste him, there's no stopping. He persuades my lips open, his groan vibrating on my tongue and sliding into my chest. He creeps one hand up and into my hair, bunching it in his fist. My hands venture under the leather jacket he's wearing and I dig my fingers through the soft cotton of his shirt into the dense muscles of his back.

He slows the kiss when we're temporarily sated, but sexual energy still powers the connection between us. He pulls back, glancing over my shoulder at Charm, and quirks love-bitten lips into a rueful grin.

"Sorry, we haven't seen each other in a while." He pulls me into his side, one arm draped over my shoulder. "You must be Charm. Nice to meet you."

Charm's cheeks are positively pink, and I'd know that flush anywhere. In college, the girl didn't have a spank bank so much as a vibrator vault. I know how many batteries she used to go through.

"Charm, you don't get to think about this tonight when you're alone." My voice is light, but I narrow my eyes so she knows I'm dead serious. Grip will not feature in her fantasies—I forbid it.

"Ahem." Charm practically floats to her feet and glides over, hand extended. If she curtsies, I'm kneeing her in the vagina. "I've heard so much about you, and none of it did you justice."

Grip's mouth tightens against what I suspect is laughter. "I've heard a lot about you, too."

"Have you heard that I really want to do a book deal with you?" Charm shifts from slut muffin to shrewd businesswoman-editor-person with whip-lash swiftness. "I suspect come December your Grammy nom will be announced. May as well start on *New York Times* bestseller, too."

"Charm, we're here to look at the apartment," I remind her. "Not ink a deal."

Who can think about business at a time like this, when I'm snuggled into my boyfriend's hard body and surrounded by his addictive scent?

"Knock, knock." A living, breathing prediction of Charm in twenty years pokes her head into the apartment entrance. "Anybody home?"

"Mother." Charm teeters on her Manolos, making her way over to Bridget Simmons, offering air kisses that come close to actually landing on her cheeks. "You look amazing."

"Oh, thank you, dear," Bridget practically purrs. "I've been doing Pure Barre."

"It shows," Charm says admiringly. "Where's Mrs. O'Malley?"

"Not far behind me, I'm sure." She smiles over at Grip and me. "Hullo, darlings. You must be Grip. Nice to meet you. Bristol, come, come."

Her hands bid me, flashing diamonds and drawing me into her Chanel-scented bosom.

"Hello, Mrs. Simmons." I do the perfunctory air kisses we were trained to perfectly execute in finishing school. "Thank you for helping me this week. This property is gorgeous."

"Isn't it just?" Bridget takes in the spacious living room and the glimpses of the city skyline it affords. "The owner wants to leave it furnished, if that's not a problem."

"Grip arrived just before you did, so we haven't had a chance to look around yet." I reclaim my spot beside him, tucking into his side, a wave of want and need slamming into me like a blow. The tension of his body tells me he's suffering from the same deprivation I am.

"Mrs. O'Malley got stuck in some traffic, but should be here soon." Bridget stops abruptly when her phone rings. "Oh, this is her now. Let me take it."

She steps out into the hall and starts a rapid-fire one-sided conversation.

"I'll be right back, too." Charm holds up her phone. "I should check in with the office. I hadn't planned to be gone this long."

As soon as she steps into the hall, Grip drags me by the wrist into the small powder room just off the entrance. I don't get the chance to ask him what he's doing before he shows me, lifting me onto the sink and slotting his lean hips between my thighs. One hand shoves into my hair and the other wraps around the side of my neck. His tongue goes deep sea diving down my throat, and who cares about breathing? Endless days and interminable nights missing him make me desperate, make my hands shake when I touch him. I scoot forward to feel him through my wet panties, my tulle skirt rasping over my thighs as he pushes it up. I roll my hips into him, seeking friction in my neediest place.

"I heard the things you said about me," he mutters against my jaw.

"Oh, God." I squeeze my eyes shut, embarrassed not because he didn't know I felt those things, but because I got caught gushing.

"Did you mean them?" His whisper over my lips makes them throb.

Forget embarrassment—he's hard between my legs, and I realize my declaration turned him on. I've been too long without him to be reticent.

"Every fucking word." I reach between us to rub him through his jeans. His breath rushes out against the skin of my neck, where his head is buried.

"Baby, I missed you." He sucks my earlobe and runs his tongue along my neck. "God, so much."

He drops to his knees, his wide palms on the sensitive skin inside my thighs, spreading me open. He tugs my panties aside and presses his nose to me, inhaling sharply.

"Grip, stop." I halfheartedly try to bring my legs back together. "We can't."

"I woke up like eighteen hours ago in Paris and couldn't remember how your pussy smelled." Lava-level heat darkens his eyes. "That's been driving me crazy."

Holy shit. We may not make it out of this bathroom alive.

Before I can even voice that fear, he's tugging my panties down my legs and lapping at me like he's parched and I'm the last glass of water for miles. He's French kissing my pussy, tunneling his tongue into my depths. I want to be discreet, want to do the decent thing and drag him up and back out into the living room so we can pretend to be upstanding, well-adjusted human beings, but I can't because, love-starved animal that I am, my fingers are digging into his scalp and pressing his head deeper into the starving center of my body. If he bites my clit ...

"Ahhh. Oh God, oh God, oh God. Griiiiiiip." In the midst of what borders on an out-of-body experience, I slam my palm into the wall for support. "Oh, please don't stop. Yes! Dammit, yes."

His mouth, right at the nexus of my pleasure, dips my inhibitions into boiling water, and they dissolve. Discretion takes a flying leap off Orgasm Falls, and I'm coming loudly and with unladylike enthusiasm when there's a startled gasp from the other side of the heavy wooden door and then an awkward cough.

Grip freezes and reaches up to cover my mouth with his hand. His eyes are laughing and his lips are shiny. "Why are you so *loud?*"

I jerk away from his hand and narrow my eyes still teary from my cataclysmic orgasm.

"You bit my clit," I hiss. "What did you expect?"

"Um, Bristol?" Charm taps the door, her voice sounding awkward. "We're, uhhhh . . . out here when you're ready to come—I mean, um, *come out* . . . here."

"We'll be right out," I reply with false brightness before lowering my voice to a whisper. "You think they heard me?"

"Seriously?" He stands, a smug grin on his face. "They heard you in the Bronx, Bris."

This isn't happening. If I pretend long enough that they did not just hear me screaming my brains out mid-orgasm, maybe it will become reality, replacing this disaster where I'm still shuddering from coming hard as fuck on a stranger's porcelain sink.

"We should get out there." Grip grabs the knob.

"Wait." I clutch his arm and hiss. I can't stop hissing because they've heard enough and anything above a hiss would only tell them more. "You've got . . . you need to . . ."

I pantomime rinsing my face off, furious when he tilts his head in confusion.

"You are not going out there wearing . . . *me* . . . all over your face," I whisper fiercely. "I'll go first. You . . ."

I motion between the faucet and his amused expression. I reach for my panties, but he holds them over his head, out of my reach, and then shoves them into a pocket of the jeans resting low on his hips.

"I hate you," I growl.

"Yeah, it sounded like it."

He has the audacity to smirk, and it's so damn sexy I'm tempted to hop back up on that sink. Instead, I draw a deep breath, reaching for the breeding my parents paid so much for, and open the door. I want to sink through the buffed-to-high-shine hardwood floors when I see a third person has joined Charm and Bridget. Apparently, Mrs. O'Malley arrived while Grip and I were indisposed. Bridget looks uncomfortable and slightly shocked. Charm looks amused and slightly jealous. She introduces me to Esther O'Malley.

The powder room door opens behind us and Grip steps out, turning his smile up to full wattage. Charm practically swoons.

"You must be Mrs. O'Malley," he says, reaching for Esther's hand. "I'm Marlon. You have a beautiful home."

"It really is," I agree. If he can recover smoothly and be all normal, so can I. "We were just admiring the powder room."

Abort mission.

Why did I remind them about the powder room? But I can't stop. My mouth runs ahead of my good sense.

"And noticing the, um . . ." What was I noticing other than Grip's head between my legs? "The wallpaper."

"Wallpaper?" Mrs. O'Malley's thick, dark brows pull center. "There's no wallpaper in there."

"Exactly," I rush to say. "I told Grip, I said, Grip . . . um, Marlon, I'm so glad they didn't use wallpaper in here."

"She did. That's what she said." Grip nods with great gravity. "What color would you call that paint, though, honey?"

The polite smile freezes on my face, and my eyes jerk to find his. He's laughing at me. His mouth is a flat line, but those eyes are *a-live* with laughing at me.

"Oh . . . gosh, well, it's such a . . . such a . . . rich color," I stammer. I'm not a stammer-er, but it's not every day I have an all-out orgasm within ear-shot of a little old Jewish lady with an Irish last name. "I'd call it . . . well . . ."

"White?" Mrs. O'Malley offers helpfully.

Damn. White. I didn't exactly take note of the walls when were in there.

"But it's such a rich white," I say, forcing my lips to stay curved.

"Well, this *is* Tribeca," Grip deadpans. "There's bound to be a lot of rich whites."

An uncertain silence blossoms among us, one of those spaces where you're not sure if it's safe to laugh or if things just got really awkward. And then the most unexpected thing happens.

Mrs. O'Malley laughs—gut-busting, bend-at-the-waist, wiping-tears laughs. It's a hearty sound, full of life. Chuckling, she links her arm through my boyfriend's and starts walking off to show him the place. I'm still standing there getting my shit together as their voices mingle down the hall, and then a goofy grin finally finds its way to my face. I knew I liked this place. Anyone who laughs like that knows how to make a home.

Charm and I pull up the rear, with Bridget, Grip, and Esther ahead of us.

"Bristol," Charm whispers. "You were right." "About what?" I ask cautiously.

"That time we had that threesome with Bumpy Dick"—a skanky smirk slides onto Charm's lips—"you definitely didn't sound like *that*."

Six

Grip

"**Y**OU CAN'T KEEP YOUR HANDS OFF HER, CAN YOU?"

Esther O'Malley studies me with a knowing grin. I don't want to grin back. I should be embarrassed that this nice old lady just heard Bristol screaming her head off, but it's hard to find the shame with Mrs. O'Malley grinning at me like a Cheshire cat.

"Um, no, ma'am." I chuckle and try to look chagrined. "We haven't seen each other in a couple of weeks, and I missed her. Sorry about earlier. That was ..."

Remarkable. Earth-shattering. World-rocking.

"Unacceptable," I say instead.

"Don't apologize. She's a beautiful girl." Esther glances over her shoulder at Bristol and Charm bringing up the rear. Bristol splits a glance between Esther and me with bright red cheeks. I've seen that girl blush more lately than I can ever remember.

"That she is," I agree.

Mrs. O'Malley leads me out and into an enclosed porch of sorts that looks like it might have been a greenhouse at some point.

"Are you two married?" she asks.

"Is that a condition for the lease?" I frown because I really love this place, more than any of the others Bristol sent pictures of this week while I was in Europe doing shows.

"Oh, no." Mrs. O'Malley releases another one of those robust laughs. "Just curious."

"We're not married." I pause to offer a one-sided grin. "Yet."

"Engaged?" Her brows climb into silver-streaked bangs. "Not yet."

"What are you waiting for? Someone else to snatch her up?"

Even as a joke, that idea feels like a set of jagged fangs tearing through the muscles in my stomach, though I know it would never happen. I know she'll never be anyone else's.

"That's not even . . ." I clear my throat. "No, I'm just waiting for the right time. There's so much transition right now, so much going on. I just . . ."

I have no idea why I'm telling a complete stranger all of this, but there's something about this lady. Ever since she busted out laughing over my joke and took my arm, a rapport has been building between us.

"I just want it to be right," I finish.

Bristol, Charm, and her mother join us in the greenhouse before Mrs. O'Malley can respond. Bristol makes her way over and slips her hand into mine while the other ladies converse about the latest gossip in the city.

I assume Bristol is over her embarrassment, but I still bend to whisper, "You okay?"

I linger behind her ear, inhaling the mingled smells of her hair and perfume, heated by her pulse.

"Yeah." She glances at Mrs. O'Malley still chatting with Bridget and Charm. "I owe you for that nasty trick you played on me. 'What color would you call that, honey?'" she mimics.

"Your face." I drop my head into the curve of her neck and chuckle. "Classic. 'Such a rich white.'"

"Asshole." When she draws back, the affection in her eyes and the smile on her face remove any sting. "Do you like this place?" "My favorite so far, by a lot."

"I don't know." A tiny grin teases the corners of her lips. "We could always go to my old stomping grounds, the Upper East Side."

"I told you it's too bougie." I laugh because we've already had this debate.

"Is bougie anything like siditty? You called me that once."

"That's because you *were* siditty." I dodge her small fist when it comes toward my chest. "And yes, kind of like that."

"But it costs just as much to live in Tribeca as it does there."

"Yeah, but Jay-Z lives here."

We both laugh at the ridiculousness of that statement.

"I really like this." Bristol studies the outdoor porch with the comfortable couches and the table set for two in the far corner. "It reminds me of our roof at home."

"Be a great place to watch the sun set," I say. "Or snow fall. You know I've never seen snow fall?"

Bristol turns stunned eyes up to me.

"Are you kidding? You've never seen snow? How is that possible?"

"I've seen snow on the ground, but never falling." I shrug. "I'm a Cali guy. We never had snow falling in LA. When my mom sent to me to Chicago that year the violence was off the chain in my neighborhood, it was summer, and any time I've seen snow, it was after the fact. I just want to catch Mother Nature in the act, see it coming down."

I glance around the renovated space that oozes charm and intimacy.

"This would be a great place to watch snow fall."

"Yeah, this is a beautiful space," Bristol agrees. "The whole apartment is really, and there's a suite on the other side for Amir."

I slant her a disbelieving glance and a quick frown.

"What the hell makes you think Amir's coming with us to New York?"

"Well, I *will* be away some, and you need protection."

Irritation rises as it usually does when someone implies that I can't take care of myself—something I've been doing all my life in rougher neighborhoods than Tribeca and SoHo.

"He doesn't need to," I say. "If I have an event or something, he can fly in, but I don't need him around the clock like some shadow."

"Grip, you're not just a local guy who made good and can—"

"I don't want that, Bris," I cut in, softening my voice when it comes out too harsh. "I said I can take care of myself. You think Amir's going to walk me to school every day? Sit in class and make sure no one bullies me? What the hell?"

"Don't be ridiculous." Exasperation pinches Bristol's lips together. "Your profile—"

"Let's not do this right now. I don't want to talk about my profile or my security detail."

I glance at Charm sitting on one of the couches, typing rapidly on her phone.

"And I sure as hell don't want to talk about a book deal." I interlace my fingers with Bristol's, tugging her close until I can see the onyx starburst in her silvery eyes. "Don't be my manager for a minute. We're about to live together, move across the country together. This is a big step for us. Let's enjoy it like any other couple taking a big step."

She blinks up at me, a small breath shuddering past her lips. I cup her neck, spearing my fingers into her hair, and have to remind myself there are other people in the room.

"Can we just do that?" Emotion makes my voice husky as the truth of my words sinks in. "These last two weeks away from you reminded me how much I hated being apart when I was on tour this summer and you stayed in LA."

She nods and squeezes my hand.

"You uprooting your life to come with me here to New York, it humbles me, Bris." I swallow the warm knot in my throat. "Honestly, if you hadn't agreed to come, I might not have pursued it and would have just let this opportunity go."

"I know." Her eyes are clear, completely at peace about her decision, about her sacrifice. "And I would hate being the reason you didn't come here for this."

I don't care that we aren't alone. I don't care that they already heard Bris screaming with my head between her legs. Let them damn well think what they like. I brush our lips together, running my tongue into the corners of her mouth, kissing her with all the tenderness she inspires inside of me, like no one ever has before.

"Don't stop knowing me better than everyone else does," I say between kisses.

It's our greatest intimacy, the way she knows me, accepts me. This is as intimate as when I'm inside her. It's a closeness that goes beyond bodies.

"I'm trying." She glances down at the flagstone floor.

"You don't have to try. You just know me."

"Well, you're changing, evolving ... coming into yourself, into your convictions." She lays one hand against my jaw. "It's awesome."

I don't get the chance to probe further because Mrs. O'Malley joins us, serving us both warm helpings of her smile.

"You two remind me so much of Patrick and me," she says. "We should have been oil and water—me, the reserved only child from a good Jewish family, and Patrick, so loud and boisterous from his Roman Catholic clan of brothers and sisters. Neither of our families were thrilled about us being together."

Her assessing glance bounces between Bristol's face and mine, and then drifts down to our joined hands.

"We didn't care." Her shoulders lift as if to say *c'est la vie.* "We knew. We loved. We did what we wanted to do."

She casts a wistful look around the enclosed patio. "This place, our home, was our last project together."

"Project?" Bristol asks.

"Yes, I was a designer and he was an architect." She laughs quietly as if at a memory just for her. "We moved here when prices were much lower. Best investment we ever made."

"So you designed and decorated this place?" I ask. It's gorgeous and modern; I never would have imagined the owners designed it themselves.

"We did. We even gutted this rooftop greenhouse and made it more functional." She leans into us, lowers her voice, and points one bony finger up. "We replaced all the glass, tinted—you can see out, but no one can see in. Comes in handy." She waggles her brows. "I'm sure you can guess why we did that considering your time studying the paint in the powder room earlier."

Something between a horrified gasp and surprised laughter pops out of Bristol's mouth at Mrs. O'Malley's boldness. I've already seen this side of the roguish old lady, so my reaction is a little milder than Bristol's. She ignores Bristol's embarrassed response and waves her hand toward the table in the corner.

"We'd have our evening meals there with candles and the view of the city." A breathy laugh. "We'd dance out here for the longest time, song after song, and then we'd ..."

Her words wait on her lips while she swallows, a telling blush rising on the parchment skin of her cheeks.

"Those were good times," she says, her voice softer, reflective.

"We love this place, Mrs. O'Malley." Bristol's voice is quiet and her eyes careful at the obvious emotion in the older woman. "We'd love to lease it, if you'd accept our offer, and we'd love to meet Mr. O'Malley."

"That won't be possible." Tears well in Mrs. O'Malley's eyes before she blinks and swipes ruthlessly at her wet lashes. "He's ... in a facility in Connecticut. Alzheimer's."

Time freezes, and even Bristol's fingers in mine feel cold, affected by the frigid stasis. Pain saturates Mrs. O'Malley's eyes again.

"He chose the facility before ..." She clears her throat. "Before he couldn't make those choices for himself anymore. I have an apartment near him, so that's why we're leasing our home."

Fond memories collect in the watery eyes cataloguing the overstuffed outdoor furniture, the small dining table, the plants lining the periphery of the space.

"I can't bear to sell it yet." The shaky line of her mouth firms, and obstinacy overtakes any sign of weakness. "And I insist on it remaining just as it is, at least until he's …"

My hand tightens around Bristol's as Mrs. O'Malley struggles with the word she doesn't say aloud but that still intrudes on her stubborn silence.

Gone. Once he's gone.

"I'm so sorry." Bristol touches her hand. "How long have you been together?"

The pain shifts on Mrs. O'Malley's face, making room for something younger, fresher, an echo of past hope.

"Fifty years." She laughs, passing a glance between my face and Bristol's. "Longer than you've been alive. I knew he was it for me the first day I met him, and he knew, too. We were married a month later."

"That's beautiful." Bristol leans into me a little deeper, a soft smile on her lips. The tightness of Mrs. O'Malley's expression eases and she looks back to me.

"Don't waste time when you know it's real," she says.

I think back to our discussion before Bristol joined us. There's nothing stopping me from asking Bristol to marry me, certainly no obstacle in my heart. We haven't been together that long, but I don't care about that. I knew Bristol was the one years before she even gave me a shot.

"Fifty years." Mrs. O'Malley lowers her lashes, blinking rapidly. "And it still isn't enough. Anything that ended would never be enough for a love like ours. A love like ours is only satisfied by forever."

She looks back up with eyes still shadowed by sadness, but direct and sure.

"Don't feel sorry for us, for me," Mrs. O'Malley says. "We have a great love. Emotion tells you about love, but hard times prove it. How can you know something is great unless it's tested? Until then, it's just an assumption. It's a question, but life has a way of answering."

I'm still absorbing the things she said, considering the great love I feel for Bristol. I wonder when ours will be tested, but I have no doubt we can withstand anything life throws at us.

"So, what do we think?" Bridget triangulates a glance between Bristol, Mrs. O'Malley, and me. "You like it?"

Bristol and I exchange a quick look and an almost indiscernible nod before I speak up.

"We love the place." I direct my words to the sweet Jewish lady with the Irish last name and naughty smile. "What do you say, Mrs. O'Malley?"

"I think we have a deal." The wicked glint in Mrs. O'Malley's eyes should warn me she's up to no good. "Just remember that I want the house to remain as it is, so I hope you like the way it's decorated. At least we already know Bristol likes the powder room."

I want to keep her around just to make Bristol blush.

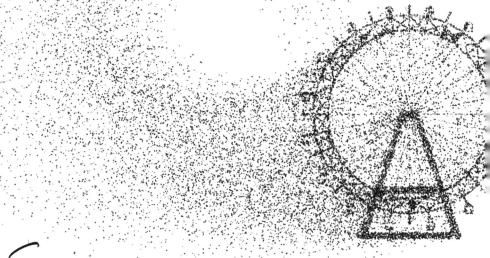

Seven

Bristol

"THIS WILL GO BETTER THAN I THINK IT WILL."

I've recited this mantra to myself all morning, hoping it's like one of those affirmations you just keep putting into the universe until it comes true. If that's the case, I'll chant it all the way to Compton for the going away party Grip's mother is hosting for him. I've been back a few times since that first disastrous Sunday dinner, and Ms. James has warmed considerably toward me.

I think she actually likes me now.

Jade, on the other hand, continues to give me a bit of a cold shoulder every time we meet. A few weeks ago, I ran into her at the studio where Grip was recording. He passed some of her songs on to a few artists, and now she's actually writing for several of them. I congratulated her, but she still looked at me like I was something she stepped in—or maybe something she wanted to step *on*, like a bug . . . a white girl bug who has no business being with her cousin. She hasn't said that outright lately, but every roll of her eyes and suck of her teeth tells me she wants to, and Jade isn't one to hold back for long. I just hope that today at this party, when I'm surrounded by strangers and already feeling like I don't fit in, she can refrain from saying what her body finds a dozen other ways to tell me.

"This will go better than I think it will," I say again when the cage door of the elevator lifts on Grip's floor—just in case the universe is listening.

I had an early meeting with an event organizer this morning. Grip hates it when I take meetings on the weekends, but with me leaving for New York soon, I have a lot to get settled in a short amount of time. It was so hard to drag myself out of the warm bed with Grip naked and at half-mast in his sleep. The white sheet, stark against his roasted caramel skin, had dipped so low I could see the muscled slashes at his hips. A little restless when I left the bed, he flipped onto his stomach, and I wanted to lick up the wide smooth expanse of his back, nip the firm rounded cheeks of his ass when the sheet slipped even more, hid even less.

I check my watch to see if we have time to make good on that morning wood he was sporting before we leave for the party, and my key is still in hand when the loft door swings open. The last person I expect to see standing there is Angela Gray.

"Mother?" Surprise quickly congeals into suspicion. "Why are you here?"

Guilt clouds her expression before she reassembles her features into the lovely indifference I've been accustomed to my entire life.

"Just stopping by." She digs around in her bag until she finds her keys.

Grip steps into view just behind her, and I'm distracted by the worry in his eyes.

"What's going on?" I ask him over her shoulder.

"I'll tell you inside." He glances down at my mother. "Thanks for coming by, Angela."

She sketches a curt nod without glancing up at him.

"I'll keep you posted," she says easily before turning her eyes to me. "We need to have lunch before you go to New York, Bristol."

I stiffen at her words. She's already told me what she thinks of me leaving LA to "chase" Grip. Apparently, it's anti-feminist to be with the man you love even when your job allows the flexibility to do so. I thought feminism was supposed to be about the power of our choices, and yet when I choose Grip, when I put him ahead of my career and convenience because I love him, that choice is denigrated. When women truly understand feminism, they see the power of knowing what you want more than anything and pursuing it.

And I want Grip more than anything.

"You *are* still going, right?" she asks when I'm silent.

"Definitely." I cross the threshold and tuck under Grip's arm, pressing into the faded scent of yesterday's cologne and the pure, raw maleness of him. "I'll call about lunch. I have a lot to get done."

She nods and walks over to the elevator, holding my stare until the doors close.

"She'll miss you." Grip kisses my forehead and closes the door. Once we're inside, he cages me against it with his elbows and forearms pressed alongside my head. "That's why she's salty, not any of that pseudo-feminist crap she spouts about you adjusting your plans to come with me."

"Why was she here?" I won't be distracted by the hard body crowding me, by the delicious shape of his shoulders straining against his T-shirt.

"Hmmm?" Grip licks at the curve of my neck and shoulder, his tongue like rough velvet.

"Don't 'hmmm' me, Grip." I slide away from his warm body, putting some space between us. "It's like being in the *Twilight Zone* for me to come home and find you with my mother, so cut the crap. What did she want? Was it about me going to New York?"

I don't wait for his response.

"Dammit." I drop my bag by the couch and flop down, eyes trained on the ceiling. "Why can't she just let me live my life?"

Grip slides his hands into the pockets of the loose lounge pants that hint at the sleek musculature of his legs. He settles on the couch beside me and captures my hand, kissing the knuckles.

"She wasn't here about New York." His words emerge reluctant, low, sober.

I glance at his sharply hewn profile, noting the muscle ticking in his jaw. "What's going on?"

His chest rises and falls with the deep breath he draws and expels before beginning.

"It's Parker."

I only have to hear that bastard's name to feel Parker's fingers probing roughly between my legs again. I chew on my bottom lip and can almost feel the sting of him biting me there, of him making me bleed. I ration a slow breath through my nose, steadying myself as much for Grip's peace of mind as my own pride. I don't want him to worry, though I know him well enough to see concern in his dark eyes already.

"What about him?" I drop my head to Grip's shoulder and wait for his response.

After a beat of silence, he speaks. "He's getting out."

My body tenses involuntarily and I turn my head to search his face. "When?"

He gathers both my hands in his and turns slightly on the couch so he can see me, pushing my hair back and cupping my neck.

"Next week or so." Grip watches me closely. "We knew this would happen, babe. He's got too much money and too many corrupt people in his pocket to hold him for long."

I swallow, my muscles tautened with tension.

"I guess I hoped for a little more time to figure out a plan."

"You ain't figuring out nothing." One brow lifts over Grip's icy glance. "Son of a bitch is handled."

"Handled?" A frown gathers on my face. "Handled how?"

"Apparently, his father has his own plans. He needs Parker free to make some merger happen. Shipping his ass off to Russia."

"Russia? Merger?" I shake my head, but all the pieces still don't make sense. "What the hell are you talking about?"

"Ever heard of SiberTech?"

"Yeah." I nod, mentally rehearsing what I know, trying to make the pieces fit. "Natasha Sukolov's family owns SiberTech. She went to high school with us in New York, but their interests still lie mainly in Russia. What does SiberTech have to do with Parker getting out?"

"They're using a marriage between Parker and Natasha to seal the deal." Grip shrugs. "His dad found the right strings, pulled them, got Parker off."

My fingers clench in my lap, anxiety twisting them. What if Parker comes after Grip again? My mind is already seeking out solutions, loopholes, anything to insulate Grip from whatever Parker might pull.

"Hey." Grip covers my balled fists with one big hand. "He's not touching you."

My eyes fly to meet his. God, we're a pair. We'd both do stupid shit to protect each other. I hadn't thought of myself, only him, and he's only thinking of me.

"We've been in constant communication with Parker's mom. She's pretty badass," Grip says, admiration filtering into his expression. "With her help, we got it all figured out."

"We?" I interject stiffly.

"Yeah, your mother and I," Grip continues smoothly, but no way he doesn't consider how un-cool it was to do all of this without me. "Mrs. Parker assures us her son is no threat. Her husband's sick of cleaning up after him. He's got his foot so far up Parker's ass, he won't piss without it being tracked. Parker will marry this Natasha chick, fly away to Russia, run their business there, and leave us the hell alone."

The tense line of Grip's lips relaxes momentarily.

"And Mrs. Parker's got so much shit on her *husband*, it's in his interest to keep Parker in check. We have layers of protection, babe. We've been monitoring it for a few weeks. Now we know Parker's getting out of prison, but also out of our lives for good."

"Why am I just now hearing about it?" I ask, irritation crowding out concern or even relief. This is all good, but they were meeting without me, discussing something that is completely my business behind my back. "Why was my mother telling you and not me? Talking with you, not me?"

"Because I asked her to." Grip's voice brooks no argument, and the arrogant brow he cocks dares me to say something. He must have forgotten who he's dealing with—I always have something to say.

"You asked her to cut me out of something that so obviously concerns me?"

"I just wanted to know first, Bris." He pulls in that patient breath, the one that says he's preparing himself in case I want to fight. "And see what we were dealing with. I was gonna tell you once everything was settled. Now it's settled."

"But—"

"I just needed to be sure. I wanted to be the first line of defense."

"In this situation or . . . ?" I let my raised eyebrows finish the question.

"In everything," he says decisively. "Do you have any idea how it felt to be locked up knowing you were even considering . . ."

His words thin to nothing, like he can't bring himself to voice what I had planned to go through with. A deep swallow bobs the Adam's apple in his throat.

Yes, I was going to fuck Parker to get Grip out of jail, and I would have done it had he and my mother not intervened. It would have gutted my soul, and maybe I would never have forgiven myself, but if I have to choose between my pride, my supposed virtue, and Grip's freedom, well that's not a choice at all.

"Don't think I'll let you wrap me in cotton, Grip," I assert. "I can take care of myself."

A scowl contracts the sharp lines of Grip's face.

"Fucking Parker for all the world to see? That's how you would take care of yourself? And you think I'd want you to do something like that to protect *me*?"

He pulls away to fold his arms across his chest, the muscles straining against the sleeves of his plain white T-shirt. I feel the distance instantly, not just between our bodies, but separating our perspectives. This is a fight we never had. We talked some after he left jail, but we were just so relieved to get rid of Parker, too happy to have dodged the bullet and we didn't air this. Now it's in the air, and it's a cold front that makes me shiver.

"I didn't have a lot of options." I lay my palms flat against my bare legs. "I won't apologize for being willing to do whatever it took to protect you."

"Then don't ask me to apologize for doing the same. Look, just be glad it's handled. It's over." He stands and heads toward the stairs. "I'm gonna shower."

"We aren't done." I rush up the steps, close on his heels.

"Bris, later. We don't want to be late for our own party."

Your party. I don't correct him, but we both know this party could go on without me. There are probably several people there who wish Grip *would* go on without me.

He grabs his T-shirt from the back and yanks it over his head, tossing it into the bathroom hamper. My steps stutter to a halt. My eyes cling to his skin, stretched like dark velvet over the balletic play of muscles in his back. He shucks the bottoms and drops those in the hamper, too, unaware that my mouth has gone dry.

I know I had a point, but the flare of his powerful thighs, the tight curve of his ass from a tapered waist—it scrambles my thoughts. When he turns to the side to start the shower, his dick juts from the flat, ridged topography of chest and abs. I lick my lips, lips that have more than once been doused with the spicy-sweet taste of him in my mouth.

Why is he so damn fine? It's not fair.

"It's not fair," I mumble faintly. That jars me, reminds me I wasn't done with this argument. "Parker manipulated *me*, Grip. It wasn't fair to keep me out of it, and I want to make sure you don't do this again."

"Fuck fair." Grip steps into the shower. "I don't care if it's fair—I care if you're safe. We can fight about this every day if you want. You aren't leaving me over it, and I'm not leaving you, so what the fuck ever. Agree to disagree. I'm done talking about it, Bris."

With that, he turns his back to me, reaching for the shower gel.

He's right. I'm not leaving him over it, but I don't want to resent him. I want to trust him. I want him to trust me. That's what we have, and I won't let him ruin it with his irrational overprotectiveness.

I stand at the shower threshold and prop my shoulder against the wall. His head snaps around, the dark eyes narrowed and connecting with mine. He's braced for a fight I'm not giving him.

"Thank you," I say, wanting to ease things between us, even though it probably won't be our last clash over this issue.

Grip's wide palms slow in soaping his biceps. The tight line of his mouth loosens some and he sighs.

"Don't thank me." He braces one hand in front of him against the tile, eyes dropped to the water rushing down the drain. "It's my responsibility to take care of you."

He slants a look at me through the steam, a groove between his thick brows.

"That's all I want, Bris." He pierces me with the intensity of his eyes. "I want you safe. I didn't get the chance to personally protect you before. All I'm asking is that you let me do it now. I didn't want you anywhere near that motherfucker, and now you won't be."

Anger, concern, and sincerity knot in his deep voice, as tangled as the emotions twisting in my belly and coiling up tightly in my chest. Even when I'm driving him crazy, there's a fathomless affection for me in his eyes. It was there all those years when he was fucking other people and I was doing the same. It's there now, as clear to me as the water flowing in rivulets down the shower door.

There's something helpless about truly being in love, the kind of love they write songs about, that inspires poetry and launches ships and wreaks havoc. It leaves you slightly off balance, controlling when you mean to cherish, smothering when you mean to hold close. Maybe it takes a while to find the *just right*. I saw that in Rhyson when he and Kai first got together, and now I see it in Grip, too.

Hell, if I'm honest, I see it in myself.

Grip loves me desperately. I recognize that in him because it mirrors my own heart. I love him desperately enough to debase myself with Parker in broad daylight if that was what it had taken. How can I be angry at Grip for reciprocating that love? For feeling as helpless and off kilter as I do sometimes?

"Okay, Grip." I draw a deep breath that's scented and steamy from the shower. "I'll give you this one, but you need to give me something, too."

He ducks his head under the water streaming over him, licking along that body the way I want to.

"This isn't a negotiation. I will protect you every time as I see fit," he says. "But what do you *think* you want?"

"Amir moves to New York with us."

"Hell no." He glowers at me. "I don't need him."

"And I didn't need you running interference with Parker, but I understand why you did that. For your own peace of mind. I need Amir in New York with you for mine."

He's quiet, staring at the tiles under his feet for a few seconds. "Grip, I know you think you're all straight outta Compton . . ." I pause for his chuckle, which I know is coming. "But you're famous now—like really famous, and you cannot assume everyone has good intentions."

"I know that, but I can take care of myself." He looks at me, the conflict of wanting to please me and needing to maintain his pride clear on his face. "I always have."

"Well you haven't always been this version of yourself," I counter. "And you'll be in situations with factors you can't control all the time. You need another set of eyes, someone you can trust."

He considers me, the stubbornness in his eyes yielding a little. "Rhyson's had stalkers," I remind him. "And he always resisted having a lot of security, but that taught him how vulnerable he is because of what he's chosen to do. Now that he has Kai and Aria, security is tight and everywhere all the time."

Grip just nods.

"Doing this for a living, it makes the stakes high," I say. "But when you love someone, it raises them even more. You have more to lose, and I don't want to lose you, Grip."

Just the thought of something happening to him is like a hot poker through my heart. I know he can see the fear in my eyes. I don't even try to hide it, and I am not above exploiting his love for me to get what I want it if means keeping him safe.

"Besides," I say, struck with sudden inspiration I can't believe I didn't use earlier. "If Amir is there protecting you, he's there to protect me, too, right?"

Grip's eyes narrow and his hands go still as he considers this.

Bingo.

"Okay, he can come," he finally says, but sets his face in stone. "But no way is he living in the same apartment. I don't care how many floors it's got."

"I thought you might say that, which is why I already called about another apartment up for lease in the building."

"You already . . ." He shakes his head, exasperation and grudging admiration in his eyes. "Okay, Bris."

I turn to go before I feel less magnanimous, glad I've found at least enough peace with the situation not to ruin what was already going to be a difficult day.

"We're good?" he asks, soaping the heavier muscles of his shoulders and his ink-splattered arms. Water skids over his chest and between the stacks of muscled abs. A trail of suds migrates south, catching in the hair nesting around his cock.

I lick suddenly dry lips and subtly squeeze my thighs together to suppress the involuntary pussy clench the sight of him incites. While I was negotiating, I could block out the absolute perfection of him, but now I can't look away from the wide head that still feels like it's splitting me open every time even after months together. I don't know if my body will ever fully adjust—I hope not, because the almost-too-much-ness reflects my emotions, like this love is almost too much, straining the seams of my heart until I think I may burst from what I feel.

"Yeah . . ." I clear the huskiness—and hussy-ness—from my voice and try again. "Yeah, we're good."

A strong hand vises my wrist and tugs me forward until I'm just beyond the shower threshold, close enough for steam to slip under my dress, but not close enough to get wet—except I am wet. I may not be in the shower, but my panties are soaked. Then it only gets worse when, with his other hand, he strokes himself languorously, lazy flicks of his wrist that lengthen him into a thickly veined, rigid column.

"Bristol."

My name on his lips pulls my attention from the steady pull between his thighs to the dark stare trained on me, his eyes narrowed with water droplets clinging to the thick lashes tangled at the corners.

"Tell me what you want."

Those are my words, the ones I used to probe about New York. I knew what he wanted then, and he knows what I want now. I grit my teeth against all my wanton urges, but the words spill out.

"You." My breath comes short and quick. "I want you."

In a quick motion, he jerks me into the shower, fully clothed. My dress plasters my skin, and water seeps into my shoes. It will infuriate me later that he has ruined a perfectly good pair of Jimmy Choos.

Eight

Bristol

"**Y**OU DID THIS ON PURPOSE."

I flip down the visor mirror to study the bright red mark on my neck. I should have left that bathroom, but no, I just couldn't resist. Grip's shower ended like so many do—with me up against the wall.

Grip lets out a salacious chuckle from the driver's seat. He's one of the few people allowed to drive my car, and as he navigates back roads on our way to his mother's house, I'm glad I trust him to do it. As nervous as I am, I'd probably run off the road.

"So, you think in the middle of shower sex, I had the presence of mind to give you a hickey?" Grip flicks me a disbelieving glance. "Just to embarrass you at my mom's house?"

"Yes, I absolutely do, because you're always looking for ways to embarrass me."

"Babe, I don't even know if the sky is blue when I'm inside you."

"You're so full of shit." My laugh takes flight on the wind with the top down. "Your sweet talk doesn't work on me."

His knowing look picks my bravado apart, because his sweet talk totally works on me and he knows it.

"As if I'm not nervous enough." I play with the cuff of my linen shorts, focusing on that small movement instead of the next few hours meeting Grip's friends and family. I've met some here and there over the last few months, of course, but with Grip on tour all summer, not many.

"Don't be nervous." Grip's frown comes quickly now that he sees I'm legitimately not looking forward to this. "Amir will be there, and Shon. You know them and they love you, and my mom is asking about swirl grandbabies every time we talk, so I'm pretty sure you've won her over. Once we procreate, you'll have her eating from the palm of your hand."

"Swirl . . . wait, what? Oh, my God." I'm not sure if my stomach flips over inside because of his mother's outrageousness or at the thought of having Grip's kids. I never saw myself as maternal—like, *at all*—but imagining myself pregnant with Grip's child is a different matter altogether. I'm assaulted with images and feelings better examined alone than when I'm heading into what feels like social battle.

"Everybody at this party," Grip says, "they're guys I grew up with, neighborhood ladies who whooped my ass when I was a snot-nosed kid, people from Ma's church."

"Church?" My hand flies to my neck to cover the bite marring my skin. "Oh, God."

"It'll be fine." He grabs my hand from my lap and kisses my fingers, not taking his eyes from the road.

"I want them to like me," I say. That's hard to admit because I can count on one hand the people I want to like me, and it's been that way all my life. I was born with a limited amount of fucks, but all of a sudden I need the approval of Ms. James and this whole group of nameless, faceless people who may hold the same views as Jade.

Ugh, Jade.

"Will Jade be there?" I ask, braced for the affirmative.

"Probably." Grip's shoulders lift and fall, quick and careless. "Look, Jade gets on board with us, or she doesn't. I don't give a damn."

He *says* that, but I know how happy it made him to restore their relationship, and the last thing I want is to be the reason it falls apart again. I'm still considering that when we pull up to the house where Grip grew up. The narrow street is lined with cars, trucks, bikes—everything from the infamous Impala to three-wheelers.

Some mix of nerves, dread, and anticipation climbs up to lodge in my throat where I can't gather enough breath. This is ridiculous. I run a record label. I make stars for a living, literally pluck people from obscurity and do whatever it takes to propel them into planetary stardom, from no-name to household name in the manner of an album release—and yet a house full of strangers on this crowded Compton street fills me with trepidation.

But it's not them. It's *him.*

Grip opens my door, the color of his skin even richer against the pink polo shirt he's wearing with army green cargo shorts. His eyes are set to simmer as he peers down at me in the passenger seat. He leans down and takes my lips between his softly, tenderly, like I'm the most precious thing in his world. His eyes say that, and he tells me all the time. He's the reason for my trepidation. Relationships, friendships—especially longstanding ones, familial ones—mean the world to him.

Would he always put me first? I know he would.

Would it hurt him if he had to make those choices?

I know it would, and part of loving someone is doing everything in your power to make sure they don't hurt.

There's barely room to walk in the driveway with all the cars slotted into the tight space. Grip weaves his way between the vehicles, single-filing us in the narrow passages, his hand wrapped reassuringly around mine. The sounds flooding Ms. James' stamp-size front porch—'90s Snoop Dogg, raucous laughter, and dozens of voices clamoring to talk over each other—reach us before he opens the screen door.

There is what must be a code-breaking number of people squeezed into the front room, running over into the hall, and presumably spilling into the back yard. The smell of grilled meat wafts past my nose, joining a tangle of other sensations. The whir of a fan oscillating in the corner of the crowded living room. The rich palette of colors—skin tones ranging from gold to bronze to copper, nutmeg to hazelnut to walnut, but none that match my skin, barely sun-kissed, stark and pale among the rich range of pigmentation.

They greet Grip, enthusiasm and undeniable pride in their words and the affectionate embraces they offer him. When their eyes latch onto me, though, they hold questions, speculation. They don't know me. They aren't sure I can be trusted with the boy they watched grow up and do better than most ever imagined anyone from this neighborhood could. I swallow my discomfort, determined to fit in, determined to shake off my sense of displacement and get to know the people Grip loves, the ones who obviously love him.

"Bristol, hey!"

I turn toward the familiar voice in the crowd, hoping there's a familiar face to go with it. I'm grateful to see Shondra, Amir's longtime crush and maybe now girlfriend.

"Shon, hi." I reach for her like a lifeline, accepting the hug she folds me into.

"You got this girl," she whispers, a genuine smile spread across her pretty face. "These folks ain't nothing to be scared of."

Shon bore witness to the carnage of confrontation between Jade, Ms. James, and me the first time I was here. She spoke up for us, for Grip and me, and I'll never forget that.

"What are you whispering about, Shon?" Grip asks, pulling her into a tight hug. "No, don't tell me. I probably don't wanna know. Where's your boy?"

"And what boy would that be?" Shon lifts her brows in challenge.

"Whoa." Grip's grin turns into a full-bodied laugh. "You got more than one? Does Amir know?"

"Gotta keep him on his toes," she says with an audacious wink. "He's out back playing bones and *losing*."

"I've never seen Amir win at dominoes. I might whoop his ass in Spades later, too." Grip laughs, but is distracted when a gorgeous girl, no higher than his breastbone, walks up and places her hand on his arm, an invitation stamped clearly on her heart-shaped face.

"Grip, hey baby," she purrs, her wide eyes and the dark hair curling around her shoulders a seduction. "Welcome home."

My discomfort and nervousness dissipate at the sight of this beautiful woman with her richly golden skin practically petting my boyfriend. I'm standing right here. He's holding my hand. We're obviously together. I suppress the possessive growl curling at the base of my throat; better to let Grip handle it instead of behaving unreasonably and alienating people any more than I have to.

"Sierra, hey." Grip deliberately lifts her tiny hand from his arm. "It's been a minute. I heard you opened that shop down off Central Avenue. Congratulations."

"Same to you." She tips her head back, the long hair winding down her spine and nearly touching her curvy backside. "You done good. Come a long way since we snuck behind the bleachers at football games."

Her sultry laugh grates on my nerves, and my fingers tighten around Grip's in a warning. If he doesn't back this bitch up, I will.

"Uh . . . yeah. That *was* a long time ago." Grip clears his throat and pulls me forward. "I don't think you've met my girlfriend Bristol."

Sierra's subtly scornful glance starts at my wedge-heeled espadrilles, crawls over my legs in mint green mini shorts, gains momentum when she searches my face, and finally is downright rude by the time she reaches the artfully messy bun I gathered my hair into.

Fuck. Her.

"Hi." I extend my hand and smile politely. "Nice to meet you."

She stares at my hand like it's palsied for a moment too long before taking it between her French manicure-tipped fingers.

"I guess you'll miss Grip when he moves to New York," she says, watching for my response.

"Not really, since I'm moving with him." I widen my eyes innocently. "Grip says this is my going away party, too, so thank you for coming."

Grip catches his half cough, half chuckle in a fist at his mouth.

"It was good seeing you again, Sierra," he says neutrally. "Good luck."

"Well maybe we could—" she starts.

"Sierra, your sister's looking for you out back," Ms. James interrupts, suddenly appearing at my side.

"But I was just—"

"I know, baby." Ms. James turns Sierra by one slim shoulder toward the back yard. "But she said something 'bout potato salad. Child, you better get out there. We *need* that potato salad."

Ms. James waits for the tiny thorn in my side to get out of earshot.

"She always was a fast tail girl." She tsks and shakes her head, her neat dreadlocks swooshing with the motion. "Been after my boy since training bra days. She don't ever give up. Marlon, why you always late? You *stay* on CP time. You can take the boy out the hood, but you can't take the hood out the boy. Bristol, come to this kitchen and help me with these greens."

And she's gone.

In a flurry of lightning-strike words, affectionate admonishments, and dreadlocks, she's gone, plowing her way through the knot of bodies slowly realizing Grip has arrived and lining up to greet him. At the threshold of her neat kitchen, she turns, one brow lifting and reminding me of her son.

"You coming?" She rests a fist on one slim cocked hip. "These greens won't cook themselves."

Grip widens his eyes meaningfully and cocks his head for me to follow his mother.

"Don't shoo me," I mutter, untangling our fingers. I can't hold back a smile, though, over what just happened. Ms. James put that "fast tail" girl in her place and chose *me*—I mean, she just chose me for collard greens, but I'll take it.

"Hey, wait." Grip tugs me back into his hard body, one hand palming the small of my back. He squats enough to kiss my nose then settles his lips over mine, lingering and taking his time to stake a claim on my mouth. "Don't be too long. I want everybody to meet my girl."

Pleasure blossoms inside me. I hope when we're half blind and soaking each other's dentures, he'll still call me his girl. I'm feeling so good, even the weight of many pairs of eyes—curious, speculative, assuming—bearing down on my shoulders and back the whole way up the short hallway leading to the kitchen can't short-circuit my grin.

They can't, but Jade does as soon as I see her leaning against the kitchen counter. Our eyes clash and our smiles fade in sync. Her hair is neatly braided into rows. The big doe eyes narrow on my face, and she doesn't try to hide her irritation when she tosses her ever-present Raiders cap onto the counter.

"Hey Jade." I brighten my voice, hoping the undercurrents that always run through our interactions won't be as strong today.

"What's up?" she responds dispassionately, not trying as hard. Apparently, I'm much better at faking than Jade is . . . or maybe I just care more.

"Put this on." Ms. James passes me a red apron with *Thug Life* printed on the front. Her full lips tip into a smile.

"That was Marlon's idea of a joke one Christmas. Just put it on so your pretty outfit won't get wet."

"Wet?" I tie the apron over my clothes and await further instructions. "You wanted me to help cook the collard greens, right?"

I try not to sound too eager. My heart should not skip a beat at the prospect of finally learning the secret to the greens she makes for Grip.

But it does.

"Oh, no, little girl." Ms. James pats my shoulder. "You ain't ready for heat yet. You're on wash duty this first time."

"Excuse me?" I glance at Jade for a clue about what wash duty means, but she's grinning down at her phone, fingers flying furiously over the keys. "Wash duty?"

Ms. James hefts several bags of greens onto the counter.

"Wash all these." She grabs a knife, using it to wave me closer. "Watch me now. You gotta take the leaves off the stalk just like this."

She demonstrates, cutting the leaves away and discarding the center stalk while I stare at the massive pile of greens.

"And *then* I get to cook them?" I ask tentatively.

"No, baby. You ain't graduated to cooking yet. Today your lane is just washing." She heads for the door without looking back. "Stay in your lane. I'll be back in a few minutes. Let me go check on this grill—you know Amir is out here grilling these links, and ain't no telling what he's messing up."

She blows out of the kitchen as swiftly as she blew into it, and in her wake, I stand clutching the knife in one hand and a bushel of greens in the other. I really wanted to cook, but sense that she's testing me. I've never met a test I couldn't pass, and this one—though I don't fully comprehend the point of it—will be no different.

While Jade continues texting, laughing under her breath intermittently, I set myself to methodically washing and cutting. The muted sounds of laughter and conversation from the living room along with the shouts of men playing dominoes in the backyard settle my nerves. I'm here, but not here. Nothing is expected of me for a few minutes. It gives me time to collect myself, and maybe that's what Ms. James wanted to happen. Maybe she saw past my serene façade to the uncertain girl floundering inside and knew I needed a few minutes alone.

Well, alone with Jade, who wears a huge grin and keeps texting as if I'm not in the room. I clear my throat to remind her I'm here and ready to be her friend. I'm an idiot. I should be glad she's not castigating me or looking at me like I'm pocket lint, but instead I'm drawing her attention. Why? Because though she's a bitch, Grip loves her. I know he wants her in his life, which means she'll have to be in my life, and I'll have to be in hers.

Thus, the trying so hard.

"Someone special?" I ask, looking up from the greens with what I hope is a natural smile.

Jade's answer is a cocked brow and dead eyes. "Huh?" she asks, voice flat. "What'd you say to me?"

"Um . . . I just saw you texting and smiling and thought maybe . . . there's a guy or—"

"I don't do dick."

My hands freeze under the stream of cold water. I can't keep my foot out of my mouth around this girl. Did Grip *tell* me she was a lesbian and I forgot?

"Oh, that's fine." I shrug and keep smiling. "I mean, I'm fine with that."

"Glad I have your permission to fuck who I want." She rolls her eyes like I'm stupid, and I feel stupid most of the time when I'm talking to her. I know people. I *get* people, I figure them out. It's part of my job to understand and charm them and, well, it sounds bad, but use them to get what I need for my artists. But, I can't understand Jade, and I sure as hell can't charm her.

"I didn't mean it that way, Jade. I just find myself grinning like an idiot when I'm texting Grip and thought—"

"So now I'm an idiot?"

I toss a leaf into the sink, frustration making my movements jerky.

"Would you stop picking apart everything I say?" I draw a calming breath in through my nose and push it out through my mouth. "I'm trying to make conversation, that's all."

The slow, sweet smile that slides onto Jade's face is incongruous and should be my first clue that she's up to tearing me apart.

"Okay. Let's make conversation, Bristol." She straightens from the counter and crosses over to stand beside me. "Since you all in my grill and up in my business, I'll tell you who I'm texting."

She pauses, eyes riveted to my face for my response. I school my features and won't give her one.

"It's Qwest."

That name should not give me heartburn, but every time I hear it, it's like a lit cigarette behind my ribs. Maybe it was seeing Qwest with Grip all those weeks and knowing he was fucking her, fearing that she was fucking his feelings for me right out and I would be left lonely and still in love with him. Maybe it was Black Twitter rallying behind her and turning on me, painting her as the victim and me as the villain. I don't know why I feel this way when I hear Qwest's name, but she is my sore spot, and Jade knows it. She's twisting her knuckle into a bruise on my heart, and even though I was prepared, I know my face doesn't hide it.

"Oh, I didn't know you and Qwest were together." I laugh, trying to make a joke of it . . . a bad, awkward joke, which is the only kind I can seem to manage with Jade.

"Oh, no. Not me and Qwest. She *loves* dick." Cruelty engraves a smile onto Jade's smooth, pretty brown face. "Just ask Grip. He knows."

These are the cleanest greens anyone will ever eat. I'm scrubbing this one leaf mercilessly, almost to the point of translucence, training my eyes on the sink so Jade doesn't gain any ammunition from the hurt I know she would see. All I want is to be this girl's friend, and she can't tolerate five minutes with me. She's carrying on an entire conversation with Qwest while I'm standing right here trying harder than I've ever tried with anyone.

"I meant that I didn't realize you two knew each other," I mumble.

"We didn't really, until recently. I'm writing some stuff for her new album." Her pause fills with anticipation of something I know will be at my expense. "Grip introduced us a few weeks ago."

The knife slips off the stalk, slicing into my finger, matching the tiny nick Jade just made across my heart. It's not a big deal; rationally, I know that. Grip is contractually bound to work on Qwest's next album, writing and producing. Hell, I negotiated the deal, but he wasn't mine then—only he's *always* been mine, even when I didn't claim him, and it screws a wrench through my eye that I'm the one who threw them together, that Qwest knows the weight of his body because of me. That glorious fullness when he swells within me—she's had that. The sweet heat of his panting breath in my ear when he comes—she felt that before I did. I can't ever take that knowledge from her, but I want to strip every memory of him from her mind, body, and heart. So, I know it's not the tiny injuries Jade inflicts now that are at the bottom of my irrational response; it's all my old self-inflicted wounds that haven't quite healed.

"You know it's just a matter of time, right?" Jade tilts her head, considering me. "He's not the first Black man turned out by some white pussy."

"Shut the hell up." I snap my eyes to her face. "Don't talk about us. You have no idea."

"You're just a high to him." Jade's full lips curl around her derision. "And just like any high, he'll come down. You'll wear off once he gets tired of explaining his Blackness and answering your dumb questions. One day he'll want to be understood, not just fucked."

"I do understand him." I'm certain of it, but in a way, she carries the same brand of charisma Grip does, the same confidence that, even twisted around a lie, entices you to believe.

"Just watch him with Qwest the next time they're together," she sneers. "They fit. Everyone sees it except you. She's just waiting for him to wake up from this dream, shake off that jungle fever. Maybe you're a Black man's fantasy, but she's real life, and when it comes down to it, Grip is nothing if not real. Deep down, you know it."

Her lies and speculation circle me like rope, slowly restricting me. For a frozen moment, I can't speak, and even though Grip's love is gospel to me, my religion, my truth, some little voice within me whispers, *What if she's right?*

Jade doesn't say more words. She's quiet, allowing the ones she's already spoken to take root. I know she's hoping she'll get under my skin, but she won't. Even with that tiny granule of doubt, I try not to let her. I'm still staring at the blood surging from the tiny cut on my finger when Grip walks into the kitchen.

"Babe, what'd you do?" He moves my finger under the flow of cold water, concern clumping his brows.

"It's just a cut." I swallow against the unreasonable hurt that he introduced Jade and Qwest.

"Well I don't like any kind of cut on you." His voice admonishes and caresses at once. "Jade, where are the bandages?"

"God, Grip. The girl's fine." Jade huffs an exasperated sigh. "It's not like she's gonna lose a finger."

Grip angles a glance at her, his frown deepening. "Would you just go find a Band-Aid?"

Jade's eyes connect with mine before she shrugs and heads out of the kitchen.

Grip watches the door for a moment, even after Jade leaves, questions queuing up in the eyes he turns back to me.

"She bothering you?" he asks. "I know she's still coming around about us."

Is that what he thinks? Jade shows no sign of coming around any time soon, but even irritated with her, I see the affection, the place she holds in his heart, and I really don't want to come between them—especially not when that relationship is so newly restored.

"No, it's cool. She's . . . just being Jade." I try to free my finger, but he doesn't let me go. "My finger's fine."

"I'll be the judge of when it's fine." He offers a lopsided grin. "And who thought it was a good idea to leave you in the kitchen with a knife?"

I know he's teasing me about my legendary culinary ineptness, but now is not the time. I'm still a little bruised from my conversation with Jade.

"I may not be a great cook, but I'm not a child." I snatch my finger back. "Like Jade said, it's just a cut."

When the words come out harsher than I mean them to, Grip grabs my finger, taking it into the warm silk of his mouth, sucking and running his tongue along the injured groove. Electric current spears me down the middle, landing in my core. He sucks all the oxygen from the room, and my lungs desperately push breath from my chest. He studies me under hooded lids, knowing exactly what he's doing to me.

"Was Jade messing with you?" he asks, his voice husky, but his mouth a firm line. He's abusing the sway he holds over my body. I know it, but he still makes me want to confess. I close my eyes and clear my head long enough to tell him only what I want him to know. I need to make my own way with

Jade, and I won't do myself any favors if she thinks I go running to Grip to complain every time we disagree.

"No." I meet his eyes steadily. "I was just a little surprised. She was texting Qwest about a song they're working on, and I didn't realize they even knew each other."

"Yeah," Grip says. "I introduced them."

His eyes are clear, free of discomfort or regret. I know he doesn't think this should be problematic at all. It shouldn't be, but I can't resist pressing a little.

"You didn't tell me they were working together."

"Should I have?" Grip bites the inside of his cheek and frowns a little. "I didn't think it was important. Qwest was looking for new material, and Jade's looking for artists to work with."

"And you thought they'd be a good fit."

"Of course." Grip's powerful shoulders lift and fall carelessly. "They have a lot in common."

"Really?"

"They both have this badass sensibility. I knew Jade's lyrics would feel right to Qwest. They've both overcome a lot, lived through a lot of the same things."

Things I have no idea about, things they can easily bond around when I basically have to negotiate a treaty just to have a conversation with Jade.

"You admire her." It's a statement, because it's obvious he does. "Qwest, I mean. You admire her."

"I respect her, yeah," Grip says. "I mean, hip-hop's a male-dominated industry where most of us call women bitch and ho without blinking, and she shoved her way to the top. Her drive and talent and intelligence have made her one of the biggest names in the business, and she takes no shit from nobody."

Grip watches me carefully, probably catching on to the fact that this means more to me than it should.

"Does it bother you that I respect Qwest?"

I could just say yes, but it's not that simple. I, too, admire everything Grip just described about her. I relate to it because in many ways, those are the challenges I face in my career, too. Those aren't the things that bother me, and I have to be honest with him and with myself about what does.

"It doesn't bother me that you respect Qwest. I think it bothers me that you fucked her."

He doesn't even flinch, and I wonder if I can still shock Grip, or if he knows me so well he anticipates my thoughts, reads them in the air over my head before they make it to my mouth.

"And I hate every son of a bitch you ever fucked," he says, his voice remaining steady though his eyes darken. "But I can't change your sexual history, just like you can't change mine. We can only worry about the future."

His hand slips between our bodies, between my legs, to cup me, his wide palm hot as a brand through the thin linen of my shorts.

"And this," he says, pressing into my pussy, "is the sum total of my sexual future."

"Are you using my body against me?" I ask, my voice sandpapered by lust.

"I will use whatever is at my disposal to keep you with me forever."

"And you think my pussy is at your disposal?"

Grip slides one finger over my clit through my clothes.

"You think it's not?" He grabs my uninjured hand and presses it to his crotch. "Because *this* is completely at your disposal as much as you want, any time you want it, and any way you want to use it."

He links his fingers with mine, careful of the cut on my pinky, and settles our twined hands over his heart.

"And this is yours, too, Bristol, all the time, whether you want it or not."

My eyes rest on our hands over his heart, and I feel some peace for the first time since I walked into the kitchen to talk to Jade, maybe since we arrived . . . maybe since I woke up today with this party hanging over my head. When things are out of control, he's always my peace, always my sigh of relief. He's the reminder that come what may, there's us, and we aren't going anywhere—ever.

I step closer, his hand still between my legs, my hand still on his dick, and rest my forehead against his chin.

"I'm sorry." I breathe the apology into the Grip-scented skin of his neck. "I just feel . . . possessive, probably even more when it comes to Qwest because I know she would never have had you if I hadn't thrown the two of you together. I love the way you love me, in and out of bed, and the idea of someone else having you . . ."

My words trail off as his dick thickens and lengthens in my hand.

My eyes zip up to his face, where his eyelids hang heavy over the dark storm of his eyes and his lips are parted on a hot breath.

"Does it turn you on that I'm possessive of you?" I ask.

"I'd fuck you in that sink right now if it wasn't full of collard greens," he says, his eyes speculating like he might follow through on his threat anyway.

Despite power surging through me from the knowledge that I affect him this way, and even with the air so thick with lust I could cut it with the knife I used just minutes ago, I laugh. It's a robust sound that scrambles from the bottom of me and climbs to the very top, like I'm a mountain and this sound scaled every challenge, every obstacle, to soar.

"Is that you laughing like a bird again?" Grip's chuckle vibrates from his chest into mine.

I slide my hands over the ridges of his abs and chest to link my wrists behind his head, peppering gentle kisses over his lips. "You're never gonna let me live that down, are you?"

"Not a chance." Grip rests his hands at my hips, pulling me into his hard heat. "You can be a bird—my pretty bird."

I lift to touch my lips to his, ready to settle into a stolen kiss before we have to get back to the party.

"I shoulda known," Ms. James says from the kitchen door, hands braced on her hips. "Sent you in here to get Bristol, and *here you go*, all booed up."

Grip and I both laugh, holding each other loosely, our bodies cooling off as his mother approaches the sink.

"I heard you needed this." She hands me a Band-Aid before leaning over to inspect my handiwork, nodding her approval.

"Good job." She starts transferring the greens into a large pot of water. "That's enough for today."

"But I just washed!" My mouth hangs open. "I didn't learn anything new."

"You gotta work your way up to my greens, girl." A quick grin creases the still smooth skin at her eyes. "Next time, you boil."

I take in her friendly face like a balm to the abrasions from my conversation with Jade. The first time I was in this house, Grip's mother and I weren't friendly. We didn't exchange smiles, and there was no affection slowly growing between us. It's been baby steps for us, both of us loving Grip and wanting to know and like each other for his sake. If I can have this with Ms. James, I have to believe one day I'll have it with Jade, too. This warmth I'm basking in between Grip and his mother, the sense of family with them in this kitchen and permeating the entire house—I want it. I never had it for myself growing up, and I'm adopting it as my own.

I lean into Grip's chest, tucking my head into his neck and smiling at his mother, who watches us with eyes warmer than I ever thought they would be.

"You're right, Ms. James." I give her a quick nod, returning her smile. "Next time."

Nine

Grip

Bristol's laugh hooks me from across the yard, drawing my attention from the abysmal hand of cards I'm holding. If you're playing Spades and all your cards are red, that's not good. These cards are bleeding, but at least Bristol is still having fun. It's amazing the wonders food and alcohol can work. With a full belly and a bottle of beer, she's seated in a circle of lawn chairs, shoes off, hair tumbled from the knot she had it in earlier. She throws her head back, the muscles in her throat contracting to push out the sound that takes over everything else, at least for me.

She's sitting with Shon and several of the girls I've known all my life. Once they realized Bristol knows everyone in the music business and manages many of its hottest stars, she became really popular. They wanted all the gossip she could divulge. Talk of music quickly shifted to her shoes, her bag collection, where we'll be living in New York, all the details of our so-called glamorous life. Bristol isn't one of those women who has lots of friends. Over the years, she has hand-picked a tight circle of people she trusts and would do anything for. Under the prickliness, and when she sets her mind to it, she's all charm. She has my lifelong friends eating from her hand and hanging on her every word.

Bristol was nervous and stiff at first, and I can't blame her. This isn't an easy group to jump into. Some are territorial, many mistrusting, and a few just downright biased when it comes to white women. But, they're also the most loving, supportive, give-you-the-clothes-off-their-back people you'll ever meet. They're my family, with or without blood. I know some of them don't like or understand that I've chosen to spend my life with Bristol, but that's all based on shit assumptions. I've seen too much good in their hearts to believe they'll hold on to those notions once they see how much I love her and how good she is for me, once they see how much she loves me, and that is one thing Bristol can't hide. My dick twitches when I remember her confessing her possessiveness in the kitchen. This party is for me, but I'm wondering how soon we can be out. I leave tomorrow for New York, and Bristol won't be able to join me there for at least the next week or so. With Kai's debut album dropping Tuesday, Bristol can't and won't leave her side.

So, I'm thinking we should probably fuck a lot before I leave.

"Man, it's getting late." I lay my awful hand of cards facedown on the table. "You guys still into this game or you wanna call it?"

Please call it so I can take Bris home.

"Oh, no. We're finishing this, *ese*." Mateo, my friend since elementary school, wrinkles the folds of skin above his brows into a frown. "You always trying to get ghost when you have a sorry hand. I know you."

I roll my eyes and, resigned to finishing this crappy game, pick up the blood-red cards.

"Maybe if you concentrate on the game," Mateo says, never looking up from his hand, steadily shifting cards around, "instead of drooling over your girl, you and your partner wouldn't be in the hole."

"I'm focused," I say, distracted again when Bristol gets up and crosses the yard toward us.

"I meant focused on the *game*. I give you a pass, though." Mateo turns his stare on Bristol, too. "'Cause your girl's fine as hell, Marl."

He's one of the few who never took to calling me Grip, which always irritated me, but not nearly as much as the fact that he's still looking.

"Matty." I lean forward to snap my fingers in his face. "Eyes on the cards and off my girl."

"Awww, you skeered I'll take her from you?" The bastard blows me an air kiss.

Mateo, half Black, half Mexican, hair loose and hanging down to his waist, is a good four hundred pounds. I have nothing to worry about, but his remark does make me crack a smile. We both laugh, but when she gets closer and his eyes drift over her long, tanned legs, the laugh clogs in my throat.

"For real, Matty, I'm gonna fuck you up you keep looking at her like that."

Our eyes connect again and I can't even hold on to my ire, not with him.

Second to Amir, he's been my ace boom since diaper days. I'd trust him with my life. Growing up in these streets, I've had to more than once.

Bristol reaches us at the table and stands beside me. I capture her hand and bring it to my lips.

"You wanna sit?" I ask her.

She looks at the full card table, smiling at the other three guys playing Spades with me.

"There's nowhere to sit."

"As long as I got a lap," I say, patting my leg, "you got a place to sit."

She laughs, flashing the guys a self-conscious smile, but settles onto my lap and rests her back against my chest. Once she's seated, I introduce the other two guys at the table and leave Matty for last.

"Babe, did you meet Mateo?"

"No." She smiles. "Nice to meet you, Mateo."

Matty inclines his head, grinning at Bristol over the splay of his cards.

"He grew up with Amir and me here in the neighborhood." "One street over," Matty says. "Just opened my business here."

"What do you do?" Bristol asks.

"I own a tattoo shop right up the street."

"He's done every tat I have," I say. "I wouldn't trust anyone else."

"Really? You do great work. Yours are beautiful, too," she adds, nodding to his arms, brightly painted with everything from the Virgin Mary to Snoop Dogg.

"Thank you. I don't see any ink on that pretty skin of yours." Matty gives her an outlandish wink. "But maybe you're hiding it."

Bristol's shoulders shake into my chest when she chuckles. "Nope." She stretches her arms out. "Virgin skin."

"Well if you ever want that cherry popped ..." The ring piercing Matty's eyebrow glints when he waggles it suggestively.

"All right," I cut in. "You ain't getting anywhere near her cherries."

We all laugh and turn back to the game and this shitty hand I was just dealt. Bristol falls back to my chest and drops her head to the crook of my neck and shoulder. Her scent, fresh and clean—shampoo, body wash, and just her—drifts up, filling the air around me. My arms frame her slim body as I study my cards, sad to see they're still just as red. I'm tempted to toss it in and drag Bristol's good-smelling ass out of here even though the other guys show no signs of stopping. I haven't seen most of these folks in a long time, though. I can put my dick in check for another hour.

Maybe. If Bristol keeps squirming, maybe not. "What game are we playing?" she asks.

"Spades." Mateo looks up from his hand, his smug grin telling me his hand is a lot less red than mine.

Bristol leans back and whispers near my ear, "If it's Spades, shouldn't you have some?"

When her "whisper" reaches Mateo's ears, he snickers, anticipating the ass kicking he's about to deliver and smiling gleefully. I toss my cards down and push an exasperated sigh into the hair at Bristol's neck.

"Babe, you just told everyone what's in my hand."

"I'm sorry," she says, but she and Mateo still laugh.

I grab her hips and pull her deeper into my lap until she feels my erection and squirms, rolling her ass over me. I barely catch the groan rattling behind my teeth.

"Keep it up," I say low enough for only her to hear. "You're gonna mess around and get yourself fucked in my mama's bathroom, and we both know you can't be quiet."

Her not-so-subtle elbow dig into my ribs has me *umph*-ing and trying to catch my breath to focus on the game.

"Aw, hell." Mateo's partner glances up from his phone, apologizing with a look. "I gotta go. Just got called in to work."

Fine by me.

"Oh well." I try to sound disappointed, leaning up, ready to slide Bristol off my lap so we can get the hell out of here and head home. "We'll call it a draw and finish next time."

"Let me play." Bristol turns her head, eyes begging. "I can take his place. I've been watching. I think I have the hang of it. I'm really good at card games."

"You don't just pick up Spades," I scoff. We take our Spades seriously.

"From what I've seen," she continues, undeterred, "it's basically a combination of strategic thinking, risk assessment, intuition, and good old-fashioned luck."

We stare at her like she's grown another head.

"Stick to games you can handle, like Crimes Against Humanity," I say, "ow-ing" slightly when she punches my chest.

"It's *Cards* Against Humanity," she corrects. "And maybe you're scared I'll kick your ass."

"Uh, yeah, that's it." I slide her off my lap. "I'll teach you Spades another time."

"She would be my partner, right?" Mateo leans back in the poor chair creaking its complaint under his substantial weight.

Bristol pauses, halfway up from my lap.

"Yeah." She nods eagerly, scrambling over to take the seat Mateo's partner vacated. "I promise I won't let you down."

"This is crazy." I shuffle the cards into a neat deck. "She's a beginner."

"I'll take her," Mateo says.

Bristol claps enthusiastically and gives me a triumphant look.

"You have the deck." She nods her head toward the cards in my hand. "Deal."

I'll never truly understand what transpired over the next half hour, but somehow Mateo and my novice girlfriend go on an epic tear that leaves us a hundred points behind in the end. I'm stunned and disgusted as Mateo lifts Bristol clear off the ground and twirls her around. They commence mercilessly rubbing in their unlikely win, and even contrive some weird victory shimmy.

It's kind of turning me on. Maybe *now* we can go.

"Partner, you gotta drink to our win." Mateo proffers a forty ounce to Bristol.

This should be fun—Bristol drinking a forty.

She takes the bottle to her lips and then screws her face up with distaste.

"Oh, my God." She wipes the excess liquid from her mouth. "Do we *have* to drink lighter fluid?"

Everyone who has gathered around cracks up. Pink floods her cheeks and she covers her face with both hands. I pry her fingers away, one hand finding her waist and the other caressing her neck.

"Hmmm, I don't know what your problem is." I drop a kiss on her lips. "Tastes good to me."

She scans the circle of people gathered around us, her face lit up and still slightly pink by the time she looks back to me. She hooks her wrists behind my neck.

"Maybe it's an acquired taste," she says.

She's the acquired taste, and I don't need to ever have another woman for the rest of my life to know she's the sweetest thing, the only thing that will satisfy me. I'm seduced by her openness, captivated by her willingness to dive into my world and find her place. She fills my vision to the very edge until I can't focus on anyone but her.

"No fraternizing with the enemy, Bristol," Mateo says, tugging her into a side hug and taunting me with a smirk.

"Find your own girl." I chuckle but pull her back to my chest, crossing my arms at her waist. She crosses her arms to hold my elbows and tilts her head into my neck.

"Now that I'm out, I can." Mateo's laughter fades, and he looks at me seriously for the first time all day. "I gotta thank you again, Marl."

I shift, tightening my arms around Bristol. I hope he doesn't make a big deal out of this, especially with everyone gathering around. Bristol glances up at me, the question in her eyes.

"Did he tell you what he did?" Mateo asks Bristol. She shakes her head and waits for him to go on.

"I got pulled over in Vegas for some shit I didn't do." Mateo twists his lips into a grimace. "Wrong place, wrong time. I got caught up in some other nigga's drama and couldn't get uncaught."

"What happened?" Bristol asks, not flinching at his use of the N word. She's been around enough now that she's used to it. I don't know if that's a good thing or not, but it won't be the last time she'll hear it while managing a hip-hop artist, and certainly not the last if she's around my friends.

"I was rotting in a Vegas jail." Mateo runs his hand over his goatee thoughtfully. "The bail was high enough for nosebleeds. I couldn't touch it— no one could." Mateo flashes me a look of chagrin. "Well, no one I wanted to call."

Surprise is evident on Bristol's face when she looks up at me. "You didn't know?" she asks.

"No." I tuck my chin deeper into the clean, sweet scent of her neck. "I was on tour, and this knucklehead didn't call me."

"I didn't want to be one of them dudes always needing shit from your homey when he makes it big, expecting stuff," Mateo says, a frown sketching his disgust. "Grip was the last person I wanted to call."

"Which is ridiculous." I roll my eyes at the proud stubbornness he's always had, even when we were kids. "This was jail, not asking me for a hookup. As soon as Ma let me know what was up, I sent a little something to help."

"A little something?" Mateo snorts. "A hundred thousand dollars ain't a little something, Marl. I'd been sitting in that jail for two months."

Indignation scratches me from the inside when I think of Mateo and thousands of others like him rotting in jail, innocent but unable to make bail.

"It's a rigged system." My voice comes out abrasive in the soft mass of Bristol's hair. "As long as there are people financially benefitting from the imprisonment of others, our justice system can't be pure. Prison should not be a business."

I clamp my lips over the other things I would say. It's not a night for my soapbox, and once I start talking about mass incarceration and the other things that affect Black, brown, and poor people disproportionately, I won't be able to shut up. It's a party, not a protest.

"And that's why you're going to New York," Ma says, startling me since I didn't notice her take the spot beside me in the yard. "To learn how you can help our boys, right?"

"Right." I stretch my arm to bring her to one side, shift Bristol to the other, and lay a kiss on the top of Ma's head.

"Okay," she says to change the subject, passing her grin around to everyone in the circle. "We ate. We played. We smoked."

She points to Mateo in the middle of a long draw on the blunt he pulled from his pocket.

"I hope you brought enough of that for everybody." She doesn't pause for the laughter that follows her words. "But I want to say a few things before we go home, before Marlon leaves for New York tomorrow."

If I could blush, I would—maybe I am under all my melanin.

"Now Marlon thought it was silly to have a going away party since he'll be back," she says, "and is only gone for the semester, but I'm just as proud of him for him doing this as I am of his platinum records. I always told him how important education was for everyone, but especially for little Black boys."

The sun has gone down, and tiki lamps around the perimeter cast patches of light in her small back yard. In the half-dark, I search my mother's face. She's changed so little in some ways, the skin at her eyes and neck still smooth and taut, but so much in others. Raising a boy in this neighborhood by herself took its toll. She always has a joke, always makes us laugh, but every person here knows the losses she's endured and the sacrifices she made, mostly for me. She focuses her intense stare on my face with the steady eyes that, for most of my life, shaped what I see.

"I'd come home from working my second job some nights," she goes on, "and Marlon would be up reading or reciting a poem for school. He was a roughneck, don't get me wrong."

My chuckle joins everyone else's laughter.

"But he was smart." Ma wears her proud smile like a badge. "This is a hard life, and a hard place to grow up. It's a rock that too many break themselves on, but you broke the rock, Marlon. You never let a place, a neighborhood, or our circumstances define you. You're a mold-breaker. You always have been."

Her eyes drift to Bristol, quiet and still against me, watching my mother as closely as I am.

"You keep living your life exactly as you see fit." She smiles at Bris-tol. "Trust your gut. Trust your heart. They haven't steered you wrong yet, and I'm proud of you."

I'm unexpectedly moved by her words, by all the support surrounding me. Every face, every smile, every person in this backyard loves me. Some of them didn't understand when I took a bus every day to another world at the performing arts school. Some of them didn't understand when I was sweeping studio floors instead of getting a "real" job or going to college right out of high school. Some of them don't really understand why, with a platinum album and a successful music career, I feel the need to go to NYU at all. Some of them don't understand why the girl cuddled against my chest, who in most ways is completely foreign to them and to this life, is the center of my world. They don't understand, but they support, and on the cusp of this new chapter in my life, unsure of what happens next, that's all I can ask for.

Ten

Grip

"**B**RISTOL!" THE BARISTA CALLS OUT, SCANNING THE CROWD FOR the person who ordered the grande white chocolate mocha. I get it every day at this coffee shop within walking distance of NYU's campus, and the drink has become my own inside joke for my relationship with Bristol.

Plus, that shit's the bomb.

"Uh, mine." I step around several other customers waiting for their orders.

Yeah, I miss Bristol so much, I give her name to the barista for my coffee. If that makes me a pussy, I don't care. I don't need caffeine. My heart is already galloping in my chest. After two weeks, she's finally joining me at our place in New York.

"Damn, Grip," says a low-timbered voice from behind me.

I turn to meet a pair of laughing eyes behind dark-rimmed glasses.

"I knew you were trying to be all incognegro in my class," Dr. Israel Hammond continues, "but I didn't know you resorted to using girls' names to keep your identity a secret."

Shock and nerves lock up my words for a second. Is this how my fans feel when they meet me? I've been in Dr. Hammond's class for over a week and haven't mustered up the nerve to approach him. It's like being star-struck, but smarter—more like mind-struck, because this guy's a genius.

"Professor Hammond."

"Call me Iz," he insists. With his close-cropped hair, Malcolm X T-shirt, elbow-patched blazer, and shell toe Adidas, he's a study in contrasts, all these cool pieces that don't quite fit but make sense as a whole. "And technically I'm not a professor. It's just for this semester. Then it's back to writing and running my organization."

After the success of *Virus*, he started an organization focused on the issues of criminal justice reform his book raised.

"Okay, Iz." I clear my throat and hope I sound like a grown man, not a fangirl. "I didn't even know you knew I was in your class."

"I've known since before the first day." He gestures to the corner with two leather armchairs. "Wanna sit?"

I settle into the seat and consider the man I crossed the country to study with. He's not your typical academic. Once you get past the glasses, he's more lumberjack than scholar. He's probably a good six five in socks with hulking shoulders and huge hands. If I didn't know he was faculty, albeit temporary, I'd assume he was a baller.

"The administration actually notified me that you'd be in my class before the semester even started," he says, taking a sip of his coffee.

"Why would they do that?" Irritation scrunches my face. As hard as I've been trying to be normal and like everyone else, the administration singled me out.

"Having someone famous in your class could be disruptive." He shrugs those massive shoulders. "If half the students will be lining up for autographs or throwing their panties across the class, I'd like a heads-up."

A smirk works its way through my irritation.

"Thank God there's been nothing like that," I say. "I don't think most people know I'm even there."

"Well you sitting at the back with that hat pulled down low isn't much of a disguise, but I guess it's working for you."

"It also helps that your class is huge."

"Yeah. I had no idea there would be such a response."

"Are you kidding?" I know I'm gaping, but I can't check it. "Your book is . . . life-changing. This is my first semester on campus. I've been an online student for the last year and a half, and I relocated from LA for the semester just for this class."

He's a stone-faced man, but surprise ripples across his rugged features.

"I had no idea." His eyes drop to his drink and then lift to narrow on my face. "Why would you do that?"

I hesitate, self-conscious in the presence of someone who has become a hero of sorts to me—not the Superman, Marvel comic kind of hero, but the kind whose superpower is reason and whose kryptonite is ignorance.

"I read *Virus* on my first world tour over the summer, and it articulated so many things I had either never considered, or knew but never put into words," I say. "I didn't set out to sell a million records. I wanted to be successful, of course, but fame is seductive. It has this way of making you forget who the real person is behind all the hype, and the bigger I get, the less I want this distance between who I am in public and who I am in private. If anything, I want people to know the things I really believe in and stand for."

I pause to look at him frankly.

"I come from nothing. Where I'm from, a life like the one I'm leading now is a fairy tale. I want to leverage my success to change things for people who don't actually believe another life is possible. Your book helped me see that."

"So, if my book did all of that," he says, taking his glasses off to clean them on the hem of his T-shirt, "why haven't you at least come to my office hours? I can't even get to my door most days for the line of students in the hall, but if we hadn't bumped into each other here, I wouldn't have ever met you."

I take another sip of my drink, using that time to collate my thoughts.

"I guess I didn't want special treatment because of . . . you know."

"You don't think you're special?" he asks.

"Um . . ." This feels like a trick question. "Well, everybody is special."

"Does everyone sell a million records?" He tilts his head, both brows lifted like he really wants to know.

"Well, no, but—"

"Do hundreds of thousands of fans across continents fill arenas to see everyone?"

"Look, I see what you're getting at, but—"

"Would you say Martin Luther King was special?"

"Yeah, obviously."

"But he would argue that he wasn't better than anyone else." He plows on, not waiting for the response I'm not sure of anyway. "And what about Ghandi? Wasn't he special? But fighting a caste system, he would have been the last to say he was in any way superior."

He and I watch each other, the sounds of conversation and lattes being slurped and coffee shop music coalescing around us as his words sink in.

"I guess my point is we are all created equal," he says. "But it's what we choose to do with what we have that makes us extraordinary."

He laughs, flashing white teeth against skin the color of mahogany.

"Or not," he says. "'Cause best believe most people don't do enough with what they're given. The fact that you did so much with the little you had makes you special. Own that."

And just like that, uprooting my life, even missing my girl to the point of aching feels worth it. Some people are a revolution and, with their words, overturn the things you thought you knew. You don't always see them coming, but once you're with them, you know the impact they have will be like a crater, deep and lasting. That's how much of an impression they will leave. Over the next hour as Dr. Hammond challenges me, pokes at my perspectives, and picks apart my preconceived notions, there is no doubt in my mind he is one of those people, and his impact on my life, unfathomably deep.

Eleven

Bristol

THIS IS MY NEW HOME, AT LEAST FOR THE NEXT SEMESTER.

It's not the pictures of Grip and me, of Rhys and Kai, Aria, and our friends sprinkling the mantel and other surfaces here in our temporary Tribeca apartment. It's not the clothes hanging on my side of our closet. It's not even my favorite cookie dough ice cream that Grip has already stocked in the freezer. These aren't the things that make this place home.

It's him.

If I'm in Antarctica, as long as Grip is there shivering beside me, it's home.

Now where is he?

I wander from room to room, checking both floors, but there's no sign of him. It's kind of anti-climactic considering I took an earlier flight to get here. That's what I get for trying to surprise him. I know his schedule as well as I know my own: he had class today then a session with Qwest's producers and writing team this afternoon.

Grrrrr.

I refuse to torture myself with thoughts of them working together while I was stuck in LA, although "stuck" isn't the right word. I was just a *little* busy making Kai's debut the freaking number one album in the country. If we thought the offers were pouring in before, now I'm flooded with movie roles, endorsement options, and more opportunities than she'll be able to handle. If all goes according to plan—mine and Rhyson's, that is—soon Broadway will be knocking, too.

"Dammit."

The muffled curse reaches me from the greenhouse, and quiet steps take me toward the outdoor retreat where I'm now sure he is. I wonder if it will always feel like this when I'm about to see him. Anticipation trembles in the air. My mouth dries and then waters with the promise of his kiss. There's a pillow fight in my belly and feathers float all around. Mrs. O'Malley's eyes still gloss over when she thinks of her Patrick, of the years they had before his illness. They made this place together. I take in the tinted windowpanes and the space they created for one another.

Great love must be tested.

Is there a greater test than your soul mate no longer knowing you? Than the memories you created together forgotten, lost to an encroaching darkness? I've seen Mrs. O'Malley clinging to what they had with all her strength, and it makes me want to cling to Grip harder and as long as I can—especially when he does sweet things like stringing fairy lights and preparing a dinner that even now prompts my stomach to growl. He stands over the table, the width of his shoulders and the strength of his arms confined in a slate-colored button-up, rolled up to his elbows. A black vest molds the power of his chest, and dark jeans fit the flexing muscles of his thighs.

"What the . . ." He trails off, clicking the lighter over the candles and looking baffled when there's still no fire.

"Need some help?"

He whips around toward the entrance where I stand. His expression shifts from surprise to pleasure and then settles into a slight frown.

"You're early."

"Sorry." I turn on my heel. "I can leave."

I don't make it half a step out of the greenhouse before a strong arm wraps around my waist. Grip presses me into his chest, inhales a deep breath of me, and kisses my neck.

"You aren't going anywhere," he mumbles into my hair.

I face him, reaching up to rest my elbows on his shoulders.

"Make up your mind. Do you want me?" I dust my lips across his, dropping my head back before he can take command of the kiss. "Or not?"

"Oh, I want you." Lust roughens his voice. Love makes it soft.

His gaze drops, a lazy, heated sweep over my body, a sweet searing of my skin. The look is as heavy as a stroking hand, but so gentle that I barely feel its tantalizing weight.

"What's all this?" I gesture over his shoulder to escape this hypnosis of passion. We could stand here all night staring at each other, and after nearly two weeks apart, I want to do more than look.

He takes my hand and walks us over to the table in the corner, the same place it was when we viewed the place a few weeks ago. Now it's loaded with domed dishes, sparkling glasses, cutlery, wine, and a bottle of champagne chilling in ice.

"Champagne *and* wine?" I ask.

"One for dinner," he says with a grin. "And one for a toast."

I grab the note propped against the wine bottle.

Eat. Drink. Dance. Love. It's all better under the stars!
Welcome! Take care of our home and don't waste one moment.—Esther

"How thoughtful" I consider the beautifully set table. "Did Mrs. O'Malley do all this?"

"She sent the champagne to celebrate your first night here." Grip plucks the note from my fingers and drops it to the table. "The food I ordered from this place up the street that delivers and makes things look fancy."

The smell of him, the heat of his proximity works on my resistance— never the strongest to begin with—and I tip up to take his lips with my mouth, stroking his tongue with mine until he growls, his hands tight at my hips.

"We are not doing this out of order, Bris," he says, his breath misting my lips. "You saw the card. First we eat, then we drink. Then we dance."

"Then we love?" I finish, sliding my hand to his belt. "Are you sure you want to save that for last? Because I don't mind flipping the script."

"You're always so horny." His husky laugh feathers against my cheek. "It's one of my favorite things about you actually, but no. Tonight, we're doing it the right way. We'll eat."

I notice for the first time that there is only one chair. My lips twitch with a barely checked smile.

"Where's the other seat?" I ask.

"I burned it," he deadpans.

Our laughs tangle between our mouths at his ridiculous statement.

"You did not burn it."

"Well it's not here." Grip sits down in the lone chair, spreading his thighs and grinning. "I guess you have to sit with me."

He grasps my wrist and tugs me forward until I'm standing between his legs. I shake my head, smiling inevitably, and settle onto his lap.

"This could get awkward and messy." I twist to get my plate and make room for all of our food on one side of the table.

"Think of it as food foreplay." He pulls me back until I feel him hard and poking in the crease of my ass. "See? It's working already."

I wiggle in his lap, drawing a laughing "shit" from him as we dig in, reaching around each other to get to our food, eating from each other's plates, one feeding the other, spilling food and wine all over the place. It's a five-course meal with all the courses squeezed onto our little table at one time. It's an orgy of decadent tastes and consuming conversation, the words flowing as smoothly as the wine.

He's asking for every detail about Kai's release, about the days we were apart, and I'm demanding everything he can tell me about Dr. Hammond's class. The name Iz peppers every other sentence, flavoring our discussion with Grip's admiration and something close to awe.

"I think I'm jealous of Dr. Hammond." I shift on Grip's lap, feeding him chicken with greasy fingers. "I hope he hears my name as much as I'm hearing his."

"More." Grip eats past the meat to capture my finger in his teeth, tracing my fingerprint with his tongue. "He's sick of hearing about how wonderful you are."

"I can't wait to meet him." I pierce an asparagus spear on my fork and shove it into his mouth. "I bet your leg has gone to sleep."

"Not my third leg." He chews the crisp vegetable, stretching to grab and tear a roll down the middle then work it past my lips, laughing when I choke a little. "It's wide awake."

I grind my ass over that third leg, satisfied by and hungry for the stiff readiness behind his zipper.

"You made a mess." Voice stripped of pretense and body tired of waiting, I tip my glass of wine toward the stain on his vest where the chicken's rich burgundy sauce has left a splotch.

"Yup," he agrees, eyes locked with mine. "I should take this off."

He slips one button and then the others from the holes until his vest falls open.

I scoop up some of the sauce with my spoon, bringing it to my lips, but at the last minute allowing it to dribble on my silk blouse.

"Oops." I breathe into the small space separating us. "So should I."

I grab the hem of the stained shirt and pull it over my head.

He swallows loud enough for me to hear it. His jaw tics and his eyes roam over my naked shoulders and stomach, over the breasts barely contained by strips of silk and lace. He takes my glass of wine from me and goes to take a sip, allowing just a few drops to land on his shirt. I reach for it, fingers fumbling at the buttons, laying bare the sculpted plane of abs and pecs.

"Are we ready for love now?" I lick the heady traces of wine from my lips.

"Mrs. O'Malley said we have to dance." His words are a dark-timbered rumble laced with want as he shifts me off his lap to stand. I press myself against his chest, grabbing his shirt by the lapels and shoving it down his arms to the floor.

"There's no music." I trap my bottom lip between my teeth and look up at him through my lashes because I know that drives him crazy.

He reluctantly steps away from the heat our bodies share and crosses over to the wall. With the press of a button, music wafts from the hidden speakers. The music is sensuous and whispers sex before the singer delivers the first lyric.

"Prince?" I ask, surprised. I recognize the iconic voice, but not the song. "What is this?"

"'Adore.'" Grip lifts my arms around his neck and hooks my wrists there. "One of my favorites."

"I've never heard it," I murmur, barely aware of saying anything. I'm entranced by the intensity of his stare. He cups my jaw, drawing me closer until all our bare skin presses together and all our covered places strain against our clothes, seeking out naked skin and heat. We sway to the music, our hands moving over each other in a dance of rediscovery. He palms my hip, sliding down to hold my ass through my skirt. My fingers wander over the ridges and dips of his torso, rendered in stone. I run my thumb across the fullness of his bottom lip, tracing the lines that are so precise it's like an artist drew them.

God, this man's mouth.

I reach up to kiss him, slowly exploring the warm silk interior of his mouth, our tongues like the tide, pushing in and flowing out. We trade moans, our mouths sharing the soft, needy sounds. Our hands pick up pace, mine urgent at his waist, undoing his belt, his fumbling at my back, unsnapping my bra. It's a quick, thorough disrobing that leaves us naked in the moonlight, half-drunk on the stars with Prince on repeat.

"Now?" I pant at the right angle of his jaw, dragging my lips over his neck and licking at the saltiness of his clavicle. "Time for love now?"

He closes his eyes and draws in a deep breath, but his body betrays how much self-control he's exerting when his dick twitches against me.

"We have to drink," he says sternly, stepping back and leaving me chilled, bereft.

"We've been drinking," I whine, every cell of my body pouting because he's denying me.

"But we haven't toasted." With a devilish glint in his eyes, he walks naked over to the table, the high, round arch of his ass flexing with every step. He pours two glasses of champagne from the bucket that has been chilling all night. My eyes drop between his legs and I force myself to stay standing when he hands me the flute instead of dropping to my knees and taking him in my mouth. Carnality courses through my veins, feral desire possessing every part of me. I want him occupying every empty space. I want to lick his sweat and bite chunks from him, swallow him whole. I grit my teeth and accept the fragile glass filled to the top with exhilaration and bubbles.

"This is a lot of champagne," I say, letting the bubbles tickle my nose. "I'll be too drunk for . . ."

I clear my throat, leaving wild thoughts unspoken and bucking in my mind.

"I think you'll manage." He lifts his glass and quirks a smile at me, even as his eyes lose some of the humor. "A toast to our first night in our first home together."

He gently tucks strands of hair behind my ear, rubbing the texture between his fingers before looking back to me.

"You didn't have to do this, Bristol," he says softly. "Move here, disrupt your life, your career for me like this, but I'm glad you did."

"No, I did have to," I disagree, surprised to find myself blinking back tears. "What I feel for you is not optional, Grip. It's a mandate, a demand I have no problem meeting. I have to be wherever you are."

He studies me a moment longer, and the intimacy and openness are almost too much, but I force myself not to look away. I've never been more vulnerable to anyone, and I've never trusted anyone else the way I trust Grip—with my life, with my heart.

"A toast then, to wherever we are." He clinks our glasses together, raising his to his lips, but at the last minute and with a wicked grin, pouring just a little onto my chest. I gasp as the cold liquid trickles over my flesh, streaming between my breasts. Before I have time to recover, Grip pours more over my nipples, which immediately bud and lift as if they're drinking in the potent liquid. Not done, he pours the rest of his champagne over my belly, wrenching a whimper from me when it drifts between my legs, sluicing into my naked folds, seeking out my core, the parts of me that silently beg to be filled.

"Grip." My voice emerges on a need-broken whisper. "What are you—"

With his lips, he answers the question I didn't get to voice, licking the champagne from my shoulders and flattening his tongue between my breasts, soaking up every drop in greedy swipes. His hands clamp around my hips and he sinks to his knees, his mouth venturing across the flat surface of my stomach like a sojourner, lost and searching. His tongue delves into my belly button then he nibbles the skin at my hips and above my pubic bone, the bristle on his chin abrading even as he withholds his mouth from me. Over and over, he kisses closer and closer, but never spreads me, never tastes me in the deeper places. The champagne boils between my legs as my body heats.

"Grip, please." His lips, torture and promise, keep relief and release at bay.

"What, baby?" His heated whisper lands on me, but he won't give me what my body is weeping for. He runs his nose over the slit dividing me, and with a deep inhale, draws in my scent. From his knees on the floor at my feet, he lifts his eyes, burning a trail of possession over my limbs. "Tell me what you want, Bris."

I swallow the words, holding out as long as I can in a sensual battle of wills I won't win.

He feathers kisses over my hips, runs his wide palms over my legs, kneading the muscles of my thighs, sliding his finger between the cheeks of my butt.

"Grip, you know," I whisper. "Just do it."

"I wanna hear." The measured control of his words is at odds with the rampage of his eyes. "Tell me what you want."

"My pussy." Tears adorn the corners of my eyes, the need is so strong. "Eat my pussy."

"Fuck yes," he growls, his fingers separating me and his tongue unleashed to spear inside. He pulls my leg over his shoulder, opening me up, and bites my clit, a double-edged sword of pleasure and pain slicing through me.

"Oh . . . oh, God." I dig my nails into his shoulders—it's the only way I can stay upright.

He takes his time, sucking the lips, biting me, licking and slurping until the champagne is gone and he's binging only on my juices, moaning at the juncture of my body. He springs to standing, grabbing me by my nape, pulling me into a kiss fierce enough, ferocious enough that my teeth cut into my lips. He's feeding me the taste of my body, rich and tangy on his lips. It's carnal and addictive. I grab his neck, too, sucking on his tongue and biting his lips until the metallic sting of our mingled blood christens the kiss.

With a growl, he lifts me up, and I lock my legs at the cleft of his ass. He walks us to the padded bench in the middle of the green-house, sinking down and fitting my thighs over his in a loose straddle.

"I'm gonna let you be on top the first time we fuck in our new house," he rasps, setting the words on fire in my ears.

"Thank you," I whisper, my voice desperate with the need to vise the length of him with my body.

"But if you don't ride me hard enough, I'm flipping you over and tearing that ass up. Got it?"

"That sounds fair." I nod frantically, no breath left for banter. I'm just ready to impale myself on him.

With one quick motion, I rise up, knees on either side of his thighs, and scramble onto him like his dick might get away from me, like he's the last train and I might miss my ride. Every time, it feels like he's too much, the blunt intrusion of his cock, but then my body remembers I was made for him. I allow myself one second to feel the pinch and then roll my hips once, slowly, letting him feel me again, the undulation of my body a promise. Each time he goes deeper, crossing any barriers my body, my heart would erect—only there's no barrier, nothing between us. I grip his knee behind me for leverage to grind deeper, roll harder. My breasts bounce in his face and he bobs his head, his mouth open and seeking until he has one in his mouth. He suckles me hard, zipping electricity from my chest to my core. It's a direct line, and with every thrust, every stroke, my heart contracts.

"I missed you so much," I say, looking him in his eyes, letting him see the ache I've carried around while we were apart. I withhold nothing from him. Not my body—he can have it any way he wants it. Not my heart—flung open like a door for him to walk through. Not my soul—twisting around his every time he hammers up into me, possessing me from the inside out.

"God, Bris," he says at my neck, scorching the skin with his breath. "I was going crazy. We can't be apart like that. We just ... we just can't."

Words of love and devotion tumble between us, swirling around us, cocooning us in the greenhouse. We are hothouse flowers, growing in plain sight, blossoming under tinted glass. Beyond the roof, stars burn light-years away, bright and already dying, but here, between us, brews a solar storm, a stellar explosion behind my eyes, a constellation of love and lust, dots connecting inside as I clench and squeeze through my orgasm. He stiffens beneath me, his fingers clutching tightly enough to bruise. I'll bear marks in the shape of his hands, bites on my nipples, stubble burns inside my thighs, sensual mementos I'll carry with me. I'll wear his touch tomorrow under my clothes. The marks he'll leave on my body will fade, but the way he's marked me as his, the way he's carved himself into my heart, that's forever.

Twelve

Grip

"**M**MMMM." THE SWEET TASTE OF PLANTAIN EXPLODES ON MY taste buds, and I squeeze my eyes shut in culinary rapture. "This food . . . damn."

"What'd I tell ya?" Iz sips his rum before diving back into the plate of oxtails in front of him. "I love Miss Lilly's."

The Jamaican diner is packed, and the asymmetrical patterns and bright, clashing colors animate the space.

"And not too far from campus," I mumble around a forkful of saltfish. "I need to bring Bris here. She would love this."

"And I need to find a way to get paid every time you say that girl's name." Good-natured teasing gleams from behind his glasses.

I could tell him that she says the same thing about him. Over the last month, Bristol has settled in at our new place, and she teases me about how much I talk about Iz. We've become friends, but there's still a level of awe I hold for him previously reserved for the likes of the MJs—Michael Jackson and Michael Jordan. It's his ideas, his perspective that impresses me, though, not his prowess on a court or in the studio.

"It's good," Iz continues when I don't answer. "You obviously love her."

"Very much." I gulp pink Ting, the cool liquid chasing the Caribbean flavors of my meal. "That's my girl."

"She's ride or die, huh?"

I pause mid-chew as the memory of Bristol in the holding room, desperate, willing to bow to Parker's sick demands to get me out of jail, jabs my brain.

"You could say that, yeah."

I consider him across the table. We haven't really talked much about our personal lives. He knows I have a girlfriend I'm serious about and that she moved to New York with me. He knows, obviously, that I'm a musician, but most of our discussions have centered on mass incarceration, police brutality, and fatherlessness in the black community—issues we're both passionate about. We've run the gamut of ills, and I admire his intelligence and insight more than anyone's, but I can't say I know much about him. He's not what I imagined he would be. He's a cool cat with his vintage kicks and elbow patch sports coats. Though I hold him in the highest esteem, he's only a few years older than I am, I'm guessing in his late thirties. There has to be quite a story behind a guy as relatively young as he is accomplishing so much.

"What about you?" I probe. "Wife? Kids?"

He drinks his rum, his face unreadable before he replies. "Divorced. One daughter."

"How old's your little girl?"

"She's six," he says. "She and her mom are still back in Philly. I see her all the time when I'm there, not as much while I'm teaching here this semester."

"You got pictures?"

I ask because I know I'll be obnoxious with my shit, showing everyone pictures of our kids once Bristol and I have them. I'll be one of *those* dads. I never had one to be proud of me, but mine will, and if it's a girl? I'll probably buy my first shotgun the day she's born.

A tiny smile cracks the impassivity of Dr. Hammond's face as he pulls out his phone to show me his daughter. I see echoes of his features in her expression, but she must look a lot like her mother.

Soft pigtails brush her shoulders, and her snaggle-toothed smile is adorable. I can't help but wonder what our kids will look like.

"Man, she's beautiful." I hand him his phone, already feeling like I know him better just from seeing her.

"Yeah." His gruff laugh lands in his glass of rum. "Fortunately, she takes after her mother."

"How long you guys been divorced?"

"Much longer than we were married." He grimaces. "Let's just say I was more ready to be a father than I was to be a husband."

I nod, leaving that alone unless he wants to elaborate. Surprisingly, he does.

"Just be sure, when and if you take that plunge. Being unfaithful . . ." He leaves that comment on the table, polishing his glasses on the hem of his T-shirt, a habit I've noticed. "I guess it's already pretty hard to stay faithful with all the ass that must get thrown your way."

"Nope." I shrug and turn my mouth down at the corners. "It's just Bris for me. If she wasn't the one, yeah, it'd be hard, but she is, so it's not."

It sounds too simple even to me, but I don't know a better way to say it.

"No side chicks?" Surprise stretches his expression. "Groupies on the road?"

"Nah." I shake the bottle of Ting over my mouth, teasing the last of it down my throat. "I couldn't do that to her. Hell, I don't even want to."

If there are laws of attraction, she has rewritten them with a one-girl clause. I'm not blind—I notice when a woman is attractive, but actively want? Think about for more than two seconds? Just Bris.

"She must be something else," Iz says with a smile. "I need to meet this girl."

"She wants to come hear you at the Prison as Business forum in a few weeks, if she's in the city. She travels a lot."

"That should be interesting." A frown settles between his thick eyebrows. "You know it's basically a debate between me and Clem Ford."

"That bigot." Distaste for the man in question sours my meal and I put down my fork. "He's making money hand over fist from prison labor."

"At least he's honest about his views," Iz says. "Most of them lobby for longer sentences but never acknowledge the racism and greed underlying those polices. He's an unapologetic bigot, and his radio show is his bully pulpit. He doesn't hesitate to say Black and Brown people should be used this way, and he has an army of followers."

Familiar frustration and anger seethe in my belly. That kind of systemic racism is blatant, and everyone else benefits—the people who lobby for longer sentences for nonviolent crimes, the businessmen exploiting prison labor for next-to-nothing pay, the bigots who believe those injustices are what we deserve. Everybody's happy except the millions imprisoned, many unjustly, and the families splintered by it.

Iz's phone buzzing on the table jars me from the thoughts darkening my mood. The name Callie flashes on his phone screen.

"Hey Cal," he says, glancing at me and lowering his voice. "Yeah. I'm at Ms. Lilly's with Grip."

I gesture to a waitress and order another pink Ting while Iz listens.

"You don't have to do that." A frown puckers the straight line of his brows. "Okay. If you're that close, then thanks."

He ends the call, running his hand over the back of his neck, agitation clear on his face.

"Everything okay?" I ask.

"Yeah, that was my TA. I left my laptop in the lecture hall, and she lives around here. She's bringing it by."

"Oh, that's sweet."

"Sweet isn't how I would describe Callie." He chuckles. "But, yeah, I guess."

Callista Garcia is a beautiful girl from what I've seen of her in class, petite with golden brown skin and a cap of silky dark hair.

"What is she anyway?" I ask.

He stiffens, his glass pausing halfway to his mouth.

"What do you mean *what is she?*"

"Like nationality." I cock one brow and watch him more closely. "Ethnicity. She just has a unique look, and I wondered."

"I think her mother is Dominican and her father is Asian, maybe Japanese, not sure."

The woman in question walks through the door, and it's fascinating to watch Iz's response to her. His fist clenches on the table, and his lips tighten.

When Callie approaches our table, even her NYU hoodie doesn't disguise the tight, curvy body underneath. Her short hair is rumpled like she's been running her fingers through it, and she looks tired with shadows under her eyes. Her lashes frame dark eyes that shine with intelligence and curiosity.

"Hey Iz," she says when she reaches our table and hands him the sleeve with his laptop. "Here ya go."

There's an ease to her, like she doesn't realize she does remarkable things. When Iz introduced her on the first day of class, he said she graduated with honors from Yale. She's a freaking Rhodes Scholar and is at NYU on some prestigious fellowship. The woman is brilliant, but you'd never know those things just looking at her. She looks like any other student schlepping around campus.

"I pulled some stats on Clem Ford's business ventures and where they intersect with the prisons he's invested in, along with some of his more incendiary comments." She nods to the laptop case. "Slipped the printouts in there for you to look at when you get the chance."

"You didn't have to do that, Cal." Iz frowns and looks uncomfortable for just a moment. "You're my TA. I don't expect you to do anything outside of class, and this debate is technically outside the purview."

"I don't get technical when I'm passionate about someone." Her eyes drop to her fingers toying with the strap of her backpack. "I mean . . . about helping someone, about doing something I care about."

"I know what you meant." Iz scratches that spot on the back of his neck again. The implications of the tension I'm witnessing between them are still crystallizing in my mind when Callie gives me her attention and requires mine.

"Hey Grip." Something shifts on her face, in her posture, and she looks even less like the scholar I know her to be and more like a thousand other girls who have stuttered when talking to me since I started performing. "I haven't gotten to tell you, wanted to give you space in class, but I loved your album."

"You've gotta be kidding me," Iz mutters, rolling his eyes.

We both ignore him, and I do what I always do when a fan says something like this: give her my sincerest smile and a few seconds of my time.

"Thanks, Callie."

"'Bruise' was my favorite." She peels back the sleeve of her sweatshirt to bare her wrist. "It inspired this."

Scripted over the fragile skin of her wrist is the most famous lyric I've ever written: *We all bruise.*

"Wow." I'm dumbfounded. Fans have done some outrageous things to prove how much they love me and my music, but there's something about this brilliant young woman memorializing my words on her skin that moves me especially. "I don't know what to say, Callie. I'm incredibly humbled by this, for real."

"You graduated summa cum laude," Iz says. "You were a Rhodes Scholar with honors. Fucking *Yale*. The administration plucked you from three hundred applicants to be my teacher's assistant this semester and you want, what? Some rapper's autograph?"

He bends a look of unnecessary apology toward me. "No offense, Grip."

"None taken." I laugh. "I *am* some rapper. I'm a lot richer than you, though. That's a small consolation."

"Asshole." He chuckles and shakes his head at the smartass comeback.

Fortunately, neither of us takes ourselves too seriously, which is probably why we get along so well.

"I can be all those things," Callie asserts, elevating one eyebrow.

"And still be a fan, still love music, still appreciate a man who stands for something, who distinguishes himself from the rest of the herd and their bullshit. It's why I wanted to work with *you*." She pauses just long enough for her words to sink in before going on. "Was I wrong, Iz?"

The amusement withers on his face, and the current passing between the two of them makes me feel superfluous, like I'm in the way of something that started before I got here, something that has happened before.

"Thanks for bringing my laptop," Iz says evenly, not addressing her question.

She lopsides him a grin that says, *That's what I thought*, turns on her heel, and starts toward the door.

"See you gentlemen in class," she tosses over her shoulder.

A hundred of my unspoken questions pucker the silence she leaves behind.

"Soooooo . . . have you two—"

"Don't." He aims a warning over the rims of his glasses.

I raise my palms up as defense against the intensity of that look. "There was just a vibe, sexual tension or—"

"There's no sexual anything." His words slice into the space of the booth separating us. "She's one step removed from being my student, and I don't fuck my students."

"Well, speaking as one of your students, I'm glad to hear it." The grin he concedes breaks the scowl on his face.

"I just wanna go on record as saying if you ever change your mind about fucking your students"—I knock back the rest of my Ting—"she'd be a great place to start."

Thirteen

Grip

"**K**AI'S ON IN FIVE."

The production assistant hands me a lapel mic and checks something off on her clipboard. "If you can have her put this on, we'll make sure it's properly positioned when she comes out."

"Uh, yeah." Leaned against Kai's dressing room door, I glance up from my iPad. "She'll be ready. Thank you."

Five minutes. The countdown on Angie Black's YouTube channel says the live feed starts in five minutes, too. I know Grip's been looking forward to this Artists as Activists panel, but I'm not as excited. Seeing him with Qwest might only further water the seeds of insecurity Jade planted and I allowed to take root, at least a little. I'll check back in a few minutes, but now I need to get Kai onstage for her performance.

"You ready?" I ask once inside her dressing room.

Kai raises wide eyes, pressing a silencing finger to her lips. Aria has fallen asleep at her breast. I've seen Kai feed my niece too many times to count, but never wearing a beaded halter top, leather pants, and full face of makeup. Her dark hair is flat-ironed and falling nearly to her waist. She carefully extracts her breast from Aria's little rosebud mouth and gently places her in a travel playpen. She literally hasn't missed a beat, dropping all her baby weight *and* her first solo album to rule the charts.

She picks up her phone and turns a pout in my direction.

"No messages from Rhyson." She sighs and faces the mirror to check her makeup.

"He hasn't landed in Prague yet. He'll call when he gets there." I consider her reflection and dig into the bag her stylist left behind. "Try these earrings instead."

"I'm exhausted. Aria was up all night teething." She changes out the earrings, closes her eyes. "And I miss my husband."

Her eyes pop open to meet mine in the mirror, and her smile teases me.

"I guess you miss Grip, too, huh?"

"Yeah." I check the iPad once more—three minutes. "He has this panel airing in a few minutes that I need to watch. Qwest is on it, too."

I try to keep my voice neutral, but something must tip Kai off because she offers a reassuring smile I don't want her to know I need.

"You know you have nothing to worry about, right?" She turns and perches on the edge of the dressing room table. "Grip has been in love with you as long as I've known him, and he's ecstatic to finally have you."

"I know." I force the words, blowing my nervous energy out in a sigh. "But he was with her, and I can't help but think she still has feelings for him. I trust *him*."

"Good, because he'll never give you reason not to."

A text message lights Kai's phone on the dressing room table. She grabs it, smiling and responding.

"Rhyson?" I guess.

"No, my sister." Kai grimaces. "Half-sister. She lives in Vegas with my dad and ... his wife."

I notice she doesn't say stepmother. Kai and I haven't talked much about her complicated history with her father, but I know they've been working on their relationship.

"She's wishing me luck." Kai sets the phone down and meets my eyes with a soft smile. "She's a great kid."

"You guys are close?"

"Getting there. We talk more than ... well, more than I talk to my father."

"Thank you for encouraging Rhyson to work on things with our parents," I say. "Seeing you do it has helped him a lot."

"I try, but it's not easy. My father ruined my mom's life for a while." Pain etches lines between her brows. "He hurt a lot of people—the church he abandoned, his community."

"You?" I venture quietly.

Kai looks up, blinking a few times and drawing a shallow breath.

"Yeah, me." She glances at Aria, a tender smile tugging at her lips. "He was my world. I think sometimes we don't realize that for our kids, we're everything. I mean, friends and family, of course, and as they get older, maybe their peers have more influence, but we're what they see most. I was a daddy's girl, through and through."

"And he left with her? With his current wife?"

"Yeah, she was pregnant." Kai licks her lips before going on. "She was the secretary at our church, where he was the pastor."

"Wow." I wrestle with surprise and disgust. "Another reason to skip religion."

Kai considers me in silence for a few seconds, crossing one ankle over the other before speaking.

"I get that." Her harsh laugh splinters in the air. "Hell, I felt that. For a while I wasn't sure what I believed because most of it came from my dad."

She drops her eyes to the floor.

"And I didn't believe in him anymore." She shrugs. "But liars *can* tell the truth. It took me a long time to figure out that just because my dad lied about his affair, it didn't mean every sermon, every Bible story, everything he told me about God was a lie."

"Is that why you're church shopping?" I give her a smile so she'll know I'm not mocking her.

Kai rolls her eyes and grins.

"Rhyson probably thinks I'm crazy. I know he's not big on faith."

"He has faith in *you*," I assure her. "He loves you more than anything."

"The woman he loves was shaped by my father," she says. "By my mother even more, but my faith was shaped by my dad. There's not a doubt in my mind that, in spite of his flaws, he understands faith. He understands God, even if he doesn't always follow. I've finally managed to sift out what was his and what's mine, what I want to keep and what I don't need. I want to pass that on to Aria. She'll have to go through the same process, decide what part of what I've shared is for her and what is not, but I want her to know that part of her mother."

Her smile wavers, bitterness leveling it out.

"The way I know that part of my father, the way I know all of his parts . . . even the ones I wish weren't there."

Three quick raps at the door interrupt and signal that it's time. Kai glances again at Aria sleeping peacefully, reluctance to leave obvious on her face.

"Don't worry, I got her." I open the door for the production assistant, who looks at me expectantly. "She'll be right out. Thanks."

When I turn back, Kai is leaning over the pen, smiling.

"Okay. I'll be back." She gives me a knowing look. "And don't be paranoid about Qwest and the panel. She's a great girl. It's no secret she and I are friends, and I feel for her, for how things happened, but Grip has never really been anyone's but yours. Remember that."

With one last glance in the mirror, she's out the door. I turn on the monitor mounted in the corner to watch the feed of Kai's performance but mute it to focus on the panel that is just starting online.

"Thank you for joining us today," the host says. "We're continuing our web series entitled Helping Ourselves. Each week we discuss an initiative or a group of people making a difference in communities of color."

Angie, her hair in its natural state, a beautiful nimbus of textured waves and curls, wears skinny jeans and an off-the-shoulder sweatshirt. Her skin is tiramisu brown, glowing with health and good makeup. She exudes complete confidence. I haven't had any interaction with her at all, but I'm already impressed by what I see.

"We're broadcasting on YouTube and Instagram," Angie continues, smiling into the camera. "We're also live tweeting, and the official hashtag is #HelpingOurselves."

She gestures to her right, where Grip, Qwest, and a few other celebrities are seated. I try not to read too much into the fact that Grip and Qwest are right beside each other.

Angie performs quick introductions for each person, famous in their own right and arena, but Grip is the best known, by far. He's not doing anything that should make you want to look at him instead of everyone else, but you do. You just do not want to take your eyes off him.

Or maybe that's just me.

A new sense of purpose rests on Grip's shoulders since he started Dr. Hammond's class and moved to New York. He's definitely still engaged as an artist, still the studio rat he's always been, but there's more to his life now, and I can tell it is deeply satisfying to him. It's significance. He wouldn't be the man I love without this passion, this thirst to do something about the things that need doing.

He's laughing at something Angie said that I missed because I've been caught mid-drool. He leans back, his casual posture a thin veil over the coiled energy always waiting to spring forth. The *Run DMC* shirt fits the lean musculature of his chest and arms. I smile at the cheap black plastic watch on his wrist that he's never without, the one I won for him that night years ago. Qwest may have more in common with him—culture, music, challenges—but that watch reminds me that Grip and I have a history and a future.

"Grip, you've always been socially conscious," Angie says. "But 'Bruise' kind of put everyone on notice and started a lot of dialogue. Can you talk a little about what went into that song?"

"Yeah, sure. I grew up with that tension." Grip leans forward, elbows propped on his knees and eyes lit by conviction. "Needing law enforcement because I lived in such a dangerous place, but fearing cops because we never felt they were checking for us. I didn't write the song to take a side as much as to represent *both* sides, and hopefully show that we're more alike than we are different, find some common ground to negotiate the most difficult things. It's not right when unarmed black men are shot in the back for doing nothing and then officers walk away with impunity, but it's also not right when good cops are judged by the same stripes as the bad ones. It's not right to ambush good cops to make a point. Nina Simone said it's an artist's responsibility to reflect their times. That's what I want to do."

A wide grin hangs between my cheeks, pride swelling in my chest. His intelligence and passion are evident every time he answers a question. Angie has assembled a great group, each of them incredibly talented and popular, leveraging their moment for causes close to their hearts. I'm even touched when Qwest talks about Our Girls, the initiative she works with to raise awareness about women of color who go missing and the fact that they receive less media coverage and less attention.

"Grip, you're here in New York now, right?" Angie asks near the end of the allotted broadcast time. "At NYU?"

"Yeah, for the semester." Grip grins. "I love New Yorkers because they don't give a damn about me most days. I walk to class and grab coffee and go home like everybody else. There's an anonymity here that I really enjoy."

"And what are you studying?" Angie asks.

"I'm taking Dr. Israel Hammond's course on systemic bias in the criminal justice system. He's a guest professor this semester."

"Now that's a woke brother." Approval shines from Angie's eyes. "I read *Virus* when it came out. It should be required reading for everyone."

"He's brilliant and cool as a fan." Grip returns her smile.

The open curiosity gives way to a calculation I've seen on faces like hers on shows like these a hundred times. Even before she asks her next question, I sense the interview about to take a different turn. Call it premonition, or call it one ruthless bitch recognizing another, but I know.

"And you've been sighted with your girlfriend here in the city," she says. "She moved here, too, right?"

Grip must recognize that look, too. He shutters his expression, but keeps smiling. "Yeah, she grew up here."

"I keep it real, Grip." Angie spreads the look to the rest of the panelists. "Every person here has been on the receiving end of my real. It's your first time, but I'm not gonna treat you any different."

Oh, God. What is she about to say?

"You sound like you understand and want to raise awareness about the issues facing Black people." The "but" is all over her face before she even says it. "*But*, really how woke can you be sleeping with a white woman?"

All the air freeze-dries in my chest, just stalls and is enveloped in cold.

"What did you say?" Grip's brows bend like an accordion into a disbelieving scowl. "What does that have to do with being woke? With wanting to make a difference?"

"I'm just saying we get sick and tired of watching men like you talk about the cause," Angie says, her polite mask falling away, the indignation she must have been hiding rearing its head. "Talk about what our community needs and esteem Black women from one side of your neck, and then go and choose a white woman as your partner. You out here playing in the snow. It's a little hypocritical."

"How is it hypocritical?" Controlled rage is evident in Grip's narrowed eyes and the fists clenched on his knees. "I don't see anything incongruent about those two things, unless you are operating under the false assumption that me wanting to end systemic racism equates to me hating white people. I don't hate white people—I hate *racism*."

Grip pauses meaningfully, tipping his chin back to study her closely.

"We gave you a pass when you chose a white woman over the Black woman you *said* was your queen," she says.

Not true. It drives me crazy when people assume "Queen" was written for Qwest, and the #GripzQueen hashtag still haunts me occasionally on social media.

"Did you hear me asking for a pass?" Grip cocks one brow, his voice even but taut with outrage. "You don't give me passes because I don't need your approval."

"All I'm saying is I bet you won't find Dr. Hammond pulling this. You may *talk* woke," Angie asserts with relish, "but your walk is broke."

Oh, I bet she's been saving that line for a special occasion.

"Oh, you wanna compare walks?" Grip sits up straight, his words sounding like a battle cry. "Check my record—I've put my resources where my mouth is. I take every chance to engage with these issues, not just throw money at them, and what exactly have you done other than start Twitter beef and host a podcast?"

"Don't throw shade at me for voicing what most Black women think," she fires back. "I just thought I should bring it up because I wasn't sure if you were ashamed of her or what. We rarely see you out or in the news with her the way you have been in past relationships. You must realize how bad it looks."

"I see no need to satisfy the curiosity of people who don't mean well," Grip replies. "Who only want to play in mud and make a mess of people's lives on Twitter and Instagram. She isn't a public figure, and I'm protective of her privacy. She chose me, but she didn't ask to live on blast. I try to honor that. Believe me, it has nothing to do with me being embarrassed."

"She may not be a public figure," Angie says. "But she's sleeping with one, and she's related to one. Her name is Bristol Gray, for those who may have missed it since you've been hiding her, and her brother is Rhyson Gray—now that's a big name. You don't mess around. Go white or go home, huh?"

"I came on this panel to talk about issues," Grip says. "Real issues that are costing us lives and compromising our future. You, however, chose to talk about shit that doesn't matter and isn't anyone's business but mine and my girlfriend's. I bet the men sitting in jail too long for petty crimes, or for crimes they didn't even commit, those looking for jobs or needing education to even compete for them, all the people I want to help won't give a damn if the person helping has a white girlfriend or not."

Grip stands, reaching to loosen the mic from the collar of his T-shirt.

"So, I say, with all due respect, Angie." He holds the mic in his hand, farther away from his mouth, but there's no mistaking his parting. "Go fuck yourself."

He flings the mic onto the couch, leaving various degrees of shock and satisfaction on the faces of those who remain.

"Peeps, you heard that." Angie turns her gaze to the camera. "Now I want to hear from you. Where do you stand on Black men pretending to be all woke, but first chance they get, going for a white woman? Leave comments on YouTube, on Facebook, tweet us, tag us on Instagram. Hashtag #PlayingInTheSnow."

She levels a more parting smile at her watching audience, the kind of smile you give when things go exactly as you've planned.

Fourteen

Grip

"**S**HIT!"

The expletive bounces off the walls of the narrow corridor as I leave the stage and head for the greenroom to collect my things. I can't believe I allowed that conniving chick to lure me into that trap.

"Grip!"

I don't turn even though I hear Qwest right on my heels and calling my name.

"Grip, stop."

I'm still not stopping. Rage pumps toxins into my bloodstream, and I might poison anyone I make contact with right now.

"Man, hold up," Qwest says louder, irritation lacing the words. "Grip."

"What?"

The word cannons from my mouth, and I turn around abruptly, Qwest slamming into my chest. Breathing like a bull, air streams from my nostrils. Angie Black is the red flag I can't get out of my head. How dare she use a panel on such important issues to create drama? And to bring Bristol into it, to call her name and imply that I'm embarrassed to be with her. My jaws hurts, my teeth are locked so tightly together.

"About what happened out there—"

"You mean the ambush?" I snap.

"Yeah. I didn't know anything about it."

"Really?" A scoffing gush of air rushes past my lips. "You expect me to believe that? Don't give me that shit, Q."

"Who you think you talking to?" The goodwill on Qwest's face gives way to irritation. "You better act like you got some sense talking to *me*."

"So, it's just coincidence that we ended up on this panel together? You're asking me to believe you didn't know things would go left like that?"

"I don't care *what* you believe." Qwest's anger clashes with mine in the tight space. "My cousin was snatched when we were twelve years old. There were no TV cameras, no vigils, no magazine covers for months wondering what happened to her. She was just gone, and we never saw her again, never got answers. That's why *I'm* here, not for your conceited ass."

Real pain etches itself onto her face, and regret pinches in my chest.

"I'm sorry. I shouldn't have questioned your motives." I blow out a frustrated breath and drag my hand over my jaw. "That was just some sideways shit I didn't see coming, and this was not the time or the place for her to pull that."

Qwest nods, something close to sympathy filling her dark eyes. Finally, we sigh in sync, each of us letting go of our anger at the same time.

"I swear I didn't know," Qwest says, her voice softer. "What Angie did out there, it wasn't cool, and I'm sorry she went out like that."

I tilt my head back to study the ceiling for a second before looking back to Qwest.

"And I'm sorry if I took any of this out on you." I lean against the wall, bending my knee and propping my foot there. "I'm just tired of this. What does me wanting to spend the rest of my life with Bristol have to do with me wanting things to improve? Wanting better for our community?"

Surprise and then something that resembles hurt flits through Qwest's eyes before she drops them to the cheap corridor carpet.

"The rest of your life?" She forces a laugh. "So it's like that?"

Dammit. I'm so Bristol's, sometimes I forget I was ever anyone else's. In this moment, I definitely forgot Qwest ever felt she had any claim on me.

"I'm sorry." I scrub the back of my neck. "I didn't think—"

"That I still had feelings for you?" Her mocking smile is turned inside out. "You're a hard man to get over."

A sheet of ice falls over Qwest's face.

"But I have," she says. "I'll admit, seeing you again . . ." She rolls a lusty look from my head to my Jordans. "You could still get it."

She tips her head up to meet my eyes, a question there, one I hope she doesn't voice.

"Qwest, come on," I say, clearing my throat of awkwardness. "You know I'm with somebody else."

"I bet she don't give it to you like I did," she says, all sass and bravado.

Actually, she does, but I choose not to make things worse by saying so. I just watch her, keeping my face indifferent.

"Let's not do this." I push off the wall, intending to step around her, but she pushes me back, leaving her hand in the center of my chest. It feels wrong to have someone else touch me, but I tamp down my unease and leave it there for now. I still feel guilty about the way I dragged her into the complex web of my relationship with Bristol. I hate that I hurt her before, and I want to handle her more carefully than I did in the past. I'll leave her hand there and leave our eyes connected until she says what she needs to say.

"If I had long, silky hair," Qwest says, bitterness tingeing her voice, "and gray eyes and a pretty golden tan, would you want me then?"

Damn.

"It has nothing to do with that, with those things, Qwest." I place my hand over hers, hoping the contact offers her some comfort. "Am I attracted to Bris? Of course, but I've been attracted to a lot of women."

"You were attracted to me." Boldness presses through the uncertainty on her face.

"I was," I agree. "But I've only ever loved one woman, and that's Bristol."

I pause, meting out my next words with care.

"And she's the only woman I plan to be in love with. So yeah, I'm spending the rest of my life with her, and I can't know what would have happened if she looked different, if she were blond, if she was Black. For me, it's a moot point, because I'm in love with the version of her that I have. That's all that matters."

Qwest flinches, like my words were a slap in her face. She pulls back, and with the tiny weight of her palm lifted, I breathe easier. She steps away and clears her throat, the uncertain woman asking questions gone. The assertive badass I'm used to seeing, the one who has all the answers, stands in front of me again.

"Love who you want, Grip." Her voice, her eyes, everything about her is resigned now. "Just be in the studio when my team needs you. I may not have any hold over your heart, but I still got your ass under contract for my album."

I manage a laugh, hoping to get us back on the footing we've had over the last few weeks I've been working on her project while in New York. "I'll be there."

My phone vibrates in my pocket, and I take it out to see Bristol's name.

"Well, I guess I should let you handle that," Qwest says, eyeing the screen. Her typical swagger is at odds with the lingering hurt I see in her eyes as she turns to walk away.

"Bris, I—"

"Why is she touching you?"

Bristol's voice is that dangerous, about-to-go-HAM quiet.

"Um, babe, what?" I'm disoriented. "Why is who touching me?"

"Qwest. She was all over you."

"The hell she was. I have no idea what you're talking about."

"Oh, maybe you should check Instagram. That's where you and I and Qwest are all tagged in a picture that shows her *touching you*."

With her still on the line, I pull my phone away from my ear and go to my little-used Instagram account.

"Well, damn."

Some intern, production assistant, gofer-ass punk skulking around here in the halls must have snapped a picture of Qwest with her hand on my chest and posted it just that fast. The moment that felt wrong when it was happening looks even worse out of context on Instagram. What was me trying to protect Qwest's feelings and not hurt her any more than I already have looks intimate, like a secret, and the caption only adds fuel.

Maybe @TheRealGrip is taking @MsAngieBlack's advice to heart and going back to black. Who is really #GripzQueen? #TheBlackerTheBerry #TheSweeterTheJuice #OnceYouGoBlack #YouWontGoBack #WokeCheck #PlayingInTheSnow

Neither Bristol nor Qwest is referenced specifically, but both are tagged. *Fuck my life.*

"Bris." Now my voice is dangerously soft. I'm good and damn tired of people in my damn business every time I turn around, poking their noses in my shit where it doesn't belong, messing with me and my girl. "You know this isn't real."

"It looks real," she whispers. "It feels real."

"Bristol Gray, if you tell me you believe this, I'm fucking you into next week when I see you."

Typically, she would say, *Is that a promise?* or offer some smartass comment, but the other end stays silent.

"Bris, come on." I bang my fist into the wall. "You know this isn't true. If she were a guy, I would kick Angie's ass."

"Well she's a girl," Bristol says, her voice hardening. "And I do plan to kick her ass where it will hurt most."

"What do you mean?"

"Meaning I'm calling her producer. That shit was way beyond the scope of what we agreed to."

"That isn't the way to handle it."

"The hell it isn't." Bristol's indignation and resentment nearly choke her words. "She thinks she can come for me—for *us* like that with no consequences? She's about to learn differently."

I squeeze the bridge of my nose, bracing myself for a fight I really don't want right now. "Bris, you're not doing that."

Her voice drops. "What did you say?"

Aw hell.

"I said you're not doing that. That's what she wants."

"Then she'll be very happy to find herself out of a job because if she wants a fight, I'm her girl, and she should know better than to bring a fucking tweet to a gun fight."

"You don't want beef with this chick. It'll only turn the tide against you."

"Why? Because I'm white? Because everyone's looking for a reason to turn against me anyway since I'm with you? Like the tide wasn't already against me."

"We're in the twenty-first century, and nobody should still hold these views, but it's just a few, Bris. They are just the vocal ones. I know it's hard. It's hard for me, too."

"I'm so sorry I'm making life hard for you, Grip."

"Stop it." Anger flares in my words. "We're not doing this. Us fighting won't make things any better."

"No, what will make things better is teaching Angie Black that I'm not the bitch to mess with. She's firing shots? I'm firing back."

"You're not," I say, barely holding on to my calm. "Not representing me, you're not."

An ominous silence swells from the other end, reaching across the country to suffocate me.

"What did you say?" she finally asks.

"Look, it's my career," I force myself to reply. "And I determine what will or won't be done on my behalf, and I say no."

"I see," she says, suppressed fury embedded in her response.

As soon as the words left my mouth, I wanted to take them back. I know this will only push Bristol away, will only make her angrier, but I will not have her embroiled in some beef with one of the most influential figures in the socialsphere. They want to come for me? Let them, but I'm not having them hurting Bristol. I should have just said that; it would have gotten a better response than this.

"Bristol, look, I—"

"I should go," she cuts in. "Kai's almost done with her segment, and Aria's here with me. She just woke up."

I sigh, resigned to not making this right until she comes home. "Okay. Can I pick you up from the airport tomorrow? What time does your flight land?"

"I don't think I'm coming." Her voice is cool and distant. "Things are still hectic for Kai. Luke's reality show starts production this weekend, and I'm thinking I should stay here for that. I'll come ... I don't know, next week."

This is bullshit. I know it, and so does she. Does she not feel how this distance is killing me? Not just the three thousand miles separating us, but the chasm opened up by this asinine fight.

"Are you sure that's why you're not coming home?" I ask, letting my frustration leak through the words.

A baby's cry cuts off her response. Aria.

"I have to go," Bristol says hastily. I hear her *shhhh*-ing our goddaughter.

"Bristol, wait."

The line dies, and there is nothing but silence on the other end, a gaping hush swallowing all the things I wish I'd said instead of all the wrong shit I spoke. I consider calling her right back, but I don't want to distract her when she's taking care of Aria for Kai. Besides, I need to get to the studio in Harlem for a session. I glance at my watch to see how much time I have to get there. I stare at the piece-of-shit watch I never take off, only to find that it has died. After almost a decade, this watch that has never failed me decides to die today. I'll never forget the night Bristol gave me this watch, the night of our first kiss, trading hurts and hearts a hundred feet in the air, stuck on a Ferris wheel. The watch may have finally stopped working, but *we* still work. We'll always work. In a world of pieces that never seem to fit, we do. We work. We make sense when nothing else does, and I have to remind her of that.

Fifteen

Bristol

MESSED UP.

As soon as I told Grip I was staying in LA for work instead of returning to New York, I knew it was the wrong thing to do. The voice in my head calling me a fool is so loud and insistent, I can barely focus on anything else. Sitting here on the set of Luke's new reality show, I'm not really needed. I mean, it's good for me to be here, sure. Luke appreciates it, but he doesn't *need* me. Grip, however, does need me. Even across the country, I *feel* his need, the desperation to make things right. I need him, too. I feel it, too. It hounds me. After yesterday's disaster, another public dragging, the only place I want to be is in his arms, reassured that we're okay and, no matter how many stupid fights we have, will always be okay. Where am I instead? Here suffering indigestion from bad craft services food.

"That sound good, Bris?"

My unfocused gaze locks in on Luke, who watches me, both brows lifted in query.

"Uh, sure." I shake my head to pull myself back in. "Wait, I didn't actually hear what you said. What are they asking you to do?"

For the next few minutes, he details a segment the producers have set up showing him in the recording booth of the studio where we're shooting.

"Yeah, that sounds great." I glance at my phone, checking for missed calls or texts from Grip. Nothing. We don't fight often, but when we do it's a conflagration, burning everything to the ground, and right now I'm charred. Grip is usually the first to apologize. He's a better person than I am, the bigger person, but not this time. I'm making the first move, and it's on the next plane out of LA.

"I need to go to New York," I say abruptly, cutting in on whatever Luke was telling me.

Luke's startled expression morphs into understanding. "Is this about that Angie Black thing yesterday?"

Oh, that's right—Luke knows. Everyone knows, because my life is an open book—and not the fairy-tale kind, more like a Stephen King novel.

Misery maybe?

"Yeah." I gather my iPad and bag. "I was supposed to be there by now, but ..."

I let him fill in the blank with my cowardice and avoidant behavior.

"You *do* realize most people don't feel that way, right?" Luke asks with a kindness not typically found in this industry. "The things Angie said ... I know there are some who agree, but most don't. Look at all the support you guys got afterward."

I was pleasantly surprised by all the flak Angie received, lots of it from black women wanting us to know they didn't agree with Angie. It came from groups Grip has donated to, from cops he's worked with who defended him. It was actually pretty amazing. There were, of course, those vocal in their support of Angie's position, but it was heartening to see the support for us, too.

That still doesn't fix the fact that I messed up.

"This is some high-profile shit, Bris," Luke says. "But you can take it."

"Taking it is easier said than done when 'it' is blasted all over every social media platform and your relationship is reduced to tacky hashtags by people who want to see it fail."

To my absolute dismay, my voice shakes and I'm blinking back tears. I hate being reduced to this weak, teary *girl*. This time it's not what *they* did to me. It's how badly I've handled things.

"Hey." Luke takes both my hands in his and dips his head to catch my eyes. "I was there the week you and Grip first met. I saw him love you for years, and I saw you try your best not to love him back. It's never been more obvious to me that two people belong together. This is a bump in the road, and not even a bump of your own making. Somebody else's biases shouldn't be causing problems between you."

Right now, Luke isn't my client; he's the friend I've known for more than a decade, since before the money and the fame, and he's right. Urgency to make things right quickens my breath and smolders in my blood.

"You're a wise man." I pull my phone back out of my bag, my mind and fingers already racing ahead while I start searching for a flight. "I'll have Sarah on set tomorrow, but I need to get to New York tonight."

"Maybe." Luke aims his megawatt smile over my shoulder. "Or maybe New York will come to you."

Before I can fully process what he's saying or turn to see what's over my shoulder, a warm, familiar weight settles at my hip. That clean skin-deep scent I've come to associate with one person envelops me. I look up and over my shoulder to find Grip scanning my face with sober eyes.

"Hey." That's all he says, like he's supposed to be here on the set of a reality TV show instead of in class, instead of in New York. His fingers tighten at the curve of my waist, though, belying the calm greeting. The tension rolls off his body and onto mine. I absorb it, feel it tightening the line of my mouth and clenching my hand around the strap of my bag.

"Dude." Luke reaches for Grip's free hand, doing that man clench hand-shake thing. "What's up? Good to see you."

"You, too." Grip's mouth relaxes into a smile for our longtime friend. "You think you big time now, huh? Now you got your own show and all."

Luke laughs, his bright blue eyes lighting up and crinkling at the corners.

"I've always been big time." He offers an immodest shrug of his shoulders. "The rest of the world's just catching up, thanks in large part to your girl here."

"Yeah, she's something else." Grip's smile dims a little, but he doesn't look my way. "Well, congrats."

Before any of us can say more, the director's assistant interrupts, her harried expression and flyaway hair conveying the kind of day it's been.

"Luke, Steven's looking for you." She sets her stress aside long enough to ping-pong admiring glances between Grip and Luke. I can't blame her. Facing one another, they're a study of beautiful contrasts, Grip's darkness and raw sexuality a perfect foil for Luke's blond hair and surfer-boy-next-door good looks.

"You said Steven needs me?" Luke prompts.

"Um, yeah." She blinks the stars from her eyes and frowns. "He wants to talk through a few things for this next sequence."

As much as I loathe the thought of leaving Grip even for a few minutes, I force myself to turn to him, prepared to ask him to wait for me, but again, it's Luke to the rescue.

"Hey, I got this, Bris." His kind eyes smile back at me. "I'm sure Grip didn't come all this way to see me."

My eyes lock with Grip's, and I already see the reprimand behind his impassivity.

"Okay," I say. "I won't leave, though, until you're done. Come find me. I want to make sure you feel good about everything."

"That works," Luke says, turning back to the production assistant. "Take me to your leader."

He gestures for her to lead the way and they're gone, leaving Grip and me alone.

"Is there somewhere we can talk?" He scans the studio's parking lot, which is doubling as our set. We've broken for lunch, and the crew swarms around the craft service table like ants at a picnic, hungry and industrious. There won't be much time for food. Everyone's focused on the meal, but not too focused to miss Grip. His star has risen stratospherically since his album dropped. They pretend not to be starstruck, but their surreptitious attention presses in on the privacy this conversation requires.

"Luke has a trailer of sorts." I flick my chin toward it, across the parking lot that has been cleared for today's shoot.

"That'll do." A thick fan of lashes hoods whatever is in his eyes. I hate not knowing what he's thinking, other than that he's not pleased with me.

I can't blame him; I haven't been pleased with me since that damn panel.

We're halfway across the lot, and the silence is suffocating. The air hasn't been this heavy between us since before we got together. I hate that I did this. He walks beside me, a gulf-sized space between us and his eyes set on the trailer like it's a finish line. Once we're inside, I walk farther into the room, setting my back against the wall and watching him across the few feet separating us. Grip leans against the small bar stocked with Luke's favorite drinks and stares back at me. Everything is heightened in the small, tight space. Tension coils between us, pushing against the flimsy trailer walls. While a thousand ways to apologize fill my head and rest on my tongue, the silence tautens and lengthens.

"I was coming to New York tonight," I finally say. As apologies go, it's pretty lame, and not quite actually one.

"I heard you saying that when I walked up."

Grip looks good. He always does, but after more than a week apart, my eyes are as hungry for him as my heart is and I can't look at anything else in the room. He's wearing dark jeans and a Kelly green T-shirt that says *JOBS NOT JAIL* on the front.

God, did I mention he looks good?

I just want to skip to the part where he's soothing this ache at my core, where he's banging me like he's a bull and I'm his china shop. His still somber eyes tell me we're not there yet, but the compulsive clenching between my thighs reiterates that I'm ready to be.

"I'm sorry I pulled rank on you." His quiet apology when I was wrong on so many levels—when by all accounts, I should be apologizing first instead of just eye-fucking him—squelches my raging hormones.

"No, you were right." The words fight to get out of my mouth. "Not confronting Angie was the right call."

"I know that." He lifts one dark brow. "It would only make things worse, but I should have talked that through with you until we agreed on it, not tried to use the advantage our working relationship gives me to manipulate you."

He pauses, hesitation evident in his expression.

"I want to be your partner, Bris," he says softly. "In everything. There's no rank between us—ever."

I drop my eyes to the hands clasped in front of me.

"Thank you for that. I'm sorry, too. I should have said it first. It seems like whenever we fight, you're always the one . . ."

I swallow my pride and set aside every insecurity that's assaulting me to give him the truth.

"I'm just glad you're here." My voice wobbles. *Dammit.* "I'm just . . .I'm sorry."

I don't look up, but I hear him taking the first steps, feel him drawing closer. I anticipate his touch, shaking with the need of it. And then it comes. The perfect simplicity of our fingers twined together, of him holding my hand. It paradoxically brings me peace and incites my senses. Even as my soul seems to exhale in relief, want and need form a blazing knot in my belly. He tilts my chin until I have to meet his serious stare, his loving eyes.

"Bris, this is all we have." His words are so low, if someone else were in this tiny room with us, they wouldn't hear. They are only for me. "Until this semester is over, our time is split, and this is all we have."

I press our palms together.

"If you legit had to stay here in LA this weekend for work, I get that," he continues. "You know I'm not that dude who wants you compromising your career for me, but if you were avoiding me because of our fight—"

"I was." The admission leaves my lips before I can dissemble. His closeness, the intimacy of our fingers clinging, of our hearts beating through our chests and straining toward each other, demands my unequivocal honesty. I don't look away, refusing to let embarrassment over my childish behavior deprive me of these beautiful dark eyes for even another second. I don't miss the flash of disappointment at my words.

"I know that." Grip's mouth tightens, and I want to lick at the seam of his lips until they open for me, until he lets me back in. "That's why you should have had your ass in New York this weekend."

With him standing here in front of me, solid evidence of his love, I'm ashamed of myself, ashamed that I let doubt and insecurity rule me. I let them keep me here when I should have been there with him.

"You're right," I state simply.

"I hate it when we fight." He drags a hand across his face. "I can't focus. I can't sleep. I can't . . ." His words straggle into a growl of frustration and his brows snap together. "Nothing feels right when *we* aren't right. You let that shit Angie Black brought up get to you when you know it means nothing, and that stupid post on Instagram . . . I get how someone else would think something was up with Qwest when they saw that, but for you to . . ."

The questions build up in the look he gives me until I'm sure the moment will explode.

"Why, Bris? There's gotta be more to this than just the shots Angie fired. We're used to that shit. What's up for real?"

The reality of him, the steady pulse of this connection we share—with him standing in front of me, all the things that kept me on this coast seem ridiculous now.

"I . . . um . . . I was . . ." I squeeze my eyes closed for a second, feeling ridiculous now. "I was jealous."

"Jealous? Of Qwest?" The heavy breath he expels breaches the air between us. The demand of his eyes is louder than the word, louder than her name in the quiet room. "Because of some awkward photo posted to Instagram? How could you possibly be jealous of anyone when you know I've looked my own mother in the face and told her I would choose you over anyone?"

Well, when you put it that way . . .

"I didn't . . ." I falter because it's true; he did that. As much as Ms. James has sacrificed for him and as much as he loves her, he told her that, for me. "Not Qwest specifically."

"Baby, I'mma need you to get specific, because not one day since we got together have I *ever* given you reason to be jealous of any damn body, and yet you tried to play me—"

"I did not try to play you."

"You tried to play me," he persists, "like I was born yesterday morning and would accept some shit excuse for you staying here when you were supposed to be with me."

He levels a hard look at me that somehow still manages to convey his love.

"Now tell me why."

How do I put into words this awkward thing when nothing is ever awkward between us? But this is. This fear that crept insidiously into my head after my conversation with Jade and blossomed while I watched that panel—it's awkward.

"I'm not jealous of Qwest specifically." I'm embarrassed to even say this, but I have to. "When I watched that panel, I listened to Angie, and even to Qwest, to the other people onstage. I listened to you, and you were so passionate and knowledgeable and . . . I'm not—not about those things. What if some morning you wake up and my curiosity feels like ignorance? And you've lost patience with the things I don't know that someone else would. What if one day you decide you want someone who's . . ."

My voice peters out because to even say it feels wrong, but it's what I've been wrestling with since my last conversation with Jade, even though I haven't acknowledged it to myself.

"What if I decide I want someone who's what?" Grip tips my chin up again to search my eyes. "Someone who's Black?"

I don't nod, but he knows. What if he decides someday that the one thing he really wants, really *needs* is the one thing I can never be?

"Bris, I get it. The more active and vocal I am about these issues, the more some people want to focus on me being with someone who isn't black, but listen." He slides his hand to cup my neck, his thumb caressing my jaw. "I won't ever want someone who isn't *you.*"

I know that, or I knew it before I was on one coast and he was on the other and everyone had something to say about us and all the warning seeds Jade dropped in my ears started taking root.

"I'm sorry I freaked out." I draw a deep breath. "I kept thinking about you guys working together on her album, having your music in common, and then both being activists . . . all I could hear were the things Qwest was saying, the things Angie was saying, the things Jade said, and I—"

"Jade?" Grip's question slices into my explanation. He narrows his eyes, searching my face for answers I didn't mean to ever give him. "What does Jade have to do with this?"

Shit.

"Um . . ." I offer a nervous laugh while I search for a way to put him off Jade's scent. "Nothing. It doesn't have anything to do with Jade. I just meant—"

"Bris, you know better than to lie to me. What did she say to you?"

"Nothing."

"Bullshit. Tell me."

I press my eyes closed against his questions.

"I don't want to come between you and Jade now that you've cleared the air."

"You won't. Me and Jade, we're good. We'll *be* good. Just tell me what she said."

He dips his head and searches my eyes for anything I might hold back.

"Tell me everything."

I lick my lips, trapping the bottom one between my teeth before I start. Grip's family isn't like mine, fractured and dysfunctional. His family, especially his mother and Jade, mean everything to him. The last thing I want to do is cause more trouble than his relationship with me already has.

"When we were at your mom's house—"

"Wait," he cuts in. "You haven't been to my mom's since the going away party. This conversation was that long ago?"

"Yeah," I say carefully. "Then."

Grip crosses his arms over his chest and studies me closely, displeasure clear in the twist of his lips before he speaks.

"So, you've been thinking like this for a while and never talked to me about it?"

"It wasn't like that, I promise. It was . . . just some of the things Jade said got to me, and when I watched the panel, it all came back."

"What did she say?" He speaks the words smoothly, but there's a dent between his eyebrows.

"Just that one day you'd get tired of me not understanding your blackness."

"Understanding my . . . *what*?"

"You know, not knowing the movies or the songs or getting the jokes or knowing the things that are such a part of the community that means so much to you."

"Hmmm. What else?"

"She said I was a fantasy, a high you'd come down from, and then you would want something real, a woman like Qwest, to cure your jungle fever."

A startled laugh erupts from Grip.

"She actually said jungle fever? Who says that? Damn, that's some '90s Spike Lee shit. I'm embarrassed *for* her."

"It's not funny."

"Babe, it kind of is." The short-lived humor fades from his expression. "Actually, what's not funny is that you bought into it and let it come between us. You're it for me, Bris. You know that."

"I do know that. I'm sorry I was an idiot."

He softens his voice. "I'm sure it won't be the last time." His hands coast down my arms, heating my skin along the way before he takes my hands between his.

Anger stirs anew when I consider the stunt Angie Black pulled.

"I still say Angie shouldn't get away with this completely. Can't I—"

"She didn't." Grip's full lips thin into a severe line. "I blasted her ass when we got off the phone."

"You did?" I hope he gave it to her good, though I would have enjoyed peeling her skin off myself.

"I did, and I talked to her producer about it. He was apologetic and said he hadn't known she planned to go there. They're suspending her for two weeks." He squeezes my hands. "It wasn't that I didn't think she needed somebody's foot up her ass, I just didn't want it to be yours."

He was protecting me. I feel worse and better at the same time. I lean up, whispering my regret to him. "I'm sorry."

"Baby, it's okay. Just don't do that shit again." He grins and pushes the hair back from my face. "Let's go home."

"Are we making it permanent now?" The half-joking question slips past my lips on a fractured breath and a broken laugh. "Is New York home?"

Grip brushes his thumb over my mouth, dipping his finger into the bow of my top lip, pressing against the bottom until he's touching my teeth and tongue. His eyes rest hot and heavy and possessive on my mouth before he captures my eyes with his, making sure he has my attention.

"I'm your home, Bristol."

He's so certain. He never wavers in his love for me, in his certainty that we belong together no matter what anyone ever says. I'm ashamed again that I let Jade's words, Angie's criticisms, and Qwest just being Qwest make me doubt even a little bit.

"And you're mine," he adds.

"You better believe it," I agree with a smile. "But speaking of our current home, aren't you supposed to be in New York? In class?"

"I skipped."

I know how much he loves Dr. Hammond's class and what this time means to him. That he would miss that class speaks volumes.

"You skipped class?" I ask, my mouth hanging open.

He's told me a hundred—a thousand times how much he loves me, but that girl who moped around a deserted mansion while her family traveled the world without her, the one who crouched beyond her brother's rehearsal room listening to the magic of his music, looking for a way in, she still treasures being the most important thing to someone as incredible as Grip.

"You came for me." I cup his jaw, my voice and my heart softening the longer we're together.

Grip cups my face, too, his rough palm a welcome abrasion, his eyes intent.

"I'll always come for you. You should know that by now." He bends to press our foreheads together, his words misting my lips. "I have no pride when it comes to you, to this. I'll chase you anywhere."

I don't have words for how secure and completely adored that makes me feel, so I don't speak. I shift my head, my lips clinging to his, just for a moment. I deepen the heated contact of our mouths until our tongues move in tandem, tangling, wrestling, tasting.

"Don't run from me again." He breathes the words into my mouth and his fingers clench in my hair. Though just a whisper, they arrest me, an imperative that grabs me by the heart.

Sixteen

Grip

THERE'S A CERTAIN SENSE OF RIGHTNESS SEEING JADE IN THE STUDIO, not the way she used to come, her eyes lit with a hidden jealousy for my success, a nurtured resentment that the shot I got—the scholarship to a performing arts school—could have been hers. She has her own shot now, and I love seeing her take full advantage of it.

The ever-present Raiders cap is on the floor by her feet. Her head, hair sectioned into cornrows, is bent over a notepad. The guy she's talking to, Skeet, an old friend who needs other people's lyrics, notices me at the door before Jade does.

"What's up, superstar?" He crosses over, daps me up, and surveys me thoroughly. I know what he sees. My clothes are casual in that deliberate, understated way you have to pay a lot of money for. We started from the bottom together, but I kept rising, and he keeps slipping. I hope Jade's clever flow can help him.

"What's good, Skeet?" I ask, wishing I didn't know him well enough to recognize the calculating light in his eyes.

"You on the come up." His laugh is a prelude to the question I see coming a mile off. "When you gon' put me on? Let me spit on a track. I need some of that Top 40, double platinum love."

"We'll see." My smile is super-glued in place, not slipping a millimeter. "I'm not really recording right now, at least not for myself."

"Oh yeah. I heard you and Qwest in the booth again." Calculation becomes speculation. "I saw that panel Angie Black put on, by the way. That was messed up, man."

I shrug, unwilling to give him anything more to work with and tired of talking about it.

"Nothing I haven't heard before. Won't be the last time somebody comes at me with ignorant shit like that."

My eyes find Jade, who sits on the couch across from the sound board, tossing her cap from hand to hand. She knows I'm here to see her, and she's just waiting for Skeet to figure it out.

"A'ight, bruh," I say, patting his back. "I need to holla at Jade for a minute. You mind?"

"Nah. We were just going over some notes before the engineers get here for the track we're recording tonight." He grabs a bag of weed from the sound board and heads for the door. "I'mma go burn one. Take your time."

He turns at the door, smiling at Jade.

"And thanks for hooking me up with your cousin," he says. "Her shit's the bomb."

He leaves behind a silence thick with my displeasure and Jade's curiosity.

"Yo, what's good, cuz?" She pounds my fist, scooting over so I can sit on the couch beside her. "Thought you were still in New York."

"I was, but I came to get Bristol. We're flying back tonight."

Irritation flashes across her face before she can hide it. I really thought we were gaining ground, but I realize now she believes Bristol is an itch that, once scratched, will be gone. She's just been biding her time.

"I'm glad to see you working with Skeet." I slouch into the cushy leather worn to buttery softness during many late-night recording sessions. "He needs the help."

"Yeah, his stuff was whack." Jade keeps a straight face for a few seconds before sharing a grin with me. It makes her look younger, carefree, and I glimpse that girl who used to ride bikes with me until the streetlights came on. It's for that girl that I want to be gentle.

"I need you to try with Bristol, J." I cut the small talk and get right to it, my voice soft enough to persuade, but firm enough to insist.

"And what'd Miss Run Tell Dat say?" She twists her lips into a grimace. "I knew she couldn't keep her mouth—"

"She didn't." I'm losing patience the more Jade lets her resentment show. "I had to drag it out of her, what was bothering her."

"And it was me?" Jade touches her chest. "I'm what's bothering her when I haven't even talked to her?"

"Not since my going away party, right? She finally told me about the conversation you had in the kitchen."

"I didn't tell her anything Angie Black didn't say in front of the whole world," Jade snaps. "When you gonna realize Bristol is not for you? You have an opportunity to make a difference, and being with her is ruining it."

"Ruining it how?"

"How much can Black lives really matter when you fucking a snowflake?" A disparaging puff of air coasts past her lips. "We supposed to respect that? Just get rid of her and find someone like Qwest, that's all I'm saying."

That's all? Jade says it easily, like it should be self-evident, like giving up Bristol shouldn't break me, when it would. How can she think she knows me and not realize that losing Bristol would crush me?

"You still think she's a trophy or a phase I'll grow out of, don't you?" I lean forward to study her face in case it tells me something different than her words do.

She just looks at me, the *damn right* so clear on her face, she doesn't bother voicing it. I reach into the pocket of my leather jacket.

"Does this look like a phase to you?" I open my palm, exposing the large square canary yellow diamond I picked up before I went to the set of Luke's show. Jade glares at the ring like the lights bouncing off the facets taunt her.

"You really doing this?" she grits out. "Wait'll Aunt Mittie sees that."

"Oh, she saw it." I slip the ring back into the safety of my pocket. "When she helped me pick it out. Now all she talks about is swirl grandbabies."

"You're gonna have kids with *her*?" Disgust wrinkles the smooth surface of Jade's face.

Now she's pissing me the hell off.

"Yeah, I'm gonna have kids with her," I snap. "As many as she'll give me. And fuck you for making it sound like some kind of violation. I found somebody I love and want to spend the rest of my life with."

"Oh, everybody says forever in the beginning."

"We've been through this before, Jade. It *is* forever with us."

Jade rolls her eyes and shoves the Raiders cap over her cornrows, resignation wrestling with protest in her expression.

"Listen to me." I take both her hands in mine and look at her until she looks back at me. "I *will* choose her over you."

Her lashes drop and blink several times, a frown drawing her brows together.

"And if you can't get over this bigoted shit, you won't be in our lives."

Her eyes fly to my face, widen and then narrow.

"I love you, Jade. You know that, but you need to understand something: anyone who wants to hurt Bristol has to go through me to get to her."

I pause meaningfully before finishing.

"And they will *not* get to her," I warn. "Keep showing your ass when she comes around, and you won't *be* around. I'm not tolerating the toxic."

An unexpected smile quirks her mouth. She reaches into the pocket of her baggy jeans for lip balm and slides the stick over her lips.

"Alliteration," she murmurs.

"What?" I exhale a frustrated breath. "Are you hearing me?"

"Yeah, 'tolerating the toxic'—it's alliteration." Her smile reminisces. "You came home one day from school. We were in like the sixth grade or something. You learned alliteration that day and couldn't stop talking about it, giving me examples, making me come up with some. You were the smartest boy I knew."

She shakes her head, something close to pride creeping into her eyes.

"You still are. Even on that panel, you stood out. You're the best of us, Grip, and I wanted you . . ."

Her rueful sigh says it: she wanted what she thinks is best for me, namely, for me to choose a black woman. I hook an elbow around her neck, pulling her into me.

"You know what?" I touch our heads together. "Even though I dated all over the place, every ethnicity, I think somewhere in the back of my mind I thought I would settle down with someone just like Ma. Maybe I assumed that meant she'd be black. I never gave it much thought, but that's not what it meant. Bris is strong and determined and loyal and as ride or die as they come, just like Ma. I didn't see this coming, but she is exactly what I need."

I kiss Jade's forehead and stand, looking down at her. "I'm not giving her up, J," I tell her. "Not even for you."

She doesn't reply, but fixes her eyes on the floor, offering no more words. I don't wait for her to say anything, just head out the door. My words should be the last because they're the only ones that count.

Seventeen

Grip

"THIS IS REMARKABLE, IZ." I STUDY THE PROPOSAL IN FRONT OF me, so excited my foot is bouncing and I can practically feel my blood zooming through my veins. I saw an early draft, and talked Bris to death about it on the plane back to New York, but the final version is even better.

"I want in," I say decisively.

"What do you mean?" Iz glances up from the stack of papers he's grading in his office. "Want in on what?"

"I want to invest in this program," I say. "The community bail fund program."

Surprise widens his eyes behind his glasses, and he tosses his red pen onto the chaos of his desk.

"Man, I wanted your opinion, not your money."

"Well you got both. Where are your beta cities?" I ask. "You say you'll launch it in five major cities—which ones are you considering?"

"LA is definitely on the list." His deep chuckle fills the small office. "If that's your next question."

"Now I really want in." I take a deep breath. "But I want a seat at the table, not just somewhere to throw my money."

"What does that mean exactly?" Iz takes off his glasses and polishes them on the hem of his Morehouse College T-shirt.

"With your organization, is there any room on the board of directors for a ridiculously rich budding philanthropist who needs to learn the ropes?" The question comes easily, but I'm holding my breath. I want this—as much as I wanted my first record deal, as much as I wanted studio time so badly I swept the floors for it. The only thing I've ever wanted more than this was Bristol. I got her, and I'm getting this, too.

"For a man with your resources," he says, leaning back in his chair and steepling his fingers at his chest. "That could be arranged."

"For real?" I don't want to sound eager, but the chance to pour my energy into something that will have immediate impact on the community where I grew up? Hell yeah, I'm eager.

"For real." Iz nods. "And when I say your resources, I'm not just talking about your money, Grip. You're a smart guy—principled, articulate. You have a level of influence, a platform no amount of money could buy."

Iz's words affirm me in a way I don't think I ever have been, in a way I don't think I knew I needed. It feels different than the things my mother told me growing up. He may not be old enough to be my father, and I may not have known him very long, but there's no one else I respect more. That was one of the few things Angie Black and I did agree on.

"By the way," I say, turning the subject partially to avoid the emotions his encouragement elicited. "Not sure if you caught that panel I was on last week, but Angie Black was singing your praises."

He picks his pen back up to resume grading papers, his forehead crinkling into a frown.

"Yeah, I saw it." It feels like the words are being pulled from his mouth with pliers. "As much as we'd talked about your girl, I never thought to ask if she was a sister. I just assumed."

"And I never thought to mention it because it doesn't matter." I suck my teeth then grit them. "I can't believe Angie turned what should have been a thoughtful, productive dialogue into a circus, and she had the nerve to question my commitment to these causes because my girlfriend is white. How ridiculous is that?"

He's especially preoccupied with the papers in front of him. He doesn't acknowledge my statement with even a grunt, and suddenly I need him to.

"Right, Iz?" I press. "The idea that my effectiveness is compromised somehow because Bristol is white—it's bullshit, right?"

He doesn't lift his eyes from the page in front of him. "Well, you do like to make it hard for yourself, don't you?"

Tension stretches across my back like a wire hanger. "What does that mean?"

"It's just an awkward time to be talking black and sleeping white." He shrugs the linebacker shoulders rebelling against his tweed sports jacket with patches on the elbows. "To be dating someone outside your community when you're emerging as such a voice *for* it."

The smartest man I know just said some dumb shit.

"You see those two things as somehow incongruous?" My question is laced with dread as I brace myself for the man I saw as a hero to show his feet of clay.

"I just think a lot of successful brothers do what you're doing." He finally meets my eyes, tossing the pen down again. "You probably don't even realize that you've been societally conditioned to see the white woman as the ideal. On some level, winning the white man's prize is a symbol that you are now equal to him. You acquire her as an extension of your success."

"*Acquire* her?" I throw my voice across the desk like a blade, honed and precise.

"It's natural really," he continues matter-of-factly. "It's the ultimate act of defiance against those who have traditionally oppressed you. She's an ideal to achieve, and we see that, in every aspect of your life, you're an overachiever."

"Bris isn't some ideal, some lie mainstream media fed me and I fell for. This is love, not politics."

"Love *is* politics," he counters. "Because love is merely a function of your values and priorities."

"If you think love is politics, then I see why your marriage failed." A storm cloud bursts on his face, raining anger.

"Watch it, Grip," he says. "You're way out of line."

"*I'm* out of line?" Incredulity and fury brawl within me. "You dare to bring this bullshit to me, insult the woman I plan to marry, insult *me* this way, and then you say I'm out of line?"

He narrows his eyes on my face at the word "marry."

"That's your decision, of course," he says. "Not one I would ever make. I believe the greatest expression of commitment to Black people and the Black family is the commitment to a Black woman. For that reason, I don't date outside of Black, much less marry."

"Oh, so I imagined the vibe between you and Callie?" A mocking laugh grates in my throat. "You don't date or marry outside your race, but you'd fuck outside of it if Callie was down."

The fury in his eyes bores into me. "Who the hell do you think you're talking to?"

"I really have no idea who I'm talking to." I grab my saddlebag and stand, my hands shaking with the rage I'm suppressing. "I can't believe I moved to New York to study under a bigot."

He surges to his feet, fists balled like a boxer. "You have the audacity to call *me* a bigot?"

"*I* have the audacity? You're the one talking to me about Gandhi and Martin then spouting this crap. Martin said we should judge people by the content of their character, not the color of their skin, yet here you are judging Bristol because she's white before you've even met her? Hypocrite."

Anger ignites in his eyes at the insult, but he runs a slow hand over the stubble on his jaw. He sighs, shoving big hands into the pockets of his jeans.

"Look, we're both upset," he says. "This is why I didn't bring it up. I knew we didn't agree on this subject, and it does no good to talk about it. We can still work together, do a lot of good. That seat on the board is yours, and I meant what I said—it's not just because of your money."

"So we can work together and do all this good," I say, "but the whole time you're looking at my wife and thinking she's a mistake? That she's some Anglo trophy I use to prove something to other people? Even worse, because of some self-hate, to feel better about myself?"

He goes quiet, his chest swelling with the deep breath he draws in. I gesture to the proposal abandoned on his desk, my excitement smothered by disappointment and disillusion.

"How do you squeeze such big ideas into such a narrow mind? You're smarter than this, Iz," I say quietly. "I thought I could follow you. I thought you had answers, solutions."

I walk to the door and give him one last sad, disgusted glance, saying what I'm fully prepared to accept may be my last words to him ever.

"Turns out you're the problem."

Eighteen

Bristol

'M IN THE KITCHEN WHEN GRIP COMES HOME. I BOUGHT A COOKBOOK, and it openly mocks me from the counter, its pages a reminder of my culinary failings. Occasionally I have these domestic urges. They typically pass, but ever since we moved into this beautiful place that has never been anything but a home since the O'Malleys drafted their first designs, the urges are harder to ignore—to buy fresh flowers for the kitchen from the stand up the street, to try cooking pan-roasted chicken with lemon garlic green beans.

That's why I'm in the kitchen asking myself how the hell to make lemon garlic sauce when Grip comes home. It's crazy that I know him so well, but I allowed Angie Black and Jade and others to get under my skin, to play on my unreasonable insecurities. And I do know him. I know how his steps sound at two in the morning when he's been at the studio laboring over a track and drags himself through the front door, or when Dr. Hammond says something that rocked him to the core, rearranges the way he thought about life. Those days his steps eat up the hardwood floor, eager to find me and share. Today's steps stutter, like someone lost and looking. They pause, wait. They're not sure.

He's on the couch when I enter the living room, head in his hands and elbows on his knees. On bare, silent feet, I pad over to him. He doesn't look up until I rest a hand on his head, caress the tight muscles in his neck.

"Hey." He manages a bend of his lips, almost a smile, but his eyes are defeated.

I instantly want to make whatever it is better, and my fix-it instinct springs into action. He pulls me down onto the couch to straddle his lap. Many days I don't leave the house because it's also my office, but today I met with Charm about Grip's book deal. The Stella McCartney dress I wore to her office inches up my bare legs as I settle over him. His hands are on me right away, caressing my calves and feet, venturing over my thighs, reacquainting himself with the shape of my back through the thin silk. He greets my body the way he typically does, but there is nothing typical about his expression as he lays claim to me one limb at a time.

"Baby, what's wrong?" I back the question up with kisses feathered over his jaw.

He surprises me, grabbing me by the neck and pulling me into his lips forcefully. He kisses me, a greedy plundering of my mouth, consuming me with both hands. His kisses spill down my chin, a delicious mess. I hate to stop this but I know him too well and love him too much to be an escape hatch.

"Hey," I say against his lips, scooting back from the stiffening length of him. "This is all very nice, but I asked you a question. What's wrong?"

He stares into my eyes, and I see hurt there. Someone hurt him. My teeth clamp down. My nails cut half-moons into my palms. All I want is a name, a name I'll find a way to erase. He leaves kisses in the hair curling at my temple from the heat of the kitchen. I just caress his jaw, giving him room to tell me what happened.

"Iz and I talked about the Artists as Activists panel." He shakes his head, a fraudulent laugh escaping. "I assumed he'd be on my side, that we believed the same things."

I already know, but I still ask.

"Believe the same things about what?"

At my question, a shadow passes over his face, like the sun playing hide and seek with the clouds. In an instant, he goes from telling me to protecting me.

"It's nothing." He shrugs and pulls me back down to lock my crotch over his. I resist, forcing resolve into my look and my voice.

"Tell me."

He sighs and licks his lips before speaking.

"Iz doesn't think we should be together," he finally says. "He doesn't believe in us."

Doesn't believe in us.

I don't think Grip realizes how telling the phrase is, how much the professor's opinion has come to mean to him. In a relatively short time, Dr. Hammond has become much more than Grip's temporary professor. Grip moved here for the social justice maven with the brilliant mind, but he's become friends with the man. He respects Dr. Hammond as much as I've seen him respect anyone ever. He may not say it, may not even be able to put into words how deeply injured he feels, but it's there.

"And to think I was about to donate to his community bail program." Grip shakes his head, disgust written plainly on his face.

I stiffen against his chest, pushing a chunk of hair behind my ear and processing what he's saying. On our flight back to New York, Grip showed me the preliminary plan for Dr. Hammond's program. His eyes lit up, passion and purpose humming through every cell of his body. I can't get that image of him out of my head, and his friend Matty is there in my mind's eye, too—the one who sat in jail for months because he didn't have money for bail, the one who hadn't really done anything wrong. For him, I have a name and a face, but how many men are in that position and worse? Men we don't know are suffering, and nobody is saying their names.

"But now you won't?" I ask. "Because Dr. Hammond doesn't approve of us, of me, you won't work with him?"

A scowl etches Grip's expression.

"Hell no I'm not working with him." The words fly from his mouth like hornets, swift and stinging. "Why am I even here? I uprooted my life, had you uproot yours, to chase a small-minded man. I feel like a fool."

I understand his disappointment, but I can't say I agree fully with his assessment. I've known Grip a long time and he's breathed his convictions since the day I met him, but I've never seen him the way he has been these last few months. There is a focus and determination all encircling this incredible sense of purpose, like he understands what he was made for. I don't want him to lose that because of me. Besides, his mother felt the same way about us not too long ago, but her heart has changed; why can't we give the professor's heart the chance to change, too?

"Imagine something with me for a minute." I trace the velvety line of his eyebrows and run my thumb over his full lips.

His eyes drift closed as he absorbs my touch, sounds of contentment stirring in his throat and vibrating against my fingers.

"Let's say I have cancer."

He opens his eyes to glare at me. "I don't like this."

"Just hear me out. I have cancer, and there's nothing more they can do for me."

He goes still, and for a moment I don't even feel his heartbeat through his chest, like the thought of my heart stopping stopped his.

"I don't have much time left," I whisper, letting him feel the possibility of me being gone. "But then someone discovers the cure for cancer."

He tips his mouth to the left and he traces the curves of my knees. "There's just one catch." I dip my head to capture his eyes. "The man who discovered the cure—he's a white supremacist."

He looks back at me unblinkingly for a second before allowing himself one blink—just one.

"Do you accept the cure for cancer?"

"What good is this when—"

"Answer the question. Do you accept the cure for cancer from a white supremacist to save my life?"

"I'd accept the cure from the devil himself to save you. You know that." He sighs. "It's not the same."

"What's the title of Dr. Hammond's book?"

He rolls his eyes. "You know the title, Bris."

"Humor me."

"*Virus.* The title of his book is *Virus.*"

"And the point is that racism is a virus that's constantly changing, constantly adapting, right?" I ask. "That it adapted when slavery was outlawed and when Jim Crow was eradicated and when segregation was legally struck down. It works its way into our systems, like our penal system, right? It's a nasty bastard that just keeps morphing and surviving like a cockroach."

Now I have his attention. He's stopped countering my every word, stopped protesting and thinking this is a useless exercise. He's finally listening.

"The person who finally cures cancer won't be perfect," I tell him. "They'll just be the person who figured out the cure for cancer, and the people who live because of that won't care that he cheated on his taxes or stepped out on his wife. They'll care that he cured cancer. Dr. Hammond has a cure, at least for part of the problem. With his ideas and your resources and influence, imagine how much good you can do."

"He doesn't think we should be together, thinks I've been societally conditioned to 'acquire' you." Grip's flinty look doesn't dissuade me, even though that is some bullshit.

"I bet there are more things you agree on than disagree." I prop my elbows on his shoulders, leaning into him and persisting. "I bet when he gets to know me, I'll go from being a 'they' to being Bristol. Isn't that what you said months ago when you performed 'Bruise' for the Black and Blue Ball? That sometimes it takes us being around each other and getting to know each other, at least giving us the chance to go from being a category to who we really are? As individuals, who we really are?"

He shakes his head, genuine humor apparent for the first time since his steps stuttered through our front door.

"So, what?" A grin tilts his mouth. "You remember *every* word I say?"

He really has no idea.

"If I only get one life with you," I mutter into his neck, "then, yes, I'm holding on to every moment and every word you say."

He pulls me away from the crook of his neck, studying my face. His eyes darken, emotion redolent in the air between us.

"You're so precious to me, Bristol," he says, his voice the perfect blend of raw and reverent.

I kiss him deeply, my tongue sliding against his, a choreographed dance between two partners, sensual and tender. I feast on his bottom lip, nipping and licking at the spot until he groans and shifts me lower again, his hardness marrying my softness, my wetness.

Not this again.

He keeps getting me off topic.

"Will you consider it?" I ask, inserting space between our lips, cutting into the hungry kisses.

"Huh?" Passion glazes Grip's eyes. "Consider . . . what?"

"Dr. Hammond." I pant between our lips, resisting the temptation to sink into another kiss. "You'll think about still working with him?"

He tilts his head back into the sofa cushion, lashes lowered over the resentment in his eyes at the mention of the professor's name.

"Yeah." He nods, but derision still twists his lips. "I'll think about it."

"Good." I startle him when I hop off his lap.

"Hey, where are you going?" He points to the situation behind his zipper, the pole in his pants.

"We'll have to handle that later, babe. You think you love me now? Wait'll you taste my garlic lemon chicken thingy." I head toward the kitchen, calling over my shoulder, "By the way, don't bother me tonight. I have lots of reading to do."

I downloaded *Virus* a long time ago, and it's well past time I read it for myself. If I used Grip's own words to prove my point, maybe I'll need to use Dr. Hammond's own words on him, too.

Nineteen

Grip

"CAN I SEE IT?"

Amir and I are in the kitchen. He's frying, of all things, bologna, and I'm on my laptop working on an assignment for Iz's class. Things have not been the same between the professor and me since our argument. He was watching the door the next day when I came in, like he wasn't sure I'd show, and honestly, I was ready to pack up my shit, grab my girl, and fly back to LA. Even sitting through his class felt like a betrayal the first few minutes, like I was telling him it was okay to think the things he does. If it hadn't been for Bristol, I would have chucked the deuces on his ass.

But during class, we dove into case after case, injustice after injustice that reiterated just how broken our justice system is, how black, brown, and poor people are clearly disproportionately suffering the brunt of it. This is bigger than even something as important as whether or not Iz approves of me loving Bristol. For me, that's a heinous bias, and I can't believe the same bright mind that produces brilliant ideas for programs and policies confines itself to that kind of thinking, but he *does* have solutions. He *does* have good ideas, and together, we can help a lot of people. Maybe we can even change things.

"Bruh, you gonna show me or what?" Amir scowls through the smoke rising from the sizzling pan.

"Not while you got my house smelling like a heart attack." I glance from my laptop to the sizzling grease in the pan. "You can't keep eating like this. We're thirty, not thirteen. You need to eat better."

"Who you supposed to be?" Amir demands, a grin on his face. "The surgeon general?"

"The surgeon gen—" I shake my head and laugh. "Also, if we're gonna get technical, you're thirty-one, a year older than me."

"Aw, hell. Here we go." Amir rolls his eyes and takes a sip of his beer.

"I mean, we can't forget you flunked the first grade."

"You know I was sick that year and missed a lot of days."

"Still." I slant him an amused glance. "First grade."

"You ain't ever gonna let me live that down, are you?" He shakes his head and adjusts the flame on the burner.

"My point is you gotta adjust that diet. You know all the shit that runs in your family."

"What runs in my family?"

"Hypertension, heart disease." I tick the afflictions off on my fingers. "Diabetes."

"Always with the 'betes," he mutters. "And that's just your mama's side."

"Don't talk about my mama," he warns, but still chuckles.

"I'm just saying, half your aunts died with no feet 'cause of the 'betes. You can't even crip walk with no feet, bruh."

"Do I have Bristol to thank for the lecture?" Amir asks. "She got you eating healthy? She cooking vegetables for you every night or something since we moved to New York?"

My laugh booms in the kitchen, and even after it fades, a grin still hangs around on my face.

"Did you ask if Bristol … *my* Bristol … has been cooking every night?" I clarify with a laugh. "Occasionally she'll get in here and try a little something. Not that I give a damn. I don't care if Bris can't boil water. She has other talents."

"Please don't talk about your sex life." Amir grimaces. "It turns my stomach to see a man so pussy-whipped."

"Least I'm getting some."

"Ooooooh. That's low."

"On the regular," I continue goading. "Daily. Usually twice a day, and it's the bomb."

"You just gotta rub it in, don't you?"

"Hey, you can't call a brother pussy-whipped then get salty when he tells you how good it is."

"You got me there." Amir laughs.

We've been teasing each other this way since eighth grade when we both got our dicks wet for the first time. I'm not one of those guys who fucks and tells, especially about Bristol, but I've never been able to take a shit without Amir knowing. That won't change any time soon.

"What about you and Shon?" I ask.

"What about us?" Amir's eyes narrow, wariness seasoning his words. "What you mean?"

"I *mean* what about you and Shon? I tell you all my business.

You've told me jack shit about you and Shon." "Nobody asked you to spill all your business."

"I'm pretty sure you *did* ask me to spill all my business."

"Yeah, but now you can't shut up about your girl." Amir offers a good-natured smile and shrugs. "Since it's Bris, I'll let you get away with it. Me and Shon went on a few dates. We're taking it slow."

"Slow?" I ask with disbelief. "Dude, you met her in pre-K. How much slower can you take it?"

"You didn't close the deal with Bristol for eight years. I think I'm on pace to do better than you."

I laugh when grease flies up from the hot pan and pops his hand. "See, that's what you get for cooking that shit in here."

"You know you love some bologna," Amir says with a grin. "Don't even try to get all new now that you live in Tribeca."

"If I'm not mistaken, you live downstairs *in Tribeca*."

"I ain't footing the bill, though. That's on *your* dime."

"You a freeloading motherfucker." I laugh at the expression on his face. "You knew good and damn well I didn't need you to move with me to New York, and you let Bristol get herself all worked up about *security*. I hope you're happy now, living in Tribeca and getting paid to do jack shit all day."

"Man's gotta make a living," he says, his grin unabashed.

My discussions with Iz about increasing enterprise in urban communities, a green revolution for people of color, come to mind.

"What do you want to do, Amir?" I flip the high-backed chair around and straddle it, folding my arms on its back.

He glances up from flipping the bologna to the other side. "Do with what?"

"Bruh, with your life." I shoot him a skeptical glance. "It's gotta be more than pretending to protect me for the next fifty years."

Amir turns down the corners of his mouth.

"I was taking some night classes before I won the lottery on your security detail."

We share a grin before he sobers, shrugs.

"I took some business courses at the community college. Maybe I'll get on the Magic Johnson tip, ya know? Bringing quality businesses to the hood, that kind of thing."

"Hey, I'm here for that, too." I hesitate before voicing the idea that has been unfolding in the back of my mind for a few weeks. "You could do what I'm doing, get a degree online, business or something. Between music and the stuff I want to do with Iz, I might not have much time for the businesses I'd like to see happen."

"So, what?" Amir points the spatula he's holding at himself. "You want me to do some black enterprise stuff or something?"

"Why not?" I ask. "You're smart. You know how to hustle and understand the hood, know what it takes for businesses to make it there. I trust you. Who better to invest with? All you'd need is some training."

Interest sparks behind Amir's eyes before he looks away to open a loaf of bread.

"I'll think about it," he says and clears his throat. "Now back to my original question. Can I see the ring?"

I let him get away with changing the subject.

"I hate that I even told you I had it." I grin and make no move to get it out.

"Stop being a pussy and show me the ring."

I reach into my bag, take out the ring I've been carrying for the last week, and walk over to the counter where he's still frying up heart disease in the form of meat product.

"Shiiiiiit." He stretches the expletive out like a Slinky, obviously impressed as he takes it from my fingers. I want to take it back as soon as it leaves my hands, not because of how much it costs—though, *damn*, it cost a lot—it just feels like he's holding my future in his big ol' clumsy hands.

"If you get grease on the ring, I'm gonna—"

We hear the front door open, and Amir's eyes go as round as plates. Bristol's heels tap on the hardwood, the sound louder as she rounds the corner. Before I can take the ring back, Amir tosses it into the sugar canister.

"What the . . . ?" I smack the back of his head.

"I panicked!" He shrugs just as Bris enters the kitchen.

"What's that smell?" She wrinkles her nose, distaste on her face.

She joins us at the counter, tipping up for a kiss. I try to think what act-
ing-normal Grip would do . . . he would cup her face with both hands and
kiss the hell out of her, so I do. She's liquid against my chest and breathless by
the time I'm done. She glances at Amir, smiling a little self-consciously even
though he's used to us.

"Is that what you're wearing to the debate?" Bristol asks.

The conversation on race and mass incarceration between Iz and Clem
Ford is tonight and being broadcast live from a nearby bookstore.

"Yeah." I glance down at my narrow black slacks, gray button-up, fitted
black leather jacket, and boots. "What? It looks busted?"

"No." She frowns at her pantsuit, not even wrinkled after a full day of
meetings. "The opposite—you look too good. I need to step up my game and
change."

She looks gorgeous. "You look gorgeous."

"You have to say that." But my compliment puts a smile on her face. "Are
you going with us tonight, Amir?"

He meets my eyes over her head, and I silently shake my head and give
him the finger-slitting-the-throat warning.

"Uh . . ." His eyes dart from her to me and back again. "Nah. I have . . .
um . . ."

"Shit," I offer helpfully. "He's got shit to do tonight. Besides, the bookstore is only a few blocks away. We can easily walk. We'll be fine."

"There'll be a lot of racist idiots there." She glances uncertainly between
the two of us.

"I said we'll be fine." I'm barely holding on to my patience now.

"You strapped, dawg?" Amir asks.

I lift my pant leg and show him the gun at my ankle.

"Is that really necessary?" The concern trebles in Bristol's eyes once she
sees the gun. "You know how I feel about guns."

"And you know how I feel about not being able to protect you—not
gonna happen. I have the license for it." I drop the pant leg and turn to Amir.
"Like I said, we'll be fine walking."

"It's cold out there." Bristol rubs her arms like she's still standing on the
sidewalk. "It's December."

"I'm the Cali dude," I tease, "and I'm willing to walk in the cold, but you
grew up here and are wimping out?"

"She's right, though," Amir says, poised to take the first bite of his sandwich. "It *is* cold."

I point in the direction from which Bristol just came.

"Why don't you take your heart attack on white bread and go back to your place?"

Bristol gives the sandwich a cautious glance. "What *is* that?"

"You never had bologna, Bris?" I ask.

"No." She offers an investigative sniff. *This I have to see.*

"You probably wouldn't like it," I say casually. "It's what we grew up on. We had to eat it in the hood—you know, us being poor and all, struggling to make ends meet. Right, Amir?"

He catches on immediately and jumps in.

"Oh, yeah," he agrees. "Some nights this was all our moms could afford, but I understand, Bristol, if *you* don't want to try—"

"Give it to me. I'll try it," she interrupts, stepping over to Amir and the sandwich in question. "I bet it's . . . well . . . I'm sure it's . . ."

Her voice dies when she comes face-to-face with the processed meat. Looking brave, she bites into it. She goes a little green for a second, like she might be sick, then she chews it quickly, determined not to ever let us know. Meanwhile, Amir has a coughing fit to disguise his laugh. I've had lots of practice keeping a straight face when messing with Bristol.

"You like it?" I ask.

"Mmmhmmmmmm." She swallows her gag reflex. "I can see why . . . see why you guys loved it. It's . . . so . . . so . . ."

"Good?" I supply.

"Yeah, it's good." She hands it to Amir like it's burning her fingers. "I don't want to take it all from you, Amir."

"Oh, *no*, Bristol." He pushes it back toward her. "You can have—"

"No, really." She shoves it back to him, looking like she needs a barf bag. "Please take it."

"I'm gonna head out then." Amir bites the sandwich, closing his eyes in ghetto rapture. "Hmmmmm. Thanks for leaving me some, Bris."

"Of course." She laughs nervously, like she's afraid she'll have to down some more. "You keep it. You eat it . . . all of it."

As soon as we hear the door close behind him, Bristol rounds on me.

"Oh, my God. Why did you let me eat that shit?"

My laugh bounces off the walls.

"That's what you get for trying to hang with them hood boys. It's definitely a meal we learned to love out of necessity."

"Next time a warning would be nice." She stretches up to grab a mug in the cabinet, smiling at me over her shoulder. "You ready for tonight? Are you gonna behave?"

"A rapper, a white supremacist, and a narrow-minded professor walk into a bar." I cross my arms over my chest and shrug. "What could go wrong?"

"It's my first time meeting Dr. Hammond." She pours this morning's coffee into a mug and pops it in the microwave. "I'm a little nervous."

"Don't be." I scowl at the thought of introducing Bristol to Iz knowing how he feels about our relationship.

"You just leave the professor to me." She reaches for the—*holy shit.*

The sugar.

I race over and slam my hand on the canister. "What are you doing?" I ask.

"Um ... making a quick cup of coffee?" She slides a perplexed look from my face to the canister. "It's been a long day, and I just need a hit of caffeine to get through tonight."

"It'll just make you jittery." I sound jittery as hell. I feel like the ring might glow through the canister and give itself away.

"I got up way too early. *Someone* woke up before my alarm and demanded sex." She cocks a chiding brow. "Twice."

"What can I say?" I lift and drop my shoulders. "A man's got needs."

"So does a woman. I *need* my coffee, and I take sugar. Move."

"You can't have this sugar because ..." I twist my brain around until I stumble on a logical explanation. "Roaches."

Judging by the horror on Bristol's face, you'd think I said Nazis. "Did you say *roaches?*" Her voice drops several decibels to deathly quiet.

"Yeah, I, uh ... saw a roach in the sugar."

"Here?" I'm pretty sure her face blanches.

"In Tribeca?"

"They get around, Bris."

"I better dump it." She goes for the canister, but I slide it out of her reach.

"I'll throw it out."

She pulls her phone from her pocket.

"I'll just call property management. They need to—"

"Let me do that, babe." I pluck her phone from her fingers and slide it back into her pocket. "You go get dressed. We need to leave soon."

"But you'll call?" She gives the sugar canister one last anxious glance. "I may not be able to sleep tonight thinking about that roach."

"I have creative ways of putting you to sleep." I lean down, lips on her, hand locked onto the canister. I pull away and turn her toward the stairs. "Go get even more beautiful for me and we'll go. We don't want to be late for the showdown."

I swat her ass, smiling when she jumps a little and laughs back over her shoulder before taking off up the stairs.

Relief slowly pushes a breath out and slumps my shoulders. With one last furtive glance to make sure she's not coming, I lift the lid and dig around in the sugar to retrieve the ring. The purity of it captures then reflects the overhead lights, a spectrum radiating from the yellow diamond.

"No roaches." I slip the ring back into my pocket. "But I did find a canary."

Twenty
Bristol

"WHY DO YOU KEEP SMILING?" I ASK GRIP AS WE WALK toward the bookstore for the debate.

"You're wearing my necklace." He squeezes my hand and slants me a smile, his eyes locked on the gold bar dangling between my breasts.

"*Your* necklace?" I touch the chain around my neck, tracing its inscription. "I distinctly remember buying this myself."

"But I inspired it," he says smugly.

The Neruda line carries such significance in our relationship, declaring, *my heart broke loose on the wind.* I can't wear it without thinking of our first kiss, without remembering him slipping under my armor, his own vulnerability tempting me to share things with him I'd never shared before.

"I love it when you wear it." He studies the sidewalk as we walk briskly toward the bookstore. "You look beautiful tonight, by the way."

"Well I knew I needed to dress warmly since you were making me walk." I laugh at his good-natured grimace.

A white sweater fits my torso closely, and cropped, wide-legged pants of the same color swing loosely from waist to mid-calf. My camel-colored leather boots and cashmere coat finish off the outfit.

"These boots are already killing me," I complain, sneaking a glance at his face.

"I don't want to hear it." He laughs and tucks my arm into his. "It's a gorgeous night for a walk, and you know it."

He's right. The chill in the air underscores the holiday cheer lent by Christmas decorations on every corner and in the store windows.

"It's our first Christmas as a couple," I say.

"Yup. Too bad we'll be back in LA. Maybe I'd get my snowfall on Christmas morning if we stayed here in New York."

"Do you want to stay?" I hope he doesn't. I miss my palm trees and my goddaughter, my brother and Kai. I think I even miss my parents. It *must* be time to go home.

"Nah." Grip pulls his leather jacket a little tighter around him. "I'm ready to go back. I'd rather have our friends and family than snow."

"Maybe you'll get it tonight. They're calling for it."

"I'm not gonna count on it." He stops in front of a bookstore with a line of people stretching from the door. "We made it, and look, your feet didn't give out."

"Very funny." I lean into his shoulder. "I'm really looking forward to hearing Dr. Hammond."

Grip's smile drops, and he glances into the store.

"Yeah, well, Clem Ford may be an ignorant ass bastard, but he's also smart and tough. Hopefully Iz can hold his own."

He more than holds his own. I'm astounded by the sharpness of Dr. Hammond's mind. His thoughts are agile, contorting and twisting to cut Ford off and anticipate his arguments before he makes them. I was impressed when I read his book that impacted Grip, but hearing him in person, I understand why we moved to New York, why this man's ideas swept through Grip like a hurricane.

Dr. Hammond is unlike anyone I've ever met. There is a restrained power to him, to the force of his intellect. Physically, he's more like a football player than a professor. Six-five or so, he's not so much wearing the dark blue suit as leashed by it. I can already tell he'd rather be comfortable than fashionable. Picture a younger Idris Elba, and you've got Dr. Hammond. His charisma is time-released, fed to you in slow, sneaky doses, slipped to you with a smile that seems like it's costing him something. His reserved demeanor, which should make him seem aloof, instead pulls you closer. It draws you in and sits you down to listen. I glance around the bookstore, crowded with his students and readers clutching copies of his book. His deep voice pitches low, and you're not sure if you're on the edge of your seat because you're straining to hear or because what he's saying is turning the things you thought you knew upside down, but either way, he has you on edge.

In contrast, everything repulsive in this world convenes in Clem Ford. I want to scrub my ears after sitting through an hour of his thinly veiled racist rhetoric. He has a brand of charisma, too, a dark pull, an undertow for bottom feeders.

He has his own supporters here, young students who follow him to the edge of blatant bigotry. As a businessman, he is convincing and astute. Unfortunately, his business is prisons. I never considered that many corporations use prison labor at a fractional cost, and having a large incarcerated population is good for business.

And bad for prisoners.

Ford and Professor Hammond personally dislike one another; it's apparent from their opening statements and the first questions they take from the audience, standing on opposite shores with an impassable body of water between them. Ford's ideas are fiscally sound, but morally bankrupt. The professor picks apart each argument methodically, persuading the audience with a formidable grasp of history and philosophy, and a compelling vision for the future.

Grip still isn't happy about Professor Hammond's perspective on our relationship, but I read grudging respect in his eyes, a reluctant pride in how well Iz—as he told everyone to call him—represents the issues they're both committed to. I squeeze his hand, and he turns to look at me.

"You okay?" he asks, head bent attentively.

"Yeah." I nod and lean over to drop a kiss on his jaw. He palms my head and brings me close enough to whisper in my ear.

"Are you bored?"

The question almost hurts my feelings. I know he's just being considerate because this isn't necessarily the world where I spend most of my time, but I want him to know I'm on the edge of my seat along with everyone else.

"I love it." I press my hand along his face. "Professor Hammond is brilliant. I'm glad I came."

Pleasure widens his smile and crinkles his eyes at the corners. "I'm glad you came, too."

He sits back and tunes in again. They're almost done with the Q&A; I missed the last question, but I listen closely to the professor's response.

"Don't feel bad for not knowing," he tells the young student still standing at the mic set up in the aisle for questions. "Feel bad for not doing once you know. The things you've heard here tonight, now that you know about them, what will you *do* about them? Ignorance is a naturally occurring state.

It's not what you feel guilty about, it's what you *do* something about. We are born not knowing, and our experiences feed us information. You limit your knowledge and understanding of not only your place in this world, but the place and plight of others by doing what you've always done and knowing only what you've always known. Position yourself socially and intellectually to know more, to understand beyond the scope of your experiences. That is how we evolve as individuals and as a society."

I want to stand up and yell, *Mic drop!* after just about everything he says, and this especially appeals to me. Jade was right: there *are* a lot of things I don't know and don't get about Grip's upbringing, his past.

I definitely don't get bologna sandwiches.

But I won't feel bad for not knowing. I'll do what the professor said. I'll keep positioning myself intellectually and socially to know more. It's no different than what Grip had to do, than what millions of people do to understand what is unfamiliar to them but essential to learn.

When the moderator thanks everyone for coming, the crowd breaks and splits, Ford's followers clamoring to speak to him and a line forming in front of the table where the professor is posted to sign books.

And they aren't the only ones people are eager to talk to.

"Yo, Grip, could I get a picture?" asks a young guy with dreadlocks.

That one request sets off a chain reaction of people realizing Grip isn't just another student, but a superstar. Within seconds he has a line of his own and is signing copies of the program we received when we walked in, taking selfies and listening to teary-eyed girls tell him how much his music has touched them. Like a good little celebrity and with much more patience than I would have, he navigates it all with a pen in one hand and my hand in the other.

"Hey." I tug on his hand to get his attention. "I'll be right back."

His smile slips and he turns to me. "Where are you going?"

I affect a cockney accent. "Can't a lowly servant girl go to the restroom while you hold court, m'lord?"

He tilts his head and scrunches his face up. "I don't even know what you're doing right now."

I laugh and pull my hand free.

"Never mind. I'll be back," I tell him, walking backward. "Deal with your ... public."

I'm still chuckling at the look of frustration on his face as I walk beyond his reach. Bigots make him nervous, and apparently, there are a lot of undercover ones here tonight. They hide behind their hedge funds now, behind profit sheets instead of white sheets, but the heart is the same.

I take my place in line behind a few other people clutching copies of *Virus*. I pull mine out of my bag and wait my turn. I can tell the professor has signed quite a few of these tonight, and his patience has started to fray. He's not like Grip, a practiced professional used to all the attention and demands. He's a brilliant man who wrote a book he never expected to do what it's done. If the frown he's wearing is any indication, having "fans" and signing autographs isn't exactly his forte.

"Who should I sign it to?" he asks brusquely without looking up from the book I handed him.

"Make it to Bristol." At my name, he looks up sharply, his eyes speculating if it's a coincidence or if I am who he thinks I am. "Yes, I'm Grip's Bristol."

A slow smile works its way onto the handsome face marked with lines of weariness.

"You certainly are." He extends his hand. "A pleasure finally meeting you."

"Is it?" I accept his hand, making my tone just cool enough for him to know I'm aware of the words he's spoken against our relationship.

"He talks about you all the time."

"I heard he left out one important detail." I pause meaningfully. "At least important to you."

He has the decency to look uncomfortable for a second, but it passes quickly, and in no time the same self-assured, self-contained man who dismantled Clem Ford's flawed arguments tonight stares back at me, awaiting my next move.

"Could you sign by my favorite quote instead of in the front of the book?" I ask. "I folded down the page and highlighted the passage."

He turns to the page, and I know he's being confronted with his own words, words I've nearly memorized.

Too many of our American systems are built on bias. The irony is that these biases are often inextricably, if unconsciously, connected to our own sense of superiority. The very biases that make those in power feel stronger, better, actually weaken them. Our biases are our blind spots, and we need others to guide us in the darkness of our own ignorance.

He contemplates the passage for a moment before signing and handing the book back to me.

"It's not personal," he says with what looks like genuine regret in his eyes.

"When you're the person, it feels personal." I lean closer, speaking for his ears only. "What you wrote in that book about bias, I believe it. Do you?"

"Touché," he says with a tired smile. "You don't pull punches, do you?"

"No, I don't, especially when it comes to Grip. Even though he knows where you stand on us, he still respects and admires you. So do I. I believe you can help each other and help a whole lot of people."

I let those words sink in before going on.

"For that reason, I encouraged him to continue his work with you." I firm my lips and narrow my eyes. "But hurt him again, and you'll have to deal with me."

For a moment, shock overtakes his expression, and I wonder if I went too far. Then something cracks. His eyes light up, and laughter—completely at odds with the sobriety he's demonstrated all night—spills from his mouth. It goes on for several seconds, and I'm determined not to join him, but my lips twitch, which only sets off another round of laughter. After a few more seconds of me awkwardly watching him laugh at me, he settles into a relaxed grin.

"Message received, 'Grip's Bristol.' Have a good evening," he says, dismissing me with a nod and still smiling. "Next in line."

I step aside with my signed copy pressed to my chest. Grip still has quite a few fans he's making his way through, and he catches my eye and mouths, "Sorry." I cross my eyes at him, drawing a wide grin before he turns his attention back to the selfies and autographs. I do what I've become accustomed to doing trailing behind superstars—my best imitation of a wallflower, posted up and waiting.

"Excuse me, have we met before?"

I glance up and can feel surprise and disgust warring on my face when I see the man in front of me. I school my features, unwilling to give Clem Ford the satisfaction of knowing my thoughts.

"I don't think so, Mr. Ford."

"Well you obviously know me." He smiles like an amicable snake.

"I'm here tonight, so of course I know who you are." I turn my attention to my phone, refusing to engage with him. "But no, we haven't met."

"Your mother is Angela Gray, right?"

Despite my inward double take, I look at him with no sign of surprise. "Yes. You know her?"

"The Hamptons." He snaps his fingers as if now he has it. "Last summer in the Hamptons. We were both at her fundraiser for some charity or another."

I nod, remembering as vaguely as he does, but enough to know I was there. "Yes, but I don't believe we met."

"Not formally." His eyes make quick work of my clothes like they aren't there and he can see what's beneath. "But who could forget a woman like you?"

Clem Ford is sixty if he's a day, and he might be a bigot and an opportunist, greedy and corrupt, but he's not a dirty old man, as far as I know … so I'm not sure why he's trying to convince me that he is. His eyes, poured into their deep sockets and surrounded by a network of wrinkles and saggy flesh, hold no real interest, at least not of a sexual nature. He's not a man who does things for no reason, so why is he bothering with me?

"Can I help you?" Grip asks from behind Ford.

If I hadn't been watching him closely, I would have missed the glint of satisfaction in Ford's eyes before he turns to face Grip. No, he didn't have any real interest in me, but he knew how to draw the person he *is* interested in. I was the unsuspecting bait in whatever trap he wants to set for Grip.

"Mr. James." With his back to me now, I'm left with the unflattering view of the balding back of Clem's head. "I'm sorry we didn't get to hear from you this evening."

Grip's eyes remain locked on Ford, assessing, picking around his intentions.

"From me?" Grip quirks one brow, but otherwise shows no response. "Wasn't my night."

"Dr. Hammond is definitely a worthy opponent in a debate." Ford slides his hands into his pockets and rears back. I don't need to see his face to know he's up to no good. "But you're the man everyone's talking about and listening to. You're the voice for this new American Dream."

Grip watches him, waiting for the point. Despite the languid posture, arms folded over his chest, he's on high alert, ready to flare barbs like a porcupine at the first sign of threat.

"I know you don't think we have much in common," Ford says, "but you're wrong. I can think of at least one thing we both seem to love."

Grip's eyes slit and he swallows, and I feel him bracing for Ford's next words. I'm sure they'll be handpicked to antagonize him, and I silently will him not to fall for it.

"And what's that?" Grip asks.

Ford steps closer to whisper into Grip's ear. I don't hear whatever nastiness he feeds Grip, but in a flash of lightning and with a thud that sounds like thunder, Ford lands beside me on the wall, pinned there by the manacle of Grip's hand.

"Say it now." Grip's voice razors through air viscous with animosity.

Even under the weight and pressure of Grip's hand, Ford forces a strangled, taunting chuckle. The chatter in the room dies down as people turn their attention to the drama playing out between these two men.

I ignore Ford and step close to Grip, placing my hand on his arm.

"You need to let him go," I say fierce and low. "Now."

Frustration bunches the muscle along Grip's jaw and his fingers tighten fractionally around Clem's throat.

"Man, he's not worth it," Dr. Hammond says, materializing on the other side of Grip. "This is what he wants—for everyone to see some violent thug when they look at you. Whatever he said, it's not worth it. Let him go before somebody turns the cameras back on or calls the cops. Or even worse, start a riot in here."

He glances at the crowd, a few of Ford's supporters making their way toward us, wearing outrage on their faces. Others inch closer, trying to catch the words flowing between us. A tall, suited man, apparently from Ford's security detail, steps forward menacingly, but Ford holds up a staying hand, stopping him from intervening.

"Is this what you wanted to see?" Grip asks Clem, loosening his fingers but not letting go. "The violent thug?"

"I knew he was in there," Ford rasps. "It's just a matter of knowing which button to push. We all have our weaknesses."

His eyes flick to the side and find me, a wretched grin sawed into his face.

"Don't look at her." The words fire from Grip's mouth. "Look at me."

Clem takes his time turning mocking eyes from my face back to Grip.

"You want to push my buttons?" Grip demands. "You're using her to provoke a response? Try me and see."

I gulp back a river of profanity. The thought of this man using me to provoke Grip unleashes a rage that I leave boiling in my belly. I can't very well talk Grip down if I'm standing on the ledge beside him, ready to jump.

"Grip, please let him go," I say, finding matching concern in Dr. Hammond's eyes across Grip's arm, a stiff bridge from his body to Ford's neck.

As abruptly as he grabbed him, Grip releases Ford.

"Get him out of here," Dr. Hammond tells me, watching as Ford coughs a little, adjusts his suit, and walks back to the group of admirers security is holding back. When I see the outrage on their faces, I realize just how ugly this could have gotten. Grip's fans and Dr. Hammond's students and followers study the smaller group of supporters who showed up to demonstrate solidarity with Ford. This has the potential of a bomb poised to blow, and I need to get Grip out of blast range.

I drag him through the door and down the sidewalk. My feet hurt in the high-heeled boots, but I ignore the discomfort, covering as much ground as possible at a bruising pace.

"Bris." Grip tugs on my hand, trying to slow me down. "Babe, hold up."

I ignore him and keep moving, as much to give myself something else to focus on as to actually get away from that scene.

"I said stop."

Grip pulls us up short, stronger and able to stop me when he wants to. He lifts my chin, forcing me to look at him. We've been practically running in the freezing cold. Exerted, we watch each other through frosted-air breaths. He scans my face under the streetlights, impervious to the steady stream of people trickling past, a few of them wearing questions about Grip's identity on their faces. It's times like these I wish he was just mine, wish the whole world didn't feel they had a right to be in our lives.

Actually, I pretty much feel like that all the time.

"Are you okay?" he asks.

"Am *I* okay?" My voice spikes with incredulity. "You're the one who just choked a white supremacist in a roomful of white supremacists, but yeah, I'm just dandy, Grip. What the hell?"

"I did not choke him. I firmly held him against the wall. The limp dick bastard could have gotten loose at any point if he'd tried hard enough."

"And why do you think he didn't try?" I demand. "Why do you think he held back his security? Why'd he grin like a maniac the whole time? You played right into his hands."

"Fuck this." He tries to start walking, but I grab his elbow.

"No, listen to me. You're there for a debate on people of color and mass incarceration and you do something like that? You know what you're up against. You have everything he thinks you don't deserve. He wants to discredit you, and you opened the door to let him. You have to be wiser than that."

"Wiser?" Anger forces a plume of breath out to freeze in the air. "So now you're telling me how to be a Black man in America? Like I haven't negotiated this shit my whole life?"

"Oh, is that how it's gonna be?" Hurt crowds my heart in my chest until it's just a small thing barely beating. "I don't get to tell you things like this? Why? Is it a Black thing and I wouldn't understand?"

"This isn't going to a good place." He runs both hands over his head and down his face. "Let's get home."

"No, I want to know." I tuck my hands, like blocks of ice, into the pockets of my cashmere coat. "Are there things that are off limits with us? When we have kids, will it be 'our' community and 'our' causes and 'our' struggle, and Mommy just gets to watch? Is that what you envision for me? Another family where I don't quite fit?"

Tears blur his face in front of me.

"Because I've done that." I swallow the painful lump searing my throat. "If that's how it's going to be, tell me now. I want to be prepared if you don't want what I thought you did—something that doesn't have barriers or boundaries. I would never be disrespectful, you know that, but don't …"

I look down at the cracks in the sidewalk, wondering if somewhere inside I'm cracking, too.

"Just don't leave me out," I whisper. "Don't make me feel like there are parts of your life I can't touch, because I don't have *anything* you can't be a part of."

He's quiet … not just a quiet that is an absence of words, but a quiet that gives him space to think. He's turning it over in his mind, the things I've said, and I've known him long enough to leave him with his thoughts for a while. He'll come back to it when he's ready.

"Look." I take his hand, loosening the tension of the last few moments. "I would never assume I know what it's like, but I know rich, entitled assholes. I grew up with them, and *that one* is after you. You gave him ground he should never have."

I shake my head, bewildered by the idea that he would allow himself to be in that position.

"Why did you get so angry? What did he say to you?"

A wall of ice falls over his face and his lips pull tight at the question, at the memory.

"Let's go."

He starts walking again without waiting for me. I stay right where I am in the middle of the sidewalk, and he's several feet ahead before he realizes I'm not trotting after him like some cocker fucking spaniel. When he glances over his shoulder and I'm where he left me, his shoulders stiffen and swell with a breath I'm sure he draws to keep himself calm.

Good luck. That shit rarely works for me.

He heads back with swift strides, his eyes a dark maelstrom, nostrils flared, and all I can think about is the amazing make-up sex we'll have after this fight.

"What?" Hands locked at his hips, the leather jacket fitted to the ridges of his chest, his expression a study of irritation. I just want to shake him up like an Etch A Sketch and jar that look off his face.

"My feet hurt."

"Your feet . . ." He shakes his head as if to clear it. "What are you talking about?"

"You said we'd be fine walking home, but my boots have four-inch heels, and my feet hurt."

"Then maybe you shouldn't have worn four-inch heels."

"And maybe you should have called for a car like I suggested."

"For four blocks?" He rolls his eyes, but the brackets around his mouth disappear. His shoulders, all rigid muscles moments before, drop just a little. "We're New Yorkers now—we're not taking a car for four blocks."

"I've been a New Yorker all my life, and I never had a problem taking a car four blocks wearing four-inch heels."

He cups my neck, his thumb caressing my cheek, his eyes filled with a familiar exasperation and affection reserved for me.

"How many fights do you want to have at one time, baby?" he asks.

"That depends." I smile and nod to his shoulders. "Are you giving me a ride?"

"A . . . a ride?"

"Piggyback."

His truncated laugh rides on a puff of frigid air. "You're joking."

"Is that a no?" I keep my face neutral. "There's only a block and a half left."

"Exactly." He throws his hands up. "You can walk a block and a half."

I look at him. He looks at me. I'd rather our wills clash over something this trivial than what we were wrangling about moments ago. Those things had weight and depth, not suited for sidewalk conversation. Those things should wait until we get home.

"Hop on," he finally says grudgingly, but with the tiniest flicker of amusement buried in his eyes.

There aren't many people out as we get closer to our place, and the ones walking past don't look too closely. They've seen odder things than some guy carrying his girlfriend piggyback.

"You're choking me," Grip says, but it's a lie. Just to tell him I know it is, I tighten my arms around his neck.

"Ow." He laughs. "As if it isn't already hard enough carrying you."

"Are you calling me fat?" I inject indignation into my voice. "Keep it up and you'll find yourself on the couch."

"First of all, there are three bedrooms," Grip says. "Second of all, if I slept on the couch, you'd be on top of me when I woke up."

I smack his head.

"What?" His shoulders shake under my arms as he laughs. "You love couch sex. I mean, you love all sex, but especially couch sex."

"Oh now I'm a nympho?"

"Only for me." He pulls my hand from where it's hooked loosely at his throat up to his lips for a quick kiss. "And that's totally acceptable."

For the last block, we don't speak much, there's less need to. We *feel* the things we need to know instead of say them. With my chest pressed to his back, forgiveness, love, understanding, and tenderness transfer noiselessly between the layers of our clothes, an emotional osmosis through blood and bone, through hurt and fear. I don't know how I realized this was what we needed, but I did. It's hard to touch when you're fighting. The anger is like a force field, keeping your bodies as far apart as your opinions. I knew if we could feel each other, my breath syncing with his, my heartbeat seeking the rhythm of his, my nose buried in his neck, his hands hooked under my legs—if we could get back here, touching, we could right ourselves.

And we have.

Even on the elevator, he doesn't put me down, like we're afraid to break the truce our hearts negotiated through these points of contact. At our door, he slowly lowers me to the floor, turning to press into me with his arms on either side of my head.

"How about a good night kiss?" he asks, like this is a date and we're parting ways instead of living under the same roof and sleeping in the same bed on the other side of that door.

A wordless nod is the only signal I give, and the only one he needs. His breath warms my lips after the cold walk home. The sweetness, the rightness of it squeezes around my heart. His mouth is familiar, the shape and texture, the soft fullness I've memorized with mine, and yet every time, every kiss is a revelation, a mystery trapped between his lips, hidden under his tongue for me to discover. I will kiss him a million times in our life together and never tire of it. My lips will always cling, curious and searching. His touch is an endless thrill. I don't know if we'll have five years or fifty like the O'Malleys, but I will never get used to this wild yearning, will never get enough of this deep contentment.

I can only hope we end every fight with a kiss.

Twenty-One

Grip

"**W**INE?" I ASK ONCE WE'RE INSIDE.

"God, yes." Bristol sits on the arm of the couch and gingerly takes off her boots like her feet might come off with them. I owe those boots new soles, a spit shine—something to express my gratitude. If it weren't for them, Bristol and I might still be snapping and snarling at each other on a New York sidewalk.

That's not to say we don't have to finish our conversation. We do, but with calmer heads and hearts back in alignment.

"Meet me in the greenhouse," I say, heading for the kitchen to grab a bottle of whatever is already chilled. When I get out there, she's curled up on one of the thick-cushioned outdoor couches. Her legs are folded under her, and her head is tipped back as she stares up at the stars through the tinted glass.

I pour us both a glass of Bordeaux and take my place beside her. There are many kinds of quiet. The kind we shared the last block of our walk home needs nothing added. Then there's silence like the one we're sitting in now, one that's primed for confession.

"That white pussy," I say, barely loud enough for her to hear. I don't want her to.

"What?" She turns her head, still tipped back on the couch, to watch me. "What'd you say?"

"That white pussy," I repeat. "That's what Clem Ford whispered to me. He said the thing we have in common is that we both love that white pussy, and that fifty years ago I would already be dead for fucking you."

I suppress the anger that immediately ignites in me again at the words he said, at the way he looked at Bristol before he said them. I'm such an idiot. I knew he was setting a trap for me, but he used the only lure I would never leave in his snare. As much as I told myself not to respond, my hand had a mind of its own as it wrapped around his fleshy throat, and in the moment, it felt like my hand had the right idea.

"Oh, my God." Bristol gulps, indignation stealing her breath. "I can't even . . . That's awful."

"Yup." I sip the Bordeaux, waiting for the expensive liquid to settle me, not feeling the effects yet. This situation may require weed.

"As much as I want to kick his ass myself," Bristol says, anger straining her features, "you know he was just provoking you, trying to get a rise out of you. You can't let him."

She turns her body to face me, but leaves her cheek against the cushion.

"And I'm just concerned. I didn't mean to lecture you." She holds my eyes with hers, takes my hand, and weaves our fingers together. "You know I would never presume to tell you anything about being Black in America."

"That was a stupid thing for me to say," I interrupt. "I was angry and frustrated. I'm sorry."

"Maybe I was being . . . I don't know, presumptuous." She fixes her eyes on our fingers twisted together. "I just wanted us to both see what he was doing and not fall for it next time."

Bristol grimaces delicately.

"And I'm afraid there *will* be a next time. There's something about you that offends him. Actually, I think it's everything about you. When there are guys like you running around, how is he supposed to sell his false superiority bullshit? Men who are smarter than he is, rich like he is, more accomplished. Famous. Well respected. He wants to think you're an aberration, but he's scared there's more where you came from."

Her assessment is spot-on. Now I have to wade into what is sure to be one of the toughest conversations we've ever had.

"When I first started at the performing arts school," I say, studying our hands caressing, mine darker and rougher than hers, "I'd never really had a white friend. Your brother was the first."

She watches me, not making a sound, so still I wonder if she's breathing.

"There were pretty much no white people in my neighborhood," I continue. "Not at my school, not in the stores where we shopped. The only white people I ever saw on a consistent basis, who were in my life, were cops, and I'd been conditioned to fear them."

I take a gulp of wine.

"That's how separate we felt. I'd go as far as to say sometimes we felt forgotten." I pause to laugh. "When I showed up at my new high school, I'd never seen an episode of *Friends*, and who the hell cared about that show? The kids' jokes weren't funny, but I was the only one not laughing, and when I tried to be funny, they didn't get it. None of it made sense to me. It was foreign, like a parallel universe where up was down."

I glance up to find her eyes fixed on me in complete concentration.

"If Rhyson and I hadn't become close, I probably would have quit. He'd never seen *Friends*, either. He knew less than I did in a lot of ways because he'd been on the road busting ass like a grown man, playing piano since he was eleven years old."

I shrug, trying to remember why I thought I should tell her this.

"I just . . . Tonight, you asked if it was a Black thing and you wouldn't understand." I sigh, unsure how to approach this, but needing to say it all without a filter, the way our other conversations have always been. We've never done eggshells, and tonight sure as hell isn't the time to start. "Is that how you feel when you're at my mom's or . . . wherever with me? With my friends?"

"Sometimes." Her voice is soft, but her eyes remain undaunted. "Like everybody understands something I don't. Like at any given moment, I'll make a fool of myself and not even know it. It's a very vulnerable feeling—that you don't even know what you don't know. I think that's why I let Jade's words get to me. You know me, I'm not the girl who gives a fuck, but around Jade, in situations like that, I find myself trying so hard—not trying to be Black, just . . . *trying*, because I want to understand."

"I'm sorry if I make you feel excluded sometimes. I don't mean to." I tilt my head to peer into her eyes. "Some things are specific to my cultural experience, and I don't know if you'll ever fully grasp them all. Real talk, I don't *care* if you don't. Ethnicity is just one part of who I am, a very important part, yeah, but just one, just like it's only one part of who you are. There are things about your job, your past, your experiences that I won't completely get, either, but I want to know about them because they make you who you are."

"You're right." She looks at me, the open love and need in her eyes burning a path to my heart. "There will be things I can empathize with, but won't ever know firsthand. Please don't ever feel there's anything you can't say or that we can't share. I want a love with no walls. This world uses whatever it can—race, politics, religion—to divide us. We can have differences, but promise me they won't be walls that divide us."

"I can promise you that." I capture her hand because I can't *not* touch her when the air throbs with our honesty.

"We're doing something hard, Grip," she says, her expression earnest. "In a culture, in a climate that would push people like us apart, we choose to be together. We *fight* to be together."

"Yeah." It's all I can manage because the passion on her face, resonating from her body, steals my words, quickens my heartbeat.

"And I will have uncomfortable conversations with you. I'll confess embarrassing things so you understand me. Whatever it takes. Listening to Dr. Hammond tonight helped me understand that even if I find bias in *myself*, if *I'm* ignorant in some way, it doesn't mean I don't love you. It means I don't know."

She reaches up, her hands trembling around my face, her eyes deep and dark and frank.

"And I want to know. I need to know because I love you. You're my end game, Grip. Any hurdle we face, we'll overcome it together. Nothing will stop us."

There's no other way to respond to that except to touch her; to physically express how her words have exploded inside of me. I lean to drop a kiss on her lips, meaning for it to be quick, but she's so sweet, so addictive, I can't let go . . . can't pull back . . . can't stop. My fingers drift into her hair and my thumb presses on her chin, opening her up to go deeper, seeking the passion that gave me those words. She shudders when I lick the roof of her mouth.

"Grip, God," she whispers into me. "It's always so good."

My lips dust over her jaw and behind her ear, the delicious scent of her hair making me dizzy, making me want her more. She tips her head back to give me access to the smooth skin of her neck.

"Oh my God!"

If she's saying that now, wait till I get this sweater off.

"Grip." She taps my shoulder. "Hey, stop for a second. Look up. I think you're finally catching Mother Nature in the act."

I drag my attention from the curve of her neck to glance up through the greenhouse glass tiles. Huge snowflakes drop from the sky, a starless black hole that stretches beyond my imagination. At thirty years old, I'm seeing my first snowfall. I doubt it will even stick or that there will be much accumulation, but the point is seeing it happen, seeing what feels like a miracle in progress. Most people have experienced this, felt this wonder when they were just kids. Having it this late in my life makes it sweeter, makes me appreciate the miracle of nature that it is.

And I know exactly how I should mark my miracle. "Close your eyes, Bris."

She swings a look around to me that asks what I'm up to. "What do you—"

"Would you just do what I ask for once without all the—"

"I will kick you in the balls if you say without the *sass*." Bristol crosses her arms over her chest. "I'm not a fourteen-year-old girl and you are not my father. I don't need paternalism from you, Grip."

"Okay, can you further the feminist cause later and just close your damn eyes?"

"I will." Bristol grins widely. "But only because it's your first snowfall."

"Why you gotta make everything hard?"

"If that's a hint that you want to have make-up sex," she says, finally obediently closing her eyes. "I *won't* give you sass on that."

I slide off the couch and onto the floor in front of her, reach into the interior pocket of my jacket.

"All right." Standing on my knees, I face her, wedged between her legs. "You can open your eyes."

She does, and they immediately widen beyond what I think is humanly possible.

"How about engagement sex?" I hold the delicate platinum band between my thumb and index finger. "I've heard it's even better than make-up sex."

Her jaw drops a few more centimeters with every second that passes. Bristol, who always has something to say, is struck dumb, and I'm about to tease her about it when fat tears slip over her cheeks.

Holy shit. I can't do Bristol tears under any circumstances, even joyous occasions.

"Babe, don't cry." I swipe a thumb over her cheekbone and cup her chin. "You're gonna give me a complex."

"How can I not … you just …"

She gives up, shaking her head and dropping her lashes into the wetness gathered under her eyes. Her forehead falls to rest against mine, and we just sit there for a few seconds. Her hand slides around my neck and she kisses my jaw, sniffing and blinking rapidly against my face. I turn my head to look at her and she stares back at me, her silvery eyes as clear as crystal, as certain as the sunrise.

"You just gonna leave a brother hanging like this?" I ask, my voice husky with emotion.

Her chuckle breezes over my lips, and she sits up straight with a red-tipped nose and damp cheeks.

"I heard you say something about engagement sex," Bristol says. "But I haven't heard an actual proposal."

My smile wavers and then drops. I can't lighten this moment any more. It has more weight than anything I've ever done, and it deserves more than I've ever given anything.

"Bristol, I've loved you so long, my heart doesn't remember life before you. For the last decade, you've been the first thing I think about and the last thought in my head." I proffer the ring. "Would you do me the honor of forever? Will you marry me?"

She swallows and fresh tears fill her eyes, but she blinks and bites her lip as if she's trying to keep it together.

"I aspire to be many things," she finally says, "but there is nothing I will ever do that will make me prouder than being your wife."

When she puts it that way, knowing her ambitions and her drive, to hear her esteem our relationship above all else as we start our life together humbles me. If I wasn't already on my knees, that would have brought me to them. I take her hand and slip the ring onto her finger.

Twenty-Two
Grip

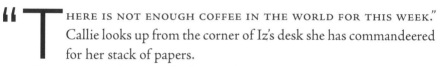

"**T**HERE IS NOT ENOUGH COFFEE IN THE WORLD FOR THIS WEEK." Callie looks up from the corner of Iz's desk she has commandeered for her stack of papers.

"I told you to focus on finals—grading mine and taking your own." Iz studies her over the rims of his glasses. "Grip and I have this proposal under control."

"Well, don't you have finals, too?" Callie asks me.

"I do." I flash her a grin. "But this is the only class I'm taking this semester. Next semester, I go back online and home to LA."

Callie tosses her pen down, sitting back in her chair and crossing her legs.

"Wait. Did you move to New York just for Iz's class?" she asks.

Iz and I have negotiated a tentative détente, but it's still galling that I moved across the country to learn from a guy who thinks I shouldn't be with Bristol. It's narrow-minded, and it makes me feel stupid for coming here, but . . . the guy *is* a genius, and this proposal we're working on is something I could only dream of being a part of before I met him.

"You could say that," I mumble, looking back to the pages I've been marking up. "So, are we set on the college campus tour?"

"Uh, yeah." Iz sounds about as uncomfortable with Callie's question as I am. "You need to run this schedule by your team or whatever?"

"By Bristol," I say deliberately, looking up to meet his eyes. "She manages everything, but this far out, we should be able to accommodate these dates."

"And just to be clear," Callie says, propping an elbow on the desk and leaning forward, "you're going to college campuses all over the country talking about this community bail fund?"

"And the community justice defense initiative," Iz adds. "For those who have been wrongfully accused or convicted and can't afford quality legal representation."

"And Grip will perform at each stop?" Callie asks.

"Yeah, a few songs, not a full concert," I clarify. "And I'll talk about the program. We want to mobilize the next generation around these issues, raise awareness, recruit volunteers."

"This will slay." Callie grins and swings her eager look to Iz. "Where do I sign up?"

"Say . . . huh?" Panic fills Iz's eyes for a moment. You wouldn't expect a woman who barely clears five feet to scare the living shit out of a guy as big and imposing as Iz, but I get the impression he always wants to beg me not to leave him alone with her. I suspect it's so he won't screw her into the nearest wall, but these are merely my speculations since he won't talk to me about it.

Not that we've talked about much outside of the program lately.

"I want in." Callie sets her mouth in a stubborn line. "I'd be volunteering like anyone else since I won't be your TA after this semester."

The stare they hold picks up where some conversation I haven't been privy to left off.

"We'll see," Iz mutters, turning his attention back to the proposal.

"Yeah, we will." Callie gathers her backpack and stands. "I need to get to class myself."

When I glance up to tell her goodbye, that same odd expression she wore the first time she went fangirl on me is back on her face.

"Not to make this weird, but . . ." she says in that voice people use right before they make things weird. "I've acted like a normal person all day and think I deserve a commendation for not bringing this up earlier."

I stifle my grin because I already know where she's going. "Yes?" I lift both brows sky high and wait.

"Oh my God," she gushes, unlike any other Rhodes Scholar you would ever meet. "Is it true? Are you engaged?"

So much for stifling grins, because the shit-eating-est grin of all time overpowers my face. Bristol was with Kai for a late-night talk show performance, and some of the production team backstage spotted her ring. A few posts and several tweets later, everyone knew—or thought they did, since we haven't confirmed anything and really have no plans to. Bristol may promote for a living, but she doesn't like that lens turned on our private life, not even a little bit, and I can't blame her. It's a pain in the ass. We'll have to eventually, but it's only been a couple of weeks, and we're right here at Christmas. Maybe after the New Year we'll draft something to announce, or maybe we won't confirm at all. In the meantime, it's no one's business that I'm the happiest son of a bitch on the planet.

"Well, are you?" Callie presses, her indomitable spirit infectious.

"If you can keep your mouth shut," I tell her, shit-eating grin still firmly in place, "then, yes, I am."

"Eeeeeep!" Callie sits back down and drops her backpack like she's got all day to hear the details. "Tell me everything."

"Don't you have a class in two minutes, Callie?" Iz asks pointedly, flicking his eyes toward his office door. "See you tomorrow."

Callie holds his glance for a moment longer before retrieving her backpack and heading toward the door.

"Congratulations," she says over her shoulder. "An engagement and Grammy nominations all in one month. You win December."

I haven't even processed the Grammy nominations. The day after I asked Bristol to marry me, I found out about the three nominations. I'm proudest of "Bruise" being up for song of the year.

"Thanks, Cal." I give her a grateful smile.

"Bristol's a lucky woman," she says softly, sincerely.

"I'm a lucky man."

"Well, I want to hear all the details when Professor Killjoy isn't around," she says with a pointed glance at Iz before she leaves. "Good luck on your one exam."

"That girl," Iz mumbles, staring at the space she just vacated like she might have left an outline in the air.

There's no doubt in my mind that Iz jerks off to thoughts of Callie defending her dissertation naked. A few weeks ago, I would have given him shit about it, but things changed after that fateful conversation. Now I pretty much stick to the things we do agree on. Otherwise, I have nothing to say to him.

"She's something else," Iz says.

"Yeah, she is, but remember—you don't fuck your students," I can't resist saying.

Iz squints his irritation at me. "I meant Bristol."

I pause in stuffing the proposal into my saddlebag.

"Even though she's white, you mean?" I douse the words with sarcasm.

"Look, you know I have nothing against white people."

"Except when they date Black people, right?"

"It's just not my preference." Exasperation cracks his calm façade. "I get to have my preferences."

"You think I give a damn what color you prefer? Date Smurfette, go blue for all I care. It's you somehow actually buying into the bullshit logic that me being with Bris is a disservice to our community that bothers me."

"All right. You want the real?" He sits back and crosses thickly muscled arms over his broad chest. "I don't think they can ever really understand us or be trusted. I'm not sure you can be white in this country and not somehow be infected by its racial history, by the collective superiority and privilege ingrained in them from birth."

"I'm not spending my life with a collective history." I brush my hand impatiently over the layer of hair I keep so low it's barely there. "I'm in love with one woman, who happens to be white and has never given me reason not to trust her, at least not the way you mean."

"And what if she slipped up and called somebody a nigger one day?" he demands. "How would you feel then?"

I remember Bristol's dismay the day we met when Skeet used that word. It was the first of many conversations we've had about the things most people avoid. Even the night we got engaged, we were still having those conversations, and we'll probably have them for the rest of our lives.

"Bristol would never use that word. If anything, she can't believe we use it to each other. If it were up to her, it would be eradicated and no one could ever use it again."

"Never say never. Do you expect her to truly understand the struggle of a Black man in America?"

"That's a fair question," I reply, glad Bristol and I already discussed this. "I don't know that I do expect her to understand everything about the struggle. I know she'll always sympathize, but maybe there will be things she doesn't completely get."

"And you can live with that?" Doubt settles on his face.

"You know better than anyone how hard it can be for us." I shake my head. "I have to ask myself when I come home, do I want someone who completely understands the struggle? Or someone who completely understands *me*? Someone I can't wait to come home to, someone who makes me laugh on the hardest days of my life? Every single decision isn't filtered through my race. Love isn't."

Iz doesn't look away from me the whole time I'm talking, and I feel like maybe some of what I say lands. He finally clears his throat and shrugs.

"I would just always wonder if I could ever really know a white woman, if she could ever really know me." He shakes his head. "Enough to trust her with my life? With my children?"

"And did your wife really know you? I bet she didn't think you would cheat on her, but you did, and from what I can tell, you're both Black."

A heavy silence follows my words, and as we sit in it, Iz slowly raises his eyes.

"I didn't cheat on her." He twists the grim line of his mouth around the words. "She cheated on me."

Damn. Now I feel like a real asshole.

"I'm sorry about that. I assumed . . ." I leave not-well-enough alone and press on. "I do know I don't ever have to worry about that and neither does Bristol. It's nothing to do with our race. I would never do that to her, and I know she would never do that to me. Have you never been captivated by someone so much that the rest of your life without them seems . . . empty? Not even your ex?"

For a moment, Iz's eyes stray to the door Callie recently walked through, and then he clears his throat.

"No, it wasn't like that with us." His tone remains even, but his lips twitch. "But it sounds a lot like being pussy-whipped."

Hearing that word takes me back to the debate with Clem Ford. I shift in my seat a little.

"I, um, I didn't get to thank you for helping Bris talk me down the other night."

"You mean when you almost ripped Clem Ford's throat out?" Iz asks with a mockery of calm. "Sure. Any time. At least I know you have your own money and won't need our bail fund. What the hell were you thinking?"

"He disrespected Bristol." Anger surges through my veins again at the memory.

"Well I hope she's worth going to prison for because you ever pull some shit like that again, that's exactly where you'll end up. You're lucky he didn't press charges."

"Oh, he has no desire to see me in jail yet." My bark of a laugh is certain and cynical. "He's just getting started with me and wouldn't want to end the game this soon."

I grab my saddlebag and motorcycle helmet, determined not to be late for my appointment with Bristol and Charm to finally figure out this book deal.

"Bristol helped me realize that I represent everything he thinks should be impossible. Based on his metrics, I shouldn't exist, much less get to choose someone from his race to spend my life with." I stand and level a disgusted look at him. "I guess that's at least one thing you two agree on."

"Who the hell do you think you are comparing me to that backwards cretin?" Iz demands, indignation pinching his strong features.

"I got a front row seat to your brand of selective progressivism," I fire back. "And at the end of the day, you both judge people you don't know anything about by the color of their skin."

"If I'm such a bigot," Iz snaps, anger darkening his eyes and hardening his jaw, "then why the hell are you still working with me?"

"Because the woman I love is wiser than both of us," I throw back at him. "She cares enough about people who don't even look like her to set aside the gross offense of your discrimination because she believes we can help them more working together than apart."

A silence falls after my bellowed words, a silence teeming with the complexity of our admiration for each other, with our resentment, our shared convictions, our differences. I watch the anger melt from his face in phases, loosening feature by feature until all that's left is a milder expression and uncertainty.

"She used my own words on me, you know," he says, a wry grin tipping the edge of his stern mouth.

"What?" I shift my bag on my shoulder, needing to go but wanting to hear what he has to say. I keep hoping he'll say something to demonstrate his perspective is changing.

"Your girl, Bristol. She had me sign her copy of *Virus* in a section on inherent bias."

We share a grin because sometimes all you can do is laugh at the things Bristol does.

"She introduced herself as 'Grip's Bristol,'" he says, his grin deepening to a full-on smile.

Damn right she's Grip's Bristol.

"Oh yeah?"

"And she said if I hurt you again, I'd have to deal with her." His smile dies off, and he looks down at the mess of papers littering his desk. "I didn't mean to hurt—"

"You didn't hurt me."

It's a lie. He did hurt me, but I haven't given any man the satisfaction of truly hurting me since my dad walked away without looking back. I won't let Iz know he held that place in my life until he said those things about Bristol.

"You're just a smart guy with great ideas," I continue, stiffening the words around any emotion left over. "I thought you were something that you're not. My bad, not yours."

If I didn't know Iz better, didn't know he doesn't give a damn about anyone's opinion, I'd think that's guilt in his eyes. Whatever it is, he blinks and it's gone.

"Yeah, well, okay. Good." He takes his glasses off to polish them on the edge of his Howard University sweatshirt. "Well I'm still glad you'll continue with my organization now that the semester is over. I'm ready to get out of the classroom and back to the real grind."

"Of course. The cause is bigger than you and me."

"Right." He twists his lips around, frowns, and releases a sigh. "Look, tomorrow's the exam, and I assume you're leaving the city after."

"Yeah, though we're actually keeping our place here for another six-month lease. Bris has some Broadway stuff popping off for one of her clients, and we love the city, love our place. We'll be back and forth."

"You still want that spot on the board of directors?" he asks as if he doesn't care, but somehow I know he does.

"Yeah, sure." I shrug like I don't care, but I want on that board like nobody's business. "If you think it could work."

"My assistant will send you details about our next meeting and papers you need to sign." He hesitates before going on. "I know it's . . . well, I'm sorry I was a . . . uh, disappointment to you, Grip."

I study the regret marking his face and his words. I don't say anything that would counter because he did disappoint me, and I refuse to make it easier for him.

"But I'm . . . well I'm honored that you moved here to study with me," he mutters. "Shocked actually. It's been really cool getting to know you this semester, and I look forward to, uh . . . well . . . what I'm trying to say is . . . fuck it."

He reaches into his desk drawer and pulls something out, something badly wrapped in plain paper.

"Merry Christmas." He practically spits the goodwill at me and extends the gift.

I just stare at it, and after a full five seconds, I accept it.

604 | KENNEDY RYAN

"I didn't get you anything," I mumble, tugging on the tatty ribbon.

"It's not much, believe me. Uh, you can open it later." He sits at his desk and pushes his glasses up his nose. "I'm getting ready for finals, if you could just close the door behind you."

Iz is a PhD, and he must hold at least a master's in dismissing people. I nod, suppressing the grin that tries to break past my restraint.

"A'ight," I say casually over my shoulder. "Merry Christmas."

I walk down the hall away from his office and down the stairs. In the stairwell, I drop my saddlebag and sit on the step, turning the gift over in my hands for a few moments before pulling the ribbon.

It's a book.

Iz *would* give me a book.

I trace the aged leather, the letters pressed into the weathered cover.

Montage of a Dream Deferred by Langston Hughes.

I flip open the front cover, and my blood stands still in my veins when I note the date—1951—and the famous poet's autograph.

A signed first edition.

I turn to the spot slotted by an index card, a crisp contrast to the worn, fragile pages. The poem is "Harlem," and the familiar refrain asking what happens to a dream deferred stings tears in my eyes.

I can't ever read this poem without remembering the day my cousin died in the front yard. There are some moments in life that will always haunt us, no matter how many joys follow, and that day is one of those. I'll never forget reciting this poem in my bedroom closet to keep Jade calm while one of her brothers shot the other.

Iz couldn't know its personal significance to me, but as I read the card, I understand why he chose it.

Grip,

Our brothers live so long with dreams deferred, they forget how to imagine another life. For many of them, all they know is frustration, then rage, and for too many, the violence of finally exploding. You symbolize hope, and I know you take that responsibility seriously. I hope you know I believe that, and that nothing I've said led you to think otherwise. Bristol's right—our biases are our weaknesses. Few are as patient as she is to give people time to become wiser. Thank her for me, for giving me time and for encouraging you to work with me. Together, I think we will restore the dreams of many.

Merry Christmas, Iz

Twenty-Three
Bristol

THIS ISN'T MY FIRST GRAMMYS, BUT IT'S THE FIRST TIME TWO OF my clients have been nominated for multiple awards. Rhyson has won several in the past, of course, but tonight, Grip and Kai are up, and I think Rhyson and I are more nervous than they are.

"I'm still not sure about that lighting." Rhyson watches a video of Kai's rehearsal from earlier today on his phone. "Can we talk to the LD one more time?"

"Leave the lighting director alone," Kai says from the corner where she and her stylist are consulting about her dress for the red carpet. "Rhys, you're doing that thing again."

"What thing?" he asks absently, eyes still fixed on the video.

"The thing where you try to control the whole universe and act like a crazy person?" She stretches her eyes wide like he should know. "That thing."

He looks up, one dark brow cocked, and stops the video, setting the phone down on the table.

"It's your performance, Pep." He shrugs. "If you feel comfortable with uneven lighting for the biggest performance of your life, who am I to disagree?"

"Rhyson!" I roll my eyes at my brother. "Don't do that. The lighting was fine."

"*Fine?*" His disgust is palpable. "Fine, not perfect. She should have perfect, Bris, and you know it."

Kai and I exchange a look that says we hate it when he's right.

"Okay." I grab my phone and bag from the dressing room table. "I'll go talk to the lighting director."

"It's the blue wash," Rhyson says with a satisfied smile. "The setting at the beginning of the second verse."

"Right. Blue wash, got it. I'll see you guys back at the hotel." I pause at the door. "And Sarah will be with you for the red carpet tonight."

"Oh, great." Kai gives me a wide smile. "What are *you* wearing for your first public appearance as an engaged woman?"

"Ugh." The sigh drags past my lips. "Don't remind me. As if I don't have enough to do without having to think about getting red-carpet ready."

"It's a big night for Grip," Rhyson says. "I'm sure if it comes down to whether he needs his manager or his fiancée more, it would be his fiancée."

"You mean the fiancée who's running off to check the blue wash before the second verse?" I give him a well-meaning smirk.

Rhyson doesn't allow himself much guilt, but I'm pretty sure that's what flits across his face. He grabs his phone and stands.

"I'll talk to the LD," he says.

"No, you won't." I wave him back to his seat. "It's a huge night for Grip *and* Kai—for Prodigy. Our little label is up for a grand total of six nominations. I can do my job *and* be fabulous for the red carpet."

"You sure?" he asks, uncertainty mingling with the guilt in his expression.

"You doubt me?" I volley back with more confidence than I actually feel.

"Okay, if you say so. See you later, sis."

I'm wrapping up my conversation with the lighting director backstage—who, at the very least, deserves a fruit basket once this is all over—when I hear a familiar voice behind me.

"No, that worked," Qwest says. "They hit it on that last runthrough. Just make sure we strike that spot onstage, or I won't hit the mark for camera two."

I stand perfectly still in the corner where the lighting director and I talked, hoping she'll walk on by and I'll go undetected.

"Bristol?"

There goes hope.

"Qwest, hey." I step forward, a smile pasted on my lips that feels like it's made of plastic. "Good to see you."

"Hmmm." Qwest waves her choreographer on her way. Her eyes roam over me as they usually do, like she sees several things lacking before reaching my face. "I guess I should have known you'd be here."

As friendly greetings go, it's not one.

"Well, congratulations on your nomination." I give her another stiff smile and start to walk off.

"Did you lobby for Grip and me not to perform 'Queen'?"

Her question startles me enough to turn around and face her again. Her one Grammy nomination is for collaborating with Grip on "Queen," for best rap performance.

"No. I-I don't remember it even coming up. The producers of the show were very clear that they wanted Grip to perform 'Bruise.'" I meet her eyes with nothing to hide. "It's up for song of the year, and it's pretty standard to ask the artists nominated for that award to perform, well, the song they're nominated for."

Qwest looks unconvinced for a moment before resignation clears her pretty face.

"It's fine." She shrugs. "I'm performing one of my other songs anyway."

"Good." I hesitate before speaking again. "I would never meddle that way, Qwest—in Grip's career, I mean."

"Awwww," she says sarcastically. "I guess that's one of the many reasons he loves you—that and your pretty hair and golden tan."

I don't reply, but instead let her stew in her own petty silence. I don't have the time or patience for this shit today.

"I'm sorry, too, about all the drama with Angie Black." Qwest watches me closely. I know she wants a reaction I'm determined not to give her. "And that picture on Instagram. I can imagine how I'd feel if I saw my boyfriend's ex with her hands all over him."

"Then why did you have your hands all over him?"

So much for not giving her a reaction.

"*There* she is." Her smile is immediate and knowing. "I figured your claws would come out soon enough."

"I don't want my claws out, Qwest. I wish you well. I know you don't believe that, but I do."

"Oh, spare me." The mask falls away, and Qwest's ire is on full display. "You wish me well because you got nothing to worry about. I'm not a threat to you, and you know it."

"You think I don't feel threatened by you?" My scoffing laugh bounces between us. "Many of Grip's family, friends, and fans would dance in the streets if he dumped me for you. Do you know how many people have told him that being with me discredits the work he does for the Black community?

And that you 'make sense' and I don't? That if he wanted to have a real impact, he would choose you?"

"But none of that is Grip," Qwest says. "You and I both know how he feels about you, that he doesn't give a damn what any of them thinks. All I hear in everything you've said is that he's willing to tell everyone to fuck off for you, and that's gotta make you feel as secure as hell."

She's right. When it comes down to it, as tired as I am of all the outside voices and influences, I don't doubt Grip's love for me. I've had moments where I let the negativity get to me, but at the center is a rock-solid faith in our love.

"Besides," Qwest continues, a touch of malice in the look she gives me, "you saw something you wanted that wasn't yours, and you went for it. I probably would've done the same thing. Game recognize game."

I see what she's doing—provoking me—but the thought of her claiming Grip when he was never really hers festers under my skin.

"You're mistaken," I say before I can talk myself out of it.

"Oh?" Qwest furrows her brow as if she's clueless about what I mean. "How am I mistaken?"

"He was never yours." I force myself to look into eyes that hold more knowledge of Grip than they should.

"He was mine when he was in my bed."

"He's been in lots of beds, but there's only been one woman in his heart."

"And that's you?"

"And that's me." I hesitate, swallowing cruel words for kinder ones. "Look, I'm trying to be gracious here, Qwest. Don't make me be mean."

Her harsh laugh scratches over my ears.

"Well, the next time you feeling all *gracious and shit*," she spits through a bitter smile, "and want to lend your man's dick out, let me know, 'cause honey, I wasn't done with it."

She steps closer, her perfume invading my space as quickly as her slim body.

"You may be the only one who's ever *'been in his heart,'* but I wouldn't have known it by the way he fucked me."

The sharp reminder of their past intimacy slides under my ribs like a stiletto and makes me draw a stilted breath.

"Like I said, game recognize game," she says. "The next time you want to throw Grip in my face, Bristol, be absolutely certain you can handle what I'll throw back."

Why am I even doing this? Why engage with her this way? I know I have nothing to worry about, but I keep letting this damn possessiveness get the best of me, and I'm tired of being jealous for no reason. With a weary sigh, I scoop the hair back from my face. The arrested expression on Qwest's face confuses me until she reaches for my hand, holding my ring finger up to the light. Hurt floods her eyes as she studies the large square canary diamond Grip placed there.

"So it's true," she says quietly. "He's marrying you."

I don't know what to say. I just stare back at her and wait for her to drop my hand. She forces a laugh.

"Well that was fast."

"Fast? If you call ten years in the making fast, then yeah."

She pulls a stream of braids over her shoulder and fingers the sleek strands. Her expression says she doesn't give a damn, but I'm not convinced, and my heart hurts. I want to hate this woman. She slept with Grip. She led a social media shade campaign against me, but it's the hurt I see just beneath the surface that keeps me from the dislike I want to give in to.

"I'm sorry, Qwest." I know she wouldn't want my pity. I respect her too much for that, and the barbs we just exchanged assure me she doesn't need it. I can't be sorry that Grip is mine, but I am sorry she ever thought he would be hers, sorry for my part in letting her believe that even for a few months.

"You said it—you're the only one who's ever been in his heart, who ever got past his bed." Quest's glassy eyes fix on my ring finger. "The rest of us he fucked, but doesn't give a damn about."

Without another word or glance, she turns on her heel and walks away.

Twenty-Four

Grip

OVER THE LAST FEW MONTHS, AT TIMES I'VE BEEN ABLE TO FORGET I'm a celebrity. I've been dragging myself out of bed and going to class, sitting through lectures, turning in assignments like any other NYU student. Besides going into the studio and the occasional appearance, life has been more normal than it has the last few years. Sure, Angie Black put my life on blast and all the drama about me dating Bristol flared up again, but it's been pretty tame, considering.

Tonight, though, I'm nominated for three Grammys, including song of the year and best new artist. I walked the red carpet with Bristol at my side, answering some questions, dodging others. She didn't wear her ring, and we remained non-committal on our engagement, instead focusing on which designers we were wearing and which performances we wanted to see. Useless things like that seem so far removed from the issues I've focused on for the last few months with Iz, but in perspective, I know this is a big deal. This part of my life lends me more leverage in the others. The higher my celebrity stock goes, the more influence and resources I'll have for the things that really matter. So, I smile and answer questions and shine as brightly as I can along with all the other stars. My mama always told me to remember that every time I step out of the house, I represent those who will never have the opportunity to step onto a stage this large.

"Are you nervous?" Bristol leans over to whisper once we're in our seats and the show is underway.

I glance at her, and for a moment, forget how momentous tonight is. All

I can see is how beautiful she looks. Her dark burnished hair is wild in that intentional way that probably takes a lot of time to make look that effortless. The dress she chose is bluish-green with vibrant splashes of color, and her feathery earrings reflect the brilliant palette of her dress.

"You're my pretty bird tonight," I say instead of answering her question directly. I touch the hair rioting around her face. "Maybe a peacock."

"Thanks, I think." She rolls her eyes, but quirks the fullness of her lips into an irrepressible smile. "But don't change the subject. Your first category is up next. Are you nervous?"

Grinding all these years, a Grammy seemed like the culmination, like winning one would be the ultimate happiness, and I won't lie, winning would be pretty dope. But, the hardware that makes me happiest isn't the Grammy, it's the one Bristol left back in our hotel room. I lift her hand to my lips for a quick kiss. I was more nervous walking around with that ring in my pocket for a week than I am waiting for my first Grammy.

"Nervous?" I repeat. "Li'l bit."

She studies me for an extra second before smiling and turning her attention back to the stage as the nominees for best rap performance are announced.

Some girl from a reality show I've never watched does the honors, her face animated when she opens the card.

"And the winner is," she says, pausing to stretch out the audience's bated breath. "'Queen,' Grip and Qwest."

This moment is pretty surreal, with the applause louder than I thought it would be, the lights brighter, more cameras capturing everything from perfect angles. It feels like a dream I had as a kid that I just don't wake up from. The only thing real in all of this is Bristol's hand gripping mine and the tears swimming in her eyes. I lean over to kiss her cheek, and she whispers, "I'm proud of you."

A part of me wishes I didn't have to go onstage or make a speech. I wish I could just stay here and bask in the fact that the woman who knows me better than anyone else and has seen this journey almost from the beginning is proud of me. I squeeze her leg and lean down to kiss behind her ear, where the smell of her perfume and the scent unique to her body are strongest.

"Go." She laughs, giving me a little push. "And don't forget to thank your mother."

Like I could.

Qwest makes it to the stage before I do, and I nod for her to take the mic first. With her long braids twisted into a knot at the base of her neck and an evening dress sheathing all that famous ass, she looks classy and composed, powerful and regal. I'm happy for her—it's her first Grammy, too.

"Wow." She turns a bright smile on the audience, and I'm glad she gets this moment for herself. "Obviously, I need to thank my team, my manager Will, Ezra Cohen with Sound Management, my family for holding me down, all the fans, and everyone who supported me along the way."

She glances back at me, her smile wavering for just a second as the feelings I suspect she still has for me congregate in her eyes. She blinks, and that vulnerability disappears, covered with the high shine of celebrity again.

"Most of all, thank you, Grip," she says after a moment. "For putting up with my crazy ass and trusting me with such an incredible song."

I offer her a quick wink and a grin before she turns back to the crowd.

"It's an honor getting to inspire young girls to respect themselves, to carry themselves like the queens they're meant to be. If a little brown girl from Bed-Stuy can stand up here, you can stand anywhere you want!"

The applause dies down before I step to the mic. I'm determined to keep this short and simple. I still have to perform "Bruise," and the sooner I get backstage, the sooner I can start mentally preparing for that, but I don't want to cheat this moment because I'll never get it back.

"This is amazing." I look out at the crowd, peers and fans and industry professionals, taking it all in. "There's a lot of people to thank. I'll try not to screw this up. Um, where's Rhyson?"

I shield my eyes from the bright lights and search the first few rows where I remember he and Kai were supposed to be seated.

"I absolutely wouldn't be standing here without you." There are a thousand memories in the glance we exchange. With all the jubilation going on around him, his eyes remain sober. He knows what this has cost me, knows how hard I've been grinding, how hard *we've* been grinding since high school. He knows, probably more than anyone, what it means. "You and the Prodigy team always have my back, and I couldn't ask for a better friend. Love you, dude, like a brother. To all the fans who humble me daily, this doesn't happen without your support. Thank you so much."

I stare down at the trophy before continuing.

"A lot of people speculate about who I wrote this song for, what I'm talking about." I pause to chuckle. "My mom will tell you unequivocally that she is #GripzQueen."

The audience laughs, and I know my mom is somewhere in the Staples Center loving this.

"A lot of people think I wrote it for Qwest." I glance at her beside me. "Writing a song like this and not having a strong woman help me perform it, give voice to it, would have been a travesty. You are an amazing representative for powerful women everywhere, Q."

She nods and smiles, but I can tell this moment is affecting her in ways she didn't anticipate. I hope the emotion in her eyes has more to do with the gravity of the achievement than with me and our past relationship.

"Some think it's for Black women or women in general." I shrug, a subtle smile playing on my lips. "You're all right. It's for my mom, who taught me what love is, what strength looks like, how to not just survive difficult circumstances, but to thrive in them. It's for women like Qwest, who dream big and work hard. It's for my aunties in the neighborhood who took it upon themselves to straighten me out if my mom, working two jobs, wasn't around when I was acting the fool. It's for all of you girls who aren't sure you're worthy of respect when we, especially in hip-hop, sometimes don't give you your due. It's fitting that my first Grammy would be for 'Queen' since I wouldn't be here if it hadn't been for all the incredible women who kept pushing me forward."

I find Bristol sitting where I left her, pride and love shining in the eyes that never leave my face. I can already see the *Coming to America* GIFs that will be everywhere if I call her my queen, so I force myself to stop short of that. She would be fine if I didn't say a word about her. Hell, she'd probably prefer it after all the media shit-storms we've been through, but there's no way this moment even happens without her.

"It's for you, Bris," I say softly, even though my words are amplified throughout Staples and in millions of homes. "You're the best thing in my life. None of this would mean anything without you."

Our eyes hold in an extraordinary recognition I could only share with her, of the sacrifices we've made and the risks we've taken together, all while falling in love. I want to call her my girl, my fiancée, my *wife* in front of the whole world, but we've agreed we don't want our engagement to be a lightning rod or some sideshow, a hot potato people toss around to gain more followers, get more likes and retweets. So, I don't tell these people anything that's none of their business. I just hold up the gold statue and don't give Black Twitter or Angie Black or any of my critics more to work with than necessary.

"Thank you."

I don't return to my seat because I still have to perform. Once I'm backstage, that tunnel vision that comes with such a huge performance consumes me completely, not just because it's so significant for my career, but because of the nature of the song, which has been significant for my cause. I've performed "Bruise" in larger venues, but this is the *Grammys*. It doesn't get any bigger than this, and I want to be a megaphone for this moment. It's a perfect convergence of my gifts and my passions, and I don't want to blow it.

From the first note, I know it's a special performance, a demarcation in my journey as an artist. The lights and imagery, a moody wash of black and blue, coordinate with typography of the song's most powerful lyrics onscreen. As many times as I've performed this song, the words have never felt as meaningful as they do tonight, with the names of slain black men scrolling behind me.

We all bruise,
It's that black and blue
A dream deferred, Nightmare come true
In another man's shoes, Walk a mile or two
Might learn a couple things I'm no different than you!

As I'm performing, the faces of the men on that wall behind me flash through my mind on a reel, their lives cut short. I remember the day each of them died—how I heard, what I was doing, how it felt to know things this fucked up could still happen in our country. The same coalition of anger and pain and hope that led me to write the song compels me to perform it like the next life depends on it. Like this song might save somebody, even though it came too late for these men. Like my art has no limits and love has no walls.

As hard as I try, I can't keep my voice from wobbling, can't keep the hurt and the outrage from reverberating through each lyric. Despite my best efforts, tears—fucking *tears* streak down my face, defying any show of strength. My tears are for the mothers and the sisters and fathers and wives and daughters and sons watching this *show* tonight with an empty seat at their table, watching me perform this song with a hole in their hearts. I shed tears for the tragedy of bias and the futility of revenge. None of it bears any fruit, and it could feel hopeless, except when I look out, I see the same emotion that's commanding me has command of the audience, compelling them to their feet and streaking their faces with tears, too. White, Black, Brown, all of them—a mosaic of the emotions warring inside of me. Though I could be cynical, though I could doubt that it means anything, that *they* mean it, in this moment, even with the hurt and the anger and the frustration, I make room in my heart for faith that one day, no matter how long it takes, we'll get it right.

Twenty-Five

Bristol

"T WO OUT OF THREE AIN'T BAD." I MEET GRIP'S EYES IN THE bathroom mirror. "You're officially a Grammy winner now."

"And losing best new artist to Kai is no loss at all." He grins at me, brushing his teeth as we get ready for bed. "Least we kept it in the family."

"Yeah, Kai had a huge night. Three trophies." I yawn while removing the makeup from my face with a wipe. "I think Rhyson was on a higher cloud than she was."

"He's proud of her, and he should be." Grip leans against the marble counter in my bathroom. "Grammys, movies, endorsements ..."

"And Broadway," I insert, running a brush through my unruly hair. "Just give me a little time."

"Yeah. Kai's on that world domination trip. She's on the come up big time."

"You are, too." I lean into him, pressing my chest to his. "Song of the year's nothing to sneeze at."

Grip palms my head and lays a kiss in the hair at my temple without acknowledging my compliment.

"And best rap song." I lower my lashes to study our feet, almost touching. "With Qwest."

He tips my chin up, searching my eyes.

"Did it bother you to see us up there together?"

"It bothers me to see you with anyone who isn't me." A tired, self-deprecating laugh rumbles over my lips. "But I was okay."

I hesitate, biting my lip before going on. "She still has feelings for you, ya know."

Grip runs his tongue over his teeth, a thoughtful frown disrupting the strong line of his eyebrows.

"Yeah, I know."

I tip up on my toes and kiss his chin, slipping a hand to the back of his neck. He rubs my back and we appreciate the closeness of each other's bodies for a minute, the silence swelling with a tenderness, an intimacy I can't imagine sharing with anyone else.

"Your performance tonight . . ." My words evaporate because I can't find the right ones to express how moved I was when he performed "Bruise." It wasn't just me, either—he ushered the entire crowd to another plane during that performance, and I still feel like I'm coming off a high. "I've seen you be amazing, but this was something else. It was on another level, from a different place."

"It felt . . . I don't know." He shakes his head and shrugs, a helplessness limiting what he can say about it even now. "It was a once-in-a-lifetime moment. I couldn't hold it together. Thinking about those guys who died and the cops who were ambushed, I just lost it."

I don't respond for a moment because I can't. The same emotion that overcame me during his performance steals my words again. Seeing those names scrolling behind him, seeing the tears rolling down Grip's cheeks, looking around and seeing that I was surrounded by wet faces and broken hearts, there was a oneness in that crowd I've never experienced before. What if we achieved that kind of unity without music? Without a stage? In our communities and in the streets? How would that feel?

"That was sweet, dedicating the Grammy for song of the year to your cousin Greg," I say, clearing my throat and shifting to something I can actually articulate. "He's a good cop."

"And to Chaz." Voice subdued, eyes somber, Grip wears the sadness that always accompanies thoughts of Jade's fallen brother.

"Yeah, and to Chaz," I slur the words as exhaustion takes its toll.

The last few days have been nonstop.

Grip links our fingers, allowing our hands to dangle between us. He caresses over my hip and down my thigh before cupping my ass possessively, warming me through the silk of my nightgown. His bare torso and long, muscled legs in just briefs stir my passion, but I'm too exhausted to do anything about it.

A first for me.

My head flops against his shoulder, and I can barely keep my eyes open. There was all this press after the show, and then we must have hit every after-party Hollywood had to offer.

"Come to bed," he whispers in my ear, ghosting kisses down my neck. "To sleep. You're obviously too tired for anything else."

I almost trip over my feet, stumbling behind him as he leads me to the bed. I climb in, grateful when he pulls the comforter up over my shoulders.

"Do you miss your loft?" I ask with the last of my consciousness. My eyes droop drowsily and I consider him in the light of the lamp on his side of our bed.

"Not really." He lies on his side, tucking his pillow in the crook of his neck and shoulder. "We don't need the place in New York and two places here in LA. The guys from Kilimanjaro subleasing the loft makes sense. Besides, I got spoiled living with you last semester, waking up with you every morning."

He pushes my hair back and runs his thumb over my cheekbone. "I can't go back now."

We share weary smiles and skim our lips in sleepy kisses until my eyelids drift closed.

"Bris."

I start awake, barely. "Wha ... Huh?"

"I need to ask you something."

"Is this something I need to actually remember tomorrow?" I murmur, eyes closed and the cool pillow soothing under my face.

"Yeah, you need to remember this."

"Okay," I mumble through a yawn. "Shoot."

"When can we get married?"

My eyes pop open to find him watching me, his expression as alert as if it's the top of the morning, not the end of an extremely exhausting, emotionally draining day.

"What?" My heart buffets my ribs, fighting against the tired body caging it. "When ... why ... *what*?"

"You heard me." He chuckles, brushing a knuckle over my brow. "We said we'd set a date after the Grammys were behind us."

"And you consider, oh, an hour ago 'behind us'?" A tiny, tired smile tugs at the corners of my mouth.

"Yeah, I do." He moves forward until our heads are on the same pillow and our foreheads press together. "When will you marry me?"

It feels like rocks are tied around my arms, but I lift and link them behind his neck, scooting close enough that the heated hardness of his body absorbs mine.

"Depends," I say, my voice weary and husky. "You want to do it tonight, or would you prefer tomorrow?"

My eyes may be barely open, but there's no doubt in my mind they are certain, no doubt he reads complete willingness in them. If he said to me that we should drag our tired asses out of bed right now to go get married, I'd do it. He knows that; his pleased smile tells me so.

"It doesn't have to be tonight or tomorrow." He leaves one last kiss at the corner of my mouth. "But it will be very soon. Just making sure you're down for very soon."

He reaches over to turn off the lamp.

"Okay," he says into the darkness. "Now you can go to sleep." With complete contentment and the promise of forever very soon, I do.

Twenty-Six
Grip

I<small>T'S OUR WEDDING DAY. F</small>INALLY.

I say "finally," but it's only been a month since the Grammy's. After that night, Bristol and I decided we would not even publicly confirm the engagement, but would move forward with our own plans, in our own way. Nobody's business. We've invited only our innermost circle of family and friends. We didn't hire a wedding planner or anything, just made some simple arrangements, and forced vendors and those involved to sign Bristol's NDAs.

And now the day is here, and I'm a horny groom. Does this actually come as a surprise to anyone? Probably not, but this semi-erect state I find myself in on my wedding day was completely avoidable. Bristol—who can barely spell "tradition"—decided we shouldn't see each other the night before the wedding, other than the rehearsal dinner. Add that to the fact that we've barely seen each other for the last two weeks being on different coasts and … horny groom. My balls are a dismal shade I like to call Bristol Blue.

I sip my coffee and take in the picturesque view of the Rocky Mountains through the hotel window. The snow-capped peaks and stretches of pristine snow are breathtaking. When Bristol suggested an Aspen wedding in honor of our snowy proposal, I wasn't sure at first, but seeing the soaring splendor of the mountains, it seems fitting. Our journey has been uphill, and in some ways, it may always be. At times, our climb has felt as insurmountable as some of those mountains. The easiest thing about being with Bristol is *being* with Bristol, and she makes all the outside pressures and criticisms worth it. So, yes, being surrounded by a line of mountains suits us perfectly.

"Are you okay?" my mom asks from across the small table in the hotel suite.

Knowing Ma, I could say, *No, I'm horny*, and she wouldn't bat an eyelash. She'd just tell me to eat my oatmeal and be patient because I'll be smashing before the night is over.

"I hate oatmeal," I say instead, flashing a quick smile.

"You always did." She swaps my oatmeal for the pastry in front of her. "I wondered why you ordered it."

"I didn't mean to. I didn't even notice."

"You're distracted." Ma spears a square of French toast. "It *is* your wedding day. You nervous?"

"Nah." I bite into the pastry's flaky sweetness, chewing thoughtfully. "Just ready. This has been a long time coming."

Ma smiles, rubbing away the condensation on her glass of orange juice.

"It's obvious you love Bristol very much." She takes a sip, peering at me over the rim of her glass. "It's a shame Jade couldn't make it."

"Couldn't?" I scoff. "Wouldn't is more like it. I don't care."

"Oh, you care." Ma reaches over to cover my fist where it's clenched on the table. "You just care more about your happiness than you do about Jade's opinion, as you should. But it's okay that it hurts, her not being here. She'll come around eventually."

But she hasn't yet, and it does hurt. The last time I saw Jade, I warned her that I'd choose Bristol over her, that I wouldn't hesitate to cut her out of my life if I had to, but I didn't actually think it would come to that. I didn't actually think Jade would object enough to cut *herself* out my life, or cut me out of hers. Either way, we haven't spoken since that day in the studio. I sent her an invitation, but she didn't respond. I want to text her middle finger emojis and let her know I don't give a fuck, except Ma's right—I do. It hurts, but today isn't for regrets or recriminations. It's for Bristol and me.

"You're okay with it, though, right Ma?" I cast a searching glance at the woman who has been the guiding force of my life. "With Bristol and me, I mean. Now you're okay?"

My mom looks back at me with deep affection in the eyes roaming my face before she answers my question with one of her own.

"How many men want to have breakfast with their mother on the morning of their wedding?" She sits back in her seat and crosses her legs.

I shrug. I didn't think about it. It just feels like I'm about to turn a corner, like the ground is about to shift beneath my feet, and my mother has always been with me for every transition, large or small. It's always been her and me against the world. Me getting married . . . it feels a little like the end of an era and the beginning of something new. Starting this day with the woman who got me where I am . . . it felt right.

"I didn't hold back my opinion when you told me you were in love with Bristol," Ma says. "You've always known I didn't want you bringing no white girls home."

My heart sinks in my chest. I'm prepared to take these next steps without the support of my friends and family, but it's bad enough not having Jade. Taking such a monumental step without Ma in my corner, especially when I thought we had come so far, it would hurt.

"But then I met *her*," Ma says. "And 'them white girls' became *Bristol.* That girl loves you, and you love yourself some Bristol."

Her humor and the relief that she does seem supportive after all coax a chuckle from my throat.

"True that," I say with a smile that lingers on my lips even after the laughter dies.

"Let me show you something." Ma bends to her purse and pulls out a small bag discreetly etched with *Chelle's*, Bristol's favorite jewelry store. She passes the bag to me, urging me to open it with a nod of her head when I just stare at it blankly. "Go on. Look."

I pull the delicate tissue from the bag, finding an ornate box inside. When I crack it open, there's a brooch tipped with a crown studded with diamonds. I'm pretty sure the brooch's stickpin is platinum, and this must have cost a small fortune.

"Read the card," Ma says, watching my face carefully for a reaction. I find the folded card hidden in the depths of the tissue.

Ms. James,

I know it's unconventional for the bride to give her future mother-in-law a wedding gift, but I really wanted you to have this. As soon as I saw this crown, I knew it belonged to you, #GripzQueen. I want to thank you for so many things, for giving me a chance though I wasn't what you originally envisioned for your son, for making me feel like part of your family, something my own parents weren't always sure how to do. Most of all, thank you for raising such a magnificent man. He is the man of my dreams. When I thought of my husband, I didn't dream in color, I dreamt in character. My own father's left much to be desired, and I only knew I wanted something different from what I saw in my parents. I have that with Grip, and it's because of the remarkable character you instilled in him. So, thank you, Grip's original queen. I would like to be a daughter to you, but I will accept friendship. Whatever we are, we both love Grip—Marlon—more than anything else in this world, and we'll always have that.

Thank you again,

Bristol

I figured I would cry at some point before this day was over, but I didn't expect it to be before it has even really begun. I'm sure my mother loved this, was pleased by it, and that's great, but I read between the lines of this letter and see all the things no one else knows about Bristol. I see all the ways she's vulnerable and never lets on, all the things she ached for growing up but never received. I'm amazed by this girl's capacity to love. She learned early on to reach out first, constantly asking for love from her parents, and even from Rhyson. She was, and many times still is, the one holding her family together, even when they don't want to be. Even though my mother rejected her at first, she has been reaching out to her every chance she's gotten. I grab my mother's mimosa, knocking it back and washing away the emotion burning my throat. I'm not crying—not yet.

I kiss Ma's cheek at the door, studiously ignoring the sheen of tears in her eyes. If I look too closely, I'll see all the sacrifices she made, all the hardships she endured for me to have not just this day, but most of the other good things in my life. With promises to see her at the ceremony, I rush to the elevator, determined to see Bristol before everyone gathers at the small stacked stone chapel where we'll exchange our vows. Fuck tradition. She won't be in her wedding dress yet—is there a specific rule about seeing your bride naked before the ceremony?

No? Thought not.

I step into the elevator, stopping short when I come face to face with the last person on earth I expected to see in Aspen for my wedding . . . unless this is a weird coincidence and he's here for something else.

"Iz." I blink stupidly at him leaning against the wall in the corner. "What are you doing here?"

He shifts his feet, a quick frown jerking his brows together.

"Well, I . . ." He shoves his hands into the pockets of his dark jeans. "I heard you were getting married."

I level a knowing look on him.

"We went to a lot of trouble to make sure that no one 'just hears' we're getting married, so I doubt that."

"Maybe my invitation got lost in the mail," Iz offers with a half-smile.

"They were digital."

"Spam?"

"Nope." I narrow my eyes at him. "I didn't send you an invitation, and you know why."

"I know you didn't." He glances at his boots with their light dusting of snow. "Bristol did."

I'm completely silent while I process this information. I don't know if I'm pleased, angry, confused, or something else altogether. While I'm figuring that out, Iz goes on.

"You're right," he says. "She is wiser than we are. I kept going back to that passage she highlighted and had me sign in my book. I must have read it a hundred times, seeing it through her eyes."

"Is that so?" I lift a skeptical brow.

"Yeah, it is." A slow smile pulls at his mouth, making him look younger, less the sober academic. "I haven't changed my mind about why most Black men who choose white women do it, but I've changed my mind about you and Bristol. I don't believe a white woman can ever really understand the struggle of a Black man in America, but I was married to a Black woman who understood the struggle but never understood me."

I'll have to ask him for the full story one day. From what I've ascertained, there were transgressions on both sides, and definitely regret on his.

"Bristol may not understand the struggle," he continues, "but she understands you. She loves you unconditionally—I've seen it—and in a world as hard as ours, unconditional love goes a long way."

His smile melts like the snow topping the mountains that left me awestruck just minutes ago.

"I would say having Bristol makes you a very lucky man, Grip." The elevator dings, signaling that I've reached the top floor where

I know Bristol's room is.

"This is me." I step out, but at the last minute, insert my arm to stop the doors from closing. "Hey. Thanks for coming, Iz. It, uh . . . well, thanks."

He nods, and with one last look, I allow the doors to close. If I wanted to see her before, now the urgency to see her, to remind myself that in just a few hours, we'll be husband and wife, burns through me. If I needed affirmation that I was doing the right thing—which I really didn't—I've had it in this morning's encounters with my mom and with Iz.

I rap my knuckles against the door a few times. When there's no answer,

I knock a little harder. Still no response. After three minutes, I'm pounding the door and saying Bristol's name maybe a little louder than the situation warrants. The door is yanked open from inside, and my beautiful bride stands on the threshold glaring at me, her hair all around her head and her face free of makeup. A silk robe is tied at her narrow waist.

"You better have a really good reason for being here." Though stern, her eyes and voice soften the longer we stare at each other. I slip into the room before she can stop me.

"Grip, no." She swats at my shoulders when I pull her into my arms. "You cannot be here. We cannot see each other."

"Bullshit." I bend to kiss her, my lips searching, seeking out her sweetness.

"You have to go," she mutters against my lips, but her fingers cling to my arms.

"I miss you." My whispered words catch fire in the air between us, and I feel her nipples bead against my chest. My fingers fumble at the tie at her waist, and I push at the shoulders of her robe.

"No!" She catches the silk lapels and pulls them tightly over her breasts, her eyes wide. "You have to go."

"Babe, come on." My hands slide down to her waist, the flare of her hips, the curve of her ass. "We got time. Don't make me beg."

"Beg?" She steps out of my arms, clenching the neck of the robe at her throat, showing me even less skin. "Yeah, right. When have you ever had to beg?"

"I used to have to beg," I remind her. "When you wouldn't give your boy a shot."

Her face softens, the tousled hair around her face and shoulders tempting me to shove my fingers into the shiny strands. A smile so sweet I want to taste it teases the corners of her lips.

"That was a long time ago, and don't remind me what a fool I was all those years."

We share a smile, and before she kicks me out, I take her hand and press it between my palms.

"I saw the gift you gave my mom," I say, my voice low with gratitude. "And I ran into Iz on the elevator."

"Two of your greatest influences." She shrugs her slim shoulders under the brightly patterned silk. "It wouldn't be the same without them. *You* wouldn't be the same without them, and for that I'm grateful."

She opens the door and shoves me into the hall. The door is closing in my face when I stick my foot in to stop it. I peer around the heavy wood, needing the last word.

"The next time I see you," I say with a smile, "you'll be Mrs. Marlon James."

She pauses in closing the door long enough to lean forward and drop a quick kiss on my lips.

"I can't wait," she whispers. "I love you."

The door slams in my face, but if those are her last words, I'll let her have them just this once.

Twenty-Seven
Bristol

'M JUST BEYOND THE ENTRANCE. I CAN SEE GRIP. I CAN SEE IN, BUT NO one knows I'm here yet, and I take in the ethereal beauty of the small chapel. A mix of artificial snow and white roses, a juxtaposition of blooms and blizzard, sprinkles the aisle from the chapel door to the altar. Potted trees march along the wall, naked of leaves, branches adorned with snow, warmed with tiny lights. Lanterns suspended from the ceiling cast a glow over the old chapel, hallowed by years and a thousand services and ceremonies before this one, but to me, none more sacred.

I absorb all the details, happy to see the small group of people assembled, our closest friends and family. This isn't a day for selfies or pictures that will be sold to magazines. It's a day for us, for Grip, me, and the people who mean the most to us.

Well, most of them. Ms. James and Dr. Hammond are here. Rhyson stands at the altar as Grip's best man, and Jimmi is already there as my maid of honor. Amir, Shondra, Kai and Aria, Luke, Charm—all here. Jade is noticeably absent, but I won't let that cast a cloud over today, not with all these people here celebrating our love.

"Are you ready?"

My father's question draws my attention. He's handsome, and Rhyson looks more like him every day. I considered not asking him to give me away, but that thing I can never shake, that need for my family to *be* family compelled me to include my father. My brother has forgiven him. My mother is in marriage counseling with him, and seems to have set his infidelities to the side. Today is a day for steps forward, and as the first strains of "Wedding March" herald my entrance, I answer my father with a nod and step forward with my arm through his.

The guests rise, some gasping when they see me framed in the arched entrance with my father, some teary-eyed like Ms. James and Kai, most smiling. It's my mother's face that almost makes my steady steps stumble. There is such pride in her eyes, like of all my accomplishments, marrying a good man—a man she didn't necessarily see for me in the beginning but has come to respect—is my crowning achievement. When I consider what a failure her marriage has been in the past, how much pain my father has caused her, maybe me marrying for love, finding the true happiness I have with Grip is more than she knew to hope for.

Finally I allow myself to look at my groom. People always talk about that first glimpse the groom has of his bride, but no one ever mentions the first glimpse the bride has of her groom. They really should warn a bride about this. No one told me my heart would float up in my chest and hover in my throat, or that the tears would instantly gather at the corners of my eyes when I saw him.

Maybe no one else has ever had a groom like Grip.

I always think of his as the face of a king, one sketched with an artist's skilled hands. A careful thumb smudged the sooty brows over dark eyes that see so much and can give so little away. The regal rise of bone in his cheek and the taut line of his jaw, the luxe lips generously drawn and precisely lined take my breath away. The closer I get, the more in focus his features become. I see the wedge of thick lashes, the softest thing in a face comprised of rugged planes and carefully hewn angles.

When he turns his head and our eyes meet on the threshold of forever, his jaw drops and he blinks quickly, like this first sight of me stuns him. The hours I spent searching for this dress when I should have been working were worth it. It's not white or ivory, but the palest shade of blush ever to exist. It's watercolor pink, so sheer a hue that it's barely perceptible as color at all. It's strapless, and the mermaid shape molds my curves, baring my shoulders, cupping my breasts, nipping at the waist, tapering down my hips and legs to flare just below my knees in wisps of organza as frothy as meringue.

When my father releases me to stand in front of Grip, I look up, uncovered and exposed for his inspection. Instead of a veil, I opted for a simple shoulder necklace, a string of Swarovski crystals clinging to a silver chain that drapes across my throat and collarbone, dips just shy of my cleavage and drips between my shoulder blades. Grip's eyes wander over my face, his smile growing wider as he catalogues the details of my appearance. When he sees my shoulders, his smile falters and his eyes zip to mine, startled and awed. Along the top of one shoulder, following the narrow bone, is calligraphy sketched so delicately the letters look like flowers blooming on my skin, proclaiming that my heart broke loose on the wind.

He looks out into the audience until he finds Mateo, his friend who is the only one he trusts with his ink, and now the first person I've trusted with mine. Mateo gives him a wide grin and a thumbs-up. A slash of white teeth is Grip's only answer before he turns back to me, and breaching the invisible wall between bride and groom, not asking for permission or waiting for the preacher to grant it, he touches me. His fingers trail along my shoulder, along the words Neruda penned decades ago brought to life on my skin. The words that, shared on a Ferris wheel high above the ground, unlocked a door between us that has never really closed. A smile widens on my face at the pleased look in his eyes, exactly the way I envisioned when I approached Mateo about the tattoo as a surprise. Keeping Grip away from me for the last two days so he wouldn't see it was the hardest part of planning this wedding.

I barely hear the preacher's words, barely register that a roomful of people is listening. It's not until I hear the word "vows" that I remember I have to speak and this isn't some dream where I soundlessly spectate. The things I've rehearsed for days are nowhere to be found in my mind. They're like spilled grains of sand on the shore, lost. It doesn't help that I insisted on going first, but Grip is the best writer I know—no way I'm going after him.

"I had so many things memorized," I say with a self-conscious laugh. "But I'm so overwhelmed, I can't think of them."

I glance up at Grip, who looks at me like every word coming out of my mouth, though unrehearsed, is pure gold.

"So I'll tell you all the things I didn't plan to say, but are true."

I pull in a steadying breath, willing my voice not to shake and my tears to wait until I get through this.

"Grip, I guarantee that I will disappoint you at some point in the next fifty years," I say. "I'll infuriate you. I promise you'll want to strangle me more than once."

A ripple of laughter through the audience makes me smile, makes Grip smile, too.

"But you'll be stuck with me," I say, the smile sliding off my face and the tears pricking behind my lids. "Because I'm never letting you go. I'd be a fool to let you get away. You're the best friend I've ever had, the biggest heart I've ever known, the one who sees me when no one else does and hears me even when I don't speak. I'm sure at some point I simply wanted you, maybe I even simply loved you, but we are well past that. Now I need you. You are as fundamental as the breath in my lungs, as much a part of me as the blood flowing through my body. To let you go would be to let go of life, and that's how long you'll have me. You'll have me for a lifetime, a lifetime of laughter, disagreements, battles, triumphs. No matter what comes, know I'll never leave your side."

I shift the simple bouquet of blushing tulips and white roses to one hand so I can swipe at the tears streaking down my face. My voice, my words hang in my throat for a moment, crowded with emotions even deeper than the words I manage to utter.

"I vow to stand with you through every circumstance. I promise to pick you up when you fall, to cherish you beyond reason, and to love you without walls."

When I'm done, I release a heavy breath, relieved to have gotten through it with just a few tears. With a kind smile, the preacher says a few words and encourages Grip to share his vows.

"I feel kind of silly now," he says with an almost bashful grin, completely incongruous on his handsome face. "After that, something so obviously from your heart, I almost regret writing my vows."

Here goes. I'm so glad I went first.

"But I know how much you love it when I write about you," he teases, squeezing my fingers. "So this is my heart given to you in the words I wrote."

His smile fades until his mouth rests in a sober line.

"My heart given to you completely," he adds so softy, I'm not sure the congregation hears before he launches into what he has prepared.

"It's called 'Still.'"

You ask me today if I love you,
if I take you as my own to have and to hold, and my heart replies yes.
Always, evermore, even after. Still.
Not just today before a crowd, but when we are alone, you and I, through
       years, through pain,
My heart will answer again and again, still.
Ask me in a million seconds, ask me in a billion years, Do you love me?
And I will say still.

Ask me when we toil, when we rest, when we fuss and fight.

With the taste of anger burning my lips, I will say still.

Ask me when your belly is full like the moon,

and our love has stretched your body with my child, leaving your skin,
once flawless,

now silvered, traced, scarred, I will worship you.

My eyes will never stray.

My heart will never wander, gladly leashed to you all my days. I am fixed
on you.

Our love is a great river,

the Amazon, the Nile, the river Euphrates, and my heart is a violent
churning

in my chest, swimming upstream,

defying every odd, accepting any dare To reach you.

To rush you, to hold you, to keep you.

You ask me if I love you? God, yes.

My lover, you are the single star

in a universe void before you came.

And when the years have passed,

and we have watched a thousand sunsets, and we are bent,

our bodies crooked with age ask me again.

In the twilight,

in the shadow of the life we have shared, ask me if I love you,

and my heart will answer before my lips can part.

My love, my life,

my heart never left your hands. Always, evermore, even after. Still.

Behind me, I hear sniffing. I'm aware that the audience is moved by Grip's words, but they cannot feel a fraction of the emotion drowning my senses until he is the only thing I can perceive with any clarity. Every other person, every other sound and sight is mist. The power, the passion of his words turned on me has left me undone, unraveled, a ribbon unspooled. I barely hear the words the preacher speaks, legally linking us together. It's such a formality. The words *we* spoke to one another are what joined us. *Our* words, *our* wills bind us, and even with so many looking on, clapping, cheering that we are now husband and wife, I can't make myself look away from him, and he can't tear his eyes away from me. We are caught in this most exquisite intimacy, and neither of us wants out. We want to revel in it, to revel in each other, for the rest of our days.

Part II

"Dwell in possibility."

—Emily Dickinson

Twenty-Eight

Grip

THE DARKNESS IS SO DEEP, SO DENSE, I CAN'T SEE MY HAND IN front of my face.

"For the record," I tell Bristol from the passenger seat of her car, "when I said we should use blindfolds, I was thinking kinkier, maybe with some cuffs . . . maybe some anal."

"Anal?" Though I can't see her face, her voice sounds horrified. "I told you your dick's too big for anal. Not happening."

"I'm gonna take that as a backhanded compliment." I laugh, reaching up to touch the thick cotton shrouding my eyes.

"Don't you dare take that blindfold off," Bristol orders. "And you can take it as a compliment, insult, I don't care, as long as we're clear that your big dick is not going in my tiny asshole."

She says that now, but over the last year of marriage, there hasn't been much I haven't been able to persuade her to do.

Except anal. It's a work in progress.

"Are we there yet?" I ask, tuning all my other senses to the environment to figure out where "there" is.

"Are you seven years old? We've been driving for a grand total of ten minutes . . . but, yes, we're almost there."

"Is this my anniversary present?" I lean back in the bucket seat of Bristol's convertible. "Because I read that year one is paper. Is this paper?"

"Um . . . in a way." The mischief in Bristol's voice tells me nothing except that she enjoys having the upper hand—for once.

We come to a stop, and my senses automatically go on higher alert. I sniff the air, wondering if we're going to a restaurant.

"You told me your mom says you have extra senses from growing up in Compton," Bristol says, a smugness in her voice that I fully plan to fuck out of her when we get home. "How are all those extra senses serving you right about now?"

I sniff again, pulling in deeper draws of air.

"I sense that you're wet and you want me to fuck you," I say with a straight face. "How am I doing so far?"

The silence that follows my outrageous comment has my shoulders shaking because even though I was just joking, I know I'm totally right.

"Bastard," Bristol mutters before I hear the driver's door open and slam closed.

My head jerks around when my door swings open, and I do smell her. The unique clean scent that is Bristol's invades my nostrils, and I want to sniff her like a stalker as she leads me by the arm along what I think is a sidewalk. Don't ask me how I know, but when you grow up with so little grass and nothing but asphalt, your feet know sidewalk when they meet it. A bell dings over a door, and I'm pretty sure ...

"I smell Mexican."

The blindfold is wrenched from my eyes, and I come face to face with Mateo.

"You're half right," he says with a grin. "The other half is black, on my mama's side. Blaxican!"

I glance around the tattoo shop where I've always gotten my ink. Bristol is already seated, a satisfied smirk on her face and an empanada halfway to her mouth.

"Mateo told me his dad has a taco shop around the corner," Bristol says around a mouthful. "And I thought this would be a perfect meal for our anniversary."

"When you said you'd handle our first anniversary dinner," I say, sitting down in the chair beside her, "I kind of envisioned something a little more upscale."

I shoot my friend a remorseless glance. "No offense, Matty."

"I got you, *ese*." He leans against the counter that holds the cash register. "But your wife knows what she wants."

Wife.

Bristol has been my wife for a year. It feels like yesterday and it feels like forever, like we're just getting started, and like we know each other more deeply than I ever thought possible. I want to slow the hours down because it's going too fast. One day I'll wake up and be at the end of this journey, like Mrs. O'Malley, and even after a lifetime with Bristol, I'll bargain with God for one more day.

"I had an idea for an anniversary gift to each other." Bristol wipes the corners of her mouth with a paper napkin. "Something that will last all our lives."

"I'm guessing it's a tattoo," I say, looking around Matty's tattoo parlor.

"You're very astute without the blindfold. I'm almost done eating so I can go first."

I frown because she has one beautiful tattoo on her shoulder of the Neruda line that galvanized our connection years ago, and I need to sign off on anything else. I mean, I have tattoos all over, but I'm a lot more careful with Bristol's body than I am with my own.

"What kind of tattoo are you getting?"

"You mean what kind of tattoo are *we* getting?" She reaches into her purse and hands me a sketch. "This one."

It's a pair of hands, one masculine and one feminine. Banding each ring finger is Matty's trademark calligraphy of the word *still*. The letters wrap around each finger, sketched to look like delicate vine.

"You like it?" Bristol asks, her voice soft, uncertain.

After the wedding, she requested that I give her my vows, my poem "STILL," in writing. I know she added it to a box where she keeps our memories—the leather book of Neruda poetry, the tarnished whistle from the carnival, and now the vows I wrote for her. I know

"STILL" holds significance, but I never saw this coming.

"You want to tattoo this on our fingers?" I ask, just to make sure I'm clear. "The word *still?*"

"Yeah. I have no problem making this permanent on my skin." She smiles, but bites her bottom lip. "Unless our first year has made you reconsider forever."

As an answer, I slip my wedding band off my finger and into my pocket then turn to Matty, who's already prepping his ink and needles.

"All right, partner, do your worst."

I've gotten used to the discomfort that comes with tattooing—hell, I got my first one when I was only fourteen. Amir and I were Matty's guinea pigs, and he had to fix that first one—a sadly disfigured angel—years later, after his skills improved. Bristol, though, has only gotten one tat, and she winces at the sharp needle pumping ink into her skin. Matty's fast, though, and as gentle as he can be. After a couple of hours, we have matching tattoo bands on our ring fingers, not huge, but present enough to see even under our wedding rings. Matty has cleaned the tats and is prepping for his next customer while we eat the last of our cold empanadas and drink flat beer in the back room that serves as kitchen, office, and occasional bedroom for Matty and his staff.

"It's not what I expected." I grin when her questioning eyes find mine. "But it's perfect."

"Good." She licks her lips and sets her bottle of beer on the small round table that's covered in drawings; the tattoo artists must use it to practice on. "I did something today that I hope you approve of. I probably should have asked you first."

"Asked me first?" There aren't too many things that fall into Bristol's *ask Grip first* category. "What'd you do?"

"I removed my birth control." She twists her lips, unaware of the freak-out she just set off with her words. "Well, technically, my doctor did. It was really simple. She just—"

"Whoa." I carefully set my beer beside hers. "Back up. You said you—"

"Removed my birth control, yeah." She peeks at me from under her lashes. "Is that okay? You said whenever I was ready—"

"We could start trying, yeah." A foot-long grin stretches between my cheeks. "So you're ... are you saying you're—"

"Ready to have a baby, yes." She worries the corner of her mouth with her teeth. "Your baby, yeah."

Being married to Bristol has made the last year of my life the best. To think of us adding children to this ... so many emotions rocket through me. A girl, a boy—could be both. Bristol's a twin, and her father and her Uncle Grady are twins.

"We could have twins!" The words fly from my mouth before I think better of it, and I can tell it hadn't occurred to Bristol, though I don't know how that's possible.

"Two?" Her eyes stretch. "At one time?"

"Your father's a twin. You're a twin," I remind her gently. "If your mom, who has the maternal instincts of a barracuda, can do it, I'm sure you'd be fine."

"Oh, God." Her dazed eyes fixate on the table. "Two."

She snatches her bottle from the table, tipping it back until the last drop is gone. Without missing a beat, she grabs mine and does the same. Before she starts raiding Matty's small refrigerator for cheap liquor, I decide to stop her.

"Baby, come here."

I hold my arms out and wait for her to settle on my lap. The mere thought of Bristol having my baby has me horny as hell, so when she squirms to get comfortable in my lap, I'm anything but comfortable as my dick swells into the curve of her ass. I had the best intentions when I asked her to come to me. I wanted to soothe her fears, wanted to reassure her that whatever we have, however many kids we have, we'll be fine.

But damn.

Now with her in my lap and her scent surrounding me and the satiny skin of her throat silently begging to be licked and bitten, reassuring her is the furthest thing from my mind.

I just want to fuck her.

"We have a couple of options," I mutter into the sweet-smelling curve of her neck.

"What are they?" she asks breathlessly, tipping her head back so I can take more of her skin into my mouth. "These options, what are they?"

"I can lock that door, and we can hope no one needs to come back here to microwave a Hot Pocket."

She pants against my lips, turning so she's facing me, her thighs splayed over mine while she grinds her wet heat into me.

"And the other options?" She feathers kisses over my cheeks and plunges her tongue into my ear.

Holy hell. I'll come in my pants like a pubescent boy if she does that shit again—and that's a promise, not a threat.

"We can go in the alley, or maybe even the bathroom, but folks use the bathroom a lot around here." My voice is so husky it's scraping the bottom octave. "What we're *not* gonna do is wait till we get home, because I can't."

Our eyes tangle, an electric charge in the air, breaths getting heavier the longer we feel each other, smell each other.

"Alley," she rasps, standing and practically running toward the back exit.

"You sure?" I ask like she has a choice now, but my hand is already at my belt. I'm already calculating how much time we probably have before someone invades our quiet alley. In my head, I'm already doing a stellar job of fucking her against that brick wall.

Small mercies, she's wearing a dress. With our eyes locked, she raises it over her thighs to show me her panties, and with slow, steady movements, she eases them over her hips and down her legs. They encircle her shoes in delicate lace and silk. She widens her stance a few inches and reaches back under the dress. I can see her hand moving at the juncture of her thighs and her eyes are still fixed on me, though they start going hazy with the pleasure of her own fingers.

"Did I tell you to touch yourself?" I ask, trailing kisses down her neck, pushing aside the collar of her dress with my chin, sucking the skin tattooed with Neruda into my mouth to make sure she is as sweet as she was this morning.

Just as sweet.

"You didn't want me to get started without you?" Her fingers slide up and down her slit under the silky material.

"Oh, you can get started." I slide to my knees. "As long as you know I'm the one finishing you off."

I duck under her dress and, as gently as I can with a dozen horses galloping through my veins, push her hand aside.

Get that shit outta here. Not tonight.

When she comes tonight, the first time we make love without a net, it'll be all me. As hot as it is to watch my wife touch herself, I'm holding myself personally responsible for all her orgasms tonight, kind of like a designated driver, except I'm already drunk on the smell of her and the liquid desire pouring from her pussy while I eat her out in this dark alley. The possibility of discovery heightens every second, like there's barely time to suck her clit. Barely time to get three fingers inside of her. Barely time to pull these lips into my mouth, except I do take my time. I'm thorough with this, and it's time well spent when her thighs tremble around my cheeks. She forces my mouth deeper into the V of her body, an act of pure desperation, primal instinct compelling her fingers into my scalp. She thrusts frantically against my face.

I love the scream that rips from her throat as she gushes into my mouth, and I don't even try to stifle the sound. Anyone who comes back here is getting an eyeful and an education. She starts sliding down the wall, her legs giving out, but I bracket her slim waist with my hands.

"Not yet, baby." I trap her against the wall with one hand and fumble to get my pants undone with the other. Her eyes are cloudy and sated, but when I jerk her legs up and around my back, she blinks and lust filters back into her stare. I thrust up, deep and hard and sudden, making her breath hitch.

"Grip." She squeezes her eyes closed, her face wreathed in pleasure. "I do need to walk tomorrow."

"Yeah?" I press into her, holding her hostage between my body and the brick wall. "Well you should have married some other guy if you need to go around walking all the time."

"Marry some other guy?" She breathes through a smile. "Never."

I surge into her again and again and again, relishing the startled sound she makes, like she had no idea I could tunnel deeper into her body than the last time, but I keep making a way. She hooks her arm around my neck for leverage, taking my lips between hers and biting hard enough to sting.

Tension stiffens my back and legs, seethes in my balls as I get closer. Every time I thrust in, those slick walls cling to me, like they don't want to let me go. Tight and perfect, even Bristol's pussy is possessive, holding on to me, reminding me who I belong to.

"Grip," she slurs, drunk on our love, like a shot of moonshine, wild and potent. "Oh, God."

And then it happens. She goes first, her body clenching and shuddering. Her head drops back against the wall and her eyes slide closed on pure passion. I'm next, and it doesn't even feel real. Every day is a fantasy with this girl, not just the sex—though ... dayuuuum, the *fucking* sex.

But it's more than that. It's the depth of this feeling, not just when our bodies lock together, but with every glance, every touch, with the things we tell each other without saying a word. It's *life* with her. I'll never get enough of the emotion careening through my heart right now. I link our hands, pressing them into the wall so I can see the calligraphy tattooed into my ring finger.

When I make love to Bristol knowing that someday soon, she'll have my child, the vow I spoke to her a year ago today echoes through my mind just as surely as it's inked into my flesh.

Always.

Evermore.

Even after.

Still.

Twenty-Nine

Bristol

I'M HAVING A BAD DAY AND GRIP IS MAKING IT WORSE.

"Would you just sign the contract?" I pop an ibuprofen for the headache from hell vising my temples.

"Nope," he answers calmly, eyes fixed on the gigantic television. "I told you I don't like those dates."

With the remote aimed at the television, he flips through several channels, all of which start with ESPN. ESPN 2, ESPN News, ESPN Classic—how many ESPNs do we need? He's the picture of relaxation, feet up on the table, and that only serves to agitate the bee in my proverbial bonnet. I've been working all day *for him*, setting up show dates, speaking with college administrators about the *Contagious* tour he and Iz launch in a few months, finalizing a new headphones endorsement deal—and that's just today, and that's just him. There's also my list for Kai, Luke, Rhyson, and Jimmi, getting things set up for Kilimanjaro's release. It's a shit ton, and I'm only asking him to do this one little thing.

"Please don't give me crap on this." I stand beside the couch, trying to remain reasonable. I've been doing a good job of being reasonable lately.

"Babe, just rework the deadlines." His eyes flick briefly from the screen to my face and back, like he's making sure it's still me, his wife, and not some irate stranger. "I don't want to be writing during the holidays, and that deadline Charm is proposing would have me doing that."

"Not if you're ahead of schedule." I perch on the arm of the sofa. "Just rework some studio time and—"

"Rework studio time?" The look he gives me is an ounce of disbelief, a quart of frustration. "But that's when I want to focus on my next album, not some stupid book of poetry."

"Stupid book of . . ." Words fail me. I've worked my ass off to secure this book deal with one of the finest publishers in the business. "Grip, this is how you diversify. This is brand expansion. This is—"

"This is getting on my last damn nerve is what this is doing. Let's talk about it tomorrow." He scowls, turns up the volume, and gestures to the big ass flat-screen taking up what seems to be half a wall. "It's the game, babe. I was in the studio till two o'clock this morning and on conference calls with Iz all day. I just wanna watch the game."

Men. Oh, my God. They slay me with their hobbies and trivial obsessions.

I plant myself directly in front of the television and put my hands on my hips. I know it's the universal bitch wife move, but I find myself pulling it anyway.

"Now," I say obstinately. "Let's get it settled tonight so when Charm gets to the office in the morning, our signed contract is in her inbox."

"Move." Grip's eyes narrow, not even attempting to look around me. "Or I'm moving you."

I fold my arms over my chest, raising one brow to dare him. He's on his feet in a flash, his hands lifting me by my waist, hauling me over his shoulder and stomping down the hall to our bedroom. He tosses me onto the bed and walks to the door.

"How about you come out when you're off the rag?" he snaps on his way out. "Because this shit is ridiculous."

He doesn't slam the door. He doesn't even close it, but in my mind, that's the sound of his anger: a door slamming shut between us. And the most galling thing?

He's right.

My foul mood has nothing to do with the contract. I can get Charm to make those changes. They're so eager to have him, they'd let him publish any time in the next century. It has nothing to do with my heavy workload, but it *does* have everything to do with my period.

I roll to sit on the floor, my back pressed against the bed and my knees up. I drop my head into my hands, and despite all the warnings I give myself not to cry, tears slip from my eyes.

Four months.

My period has come like clockwork the last four months. I know people try for years before getting pregnant so I shouldn't be this discouraged after a few months, but when I woke up this morning and realized my cycle was here again, it just soured my whole day.

My head is down, my face covered, but I know as soon as Grip sits on the floor beside me. He's noiseless, and it's not even his scent that gives him away. It's that thing tucked away in my heart, hidden in my soul that responds to him every time he's near. Emotional, sensual, primal, it's a call and response that I never asked for, but it's undeniably there. It always will be.

"Hey." He pushes the hair back from my hot face. "Look at me."

I don't want to. My nose is probably red. My cheeks are wet. I've been an idiot and a bitch all day, and *again* he's the one making the first move to fix things. I don't want his kindness right now. I don't deserve it.

With gentle fingers, he pries my hands away from my face. I still don't look up when he brushes a thumb over the tears pooling under my eyes. He pulls me over to him, settling me sideways on his lap and tucking my head into his neck.

"My period came again," I mumble.

"I know." He kisses my eyelashes. "Isn't that supposed to happen? Like to keep all your girl parts working the way they should?"

"I'm a grown woman." I smile into his T-shirt, which is damp with my leftover tears. "I don't have *girl* parts."

"Grown woman, girl, I don't care—I like your parts healthy." He tips up my chin. "So, from what I understand, this is normal, healthy female stuff. So, what's the problem?"

"I'm disappointed." I sigh and trace the calligraphy peeping out from under his wedding band. "I was hoping this month . . . well, you know, that my cycle would *not* come."

I swallow fresh tears. Rationally, I know it hasn't been long. I know there's sometimes a delay when you get off birth control. I have no idea if I'll be a good mother, but I want to try. With him, for him, I want to try. There was a time when I saw marriage as just a formality. We had everything else: we lived together, we made love, we shared every aspect of our lives. Really, what could a piece of paper add to what we already had?

But it did. It does.

Marrying Grip transformed our love, anchored our commitment in a way I hadn't understood and could not have anticipated. I couldn't imagine a deeper devotion than what we shared before we married, but marriage to him uncovered fathoms. Instinctively, I know having his children, raising them together will do the same. It will test us in ways, stretch us in ways, *bind* us in ways I want to explore. I'll seek out anything that will grow our love.

"I wanna give you a baby, Grip."

Even in the inky depths of his eyes, my comment sparks light. An answering desire glows back at me. The intensity is magnetic, drawing me in and holding me captive. He wants it, too, but I can tell he deliberately tamps it down.

"You're just planning to push it out and drop it off?" Grip's smile lures me even further out of my funk. "What do you mean give *me* a baby? Are you not sticking around for the next eighteen years?"

"Shut up." I snuggle deeper into the corrugated plane of his chest and abs. "You know what I mean."

"This is for us, Bris." He pulls back only far enough for me to see his face. He's teasing me into a better mood, but his eyes are serious. "A baby would add to what we already have, yeah, but what we already have is *amazing*. It's more than most people ever get because I'm completely content with just you. Do you know how hard it is to be content, to be satisfied in this life? And I found someone who is more than enough to make me happy forever."

I nod, convinced, but still shaking off the vestiges of my disappointment.

"I don't want you feeling pressure." He holds my chin steady between his thumb and finger. "There's no pressure. I don't care if you're not pregnant next month or next year. It's you and me. Do I want kids? With you? You know I want to see your eyes and my nose and my lips and your whatever all mixed up in beautiful babies."

My bones, my heart, my muscles—like candles of wax, they melt under the tender heat in his words, the warmth of his stare.

"But if it never happens, I have you," he says. "Do you understand? You're it, period—no pun intended."

He does this every time. He untangles my snarls, uncoils me when I'm tightly wound. Not even five minutes ago, I was teary and sullen, rigid in my hurt and disappointment. Now I'm soft as butter oozing into bread. I'm clinging to him.

"I guess another month, another period." I hazard a grin when we stand to face each other. "And you're right, it's okay."

"And since you got your period, are you thinking what I'm thinking?"

We offer our very different responses at the same time.

"Ice cream."

"Anal."

"Well, this is awkward," Grip says with an unabashed grin.

"Did you say anal?" An astonished, confused laugh pops out of my mouth. "My period comes on, and you go straight to anal? Why?"

"It's a different . . . door, baby. It's the back door." His hand works down my spine, over the curve of my ass, his middle finger slipping into the divide down the middle of my butt. "This month gave us lemons. I'm just making lemonade."

"In my ass? You're making lemonade in my ass? That's your metaphor?"

"More like a segue. I think your period is a great *segue* into anal. Lots of people do it as a monthly alternative."

"Um . . . that's above my lay grade," I joke. "We're not doing that."

"Like never? You don't want to do anal *ever*?" Horrified panic extinguishes the teasing light in his eyes. "But I've put my thumb in your ass."

"So?"

"So that was a step to ease you in. Step one, thumb. Step two, cock. My thumb in your ass is like one hard sneeze away from anal."

I snort, skeptical and unladylike.

"It would take more than a sneeze to get your dick in there." "Bris," he says, patience in his tone and expression. "What's the difference between my thumb and my dick?"

"Um . . . several inches in sheer girth actually. You are not putting that thing in my ass. You like anal that much?"

"That's like asking do I like cherry Kool-Aid."

"Ew! You like cherry Kool-Aid?"

"Okay, it's like asking if you like cookie dough ice cream."

I would have cookie dough ice cream delivered in crates if I could. My anus clenches in protest.

"Oh, God," I whisper. "You *love* it."

"Don't knock it till you've tried it."

"I didn't say I haven't tried it."

"You've done anal?" Displeasure darkens his eyes. "Who the hell'd you do anal with?"

"Excuse me." I tilt my head and rest a fist on my hip. "Did I ask who *you've* done anal with?"

"You're right, we don't wanna go there." He shakes his head and turns his lips down at the corners. "You didn't like it?"

"It was messy and it hurt."

"Well, yeah, it can be messy, but he probably didn't do it right."

"He definitely didn't do *something* right."

"I promise you I'll do it right." He cups my ass and squeezes, his pinky fingers delving into the slit of space separating the cheeks. "Can I tell you how I would make it better for you?"

Resist. Resist. Resist.

The chant in my head grows fainter the more his hands explore my body, seeking all my needy places. It's not just the curve of my breast or the plane of my belly where he's seducing butterflies, but my heart still feels unreasonably bruised by something as silly as menses.

"Not that I'm open to it," I say, my voice slightly lust-rough. "But if I were to—"

"First I'd get you really wet," he cuts in, eyes and voice a little too eager to be merely hypothetical.

If he continues, I will be ass-full of Grip by the end of the night.

"Um, forget I asked." I laugh when his face falls. "I'm just saying . . . what about the game?"

"Game? There's a game?" His lips ghost the ink on my shoulder, licking at the delicately sketched letters. "Do you *bathe* in sugar? Damn, you always taste good."

"I can't get through a shower without you barging in and violating me against the wall, so I think you would know if I bathed in sugar."

"Is that a complaint?" He steps back like he's abandoning the hunt, and I'm not quite ready to end the chase. I pull him back to me, slipping my arms up and over his shoulders, linking my wrists behind his neck to caress the smooth skin there.

"Definitely not." I kiss his chin. "I personally can't think of a better way to start the day than wet sex against a wall."

"Mmmmmmm." The hungry rumble vibrates into my chest. "Keep it up and I'm knocking on that back door tonight."

We laugh into a kiss that starts soft and sweet, surges to hot and urgent, and settles into tender longing. He always knows how to get me back, how to pull me back from the brink, and I hope I do the same for him.

"Better?" he asks in between nips of my lips.

"Much." I rest my forehead against his chin. "I'm sorry about the bitchiness earlier."

"Don't even think about it. We both know I can be an asshole," he says, a rueful twist to his lips. "I'm sorry I called the poetry deal stupid."

"I can change the dates with Barrow." I look up to meet his eyes. "Can we chock it all up to the hormones?"

"Sure, but what's your excuse the other three weeks of the month?" The twinkle in his eye saves him from a junk punch.

"You're pushing it, Grip."

"Oh, I can push it, all right." His playful hip thrust has me giggling like a schoolgirl and shoving him toward the door.

"Go watch your game. I'm gonna take a nice hot bath and then drown my hormones in ice cream."

I head to the bathroom, already peeling off my tank top when his voice stops me.

"We don't have to go through this every month, Bris."

He's got one hand on his hip, an arm stretched up as he grabs hold of the doorjamb overhead. His T-shirt lifts to peekaboo soft-as-velvet skin stretched over a slab of granite abs. The humor has faded from his voice, from his eyes. All that's left is lingering concern and unconditional love.

"I'm telling you there's no pressure," Grip says. "I'm gonna be ecstatic and obnoxious when you get pregnant, you already know that, but until then I'm ridiculously happy with just you."

My words are stolen again by his consideration. I'm the luckiest woman on the planet. Minutes later, Grip's in the living room cursing and yelling at the television while I sink into almost unbearably hot water and mile-high suds to soothe my cramping stomach muscles, wearing nothing but a grin because I'm ridiculously happy with just him, too.

Thirty-One

Grip

"I THINK I'LL RUN TO THE DRUGSTORE."

Bristol's standing at the door of our office. Technically, it's Bristol's office in her cottage. My place a few miles away is occupied by a couple of the Kilimanjaro guys, and our place in New York isn't actually ours. It's Mrs. O'Malley's, but we're still leasing it. Lately I keep thinking about getting a bigger house here, a place that's *ours*, hers and mine, a place big enough for us and our kids. *Dammit.* As much as I keep telling myself not to think about our kids, I do. I meant it when I told Bristol there was no pressure. There absolutely isn't, but man do I want to meet these kids we'll have one day.

I check the time on the piece-of-shit watch I can't bring myself to get rid of. When I took it to the watch repair shop, they looked at me like the screws in the watch might not be the only ones loose. Bristol won it at a carnival over a decade ago, for God's sake. We never even paid for it, but I paid the shop to make it work again.

"It's late, babe," I mumble around a yawn. "Lemme go for you."

"No, you have that assignment to finish." Bristol comes into the office and sits on the edge of the desk. "It was due two days ago, right?"

"Don't remind me." I scowl at my laptop and the assignment on criminal justice reform legislation. "The professor gave me an extension, but I'm on the verge of missing this deadline, too, if I don't buckle down."

"It's been a lot the last few months." She steps behind me and sinks her fingers into the muscles along my neck, the shoulders locked with tension. "School, working on your next album, all the stuff for Qwest's single."

"I had no idea that song would do what it's doing." I cover her hand with mine, running my finger along her tattoo and wedding ring. "You never know what people will respond to."

"They always seem to respond to the two of you together," Bristol says easily.

I poke around in the air, searching for agitation in Bristol's statement. She's possessive on the best of days, but with Qwest, it's on another level. I'm pleased to report clear skies, from what I can tell.

"Well the video's in the can, the single's out, and the first round of performances is behind me," I say. "Now I can focus on . . . everything else."

Like the book of poetry I haven't even started. I won't mention that, because if Bristol says the words "brand expansion" again, I'm going through my eye with a selfie stick.

"You have knots in your neck," Bristol whispers, slipping her tongue inside my ear. She knows what that does to me. She must be prepared to face the consequences. I reach around and snatch her off her feet and onto my lap.

"No!" She squeals and laughs, but doesn't budge. "I told you I have to go to the drugstore."

"And I told you," I say, trailing kisses over her collarbone, "that I'll go. I don't want you out this late."

"It's only ten o'clock."

I shrug and keep kissing the hollow at the base of her throat.

"I thought guys hated buying things like tampons," she says, pausing significantly. "And pregnancy tests."

"I'll buy whatever the hell I . . ."

My voice evaporates as her words sink in, and I gulp down the hope that immediately springs up in my chest. I've been careful not to make Bristol feel any pressure. I meant every word I said—if we never had a kid, I'd be disappointed, heartbroken, but any man who's not satisfied with Bristol alone doesn't deserve her.

"Pregnancy tests?" I search her eyes, finding teasing and hope and trace amounts of fear.

"I'm late."

"How late?"

"Three weeks."

"Three . . ." I run my free hand over the back of my neck. She thought it was tight before; my neck's a bowstring now. "Why'd you wait this long?"

"I dunno." Bristol lifts and drops one shoulder. "I think I was scared to get excited. It could be stress making me late."

Or you could be pregnant.

"But now I have to know." She laughs nervously. "I'm going to the drug-store because I can't sleep tonight until I know for sure. We can even go to-gether if that makes you feel better."

"I don't think we'll have to go at all actually." I shift her off my lap and head out of the office, calling over my shoulder, "Gimme a sec."

Maybe thirty seconds later, Bristol looks from my face to the items I laid out on the desk with wide eyes.

"You just happen to have a pregnancy test?" Bristol lifts one of them and an eyebrow. "Or six? When did you get these?"

"Um … March?" I pretend to have to think about it. "Yeah, March."

"March, as in, our anniversary when I told you I was ready to have kids, March?" A knowing smile spreads across her face.

"I didn't buy six pregnancy tests that day. That would be weird."

"Right."

"I bought one each month."

"Which is even weirder." She laughs. "But okay."

"I know." I can't believe I'm embarrassed about this. "It was some kind of ritual or something. That first day of your period when you realized you weren't pregnant, you would always be kind of …"

"Psychotic?"

"Your words, not mine." *Though … nailed it.* "Maybe it was a hope thing, but I would go out and buy one of these. Don't ask me why."

I nod to them, a smile pressing through.

"But now we need them. I think 'thank you, Grip' is the phrase you're looking for, and you're welcome."

"Well, no time like the present." Bristol scoops up all six of the tests and heads for the bathroom.

I meet her there with a glass of water.

"I'm not thirsty, but thanks," she says, pushing the door as if to close it.

I stick my foot in to stop her.

"That's a lot of tests, and a lot of pee." I slide fully into the bathroom, hand her the water, and hop onto the bathroom counter. "Drink up."

Bristol circuits a glance from me to the door to the glass of water in her hand a few times.

"Get out." She takes a few gulps of the water and narrows her eyes at me. "You aren't watching me pee."

"So, I can eat you out but I can't watch you pee? That makes sense."

"Get out," she repeats, pointing to the door. "And give me some privacy to do my business."

I blow out an exasperated breath, head for the bedroom, and hover outside the closed bathroom door. I'm being an idiot, I know it, but I can barely breathe I'm so excited. The possibility of this actually happening, of my DNA and her DNA making something unique to us has me tripping.

After an eternity … or ten minutes … the door opens, and Bristol gestures me inside the bathroom. She has all six tests lined up on the counter. I don't even glance at them, but search her expression for the verdict. Her face is blank, downright miserly, it's giving away so little.

"So?" I hop back up onto the counter, still not looking at the little pissy sticks. "What we got?"

Bristol leans one hip against the counter to face me.

"You bought the first test in March, right?" she asks instead of getting on with it.

"Yeah." I give a jerky nod, hoping she doesn't make me feel like even more of a sentimental pussy than I already do.

"Your March test says . . ." A grin, infinitesimal in width but huge in impact on my heartbeat, quirks her lips. "I'm pregnant."

We stare at each other for a few seconds, the moment swelling with all the possibilities. It could be a fluke. The other tests could negate that one.

"Your April test says I'm pregnant, too," she says. "And your May and June tests agree."

She slides three more sticks to me. I glance down to see four tests confirming what I'm almost afraid to believe in various shades of pink and plus signs.

"Apparently, July and August concur." She pushes the last two tests to join the others, six sticks all saying the same thing.

"You're pregnant." My smile feels like it's spilling over the sides of my face. "It's definite."

"I'd like to have a doctor confirm," she says as mischief, awe, and tenderness swirl in the look she gives me. "But six tests probably don't lie."

I was determined to show restraint until we knew for sure. If she wasn't pregnant, if even half those tests read negative, I would have maintained some kind of reserve, but she's right—six tests don't lie, and my resolve goes to hell. I eliminate all the space between us and scoop her right up off her feet. Her legs lock behind me, and a peal of laughter slips free, echoing in the bathroom.

"Is that your bird laugh again?" I smile my way into a kiss against her lips.

"It seems to pop out when I'm happier than anyone has a right to be." Her cheeks are as wet as my eyes, and she presses our foreheads together. "We're having a baby, Grip. I can't even tell you what I'm feeling right now."

For once, I'm in the same boat. Words are my business, but the feeling taking over every part of me leaves me speechless.

Thirty-Two
Bristol

"IT'S SNOWING IN NEW YORK."

Grip's low-voiced comment from beside me at the dinner table makes me smile. Christmas in LA is not Christmas in New York. I've done it on both coasts, and a balmy Christmas doesn't quite feel the same. Our friends and family are here, though, and we're eating dinner with Ms. James then heading to Rhys and Kai's. That first awful time I came here for dinner, I never would have imagined that this place would feel like a haven and my brother's house would feel like hell, but Rhyson has invited my parents over for Christmas.

Armageddon, people. Armageddon.

This is something I've wished for and worked toward for a long time. I should feel less dread now that my parents and my brother will be at the same Christmas table again. The last time that happened, Uncle Grady, my father's twin brother, hosted what I like to call Bloody Christmas and they nearly came to blows. Rhyson stormed off to spend the holidays with Kai, as if he needed motivation to abandon the family.

Christmas dinner with Grip's family couldn't be more different from the stiff affairs our holidays always proved to be. There is Christmas, I've had some pretty amazing highlights—my first recording contract, a double platinum album, Grammys."

When he looks to me, all the improbable dreams I had about happiness, about love, stare back at me.

"A wife," he says softly. "This year, many great things have happened, including my first book deal."

Those around the table cheer and clap. I even hear a few *Thank you, Jesus*-es. I haven't visited the church where Grip grew up and that his mom still faithfully attends, but I am fully anticipating a once-in-a-lifetime experience.

"But the thing I'm most excited about this year, the absolute highlight"—Grip's grin is like a horizon, bright and wide—"is our baby. Bristol's pregnant."

The room erupts with good wishes, high-fives, pats on the back, even some tears. Their goodwill, their love for Grip—and by extension, for me—crashes over me like a wave, and for just that moment of impact, I can't breathe. My throat constricts around happy tears, around joy. I coveted this growing up. I didn't have a tribe, a unit of people surrounding me, cheering me on every step, but Grip did. Though I had a rough start with some, fraught with mistrust and confusion, and yeah, in some cases, prejudice, they've embraced me. Their warmth is as sure and as solid as arms around me.

I didn't grow up dreaming of stardom, of making my mark on the world the way Grip and Rhyson and Kai and Luke and Jimmi did. All my friends ate a constant diet of ambition, and even today, I still feed that appetite. Those weren't my dreams though. No, I dreamt of a home, of people who loved me whether we had a little or a lot, who were *there*. For a girl who grew up in big houses with empty rooms, this was my dream. Grip has tried to buy his mother a huge house, but she refuses to leave this one. I wondered why, but now I know. She is planted at the center of a garden with roots that go so deep, she wouldn't think of pulling them up, of leaving this neighborhood, this nucleus of people. Maybe this was her dream, too, and I find that seeing it come true for me through those who love Grip makes me a blubbering mess. I don't know if it's hope or hormones or a little of both, but it's too much. As soon as I've been congratulated, squeezed, and teased by so many I lose count, I slip off into the kitchen.

I'm facing the sink when the door swings open behind me. A soft touch on my shoulder has me swinging around with a bright smile pinned to my face.

"You okay, Bristol?" Ms. James asks, her wise eyes searching me.

"Of course." I return the gentle pressure when she squeezes my hand. "I just ... I'm ..."

To my mortification, I lose it. Sobs shake my body as a release of emotion I thought I had under control spills messily over my face, down my neck, and all over my mother-in-law. Her arms go around me, her hand moving in reassuring slides over my back, the maternal monosyllables I never heard as a child breaking me into little pieces. When Grip enters the kitchen, his mother is still putting me back together.

"What's wrong?" The smile on his face vanishes little by little until it's gone altogether. Concern radiates from him, worry in his eyes when he sees me in his mother's arms.

"Nothing wrong, baby." Ms. James pulls away enough to swipe my tears, the kind smile in her eyes matched by the one on her face. "This is an emotional time for us mamas."

"Hormones?" Grip glances between us bravely, like he needs to gird his loins if it's hormones.

Ms. James and I look at each other, roll our eyes, and promptly laugh at him.

"What?" Grip tries to look indignant, but his lips are twitching. "I can handle hormones."

"Crisis averted." I sniff and wipe away the last traces of wetness from my cheeks. "Hormones are in check."

Relief and love mix in the look he divides between his mother and me.

"Okay, if you say so." With one last lingering glance to make sure I'm okay, he shifts his attention to his mother. "Ma, Ms. Green's son is here. He says you wanted to take her a plate or something."

"Yes!" Her face lights up, but then falls. "Marlon, she ain't doing good. She's on oxygen and been in and out of the hospital."

"Man, sorry to hear that." Grip's brows bunch. "Does she need anything? Help with medical bills or something?"

She looks thoughtful for a moment before grabbing his chin.

"My sweet boy," she says. "What would do her wonders is to see your face. She asks about you all the time. She used to keep you when I got called in to work. It's just up the street, won't take long."

"Sure. I'll come." Grip checks my face, looking for signs of distress. "You wanna roll with us or—"

"No." I lean up to kiss his cheek, making sure my eyes are clear so he feels good about leaving me. "You go on. I'm gonna sneak a piece of sweet potato pie and just rest a little."

"If you need to lie down, just go in my old room." Grip brushes the hair from my face and looks at his mom. "She sleeps all the time."

"A situation I need to change," I say with a laugh. "I can't get all my work done sleeping like normal people do."

"Normal people do not sleep as much as you been sleeping," Grip says, his grin teasing me.

He drops to his knees in front of me and whispers to my stomach, laying a quick kiss on the barely perceptible roundness that is the only visible sign of my pregnancy. He does this all the time, and though I've asked him more than once what he's saying, he always tells me it's between him and his baby.

He stands, looping an arm around his mother, who barely reaches his shoulder.

"Ready, Ma?"

She nods briskly, balancing two plates covered with aluminum foil.

"We'll be back in a little bit, babe."

When I have the kitchen to myself again, I blow out a long breath. With my emotions once again under control, I really do want that slice of pie. The door swings open as I'm taking my first bite, and I almost choke when I see Jade. The last time we stood in this kitchen, she revealed just how much resentment she still harbored about my relationship with Grip. I'm sure she blames me for how things have been between them.

"What's up?" She flicks her chin like she would to a stranger on the street, not like we're family—because I guess we aren't. I smile a little uneasily as a reply.

She makes a direct line for the sweet potato pie I just sliced into, and it's silent in the kitchen while she plates one for herself. She's on her way out, plate balanced in one hand, back to the door pressing it open when she pauses and looks at me from under the brim of her baseball cap. Even today she still wears her typical uniform of baggy jeans and Raiders gear.

"I guess you got him now." A bitter twist of her lips accompanies the words.

"What?" Confusion stills my chewing mid-bite. "I don't know what you mean."

She takes a few steps back into the room and looks me over, dislike plain in her eyes.

"Once you got a kid with a man, you're linked to him forever," she says. "Can't fault you for that, I guess. Well played."

"Wait a minute." I set my fork, loaded with a hunk of sweet potato pie, back onto my plate. "You're saying you think me getting pregnant is strategic somehow? So I can stay in Grip's life even if we—"

"When you break up, yeah."

I cling to the fraying strands of my patience with the tips of my fingers.

"You can be such a bitch." It's not what reasonable Bristol had planned to say, but she left the building as soon as Jade started spouting this nonsense, and I can't for the life of me get her back.

Vodka could get her back.

I need a drink badly, and that is one thing I can't have in my current condition.

"What'd you say to me?" Jade's expression shifts from disdain to outrage.

"What I should have said a long time ago." I stand to face her eye to eye. "I've been patient. I've bitten my tongue when you've said rude, judgmental shit to me, all because I know what you mean to Grip, but you won't get away with accusing me of trapping my own husband."

"I didn't say trap." She grimaces, looking as close to contrite as I can expect. "I just meant—"

"I know damn well what you meant." My voice elevates with the emotions still close to the surface. I swallow some of my indignation and try to rein my temper. I will gouge my tear ducts before Jade sees me cry.

"I'm not, nor have I ever been, afraid of or intimidated by you," I say. "In case you were wondering if your bullying tactics work on me, they don't. The only thing I was afraid of was coming between you and Grip."

We stare at each other unblinkingly, perpetrating the same war of wills that began the day we met.

"He loves you." My voice is softer because I know it's the truth. My husband has a soft spot for his cousin. He lets her get away with things no one else would, but I was the line he drew in the sand, and things haven't been the same between them since she crossed it. "He hates it when there's distance between you."

"He doesn't hate it that much." She shoves her hands in her pockets. "He said he would choose you, would cut me out of his life if he had to."

Her throat moves with a gulp of emotion.

"And he did that," she says, glancing down to her Chuck Taylors. "He showed me."

"He doesn't want this any more than you do, Jade, especially now when you both have great things going on. Don't you want to share it?"

"So, what?" She cocks one skeptical brow. "You want me to try for the sake of the baby?"

"No, I want you to try for the sake of *trying*." I haul in a frustrated breath. "Try because maybe you're wrong about me. Maybe your preconceived notions about me are just that—notions, not even true. I love Grip more than anything. If we have nothing else in common, we have *him* in common."

Jade shifts from one foot to the other, the same look on her face that Grip gets when he's wrapping his mind around something new.

"I guess." She gives a subtle shrug and meets my eyes with lingering ire. "It'll be easier if you ain't one of them white folks raising Black kids who don't know where they come from, who don't understand their own culture and can't even stand to be with their own people."

I toss an arm toward the kitchen door, where on the other side is a houseful of people Grip has known all his life.

"Does Grip seem like he's forgotten where he came from?" I demand, fire licking under my words. "Like he doesn't understand his culture? Like he's running from it?"

Her lips part to reply, but I don't even wait for her answer, because what can she say but no?

"Well, all right then," I barrel ahead. "Our kids won't be that way either. I haven't once tried to take Grip away. If anything, I'm constantly trying to get in. Can't you see how much that matters to me?"

I pause, hesitant to say my next thought, but I press on since I'm already in the deep end.

"And by the way, our first Black president is half white."

"Huh?" Confusion puckers her expression. "What the hell does that mean?"

"It means that his mother was a white woman from Kansas, but who would know that looking at him? He looks like any other Black man, and there's a good chance that my children will, too. They'll have to navigate this world as Black people, and you know what that means a lot better than I do."

I pause while my words settle in the air and hopefully change her mind.

"Instead of criticizing me for mistakes I haven't even made yet, waiting for me to fail at raising Black children, why not help me get it right?" I ask. "They'll be your family, Jade, just like Grip is. You may not think of me as your family, but they certainly are."

She doesn't get the chance to respond because the door swings open and Grip walks through. Stopping short at the threshold, his eyes do a slow sweep between the two of us, like we've probably been fighting and he's checking for bruises and bald spots.

"Uh, hey," he says with deceptive ease. "All good?"

I bend an inquiring look on Jade, asking her silently if we are indeed all good or not. She sighs, adjusts her cap, and tips her head in a nod.

"We good." The cousins hold a stare for a few seconds before relinquishing grins simultaneously. Grip walks over and hooks his elbow around Jade's neck, stealing the cap from her head and playing keep-away for a few laughing seconds.

"I'm hearing good things about you," he says, his smile lingering and wide.

Jade shrugs and replaces the cap, playfully swatting at his head when he tries to kiss her face.

"Well I'm doing good things." She laughs at her own cocksure response and huddles deeper into his chest.

"I missed you, girl." A serious inflection strips some of the humor from his voice.

"I missed you, too." An impish twinkle leaps in Jade's eyes. "We gon' exchange recipes or some shit next? Bristol got you so whupped you talking like a chick now?"

Hearing my name in the context of a joke, of her teasing him, jolts me into the conversation. It's an olive branch of sorts, the first she's ever extended to me.

"Don't blame me." I lean against the sink, folding my arms over my chest and laughing. "He came to me like that."

"I came like what?" Grip asks, trying to appear affronted.

Sweet. Considerate. Kind. Thoughtful.

All the things I'm thinking, I see reflected in Jade's eyes, too, as she looks up at her cousin, still tucked into his side.

Yes, we both love him. We have him in common, and maybe one day, it will be enough.

Thirty-Three

Bristol

WEAK LIGHT FILTERS THROUGH A GAP IN THE DRAWN DRAPES, illuminating a sliver in our darkened bedroom. Dawn bathes the room in gray. There's no color in the sky yet, no brightness. Hundreds of mornings like this already stretch behind me, with Grip asleep at my back, folded around my body in protection, in possession, and I can only hope for a million like it to come. Some of those mornings, I'll hear banging on our bedroom door. I'll see little legs flying across the room and feel little bodies sliding between us under the covers. Having Grip's children and sharing his life is a privilege that, years ago, I never imagined I could have, and now every morning I wake up envisioning it.

"You awake?" Lingering slumber roughens Grip's voice, deepening the timber.

"Yeah, a little," I slur sleepily.

His chuckling breath skitters over my neck, waking up parts of my body moments ago at rest.

"What's 'a little' awake?"

"I'm awake, but I'm trying not to be."

"Oh." Disappointment coats his whisper. "Go back to sleep then."

I roll over to face him, picking out the planes of his handsome face hidden in the shadows of half-light.

"What is it?" I ask. "You wanna talk?"

"No." The smile I can't see is easily heard, and a warm hand traverses the curve of my hip. "I wanna fuck."

I'm immediately ready, my nipples tightening and my toes curling at the crude answer. I wrap my hand around the stiff length between his legs.

"Is that a yes?" He feathers kisses over my shoulder, licking at the ink he can't see but knows by heart is there.

"Whatever you want," I whisper, my hand setting a steady, tugging pace.

"Oooooooh." Grip's breath mists my nipples. "Even anal?"

My hand stops abruptly, apparently striking into him fear that I will abandon the mission.

"Just kidding, just kidding," he says hastily, laughing over a nipple. He suckles vigorously then languorously, the varied pace driving me wet and crazy. "You're gonna breastfeed, right?"

I gasp when his teeth lightly graze the sensitive underside of my breast.

"Is that really what you want to talk about right now?" I ask breathlessly. "My breasts as a source of nourishment?"

"I'm down to talk about these breasts twenty-four seven."

His tongue flicks over my ribs, and he slides lower until all I can make out is the shape of his head under the covers. He licks into and then blows over my belly button, and I feel his breath whispering over my stomach. He's having a conversation with the baby again, but before I can demand to know what he's saying, he lavishes openmouth kisses over the small mound above my pelvis. He scoots even farther down, gently lifting my legs over his shoulders and opening me up, pressing his face into the weeping center of my body.

I hear him draw a long sniff. I stopped being self-conscious about that a long time ago. Now it just turns me on that he loves the way I smell. His big hands cup my ass and he brings me to his mouth, tasting me with lazy laps of his tongue like a big cat and I'm his sugar-rimmed saucer. My hands wander up to my breasts, circling my palms, massaging them the way he does. The darts of pleasure radiating from my nipples in harmony with the unbearable pleasure of my pussy make me drip. The stubble coating his jaw, an erotic scrape, leaves an illicit burn. He moans against me, hastening the pace of my hips. He flattens his tongue on my clit, spreading the wetness all along the slit, dipping lower to lick that tiny puckered hole. His tongue there sets fire to nerve endings that have been cloistered away, sensations I've never felt. One thick thumb slides in and I lock up, unsure of what he's about to do.

"Relax," he whispers, raining kisses across the lips. "I got you."

Before I can think more of it, his thumb starts moving in tandem with his lips and teeth feeding on my clit.

"God!" All the air whooshes from my body and I buck, my torso and hips lifting under the covers. He ruthlessly lays an arm over my waist, keeping me in place while his thumb and mouth conspire, driving me to madness, a mindless creature gnawing on her fist, clawing at the sheets, and wailing into the dawn. His thumb works its way into some heretofore undiscovered inner sanctum, and the pleasure is pyrotechnic. It explodes, its wick burning through my belly, up my back, and lighting up the muscles of my thighs. Just like a firework, once ignited, I streak across the sky, bright and flaring, then land motionless ... still ... spent.

He handles me tenderly, turning me to my side, enveloping me, chest pressed to my back. He palms the shallow valley between my breasts, sandwiching us together until there's room for nothing. Only love could slip into a space this small. He lifts my leg and passes his dick between the cheeks of my ass and over my pussy repeatedly, a sensuous prelude that elicits moans from my throat, tight with unshed tears.

"Grip, please." I'm literally panting, begging, reaching behind me, grasping at his neck and head, desperately reaching for something to anchor me. I don't care which hole he's about to fuck, I just need him inside. The space between us throbs with need. My nerves are stretched to gossamer, the anticipation blazing through my patience, and I'm pressing my ass into him. I thrust back in a rolling rhythm meant to tempt him, meant to hurry him, but when he finally slides inside, it's slow and measured. He's feeding himself to my body in stiff inches, in short pumps, agitating me.

"Faster." I twine my fingers with his between my breasts. "Please go fast. I need it fast."

He doesn't answer, just maintains the steady pace, and my body clamps around him with each withdrawal, afraid he won't come back. I'm a seaside fire he's methodically building, taking his time with. Soon I'm a roaring bonfire, flames tossed by the wind and licking high into the air. My moans and whimpers dance with his grunts and groans in the early morning quiet.

His lips coast over my nape as his other hand cups my small belly.

"Bris, you have no idea," he whispers into my hair. "The thought of you, the sight of you pregnant ... I'm hard all the time. It's the sexiest thing I've ever seen. I don't want to be rough, but—"

"You can be," I insist, pressing back into him, luring him deeper into my body. I contract my inner muscles around him, a deliberate provocation.

"Shit, Bris." His forehead pushes into the base of my skull.

I've pulled a lever within him and he turns fast, his tempo feverish. Every time I think he must be almost done, he changes the angle, setting off another constellation of stars behind my eyelids. He's in full heat, full rut, the instincts of his body dictating every thrust and moan. Light creeps through the drapes, and the vibrant colors of sunrise quietly invade our room while sweat runs freely over our skin, adorning his chest and my back, a wet, sensuous slide that our bodies lap up. I've lost count of my orgasms. I'm limp, my muscles and bones loose and liquid even as he still hammers into me.

"Are you okay?" His words are staccato, punctuating between heavy breaths.

"Yes. Baby, don't stop." My words are sloppy in my mouth. I'm pillaged.

"I'm close … I'm gonna … *dammit*, Bris."

His growl quakes through my back as he releases. I work my hips, struggling to keep up with the heavy, frenetic piston of his body until he stiffens behind me, rigid as pleasure conquers him. Our breaths fill the air in symphony, his and mine. We come down slowly, his possessive grip on my hip easing, our heartbeats pounding in unison, neither of us wanting to stop. Our bodies still rock as the tumult of the waves gradually gentle. By the time our breathing regulates, light fully intrudes, introducing another morning.

"I really did want to talk," he says with a husky laugh, walking his fingers down my arm to caress my fingers.

"Hmmmm?" The day is fully lit, but my alarm must have another hour left. Our lovemaking has left me speechless and exhausted before the day has begun.

"I had something to ask you."

"Ask," I mutter, eyes half-closed.

"Are you nervous?" he asks. "About today, I mean? Finding out."

"Are we finding out?" Even half-dead and listless, I manage a wicked smile. Grip wouldn't be able to hold out. He told me from the beginning, even if I didn't want to know if we're having a boy or girl, he would have to.

"Bris, we already talked about—"

"Just kidding," I cut in with a wisp of a laugh. "No, I'm not nervous. Excited, but not nervous."

He rests his hand on my hip, fingers twined with mine, and presses kisses between my shoulder blades.

"Dwell in possibility," he says between kisses.

"Hmmmm?" I turn my head the slightest bit, not enough to see him, just enough to hear him better.

"That's what I whisper to our baby, to your belly. It's from a poem."

"Neruda?"

"Dickinson. It's a poem called 'I Dwell in Possibility.'" He pauses, giving me space to ask questions that I don't pose because I know he'll keep going. "I want our kids to grow up believing in possibilities, not because we have money or the advantages that come with it, but because of *themselves*. They can chase possibilities with nothing stopping them. If my mom hadn't made me feel that way, like if I could dream it and would work hard, it could be mine, there's no telling where I'd be today. I don't want other people's biases and this country's broken systems and roadblocks to get in their way."

Passion, conviction, and cynicism mingle in his voice.

"Hell, it didn't get in my way, and I had nothing. I want them to be way-makers, Bris, people who explore this world, never thinking it can't be theirs. That's what I tell him . . . or her."

I close my eyes, not to sleep, but to relish this man, this wonderful man who is the epicenter of my world.

"You're gonna be an amazing father." I drop my head back to rest in the curve of his neck and shoulder.

"I want to be," he says. "My dad sucked."

I don't hear any pain or bitterness. I've never seen holes in Grip that his father should have filled.

"When I was little, I did wonder sometimes why my father didn't stick around," he continues, as if answering a question he heard my mind forming. "But my mom didn't give me time to personalize it. She didn't keep it a secret or avoid talking about it. She just always made it about him, not a reflection of me. She used to say, 'Poor thing. That damn fool is missing out on you. Oh well, his loss. More Marlon for me.'"

I lift our hands to my lips, smiling and kissing them.

"She'd say he was gonna look up one day and see a star in the sky that was so far out of his reach, and he'd know that was his son, that could have been his. She assumed from the beginning I'd be something great."

His takes our hands, still linked, and rests them over the small protrusion of my belly.

"Dwell in possibility," I whisper, understanding it better now. Grip's mouth curves into a smile against my neck as he speaks. "There was never any doubt."

Thirty-Four
Grip

I THINK I BROKE HER.

Bristol fell asleep almost as soon as she climbed onto this examination table in the doctor's office, and she hasn't even twitched. Me and my randy ass, hard before the sun was even up, wanting to have sex instead of letting her sleep.

We didn't use the main entrance, but arranged to enter through the back and come in here instead of the waiting room, but we still have to wait like everybody else for Dr. Wagner, Bristol's OB-GYN, to finish with the patient before us. While we wait, Bristol sleeps. I'm mentally lecturing me and my dick on being more considerate in the future when Darla the ultrasound technician comes in.

She's spreading some kind of clear jelly on our little baby bump. Bristol's eyes pop open for a second, but then she drifts right back into deep sleep.

"She's really out, huh?" Darla asks with a smile.

"Yeah." I crook my mouth into a grin. "I've never known her to sleep this much. She usually works around the clock, but can barely get through the day without a nap now."

"Not unusual." Darla rolls the wand over Bristol's belly, eyes trained on the screen. "Most mothers ..."

Her words and her smile dissolve, her gaze sharpening on the ultrasound.

"Everything okay?" I ask, unease crawling over my skin.

"Um, sure." Darla blinks a few times and shoots me a farce of a smile.

She reaches up and presses a button that takes the screen dark. "I'll be right back."

"What's going on?" I demand, keeping my voice low, not wanting to disturb Bristol, but she wakes anyway.

"What'd I miss?" she asks drowsily, rubbing her eyes and sitting up. Darla gently presses Bristol's shoulder back until she's lying down again.

"Nothing yet. I just need to check on one thing. I'll be right back." She stands and crosses over to the door. "We'll wake you when it's time."

And she's gone.

The hell.

"Is everything okay?" Bristol is now fully alert, her eyes darting from my face to the door Darla closed behind her. I'm up on my feet and at the door, too. "Where are you going?"

"Piss break." I glance at her over my shoulder, ordering my face at ease. "I'm gonna drain the snake before Darla gets back."

She rolls her eyes, but her brows bend with lingering concern. "You sure everything's okay?"

"Yeah, babe. I'll be back."

I walk swiftly up the hall, stopping when I see Darla and our doctor talking outside what I assume is her office or another examining room.

"Hey," I say, walking up on them. "What's going on?"

Two startled faces turn to me.

"Mr. James," Dr. Wagner says, pulling a guard over her eyes, but not before I see the deep concern. "You should go back to the examination room. I'll be with you shortly. Sorry for the delay."

"Don't bullshit me." I don't have time to be polite, to apologize for the shock I put on their faces. "Darla, your face changed when you looked at that ultrasound. Is something wrong with our baby?"

Darla blinks at me stupidly, a swallow moving her throat. "Mr. James, I don't—"

"Don't lie to me." My voice cracks like a whip into the tight air of the hallway. "If something . . ."

I draw a calming breath, blowing out anxiety and fear.

"If there's something wrong with our baby, I want to know."

"I'll join you and Bristol in a moment," Dr. Wagner says evenly. "I'll talk to you together."

She doesn't deny that there's a problem, and that fact cuts through my protests like a shard of glass.

"Wait . . . I . . . okay. If we could just . . ." The possibility of something being wrong with our child has me stumbling. "If you could just tell me first."

"Mr. James." Dr. Wagner's reservations come to life on her face. "I'd prefer to discuss everything with you and your wife together."

I want to be the first line of defense for Bris. I've always been protective of her, but the shit that went down with Parker ramped up my need to shield her from danger, from pain. Anything wrong with our baby is pain like I can't imagine. A premonition of it skims across my nerves. It's times like these I hate those extra senses Ma says growing up street gives us, the ones that dig between Dr. Wagner's words, the things she says, into all the things she doesn't.

"I'll be there shortly," she says, finality in her voice. "Thank you, Mr. James."

Darla's biting her lip, anxiety in the eyes she slides between Dr. Wagner and me. If I had one minute alone with Darla, I'd get it out of her, but with Dr. Wagner standing guard over whatever secret they're keeping, I'm getting nothing. Resigned, I head back to the examination room. I open the door tentatively, not sure how I'll handle Bristol's questions on the other side.

But there aren't questions—she's fallen asleep again. Between the sleep her pregnancy demands and me interrupting her sleep this morning, she's exhausted. Her head droops to the side, her long lashes shadowing her cheeks. Her hand rests over the small bump, even in sleep, protecting our baby. I slide the chair beside the exam table and dip my head to kiss the baby through Bris's clothes. I do what I've been doing ever since we found out, and the ritual gives me some comfort. These words about what's possible ease my mind as I wait to hear what left Dr. Wagner's eyes so grave.

"Dwell in possibility, baby."

Thirty-Five

Bristol

SOMETHING'S WRONG.

If Grip's abrupt departure and lame excuse didn't give it away, Dr. Wagner's expression does, even though she tries to hide it beneath a mask of professionalism when she enters the room without the ultrasound technician. She goes through the same process Darla did, running the wand over my belly and studying the screen. She turns the ultrasound away to look at it, her mouth firming into a grim line.

She indicates that I can leave the examination table and take a seat beside Grip.

"Okay. What's going on?" Grip asks. "We'd like to find out the sex of our baby. Is there a problem?"

A brochure of some kind rests facedown in Dr. Wagner's lap. Anxiety ratchets up, plucking at my nerves. I just want her to blurt it out if there's a problem. This delay only stirs fear inside of me.

"When Darla looked at the ultrasound," Dr. Wagner finally says, "she noticed something about the fetus."

"What?" Grip demands. "What did she notice?"

"Based on what we see," Dr. Wagner says, her voice careful, like she's measuring the words out in a recipe that has to be exact, precise portions of brutal honesty and compassion. "We suspect anencephaly."

Should that mean something to me? For all I know, that could be anything from a rash to . . . I can't play that all the way out. This baby isn't even born and I haven't seen the 3D ultrasound, but I've felt flutters under my heart. My shape is changing and my body is working overtime to grow this baby. Anything that endangers my baby's life could cleave me into un-mendable pieces.

"Ance-what?" Grip's eyes don't leave Dr. Wagner's face, but his hand bridges the small space between us until our fingers twist into a knot of solidarity. "What is that? How do we fix it?"

"An-en-sef-*uh*-lee," Dr. Wagner sounds out slowly. Her face still wears that impassive mask, but her hands clutch the brochure like she's steeling herself to say what needs to be said. "And you don't … well, you don't fix it. Anencephaly is a terminal diagnosis. I'm so sorry."

The word "terminal" multiplies, flying around my brain over and over until my mind is a hive of bees swarming, stinging. I struggle to pluck one lucid thought from the buzzing in my head.

"But … but how can you know?" My voice emerges from its hiding place high and thin. "You just look at the screen and hand down a terminal diagnosis? That can't be right. There have to be tests or—"

"Yes, we'll run an amniocentesis as a . . ." Discomfort crinkles Dr. Wagner's face. "As a formality, but I'm certain, Bristol. It's apparent even in the ultrasound."

I can't even cry. My arms clasp my little belly protectively and my hands shake. My extremities have frozen like I'm in shock. How could I not be in shock when she just ripped the rug, the floor—the *earth* from under my feet? I don't have a leg to stand on.

"What exactly is this condition?" Grip's voice doesn't sound like it belongs to him. He has one of those voices, so warm it draws you in, but right now, there's distance, distance and desperation. "You said it's terminal, but we don't know anything about it yet."

"Yes, of course." Dr. Wagner allows sympathy into her eyes.

"Anencephaly is a serious birth defect in which a baby is born without parts of the brain and skull. Normally, as the neural tube forms and closes, it helps form the baby's brain, skull, spinal cord, and backbone. Anencephaly occurs if the upper part of the neural tube does not close all the way, thus leaving parts of the brain permanently unformed."

The compassion deepens in Dr. Wagner eyes and she licks her lips, presses them together before continuing.

"This often results in a fetus being born without the front part of the brain, the forebrain, and the thinking and coordinating part of the brain, the cerebrum. The remaining parts of the brain are often not covered by bone or skin."

"Not covered by skin and bone?" The words forcibly eject from my mouth. "What does that mean?"

"It's why we can tell from the ultrasound that the fetus has anencephaly. Let me show you," Dr. Wagner says, turning the screen around for us to see. "Here, we can see that the top of the head and the brain are ... missing, and there is only a thin membrane covering that portion, no skull or scalp."

A moan slices into her explanation, and I'm startled to realize it came from me. I cover my mouth, but I can't cover my heart. I can't silence the scream ricocheting in the chambers of my soul. It's piercing. It's painful.

"Many are stillborn." Dr. Wagner presses on despite flicking a concerned look my way. "Those who are delivered as live births will live minutes or hours, in rare cases, a few days."

"No," I mutter under my breath. "This can't be right. A test—there has to be a test, a second opinion."

"Yeah," Grip pipes in. "A real test, not just a blurry picture telling us our baby *might* have this condition."

"Like I said, we'll perform the amniocentesis, certainly," Dr. Wagner agrees.

Her pause drops heavily into the waiting quiet.

"I know this is a lot to take in," Dr. Wagner says. "But we'll need to discuss your options."

"We have options?" I ask, a harsh laugh cutting the inside of my jaw.

"Yes, options." Dr. Wagner looks from Grip to me and back again. "Decisions."

The word "decisions" sends a chill up my spine. *Oh, God, no. She can't* seriously be asking me to do that.

"More than ninety percent of parents with this diagnosis terminate the pregnancy," Dr. Wagner says quietly. "I know that's hard to process, but the fetus—"

"Stop saying fetus," Grip snaps. "It's our baby. Call it our baby."

Dr. Wagner nods, meeting the frustration and naked pain in Grip's eyes head on.

"I understand," she says, her tone simultaneously soft and firm. "But you will have to deal with these decisions sooner rather than later. We are ... well, certain options are time-sensitive."

My fingers are numb. Tears swim in my eyes, suspended but refusing to fall, frozen there by the chill creeping into my bones and through every cell of my body.

"We'll take the amniotic fluid today to test," Dr. Wagner says briskly, standing. "And discuss . . . next steps once we have those results. It typically takes about ten days for NTDs, neural tube defects."

She's moving on, and I'm still dazed, shaken, shocked.

"Is the . . ." The word "fetus" stings the tip of my tongue. "Our baby, what is it?"

Dr. Wagner frowns, shaking her head.

"Until you decide how you want to move forward," she says, "I think knowing the gender will only make it more difficult."

"Let me get this straight." Grip tilts his head and runs his tongue over his teeth in that way that means he's nearing the end of his tether. "You give us a death sentence for our child—"

"Mr. James—"

"No, I get it," he cuts in. "It's not your fault. You're just doing your job, but if you think us knowing whether it's a girl or a boy is going to make this decision any harder, you're wrong."

"It . . . humanizes the decision in a way that only complicates it for the parents."

"You think the semantics of this situation complicate our decision?" I ask hoarsely. "They don't. What complicates our decision is that we love this baby as if he or she is already here, already ours. What complicates it is the roomful of nursery furniture we've bought, every piece chosen with . . ."

My voice breaks, tears dampening my words.

"With love," I resume. "What complicates it is that I feel flutters in my stomach, and I've been waiting any day now for them to be kicks. This is our *baby*, and it's been the center of our world for months, and now you say I may have to end its life or carry it to term and then watch it die in my arms. Please. Just tell us."

I raise my eyes to her, and a tiny portion of my torture is reflected in her stare. She nods, resignation on her face when she says, "It's a girl."

Grip's sharply drawn breath matches mine, and my eyes, my hands, my heart—every part of me seeks any part of him I can get to. With our fingers tangled together in my lap, we just nod, both of us too cut up to speak, the moment so raw we hemorrhage in the silence.

In a daze, I submit to the needle slowly drawing fluid from my belly. I don't even hear the things Dr. Wagner and her staff say from then on. Agony unimaginable rises over my head, disbelief muffling all the words around me, muting my responses. My lungs constrict painfully as I go under over and over, drowning but unable to die.

And I want to die. I think I could die without complaint if it meant avoiding these "decisions," accepting one of these impossible options, if it meant not breathing and living for the next four months growing this child only to watch it die before it's ever even lived, a manifestation of our malformed hopes.

When we get to the car, Grip and I just sit there for a moment, steeping in hot water, boiling alive in our suffering.

"Fuck," Grip finally mutters. I glance at him from the passenger seat, unable to even curse. I *am* a curse. I *feel* cursed—how can I not with the things the doctor said?

"Fuck," Grip repeats, slamming his hand on the steering wheel again and again and again. I flinch at the percussion of his fist into the unyielding leather and plastic, flinch every time he strikes it.

"It can't be . . . we can't . . ." He stops abruptly, and one tear streaks down his handsome face, the face I dreamt would stare back at me in a little boy or a little girl.

"It's a girl," I whisper.

Agony ripples between us where our fingers intertwine, and Grip brings our hands to his lips.

"We can't give up yet, Bris. There's still the test. Maybe she's mistaken. Anything's possible," he says, his mouth settling into that firm line I've seen every time he's faced and conquered a challenge.

But this isn't a tough industry, a ladder to climb. It's not bias based on the color of his skin. If the tests confirm what Dr. Wagner suspects, this is insurmountable. There's no climbing out of it or working our way around the impossible choices we'll have to make.

I can't help but think of how this day began, with the heat of our love-making, with our dreams and speculations about this baby whispered as dawn broke. We were sure it would be just as we wanted, that anything was possible.

Dwell in possibility.

I can't think of what's possible as I replay the conversation with Dr. Wagner like a horror movie I can't un-watch, the word "terminal" clanging like a bell over and over in my head.

Possible? Not when all that is weighing on me, waiting for me, is death.

Bitterness pools in my heart, a fast-filling well of poison choking me. I don't speak for the rest of the ride home. I think about how certain Dr. Wagner seemed, how she called the test Grip is pinning so much on a formality. I stew in my fear and anger and frustration until it runs over, leaving little room for hope.

Thirty-Six

Grip

THE NURSERY IS DOUSED IN SHADOWS. THE ONLY LIGHT COMES from Bristol's phone, illuminating a small sphere in the dark, showing her high cheekbones, stark in the diminished light, and the full curve of her mouth pulled thin with tension. She's sitting on the floor, her dark brows contorting into a frown as she scrolls down the screen with her index finger.

The last ten days of waiting for the test results have been harder than anything I've ever experienced, but not harder than what lies ahead.

Our baby will die.

Whether because we terminate the pregnancy or decide to let it run its course, her death is an inevitability for which I have no idea how to prepare. I can't, and I have no idea how to help Bristol because I can't help myself. I thought I could protect her from anything, from anyone. I called myself her first line of defense but I'm blindsided, never suspecting that the enemy— death—had already breached our gates.

We always talk about everything, Bristol and I, but a heavy silence hung over us on the way home, like a rain cloud poised to pour. We were silent as if our words would trigger the storm, and the deliberate, unnatural quiet followed us across our threshold. Maybe by unspoken mutual agreement, we decided it isn't real until we talk about it, until we weigh our shitty options and are forced to make impossible choices.

"Couldn't sleep?" I ask from the door, my voice scratchy from lack of use. I've barely spoken since we left the doctor's office.

At my question, Bristol's head jerks up, her attention wrested from the phone. With a click of her finger, she turns it off, losing the light and plunging the room into darkness. The overhead light would show too much, would be too bright. I step carefully in the general direction of the lamp on a table in the corner. I fumble under the shade until I find the little button that will show me Bristol's face, but not much else. Her thoughts will remain a mystery until she's ready to talk, and as much as I don't want to, as much as I've avoided it for the last few hours, we have to talk.

The soft, lambent light shows me the broken heart in her eyes, killing me at a glance. They aren't teary or red-rimmed or puffy. There are no telltale signs of distress, but that secret joy that lit her eyes to precious-metal silver for the last few months has been snuffed out. They're dulled to pewter, an alloy of pain and grief, a mixture of mourning.

I take a tentative step, only to freeze when I spot the things flanking her on the floor. To her right sits a tub of her favorite cookie dough ice cream. The lid is off, and a large serving spoon spears the creamy, untouched surface. To her left is a half-full bottle of her favorite liquor, vodka. No glass, so I assume she'll be taking it to the head, if she hasn't already. My heart thuds behind my ribs because that must be a sign. Bristol hasn't touched a drop of alcohol since she found out she was pregnant. She would never endanger our baby, unless the point is moot, unless she has already decided something I thought we would decide together. My heart painfully draws its own conclusions, even though I can't make myself ask her the question.

What do you want to do?

Each word of the unspoken inquiry is like a drop of acid burning through my tongue. I can't ask. I haven't even gotten up the nerve to ask myself. I poured my pain and anger and frustration out on the only place that ever seems to offer me any relief, besides Bristol—on paper. I wrote an embittered manifesto that no one will ever read, but I haven't asked myself what I *want*. I'm afraid I already know, and if Bristol wants something different, that's what we'll do.

And it will kill me.

It's Bristol's body. *She* would have to carry and nurture this unspeakable tragedy to its inevitable end, not me. I know I have a voice in this, but I can't ask that of her. I've been afraid all afternoon to ask myself if I even want to. There are no right answers. Everything is wrong. We have door number one and door number two, and they both lead to hell, one just faster than the other.

I settle beside her on the floor, mirroring her posture—knees pulled to the chest, back to the wall. The half-empty bottle of vodka draws a line of libation between us. She blinks, still not meeting my eyes, tracing patterns on the darkened screen of her phone before placing it carefully on the floor.

"Your ice cream is melting."

"Yeah." Her voice scrapes into the quiet, giving me nothing. "I don't need it anyway."

She always says that before she eats half the pint.

"And the vodka?" I keep my voice even, free of condemnation.

"That I need." She flicks a side-glance to me, searching my face for judgment, I assume. "I need a drink, and I've been sitting here wondering if it matters anymore if I have one."

"Did you have it? The drink, I mean?"

I'm asking more than this. She knows it, and her slim shoulders stiffen.

"Not yet." She shakes her head, bites her lip. "Does it matter if I do?"

I'm still not ready.

"What were you looking at on your phone?" I dodge her question, avoid my answer.

Her eyes are windows with bars. Showing me just slices of what she's feeling before she tucks it away behind her lowered lashes. One shoulder lifts and falls. I grab her phone from the floor beneath the arch of her knees and press the home button, bringing up the last thing she saw.

"Grip, don't look—"

"Shit." The strangled curse garrotes my throat. I blink over and over, but the images don't disappear. Stubbornly, they barely blur as the first tears sting my eyes. It's a page of horrors: bulging eyeballs straining from babies' faces, rounded backs and the exposed gray matter coils of brains, heads half gone, tiny bodies twisted into a mangle of flesh and bone.

"This is how she'll be?"

They aren't my words. It's not my question, but it takes over and barges past my lips. It uses my voice. It possesses me, this demon question I hope she won't answer.

"Maybe." Bristol swallows audibly, her mouth unsteady before she disciplines it into a straight line. "Probably."

There is nothing I've ever experienced that prepares me for these images, for the possibility that this will be my daughter and then she will die. Looking at these pictures, I can't help but ask if death would be a mercy. Am I merciful? Am I selfish? Shallow? Weak? These are just words, assigning no value to the emotions rioting inside of me. I am under siege. Terror, rage, and hurt are a fevered mob, torches lit and setting my heart on fire. It's not fair. All my life I've been tuned in to injustices, to inequities, but at this moment, they all fade to nothing. They are dust compared to this. This . . . *this* is not fair, that a baby, not even fully formed, has a death sentence waiting for her, that this world is already tuning its instruments for a dirge, a requiem for her life before it begins.

This is injustice.

"What do you want?" Bristol finally asks.

And there it is. She's braver than I am. She asked me the question I came to ask her but haven't been able to. It's the same question she asked me before I moved to New York, when I wanted her with me but didn't want to pressure her. I find myself once again possessing power I don't want to use.

"Bris, you have to decide that."

"This is just as much your baby as it is mine." Her voice is a thin line that wavers then draws taut. "Don't abdicate this to me. Don't do that."

"I'm not abdicating."

"We have to decide together."

"We will. I just . . . you heard what Dr. Wagner said."

She said Bristol's body will keep preparing for what's supposed to happen. It doesn't know to stop. Her pelvic bones will still stretch. Her ankles will still swell. Her milk will come in. Her body will ready itself for a child whose death is a foregone conclusion. No matter what course of action we choose, she won't live. If she does come into the world, these pictures on Bristol's phone, heavy in my hand, are her short-lived destiny.

"It's your body, Bris." I grit my teeth, but the words escape and I prepare myself for whatever she decides. "I want you to . . ."

The words hang in my throat, choked and unsaid.

"What do you want to do, Grip?" She moves quickly, settling on my lap, facing me with her knees on either side of my legs. I stare down at the little mound of baby taking up the small space between us.

Dwell in possibility.

It's a practical joke now.

"What do you want?" Bristol dips her head to catch my eyes in the weak light.

"Dr. Wagner—"

"Is not my husband." Bristol's words cut over mine. "Tell me what you want."

"This decision—"

"Is ours, not just mine." She leans forward until our foreheads press together, the contact reminding me of who we were before this thing took over our lives, reminding me of our honesty, our intimacy that transcended flesh.

"Please tell me, Grip," she whispers, her cool breath fanning over my lips like a kiss, begging for entry.

"I want her."

The words fly from my mouth like arrows, aiming for Bristol's heart. If she wants to know what I'm feeling, I'll tell her and hope that she feels it, too.

"I want to meet her and hold her." Tears flood my throat and then spill hot down my cheeks. "I don't give a damn if she's here three minutes, three hours, three days. I want her to know that as long as she is in this world, her parents love her unconditionally, that we loved her so much, we *had* to have her . . . even if we knew it couldn't last, even though we knew it would kill us to lose her, we had to have her."

I immediately regret saying it. I understand the power Bristol has over me, that what she wants, I want to give her, and I hold that same power over her. If she goes through with this because of what I just said, and it's too much . . .

"Yes." For the first time, Bristol meets my eyes squarely. A new fire has burned away the haze. They're lit again, lit with determination and the fierce love few are capable of. "I want that, too."

"Are you sure, Bris?" My question is a raggedy-roped bridge between us. One wrong step and it could fall—*we* could fall.

"I'm sure." She shifts until she's no longer straddling me, and presses her shoulder into my chest. Her head tucks under my chin. "I can't terminate, Grip. I wouldn't judge another woman who did—I've always been pro-choice, you know that."

She looks up, her lashes damp, her lips stung and swollen from her teeth. God, she's breaking my heart. I thought Dr. Wagner's diagnosis drove a stake through me, but seeing Bristol suffer through this is a level of agony I can't even put into words.

"But this *is* my choice," she says, eyes locked with mine, searching mine. "This is our baby, and I want to have her."

I can't resist rubbing the subtle roundness of her belly, twin shafts of pain and joy coursing through me at the contact. *Our little girl.* If we do this, every moment of joy will be shadowed by pending pain. Can we do that? Endure that?

"Bris, this isn't something you can un-decide later." I push unruly tendrils of her hair back, needing to see her face clearly. The eyes that stare back at me are clearer than I've seen them since Dr. Wagner first told us what she suspected. Bristol's backbone is reinforced with steel, and I see evidence of it in her eyes: a steely determination, a certainty I can't argue with.

"I understand what this means," she says, closing her eyes briefly. "That once she's born, there'll be more pain than we can fully comprehend right now. I'm going into this with my eyes wide open."

Stretching to grab her phone from the floor, she opens a new browser window, quickly bypassing the photos that disturbed me when I first came in.

"Tell me again what you used to whisper to her," Bristol says.

The words "used to" grab me by the throat. Ever since we found out Bristol was pregnant, I talked to our baby every day, several times a day, every time I got the chance. For the last ten days, I haven't said a word to the baby. It's like I was preparing myself for the fact that she was already gone, or that she would never come. Shame spears me.

"Um, I used to say . . ." I lick my lips. "I tell her to dwell in possibility."

"What's possible, Grip?" Bristol asks. "I mean, we know what won't happen."

The fierce light that has entered Bristol's eyes dims for a moment.

"She won't live a long life," she says softly. "She may not even live at all outside of my body. We know what isn't possible, but what is?"

"I don't know, Bris," I confess. Our options seem narrow. Our choices are crap. I'm the guy who defied every odd to achieve the things I have, to build the life I have, but I've finally met a mountain I can't conquer. "What's possible?"

"Life," she whispers. "Maybe not for our little girl, but for someone else's. For someone else, she could save a life. She could do a lot of good whether she's here for a moment or for . . ."

Bristol looks down at the phone in her hand and shows me the screen.

It's a website dedicated to neonatal organ donation. I read through the information, shocked to see the organization was founded by parents who lost their baby to anencephaly.

"This is a possibility." Bristol cups my jaw and lays her head against my face. Her damp lashes blink on my cheek. "I can't terminate this pregnancy. I can't make myself do it, and I need to feel that it's not in vain."

I get it. I feel the same way, and this route feels like the only thing close to possibility in this scenario, but it will carry a heavy price, one we can't even begin to calculate.

I hope we don't regret it.

Thirty-Seven
Bristol

I'VE LIVED A PRETTY PRIVILEGED LIFE.

I know that. I get it.

Beyond the top-percenter privilege my family's wealth afforded, there's that layer of privilege that's almost become a buzzword: white privilege.

Confession.

Honestly, I used to get defensive about this somewhere inside. I didn't ask to be born white, or for the intrinsic advantages that come with it living in this country. Hell, at first I didn't want to believe it was real. It's much easier to believe you *don't* have these immense advantages through accident of birth than to figure out how you can balance the scales.

Grip and I managed to get beyond labels like "privilege" or "minority" or even black and white. Beneath the labels, we found who the other person really is and how they'll love you in good times and bad. Unconditional love, by definition, doesn't give a damn about those labels.

Life is the grand equalizer. It has a way of stripping those privileges, rendering them inconsequential. Black, white, rich, poor—when it rains, we all get wet. When it rains, it pours, and sometimes, there is no shelter. I'm in the storm of my life, or rather a storm is in me, brewing in me, growing in me ... a storm of heartache and tragedy for which there is no privilege, no escape. Not my family's money. Not my husband's fame. Not my expensive education or my ambition. The hardest things in life have no escape, no workaround. There is no *around*, only *through*. We trudge *through* those storms. They toss us to and fro. They drench us and change us and strip us of the protection we thought privilege allowed, only to find in the end that we all bleed. We all suffer. We all die.

God, I'm morbid. And philosophical. In short, I'm a bore.

But so is this guy droning on for the last forty-five minutes. It makes me appreciate how gifted an orator Dr. Hammond is to make prisons and criminal justice reform sound fascinating, because this guy doesn't.

Dr. Hammond leans over to whisper in my ear, "Glad I'm not the only one struggling."

I snap my head around to meet the amusement in his eyes with a chagrined smile.

"Was I that obvious?" I whisper back. "I thought I looked engaged."

"If that's engaged," he says with a grin, "I'd hate to see checked out."

I pretend to wince.

"I need to work on my fakery. I'm not very good at phony, never have been."

Grip leans over to see me and Dr. Hammond, who sits to my right. "What the hell are you two talking about?" he asks. "You *do* realize this banquet is to honor *us*, right, Iz?"

"Do you feel honored?" His dark brows crest over the rims of his glasses. "If you honor me by holding me hostage to a bad speech for an hour and serving me rubber chicken, I'll pass."

A laugh, along with a little water, snorts through my nose. Grip does his damnedest to chastise me with a look, but he can't hold back his smile. It's brighter than I've seen in weeks. We needed this—to get out of LA, away from home. We can't escape the pain. I carry that with me. Even the little joys, like feeling the first kick, will be overshadowed by the inevitable outcome, but something about packing a bag and flying out here to DC lightened things for us some.

Grip and Dr. Hammond are being honored for their work with community bail funds. I wasn't going to come, but I haven't seen Dr. Hammond—he keeps telling me to call him Iz, but I'm not quite there yet—in such a long time, only a few times since the wedding. He and Grip haven't really revisited his views on interracial relationships, but it's obvious that his perspective has evolved, at least as far as Grip and I are concerned.

An hour later, the three of us are in the hotel suite Grip and I booked. Iz does the honors behind the bar because apparently he put himself through college bartending. He makes a Godfather for him and a vodka martini for Grip. Meanwhile, I'm sipping yet another water.

I miss liquor. I mean, liquor has been good to me in hard times.

Hello, vodka, my old friend.

I take a deep inhale from the bottle behind the bar, and Grip looks at me like *Don't even think about it.*

"Just sniffing." I laugh and reluctantly replace the bottle.

"Since you can't drink, did you at least make Grip give up weed?" Iz asks from the leather couch in the suite's sitting room.

"I volunteered, thank you very much." Grip settles onto the couch facing Iz with his drink in hand. "No easy task in my line of work where you get high walking into every studio."

"Well Bris has the hardest part." Iz offers a sympathetic smile.

"And then even after delivery you still can't drink for a while. I assume you'll breastfeed? Hope it's not awkward, but I'm in the daddy club. Ain't no going back after being in the delivery room."

He chuckles, not noticing that my smile and Grip's have slowly faded to ash, burned by reality crashing back in on us. I won't breastfeed. My breasts are the biggest they've ever been, and my milk will come in ... then dry up. It will come and go, just like this baby.

"I'm gonna ... um ..." I stand, adjusting the neckline and the hem of the dress I wore to the banquet, keeping my hands busy while my heart recovers. "I'll be back. Just need to ..."

I can't. I speed walk faster than a woman six months pregnant probably should, going back to the bedroom and flopping onto the bed, spread out like a starfish on the luxurious comforter. I stare up at the ceiling, hot tears flowing freely from my eyes and puddling in my ears. The sadness hovers over me. I've never lived with a constant promise of heartbreak, and many days, it's too much. I often slip away to indulge in something my mother-in-law encouraged me to do when she first heard the news about the baby's fate.

I count my blessings.

It is a well-documented fact that I'm not religious—never have been, and probably never will be, but I understand why some turn to it. I see why it is such a shaping force in Kai's life. Believing there is something bigger than you must be comforting when you feel small, dwarfed by circumstances out of your control.

Blessing number one: Grip

Blessing number two: Grip. *He's so good, he counts twice.*

Blessing number three: friends and family who love me. Rhyson and Kai and Amir and Shon and Ms. James and even my parents—all have been a source of comfort for us. My mother didn't understand my decision and urged me to terminate. At first I thought it was the automatic feminist response, that she assumed I was keeping the baby for reasons that I'm not. Pro-choice is just that: I get to choose. It's my body, which I've chosen to share with Grip, and we get to choose. Yes, the path we're on is painful. To some, unnecessarily painful, but it's what we've decided to do with this body. We have our reasons, and they're just that: ours. I kept wondering how my mother could be so cold about her own granddaughter. Of course, it took Grip pointing out my mother's fear for me to understand, noting that her concern for me far outweighed her feelings for this baby. She sees how hard it will be and doesn't want me to go through what's ahead.

"You and me, both, Mother," I mutter.

The ceiling hasn't changed, but my perspective has . . . some, enough to gather my emotions and go back out. I don't get to see Dr. Hammond much, and I don't want to spend the rest of the night in here brooding.

"I'm back." I settle beside Grip, huddling under his shoulder and taking in his scent. When neither of them responds, I feel the heaviness weighing the air and note their somber faces. I know what they discussed while I was gone.

"You told him?" I ask Grip, vulnerability softening my voice.

We don't tell everyone. It's bad enough this shit cloud hangs over the next three months and dampens so many moments that should be reasons to celebrate. We don't want to field everyone's awkward questions and responses the whole time, and we also don't trust everyone to understand.

"Yeah." Grip scatters a few kisses along my hairline and squeezes my shoulder.

"I'm sorry this happened to you guys." Iz grimaces. "Dammit, that came out wrong. I can't believe I'm one of those awkward people who says stupid things at a time like this."

"It's okay," I say. "We'll be okay."

I muster a smile to make him feel more at ease, something I find myself doing all the time lately once people know. I didn't realize how much time and energy you expend making others feel better about how bad things are for you. Things are heavy enough without the burden of their discomfort and pity.

"I know you will. The two of you . . . you guys have something most people never find. My ex and I certainly didn't have it." Iz drops his eyes to his drink, rolling the tumbler between his palms before looking back up to split a glance between us. "I've never apologized for my views before you married, for the things I thought."

A gruff laugh struggles past his lips. "The things I *said* to you, Grip."

He shakes his head, self-derision twisting his expression.

"I thought I knew. I . . . assumed, I guess, assumed things about you, Bristol. You, too, Grip. You were right. I was no better than the people we call bigots, and I'm sorry. No one could look at the two of you and think your love is based on anything but . . . each other."

It's quiet for a moment. In that slice of silent space, I add Iz to my blessings column. That someone so set against us, after seeing us and knowing us, had a change of heart—that's a little bit of a miracle, and right now, I'll take every miracle I can get.

"Apology accepted." Grip takes a sip of his drink. "I just have one question."

"Sure. Go for it." A degree of wariness enters Iz's eyes, like Grip might challenge him on his past beliefs and the way he insulted us before, even if he didn't think of it that way.

"Well now that you believe a Black man could legit fall for a woman who isn't Black," Grip says, "you gonna break Callie off or what?"

Iz's eyes stretch wide and then crinkle at the corners with his smile and the laugh that booms from his throat.

"Motherfucker!" He slams his drink down on the glass table. "Technically, Callie is a woman of color, and what I tell you about sticking your nose in my bedroom?"

"As little action as you get, brother," Grip says, a crooked smile on his full lips, "ain't nothing to see in there."

I sip my water and laugh while they rib each other mercilessly for the next hour, until sleep takes me hostage, like it always seems to these days. I don't even stir until Grip removes my dress and panties. Even walking through this difficult time, Grip manages to make me feel sexy, wanted. He loves my body pregnant, and hides my nightgowns. He is my brightest spot, my greatest blessing. Even now he leans on one elbow, hovering over me protectively, searching my face for sadness, for distress, for anything he can fix in a sea of things he cannot.

"Sorry I fell asleep." I grab his wrist to look at the crappy watch I won for him years ago. "It's late. What time does our flight—"

"I delayed it." He brushes my unruly hair, which started the night in a neat twist, out of my face. "I want you to sleep in. You need rest."

He disappears under the covers, and I feel his breath, his lips whispering to our daughter. I've never asked if he still whispers to her of hope, of possibility. I have no idea how he can when most days I can't find enough hope for me, much less anyone else.

And then it happens.

A kick. From inside my belly, a jolt, a sign of life.

Grip and I gasp together, a set of startled breaths and broken hearts finding a moment of joy to share. He pulls the comforter back to show the rising curve of my stomach, clearly seen even in the dim light.

"Did you feel that?" His voice is hushed with awe dipped in sorrow.

"Yeah." I swallow the tears I'm tired of shedding. I don't want them falling on this moment. I want this one thing we have that couples always want to be free of the shadow of what's to come.

"It's incredible." Grip's smile, wide and beautiful like a stretch of morning sky, takes my breath. "You're incredible."

He bends his head, ghosting his lips over my nose, my eyes, my lips.

"Thank you, Bristol." His voice comes rougher with emotion. "Thank me for what?" I caress the warm skin of his neck, the sleek slope of his shoulders, the strength of his arms.

"For carrying our child. I know men say that all the time to their wives, but this . . ." He swallows, squeezing his eyes tightly shut. "God, if it's too much for you, Bris, I'll never forgive myself."

"No." I shake my head, overcome that he feels guilty, responsible for where we are, between this rock and impossible place. "Grip, no. I wanted this. I mean, of course, not *this*, not this way, but presented with our choices, this is what I choose. It's right for us. Baby, please don't . . ."

When words fail me, I lift my head to kiss him, opening up just enough to sample his love, to savor his concern. I want him to know we're in this together of my volition. He returns the kiss with a begging passion that flares into the solace we find only in each other—not the storm we're walking through, but the one we make with our love. It's an extravagant intimacy reserved for this bed and these bodies, and like I have many nights before, I fall asleep in his arms with the taste of him on my lips. It's enough.

In the eye of the storm, it's a blessing.

Thirty-Eight

Grip

"**S**URPRISE!"

Bristol wide-eyes the cluster of women at our front door even as a smile overtakes her face. At eight months pregnant, she's bigger than I've ever seen her.

And more beautiful.

This pregnancy is unusual, atypical in most ways, but that legendary glow women supposedly have—Bristol has it in spades. I beat her to the door when the knock came because I knew who was on the other side. Kai came to me weeks ago about a shower for Bristol—not a traditional shower, obviously, with gifts for the baby and all the items we would need if this was happening as it should. Kai wanted to do something for Bristol to express the support from the women in her life, to show that they love her and want to walk with her through the hard part that lies ahead.

I hug each of them as they file in. There's Jimmi and Kai, Shon and Charm, who flew in from New York, and my mom and Jade.

"Jade?" I don't try to hide my surprise. "Wow. I mean, it's good to see you."

Things have improved between us and thawed some between Jade and Bristol, but she's not exactly a fixture in our lives. I told her about the diagnosis soon after we found out, but we haven't talked much about it. I don't think she knew what to say. Most people don't.

"I wasn't gonna miss this girly shit." She adjusts her Raiders cap and scoffs. "You know they actually doing pedicures and facials up in here?"

"Yeah, well I heard girls like that kind of thing." I shrug carelessly. "I'm watching the game in the other room if you need to get outta dodge."

"I'll be in there by halftime." Jade's smile disappears and her eyes sober. "How you holding up?"

"We're all right." I look over at Bristol, surrounded by laughing women and nail polish and Cards Against Humanity and overpriced cupcakes. "I hope it's not too much for her."

I haven't said that aloud to hardly anyone, but Jade's not just anyone. We bonded around the hardest times of our childhood. The day that cop violated her on the playground. The day one of her brothers killed the other in my front yard. We stood witness to each other's worst moments; we share the intimacy of tragedy. Our relationship has always been a pendulum that swings from reticent to confessional.

"She'll be cool. You were right—that girl's ride or die. She's a fighter." Jade tips her head back to study my face. "It's you I'm worried about."

"Me?" I touch my chest and shake my head. "I'll be fine. I mean, it's gonna hurt to the white meat, but I'll hold as long as she's okay. If this breaks Bristol . . ."

My words disintegrate. Our love is a tensile thread, stretched beyond even the bounds I thought possible. It connects us in a way that may be invisible, but is more real to me than anything I can touch or taste. I told her once that if I break her heart, I break mine, and it's true. Our hearts are wrapped around one another, joined. I honestly believe I can survive anything if Bristol is by my side. It's the closest thing to faith I have, and I cling to it. I cling to her. She thinks I'm the one holding us up, but my strength is tangled in her. If I lost Bris . . . not physically, but what we have, it has to stay intact. It's my cornerstone, and from what I've read, the hardest thing for a couple to survive is losing a child.

Kai walks up and says a few words to Jade before my cousin drifts off. Not sure how long she'll be able to stay in here with the estrogen as thick as it is.

"Thanks for letting us do this, Grip." Sadness shadows Kai's eyes, but a smile rests obstinately on her lips. "We're with you guys. I know this is unimaginably hard, but you're not alone."

"Thanks for letting me stay," I say. "For understanding."

This whole thing is sweet, and I'm glad Kai wanted to do it, but it, like everything in this pregnancy, has a bitter side, and I want to be close if things take a turn and Bristol needs me.

"Well you can stay, but you did agree to be out of sight, so . . ." She waves a slim hand toward the living room and the mammoth flatscreen television waiting for me. "Off you go."

"I'm going," I fake grumble. All this nail polish and tarts and shit are actually starting to make me itch.

On my way out, I stop to kiss Bristol's cheek.

"You knew about this." She narrows her eyes, but a smile breaks through. "A co-conspirator."

"You can punish me later."

"Oh, I plan to." She tips up to whisper in my ear, "We can have beached whale sex when everyone leaves."

"My new favorite position," I joke. "However I can get it in."

"Ugh." She scowls and smiles at the same time. "You're awful."

"I'm in love." I cradle her face in my hands.

"So am I." She puts her hands over mine, her eyes locking on me. "Thank you for this."

I nod and bend to kiss her belly, no longer just a bump. Now that we're at the end, she can't see her toes anymore. I'm gonna miss this belly, and a sudden pain harpoons me at the thought, nearly taking my breath. Once this belly is gone, so is our little girl.

Over the next hour, I try to lose myself in the soccer match, but I keep finding my ears straining to hear what they're doing in there. I figure I can ask Jade when she joins me, but she never does, and that's got me curious. I pad down the hall and surreptitiously poke my head around the corner. Jade's still there. Matter of fact, she's adding her words to all the other pen markings covering Bristol's belly. Right across the middle is scrawled the name we chose for the baby.

Zoe.

It means life. That's what's possible: that Zoe's life and death will save someone else. Bristol laughs and squirms as Jade puts the finishing touches on what looks like a baby panda.

"It tickles!" Bristol screeches, tossing her head back, her dark hair swinging behind her.

She's so beautiful and so happy. I want to freeze this moment and store it in a time capsule, bury it for safekeeping, for posterity, to show the other children we'll have a picture of their mother fierce enough to find joy in the most difficult time of her life.

What feels like days later but is only a few hours, the cupcakes are gone, the games are stowed away, the facials are done. These wellmeaning women have taken Bristol from me all day, and as much as I love them, I want her back. I want her to myself. There's a strength we draw from one another that comes in the quiet at the end of the day, holding each other, talking about everything, reassuring each other. It's not much, but it seems to be the only thing that truly soothes the ache that's grounded itself immovably in my heart.

I wander into the kitchen, hoping maybe one cupcake survived, only to stop at the door. My mother and Bristol are huddled together against the sink, a tangle of arms and tears and grief and strength. Every primal instinct in my body blares for me to protect the two most important women in my life, to stop whatever is hurting them, but reason filters in and I feel more helpless than I ever have. It's just life, just death, an inexorable cycle that has shattered my illusion of control, and there is truly nothing I can do to stop the pain.

Bristol glances up from their weepy embrace, a subtle curve tweaking her lips.

"Hey babe." Her voice, husky and raspy from tears, strangles in her throat. "I was just telling your mom Zoe's middle name."

It's Millicent, Ma's name. Everyone calls her Mittie, but that's because Jade couldn't say Millicent and started calling her Aunt Mittie. It stuck, and we all adopted it, but her given name is Millicent, and like a precious heirloom, we're passing it on to Zoe.

My mom has talked so much about grandkids in the past, I'm sure these weren't the circumstances into which she envisioned her first one being born. I insinuate myself into their tight circle, enveloping them both in my arms and trying to give them strength from my depleted reserves.

"I love you," Ma whispers, pulling back to put her right hand on my cheek and her left on Bristol's. "Both of you. We'll get through this. God'll get us through it. Y'all got my prayers."

My mama might love her bottle of Ace of Spades and I may have even seen her toke a couple of times growing up when things got hard, but she never misses a Sunday. I know it bothers her that the faith she tried to cultivate for years when I was younger holds no real place in my life anymore.

"Thank you for that. We can use all the prayers we can get," Bristol replies, shocking the hell out of me. Since when did she care if somebody was praying? I guess tough times can do that to you.

I walk Ma to the door, nodding while she prattles, assuring her that I'll make sure Bristol gets some rest and promising we'll eat the food she left in the refrigerator for us.

"Marlon, look at me." She reaches up to grasp my chin, holding my eyes with an intensity I've never seen before. "Bristol is a survivor, we both know that, but she's not ready for this."

"She'll be—"

"Neither are you," she cuts in, her throat muscles working to hold back tears. "I know you're trying to brace yourself for it, but I want you to accept that you can't be prepared for this kind of pain, even when you know it's coming."

I stop trying to talk, to defend, to reassure, and instead just absorb her wisdom.

"It's obvious how much you love your wife and how she adores you, but this will change things." Ma's brows gather over troubled eyes. "You don't come out of this kind of battle without some scars, and as much as it's gonna hurt you, it's Bristol who has carried Zoe all this time, felt her move and shared her very body with her. Just remember when the time comes that it's a little different for her, maybe a little deeper, even closer to the bone. Fathers don't like to hear that, but listen to your mama, Marlon."

I don't trust my voice, but just nod. Mama is the last to leave, and I lean against the cottage door for a minute, letting the sudden silence sink into my overworked senses. I understand what my mom meant about not being ready even when I think I am, but I'm glad I at least have the next month to try.

They say God laughs when we make plans. When I go back to Bristol in the kitchen, I think that must be true. She's at the sink, right where I left her, eyes wide and red-rimmed, cheeks tear-streaked, hair rioting in thick dark and dappled waves down her back. It's not how she looks that brings that proverb to mind, it's what she says on a startled gasp of breath.

"My water broke."

Thirty-Nine

Grip & Bristol
Birth Plan for Zoe Millicent James

OUR BABY GIRL HAS BEEN DIAGNOSED WITH ANENCEPHALY. HOWEVER imperfect she appears to some, she is ours, and we already love her deeply and will treasure any time we have with her.

Please call her by her name, Zoe. Please ask us how we feel, if she has been active, and other things we've experienced that make this pregnancy special. This validates and honors Zoe's life.

We understand that after the birth, situations may arise that were not anticipated and decisions will need to be made. Please keep us informed so we can participate in the decisions. Please take no intervention without our approval, other than what is outlined below. We trust you will respect our wishes.

In the delivery room, we would like Zoe's father, Marlon, to be present, and the doctor who will be delivering Zoe. Other family members and visitors will wait in the waiting area.

I, Bristol (mother), would like to give birth vaginally, unless strongly advised for a C-section.

We would like to receive a birth certificate and death certificate for Zoe.

We would like her footprints and handprints. We do not wish any testing to be done on Zoe.

If our baby's heart stops prior to delivery, we do want to be informed.

We do not want the birth videotaped, but we want plenty of photos afterward.

Any drugs given to Zoe should be approved by the parents and should be given in doses to provide maximum comfort while allowing her to be alert to meet her family and visitors while she can.

Zoe's father will cut the umbilical cord.

We would like oral and nasal suctioning for Zoe's comfort only and no intubation without our permission.

After Zoe is born, we ask that she be wiped, suctioned (if needed), wrapped in a blanket, and whether alive or stillborn, handed to us.

We would also like to give Zoe her first bath.

Please hand her first to her father Marlon, as we wish to cuddle our baby immediately. We ask that vital signs, weight, medications, and labs be postponed, if possible.

If Zoe has fewer problems than expected, please discuss all possible testing and treatment options with us.

Other than routine post-delivery care, we wish for private time with our baby. We will discuss any exceptions that should be made. We want Zoe to be with us in the room at all times.

Zoe's grandmother Millicent James will serve as liaison with family and friends, periodically providing updates and managing the flow of people that she escorts into our room, at our request only, and will help us with phone calls.

We have reserved a section of the maternity wing, and only authorized personnel and approved friends and family are allowed access. Under no circumstances should members of the press be allowed access to the area.

Memorial/funeral plans have been made for Zoe at La Casa Memorial Gardens and Funeral Home.

We wish to hold Zoe as she is dying or after she has died. Zoe will be donating her organs for transplant. Based on the circumstances of her birth and death, she may be capable of donating heart valves, corneas (both tissue donation), and possibly kidneys and liver cells. As soon as she passes, Zoe will be taken directly to recovery surgery in preparation for organ donation. A burial garment will be provided. We would like to keep the following items as keepsakes: lock of hair, ID bracelet, crib card, handprints and footprints (molds if possible), weight card, hat, blanket, clothes, family handprints, and photographs, both color and black and white. We have a memory box to store any items collected.

We do not want an autopsy done.

Thank you for helping us make this bittersweet time as bearable and memorable as possible.

Bristol & Marlon James

Forty
Grip

"WE NEED TO ADJUST THE PLAN."

Dr. Wagner's words are not the ones I wanted to hear. It feels like the plan is already adjusted enough since we're delivering a month earlier than we're supposed to.

"She doesn't want a C-section." I keep my voice low enough for just the doctor to hear. "You know how important that is to her."

I hazard a glance to where Bristol rests between contractions. She scraped her hair back from her face, but tendrils have insisted on loosening from the restraint and cling to her face. Her hospital gown is drenched, and her head flops to the side in exhaustion. I've lost track of how long she's been in labor, but apparently, Dr. Wagner thinks it's been long enough.

"Her labor isn't progressing." Dr. Wagner's eyes soften with compassion, but her jaw sets with resolve. "The baby's heart rate is dropping. Given that you wanted as easy a passage for Zoe and as much time with her as possible, we need to adjust, and *now*. I can tell Bristol or—"

"No." I shake my head decisively. "It needs to be me. I'll tell her." "Good." She signals to a nurse hovering nearby. "We need to start prepping her for surgery. I'll give you a minute to explain the situation."

Dr. Wagner, in a rare lowering of her professional guard, grabs my hand and squeezes.

"You've come this far, Grip," she says, her eyes sympathetic and grave. "You and Bristol set this course that most can't or don't follow. It's time to see it through to the end."

I rein in fear and frustration and rage and helplessness, trying not to panic while a propeller spins out of control in my chest. I never had a father to teach me what it means to be a man, how to lead a household, support a family, love a wife. Most of what I know about love and about leading, a woman taught me. My mother taught me, and every lesson, every bit of advice, everything she tried to impart to me, I'm grappling for, struggling to remember as I approach the hardest thing I've ever done and will probably ever do.

"Bris," I whisper, brushing the wet strands from her forehead. "Hey babe."

Her eyes open and roll a little with fatigue and the medication she's been given for pain before she focuses on my face.

"What's wrong?" she asks, her voice thinned by the long hours. "The baby—"

"She's fine. You're doing great, but we ..."

I hate to do this knowing how badly Bristol wanted to deliver naturally. It's one more thing from this experience that won't be as we wanted it, one more thing I have to take away from her.

"We need to do a C-section, Bris." I watch her face, and my heart contracts when a solitary tear streaks over her cheekbone.

"No, Grip, I ..." She swipes at the tear impatiently and compresses her lips. "Why?"

"Your labor isn't progressing. It's been too long. We were hoping it would happen quickly, naturally, but if we want Zoe to have the easiest passage, want time with her, we need to do it now."

"Now?" Her eyes widen and she saws at her lip with her teeth. "I ... now."

"Yeah." I glance over my shoulder as Dr. Wagner and her team enter the room. "They want to start prepping you."

She grabs my hand, squeezing it hard enough to draw blood. "Grip, I'm scared." Tears swim over the terror in her silvery eyes. "I ... I can't do this."

I can count on one hand the number of times Bristol has told me she feared anything. We hadn't really talked about surgery much because we weren't planning on it, but I know enough to ease her mind, and anything I don't know, Dr. Wagner can fill in.

"It's a simple surgery," I reassure her. "They'll just—"

"No, not the surgery." She squeezes her eyes shut. "I mean ... what comes after the surgery."

She looks back at me, fear obscuring the confidence, the fearlessness I'm used to seeing.

"I can't do this." Her lips tremble as her nails slice into my skin. "I don't think I can let her go."

Fuck.

I don't think I can do this either, but we have to. The team is hovering, and Dr. Wagner's urgency is quickly becoming impatience, breathing down the back of my neck.

"Bris, it's gonna be . . ." The word "okay" congeals in my mouth. Bristol and I don't lie, not to each other. Our relationship is built on uncomfortable conversations, shitty odds and, in Bristol's words, love without walls. I'm not erecting walls between us now with anything less than the truth.

"I don't know if it's gonna be okay," I admit quietly.

Her weary eyes spark and latch onto my confession, to my unexpected honesty.

"I've never made you promises I can't keep, Bris, and I'm not gonna start bullshitting you now."

I gulp back the trepidation that would keep me from saying what has to be said before they make the cut that will bring Zoe to us, for minutes, hours, or days.

"Shit's about to get real," I say. "And the only thing I can promise you is that I will love you for the rest of my life, and I truly believe we can survive anything together. Do you believe that?"

I'll never forget this moment when, through the abject fear and despair and exhaustion saturating her eyes, I glimpse her trust in me. It's the greatest gift I've ever received.

"Yes." Her voice comes out frail, but that steel that reinforces her character. It's there. It defies the shitstorm we're flying into. I like to think it defies it because we are flying into it together. I'm not God—I can't promise her miracles, and as badly as I wish I could, I can't save Zoe. When it's time to let her go, I'll be as shredded as Bristol. I am her husband, though, and she's the only woman I've ever loved. All I *can* promise is that through everything, we'll have each other.

Forty-One

Bristol

WAKE UP DISORIENTED AND NUMB IN SOME PLACES, VAGUELY ACHING IN others. My last lucid memory is the concern etching lines into Grip's face as he promised me everything would be okay.

No, that's not right.

He didn't promise everything would be okay during the C-section or afterward. He promised to love me, and I know he still does.

But *is* everything okay?

"Grip?" Briars clot my throat and make my voice rough.

"Hey." He comes into view, and my heart pounds at the sight of him and then stops when I see him holding a tiny swaddled bundle. "You're back."

I remember now. My mind fights through the haze of drugs and exhaustion. I remember struggling to stay awake. Between the drugs and fatigue, I just needed to hear her cry. There was an incredible pressure below the curtain that blocked the lower half of my body, and then a sharp cry. Then, as if my body had held out as long as it possibly could, as soon as I heard that cry, everything went dark.

"Is she . . ."

Alive? Still here? Did I miss her? Is she already gone?

The questions clamor for first place in my head, muddling my thoughts. Tears aren't far behind, burning my eyes and making my lips tremor.

"She's right here." I can't figure out if Grip's eyes are more tender when he looks down at our baby girl or back to me. "You wanna hold her?"

Syllables and sounds jumble in my throat, and something close to a whimper then an uncertain nod is all I can manage.

"Zoe," Grip says, leaning down to the bed with his little bundle. "Meet your beautiful mama."

He transfers the sweet weight to my arms, leaving a kiss in my hair, which I'm sure is mangled and matted all over my head, but he doesn't seem to care. If anything, his lips linger.

The tip of a tiny hat peeks from beneath the striped blanket. I hesitate, knowing when I pull the blanket back, when I see her, there's no going back. I slowly peel the cover away. My heart was braced for something gruesome. The pictures I found online promised nothing like what I'm holding. Her eyes may bulge a little more than typical, but they're the same gray that stares back at me each morning in the mirror, and her little mouth, even at this stage, bears the wide fullness and sculpted lines of her father's. I know what Dr. Wagner told me, what all the research says—that she has no cognitive function. How could she, missing most of her brain? I know any movement is just instinctual twitches, reflexes, not responses to stimuli. Maybe my heart just wants to fool itself into thinking there's an awareness simmering in her eyes, that somehow she knows I'm her mother. I faced the fires of hell to meet her, to have her, even for just minutes or hours, and Grip and I have risked our hearts to hold her.

She was worth it.

I know it's unwise and I'll pay for it soon, but I open my heart to this little girl, and like a flood, she rushes in. She squeezes herself into every inch, pervading any available space until a pressure builds in my chest and explodes in a sob.

"Oh, God." Tears sluice down my cheeks, imprinting joy on my face. "She's beautiful."

I look up to find Grip looking at me the way I must be looking at her—like she's a miracle I'm going to hold on to as long as I can.

"Beautiful," he agrees, the tips of his long lashes damp with tears.

"I can't believe I passed out." I look back to Zoe, determined to absorb as much of her as I can while I have her.

"Between the drugs and the fatigue, I'm surprised you weren't out longer. It was just for a few minutes, not long at all." Grip eases himself down on the bed beside me, sheltering us with his arm over our heads on the pillow. "The nurses said it happens."

"You cut the cord?" I pry my eyes away from her long enough to catch my husband's smile, pride shining from every pore.

"Yeah, I did," he says softly. "It was amazing."

"Good."

We both turn when the door opens. Dr. Wagner enters, her face a careful mask of polite concern. A nurse follows closely behind.

"How are we doing?" Dr. Wagner asks, picking up the chart hanging at the end of my bed.

"Okay." I meet her eyes frankly, gratefully. "I know you weren't sure we made the right decision, but thank you for getting her here."

"It wasn't that, Bristol." A smile breaks through her professional façade. "That decision can only lie with the parents. It's my job to make sure you have all the facts and know exactly what a decision entails."

I glance back down at Zoe and then to Grip. The reality presses in on us. We can't hide from the end that looms somewhere in the distance, though we don't know how close.

"With that said," Dr. Wagner continues, "you know time is short."

Her words, though true, puncture the joy I managed to find holding Zoe. Some part of me wants to pretend this is a normal birth, that any minute now, my baby will start rooting around, searching for my breasts, already heavy with milk. I want to believe we need to scramble to get a car seat because she came a month early and we were caught off guard and now we have to take her home, but we won't get to take her home.

"I know your family is outside waiting. As soon as you're comfortable, if there's anyone you want to meet Zoe," Dr. Wagner says gently, "you should bring them in soon."

"We will." Grip brushes a thumb across the plump curve of Zoe's cheek. "Thanks, doc."

"She's beautiful," the doctor says, her eyes on Zoe. "I better go make my rounds. If you need anything, let me know."

When she leaves, I notice a purple feather on the door.

"What's the feather for?" I ask the nurse checking Zoe's vitals.

"Pardon?" Her eyes flick from me to Grip in that carefully calm way that tells me she knows who we are, or rather who Grip is. Nobody cares who I am, and that's fine by me. We secured this whole section of the wing to ourselves, and there are no other patients nearby. This day is hard enough without the threat of cameras or other patients stumbling into our privacy.

"The feather," I repeat, pointing to the one hanging on the knob. "Does it mean anything?"

The nurse shifts her feet and her eyes, avoiding the probing look and the question.

"It's just something we do so the staff knows how to conduct themselves," she says evasively.

"Knows what?" Grip asks. "I walked the halls some earlier and didn't see it on any of the other doors."

She glances at Zoe before answering.

"We hang a purple feather on the door when the baby is a demise so the staff all remain sensitive to the situation," she says, her voice soft with sympathy.

A demise.

It sounds cold and final, when my baby is anything but as she lies in my arms. She feels warm and alive. It feels like the whole world is waiting for a *demise* when I'm begging for a miracle.

"So would you like to start bringing in family and friends?" she asks, obviously wanting to move past the awkward moment that still has me squirming painfully like a deer caught in a sharp-toothed trap.

"Hold on one second," I say. "I want to do something first."

With a glance at Grip, I gently lift the cap away from Zoe's head. I don't hide my flaws from Grip, and he loves me unconditionally. He doesn't hide his from me because he knows I love him with the same immutable heart. Our daughter, for as long as she's here with us, deserves no less.

I want to see her flaws because I know I'll love her just the same. It's hard to look. Without the hat, the illusion that she's like every other newborn disappears with a cruel sleight of hand and confirms what the ultrasound showed us months ago. There are parts of her missing. A thin membrane covers the parts of her brain that developed, but it's not pretty.

Even so, she's ours.

"You okay?" Grip asks, his shoulders tight as if he's braced for a blow.

"Yeah." I pull the little cap back into place, even though I'll never forget what lies beneath. "She is beautiful, isn't she?"

Relief loosens the muscles in his neck and shoulders, loosens the frown from his face.

"She is." He drops a kiss on the little cap on Zoe's head. "Now let's introduce her to everybody."

It's not everybody, but it's that nucleus of people who have supported us. It's Ms. James, of course, Rhys, Kai, Amir, Jimmi, Luke, and even Jade. The nurse takes pictures of them all holding Zoe, some wearing tear-dampened smiles.

When my parents come, Rhyson stiffly greets them before stepping out of the room. Christmas dinner was okay. He and our father are doing better; he and our mother …better. The family counseling sessions have helped, but there is enough tension in the room without their unresolved issues adding to it.

My mother watches the door close behind Rhyson and sighs before turning her attention to me.

"How are you?" she asks, her eyes dry and steady on my face.

"As well as can be expected." I shrug, running a self-conscious hand over my nest of hair, licking my lips and wishing for a little color. An army of friends, family, nurses, and doctors have come through and I haven't thought twice, but without a word, this one woman reminds me that I'm probably not presentable. She's flawless as usual.

"You want to hold her, Angela?" Grip asks. "Your husband just took his picture."

"Where is he?" Mother looks around the room.

"He went to talk to Rhyson." Grip clears his throat when my mother's face falls. It's a sore spot for her that Rhyson has extended forgiveness to my father but still barely tolerates her. Of the two, she cracked the whip hardest when Rhyson was a child. She gave him prescription drugs to cope with his anxiety, and when he was addicted, she delayed getting him help because she didn't understand how serious it was.

"Yes, let's get the picture." She takes Zoe, and at first her arms are wooden, her posture arrow straight. Then, when she looks down at her granddaughter for the first time, maybe for the last, her face softens and her mouth quivers. Her body curves protectively around the little blanketed bundle. I'm astounded to see a tear skate over her powdered cheek. Then my mother does what no one else has dared to do. She inches the hat back to see Zoe just as she is. She looks up at me, and tears spring to my eyes at what I see on her face—not the agony I've seen with some, not the shadow of death, but awe.

"She's wonderful, Bristol," she says, blinking rapidly against more tears. "And of all the things you've done, I've never been prouder of you than I am right now."

I can only nod because my throat is clogged, my lips sealed. My mother is flawed, but I stopped my running tally of her mistakes long ago. The list got too long and just became a record of my bitterness. Despite all of that and as much as we've clashed through the years, I am an offshoot of this tree. I hope I grew straighter and that my roots have gone deeper. I hope my branches will reach wider, offering shelter that my mother often with-held, but if I ever have the breadth of a sequoia or the strength of a sycamore, watching her study my daughter with unflinching love, I know Angela Gray is the tree where I began.

The nurse patiently takes more pictures with everyone while they hold Zoe and some with Grip and me.

"We'll put these in Zoe's memory box," she says when the room is empty of everyone except Ms. James, Rhyson, and Kai.

"Thank you." An ache fists my heart in an ironclad grasp as I take Zoe from Ms. James. A sharp, deeply drawn breath lifts Zoe's chest, and everyone in the room goes completely still.

"Is she okay?" I ask the nurse, fear icicling my blood. "What was that?"

"It's what we call an agonal gasp." She steps closer, pressing a stetho-scope to Zoe's tiny chest. "It's not out of the ordinary."

Agonal? How can it be considered ordinary for an infant to be in agony?

"Can I listen?" I ask, eyeing the stethoscope.

She hesitates before nodding and passing the instrument to me. I put one earpiece in my ear and Grip grabs the other, with the chest piece rest-ing on Zoe's tiny torso. We listen to her heart in stereo, our eyes meeting in shared awe that we made her together, in shared fear that, any minute now, she'll be taken as quickly as she came. We fear that this little mallet in her chest pounding a steady rhythm is the only thing standing between our hap-piness and complete destruction.

The defiant little *thump thump thump* of Zoe's heartbeat caresses my ears. It's the sound of her life persisting, surprisingly strong, but I know how fragile she is. It's written on the nurse's face in lines of sympathy.

"You said . . ." My courage falters, but I gather it between my lips again and force myself to ask the question plaguing me. "You called it an agonal gasp. Is she in . . . well, is she in pain?"

As if we're one, I feel Grip holding his breath just like me as I wait for her response. If Zoe's in pain, I did this. If she's in pain, was I selfish to want her? To want to meet her? To hold her?

"Research tells us that an anencephalic infant feels no pain because the part of the brain that communicates pain isn't developed," the nurse replies, stowing the camera on a side table and turning to face us. "Doctors will tell you they are just reflexive, vegetative, and feel nothing at all."

She leans forward, looking around like she's about to share a secret. "But I don't believe that," she whispers.

"You don't?" Grip's question is covered in the same dread that lines my insides as we wait. "You think they feel?"

"I know they do." She smiles even as tears fill her eyes. "They feel your love."

Grip looks down at me, a slow smile flowing from his eyes to his lips, and nods to her.

"Thank you," he says.

"If everyone has seen her," the nurse continues, her tone pivoting back to kind professionalism. "I need to ask if you want . . ."

Her words stall, but then she takes a deep breath and goes on. "Do you have a family priest or minister? Your birth plan didn't reference one, but I thought I'd ask." Her face is gentle but deliberately blank. "Do you want last rites?"

Oh, God. I can't do this.

The realization pounds from inside my head, slamming against my temples, pushing against my chest, banging at my lips from the dry interior of my mouth. The words want *out*. They want all these people who think I'm capable of letting my baby go to know it's a lie.

I cannot.

Who the hell did I think I was? Why did I assume I was strong enough for this? I'm contemplating how exactly to let them know I can't do this, that we need to find a way to stop this spiral. I need off this ride, out of this nightmare. I need to wake up in a cold sweat beside my husband in our bed, pregnant. This bad dream can't be my life because I won't survive it.

"Um, we don't really have a minister, per se," Grip responds to the nurse. He glances at me, and even though his voice remains even, the same panic rises in his eyes, unvoiced. "We . . . I guess we could . . ."

"I'm sure there's a hospital chaplain," Kai speaks up, reminding me we're not alone. She, Rhyson, and Ms. James watch us carefully, like we might blow at any minute.

"I could call Pastor Robinson," Ms. James volunteers. "He baptized you, Grip, when you were a little boy."

Grip looks uncertain, wrestling for a moment and then looking to me.

"What do you think, Bris?" He searches my face, eyes tortured and voice low. "What do you want?"

We painstakingly crafted that birth plan, taking every step and every minute into account, but neither of us really have any faith. Last rites never occurred to us, and it never came up. I haven't given much thought to what happens when you die. You die, you're gone. But as I look into Zoe's eyes, the exact color of mine, and as I see my DNA mingled with Grip's in this little girl, that's inadequate.

I search the circle of faces waiting for me to express something I'm not sure of, until my eyes land on Kai. I don't have faith. I've never pretended I did, but today, I need to believe in something. I need to believe this isn't the end for my baby girl, that when she breathes her last and she's lain in the ground, she doesn't just go to dust.

"What do you think happens next, Kai?" I ask, my eyes locked onto hers for any sign of doubt. "What do you think happens if Zoe dies today?"

Her eyes widen, but never waver, and I realize how easy it is to under-estimate her. I know she has soaring ambition, of course; I'm her manager. I know her drive would put anyone to shame; I've seen her work ethic in action. What I didn't realize until right now is what drew my brother to her, beyond the talent and her beautiful face. At her core, there's something un-shakeable, something that if tested, holds, and I need it right now.

"I think she goes to heaven," Kai says, her voice strong and sure.

"Your daddy told you that?" I ask, lifting one brow. "You said he taught you most of what you believe about God."

"Yeah, he did." She looks at the floor and then up to the ceiling, exas-peration twisting her lips before she returns to me. "He may not have lived everything he preached, but I never doubted that he believed it, and I do, too."

"What did he say . . . I mean, well, did he have anything to say about babies like Zoe?"

Kai's eyes don't leave my face, but I can tell her mind turns back, back to some memory.

"When I was a kid, my best friend's little sister only lived for a day." Kai bites her lip before continuing. "We were so excited all those months her mama was carrying her, and for days I cried after the baby passed away."

I glance down at Zoe, noting how still she's gotten, how shallow her breaths have become, and my heart rests on the jagged edge of Kai's faith, on her next words . . . borrowed faith for a little girl on borrowed time.

"Daddy told me this world is dark and dirty and hard." She huffs a laugh comprised of cynicism and grudging admiration. "That's how he talked to me, a little girl, about faith. He was ruthlessly honest about it, and he said these babies were the purest thing God had to offer. They never got tainted by this world. They're here just long enough to give us a glimpse of heaven, a glimpse of glory. He called them glory babies."

Tears slide into the corners of my mouth, drowning the sad smile. The nurse's lips purse and her eyes pinch with the effort to keep her face neutral, but I know. I don't need her stethoscope to tell me what my heart already knows: Zoe's leaving me.

I huddle deeper into Grip's shoulder. Beneath my head he's solid ground, but his chest quakes with a tremor and his tears dampen my hair when he buries his face in my neck. He always says he can't take my tears, but the sound of the sobs he's restraining, trying to protect me from his own heartbreak, rends my soul.

We're a mess.

And I suspect this is just the beginning. We got her here, but I'm not strong enough to live in the empty space she'll leave behind.

"Glory babies," I whisper, sniffing and pulling Zoe's little cap back and off, not caring if Ms. James or my brother or Kai aren't prepared for what lies beneath. Her last moments on this earth will be in my arms just as she is, in her purity, in her glory. As she came into this world, that's how she'll leave. She has nothing to be ashamed of, nothing to hide.

Our glory baby.

"Would you say the last rites, Kai?" The words cling to the inside of my throat, fighting against being spoken.

"I'm not a . . . well, that's to say, I can't . . ." She looks over her shoulder at Rhyson, whose eyes are as wet and tortured as ours. He nods his encouragement, but Kai's expression remains helpless when she turns back to face us. "I'm not a priest, Bristol."

"I don't want a priest," I snap, the fierce response rearing from my weariness. "I want someone who believes what they're saying. Do you or do you not believe my baby is going to heaven? To glory?"

Kai firms her chin, high color painting her tear-streaked cheeks.

"I do."

She says it like a vow, and her faith shines, a beam I grab hold of as darkness approaches.

Ms. James, Rhyson, and the nurse encircle the bed when Kai steps close to lay her hand on Zoe's forehead. There's no squeamishness, no revulsion or disgust on Kai's face when she touches that most unappealing part of my baby girl. With face solemn, her hand steady, and her words sure, Kai whispers to Zoe of glory, of divinity and perfect peace. She tells her that the God who sent her with His hand is waiting for her return with arms wide open. Kai's words breathe serenity, but when Zoe's little chest rises and falls with a final gasp, my heart revolts and I shatter into infinite pieces. I will never be the same. I'll never be smooth again. I'll be cracked in all the places Zoe touched in the few hours I had with her. I'll have to make myself all over with ragged bits of soul and flesh and heart, and as Kai whispers the last words to send Zoe on her way, all I can do is weep and wail and wish I was going, too.

Forty-Two
Grip

> *"I don't want so much misery."*
> —" Walking Around," Pablo Neruda Grip

THE LINE FROM NERUDA'S POEM "WALKING AROUND" IS A DAILY refrain. I wake up with it threading my thoughts like a needle, beaming through my windows with the morning sun. It has been nearly two weeks since Zoe came and went, and the grief is unrelenting, a deluge of despair. It's the rainy season, a monsoon that never lets up. Like drenched clothes, I'm heavy and dripping everywhere I go.

But at least I go.

Not much, not many places, but I've left the house. Bristol can't. She won't, and she won't see anyone. She's turned away Kai, Jimmi, my mother, calls from Charm. No one has gotten through, and everyone's worried about her ...about us.

And they should be.

I keep telling myself this is to be expected, but it freezes my blood when I look into Bristol's eyes that have always shone with vibrancy and spirit and find them lifeless.

I prop the door to our bedroom open with my back, balancing a tray in my hands. I can't remember the last time I saw Bristol eat. Knowing she loves this lemon coconut French toast from a place up the street, I grabbed an order of it, hoping I can tempt her to at least try. I set the tray down on the bench at the foot of our bed and settle beside her with my back against the headboard. I placed the huge bouquet of flowers Mrs. O'Malley sent beside the bed, but even that hasn't coaxed a response from her.

We didn't tell many people what we were dealing with during Bristol's pregnancy, but we released a statement later. The pregnancy was common knowledge. We walked red carpets together, were photographed out walking, living. People assumed everything was normal, which at the time, was simpler for us. Now nothing is simple, and awkward questions about how we're doing with our newborn will only make recovering harder. So, everyone knows what happened, but no one can really know what we're going through.

I bend to the pillow where her head rests and push the tumble of hair back from her face, surprised to find her eyes wide open and tearless, staring vacantly as she lies on her side.

"Hey babe." I touch her chin, waiting for her eyes to meet mine. "I brought you some breakfast."

She shakes her head, her eyes drifting away from my face again.

"Not hungry." She rolls over, giving me her back and huddling under the comforter. "You should eat."

"Said I'm not hungry." She pulls the pillow over her head. "Could you close the blinds on your way out?"

I stuff my frustration and general rage at the world down another inch. I'm afraid of what else is down there, buried beneath the thin flooring of my civility. It feels like some wild animal will leap out roaring and clawing and baring its teeth when I least expect it. There's a pack of feral beasts caged in my belly, in my chest, and I'm not sure how much longer they'll stay stuffed away before they come out raging.

"I'm not closing the blinds, Bris. Some sun would do you good. It's spring."

Her head makes a slow rotation until she's looking at me over her shoulder.

"It's spring?" Her eyes spark with the first emotion I've seen since the hospital. "Well whoop dee fucking doo, Grip. Now all's right with the world because it's *spring*. Who do I look like? Fucking Mary Poppins?"

I wanted emotions, yeah, but not the bitchy ones.

"Okay, Bris," I say as patiently as I can. "I'm hurting, too, but—"

"Are you?" The naked misery in her eyes breaks my heart in places I assumed were already broken. "Yet you somehow manage to go for long walks and zip to grab breakfast and eat food? And tolerate *light*?"

"I won't let this happen, Bristol," I say. "You know I won't. It's been ten days and—"

"Oh, I'm sorry." She snaps to a sitting position, the T-shirt she slept in bunching up with the covers, her hair tangled and matted and disorderly. "Has it been ten days already? Am I late? Was I supposed to be all better by now?"

"I get it. The only thing that drags me out of bed every morning is *you*." I lean over to cup her cheek. "I love you too much to let this go on. Ten days is no time in the grand scheme of things, but you can't *not eat*."

I lean closer, catching a whiff of my T-shirt she's wearing, which could probably launder itself by now.

"Damn, babe." I screw my nose up, hoping she'll allow me to tease her some. "You can't not *bathe* for ten days either."

Her lips don't twitch. Her eyes don't glimmer with humor or interest or life. She just stares at me unblinkingly.

"I can't do this, Grip," she whispers, her anger fading as quickly as it came. She presses her cheek deeper into my palm. "You keep thinking I can do this, that I'm stronger than I am, but . . ."

She shakes her head, helplessness loosening a tear from her lashes and spilling it over her cheek.

"I'm not strong enough either, baby." I dip to press my forehead to hers. "Not by myself, but remember what I promised you?"

"What?" she asks.

She doesn't remember? I console myself with the reminder that she was exhausted and on drugs before her C-section, but my heart still winces that she doesn't remember what I promised.

"I said—"

"That you would love me for the rest of your life," she whispers, eyes closed. "And that you believed we could survive anything together."

There's my girl. Hope flares in this dark room that is our life right now. It's the smallest thing, her remembering those moments, our hardest, but it's the only thing I have.

"Yeah, that's it. The only way we get through this is together." This one thing encourages me to broach a topic I know we need to address. "I, uh . . . was talking to Dr. Wagner."

Her eyes narrow.

"I just had the checkup and was okay," she says, slowing her words as if she needs to process them. "I'm not due back until my six-week appointment."

"I know." I nod my agreement. "But I called her office and we talked—"

"About me?" Her words come fast and outraged. "Without me?"

"Bris, just listen." I sigh, dreading this. "She thinks you should reconsider the prescription she suggested."

"For the milk?"

Dr. Wagner mentioned a prescription that would expedite the milk drying up, but Bristol refused. I wish she would take it. Nature is cruel, preparing Bristol's body to nurse and nurture even though her arms are empty. It's a constant reminder of what we've lost burgeoning in her body.

"No, not those." I clear my throat unnecessarily. "The, um . . . the antidepressant."

"I don't want that." Bristol tosses the comforter back, throwing her legs over the side with more energy than I've seen. It's a shame the only thing that seems to enliven her is anger. "It hasn't even been two weeks."

"True, but not only do you have the . . . grief," I say, the word getting snagged in my throat. "But all the hormonal changes that come with having a baby, too. When Dr. Wagner heard you weren't eating and were sleeping all day—"

"And she 'heard' this during your secret conversation about me behind my back, right?" Bristol stands and faces me, arms folded under her breasts.

"I'm not going to watch you get worse. Don't ask me not to help, Bris."

"You can't fix this. Pills won't fix this."

"Neither will not eating or lying in bed all day with the curtains closed." My voice comes out sharper than I intended, but those are the words I meant to say, ones I'm not taking back. I notice for the first time that she's wearing my Dave Chappelle T-shirt, *HABITUAL LINE STEPPER*. I can't help but think about that night, years ago, when she wore it while we ate on the roof, before we made love. My eyes wander over the long legs and tangled hair. Even grimy, bitchy, depressed, and despondent, she's the only woman I want.

"Is that why you want to fix me, Grip?" she asks, scorn curling her lip as she watches me watch her. "You wanna fuck? Is that what this is about? Popping some pills in me so I'll be in the mood to suck your dick again?"

"Dammit, Bris!" The words combust in my mouth, and I roll off the bed to face her, a king-size sea of rumpled, unwashed sheets separating us, a chasm of shared pain somehow keeping us apart. "How could you . . . why would you say that to me? You know it's not true. Are you *trying* to push me away?"

"If that's what it takes for you to stop poking and prodding and trying to medicate me out of this, then yeah, I'll push you away."

She drops her head forward, the mass of dark waves obscuring her face and rioting past slumped shoulders.

"You can't fix this," she moans, twisting her head from side to side and cradling her waist with folded arms. "None of that will bring her back. You can't bring her back."

I can't stay away from her. I never could, and her pain, her tears draw me, the same way her vitality and her beauty always have. There is nothing about her that repels me, even when she tries her best to push me away. I step close, cautiously slipping my arms around her, resting my hands at the small of her back. She's stiff, resistant to any comfort I offer, but after a few moments of stroking her back, she goes limp against my chest, almost pliant. This is the closest we've been since Zoe died, and I don't want to shatter it by bringing up the meds, or the support group or the grief counseling—all things Dr. Wagner says will help us—but I can't let this go on. It's not good for either of us.

The ringing phone in my pocket intrudes on the words I need to say. Bristol stiffens and pulls away, the guard dropping back into place over her expression. She retrieves it from my pocket, studies the screen, and hands it to me.

"You should take it," she says hastily, grabbing the excuse to get out of this conversation. "It's Charm. Your book is due soon."

"It can wait. We need to finish this."

"Let's make a deal." She forces a smile that she probably thinks fools me. "You answer the phone, I'll go shower. How's that?"

Does she honestly think she can fool me? Hold me off? Shut me out? No way in hell I waited eight years for her only to settle for some imitation of intimacy, some facsimile of the woman I know she should be.

"I'll take her call," I say, pressing accept. "But you better be in the shower when I'm done."

Her smile looks awkward, like her mouth forgot how to do it, but she takes a few steps toward the bathroom. I feel a momentary sense of accomplishment. She's out of bed, headed toward the shower, but I know the real problems won't wash away. The anguish Bristol's waking up with every day is subterranean, deep below the surface. It's infected the very core of who she is. I can say that for sure because mine goes just as deep.

Forty-Three

Bristol

THE DARKNESS IS HEAVY. IT'S TANGIBLE, LIKE A WEIGHTED BLANKET trapping me beneath my stale sheets. It's a living darkness, thick with blood, wet with tears. Deep, so very deep. It's a ravine, and I'm at the very bottom. It's toxic, and I breathe great lungfuls of it, like a miner in a cave with no light, no air. Every morning I promise myself I'll do better. I'll get better. I'll eat. I'll shower. I'll be kinder to my husband. I won't take this pain out on him. As soon as my mind surfaces from fitful sleep, though, I hear Zoe's heartbeat again, trapped in her chest like infant fists banging against the fragile cage of her ribs, longing to be free.

Thump, thump, thump.

A drum in the thicket of dense forest, her heartbeat reaches my ears, drawing me—an auditory illusion, I know, but it's the only real thing I can find in the dark to hold on to. I run toward it, desperate to see her, to hold her one more time. Branches bite my face, rocks shred my feet as I follow the sound of that heartbeat, the drum in the jungle. I stumble and fall face first into an empty clearing. It's deserted, desolate, and every morning, bamboozled by that sound, I pull the covers over my head again.

Even my body plays tricks on me. It betrays me. My breasts surge with life, engorged and ready to feed, but it's a joke in bad taste because no one eats from me. I'm unessential. No one needs me to survive, and what I need, I can't find.

My body is a haunted house. Those who lived here are dead and gone, and my soul is riddled with ghosts. Phantoms travel the halls, walk the rooms, raising the hairs on my body, but when I look, there's no one there.

As I face myself in the bathroom mirror, I feel guilty about the things I said to Grip. I'm aching with the memory of what we should have, but lost. When I meet my reflection, I see a shell of myself, a husk of who I used to be. Living with this dense darkness, this haunted house, this abandoned womb, I don't think I can be that girl again.

Forty-Four

Grip

"**O**KAY, I'M ACTUALLY DONE WITH THE FIRST DRAFT." I sit on the unmade bed and press the phone to my ear while I talk to Charm. "I finished all but one before Zoe …"

I was going to say before Zoe came, but all Charm or anyone who knows our situation would hear is before Zoe died. I let the words dissolve in my mouth. That's what she is to others: an epitaph with no dashes, not a year she was born and a year she passed away, but a solitary day, mere hours.

"Okay," Charm says, that hesitation in her voice like everyone else's, like she's not sure it's safe to talk to me yet. "Look, Grip, we can delay this again if we need to."

"No, it's fine. Your production team has been really patient, and I appreciate that." I glance at the stack of printed pages splayed on the bed. "All the poems are finished. I was just doing a final read-through."

"If you're sure," Charm says, a bit of relief in her voice. "That's great. Just email it."

"Cool."

Silence pools on the line, and I'm not sure if she has more to say or if she's waiting for me to go.

"Um, how's Bristol?" Charm asks. "I called her, but it went to voicemail. I haven't heard back, but I figure she'll call when she's ready. I don't want to bother her."

I didn't want to bother her either, the first day, the second, the third …
but we're at day ten, and I think it's time someone bothered her and shook

712 | KENNEDY RYAN

her out of this. I'm probably the only one who can reach her, but who's gonna reach me? I run a hand over my head. I need a haircut, a shave. Have I showered today? Have I eaten? I'm as bad off as Bristol is, but afraid to express it, to let her know. This kind of grief, it's impossible to bear, but this, what Bristol is allowing, what she's doing to herself—it's unsustainable. I love her too much to let it go on.

"Grip?" Charm prompts. "Bristol? How is she?"

"Oh, well, not great." A heavy sigh falls between us over the phone. "I mean, we're not great, but I guess that's to be expected. We'll get through it, but it'll take time."

And I'm not sure how.

"I've known Bristol a long time," Charm says. "Longer than you have, actually, and I've never seen her the way she is with you. She's almost unrecognizable, honestly. As long as I've known her, she was great at putting up walls, keeping people out, but she doesn't have that defense with you. Just don't give up on her."

I let her words wash over me, cleanse my discouragement away, and renew my commitment to reaching my wife.

"Giving up on Bristol is not an option," I say, swallowing my doubts. "But thanks for the encouragement."

"And how are *you* holding up?" she asks, her voice a little lighter. "Who's going to take care of you?"

"Bristol will," I reply. "We take care of each other."

My response comes before I even have time to think about it. I wondered who would reach me if I'm occupied with reaching Bristol, who would take care of me if I'm taking care of her, but that's the answer: we take care of each other. We always have, and if we meant our vows, we always will.

"Charm, I need to go." I consider the closed bathroom door. I don't hear water running or any movement.

"Of course. I'll be on the lookout for your email. This book is going to be amazing, Grip."

I don't give a damn and don't even bother responding, just hang up. Charm will cut me some slack for my rudeness. Being around people is hard because there are all these rules, all these things you have to do, and the only thing I want to do right now is hurt, hurt and hold my girl and *heal.*

When I enter the bathroom, the shower's not running and there's no steam fogging the mirror. Bristol's on the floor, her long legs stretched out flat along the tiles, her back to the tub. She cups her breasts where two huge wet spots show through the T-shirt. Her head is bowed and tears run unchecked down her face. I rush over to squat beside her.

"Baby," I whisper, gently moving her hands away. "It's okay."

It's not fucking okay. I'm an imbecile saying asinine shit. My inadequacy overwhelms me in the face of her brokenness, in the reality of mine. She gulps in air like she's drowning, going under. I want to be her lifeline, but I'm sinking, too.

"My milk is drying up." She squeezes her breasts, pressing her eyes shut and cutting into her bottom lip with her teeth. "Soon it'll all be gone and I'll have nothing. It'll be like I never carried her . . . like she was never here."

She opens her eyes, meeting mine with dark humor, her lips tilted to a bitter angle.

"You know I don't even have stretch marks." She tugs the shirt up and the edge of her panties down. "Except these."

She lovingly caresses a small patch of faint stripes at her hip. Her fingers drift to the relatively small but still-red scar from her C-section. "And this."

I was there for that scar. I watched them reach in and pull Zoe out. I'll never forget cutting the cord, hearing that first squawk confirming that our mission was accomplished, that Zoe had made it.

"I wish I'd seen that," Bristol says, watching me with watery eyes. "Seen you cut the cord."

Only now do I realize I spoke my thoughts out loud. I didn't mean to; I try to keep my pain to myself. Some days I can barely stand under the weight of it, but I look over at Bristol, hear her crying in her sleep, and I muzzle my own misery. She carries so much already. The last thing she needs is me being a pussy, weeping all over her. I want to be strong for her and more than anything, to protect her. I'm supposed to be her first line of defense, and watching her sobbing on the floor, caressing her scars, and clinging to her grief, I can't help but think I'm failing colossally.

"Let's get you cleaned up." It's not really what I want to say. I just want to join her on the floor and weep, but one of us has to be strong. I tug at the hem of the shirt but she folds into herself, keeping the shirt in place.

"No, I don't want to get cleaned up." Her head drops back to rest on the lip of the tub.

"Well I'm not letting you sit on the floor all day in a sour T-shirt and . . ." My voice fails.

"And what?" she demands. "Cry? Wallow? Why not?"

"This situation—"

"This situation is grief." Her strident voice ricochets off the bathroom walls. "Stop trying to fix me."

"I don't need to *fix* you," I bellow back, my restraints snapping. "I *need* you, Bristol."

"What?" she whispers, uncertainty shadowing her face. Did she think I wasn't suffering? I know I protected her from the worst of it, but she has to realize I'm as gutted as she is.

"Fucking newsflash: Zoe was mine, too. I'm her father. I'm broken." Tears set my throat on fire, and these words are the match. "It's killing me that she's gone, and it's killing me that you won't let me in."

"I don't know how." Tears paint her cheeks. "I'm in the dark."

"So am I." I grab her hands between mine. "You're my light. I'm your light. We only get through this together, Bris."

"I just feel so . . . alone." The word comes out on a gasp of desperate air, a hammer falling on my heart.

"Alone?" I bow my head, momentarily squeezing my eyes shut against the sight of her loneliness. "God, Bris, you're killing me. You feel alone? When I'm right here?"

"I didn't mean it like that, Grip." She shakes her head and tries to catch the tears sliding over her cheeks, but they're too many and too fast. "I meant—"

"This," I interrupt her, holding her ring finger up between us. "Means something to me."

I caress the word Matty inked into our skin. *Still.*

"*When we are alone, you and I, through years, through pain,*" I say, quoting my vows, my voice wilting and wet. "*My heart will answer again and again, still.*"

She looks at me, her eyes wide and wounded, my words seemingly having no effect on her. I can't do this, not right now. The only thing that hurts more than Zoe being gone is Bristol not sharing this burden with me, not letting me in.

"Fuck it." I heave myself off the floor, avoiding the pain in her eyes that I obviously can't comfort. "I'm, uh . . . going to get a haircut and a shave. I just need to get out. I'll be back."

"Grip, wait."

"I can't. Just . . ." I walk to the door, tossing words over my shoulder. "I'll be back."

Before I make an even bigger fool of myself, I get out of the bathroom, out of our bedroom, but I can't make it to the front door. I collapse onto the couch, drop my head in my hands, and cry like a damn baby, an ocean's worth of salty tears. I was counting on those vows. That she meant them the way I meant them was my only hope of surviving this. In the hospital, I told her I believed the only way we could survive this was together. If she won't let me in, I'm out here on my own. I hoped she would trust me with her pain because she's the only person I trust with mine. If I don't have Bristol, I ain't surviving shit.

Forty-Five

Bristol

When we are alone, you and I,
through years, through pain,
my heart will answer again and again, still.

O UR VOWS DROWN OUT THE TORTURED THOUGHTS THAT HAVE crowded my head for days, finally penetrating my consciousness the way nothing else has since Zoe passed. Grip wants me to let him in, but stumbling in the dark, I can't even find my way to the door and its slippery knob. I've never told Grip about my nightmare, waking up with our daughter's heartbeat in my ears. I'm covered in the hot breath of horror every morning and I've never told him. The panic that assaults me when I think about the first time I'll see a mother out with her newborn—at a coffee shop or the grocery store or the park—he doesn't know.

The hurt in Grip's eyes, it wasn't because Zoe's gone, it was because I'm gone. He misses Zoe, too. As I pull my head out of my own ass for the first time since we came home, I see that, but the hurt I just saw wasn't about her. It was about me.

I drag myself off the floor, standing as straight as I can. I can't seem to pull my spine straight anymore. I lean, I bow, my body reflecting my bent spirit. When I step into our bedroom, he isn't there. He did say he was going out. I'll at least shower and change these sheets. I've negotiated eight-figure deals with ease, but now these two simple tasks daunt me.

When I pull the sheets from the bed, papers go flying in the air. I hadn't noticed them, and now they're all over the floor. I bend to collect them, jarred when my daughter's name catches my eye.

For Zoe, our glory baby.

"What is this?" I ask the empty room, my breath seizing at the dedication.

I shuffle through a few more pages before I realize it's Grip's poetry book for Barrow. Maybe I'll read through them when I'm feeling more myself. Right now, I'm not in the mood for beautiful words skillfully strung together, not even from Grip. I'm stuffing the pages in the drawer of the table on his side of the bed when I see my name.

Not my actual name, but the title I know was inspired by me.

"Pretty Bird"

That's what he called me, how he teased me when I said my laugh sounded like a bird. That day, years ago, I had no idea how fragile joy is, that in a moment, with just a few words, everything can capsize. You can sink. One day the wind is in your sails then in no time you're the *Titanic*. I sit on the bed and read the poem attached to that distant memory.

My pretty bird,
Like a peacock, spread yourself for me.
Awe me with your plumage.
We're birds of a feather, you and I.
I hear your cry, do you hear mine?
A mating call before you fall, your holla never heard.
My moaning bird,
One by one, I'll count your feathers.
Let me try to make it better.
Can I kiss your scars?
I want to give you what you're needing
Use my heart to staunch the bleeding
And for your broken wing, my arms will be the sling
Where you go, I go, even due south
Borrow my breath, mouth to mouth

Resuscitation
A flock to ourselves, a murmuration
Just us two in our love nest
Hide in my love, take your rest
Till you're ready to fly again
Fly into my arms,
A safe arrival, a sure survival, a glorious revival
Then we'll leave this nest together
Two birds, we'll soar above the past behind us
A path we can't un-fly
A death we can't un-die
But we ain't at death's door
Nah, it's time to leave.
Our hearts can do the impossible
Do you believe?
Then fly, my love! Soar!
My pretty bird, fly with me and cry no more.

I read it again and then again. Each time through, the words find spots inside me that need soothing. I finish storing the other pages in the drawer, but can't make myself let "Pretty Bird" go. The sheer vulnerability of it, the need and love infuse every line. I'm about to call Grip, to ask him to come home, when I hear a muffled sound from the living room. I let the sound lead me, and my heart finds new ways to break when I see my husband, seated on the floor, back to the couch with his head in his hands, shaking with sobs.

I hear your cry, do you hear mine?

I haven't. I've been so consumed with my own grief, turned inside out in my pain, I didn't see his. I didn't hear his cry.

"Grip," I say in a voice I can barely hear myself but that grabs his attention immediately.

He stiffens, his head jerking up as if he's been caught. When our eyes connect, he tries to pull it together, tries to pull his strength back in place, but it fails him like a broken gate hanging off its hinge—the same way mine fails me every morning when I wake up and roll back over, unable to face the day. His rugged features crumple, a broken dam of tears running over his face.

"God, Bris." His voice falls apart like wet tissue. "I need you, baby. I wish I could do this without you, for you, but I meant it: we don't survive this unless we're together. If we're together, I know we can."

"Our love can do the impossible," I quote from "Pretty Bird." "Do you believe?"

His eyes narrow, recognition of his own words sinking in. Before he can ask, I answer.

"Your poem was on the bed." I sink to the floor beside him, reach for his hand, linking our fingers and placing them in my lap. "I hope it's okay that I read it."

His glance shifts away from me, eyes squeeze closed, long lashes wet against his cheeks. His cocksure bravado, the confidence he wore like skin drew me before. His vulnerability woos me now.

"I've never felt this lost," he confesses, his broad shoulders shrugging helplessly. "You said I want to fix you. In some ways you're right, but not to make it easier for me. I'd do anything to stop your pain, but I can't seem to find the solution. I only know that if we're together, there is one. Grief counseling, therapy, whatever it takes—I just need to know at the end, we'll still have each other."

I blink, swiping uselessly at my own tears. I've been looking for light, and it's been right here the whole time.

"You can start by just holding me," I whisper.

"God, yes." He breathes into my hair and pulls me across his lap, long legs stretched out over the floor. I huddle into the breadth and strength of his chest. How could I have forsaken, forgotten this comfort all along? For long moments, we just hang on to each other, both crying, grieving what we've lost and clinging to what we still have. There with my head against his chest, I hear it.

Thump, thump, thump.

His heartbeat. Every day the sound of Zoe's heartbeat lured me deeper into darkness, but as I wrap my arms around him, the percussive rhythm of his love and devotion and unwavering commitment beating into my ears, I know it's Grip's heart that will lead me out.

Forty-Six
Grip

"**C**AN YOU GET CARPAL TUNNEL FROM SEVERE MASTURBATION?"

Amir glances up from whatever game he's playing on his phone. "I don't want to know this," he answers distractedly.

"No, it's a real question. I'm gonna WebMD that shit." I pull out my phone and lean against the kitchen counter in our Tribeca apartment. "It's like this sharp pain in my wrist whenever I—"

"Man, you broke my concentration." He scowls down at his phone. "Asking me dumb questions."

"Remember that Dave Chappelle episode when he was teaching the kids about STDs?" I ask him.

He looks up to catch my eyes, already laughing over the infamous episode.

"I'll beat my dick like it owes me money," we quote together. The laughter dies down, but I'm not done teasing him.

"I figure if anybody would know about jerking off too much, it would be you," I say, shrugging casually, fighting back a grin. "You know, since you never get any."

"Not that it's any of your *damn* business," Amir says smugly, "but I'm getting plenty, and Shon ain't complaining."

"I just threw up." I point to my mouth. "In here a little bit."

"You told me about the stuff you and Bristol did all the time."

"Yeah, but I'm me, and you're you." I grab an energy drink from the refrigerator and toss it to him. "You see the difference?"

We both laugh, and it feels good. I laugh less than I used to, not gonna lie. The last month has been the hardest of my life, certainly of my marriage. That day when Bristol cracked the door to let me in, when she read my poem, it was a turning point, but it was just a beginning. It feels like we begin something new every week. Bristol started taking the prescription Dr. Wagner suggested, and her moods stabilized and her hormones evened out some. We've been seeing a grief counselor and attending a support group for bereaved parents. Now that we're back in New York, we'll have to start with a new group since we'll be here for the next few months. Another new start—Kai's starring in her first Broadway show. Bristol is just getting back into the swing of things, and she wanted to base here for a little bit.

"Your little problem should be over soon, right?" Amir raises his brows, gulping down the energy drink.

"My little …" Realization hits me, and I offer a frown instead of the smirk he probably expects. "Oh, yeah."

He knows Bristol had her six-week checkup yesterday, right before we flew to New York, clearing us for takeoff, you could say. I never thought I could go six weeks without sex, but that's been the least of my problems. I mean, I had to jerk off *a lot* to function in polite society, but I didn't mind. I waited years to have Bristol, and I have the rest of my life with her. Six weeks is a drop in the bucket. Do I want her? Hell yeah. Maybe it's different for guys, or maybe just different for me, but grief doesn't suppress my sex drive. The fucking Jolly Green Giant could sit on my sex drive and it wouldn't be suppressed, but it's been different for Bristol. She's not the same. She may never be. We may never be.

I feel it, too, that tectonic shift in the fundamental structure of who I am. My very nature rearranged to accommodate Zoe, and even though she's gone, that space I made for her in my heart, it won't ever close. It's a wound that's nowhere near healing—if it ever will—but life has a way of herding us back into its fold, of returning us to the flow of things that keep us moving forward. Bristol's just getting back to work. Between Kai's stint on Broadway and deals she's working for Jimmi—who's here in New York, too—her work pace is as demanding as it's ever been. I think she needs that to distract her from some of the real shit we probably aren't ready to face.

I'm finalizing my next album, starting promo for the book of poetry with Barrow, and have a few dates left on the *Contagious* tour with Iz.

Speak of the devil—my phone buzzes, and Iz's name pops up.

"Dude." I walk through to the living room with Amir and flop onto the couch. "What's good?"

"You're coming tonight?" Iz asks without preamble, a rare urgency in his voice.

"Yeah, I ..."

My next thought leaves my head when Bristol comes down the steps looking rather scrumptious. She's been pretty low key over the last six weeks, but tonight she's got a dinner engagement with Jimmi and she's pulled out all the stops. Her hair grew longer when she was pregnant and falls to the middle of her back, dark, streaked, wild. The dress is simple, relying on the shape of her body for its provocation and seduction, and let's just say Bristol's snap back game is on point. Between the grief starvation diet and her previously active life, you'd never know she just had a baby six weeks ago. The dress is white and strapless, clinging to all the curves that are riper now. The milk is gone, but I know her breasts by heart—and by hand—and they're fuller than before. I love Bristol any way I can get her, but I'm not gonna complain about bigger breasts.

Not never.

"Grip?" Iz prompts, voice still anxious. "You *are* coming to the town hall?"

"Sorry. Yeah." I drag my eyes away from Bristol as she smiles at Amir, greeting him with a kiss on the cheek. "I'm coming. I wouldn't miss you taking down Clem Ford."

Bristol's head jerks around at the mention of that man. Her eyes meet mine, and I can tell she's on high alert.

"My daughter's been in an accident," Iz says abruptly.

I sit up from my indolent slouch on the couch, elbows to my knees and the phone pressed tightly to my ear.

"Man, Iz. I'm sorry to hear that. Is she all right?"

"Yeah. I mean, I think so." His heavy sigh raises my level of concern. "I don't know. She's in Philly, I'm here. My ex was in a hurry and didn't give a lot of details. She would have told me if it was life-threatening but ... I just feel like I should be there."

"Of course. How can I help?"

"Debate Clem Ford."

What you talking 'bout, Willis?

"You want *me* to debate Clem Ford?" I glance up at Bristol, who now stands right beside me, her brows knit into a frown. "I'm not ... you. I'm not qualified for that."

"The hell you're not." He sounds a helluva lot more confident than I feel. "You got this, Grip."

His urgency and my doubt wrestle in the silence between us. "Please," he says, and with his pride, I know what that costs him.

I run a weary hand over my face.

"Yeah, sure. Whatever you need, of course. Is there anything I should know?"

For the next few minutes I jot down contacts and details the organizers sent him. By the time I hang up and let him go to his daughter, the initial panic has passed. I'm feeling slightly better.

"It's on you?" Amir asks, the game abandoned on the couch beside him.

"Looks like." I glance at my watch, a quick smile quirking my lips that the piece of shit is still telling time after all these years. "It's not far, but let's take a car. We need to roll soon."

I stand, bringing my body just inches from Bristol's.

"You look beautiful." I forego her lips, careful not to smear the vivid line of her lipstick, and opting to kiss Neruda's scripted words running along her shoulder instead. I lift the gold bar necklace hanging between her breasts bearing the same inscription.

"Is Dr. Hammond's daughter okay?" Worry pinches her expression.

"I think so." I caution myself to keep it casual. Any talk of danger to a kid hits too close to home, brings up too many things we're trying to get past. "He didn't have all the information and was on his way to Philly."

The longer we stand here together, the less I think about anything but us. I hope Iz's daughter is okay, and I'm nervous about debating Ford, but Bristol's scent, her proximity make everything else fade. We haven't even talked about what the doctor said at her six-week. It was such a whirlwind getting out of LA and arriving here, and now we've both been pulled into commitments. At this rate, it'll be tomorrow before my sore wrist goes into retirement. I rest my hands at her hips, rubbing my palms along the silkiness of her dress, imagining her skin, even silkier beneath. I turn a pointed glare on Amir, not so subtly signaling him to get ghost and give me a few minutes with my girl before we have to go our separate ways for the night.

"Uh, I'll meet you downstairs in ..." His expression inquires as he heads for the door.

"Twenty minutes. I need to get there a lot earlier now."

"K. I'll call for the car."

"Bye Amir," Bristol says. "We'll see you in a little bit."

"*We?*" I eat up the inches separating us, leaning down to run my nose along the satiny curve of her neck. "Damn, you smell good, Bris."

"Thanks." She pulls back and grabs her phone from the couch. "If you think for one second I'm leaving you in the same room with Clem Ford without me, you have another thing coming."

As much as I want her with me, I don't want her babysitting or feeling like I can't handle my shit with this idiot.

Okay . . . I did lose my shit a little that last time, but that's beside the point.

"That's not necessary," I tell her.

"Okay, it's not necessary." She doesn't look up while her fingers fly over the keys of her phone. "But I'm still coming."

"Speaking of coming . . ." I pluck the phone from her fingers and hide it behind my back. "We didn't get to talk about what the doctor said yesterday."

I can't read her face, but she stops reaching for the phone.

"Oh, she said I'm fine." She licks her lips, her brows jerking together and her eyes shifting away. "I mean, we can . . . ya know."

My arm drops to my side and I hand her the phone without a word. *We can ya know* wasn't exactly the response I was hoping for. I mean, it's great that we can . . . ya know . . . but she doesn't sound too enthusiastic about it, certainly not desperate for it like I am. I swallow my disappointment and smooth over another layer of patience.

"Great." I clear my throat and glance down at my dark jeans, button-up, and Jordans. "I look okay? I wasn't planning to be onstage but I—"

"Grip, I'm sorry," she interrupts. "You've been really patient, and I know it's been hard."

It's *hard* right now with the double addiction of her scent and her nearness seeping into my veins and smoldering in my blood and headed for my cock like a cum-seeking missile, but I play it off.

"Babe, it's okay." I cradle her face between my hands and caress her cheeks. "However long you need. I'm not some horny beast."

She gives me a look that says, *I know you.*

"Okay, I'm a horny beast." I laugh to keep from crying because I'm as hard as Skid Row right about now. "But we have the rest of our lives."

If I say it enough, maybe this hard-on will believe me.

"Tonight, when I get home . . ." she starts.

"Tonight? Yeah, we can do tonight." *Eager bastard.* "Or tomorrow. Tonight works if you want."

"I was *going* to say it'll be late when I get home tonight." Bristol's smile loosens because she's not so secretly laughing at me. "I have to meet Jimmi when I leave the debate, and there's no telling what time I'll get home."

I've fucked on less than two minutes of sleep before, but I don't point that out. If there's a curfew on our new sex life, we can ease into this.

"I'm . . . I don't know . . ." She shrugs. "Nervous? I know that sounds crazy. Are you nervous?"

"About sex?" I cannot wrap my mind around this concept. "Uh, no. Not even a little bit."

"Grip, oh my God." She laughs, and it does sound nervous, unsure, which she's never been. What we've been through changed me, and it changed her, maybe in ways I wasn't prepared for, but our vows didn't come with conditions, and neither does my love.

Ask me when your belly is full like the moon, and our love has stretched your body with my child, Leaving your skin, once flawless, now silvered, traced, scarred, I will worship you.

My eyes will never stray. My heart will never wander, gladly leashed to you all my days. I am fixed on you.

It's all still true and always will be. I couldn't have known to write about losing that child, about losing bits and pieces of ourselves. You don't see things like that coming, and you have no idea how it will affect you. You can only choose the right person, the person you want to go through shit with. Bristol is that person for me. I've always known she could endure anything life threw at her, that she would fight right alongside me. There's always been a strength in her, but now it's titanium core.

"I'm not nervous because nothing has changed," I tell her, bending to align our eyes, our lips, our hearts.

"Things *have* changed." She lowers her lashes, trying to hide from me. "My body and—"

"I love your body because it has you in it." I drag my lips over the curve of her jaw, groaning at the taste of her along the way. "Sweet Jesus, Bristol. How could you think anything has changed for me?"

"Not just physically." She glances up at me. "I don't feel the same."

At those words, my heart stumbles in my chest. A tundra inches over my whole body.

"About . . . me?" I can't regulate my breathing. "You don't feel the same about me?"

"Oh, God, no. Not that, Grip." She reaches up to touch the side of my face, her eyes earnest. "I feel the same about *you*. You know I'm . . . it's just . . . I'm all over the place. I've always been uninhibited with you, and now I feel caged, like I've had to keep my emotions on such a short leash lately, and there's something in me that's not free."

She spreads her hands and shakes her head, helplessness in the look she aims up at me.

"I'm not doing a good job of articulating this, but I'm—"

My phone cuts her off, and I want to hurl it and Amir across the room.

"Dude, what the hell do you want?" I snap.

"Put your dick up and get down here," Amir replies calmly, used to me. "Unless you want to be late and leave Iz hanging."

Shit. Have I mentioned that I hate Amir?

"Oh, and I got you a brace," he says. "A brace? For what?"

"That carpal tunnel." His deep chuckle taunts me and my stiff dick and my sore wrist.

"Fuck you." I hang up and turn to Bristol. "Car's ready. You sure you want to go?"

"There's no way you're going—"

"A simple yes would suffice." I grab her hand, pausing to let her scoop up her clutch from the side table.

The town hall is being held at that same bookstore, and it's being televised again. The magnitude of this hits me as I'm riding in the back of the SUV, cramming like this is some quiz.

"I'm not Iz," I mumble, caressing Bristol's hand absently while Googling stats on my phone. "Ford's gonna eat me alive."

"Ford will *wish* he was facing Iz tonight instead of you." Bristol stretches her eyes at the skeptical look I offer in response to that bit of ridiculousness. "I'm serious. Iz may have the degree and the books and the credibility and the—"

"Let me know when you get to the reassuring part, babe."

"And all those things." She pauses, leaning her head onto my shoulder. "But you have passion. You're brilliant. You know these issues. You've *lived* these issues. Just tell them what you know, what you've experienced."

Her confidence soothes my tattered nerves, and her reassurances give me peace in a way no one else can. She's always done that. Her eyes glow with pride and love and confidence in me. This feels like us. It's been months since we felt like *us*, since there's been any ease around us, *between* us. Maybe it's being in a different city. Maybe it's knowing we're rounding a bend with Dr. Wagner loosening the chastity belt. Whatever it is, it feels good. For the first time since Zoe died, it feels right.

Even before we lost Zoe, the shadow of loss hung over us for months. I know we'll never be the same. We'll bear the scars of the ordeal we've suffered, but we'll still be us. It's not about *what* we endure, but *that* we endure, the fact that I ain't going nowhere, and neither is she, no matter what's tossed our way.

"We're here," she says, studying the line of people crowding the sidewalk. "You ready?"

"Hell no." I bring her knuckles to my lips. "But are you with me?"

"Hell yeah," she whispers, dotting kisses along my chin.

"Then I'm good."

I capture her lips, wanting just a taste to hold me over, but dammit she's so sweet and I can't stop. Hunger breaks the surface of my control and makes me sloppy. Deep licks, sharp bites. I'm sucking her chin, nuzzling her neck. Without my permission, my hand wanders to cup her breast, to pinch her nipple, her sharply drawn breath making me even harder. I need it in my mouth. I'm sliding to my knees in front of her when everything crashes and burns.

"Ahem." Amir, not looking even a little shamefaced, grabs our attention. "Like your mama always says, if you didn't bring enough for everybody, put it away."

"You vibe-killing, cock-blocking motherfucker," I say as goodnaturedly as can be expected with a saber poking through my jeans. Bristol's throaty, unabashed chuckle doesn't help matters. *Inhibited, my ass.* I don't care what time she gets home, I'll be up and ready to show her how uninhibited she still is.

"Let's go kick some racist ass," I say, struggling to refocus.

"Kicking racist ass" may be overstating my performance, but I hold my own against Clem Ford. I'm not Iz. I don't have the epidemiological substantiation for my responses. I know fewer statistics than Iz does, and God knows I'm not as polished, but every bullshit reason Ford trots out for his corrupt system and avaricious worldview, I have an answer for.

"Are you saying crime shouldn't be punished?" Ford asks after we've been at it for an hour. "That Black men deserve special treatment?"

"Special treat . . ." Disbelief traps the words in my mouth. "You think we get special treatment?"

"It sounds to me like that's what you're asking for, that crime be overlooked."

"No, I'm asking that justice be blind and that punishment fits the crime the same for everyone," I say, outrage stiffening my voice. "That a Black man with a busted tail light not spend weeks in jail because he doesn't have bail money when someone snorting coke is given a slap on the wrist and set free. Prosecute a man for being guilty, not for being Black, Brown or poor."

"Oh, not this argument again." He rolls his eyes.

"Which argument are you anticipating exactly?" I demand, heat licking up my neck in the face of his derision. "The systematic criminalization of Black and Brown men in America? Or maybe you think I'll point out that when crack ravaged communities of color in the nineties it was a crime, but now when we have widespread opioid abuse in suburbs and rural areas it's a health crisis? I'm not saying it's *not* a health crisis, but where was that perspective, that compassion when drugs eviscerated a generation of Black people and their communities?"

"I'm only saying—"

"Oh, no," I cut in over him. "You probably thought I'd regurgitate facts about men of color serving three, four times the sentences for possession of marijuana as other groups for possession of cocaine and heroin. Are those the arguments you were expecting?"

For a silent second, hatred rears from behind the polite mask covering Ford's face. His fury is fire, but my composure isn't even singed. And before he can hide it, I see that my even keel only makes him angrier.

"The courts determine the appropriate punishment for the crime, Mr. James," he finally replies, his voice smooth and restrained.

"And when there is no crime, Mr. Ford?" I ask, not waiting for his response. "When black men, Hispanic men are pulled over and arrested for bullshit reasons and then languish in the system for months because they don't have money for bail for their non-crime? What's their crime? Their skin color? Their poverty?"

"I don't think—"

"No, you don't have to think about it, do you?" I punch the words for emphasis. "When corporations like yours set lock-up quotas, demanding ninety percent prison occupancy rates, securing cheap labor for your businesses, to do your work, you don't think about the charges the system has to trump up to meet those quotas, do you?"

"We don't—"

"What if people in certain states start paying attention to the fine print of their tax bills? How outraged will they be when they realize they are penalized for fewer prisoners? That they pay for empty beds? It's outrageous."

"What you call outrageous, we call capitalism," he says, looking into the audience for understanding, because the word "capitalism" always works.

"I'm a capitalist," I interject before he can garner much support. "Ask me how much money I made on my last tour."

I look out at the audience, playing into the curiosity on their faces.

"I have no idea." I shrug. "Too much for me to keep up with."

A smattering of laughter emboldens me to finish my point.

"I bleed green like the next American." I look out to the audience instead of at Ford. "But I won't stand by counting my money while innocent men sit in jail for months, years because they don't have the resources to prove their innocence. Men like Kalief Browder. At sixteen years old, he was wrongfully accused and imprisoned for stealing a backpack. This innocent young man rotted in jail in Rikers Island for three years without a conviction—without a *trial.* Two of those years he spent in solitary confinement. He was little more than a child himself."

I choke back anger and frustration at the miscarriage of justice. I can still see him in my mind, his young face and bright, intelligent eyes.

"He was never the same," I continue quietly. "And when he was finally released—after three years, no trial, and no conviction—he later took his own life."

Quiet descends over the crowded shop.

"I'm not asking for special treatment," I say, looking back to Ford. "I'm begging for reform, working toward it, so our justice system won't have the blood of boys like Kalief on its hands."

The applause, loud and spontaneous, startles us both. We've debated for well over an hour in relative quiet because the moderators requested the audience hold their response. Red crawls up Ford's neck and jagged displeasure seeps into his face. I look out, searching for Bristol in the crowd. She's on her feet, applauding with a smile wider and brighter than I've seen in months. It was worth it. Sitting in this hot seat, unprepared and scared pissless that I'd let Iz down—it was all worth it to see that smile on her face.

"You were amazing," she whispers when I come off the small stage.

"Thank you." I kiss the corner of her mouth, wishing all these eyes weren't trained on us. "You 'bout to bounce? To meet Jimmi?"

"Nope." She shakes her head, eyes locked with mine. "I asked her for a rain check. I wanted to spend time with my husband."

I really hope "spend time" is a euphemism for "screw my husband till we pass out from exhaustion," but I'll get clarity later. I just nod and keep her close to me as I sign autographs and take selfies and whatever else fans and people from the audience come up with for me to do. I twist our fingers together and pull Bristol into my side. She tends to wander off for this part, gets impatient and fidgety and wonders how I put up with this long line of people. I'm a patient man. Waiting on *her* taught me to be patient. All those years when I wasn't sure we would have this life together, that taught me patience.

Feeling this familiar closeness that I've missed, the closeness tragedy tried to steal from us, I'm not letting her out of my sight. Matter of fact, I'm tempted to send Amir in the car home ahead of us. Last time, we walked home from this very bookstore and were engaged by the end of the night. I'm considering shutting down the long line when someone taps my shoulder.

I turn to meet the cold calculation in Clem Ford's eyes. Bristol's fingers tighten around mine, a silent encouragement and warning. I tip my head slightly in her direction and nod, acknowledging her message: *play it cool.*

"Good job tonight, Mr. James," he drawls, looking mighty self-satisfied for a man who ended the night with most of the room opposing his views.

"Thank you." I can't bring myself to lie and say he did a good job—a good job doing what? Being an entitled asshole? We'll just leave it there.

"I didn't want to leave without saying I was sorry," he continues, even though my back is already half turned away.

"Sorry?" I glance at him over my shoulder, one brow lifted. "For?"

"For your loss, of course." His voice pitches too low for the line of people waiting to hear. "I heard about the condition your daughter suffered from. It's tragic really, but you know what many have long held about children from . . ."

His eyes flick in Bristol's direction and then back to me. "Marriages like yours." He pauses, a demon's gleam in his eyes. "Some think those children are abominations. I haven't seen pictures of her, but I've heard she—"

My fist is already arcing toward his face. I know it's a cruel, clever trap. I know he's pushing my buttons in the worst situation possible—with the cameras probably still rolling and in front of all these fans. He wants me violent, not civilized, educated, articulate, certainly not putting his flabby, pasty, bigot ass in its place, but knowing his agenda and letting this go are two different things. It's too much for him to speak about Zoe like that. Before I can reach him, a blur of white separates Ford from me, and a *crack* sounds through the space. Collective shock ripples through the crowd as they watch my wife glare up at the shit bag destined for the hard end of my fist.

"You aren't worthy to speak my daughter's name," she says, low enough for no one else to hear, fiercely enough to strip bark off trees in Central Park. "She did more in one day than you'll do in your whole miserable life, you racist asshole."

Ford's hand touches the livid mark on his face and he sputters, but Bristol charges on before he can speak.

"You want to send someone to prison?" she asks. "Send me. Press charges against *me*."

His eyes, narrowed and angry, telegraph his outrage as the event organizers, with Amir's help, hustle everyone outside, even though people continue to look curiously over their shoulders at the drama unfolding. His supporters try to press close, but the event security herds them through the front door while a few stay close to us.

"I will press charges and—"

"Oh, please do," Bristol interjects. "Then I can tell the whole world that you told a recently bereaved mother that her child was an abomination. Let's see how quickly the sponsors for your radio show disappear then, Mr. Family Values. And the super PAC raising money for your future political aspirations—how long would it take them to withdraw their support?"

He blanches, licking nervously at the spittle collected in the corner of his mouth.

"It would be your word against mine," he says with false calm. "And who would people believe?"

Bristol tilts her head to a pitying angle. "Do you know who my brother is? The people I manage and represent? Who my father is? The power my mother wields in this town? Do you know who's mentored me since college? You don't have nearly enough influence or firepower to fight me."

She takes a step closer, and I step with her, grabbing her arm, hating to see her any closer to him.

"Bristol, let's go," I say, reflecting the words she used to calm me the last time we had an encounter with this man.

Her eyes plead with me to let her handle it this time, and after a moment, I reluctantly nod, linking my arm around her waist in case something pops off. I know why she did it, but it's galling and I abhor the fact that she put herself in danger—again, for me, but I'll deal with that once we're done.

"It's not all those people you should worry about," she continues, pressing her arm over mine at her waist, twining our fingers. "It's me you should fear, because of the three of us"—with her free hand, she gestures to herself, Ford, and me—"you and I are the thugs. My husband is an honorable man.

You won't bring him down, and the next time you try, I'll show you what an abomination looks like."

Ford's eyes slit with blood-thirst and he practically bares his fangs at Bristol. The air chills around us, his malevolence sweeping in like an icy wind.

"You keep looking at her like that," I tell him through gritted teeth, "I'll undo all her hard work convincing these nice people I wasn't half a second off whipping your ass."

"You think too highly of yourself, boy," he spits, a gnarled smile on his face. "Upstarts like you, imposters. Your day is coming, though."

"Oh, my day is here." I struggle to maintain my composure. He's pushing every button, and I need to get out of here before things get worse, before he says something else that will make me want to squeeze the life from his body.

"You take our jobs, our opportunities"—his narrowed eyes shift to Bristol—"our women, and you weaken the country my ancestors built, but we *will* take it back."

"They built this country on my ancestors' backs, motherfucker." We go from me restraining Bristol to her restraining me. "None of us were here first. Unless you're Native American, you're an import just like me. We didn't ask to come here, but we're here now, and I have just as much right to it as you do. It's as much mine as it is yours, maybe more, because nothing about you, what you believe, looks anything like the America I believe in."

We're a trifuckta, three sets of horns tangled up, when Amir steps in to break the tension.

"Car's here," he says tersely with a belligerent glance at Ford before he looks back to me. "You ready?"

I can't even look at Ford for another second, the muscles of my arms straining and my fists clenching with the need to pound his face until it's unrecognizable. I help Bristol into the car and immediately fling myself into the corner of the back seat, chin in my hand. Fury hounds me as I consider the city lights, unable to look at Bristol, much less speak to her.

"Grip, if you could—"

"Don't." It's the only word I can manage without tearing into her. "I know you're upset I slapped him, but—"

"Bristol, be quiet."

I close my eyes. I count to ten. I try to visualize a serene locale, but there is not enough *woosah* in the world to calm me down right now. It's silent for a few moments, my harshly drawn breaths the only sound in the car.

"But if you would just—"

I snap my head around and pin her to the leather seat with a glare. "What did I say? Not another word until we get home."

"I'm not some child you can silence when you don't like what I say," she fires back, irritation pinching her pretty features.

She doesn't realize her indignation is a puny thing compared to my wrath.

"One more word outta you, Bristol James, and you're getting spanked or fucked in this back seat," I snap. "Amir can never un-see either of those things. You decide what it's gonna be."

She blinks a few times, her eyes narrowed but a little nervous because she knows I mean every word. She huffs out a breath, sitting in her little corner and folding her arms over her chest, rolling her eyes in Amir's direction.

What the fuck ever.

Pout, throw a tantrum and flail on the floor for all I care, but she better not say another damn word to me.

"Let us out," I tell Amir when we reach our building. He and the driver take the SUV to the underground parking garage while we go through the lobby. In the elevator, I still cannot stomach looking at her. I'm so pissed right now, and the worst part? I'm harder than a motherfucker. There was a time when I'd know how this night would end. We'd have a knock-down, drag-out, we'd resolve the issue, and then we'd fuck the night away with makeup sex—but we haven't had sex in six weeks, and the things I have to say to her may not be resolved tonight.

As soon as we're inside, she takes off her shoes and stomps up the steps like we're done.

The hell.

She makes it halfway before I catch up to her, grabbing her arm.

"Where do you think you're going?" I demand, eye to eye since she's on the step above.

"To bed," she says. "You're being ridiculous about this, and, apparently, you need space to calm down."

"Oh, I need space to calm down?" The anger I've been checking busts the seams. "Is that what you think I need?"

"Yeah. I think so."

"No, Bristol, what I need is for you to stop hurling yourself in front of Mack trucks every time you think you're helping me."

"I *was* helping." She throws her free arm out to the side. "If you had hit

Ford after all the things you said tonight, it would have undermined everything. That's exactly what he wanted."

"So you *slapped* a powerful, evil, dangerous man like Clem Ford? That's your answer?"

"You have a better one?"

"Anything that doesn't involve you making an enemy of someone like him is a better solution, but that seems to be your forte—making dumb decisions to *save* me."

"Don't you dare bring up Parker," she says with heat.

"The same recklessness you demonstrated with *Parker*," I reply through gritted teeth, "is the recklessness you showed tonight when you slapped fucking Clem Ford."

"Don't ask me not to protect you," she says, her body taut with frustration and anger.

"You don't protect me, dammit!" My voice shatters the quiet of our home, splintering any chance for peace. "I protect *you*."

"That is the biggest load of chauvinist crap I've ever heard," she yells back, the veins in her neck straining with the force of her anger.

"This isn't about chauvinism or you being my equal, or whatever feminist *shit* you want to trot out. Call me a caveman, I don't give a fuck. You will never put yourself in that position again."

"Yes. I. Will." The delicate line of her jaw juts out. "If the situation calls for it."

"The situation won't call for it."

"You have a target on your back, Grip." The concern in her eyes overpowers the anger. "Don't you see that?"

"You think I don't know?" I blow out an exasperated breath. "The more I do this, the deeper I get into these issues, the bigger the target gets. I can live with it, but what I cannot live with is you jumping in front of me every time you think I'm in trouble."

"I won't even think twice."

"Bristol, no." I clutch my head in both hands and look up at the ceiling. "You don't get it."

"No, *you* don't get it." Some of the anger melts from her face. "You're right, this isn't about me being a feminist. It's about me being your wife, your partner. I'm not some damsel in distress, Grip. I don't need rescuing, but if I ever do, I know you'd do whatever was necessary to protect me. All I'm asking is that you expect the same from me, and not lose your shit when I do it."

I was right. This won't be resolved tonight. I'm always going to want to protect her, and she's always going to risk everything to protect me.

"You protect me all the time," she adds softly. "You saved me."

"When?" I scoff. "When have you ever sat your ass down long enough for me to save you?"

"When I was in the dark, unable to shower or eat or get out of bed . . . unable to imagine living again. That's when you saved me."

I wasn't prepared for that answer. Her honesty and the naked need in her eyes chip away at my frustration.

"We saved each other," I finally reply.

"That's my point." She pauses long enough for the words to reach my head and then my heart. "Yeah, I'm reckless. When you're threatened, I don't always think it through. I promise I'll work on that, but I will save you if I can. That's what this is: you and me spending the rest of our lives saving each other, supporting each other, loving each other. You say I'm precious to you, right?"

"The most precious thing in my life, yes." I cup her neck with one hand and wrap the other around the curve of her waist. My hands are ready to make up, finding her hips, fingers spreading over the top of her ass.

"We've been through a loss no parents should ever have to experience," she says, her voice wobbling, her eyes watering. "I know I wouldn't have survived losing Zoe if it hadn't been for you."

"I feel the same way." I drop my forehead to hers.

"I love you," she whispers, angling her head until our lips brush together. Just that contact is kindling, and after six weeks, I'm a dry bush ready to burn. The fire in my belly could quickly roar out of control.

"I need to make love to you." I dot kisses over the slant of her collarbone, lick into the well at the base of her throat, suck the gold chain and the skin beneath into my mouth.

"Yes." She licks her lips, dropping her eyes but sliding her hands up my chest and linking her wrists behind my neck. "I want that, too."

"Bris." I groan into her neck, nudging the strapless dress down to expose one breast. I circle my nose around her nipple, blowing on it but not yet taking it in my mouth. It blossoms, stiffens, straining toward my lips. "I want to be gentle, but—"

"Don't be." Need ignites in her eyes. "I've been numb for too long. My senses have been muted, I guess by depression, drugs, I don't know, but everything has been a shadow of what I felt before. This, now, us together, it feels rich. It finally feels right again."

She seizes me by the jaw, pulling me close and forcing her way into my mouth, sucking on my tongue, her cheeks hollowing with the forceful suction.

"Fuuuuuuck." I squeeze my eyes shut because I know I won't be as gentle as I mean to be. "I don't want to hurt you this first time."

"I feel like someone who cuts just to feel." Her eyes find mine. "That's how numb I've been. I don't mind if it stings a little."

"You've been numb? You want to cut to feel?" I slide her hand down to my cock, nearly poking a hole in my jeans. "Here's your knife."

She squeezes my dick, her hand sliding up and down over the jeans, her eyes entangled with mine.

"Tell me what you want," she whispers, echoing the words that have been so pivotal in our relationship, one of us always trying to out-please the other.

"I want you right here, spread on these steps." My words are rough with desperation and lust.

Wordlessly, she drops to sit on the step, elbows behind her on the step above, the motion pushing her breasts forward. One nipple is already out, the dress still half off, half on. She's obeyed every command, but I have one more.

"Panties off."

Forty-Seven

Bristol

GRIP'S SMOKY WORDS HEAT THE AIR, AND WITHOUT BREAKING EYE contact, I reach under my dress and slide the wisp of silk off, tossing it behind me farther up the staircase. I tease the dress up my thighs and spread my legs for him.

I'm gloriously wet. Since Zoe died, I've been practically asexual. There were days I felt nothing. Even when I looked at Grip, I would feel love, but passion was elusive, like my heart, my body could only accommodate so much emotion at once, and grief consumed everything. Six weeks later, my heart is still broken. There are some places that may never quite heal, but the passion, the want, the scorching need I've always felt for this man alone is finally blazing a trail through my body again, and it starts between my legs.

"I want you wider," he says, his voice pitched low and dark and tortured. His eyes never leave my pussy as he methodically undoes his belt, unbuttons his pants, slides down his zipper, jerks his shirt over his head.

I yawn my thighs open, propping my heels on the step. I'm spread like a buffet for him. He licks his lips, a tell of his hunger.

I run a brazen finger down my slit. He drops his long body in front of me, stretching down the staircase below, elbows propped on the step. His head is between my legs. I reach down, spreading it, serving myself to him. He groans into my pussy, slurping and biting and licking and running his nose through my folds. Arms lengthened down my body as I keep the lips pulled back for him, my head drops to the step behind me. Pleasure long forgotten exults through me, winding between my toes like steam, circling the tense muscles of my calves, the quivery line of my thighs. My spine bows and my hips buck into his mouth. I lift one foot off the step, curling my leg around him, digging my heel into his back and thrusting over his face. Nothing exists for me except the starvation of his mouth against me and his thumb—*dammit*, his thumb in my ass, working its way into the spindled hole and finding neglected nerve endings.

"Oh, God," I scream. "Yes, yes, yes, yes. Yes. Don't stop, Grip. Baby, don't stop."

Ever since that day I heard Grip's heartbeat, I've been living by proxy, leaning on his heart to beat for mine. Grief handed me a heart of iron, and I rusted it with my tears, a muscle not made of flesh, not pumping blood. Ever since that day I've been a lament in limbo, no longer in the dark but not fully in the light, but here, now, Grip's touch drags me into the light.

I pop, like an incandescent bubble. The pain, the grief, the desolation, the darkness of the last six weeks unfurls from me in a low keening moan. It hums in my throat and explodes until I'm a deranged thing, bucking and flailing and weeping, tearing at my hair, pinching my breasts, scratching Grip's back, feeling his skin beneath my nails. My body is making up for lost time, demanding satisfaction, expecting its due.

"Fuck me." The plea trips over my bitten lips. "Any way you want, I don't care."

The dark, unspoken demand of his eyes, the shiny wetness on his wicked mouth, the scent of me hanging from his lips leaves me completely willing and wanton.

"Yes, that," I gasp. "You can do that."

"Babe, I don't want to hurt you." Even as he says it, I see a hot hope, a fantasy coming to life in his eyes.

"You won't," I tell him, my voice hoarse. "I want to feel you as deep as you can go, wherever you want to be. Make me feel it, Grip."

"I have lube upstairs," he says, his eyes drifting up the staircase.

"I have lube right here." I run my fingers through my dripping slit. "Work with what we've got."

"Damn, Bris."

A shudder rolls over the muscled slope of his shoulders, tensing the ridged plane of his stomach. With my feet I coax his pants and briefs over his hips, pushing them down the carved line of his thighs. He shakes them off, his eyes fixed on my fingers at the hidden zipper in my dress. I pull it down the side until the silk falls away, leaving me completely bare and laid out for him, wearing nothing but Neruda on my shoulder and around my neck.

"Flip over," he rasps. "On your knees."

Unhesitatingly, I turn over, placing my elbows on the step above and my knees below, my body a perfectly fuckable right angle. He doesn't tell me what he's about to do, and the questions, the wondering adds an erotic layer of suspense. He runs his cock through my folds over and over and over, wetting himself with my juices, all the while stretching me out on a rack of sensual torture. I'm mindless, catching his cadence and pumping my hips in time with his. His fingers at my nipples and his lips raining kisses down my back make me whimper. One finger and then another spear my pussy, varying the rhythm from swift to languid, surprising my flesh, keeping me on edge as I wait for him to take me where I'm not sure he'll fit, but I can't make myself care anymore. My pussy is convulsing around his fingers and I'm reaching behind me to claw at his neck when I feel the first enormous probe. I tense, but his hand at my nipple and fingers moving inside me scatter my reservations.

"Relax, baby," he says, even though passion and anticipation tighten his voice. "I got you. Tell me if we need to stop."

I won't stop him. I'm so desperate to be penetrated. I need him thrusting into me—I can't breathe without it. I'm not sure I can endure another second of this empty body. I'm a void waiting to be filled, and I don't care how. Then he pushes forward in excruciatingly slow, slippery inches. The pressure and the width of him are momentarily unbearable, and I gasp. He goes still behind me.

"Don't stop." I drop my forehead to the step above me.

"Are you sure?" His words singe the delicate skin of my neck.

I just nod my head and bite my lip, trusting him to make it good for me. *And, oh God, he does.*

He slow-slides in deeper, all the while working my nipples and thrusting into me with his fingers, stoking me like a fire, tendrils of smoke spiraling from my core and fanning out through my limbs.

Grip's enraptured grunts and curses in my ear, the rhythm of his body, at first careful and then frenzied, trigger some ancient need in me, and my flight-or-fuck instinct kicks in. I push back into him, opening myself more, spreading my legs, giving him an all-access pass to the inner sanctum he's been wanting.

"This is so good," he rasps in my ear, one palm at my breast, the other between my legs. "I want to stay here, fuck your ass all night, but I'm gonna come."

With every thrust, he abrades nerves I never knew existed, mysteries and sensations my body tucked away and hid from me, but Grip has found them. I'm panting, I'm screaming. My body is an outcry, and he spills his response into me, going rigid behind me, inside of me.

Our harsh, heaving breaths punctuate the quiet as we lie in a sweaty sprawl on the staircase. Grip eases out and gently turns my body over. The lip of the stair digs into my spine, but I don't care. He rains kisses over my shoulders, suckling my breasts, fingers invading my hair and caressing my scalp.

"Thank you, Bris. God, I've missed you so much. I love you," he whispers over my lips, sending his tongue in to taste me. "I can't stop touching you. I thought I might lose ..."

His voice breaks. He buries his head in my neck, and I feel his tears mingling with the sweat sheening my body. He reaches up, looking at me with wet eyes, and brushes away the tears I didn't realize were streaming over my cheeks, too.

"We made it." He smiles at me, eyes tender. "I told you we could survive anything together."

He never doubted us. When I wasn't sure I could make it, when I couldn't find my way out of the darkness entombing me, he came for me.

"Don't ever tell me not to save you," I say, tears rolling between my naked breasts and over the gold that binds our hearts together. "You saved me, Grip. You came for me."

He looks at me curiously, like it's something he can't believe I'm surprised by, like he wonders if I'm still figuring it out. He bends to lick at my tears and lifts the wild hair from my eyes, the look he rests on me devoted and sure.

"I'll always come for you, Bristol."

He said it after eight years of waiting for me. He said it when he came to LA after our fight. He's said it in a million ways with and without words. He says it with his heart, and I have to believe him because when I was at my lowest and thought all was lost, he found me in hell and brought me home.

"Hope" is the thing with feathers—That perches in the soul—
And sings the tune without the words—
And never stops at all."
Emily Dickinson

Grip

"WHY DO I LET HER TALK ME INTO THIS SHIT?" I MUMBLE, staring at the instructions I thought were in English, but may as well be Greek.

"Shit!"

I turn horrified eyes on my eighteen-month-old daughter's cherubic face. She's triumphant because she said a word.

A really bad one.

I squat down to the floor where she's playing with the Sesame Street app on her iPad.

"We don't say that word, Nina," I tell her gently, running a hand over the dark coils of hair springing with life and health. Bristol takes such pride in finally figuring out how to do our daughter's hair. Jade, of all people, who wore cornrows to the prom, helped her, Jade and YouTube—and my mama, and Shon. Apparently, it takes a village to do Nina's hair.

"Shit!" Nina says again, her delighted eyes startlingly silver against the copper of her skin.

"No, baby." My panic rises. The kid can't say "dog," but manages to say "shit" twice in ten seconds. "Bad word."

"Shit!"

"Dammit," I say under my breath. "Bristol's gonna kill me."

"Dammit," Nina parrots absently, her attention already back on Sesame Street.

This is bad. I'm devising how to make this *not* my fault when my cell phone rings. Splitting a look between the directions I won't understand without Rosetta Stone and the toddler I'm corrupting, I glance at the screen.

"Mrs. O'Malley, hi." Pleased to hear from her, I slide my back down the newly painted wall to sit on the floor. "Happy belated birthday. I hope you got the flowers we sent."

"Yes." The one word comes over the line faintly but carries her distress. "I . . . thank you. It was sweet."

"Is everything okay?" I frown, wondering what could have the usually upbeat owner of our place in New York upset.

"No, I . . ." Her voice collapses, and her pain reaches across the miles. "He's gone, Marlon. Oh, God. Patrick's gone."

For long seconds, her tears, the sound of her grief, shreds me. I'm at a loss, searching for the right words to say, but if Bristol goes first, there won't be any right words. The whole world will be inadequate if I lose her. I won't insult Mrs. O'Malley with my platitudes. I respect her devastation, letting her weep for a few seconds until she can speak again.

"It was peaceful," she finally says, her voice still not strong, but clearer. "I knew it would happen soon, but I wasn't ready."

How can you ever be ready to lose the love of your life? The question, even theoretically, accelerates my breath and pricks my heart in sympathy for her and in resignation that one day, we'll all taste this pain. Death is the most inevitable thing in this life.

"It was the strangest thing," she continues, fine with me not speaking. "I went to visit him last week, and he said my name."

A fresh bout of tears floods the line before she continues.

"He said my name in that way only he ever said it." Her voice sounds wistful, younger even. "Esther. That was it, but he looked right in my eyes and he knew me, Marlon. I know he did. It was really our last moment together. I wouldn't trade it for anything."

"Mrs. O'Malley," I finally say. "I'm so sorry. I . . . is there anything we can do?"

For the space of a heartbeat, she's silent, and then her voice comes strong, like I'm used to hearing it.

"Yes. Yes, there is," she says. "Keep sending me pictures of that beautiful little girl. We never had children, you know, and . . ." Her words fade into a trail of memories, a path of regrets.

"Of course," I reply immediately. "We'll bring her to see you when we're back in New York."

"Yes, do that." She pauses before saying more. "And the apartment is yours if you want it."

Even as my heart contracts for her loss, I can't deny my excitement. Bristol and I have leased that apartment for years, hoping one day it would be ours. We've made love under the vivid city skyline in that greenhouse, and Bristol made her first pot of edible collard greens there.

It's where I proposed and where Nina was conceived. "I . . . yes. We want it, of course."

"I'll send all the paperwork to your firm."

"Sounds great. They'll take care of it."

"And one more thing, Marlon."

"Yes, ma'am. Anything."

"Remember what I said the first day we met." Her voice is a thin thread strained to the point of snapping. "Don't waste one minute."

Before I can respond, she hangs up. I hold the phone for a few extra seconds, still pressed to my ear like she might share more wisdom. I finally slip it into my pocket, not pulled from my stupor until I feel something wet on my toe.

"Nina, baby." I scoop her up and rest her on my hip. "Don't eat Daddy's feet."

I walk down the stairs to find Bristol. We've been in this house for less than a year, but it felt like home immediately—Bristol made sure of that. She insisted on decorating it herself, thus me going gray trying to read Japanese instructions for something that could have been delivered fully assembled. *I'm too rich for this shit.*

She's in her office, wearing a frown, ripped-knee jeans, a paper-thin ankle-length cardigan, and a tank top that simply says PERSIST.

It's tight and strains over her swollen breasts and belly. She massages her side, eyes glued to the screen of her laptop.

"Hey." I put Nina on the floor, lift Bristol from her seat, take her spot, and then pull her back down to sit on my lap.

"Hey." She turns her head, looking around until she spots Nina, who has taken her post on the floor with Elmo.

Mrs. O'Malley said not to waste a minute, and I won't. Before Bristol can say another word, I grab her chin and pull her face around to me, delving between her lips, caressing the soft hair escaping from her topknot. She kisses me back, hunger sparking between us like a flare. She turns to face me, splitting her thighs over mine, straddling me with our unborn child sandwiched between our torsos. The kiss slows then stills until she tucks her head under my chin and slides her hand under my T-shirt, caressing the muscles of my stomach.

"What was that for?" she asks huskily, looking up with a smile, her eyes the same silver as Nina's. "Not that I'm complaining."

"Mrs. O'Malley's husband died," I tell her without any lead-up. "I just got off the phone with her."

"Oh my God." Bristol sits back, one hand going to her chest. "Is she . . . how was she?"

"Devastated."

"I would be inconsolable." Bristol looks at me, her eyes softening and saddening in empathy. "We'll send flowers and make sure to visit her when we're back in the city."

"That's what I told her." I watch for her reaction to my next statement. "She says we can have the apartment."

"What?" Bristol's head pops up, her eyes widening. "We can?"

"Yeah, if we want it."

"We want it!" Bristol bends her brows with a sudden thought. "We'll have to set up a nursery there, too."

"Yeah, about the nursery—I'm not assembling any more furniture. That shit's in German or something."

"Shit! Shit! Shit!"

Bristol's narrowed eyes shift from me to our daughter clapping and happily cussing on the floor. My wife pokes a finger in my chest.

"Marlon James, you better fix her."

It takes the rest of the day to reprogram Nina, and I'm still not convinced she won't say "shit" at inopportune times. I'm plating steaks from the grill for dinner when I realize it's been a while since I heard any sounds from Bristol's office. She's negotiating a new deal for Jimmi, a Vegas residency, and it's been more complicated than she anticipated. Kai's in another Broadway show, and Rhyson wants Bristol to set up a Prodigy office in New York. I have to keep an eye on her because she acts like she's not seven months pregnant.

When she's not in the office, I check the nursery because that's where she seemed to always be when it was almost time for Nina to come. We don't know gender, don't know names—we'll figure it out when the baby gets here. With our first pregnancy, we knew too much. We even knew that our baby wouldn't make it. We decided with Nina to take whatever came, and we're doing it again with this one.

As I expected, Bristol's in the nursery, but not setting things up or preparing for Baby Question Mark's arrival. She's sitting in the glider, where she'll nurse this baby the way she did Nina. In her lap is a box I haven't seen in years.

Zoe's memory box.

We only held Zoe for a day, but I think about her all the time. She lives on in our hearts, but also in the three people who received her organs.

Bristol looks up, eyes as wide and wounded as the day we lost our baby girl.

"I miss her." She shakes her head and bites her lip. "I think I always will."

"Of course, we always will." I go to my knees beside her to study the items in the box on her lap—Zoe's tiny handprints and footprints, the lock of her hair, pictures of our family and friends holding her, joy and heartache evident in every shot, the purple feather that hung on her door.

"She's a part of us," I finally say after we caress all of our memories. "As much as Nina is and as much as this one will be."

"Yeah." Bristol nods and tears trickle down her face.

"Dwell in possibility, baby," I whisper against her belly. Bristol lifts my chin until I meet her eyes.

"Dwell in possibility, baby," she says to me, her eyes tender, loving, secure.

"Do you think it's a boy or a girl?" I ask.

"A boy, definitely."

"Definitely?" I cock a brow at her apparent clairvoyance. "How would you know?"

"I just have a feeling." She shrugs and runs her hand over my head as I lay my lips to her belly. I push the tank top up to see her stomach, hoping for a kick or some signal that our baby is active and healthy. Bristol's beautiful pregnant. She thinks I say that to make her feel better, but I love how her body blossoms, her breasts full and heavy, her skin glowing.

"Ask me when your belly is full like the moon, and our love has stretched your body with my child," I say, quoting the vows we took years ago. "Leaving your skin, once flawless, now silvered, traced, scarred."

I look up, meeting her eyes, swimming again with tears, and I caress the faint striations at her waist, on her skin—from Zoe, from Nina, from this baby she's carrying now.

"I will worship you," I remind her, taking her hand and tracing the letters tattooed beneath her wedding band, linking our fingers, showing her the ink beneath mine.

"Still?" she asks with a watery smile.

"Yeah."

Always. Evermore. Even after.

"Still."

Author's Note

STILL is fiction, but the difficult issues raised in FLOW, GRIP, and STILL are fact. Many ask if the story Grip tells about Kalief Browder, an innocent young man who spent years behind bars without trial or conviction and who eventually took his own life, is true.

It is.

Thank you so much for going on Grip & Bristol's journey.
I hope you enjoyed it.
Read on for a Grip series short story entitled All!

Rhyson and Kai have three books of their own,
The Soul Trilogy!

A GRIP SHORT

One

Grip

I HATE WAKING UP TO AN EMPTY BED.

Scratch that.

I hate waking up without my wife. I draw that distinction because there was a time when I loved stretching from one corner of a California king to the other. After growing up in tiny, cramped spaces—which were sometimes shared with various family members, depending on their "situation" at the time—when I had my own space, my own bed, I luxuriated in it. But it only took sleeping with Bristol once to make any bed she's not in feel just . . . empty.

It isn't even light outside yet. Shadows cloak our bedroom. I press the little light on the cheap ass watch Bristol won for me so many years ago. This thing has been to the shop a lot, but it's still ticking enough to show me it's four in the morning. I've only been asleep two hours after a long night at the studio.

With the drapes drawn, barely a sliver of moonlight penetrates the darkness. I caress the rumpled, still-warm spot where Bristol should be and stare up at the ceiling. What my eyes can't see, my memory paints on the dark canvas overhead. A Ferris wheel with us at the top sharing our first kiss, Bristol's short, sweet breaths and urgent hands intoxicating me. I see Bristol, gorgeous against a backdrop of scarlet sand in the Dubai desert. Bristol under a night sky spilling snowflakes like secrets, and me on my knees, asking her—shit, *begging* her—to marry me. I see her standing in a mountaintop chapel with majestic, white-capped peaks outdone by the devotion shining from her eyes as I lay my heart at her feet, verse by verse in the vows I wrote for her. I see her weeping, broken, devastated on the hardest day of our lives. And I see her joy-lit face when she gave birth to our children

Our life together is panoramic, stretched wide in ugliness and pain, vast in love and passion. I wouldn't trade one minute of it and I savor every day we have together. Not everyone gets to spend this life with their soul mate. Some walk all their days with half a heart, with the ache of something missing. I know how that feels, and I hope to never feel it again.

Despite the exhaustion weighing me down, I swing my legs over the side of the bed, scrubbing a weary hand over my face. Not bothering to grab sweatpants, I walk from our bedroom and down the hall in my briefs. First stop is Nina's room. Our little girl sleeps like a log. She zips all over this house with boundless energy, a two-year-old tornado, leaving a trail of toys, soiled clothes, and hair bows in her wake. Every night it's a fight to get her to bed. Once she's asleep, though, not a peep.

Her nightlight illuminates the plump curve of her cheeks and the soft cloud of dark, curly hair fanned out on her pillow. I draw a sharp breath through the emotion tightening my chest. What I had with Bristol was all-encompassing before, but having Nina added another dimension to our love, to our lives, that I couldn't have conceived before my daughter. Words are my creative currency, but this feeling defies words, goes beyond the scope of what I can articulate. It didn't exist until this little girl did. It was born with her. Family has always been important to me, but this is another level. The people under this roof are my whole world. Not the Grammys or the fame or the money—none of it counts for shit without them.

I'm still smiling about my daughter's out-like-a-light state when I pad down the hall to find Bristol. She's in the nursery feeding our five-month-old son Martin. I hope I never get used to this, to the way my heart contracts when I see her breastfeeding. Or cooking dinner. Doing Nina's hair. Brushing her teeth. Putting on makeup. Practicing yoga poses. Bristol doesn't have to be doing anything monumental to make my heart stop. Just the fact that she's in my life, the center of my world, makes me count my blessings.

She looks up from her seat in the glider and smiles at me as I lean one shoulder against the doorframe.

"Hi," she says, her voice and eyes warm and soft. I smile back but don't speak. I just take her in. She recently cut her hair to just above her shoulders, and it halos around her face in dark waves and coppery streaks. Martin has fallen asleep at her breast, idly suckling every few seconds even though he isn't awake to enjoy it.

But I'm enjoying it.

Bris wore one of my shirts to bed, which she does on purpose because she knows how damn sexy I think it is. The buttons open to her navel, and one panel of the shirt covers her left side, but the other falls away to bare her right shoulder and breast where Martin's lucky little mouth wraps around a nipple.

"Hi," I finally reply, my voice a little hoarse and my dick stiff in my briefs.

"I tried to stay awake," she whispers. "But I was too tired. How'd the recording session go?"

"Not great." I push out a frustrated breath. "Everything feels forced."

I walk deeper into the room until I reach them, bending to take Martin from her, careful not to wake him. Her nipple, distended, shiny and wet, pops from his mouth. I lean down to her ear, sucking the lobe between my lips.

"Grip." Bristol's breath stutters and her eyes drift closed.

Holding Martin to my chest, I trail kisses over her jaw and down to her collarbone.

"Go wait for me," I say, my voice low and lust-rough. "I got him."

She stands and quickly leaves the room while I lay my son in his crib.

He squirms and twists as soon as his little body hits the mattress.

"Missed you today, handsome boy," I say softly, pushing thick curls off his round face.

His eyes, dark like mine where Nina's are gray like Bristol's, snap open. I catch a curse, hoping he goes right back to sleep so I can go fuck his mother. Our gazes lock in the lamplight for a few seconds before his long lashes flutter, his head lolls to the side, and he falls back asleep.

Who would believe such a little person would require so much work? So much vigilance? Bristol is back in the office for half days, but the rest of the time she's here with Nina and Martin. I'm here when I can be, and a nanny, whom Bristol vetted like the FBI, helps for a few hours a week. Sarah, Bristol's assistant, is at our house all the time working. Bris is constantly in Zoom meetings and on teleconference calls. She works harder than ever.

I help, of course, but I'm preparing for the next album and a tour. I've been more absent than I like to be. On the surface, everything is working, but there's a restlessness I've been trying to ignore so I can go through the motions of managing this complicated life of ours. I miss my time with Bris. I need more of her. If I sound like a whiny, needy wuss, I don't really care. If there is one thing I'm in tune with, it's my most base needs. And there is nothing more essential, more fundamental to my happiness, than my wife.

When I make it to our bedroom, I'm still considering her heavy workload, the time she devotes to our kids, and most of all—most selfishly of all—how little time I've had with her since Martin was born.

Those thoughts fly away on a horny breeze when I see Bristol naked in Lotus pose in the middle of our bed. Her breasts are bigger. Ass is fuller. She's always been slim, and still is, but there's a ripeness to her body after Martin that is sexy as fuck. She keeps trying to Pilate it away and yoga it off, but I love it.

"Did Martin wake up?" she asks.

Our bedside lamp casts light over the supple lines of her body, showing me the wide, sensual curve of her mouth. The thick, rosy lips exposed between her legs. The delicately muscled plane of her stomach. The small scar from the C-section she had with our first child.

"He's asleep, yeah." I stand at the side of the bed and brush my thumb under her eyes, evidence of just how hard she's been working and how little rest she's getting. "Which is what you need to do."

I should let her sleep. Guilt reaches every part of me . . . except my dick, which obstinately remains erect, undaunted and unsoftened by guilt.

"What I need to do," she says, eyes locked with mine while her hand latches on to the pole poking through my briefs, "is take care of my husband."

I haul air through my nostrils and expel it harshly through my mouth at her touch. I train my eyes above tit level because, if I look any lower, I'll be all over her, all up in her, ramming from behind, from the side, from any angle I can get it.

Don't look down. Don't look down.

I mentally repeat the mantra like I'm walking a tightrope.

"I'm all right, babe." I lie through gritted teeth. "Really. Get some sleep."

Disappointment flashes across her pretty features, quickly followed by determination. She leans back on one elbow and spreads her legs, slipping a hand between them.

"You go on to sleep, Grip," she says, dropping her head back and moaning. "I'm just gonna come at least once before I turn in."

Motherfucker.

Literally.

Without acknowledging her dirty trick, I grab behind her knees and drag her to the edge of the bed. Her husky laugh floats around us in the dimly lit room.

"Changed your mind?" Her eyelids fall to half-mast over smoky gray eyes.

"You changed it for me," I reply, tipping one side of my mouth. "Touching my pussy."

"*Your* pussy?" A lift of her brows challenges my possessiveness.

I shrug and drop to my knees, putting my face on level with the pussy in question.

"You be the judge," I say before lowering my head, widening her thighs with a press of my hands, then spreading her lips with my fingers and burying my tongue in her wetness.

We both groan.

There is nothing like this pussy. I run my nose along the slick slit before swiping my tongue through her juices.

"Oh, good Lord," Bristol breathes, rolling her hips into my greedy mouth. "Fuck, yes, Grip. Don't stop."

To quote GRiZMATiK . . . as we proceed.

Two fingers plunge inside, and I suck on her clit. She bucks against my face and loops her long legs over my shoulders, digging her heels into my back. I tug until her ass hangs just off the bed and she's supported by the grip I have on her thighs. I devour her, table manners discarded. Grunting, slurping. She comes once, and I want seconds.

"Grip, stop!" She gasps. "I can't take . . . please."

"Whose pussy is it, Bris?" I ask, biting one plump lip and then the other.

Silence. Stubborn woman makes this so much damn fun.

I apply my mouth with more enthusiasm, and then run my thumb through the wetness before plunging it into her ass to the knuckle.

"Ahhhhhh! Shit!"

Her scream pierces the quiet. With my thumb working her ass like a job, I reach up to cover her mouth.

"Whose pussy, Bris?" I demand, my tongue darting into one hole and my thumb fucking the other.

"Y-yours," she mumbles under my hand, the word breath-starved and choppy. "It's your pussy."

I plunge my thumb in deeper until my palm touches her ass, and she bucks wildly, her hand gripping the back of my neck and holding me in place while she thrusts against my lips. Once the tremors racking her body die to twitches and her moans settle into tiny whimpers, I carefully lift her, taking her place on the edge of the bed and turning her to spread her thighs over mine. She snuggles into my neck, the scent of her skin and shampoo mingling with the sweet muskiness covering my face and coating her thighs.

"Holy shit," she says, her deep-throated chuckle rumbling into the curve of my neck and shoulder. "I can't think straight. Did you suck my brain out when you were down there?"

"Focus. I think you mentioned something about taking care of your husband." It's my turn to lean back on one elbow. I gesture to the briefs I'm still wearing and the obviously eager erection straining to get out and in.

"It's all coming back to me." She shoots me a mischievous glance from under long, curly lashes.

"If it 'comes' any louder, you'll wake the neighbors *and* the kids," I warn her, my grin smug. "And the way I feel right now, Martin will just have to cry until Daddy's done."

"Ah, speaking of Martin," she says, her smile and the look in her eyes devolving into something baser.

My dick gets even harder. She grins. She knows. She leans up and cups her breasts, her thumbs stroking the fat nipples.

"You can taste. It's just us, Grip."

She caresses her breasts in hypnotic circles, and I'm mesmerized by how the nipples peak and harden. I grip her back, my fingers meeting on her spine, and I pull her breasts to my face. They're slightly damp when I pull one into my mouth and suck so hard that she draws a sharp breath above me, but I don't stop. I find a rhythm, my mouth and tongue and teeth cooperating to get what I want. When a few drops of her milk hit my tongue, it drives us both into a frenzy.

"That is so fucking hot," she gasps, scrambling to get my briefs down and off before she scoots as close as possible on my lap, the smooth skin of her thighs dragging over the rougher skin of mine.

She holds my cock in her hand, fisting it tight, pushing up and down, her thumb caressing the head.

"Don't play with it, babe," I say abruptly. "Take it."

I need to feel her tight and wet and hot around me. Beyond the horniness—*which let the record show, is at an all-time high*—I need that connection. The one we've forged through years, through pain, through unimagined highs and heart-crushing lows. So much in our lives is changing, but this never does. This scorching slide of her flesh on mine, of her taking me in so tightly, is a sweet chokehold on my cock that makes me hiss. I would know this pussy in the dark. I could be blind and half-dead, and you couldn't fool me with another woman. Just this one. This fit. This perfect friction. The grooves of our souls fit as tightly as our bodies do.

Her forehead drops to mine, panting breaths misting my lips while she rides me, her arms hooked behind my neck. The pace grows more frantic as I thrust up aggressively, meeting her pussy halfway. I grab her ass cheeks, spreading them and taking over the rhythm so I can slam her body down onto mine over and over, deliberately. We're grunting, rutting animals mindlessly taking our pleasure by force. Our guttural sounds bounce off the walls. Bristol's head tips back and then down, tears sliding over her cheeks and onto her bouncing breasts. I lean forward, lapping at the mixture of her milk and her tears before sucking her nipple hard. Biting her breast hard.

"Grip!" Bristol comes like a rocket, flattening her hand against my chest for support.

The sound of her coming undone, the contraction of her body squeezing every ounce of pleasure from me, sends me over the edge. I swallow my shout, having just enough presence of mind not to wake the kids. It doesn't matter if I own Bristol's pussy. This woman owns my heart. She's got my mind, my will, my soul, my emotions—all of it on lock. Happily trapped in the palm of her hand.

She's still trembling against me when I pick her up and lay her against the pillows. Now that we fucked the edge off, there is room for other things. Like exhaustion. She's already half asleep.

"Love you," she murmurs, turning onto her side and tucking her pillow between her head and her shoulder.

I *was* exhausted, but now I'm wound up, unable to sleep. Mind-blowing sex opens the floodgates. Everything pours into my mind at once. Possible fixes for the song that wasn't working tonight in the studio. The memory of my kids up the hall, snug and secure in their beds, and almost too beautiful for words. The sounds of Bristol coming, her whispers fueled by pleasure.

The shadows under her eyes.

As much as it feels like the planet shakes when we make love . . . that the very foundations of the earth shift, tectonic plates sliding to make a whole new world, it isn't. Those dark circles under her eyes remind me that the things I was concerned about before we made love still need to be addressed.

First light filters in through tiny cracks where the drapes aren't completely drawn tight. I hook a leg over Bristol's hip and an arm around her waist, possessively anchoring her back to my front.

Tomorrow.

I'll ask about the shadows under her eyes and work and the kids, and the question I asked her once before and have to ask her again.

Did she mean it when she said she would follow me anywhere?

Two

Bristol

I DON'T THINK MY BOOBS WILL EVER BE THE SAME.

Seriously. Why are they so big? I alternate between fear that they will never return to their original size and dread that they will deflate and hang low and be saggy balloons with nipples. I was still breastfeeding Nina when I found out I was pregnant with Martin. Back-to-back babies meant very little recovery time for the rack.

And I know for a fact my feet will never return to pre-baby proportions. A half size up, and I can't wear any of my Louboutins. Also, I am not above re-vagination if things start feeling loose down there. I need a tight-fit fuck. Though given the size of Grip's cock, I don't think that will be a problem anytime soon.

Damn, he fucked me into a coma last night.

Not complaining. I can attest to the fact that a good slumber fuck is waaaaaaay better than melatonin. With all that I have going on, you'd think sleep would come easily, but mine has been sporadic. No rest for the weary.

Or the busy.

I can't seem to turn my brain off even when my body is ready to tap out. Between feeding Martin in the middle of the night, trying to keep up with the warp speed of Prodigy's expansion and growth, and keeping Nina's little adventurous self *alive*, I'm half-zombie. I'm just really good at covering it. Lots of concealer. Lots of yoga. Lots of juicing.

What's LA without juicing?

I'm doing everything I can to keep all the balls in the air, and I think it's working. Sure, I'm exhausted and smell faintly bovine most of the time, but the kids are healthy, happy, and spend more time with me than anyone else, which is important to me. My clients are all flourishing, climbing and succeeding. Prodigy is a force. I set up the New York office before Martin was born, but I really wanted to be in LA for the birth, surrounded by my family. Now the New York office needs some TLC, so it may be time to head back. I have to talk with Grip about camping out on the East Coast for a while, and I'm dreading it. I'm thinking, though, if the kids and I stay in New York when he goes on tour in a few weeks, it should be fine.

I'm feeling especially good today. Frieda, our nanny, came early because I have a meeting this morning. So she has the kids for a few hours. After Martin's first feeding, a nice long shower has me relaxed. I'm wearing my favorite knee-length cardigan, and I actually fit into a pair of pre-Martin jeans. The sex last night has my blood singing hallelujah as it flows through my veins. I didn't realize it has been over a week since we had sex. That's a long time for Grip.

Hell, I guess it's a long time for me, too.

I tiptoe through our bedroom, trying to be quiet and keep the room dark so Grip can sleep. Between working on the new album, and prepping for the tour, he's been stretched as thin as I have.

I walk into our closet to study the shelves of shoes, half of which I'm not sure I can wear anymore. I'm considering a pair of Gucci stilettos when Grip walks in.

"Morning," I say over my shoulder with a smile. "I hope I didn't wake you.

"Nah." He sits on the tufted ottoman in the middle of the closet, running a hand over the back of his neck. "I wanted to talk before the day gets away from us."

"Talk?" My hand freezes over three pairs of red pumps. I turn to face him, temporarily distracted by the stacks of muscles flexing in his stomach and rippling under the taut skin of his chest. A thin, silky trail of hair bisects his abs and arrows down to the drawstring of his sleep pants. I can see the morning wood-ish outline of his dick. My mouth waters. When was the last time I gave Grip head? I can't remember.

Oh, God, I can't remember.

"Bris?"

"Huh?" I jerk my eyes from his crotch to find one thick brow quirked over amused dark eyes.

"You know you can get it," Grip drawls, leaning forward to grasp my wrist and pull me down to his lap. He cups my jaw with one big hand and takes my mouth as a willing hostage. Our tongues twist, and I taste toothpaste and his natural addictive flavor. His hands wander beneath my tank top, and he finds my nipple, squeezing gently.

"Baby, I have to go," I mutter against his lips and then move to stand.

"No." He spans my waist and firmly pulls me back down. "We need to talk."

"We can." I drop a kiss onto his lips and get up, grabbing the Gucci heels and wiggling one foot in. "Later. Gotta go."

"Where are you going?" He frowns. "I thought you weren't in the office until this afternoon."

"Yeah, I had to flip my schedule for this meeting. A producer for that big new period piece wants to cast Kai."

"Is there nudity?" A grin lights his handsome face. "Because you know Rhys is not about that life."

"There is a little nekkid." I lean one hand against the wall and balance to put on the other shoe. "And Rhyson will have to grow the fuck up and get over it."

"What's that mean?" His grin drops.

"It means this is a great opportunity for Kai, one she wants to take. She shouldn't let his outdated caveman hang-ups stop her."

"Last I checked," Grip says, "that isn't how they run their marriage."

"You're right. I'm sure he'll manage to convince her it isn't right for *them* and she'll turn it down." I roll my eyes and walk back toward our bedroom. "I hope not. That's why I'm going to this meeting. To salvage any of the offer we can and see what compromises can be made."

"Maybe we have some compromises of our own to make," Grip says softly from behind me.

I stop and turn, one hand on my hip and head cocked to the side. "Now what's *that* mean?"

He sketches a quick frown and shakes his head. "We can talk about it tonight. I don't want to make you late."

"Is everything . . ." I search for the right word. "Okay?"

Are we okay?

We've known each other more than fifteen years, and half that time we weren't even close to okay. I was scared to risk loving him for a long time. I never want to be *not okay* with him again. We had amazing sex last night, but I know with our schedules, we haven't been nearly as close as we're used to.

"It's fine, Bris. I just . . ." He licks his lips and blows out a quick breath before meeting my eyes. "I miss you."

My heart slams to a stop. I know this man like I know my own skin. Something's not right. I take a few steps back inside the closet until I'm standing in front of him. I step between his legs, forcing the muscled thighs to widen and bracket me. I slip one hand behind his neck and the other cups his jaw, tilting his head up until our gazes lock.

"Tell me," I whisper, searching his eyes for the answer he hasn't offered yet.

"I thought you had a meeting." His hands slide up my thighs and he squeezes my ass.

"Five minutes. I can give you five minutes."

He nods but gently pushes me away before standing and heading toward our bedroom.

"We need more than that," he says. "I'll wait."

"No. Tell me." I'm nipping at his heels, and grab his elbow, turning him back to face me. "Baby, what is it?"

"It's what I said." He reaches up and spears his fingers into the hair brushing my shoulders. "I miss you."

"But I'm right—"

"Don't say you're right here. You know that isn't what I mean, Bris."

"Sex?" I ask, a frown knitting my brows. "Is this because we went a week without having sex?"

"That's just a symptom." He caresses my cheekbone with his thumb. "This is not what I signed up for, babe, and I'm not gonna tolerate it."

"Not tolerating what?"

"Half measures. Glimpses of you. Snatches of time. Weekly fucks. That is not who we are, and I won't settle for it."

"It's a *season*," I say gently. "Everyone has kids and a job and commitments that pull them in different directions for certain seasons."

"We don't have to. I love our kids. I'd give my left nut and my whole life for them. You know that, but they aren't the reason I married *you*."

"But, Grip—"

"And I love my career. Love performing and doing all the things I get to do, the things you help make happen for me, but I don't want those things more than I want you."

"I get that, but—"

"If we aren't first, nothing else feels right, and I want to adjust things before they ever feel wrong."

"Agreed." I finally get a word in. "After the tour—"

"No, before the tour," he cuts in softly. "On the tour."

I tip my head back to study the implacable lines of his face.

"What do you mean *on* the tour?" I ask. "I was thinking I would work from New York while you're away. So what do you mean *on the tour?*"

His beautifully sculpted mouth tightens and turns down at the corners.

"I want you and the kids to come on tour with me."

My eyes widen and a frown pulls my eyebrows low.

"Babe, there's so much going on. I can't possibly drop everything to trot off after you around the world."

"I'm not asking you to drop everything, and I sure as hell would never ask you to *trot*, but you have to admit we've been seeing less of each other."

"I've got shit to do, Grip."

"So do I, Bris, but none of it is more important than this." He presses my hand to his heart, which thuds the rhythm of his love and devotion against my palm. "More important than us."

"Of course not." I step closer, resting my forehead against his chin. "Of course not, but we have responsibilities. We can't just—"

His thumb lifts my chin so we're staring at each other. "We can do whatever the fuck we want to do."

He dips his head and seals his lips over mine, invading my mouth with powerful strokes of his tongue until my knees go weak and my bones melt. By the time he's done, only his wide hands holding my hips and my fingers clinging to his shoulders keep me standing.

He bends to leave kisses on my neck. I tilt my head back so he can lick me, bite me, whatever he sees fit to do. His lips brush my ear with feather-soft words.

"I pulled out of the campus tour," he whispers, sending a shockwave over me.

I jerk back, peering up into his face. He and Dr. Hammond, his former professor, have continued the *Contagious* campus tours, raising awareness and money for community jail funds and legal representation for the wrongly accused. It's vital work that I know gives Grip a sense of purpose like nothing else does.

"No." I shake my head. "It's important. You have to do it."

"It is important," he agrees. "And I will do it. Later."

"This is just a season, Grip."

"Exactly. For this season, I can't do the tours. Not and grind in the studio for this record and prepare for this tour and be the father I need to be." His dark eyes caress my face. "Be the husband I need to be, which of everything, is my most important role. We only get this life together, Bris, and I don't accept that there's a season where you and I aren't as close as we can possibly be. There can be a season where I'm less active in the issues that I care about. There can be a season where I don't record as much or where I don't tour. But there will *not* be a season where we miss each other."

A dark chuckle vibrates from his chest to mine before he adds, "Or only have sex once a week."

I swallow, emotion scalding my throat. There are so many things I'd have to adjust to take our family on tour with Grip. So many responsibilities I'd have to delegate. So many opportunities I might miss.

"Just think about it." Grip drops a kiss onto my lips and swats my butt lightly. "Don't be late. Go get Kai that movie."

I'd forgotten all about the meeting.

"Okay, yeah." I step back, slanting a glance up at him. "Tell me we're okay, Grip. I can't—"

I look down at the floor and shake my head, unable to wrap my mind or heart around us being on the outs.

"We're okay," he reassures me. "Hey, look at me."

When I do, I see the open honesty in his face.

"We're okay, but I'm gonna make sure we stay that way. I don't want to drift, Bris. This business breaks marriages. You know that. I'm protecting us. I've pulled out of the campus tour. I'll do whatever it takes."

I nod, stepping away to grab my purse and my iPad from the bedside table where I left them.

"Frieda's here for the kids," I toss over my shoulder.

"Oh, I'll send her home."

"Send her home?" I stop and turn. "I thought you had a meeting this morning?"

"I told them I'd call in." He shrugs and offers a rueful grin. "I need some time with the kids. I've been gone too much."

I nod, wondering if maybe I've been gone too much, too.

Three

Bristol

"YOUR BOTHER'S GONNA KILL YOU." KAI LAUGHS WHEN WE REACH our cars in the parking lot. "He loves me too much, and we have sex a lot, so I'm safe. But you? You, he's gonna kill."

I chuckle, clicking my car unlocked and propping my hip against the hood.

"Hey, you just scored a role in one of the biggest movies of the year," I say. "Rhyson will be proud and happy for you."

Fingers crossed.

"I Ie will be." Kai nods, her dark hair blowing across her face. "You got them down to partial nudity, which is more of a concession than I expected."

"Well, the director really wants you for this role." A cynical grin tweaks my lips. "And he doesn't want to alienate one of the most powerful men in this town, your husband."

Kai smiles and rolls her eyes.

"Well, Rhyson will be happy for me," she says. "That's part of loving someone, right? Wanting to see their dreams realized. I want everything for him, and he wants everything for me, as long as there is no full-frontal involved."

It occurs to me that Rhyson and Kai are two high-powered entertainers making their family and their careers work. Maybe she has some insight.

"Kai, can I ask your advice on something?"

She looks at me curiously. I'm not really one to seek advice from people. I'm usually barking orders and telling everyone else what they should do. Know-it-all is a prominent strand in my DNA.

"Sure," she says, an eager note in her voice. "What's up?"

"You had a hit album and were doing Broadway shows, and Rhyson had so much going on with his career. Did you ever feel like you were … I don't know. Missing each other?"

Her eyes narrow at the corners, but her lips twitch.

"Yeah. I thought I had it all under control. The baby was taken care of. I never missed a rehearsal. Knew my lines cold. Executed all my numbers flawlessly." A husky laugh shakes her shoulders. "But, apparently, I didn't have *Rhyson* under control. We had, what we in the South like to call, a come to Jesus meeting."

"Yeah, I think Grip and I just had one of those this morning," I say wryly. "He wants us, the kids and me, to go on tour with him."

"Wow." Surprise widens her dark eyes. "That would be hard for you, huh?"

"Very." I sigh and run my hand through my hair. "I was going to focus on the New York office while he was on tour. I knew we were missing each other, but I just thought it was a season. I just don't want to let anyone down, especially not Grip."

"You're helping run one of the fastest-growing record labels in the country and managing some of the biggest stars on the scene," Kai says gently. "You have a two-year-old and an infant who's still breastfeeding and not quite sleeping through the night. Cut yourself some slack."

After I had Nina, I had so much to do at Prodigy that I threw myself into work. Then I got pregnant with Martin and ran myself ragged preparing for maternity leave. I cut leave short to get back and make up for lost time.

"Yeah, you're right." I smile weakly. "I just thought everything was running smoothly. For Grip to feel that we're drifting …"

I link my fingers in front of me and shake my head helplessly.

"Bris, we're married to brilliant men. They're possessive, intense, demanding. They want *everything*."

"Yeah, I'm aware."

Kai's smile is wistful.

"But they give everything, too," she says. "There isn't anything Rhyson wouldn't do for me. Nothing he wouldn't give up for me. Loving him, living with him, is like standing in a storm sometimes, but I wouldn't have it any other way. Our guys are rare. I hit the lottery when I met your brother, and I don't mean because of his money. I wouldn't trade him for all the movie roles in Hollywood. I'm a lucky woman."

Her phone rings from her purse, and she reaches for it, but holds our stare.

"And so are you," she finishes, glancing at the screen. "Speak of the devil."

"Rhyson?" I ask with a smile, because he's probably waiting at home with a ruler to measure how much skin they're allowed to show in this movie.

"You guessed it." She puts the phone to her ear and grins. "Hey, you."

"I'm gonna go," I whisper, leaning over to kiss her cheek.

She nods and waves.

"Yeah, we insisted on the no nipple clause you wanted," she says, rolling her eyes at me.

Demanding. Intense. Possessive.

That's Grip, but Kai's right. I wouldn't have him any other way, and I'm all those things and more. I give as good as I get. I have big decisions ahead of me. I can't lose him, but I can't lose myself either. I don't want to resent him down the road because I feel like I missed out on something. I *do* have two young children. I *am* running a booming record label.

And I *can't* remember the last time I gave Grip a blow job.

That's kind of my thing. I'm really good at it.

But I also can't remember the last time we watched television together or discussed politics or something he's written. I'm driving home and combing my thoughts for those missed moments when the phone rings.

"Mrs. O'Malley," I say, using the car's phone connection so I can remain focused on the road. "How are you?"

It's been months since I spoke with the woman who sold us our place in New York, but I'm always glad to hear from her.

"I'm not . . ." Her voice breaks. "Bristol, I'm sorry to bother you, but I need to get into the apartment."

I frown and get off on the exit that takes me home.

"What's wrong?" I ask. "You sound upset."

"There's a letter," she says, tears soaking the words. "From Patrick."

My heart stumbles in my chest at the name of her husband who lost a prolonged battle with Alzheimer's a few months ago.

"Where?" I ask, feeling her urgency reach me across the phone and across the country. "What letter?"

"The home he lived in at the end, the staff found some of his things that had been left in another room. Before he . . ."

She breaks off again and her small sob tears at my heart.

"Go on, Mrs. O'Malley, please."

"At the end, he lost speech and wasn't even connected to this world, but he must have had a flash of memory before he died," she continues with difficulty. "He wrote a note telling me there was one letter I never found. We used to leave letters for each other all over the house, and there's one I never found."

"We've done significant renovations, Mrs. O'Malley." I rack my brain for anything we could have unwittingly discarded. "I haven't seen anything. I'm not sure if it would still be there."

"Is the tree still in the greenhouse?" she asks, hope pinned to every word. "On the roof?"

"Yes! We haven't touched the tree."

"Good," she breathes. "When I was working on a difficult design, I would go out there to plant flowers. Dig around until things made sense. There was a bed of roses at the base of that tree."

"There still is," I assure her.

"He buried it there," she says tearfully. "It may only say don't forget the wine for dinner. I don't care. Any word from him, anything. I'll take anyth—"

Her words are lost in tears. I allow her space, not knowing where to begin comforting her. I've only had a few years married to Grip and I would be inconsolable if he died. She and Patrick were married fifty years.

"I'll call and let building security know you're coming," I say after a few moments. "They have all our codes on file and can get you in."

"Thank you, Bristol," she whispers. "Give Grip and the kids my love."

Grip and the kids.

"I sure will," I promise with a tearful smile.

Four

Grip

HEAR THE GARAGE DOOR OPEN AND CLOSE, FOLLOWED BY THE CHIME OF the security system when someone enters the house.

Bristol's home.

I glance at my watch, noting how late it is. She's been gone all day. Other than a text telling me she had something come up, I haven't heard a thing from her. After our conversation this morning, that doesn't bode well.

I pull the cover over Nina's narrow shoulders before turning out the "big light" as she calls it. I poke my head into the nursery to make sure Martin is still asleep. He'll be up for a feeding in a few hours.

A few hours. With my wife, who I hope didn't bring any work home. I canceled tonight's studio session so we could have some time together. It was an easy call for me, just like pulling out of the campus tours. I'm willing to sacrifice as much as I'm asking Bristol to. I don't want to come off as the guy who expects his wife to set aside her ambitions to follow me. It isn't that. It's just not the right time for us to be apart. And if we can arrange it so she and the kids can come with me …

Of course, we can. I have lots of money and so does Bris. Prodigy is her brother's label. If there was ever a recipe for flexibility, we've got it. It's a matter of priority. I know what my priorities are. Will ours align?

When I enter the kitchen, she's transferring food from take-out containers to plates. She looks up with a wary smile when I enter.

"Hey," she says softly, pulling silverware from the drawer. "Did you get my text that I was picking up dinner?"

"Yeah, sorry I forgot to reply. I was giving Nina her bath."

She sets the plates onto the marble countertop and perches on one of the bistro stools, nodding to the seat beside her.

"Sit? Eat?" she asks and pulls out a bottle of wine, pouring herself a glass. "Wine?"

I don't answer but I take the other stool and pick up a fork. I don't realize how hungry I am until I have my first bite.

"Hmmm." I chew the succulent chicken and the fresh vegetables. "That new place up the street?"

"Yup." She takes a sip of wine and says, almost defensively. "Just a little wine won't hurt. It's been a long day. I have some milk I pumped if Martin wakes up."

"It's fine, Bris." I take a sip of my wine and shrug. "I trust you to have it all worked out."

Her smile comes after a few seconds of silence, and then she resumes eating. I don't know what this silence is about. After spending all day with Martin and Nina, I'm so bone tired I don't have much to say. I don't know how Bris does so much for them and still manages to be a boss at work. Every time I step into her shoes, even if it's only for a little while, I gain respect for how amazing she is.

"Mrs. O'Malley called today," she says when we're done with our food.

"Yeah?" I bend an inquiring look on her. "What's up?"

We make our way to the living room while she tells me about this letter Patrick buried in the garden. Possibly the last thing he ever wrote to his wife before he lost his grasp on reality and time.

"God, Grip, if you could have heard her," Bristol says, sinking into the overstuffed cushions of the sectional and tipping her head back to stare up at the ceiling. "She was crying, and she sounded so . . . lost. So lonely."

"Well, it hasn't even been a year since he passed." I settle beside her, deciding to ignore any awkwardness and squeezing in as close as I can. "They were together fifty years. I can't imagine."

I'll never forget Mrs. O'Malley calling to tell me her husband had died. She sounded lost and lonely that day, too. I guess it takes time. I glance at my beautiful wife, eyes closed and long lashes fanning over the shadows under her eyes that bother me so much. I wouldn't ever recover if I lost Bristol. Not really. I could probably pick myself up and go on. But "going on" is not the same as what I have now, which is *living*. Absorbing every experience with her at my side. Understanding that everything is sweeter, richer, brighter when she's with me. Even so, maybe I pushed her too far when I asked to bring the family on tour.

"We'll come," she says softly, eyes still closed.

"Huh?" My head swings around to study her delicate profile and stubborn jaw. "Come where?"

She turns her head and meets my eyes. Her hand covers the few inches separating us and tangles our fingers.

"On tour," she says, biting her lip and smiling. "The kids and I will come on tour with you."

"Seriously?" I bark a surprised laugh. "What . . . for real?"

"Yes, for real." She scoots a little closer and drops her head to my shoulder. "That's where I was all day. Sarah and I had an emergency meeting to see how we can make it work. What we need to do and shift and adjust."

"Can you?" I rub my cheek into the silkiness of her hair. "Make it work, I mean?"

"I think we can." She nods and angles her head so our eyes meet. "We will because we have to."

"*Have* to?" I lean forward to rest my elbows on my knees and look back at her still pressed into the cushions. "Babe, if I pressured you—"

"Of course, you pressured me," she says with a laugh. "You pressured me for years to be with you. You pressured me to move to New York when you went to NYU. You pressure me every time you think you know what's right for us."

Put like that, I sound like a domineering prick.

"And you know what?" She leans forward to rest her elbows on her knees, mirroring my posture so our lips are mere inches and a breath apart. "You're right."

"I am?" I can't resist. I close the space and kiss her, reaching up to gather her hair into my fist while I trace her lips, slip inside and suck her tongue.

"Hmmmm." She moans into our kiss. "You are."

She slides off the couch to the floor and scoots between my knees. Her fingers nimbly undo my belt buckle and unfasten my jeans, brushing my cock as she goes.

Okay. I'm intrigued.

"Mrs. O'Malley's call persuaded me, and a conversation I had with Kai today helped, too," she says huskily, her eyes blazing into mine. "But you know what really convinced me we aren't spending enough time together?"

In an economy of words, I lift my brows since obviously her question is rhetorical and the sooner she tells me, the sooner we'll fuck.

"I couldn't remember the last time I sucked your dick."

Said dick goes steely in my pants.

"That *is* a sad state of affairs," I agree, helping her out by shucking my jeans and briefs off and spreading my legs to make it easy for her to reach my dick.

"I'm about to rectify that," she says, lowering her head and taking me into the hot wet heaven of her mouth.

"Damn it," I hiss, my hand palming her head and shoving my fingers through her hair. "You give good head, Bris."

"Hmmmm," she hums, sending a vibration from one head to the other until I think my brain may explode from pleasure.

I sit up and take control, holding her still and thrusting in, fucking her face until I'm just shy of coming in her mouth. Oh, no. I have better plans for this load. I pull out, swiping my thumb across her swollen shiny lips and joining her on the floor.

"What are you doing?" she asks breathlessly.

It's my turn to undress her, shimmying her jeans down along with her thong. Disposing of her tank top and cardigan.

I bend her over and suck the curve of one round cheek into my mouth, working it until I know it's marked.

"Jesus, this ass, Bristol," I say against the reddened skin. "I love your body so much. I love you so much."

"I know, baby," she breathes out.

I turn her so her elbows are on the couch and settle behind her to take long swipes of her pussy with my tongue.

"Oh, my God, Grip." She clenches and a shudder rocks her body. "Again."

I love it when she thinks she can tell me what to do. I widen her legs and take to her pussy again, licking and biting and sucking until her juices run down the inside of her thighs. That's what I wanted. I sit up on my knees, running my cock through her wetness and dipping my thumb in, smearing it on her asshole. She knows what that means.

"Yes," she pants, reaching back to spread her cheeks, "In the ass, Grip."

We've come so far.

"You want it in the ass, Bris?" I ease my thumb in her ass and pass my other hand over her breasts, pinching her nipples. "I've only got two hands here. Division of labor. Can you touch your clit for me?"

"Yes," she chokes, reaching between her legs to touch herself.

"Finger it for me, Bris."

Her breath is ragged, and I hear the wet sounds of her finger passing through the creaminess between her legs.

"That's my girl." I line my dick, shiny with her juices, up with the hole I've owned so many times now. I plunge in and almost blow it at the first stroke. I stop and hold, giving myself time to pull it together.

"Grip, move. Fuck me." Bris grabs a cheek in each hand, spreading her ass for me, thrusting back. "I need it hard."

I think that's the only way I can give it at this point. I grab her hip and thrust forward again and again, over and over until I'm lost in a fury of pounding and grunting. I pull her up so her back is to my chest and keep working her ass and pinching her nipples. Bristol's fingers stroke frantically over her clit, and she keeps thrusting back to meet every aggressive stroke. Her moans dissolve into sobs and she shakes with an orgasm as I empty myself inside her, burying my face in her hair to muffle a roar.

We stay like that for a few seconds. On our knees. One of my hands cupping her breast, the other wrapped around her hip. My dick in her ass. I refuse to move. This is Nirvana. Not just anal sex and the blow job.

Though, let's be honest. It gets no better than that.

Our scents mingle in the air. Deep breaths heave our chests. I press my palm over her heart, feeling the hammer of it. This is peace. My wife in my arms. My kids asleep upstairs. I'll have them with me on a tour I was dreading because I hated the thought of leaving them.

"Thank you, Bris," I whisper into her neck.

"It was my pleasure," she chuckles, turning to face me and frame my face between her hands. "And it had been too long."

"Not the blow job." I meet her raised eyebrows head on. "Okay, yeah that, but before that. You bringing the kids on tour with me. Thank you for that."

The striking lines of her face relax.

"Mrs. O'Malley was desperate for even a crumb from her husband now that he's gone," she says, looking into my eyes, showing me her love. "I have you. I have our kids. I have this life with you, and you're right. There shouldn't be a season when we miss each other. I'll make it work."

"*We'll* make it work," I correct gently, brushing the hair back from her face. "I don't expect you to make all the sacrifices. I just expect us both to want it more than anything. To want each other more than everything else."

I grimace at the demand of my words, at the mandate of my heart. I don't know how to halfway want Bristol. How to halfway love her. I need to have everything and all the time. I have only one gear when it comes her.

All.

But that's what I want to give her, too.

All.

She smiles up at me, face flushed, her hair a disorderly halo from my fingers and fists. In her eyes, I see it all. Our past and our future. I see us looking down from the top of the world, painfully young with reckless hearts. That was the start of us. Sometimes you don't know you're at the beginning when it's happening. And even though Patrick had been sick for so long, the last time she saw him, Mrs. O'Malley had no idea that it was the end. That's why we relish every moment. That's why, even though I may seem selfish or chauvinistic or whatever someone looking in from the outside might call it, I will fight for every second I can get with this woman.

I believe in all the things cynics despise. First kisses on Ferris wheels. Soul mates and once-in-a lifetime loves. I believe in fifty years and forever. I'm sure Neruda has a poem, a line, that would fit this moment perfectly, but I can't think of it. I can't think beyond the woman in front of me, and the word "still" tattooed on her ring finger and mine. I only hear the vows poured in cement over my heart.

I said the words that day in a church on a snowcapped mountain, and I'll say them every day for the rest of our lives.

Always.

Evermore.

Even after.

Still.

And today, I add another word. The one that encircles and seals everything else.

All.

Splendid Happiness

A GRIP SHORT

Grip

I F YOU'RE AN ARTIST, THERE'S NOTHING WORSE THAN BEING UNABLE TO create. That's been me for months. Like a bottle of champagne, bubbling and ready to pop, but just . . . corked. I have ideas, vision, inspiration, but can't seem to express any of it in a decent song with lyrics that actually mean anything.

"Shit." I run a hand over my hair. It hasn't been this long since I was growing it out for dreadlocks years ago. It's as wild and tousled as I feel inside. I haven't bothered cutting it and I see even less reason to while we're vacationing in Hawaii.

Bristol might challenge the word "vacation" since I've shut myself away so much working on this next album. This villa in Kailua belongs to a friend. It butts up to the Pacific Ocean and boasts a strip of pristine beach, perfect for us to relax and for the kids to play. It's also outfitted with a state-of-the-art basement studio, making it ideal for the work I need to get done if I want to stay on schedule for my upcoming release.

Speaking of which . . .I pick up the writing pad again, its blank page looming as a reminder of how little I've gotten done. I've finished one song and, objectively . . .it ain't shit. It felt like I had to carve every word out of my skin and write it in blood. Lately nothing's been easy creatively. I miss the urgent roll of ink over an open page, watching my words spill onto the paper in a harried, barely legible scrawl as my fingers chase my thoughts. Struggling to keep up.

A peal of laughter interrupts the semi-trance I've fallen into, staring at the blank sheet of intimidation taunting me. I look to the wall of windows and an involuntary smile tugs up the corners of my mouth at the sight down by the shore. Nina is chasing Martin to the edge of the ocean, and every time the water splashes up on his little legs, he squeals and runs back, his face animated with some mix of terror and delight. He can't make up his mind how he feels about the ocean. It's vast and scary, majestic and alluring.

"The whole world's like that, lil' man." I sigh, tossing the pad and pen onto the table beside me. "You'll get used to it."

A deeper laugh harmonizes with my children's high-pitched humor, and Bristol walks into view. Her dark, burnished hair is scooped up into a messy bun and she's all long, sun-kissed legs and rounded baby-belly in her black bikini. It will never get old, how my heart thumps a little harder when I see her, like it's pounding on a door, demanding to get out.

To get to her.

It seems like that was my heart's mission from the day we met. Get as close as possible to Bristol, to barrel through flesh and bone, reservations and inhibitions, secrets and drama. As so often is the case, Neruda's words rise in my mind. On the surface, the similarities between me and the Nobel Prize-winning poet may not be apparent, but I see them. I *feel* them in his calls for justice and his musings on fate and life and death. But it's his words on love that rouse my thoughts when I consider Bristol.

Only a burning patience will lead to the attainment of a splendid happiness.

"Preach, bruh," I mumble, standing, walking barefoot and bare-chested over to the windows and sliding door.

Bristol and I wasted too many years and made too many mistakes before we came together. We both had a lot of growing up to do, but seeing her with our children chasing the waves, seeing her pregnant again, this good life was worth the toll of patience. *She* was worth the wait.

I press my palm to the cool glass and let years of memories wash over me, a tide of blessings and banes, tears and triumphs. Being with my family always provides perspective. The page may be stubbornly blank, but my heart, my life is full. I'll get it done. I always do. I can adjust the deadline if needed, but what *doesn't* move, what remains fixed and immutable, is the axis of my existence. It's those three people down there frolicking in ocean spray like they don't have a care in the world. Seeing that, at least for the moment, lifts my burdens, too.

"Thought you s'posed to be working, cuz."

I turn at the words, already grinning before I spot Jade standing in the studio doorway. Her hair is shorter than mine now, with just a froth of blonde-tipped waves on top, contrasting with the rich brown of her skin. It suits her. Most of the time she tries to act so hard, but there's something warm, even tender underneath all that toughness the world forced her to acquire. It's in her wide smile and the affection suffusing the dark eyes that meet mine. I've seen more of it since she fell in love for what I suspect is the first time. It's not just the hair that suits her. Love does.

"Where's Kenya?" I ask.

Jade rolls her eyes, but chuckles, a sound wrapped in contentment. "Upstairs battling it out with Aunt Mittie, Shondra, and Amir."

"Spades? Still?"

"What else? Your mama is the most competitive person I've ever met. Shondra and Amir didn't know what they were getting into when they beat her last night. She won't rest till she evens that score."

"Sounds like a hostage situation. You should rescue Kenya."

"Rescue her? Hell, she's having a ball. She's as competitive as your mama. When she ain't balling, she's looking for somebody's ass to kick in *something*. You should see her and Kenan on the court together. Both of 'em ballers. Neither of 'em ever cries uncle."

"Yeah, Kenan *is* just as bad," I agree. "You guys seem to be getting serious. I mean, vacationing with the fam. You never brought anyone around like this."

"She's different, yeah. I like her." Jade sketches a quick shrug with tighter shoulders, and I know her well enough not to press. She's softer with Kenya, but there's still a shell she slides back into if she feels like shit is getting too real. I can see Kenya slowly cracking it.

"What you working on?" Jade asks, classic change of subject.

"What work? I got one song and it sucks."

"Your stuff never sucks. Lemme hear."

Reluctantly, I cross over to the soundboard on the other side of the room, cueing up the solitary track I have to show for weeks of ruminating. Jade is quiet while the song plays, her features smooth and impassive, her brows knit as she listens. At the last notes, I flop onto the couch and brace myself.

"So, what'd you think?" I try to keep my voice careless.

"It's not . . ." Jade sits beside me and twists her lips from one side to the other like she's swishing the words around before she delivers them. "It's not exactly whack."

A dry laugh rattles in my throat and I drop my head back to rest on the couch. "Wow. I'll be sure to pass that on to publicity. New music from Grip. It's not exactly whack."

She drops her head back, too, staring up at the ceiling with me.

"It doesn't sound like you," she says after a few moments. "It sounds like you're trying too hard. Trying to sound like someone else."

"I think I'm trying to sound . . .relevant, but I don't know who I'm supposed to be relating to or doing it for."

"Then just do it for yourself like you always have."

I squeeze the tight muscles at the back of my neck. "Dude, I'm almost forty, and the music I grew up on, the sounds I loved and that shaped me, it's like I don't see a place for it as much anymore. That passion. That fire and conviction. I don't *hear* it much anymore."

"Oh, it's rare, for sure. You know I'm working on Qwest's new one, and she's looking, too." Jade shoots me a speculative glance. "Matter of fact, she'll probably be reaching out to you for a feature on this one jawn. It's hot, but she wants more than hot."

"She knows I'm always down. That's my girl and I love seeing her happy." I pause, mentally running through the twists and turns of my history with Qwest. "So you like her fiancé? I haven't met him."

"It all happened fast, so I've only met him once myself, but, yeah. He good people."

"That's great. Well, she knows where I am if she needs me in the booth." I cast a disgusted glance toward my writing pad. "Not that I'm much use to anyone on a track right now. I'm just . . . stuck."

"Stuck *inside*. Bruh, you're on vacation." Jade nods toward the sheet of glass exposing vibrant turquoise waves licking at the salt-colored shore. "Your inspiration is out *there*. Your girl and them rugrats of yours, they out there. Get your ass up."

In the distance, I see a breeze teasing tendrils of Bristol's hair around her face, but I can't feel its balmy caress. The tide splashes onto Nina's bare legs, but I sit here dry and can't taste the salt in the air. The alluring scene on the beach may as well be another world for how little it touches me. And Jade's right. I need to be touched.

"All right." I hook my arm around her neck and kiss her forehead, laughing when she jerks back, our years-long loving tug-of-war. "I hear ya. I'm outta here."

I stand and so does Jade, making her way over to the soundboard.

"You don't mind if I, uh, fiddle a little bit?" she asks, brows and the corners of her mouth lifting.

"Have at it, but take your own advice. Rescue ya girl from Ma and get some sun yourself."

"You worry 'bout you," Jade says, her tone already distracted, eyes locked on the soundboard lighting up as she twists knobs and presses buttons. "I got my shit handled."

I chuckle and cross over to the sliding door, slipping out and not bothering with shoes or anything other than the board shorts I'm already wearing. As soon as the door opens, the breeze licks around my body, simultaneously soothing and stirring all my senses. Bristol has waded out into the azure shallows, laughing as Nina tries to hoist Martin and they both collapse into the water. I stroll toward them, silent until I'm close, and then jog past Bristol, playfully slapping her ass. She squeaks, jumping a little, her face lighting up when she sees me.

"Where'd you come from?" She laughs.

I back my way into the cool waves and blow her a kiss as an answer before turning to scoop up both my kids, one under each arm.

"Daddy!" they squeal in a sweet-voiced duet.

I keep running until the ocean churns around my waist and dunk them both to the neck, making sure to keep their faces out of the water. Their gasps and squeaks and calls for *more* occupy the next five minutes of what suddenly feels like a perfect day.

"I was wondering when you'd come," Bristol says from beside me.

I glance over, pausing for a moment as the impact of her silvery eyes hits me again like for the very first time. We've only been in Hawaii a couple of days, but the sun has already coaxed a few freckles to the surface, and they adorn her nose like sprinkles of cinnamon.

"Jade confirmed that my song sucks," I tell her. "And then ordered me out here, which was a smart move, by the way."

"Of course, it was. Any move that brings you to me is a smart one."

"You ever get tired of being the center of my world?"

"Sometimes it's exhausting," she drawls, rolling her eyes. "But I've managed to adjust through the years."

"Daddy," Martin interrupts plaintively. "Put me up on your shoulders."

Bristol takes Nina so I can hoist Martin up. The soft heels of his little feet kick against my chest and he squeezes my neck as we wade deeper into the water until it laps around his legs.

"I can swim, Mom," Nina says from behind us. "Put me down."

Nina's five, and while she still likes for me to toss her around, she doesn't tolerate it from her smaller-in-stature mother as much. I'm not crazy about it either considering Bristol's six months into her pregnancy.

"It's deeper than you think, Neen," Bristol says. "Be careful."

My baby girl is a tadpole, though, and sure enough, in seconds she's zooming past me, her skinny arms and legs slicing through the waves, her hair stretched out behind her in a wake of copper-laced curls.

"Baby, that's far enough," I call out. The ocean isn't turbulent today, but I grew up on the Pacific and have a healthy respect for how capricious it can be. Placid one minute and treacherous the next.

Nina turns, doggy paddling to stay afloat, her face wet and frowning. "But, Daddy—"

"Do I repeat myself, Nina?"

Her frown clears, the gray eyes so like Bristol's widening. She shakes her head. "No, sir."

"Then that's far enough." I gentle the words with a smile, take the few steps separating us and tap her head with Martin's foot. She giggles and swims a circle around me, disappearing for a second underwater and then popping back up, hair plastered to her small head.

"I need to learn that trick," Bristol says wryly. "I tried last week, asked her if I repeat myself and she just looked at me blankly and said, 'What'd you say, Mommy?'"

I can't help it, I laugh, and Bristol gives me a mock-withering glare.

"You know she loves pressing your buttons, right? Every time she finds a new one, she just has to push."

"So much to look forward to in the terrible teens. I just hope she's not as bad as I was."

I pull her close, anchoring Martin by one leg and looping an arm around her, cupping her stomach. "She's gonna be magnificent like her mama."

Bristol leans her head on my shoulder, covering my hand with hers on her stomach. There's a subtle movement beneath my fingers, as gentle as the water undulating around our bodies.

"Bris," I breathe, swallowing my own awe. "Did you feel that? They're moving."

Of course, she felt it. It's *her* body, but she just laughs. It's not the first time the twins have moved, but I always seem to just miss it, so it's the first time I've felt the life growing inside Bristol for myself.

"One of them is moving." She guides my hand to the other side of her belly. "This girl has been quiet all day."

"Girl?" I raise one querying brow. "I thought we agreed we wouldn't find out. You go behind my back or something?"

She shrugs, lowering her eyes to the water and brushing her fingers through the waves. "I just have a feeling they're both girls."

"God save me. Martin and I would be outnumbered." I pull my son down from his perch on my shoulders and hold him under his armpits, dangling him in the water. "You hear that, lil' man? Your mom says we're getting two girls. What do you think?"

"Brother!" His eyes, dark like mine, stretch with excitement. Our kids can't wait for the new arrivals, and not knowing the sex of the babies makes it that much more fun for them. Every day, each of us changes our minds about what Bristol's having.

"You heard the man," I tell Bristol. "There's at least one boy in there."

"I honestly don't care." She grimaces and rubs the small of her back. "I'm so big this time, I just want them *out*. I've already gained as much weight as I had by the end with Martin. I'm huge."

I lean over to whisper in her ear. "You're sexy as hell, Bris. Always."

She turns her head so our faces are mere inches apart, our lips separated by a single breath. "You think so, huh?"

"I'll show you tonight," I whisper over her mouth. "Massage?"

"Oh." She tips her head back and releases a sultry laugh. "I've had your 'massages' before."

"You love them."

"I do." She narrows her eyes and bites down on her bottom lip. "After dinner?"

"Why wait? We can pack the little monsters up and go to the house right now."

"Grip!" She widens her eyes and her smile.

"Kiss! Kiss! Kiss!" Martin chants.

We glance down at our son, his eyes shifting avidly between us, and both laugh.

"You kiss all the time," Nina mutters from a few feet away.

It's true, tho.

"Nina, we need to get back inside," Bristol says. "We've been in the water all day, and your grandma probably has lunch ready. After lunch we can get shave ice from Island Snow."

"A few more minutes, Mommy, please? So Daddy can swim with me?" Nina asks, lips pouty and eyes pleading under a mop of hair. If she figures out she has me wrapped around her little finger, we're doomed. Who am I kidding? This kid was born knowing.

"You think *you* can keep up with *me*?" I hand Martin to Bris and walk through the water to Nina, surprised at how deep the water gets. "Okay, little fish. Let's go."

Thank God Jade convinced me to drag my ass out of the studio. This day, blessed with puckered clouds kissing a cerulean sky and sunshine that dries our bodies almost as soon as we leave the water, is exactly what I needed. Once we've packed up, we trek through the sand back to the villa, which has seven bedrooms, a pool and sauna, game room and plenty of alcoves and nooks for privacy despite all the folks who came with us. We follow the path that leads straight to the large patio where Ma has lunch ready, as Bristol predicted.

"I see the sun all over you," Ma says, bending to drop a kiss on each of my kids' damp heads. "Coming in here two shades darker."

They scrunch up their noses and lean into her affection. The same unconditional love and discipline my mother used to shape me, she pours into my children. She finally accepted a car and a house, which is in Compton because she refuses to leave her beloved neighborhood. I can't blame her on that score. There was a lot to be scared of when I was growing up, but that community raised me, and you'd have to crowbar my mother out of it.

"I don't want you cooking the whole time," I tell her, kissing her cheek. "There's a local chef I can bring in if you want."

"And I told you I can cook some, too," Bristol pipes up, setting a sketch pad and crayons by Martin's plate. He loves to draw and we keep materials within reach for him all the time.

Ma looks at her like *for real, Bris?*

Not that Bristol hasn't improved in the kitchen. She definitely has, but my mama doesn't eat everybody's food, and if she's able to cook, she prefers to eat her own.

"I'll manage, baby," Ma says dryly. "Let's save the chef for a special night. Now we got wings from the grill and potato salad and sweet tea for lunch."

"I'm just in time," Amir says, stepping through the French doors leading into the living room. "I could eat a—"

"You ain't eating nothing." Ma sucks her teeth. "March your raggedy self right back in that house and eat you some Corn Flakes or somethin'. I don't know what to tell you, but you ain't eating my food."

"He beat you in spades again, huh?" Bristol laughs, scooping food onto the kids' plates.

"You ain't gotta eat either, Bristol," Ma snaps, fighting a grin. "Me and these babies'll be the only ones eating, ya'll keep it up."

"I told you we shoulda thrown the game," Shondra mutters, walking onto the patio in a floral maxi dress. "But nooooo. You just had to win again."

"Shondra, sit down and eat," Ma orders, filling frosted glasses with tea. "You'll need all your strength for that re-match tonight."

Shondra's eyes stretch and then narrow when they meet Amir's as he sits down at the table beside her. "I tried to tell your ass," she hisses at him.

"Y'all hating on all this Black excellence." Amir shrugs, loading his plate with wings and potato salad. "I think I need something stronger than tea. Shondra, there was some beer in the fridge."

"I'm drinking tea," she says. "You can take that Black excellence right in the kitchen and get your own beer."

We're still laughing at that when I notice two empty seats at the table. "Where's Kenya and Jade?"

"Down in that studio." Ma tsks, finally preparing a plate for herself.

"They're so cute together," Shondra says.

"Don't let either of them hear you call them cute," I say.

"It's just nice to see Jade happy," Ma says. "I mean, making her music and in love and at peace with herself."

And with me.

Ma doesn't say it, but when our eyes meet across the table, I read the same pleasure I feel that Jade and I are closer than we've ever been. And happier than we've ever been. Now if I could just translate that to *my* music.

"When's Aria coming?" Nina asks, potato salad smeared on her little chin.

"Uncle Rhyson's finishing up some work." Bristol passes her a napkin. "But they'll be here in a couple of days. Maybe even tomorrow night."

Nina claps and rolls her shoulders, some little move she and Aria made up. The cousins are thick as thieves already. Aria's at our house as much as Nina is at Rhys and Kai's.

"What's that you're drawing, Martin?" Shondra asks. We're finished with lunch, and she and Amir volunteered to clear away and wash the few dishes.

"It's us!" Martin grins, showing off his little square teeth.

"Lemme see." I reach for the paper. Bristol walks up beside me and peers down at the drawing in my hand.

It's a brown man/stick figure with something close to afro-shaped hair, obviously me in need of a haircut. A shorter woman/stick he's colored peach and who has brown lines drawn around her shoulders for hair. Martin made Bristol's stomach a circle and there's two pink round things inside.

"Grapefruit," Martin says. "You said the babies are like grapefruits now."

"Ahhhh." Bristol purses her lips against a smile. "You got them exactly right, baby."

In his drawing, Bristol and I are sandwiched between the kids, Nina holding my hand and Martin holding Bristol's. They're both brown stick/kids with zigzags for hair.

I tilt my head, staring at what Martin's holding in the drawing. "What's that purple thing in your hand, son?"

"It's Zoe!" He says, his smile wide and proud. "It's the feather in her box."

Zoe's name, offered so unexpectedly, causes the adults on the patio to collectively draw and hold a startled breath. Bristol goes perfectly still beside me, and her hand goes instinctively to her stomach. She's carried two pregnancies to term with typical deliveries since Zoe, but that fear niggles in the back of both our minds. We didn't really talk about the relief we felt when there were no indications of anencephaly, or any other birth defect at this point. We'll love our babies regardless. That's not just a platitude for us. It's been tested in fire, honed in sorrow. As much as losing Zoe hurt, we talk openly about her to our kids, making sure they know they have a big sister looking out for them all the time, even though they never met her.

"You can have it, Mommy," Martin offers, his smile slipping, his childish intuition untried, but sharp enough to pick up on the shift of emotions. "I-I drew it for you, so we can put it in the twins' nursery."

"It's so good, Martin. That's a great idea," I say, glancing at Bristol, who stares down at the paper. Even though she isn't crying, her eyes have that look of shattered glass she gets sometimes when she thinks of our little glory baby. She did therapy. We both did, but therapy doesn't always eradicate hurt. Sometimes it just helps us carry it better, teaches us how to best bear our burdens.

"This is your most beautiful drawing yet, son," Bristol says after a deep breath, reaching down to caress the purple stick/feather. "I love it very, very much. It will look perfect in the nursery."

She bends to kiss his hair, closes her eyes tightly and then cups Nina's little head and kisses her forehead, too. She clears her throat and pulls back to spread an overbright smile between our children and says, "Who's ready for shave ice?"

Bristol

DEMISE.

That's how the nurse described what was happening to my baby, the significance of the purple feather hanging on Zoe's door in the hospital. The feather that rests in her memory box now, along with all the other keepsakes from her brief time with us.

A demise.

It does hurt less than it used to. At first, I couldn't think about Zoe without aching and tumbling into a black hole. A witless Alice in an arid Wonderland. I would flinch at the sound of Zoe's name, not because I didn't want to hear it, but because I wanted to hold her so badly. It's been years, but my body perfectly recalls the sweet little weight of her in my arms. Her new baby scent still fills my nostrils if I draw a deep enough breath. I remember the dark tangle of downy curls brushing against my cheek. Some days my senses are locked in a room with those memories, and I don't want to leave because she's still there. As difficult as that day was, in that memory, she's still there.

But life goes on. It *has* moved on, and I'm at baby three and four. I'm years into a marriage I grew up thinking wasn't even possible.

"You okay?"

I glance up from the table, from Martin's drawing, which I've found my-self pulled back to all day, to see Mama James, wearing concern on her un-lined face. The dining room is clear of dishes from tonight's meal, and every-one's gone to their respective corners. It's just Mama James and me.

"I'm fine." The smile I give her is genuine because after all we've been through, Grip's mother is one of the people who always makes me smile. The same way I couldn't imagine being married to someone as wonderful as Grip, I couldn't have imagined having a mother-in-law like Mittie James.

The concern on her face stays put.

"I promise I'm fine," I say. "Just thinking. Remembering."

"Anything you want to talk about?" Her voice is soft. Her eyes, as usual, are knowing.

"I'm all talked out. A lifetime of expensive therapy will do that to a girl. I guess I'm feeling more than thinking, but I'm good."

"Okay. I'm here if you need me."

"You've done more than enough. This is your vacation, too. Let Shondra and me cook tomorrow. We can at least handle lunch."

"I think I *will* get me some sun."

"Now you're talking." I sigh and stand from the table, kiss her cheek. "I'm gonna turn in. Take a quick bath since Grip's putting the kids to bed."

"Alright. I'll see you in the morning." She gives me a wry grin. "I may even let you cook breakfast."

"Oh, well, I definitely need to get some sleep," I laugh.

"Lemme get on in here and whoop Shondra and Amir's ass."

It's gonna be a long night down here and the squabbling will be *loud*. Mama James takes her spades very seriously, and Amir does not back down from Mama James. Poor Kenya and Shondra will be caught in the cross hairs of their bluster.

"Definitely a bath for me," I say, grabbing Martin's drawing and turning to head up the stairs. "Goodnight."

I run water into the deep porcelain extravagance of the master suite's bath tub, but I don't soak as long as I planned. There's a restlessness no amount of candles and bath bombs can dispel. After just a few minutes, I dry off and belt a terry cloth robe over my nakedness, smiling when both babies move.

"Hello, girls." I don't care what Grip says, I know what I feel. There is double girl power in here. "I'd love for Daddy to feel both of you move. Can we make a deal that you'll let him feel you both at some point?"

"Daddy would love that, too," Grip says from the doorway.

Leaning one shoulder into the doorjamb and wearing a Muhammad Ali t-shirt, he's a wonder, my husband. The chiseled planes of his face grow more handsome the older he gets. He has that damn *man-ness* that somehow converts years into magnetism. As the girl smoothing creams on my neck, serums around my eyes, and fighting gravity with every exercise imaginable, I should resent that undiminished masculine beauty. Except he's mine, so there's really no loser here.

I walk over and reach up to caress his jaw, shadowed with stubble. "You have a little gray in your beard, Mr. James."

He grins, capturing my hand against his face. "Does it make me look distinguished?"

I reach between us, grabbing his cock through his shorts.

"This dick makes you look distinguished." I squeeze and tug, chuckling at his sharply drawn breath.

"Fuck, Bris," he rasps, dropping his forehead to rest against mine.

"Exactly," I whisper, tipping up to nip at his earlobe. "You need to fuck Bris. I think you promised me a 'massage'. I'm collecting."

"Didn't you just have a bath?" He eyes my robe and damp hair. "The oil—"

"I want it. I want the oil and the massage." I give him another squeeze. "And the happy ending."

He grunts, closing his eyes and leaning into me, his hardness pressing into my belly. Amorous heat rises inside me like steam and I want him so badly, I'm not sure we'll make it through the massage. Grip's massages are not professional grade. They're mostly slick, deep tissue foreplay, but I love them. The restlessness I've felt most of the day could use it.

"Lie down," he says, leading me to the California king.

My hand goes to the belt of the robe, but he stops me.

"I want to unwrap you myself," he says.

I lie on my back, and he hovers over me, connecting our eyes. I see desire there, yes, but concern, too.

"Baby, I'm okay," I tell him, grabbing his hand and kissing his knuckles.

"You sure?" His dark brows pinch into a frown. "The drawing—"

"It took me off guard, and it takes me a while to re-center." I pull his hand into the neck of my robe, passing his palm over my nipple until it buds beneath his fingers. "But now I want the massage you promised."

He hesitates, scanning my face and searching my eyes before nodding. He pushes the neckline away, exposing my breasts and shoulders to the cool breeze drifting in through the French doors opening to a private balcony. Our eyes tangle, and beneath the desire filling his stare, a question lingers.

"Grip." I place his hand on my stomach. "Massage."

He bends to kiss my stomach, the underside of my breast. "I'll get the oil."

Being Grip, he called my massage therapist and asked for tips, things he shouldn't do or should, to give me a very basic, but safe, prenatal massage at home. I much prefer his over the professional one because I get fucked when it's over.

I stare up at the ceiling, and that restlessness, the unsettled parts of me, clamor for attention, try to disrupt my desire, but before I can allow myself to be truly distracted, the lights in the bedroom dim and my husband's hands are on me.

Grip peels the robe open, letting the panels fall to the side beneath me on the bed.

"You want music?" he asks.

"No," I answer, closing my eyes so my senses are completely overtaken my him, his scent and the warmth of his hands, the sound of him breathing. "Just you."

Big, oil-slick hands seek out all the knotted places in my shoulders and neck, the rough pads of his fingers so thorough, but tender as he turns me and works at the small of my back. He tends my slightly-puffy feet and ankles, pressing his lips to the arch of my foot and behind my knee as he goes. These little kisses are promises he makes to my body, and every one of them sinks through my skin and caresses my bones. We've only been here a few days and it takes a while for me to truly unplug. Traveling with young children and a group this size, there are always a million things to consider. And all my life, I've been the consider-er. The one who plans and thinks ahead and fixes when things go wrong. Making sure everyone enjoys themselves can be exhausting. All my life I thought I was preparing to be a high-powered entertainment executive, which I am, but more than anything, I was preparing to be a mother. It's the most demanding job in the world.

Grip glides over my shoulders and cups my breasts to toy with the nipples, squeezing, kneading. My breath catches, and my legs, of their own accord, fall open. I can't keep my legs closed around this man, obviously since it seems I've spent half our marriage pregnant.

"Stay here?" he asks, his own voice husky. "What do you want next?"

"Whatever . . ." I swallow, lust making my tongue heavy and my mouth dry. "Whatever you want."

"Oh, you know what I always want." He rolls his palms over my belly and moves to my hips, paying special attention to the muscles there, strained from the stretch of accommodating our babies. After a few seconds, he moves to my thighs. They're already open, but he shifts to stand at the foot of the bed and pushes them further apart. I close my eyes, suddenly self-conscious of how radically different my body looks and feels even than previous pregnancies. With the other three, I managed to stay slim and tight. From the back you could never even tell I was pregnant.

Yes, I was one of those.

But it's my body's third time doing this, and I'm closer to forty than thirty. And carrying *two* babies. The twin gene, so persistent in our family, finally found me. I have a few dimples in my thighs and some stubborn stretch marks that seem completely resistant to all the salves and butters that usually make them go away.

He's quiet standing between my legs so long that I finally open my eyes. His expression above me is rapt and his mouth is slack. Shallow, panting breaths pass over the gorgeous fullness of his lips.

"Grip?" I whisper, not wanting to break the avid desire of his eyes on my body, but needing to say his name.

"I wish you knew what it does to me." His voice is lust-rough and graveled with emotion. "To see our babies inside you like this and your pussy all wet and pretty."

My breath catches, and I close my eyes again, tipping my back and arching my neck like he thrust those words inside me. I relish the caress of his spoken love, and grip my inner thighs to spread my legs open as wide as they'll go, silently beckoning his fingers, his mouth, his cock—whatever he wants to take me with first. In the basest of ways, I signal that he can get it.

The anticipation draws my nerves taut. My heels dig into the mattress. My tight nipples pique in the tropical breeze. My legs gape for him, but he doesn't move. Even with my eyes closed, I feel the weight of his stare; feel it roving my body like a hungry predator unsure where he wants to start eating. I help him decide, allowing my fingers to stray to the lips of my pussy, swollen and wet, dripping with the want of him.

"If you won't take it," I say. "I will.

I push two fingers inside and stroke my clit and moan. It feels incredible, but I know any sensation I arouse will pale next to the touch of my husband's hands. After a few writhing, panting seconds of pleasuring myself, I feel his fingers tangling with mine between my legs. He doesn't slip inside, but rolls his hand between the lips and over my clit. My pussy makes wet, slippery sounds of approval.

"You take the top," he says, pushing my own fingers deeper into my body, his voice husky as he invades my ass with one soaked thumb. "I'll take the bottom."

"Fuck," I gasp. My fingers fly, thrusting to match the aggressive shove and pull of his in the tiny, tight hole below. We make music together between my legs. He's the conductor, and I follow the lead of his fingers, the command of his touch.

With my free hand, I reach up and roll my nipple. Grip pushes my fingers aside and thrusts three fingers into me.

"Jesus," I shout. "Grip, cover my face with the pillow. I'm gonna be so loud."

"We're the only ones on this floor. The kids are asleep, and everyone else is in the basement playing cards." He goes to his knees and pulls me until my bottom rests at the very edge of the bed. "Lemme hear you."

Further protest freezes on my lips when he hitches my legs over his shoulders and buries his face in my pussy. He's not quiet, releasing a symphony of grunts and groans as he sucks my clit, the lips of my pussy, and laps at the juices flowing out of me.

"Wanted this all damn *day*," he mutters against my opening before thrusting his tongue inside.

"Godddddddd," I scream, not caring who hears. I *need* this, dammit. Every touch, kiss, and dirty word that falls out of Grip's mouth liberates something that has been locked away, tightly coiled in me for hours. Under his ravenous mouth, that coil loosens. I unfurl like a bright banner and come for him in a long string of curses and cries. My legs flop open, my arms fall to my side, heavy, yet weightless. He's so patient, so thorough, still lapping at the wetness my body offers it to him, rolling his tongue over the insides of my thighs like he's licking a plate clean.

"You ready?" he mumbles, squeezing my ass and tonguing my pussy again.

Jesus, this man.

I nod and turn on my side, the position I find most comfortable lately. I'm not just bigger, I'm heavier. I feel the extra weight of a second child. I hear the jangle of his belt behind me.

"Grip," I whisper, not bothering, too listless, to turn over. "I want to see you."

I can almost hear the pause before he crosses around to where I can see him, his smile brightening the dimly lit room.

"What do you want to see?" he asks, hands hovering over the unbelted waistband of his shorts.

"You naked."

Grabbing the collar of the t-shirt from the back of his neck, he wrenches it over his head and tosses it to the floor. His shoulders, chest, abs, arms—a map of sculpted muscles. If possible, he's more beautiful than when I first met him. Sometimes the things we take for granted in youth, we have to work for as we age, and the intention, the work, yields an even better result. That's Grip. I don't remember him working out much before, though he's always been in good shape. Now he lifts and runs daily, and it has chiseled his body even more.

The shorts and briefs follow the shirt, and my mouth waters when I see his dick fully erect, the head glistening. I lick my lips, and I swallow, imagining his thick, salty rivulets sliding down my throat. He comes closer and rubs the tip over my lips. My mouth opens immediately, hungry to take him whole, but he pulls back.

"Not tonight." He laughs and groans. "Believe me, tomorrow you can suck my dick all day if you want. Tonight, I just need to be . . ."

He finishes the sentence with a look.

Inside you.

In our years together, bonding through fire and trial, sometimes emotion surpasses words. We've evolved, as creatures do, developing a language not made of syllables, requiring no more than a look or a touch. Grip lies down to spoon me, brushes my hair aside and kisses my nape. I drop my head back into the curve of his shoulder and neck and sigh. Grip is my harbor, his body enfolding me, his heart pounding into my back, like Morse code, sending a message every particle of me immediately comprehends and answers. A shared urgency pulses between our flesh and demands of our souls. Whatever I need from him tonight, he needs it from me, too.

He slips one hand under me, cupping my breast and tugging the nipple until it buds for him. He runs his other hand along my hip and then over my stomach.

"You okay?" he asks.

I know Grip well enough to hear the restraint he's exercising. He needs wild, ungoverned fucking, but he doesn't want to hurt me or the babies. As many times as I reassure him, it's hard for him to believe it's okay to be as rough with me as usual.

"Grip, you better fuck me hard. I need it as much as you do."

"Babe," he rasps, dropping his forehead against my hair. "Don't . . .I can't . . .the way I feel right now . . ."

I hook my leg over his behind me. "Show me."

He grips me tighter to his chest, his hand pressed between my breasts. Burying his face in my hair, he adjusts my hips to the right angle before plunging in.

"Yesssssss," I moan, pushing back and gripping one of my ass cheeks to spread myself more for him. He's so thick and goes so deep so suddenly, my breath suspends in my throat for a second, then whooshes out in a stream of relief. I've needed this, craved the rightness that comes when we do this, when we're like this, when we have this together.

When he's inside me.

At first, it's a steady slide in, out, slow, measured, and I can tell he's still checking the beast scratching to get out. His breaths truncate in my hair, frantic puffs of air as he struggles to hold onto the control I want so desperately to break. I reach back and grab his neck, anchoring myself to him, grinding back and giving him more.

"Jesus, Bris," he rasps. "I love you."

Tears sting my eyes. The tears I wouldn't allow myself earlier because Zoe was years ago and I should be over it. I could hide that from myself, but I can't hide anything from his love. It seeks out my needy places and lavishes me, comforts me, consumes me. The tears slide into the corners of my mouth, and they aren't all old sorrow. They're tears of gratitude for my children sleeping up the hall. Tears of hope for the babies growing inside of me. Tears of awe for the love of a man like Grip.

"God, Grip," I sob. "I love you. Baby, I love you."

And he snaps. His control breaks just like my voice does, and he's clenching my thigh, pumping inside of me with a vigor that rocks the bed and makes my breasts bounce. I claw at the sheets with my free hand, balling the cotton into my fist and holding on while he charges into my body over and over. I reach between my legs to rub my clit, meeting his fire, rising with him, building until the passion burns my thoughts alive.

I think nothing.

I am sensation.

A bundle of nerve endings and longing.

A storm of molecules clashing, exploding. My cries and his become indistinguishable. Our limbs twined and twisted and melded by the heat of our lust into one beam of love. Even after a powerful climax shudders through me, he doesn't stop. He clings to me, his heart thundering into my back and his hands all over me everywhere until he stiffens and releases a roar that surely cracks the sky.

***

I wake groggily, at first disoriented and searching the strange room for something familiar. The only thing familiar is the man asleep at my side. I sit up, careful not to wake Grip. In light lent by the bedside lamp and a solitary moonbeam shining through the open balcony door, I observe him. His hair and skin contrast with the starkness of the pillowcase. His strong features relaxed in slumber, a crescent of long lashes casts shadows under his eyes. By inches I scoot out of bed, grab his t-shirt from the floor and slip it over my head. I pad over to the balcony and close the door. On my way back, I spot Grip's open notebook on the floor on his side of the bed. He's felt so stymied lately and was hoping this trip to Hawaii would inspire some creative breakthrough, but that hadn't happened.

Maybe now it has.

I tiptoe, holding my breath so I don't disturb him, and slowly lower myself to the floor, back against the bed, and pick up the pad. This morning it was full of blank pages, but at a glance, I see much of the notebook is now graffitied with Grip's characteristic scrawl. His handwriting isn't that bad under normal circumstances, but when ideas and words and lyrics explode in his mind, it's not normal and it all spills in an ungainly, illegible heap to the nearest available surface. I've seen Grip write number one hits on his palms and arms, inking his skin with words that would eventually climb to the top of the charts.

He doesn't mind me reading his work. Never has, but I don't want to invade his privacy. Still, I flip through a few pages and words he's bolded and underlined leap out at me.

Justice.

Freedom.

Equality.

Hate.

Resistance.

Reform.

My warrior poet.

He fights with his pen. Always has. It's one of the things I love most about him, his conviction and the principles that drive him. He'll share the full songs with me when he's ready. I'm closing the pad, when a strip of paper torn from the book and slotted between pages catches my eye.

When I'm parched, I drink from your love

You scatter seeds over my heart, water my soul, quench dry places until my mind is lush and overgrown with thoughts of you.

"See anything interesting?"

I drop the pad, startled by Grip's sleep-roughened voice.

"I'm sorry," I say. "I didn't mean to snoop. It was just—"

"Bris, you know I don't care." He slides from the bed and onto the floor to sit beside me. He must have gotten up and written while I was asleep and then come back to bed. At some point he donned gray sleep pants. The muscles of his stomach bunch and release as he stretches his long legs out in front of him.

"Ask and you shall receive," he murmurs, grinning. "You looking at me like you ready for round two."

My cheeks burn. After all these years, Grip occasionally finds a way to make me blush. I ball my fist up and pound his chest lightly. He drags me onto his lap.

"Oh, God, Grip." I wiggle, trying to slide back off. "I'm huge."

"Be still, babe." He wraps his arms around me, and flattens his palms over my belly, caressing me through his t-shirt. I snuggle into him, absorbing the warmth of his bare chest and the sweetness of his touch.

"I needed this," he says, softly, his words stirring my hair. "Needed today with you and the kids. Needed my friends and family."

He kisses my jaw, nibbles my ear. "To be with you. Tonight, something cracked open in me. Something I've been suppressing, stuffing. This helpless anger at the world. At how shitty so many things are, how unjust. Usually it drives me into the booth, but this time was different. I haven't been able to write at all."

He squeezes me, rubs my belly again. "Until tonight. I woke up and my brain was flooded with ideas and words."

I turn my head to look at him. "So what you're saying is I have a magic pussy."

We both laugh at that, and he tickles me, making me squirm in his arms. And then we both go still, feeling the movement beneath my t-shirt at the same time. Like little synchronized swimmers, one baby moves on my left and the other on the right.

"What the—" Grip's wide eyes meet mine. "Both of them are moving in there. That's . . .that's fantastic, Bris."

"It is." I sniff, tears rising in and burning my throat. "It really is. I wanted you to feel that so badly. I feel them do that all the time, but I wanted . . . I'm so glad . . ."

I falter, emotionally drained by nothing I can name. I'll blame hormones for the tear that slides down my cheek.

"What you wrote," I say haltingly, toying with the string on his sleep pants. "What you wrote about drinking from love and—"

"From *your* love," he says, kissing the top of my head. "What about it?"

"I'm not good with words like you, or a poet. Not a writer or anything, but . . ." I reach up to touch the little flecks of gray in his stubble. "I'm so glad we met when we were young. That we get to grow old together. That I'll have a *life* with you."

"Neruda called it a splendid happiness," Grip says softly. "Said it required a burning patience."

My laugh cracks in the quiet intimacy of the bedroom. "You definitely had that with me."

"We were both patient, but this life, our marriage, those kids." He rubs my belly. "*These* kids, all worth the wait."

"And no matter what comes, we'll face it together." I brush the back of my hand over his soft lips and rugged jaw, caressing the few silver threads. I kiss him and whisper against his mouth, "And we'll be splendidly happy."

What to Read Next

The SOUL Trilogy
My Soul to Keep (Soul 1)*
Down to My Soul (Soul 2)*
Refrain (Soul 3)

ALL THE KING'S MEN WORLD
The Kingmaker (Duet Book 1: Lennix + Maxim)
The Rebel King (Duet Book 2: Lennix + Maxim)
Queen Move (Standalone Couple: Kimba + Ezra)

The Killer & The Queen
(Standalone Novella—Grim + Noelani)
Coming Soon!
(co-written with Sierra Simone)

HOOPS Series
LONG SHOT (A HOOPS Novel)
BLOCK SHOT (A HOOPS Novel)
HOOK SHOT (A HOOPS Novel)
HOOPS Holiday (A HOOPS Novella)

THE BENNETT SERIES
When You Are Mine (Bennett 1)
Loving You Always (Bennett 2)
Be Mine Forever (Bennett 3)
Until I'm Yours (Bennett 4)

About the Author

Connect With Kennedy!

I'm in my reader group on Facebook EVERY DAY and share all the inside scoop there first.
I'd love to meet you there: bit.ly/KennedyFBGroup

Mailing List
Like On Facebook
Instagram
Twitter
Bookbub
Follow on Amazon
Book+Main
Goodreads
New Release Text Alerts

A RITA® Award Winner, USA Today and Wall Street Journal Bestselling Author, Kennedy Ryan writes for women from all walks of life, empowering them and placing them firmly at the center of each story and in charge of their own destinies. Her heroes respect, cherish and lose their minds for the women who capture their hearts.

Kennedy and her writings have been featured in Chicken Soup for the Soul, USA Today, Entertainment Weekly, Oprah *Magazine*, *TIME* and many others. As an autism mom, she has a special passion for raising Autism awareness. The co-founder of LIFT 4 Autism, an annual charitable book auction, she has appeared on *Headline News*, *The Montel Williams Show*, NPR and other media outlets as an advocate for ASD families.

She is a wife to her lifetime lover and mother to an extraordinary son.

Acknowledgments

I first must thank all of the readers, bloggers, authors—everyone who supported GRIP and FLOW. Those books explored difficult issues our society continues to wrestle with. We are sometimes so divided, and when we should be standing together, we find ourselves torn apart. I wanted to raise my one voice using my little love story, and so many of you responded.

Thank you for loving Grip & Bristol enough to want more.

Thank you to my beta readers—Michelle, Margie, Mary Ruth, Teri Lyn, Shelley, Chele and Sheena. You ladies are so valuable, and if this book is in any way great, a huge portion of the credit goes to you.

Joanna, thank you for the 1am messages, the fine-tooth comb through this manuscript over and over. For being exacting, and when I need it, eviscerating. I lean heavily on your brutal honesty and constructive spirit. Don't ever be afraid to tell me the truth.

To J.A. Derouen, thank you for all the consultation, and making sure I didn't screw things up too badly. Most of all, thank you for the compassion you demonstrated, which I hope saturates these pages.

The *feather* belongs to you.

To Imani of Enamored Reads, girl you awed me with your unwavering support, monthly re-reads and generous giveaways. I'm humbled and grateful beyond words for how you have advocated for these stories. You were so in tune with Grip & Bristol that you knew what they needed even when I wasn't sure. You know the scene I'm talking about! ;-)

To my peeps in my Kennedy Ryan Books group and on my ARC Review Team, my team admins and just everyone who is in my corner every day, thank you!

Thank you to my family, specifically my brother-in-law Reggie who gave me just the right idea at just the right time, and shaped crucial aspects of this story.

I have too many author friends to thank, but everyone has an inner "squad" who puts up with them in times of self-doubt, bad cover photos and dead-line madness. Mine includes Dylan Allen, Corinne Michaels, Mandi Beck, Adriana Locke, Stephanie Rose and too many more to name. But these chicks get the brunt of it, and you're invaluable to me.

Thank you to Jenn and Social Butterfly for being hustlers. It's hard out here, and working with such a diligent, dedicated, grinding team made it a little easier. Your enthusiasm and commitment to excellence does not go unnoticed or unappreciated.

Finally …lastly …always thank you to my boys, my son and my husband, for sharing me with the worlds and characters I create …for months at a time. A story like STILL is best written from first-hand knowledge. My grasp of a great love tested, of surviving and managing to stay in love during difficult times, is not theoretical. It is actual and has been with the love of my life for the last 20 years.

To you, my darling and my greatest inspiration, I say
Always Evermore Even after Still